DISSONANCE

SHIRA ANTHONY

Dreamspinner Press

Published by
DREAMSPINNER PRESS

5032 Capital Circle SW, Suite 2, PMB# 279, Tallahassee, FL 32305-7886 USA
http://www.dreamspinnerpress.com/

This is a work of fiction. Names, characters, places, and incidents either are the product of author imagination or are used fictitiously, and any resemblance to actual persons, living or dead, business establishments, events, or locales is entirely coincidental.

Dissonance
© 2014 Shira Anthony.

Cover Art
© 2014 Catt Ford.
Cover content is for illustrative purposes only and any person depicted on the cover is a model.

ISBN: 978-1-63216-181-9
Digital ISBN: 978-1-63216-182-6
Library of Congress Control Number: 2014943224
First Edition August 2014

Printed in the United States of America
∞
This paper meets the requirements of
ANSI/NISO Z39.48-1992 (Permanence of Paper).

Readers love *Blue Notes*
by SHIRA ANTHONY

"In Blue Notes there are all of the classic elements that make passion come alive in an enchanting backdrop."

—Prism Book Alliance

"*Blue Notes* by Shira Anthony is a lyrical song of finding faith in oneself and allowing love to blossom for the first time."

—The Novel Approach

"This was a wonderfully written romantic, sexy, and enjoyable escape to the city of love, with a beautiful HEA. The writing was smooth, and painted a wonderful picture for my imagination."

—MM Good Book Reviews

"A beautiful love story by Shira Anthony, I hope to see more of Jason and Jules in upcoming books in the series."

—Mrs. Condit & Friends Read Books

By SHIRA ANTHONY

The Dream of a Thousand Nights

BLUE NOTES SERIES
Blue Notes
Melody Thief
Aria
Prelude
Encore
Symphony in Blue
Dissonance

MERMAN OF EA
Stealing the Wind
Into the Wind

With VENONA KEYES
The Trust

With EM LYNLEY
A DELECTABLE NOVEL
Lighting the Way Home

Published by DREAMSPINNER PRESS
http://www.dreamspinnerpress.com

FOR THE child victims of abuse and neglect who suffer through no fault of their own. For the adult survivors who every day live with the physical and emotional scars. For those who dedicate their lives to helping children in need, and for those who protect children and keep them safe.

More than you know, more than you think, there are survivors out there, trying to get by. Your friends, your colleagues, your relatives. All around you are adults who struggle daily with the devastating and sometimes crippling aftereffects of child abuse and neglect. Open your eyes and your heart. Stop child abuse. Speak up. Report abuse and neglect. Be an advocate for abused children. We owe it to ourselves to make a difference. We owe it to our children. They *are* our future.

ACKNOWLEDGMENTS

SPECIAL THANKS to Rebecca Cohen for keeping my little British toff from sounding like a Yank. Thanks also to Tali Spencer, Cody Kennedy, Venona Keyes, and Jase Glines for keeping me on the straight and narrow. All y'all rock!

CHAPTER

Late September
New York, New York

"NOT HAVING breakfast this morning, my lord?" Luisa asked as she turned from the mirror she was diligently cleaning.

Cameron Sherrington cringed inwardly as he breezed into the foyer. He'd come to abhor the title with a passion. And although he could hardly deny that the money that came with the title paid for his life in New York, he felt a bit removed from all it represented. He loved spending time in the penthouse towering high above East 57th Street. It was his escape from days spent in long meetings arguing with board members over transactions they shouldn't even bat an eye over.

He knew Luisa liked using his title. She liked to brag to her friends that she worked for royalty, which suited him just fine. Though he did have noble blood, it wasn't worth shit. He'd met the queen once when his father had dragged him to some gala fundraiser, but it wasn't as if he could simply ring her up on a whim and ask her to join him for tea. But Luisa didn't need to know that.

"Not today. I need my cashmere scarf," he snapped.

She immediately dropped what she was doing, opened the coat closet door, and reached for a scarf.

"Not that one, the beige one," he snapped again as he snagged it from the shelf above her head.

She closed the door softly and stepped back as Cam checked his reflection in the mirror. He worked his fingers through a particularly stubborn curl that insisted on flopping into his eyes. He frowned at his reflection. He was meeting friends for lunch at a restaurant downtown and needed to look his best. He'd chosen a pair of D&G jeans, a button-down Armani shirt, a light blue hand-knitted Burberry sweater that matched the startling blue of his eyes, and a tweedy Fendi jacket he'd picked up in Italy a few months before.

"Very nice, Lord Sherrington," she said politely.

Cam shot her an irritated look. What the bloody hell would she know? "Where are my Oliver Peoples?"

She opened the drawer in the small cherrywood table that stood sentry in the foyer and handed the sunglasses to him. "Will you be dining in tonight, sir?"

"No. But make some of that leek and potato soup before you leave for the weekend. I'll have it for lunch tomorrow."

She nodded timidly as she waited to return to cleaning the mirror. "Of course, Lord Sherrington. I'll see you on Monday."

He finished fiddling with his hair, donned the sunglasses, and pressed the call button for the private lift. "You will. And make some of that greek salad."

He paid her well—Sherrington Holdings paid her well, more accurately— even paid her when he wasn't staying at the penthouse, just to keep it up and water the plants. The least she could do was make enough food for the weekend.

"Certainly, Lord Sherrington."

He stepped onto the lift without a word, exiting into the lobby a minute later as his mobile buzzed. He pulled the phone from his breast pocket, glanced at it, and tapped the screen.

"Uncle. So good to hear from—"

"I'm late to a meeting," Duncan Sherrington said with obvious irritation. "You asked for an update."

The clipped response stung. Since Cam's father's death, Duncan had been like a father to him, and Cam had tried to make the man happy. Make him proud. But no matter what he did, he never met Duncan's expectations. He was never good enough, never smart enough, never dedicated enough. He was yet another annoying gnat his uncle was forced to deal with, and lately it seemed an entire swarm of gnats dogged Duncan's every move.

"Calling with good news, then?" Cam said.

"If nothing new is good news." In many respects, Cam appreciated Duncan's forthrightness. Blunt was always better than bullshit. Still, the only interactions he had with Duncan were in the form of verbal swats. Cam stifled his disappointment and bucked up.

"Might be." Cam waved at the doorman and strode into the bright sunlight.

"I've had Henry contact his friend. Nothing more about rumors of an investigation here. Seems Revenue and Customs has better things to do with its time."

Cam figured as much. He could handle rumors, or ignore them, if he chose to. "Glad to hear it."

"Are you staying in New York until the end of the month?" Duncan asked.

Cam got the distinct impression that Duncan would be pleased if he stayed. *One less irritation.* He'd originally planned on staying a week, maybe two. He'd used the excuse that he'd pay a visit to their US subsidiary, Raice Corp., headquartered in New Brunswick, New Jersey, when he'd actually come for Aiden's Metropolitan Opera debut. He supposed he'd need to make an appearance at Raice's offices before he headed home. Not that he was in a hurry to return to England—Duncan was more than capable of running Sherrington Holdings. Best damn decision his father had ever made, to appoint Duncan CEO of the company should anything happen to him. And there was no better time to be in New York City than late September. The days were warm and the evenings cool and breezy. Cam had been for a run in Central Park that morning, and the trees were a riot of color. Perfect.

"Possibly," he answered at last. "Next board meeting isn't until October. Unless you think you might need me to—"

"We have things under control here. Take your time."

"Thank you. I will." Fine. If that was how Duncan felt, he'd stay. Duncan clearly didn't need him. He tried to brush off the deepening insecurity. What did it matter if Duncan or anyone else at Sherrington Holdings didn't need him? He liked the idea of staying in New York a few more weeks. Maybe by the time he got back to London, his mother would have fled to warmer climes and he'd spend a peaceful few weeks at his family's estate in Surrey before the board meeting. Time spent with Lady Vanessa Baines Sherrington anywhere, especially at the estate, which his ex, Aiden, had affectionately referred to as "the castle," was downright grueling.

Cam heard the sound of rustling paper through the phone and a woman's voice in the background.

"Good. We'll speak later, then," Duncan said curtly.

Duncan disconnected the call before Cam could respond.

Happy bloody birthday to me. Had he really thought Duncan would remember? *Fuck him.* When had his life become a fucking cliché? *Poor little rich boy—no one remembers his birthday.* No doubt his mother would forget as well. She usually did. He'd enjoy himself more without a lecture about what he should be doing with his life, anyhow. Maybe turning thirty wouldn't be so bad. He would rather have celebrated with Aiden, of course, but he'd spend the evening at an impromptu party at a friend's instead, and he hoped he wouldn't be going home alone. Aiden would be spending time with Sam. *As it should be.* After cheating on Aiden—on several occasions—Cam couldn't expect Aiden to stick around, could he?

A quick glance at his watch told him he had time to take the subway to the restaurant. He loved the subway. He'd ridden it for the first time when he'd visited New York City with his mother twenty years ago, on a school holiday. Not that his mother had known about it. He'd managed to escape his mother's grasp (which wasn't all that tight since she preferred to spend as little time with him as possible) and he'd slipped under a turnstile and ridden the Lexington Avenue subway for hours by himself. Before then, he'd ridden the London Tube with his father a few times. His father had preferred it to negotiating London traffic when he stayed in the city. He'd enjoyed that, but riding alone had been far more exciting.

As it always was this time of day, the 42nd Street subway station was filled with people headed in a dozen different directions. Cam had always thought of this station as the heart of New York. The first time he'd come here, he'd gotten lost in one of the underground passages and ended up on a train to Brooklyn. Since then, he'd learned his way around the twisting tunnels so well he could navigate them in his sleep.

He headed for the Uptown platform, mixing in with the stream of people coming from Grand Central and managing not to get jostled. The woman ahead of him wasn't as fortunate. She pivoted to avoid a couple of schoolchildren and fell, dropping her shopping bags on the dirty concrete floor right in front of him.

Cam didn't have time for this. He looked around, hoping someone would come to her aid. No one did. *Bloody hell.* "Are you all right?" He offered the woman his hand.

She smiled at him with blue eyes and a face full of wrinkles, took his hand, and got to her feet. "Thank you," she said with a self-deprecating laugh. Cam helped her straighten her coat, which was open and had fallen off one shoulder. "I'm not much of a ballerina."

"Not a problem." He gathered up a few stray grocery items that had fallen out of the bag when she'd taken her tumble, waited until she dusted herself off, and handed the bags back to her. "It's a bit like entering a race course," he said as he reciprocated her smile.

"You're English, aren't you?" she asked.

"Indeed, I am." He glanced at his watch. He'd be late for lunch at this rate.

"I visited London a few years ago with my husband." Her expression grew wistful. "Before he died. We always said we'd make the trip."

Cam stifled his rising impatience with the woman. "Did you enjoy it?"

"Very much so. We saw the changing of the guard at Buckingham Palace and spent a few afternoons at the British Museum. We took a train to—" She stopped herself. "I do babble on sometimes."

He offered her a false smile. "It's quite all right."

"Thank you, young man," she said. "My son says I should take the bus, but I like the subway. There's music too."

"Music?"

She nodded. "Listen." She inhaled, pressed her lips together, and began to hum "Ain't No Sunshine." For the first time, Cam heard the sound of a trumpet through the noise of the passengers and squealing brakes of an incoming train. He vaguely remembered seeing someone playing for loose change not far from the passage to the S train.

"Oh, but I shouldn't keep you," the woman was saying as Cam came back to himself. "I'm sure you have somewhere you need to be." She patted him on the arm. "You've been very kind to an old woman."

"It was my pleasure." He wanted to make his escape. He'd wasted enough time with the woman, but she'd piqued his curiosity. Instead of rushing to catch his train, he walked over to where the musician was playing and stopped to listen.

CHAPTER

AROUND NOON, Galen Rusk finally found a parking spot after circling for nearly twenty minutes. He didn't mind—he was used to parking in New York on a weekday. On the weekend, he'd have taken the train into the city, but on Fridays the commuter lot near his house required permits, so it made more sense to drive.

He reached into the backseat of his beloved 1991 Honda Civic and pulled out his trumpet. Some of the music he'd stacked next to the case had shifted as he drove, so he straightened the piles, making sure none of the edges were bent. He'd considered buying some sort of file for the car, but each time he went to the office supply store, he seemed to forget he needed it. A stray bit of fur caught his eye, white against the black interior. He plucked the offending fuzz from the pristine vinyl with thumb and forefinger and flicked it into the street. He'd need to vacuum the interior again; Max's hair had migrated from the front seat.

No. Let it go. He remembered years ago how his therapist had told him that it was okay to let things go sometimes. Ignore a bit of dust here; leave something a bit askew there. He still struggled, though.

He sighed and zipped his leather jacket before picking his trumpet up. Until a few days before, the weather had been mild. Now he felt autumn in the air. He'd need to rake leaves over the weekend. The thought made him smile—he loved this time of year and took great pleasure in perfecting the appearance of his front yard. Tomorrow morning he'd get outside and do his fall trimming of the bushes and trees around his house.

He walked to the 42nd Street subway station, reaching it a half an hour later. He waved at the attendant in the ticket booth. He and Tyra often chatted when she finished her shift. Sometimes she'd even bring him tea when it got cold.

He reached into his pocket and pulled out a battered MetroCard, swiped it to open the turnstile, and walked through. After taking a moment first to watch the blur of activity as riders climbed steps and headed down the various tunnels that snaked around Grand Central Station, he walked to the alcove just short of the entrance to the S train. This time of day, he preferred to play here. Even though the area was cleaner and the acoustics better near the ticket booth, he liked to people-watch. Later, when the evening commute died down and the weekend took hold of the city, he'd move to his favorite spot by the turnstiles.

He inspected the concrete at length. He'd worked hard to keep his favorite areas clean, and was annoyed when someone carelessly littered. He picked up a bubblegum wrapper, a cigar band, and a used napkin and placed them in a nearby trash can. He set his trumpet case down on the concrete, shrugged off his jacket, then opened the case and pulled out his instrument. The metal felt cold against his fingers, so he pressed the keys to warm them, cycling through each in a rhythm reminiscent of someone drumming fingers over a desk. Over and again, he moved his fingers until they too warmed. Only then did he pull the silver mouthpiece out of the case and insert it into the end of the instrument. He played scales and arpeggios at first, then variations on those until his lips vibrated of their own accord.

As always, these preparatory gestures caused his body to tense. Whether from the memory of years past or from the excitement of playing in public, he never knew. He'd long ago realized it didn't matter why he felt nervous. The only thing that mattered was awareness of his fear. He'd been living with it for years. It was a part of him. A part of him that he'd mastered with determined effort, his tranquility hard earned.

Breathe. Relax.

He had no particular plan, no order of pieces in mind. He played what his heart told him to, and he allowed his emotions to guide him. Today he felt the mellow, slightly melancholic calm that seemed to accompany the changing of the seasons. Something soft and sensual. "Night and Day" by Cole Porter. One of his favorites. The trumpet became the voice—his voice—singing the words. *Night and day, you are the one.... Only you beneath the moon and under the sun....*

A bevy of high school girls walked by, giggling and whispering to each other as they passed. He caught the word "cute" before they vanished down the stairs. He'd gotten used to that over the years he'd been teaching. Students of both sexes flirted with him from time to time, despite the fact that he never denied he was anything but gay. He watched them as he watched most people: from a distance. It was safer for him. He'd learned that the hard way. He mentally pushed the disturbing memories away and remastered his focus.

At the entrance to the area where he played, a man entered and glanced at his watch. Light brown hair fell in soft curls around his face. Full pink lips and pale skin. Well-dressed in clothes that fit his lean, almost feminine body as though they'd been custom-made for it. Galen had noticed him before. He might not be interested in relationships, but he couldn't deny he wanted this man. Galen had seen many men who tried to appear as though their looks were casual and natural and failed miserably. This man was gorgeous.

Galen tried to remember the last time he'd spent the night with someone. Had it been more than a year? It had been far longer since he'd been in a relationship. Again, he pushed away the memories and focused on the music. *Let it go.* He took a slow breath, imagined his body relaxing, and the tension abated. He'd become quite good at that. His life was good now. Simple and worth living.

He began to play the next piece. *"Ain't no sunshine when she's gone… and she's always gone too long any time she goes away."*

The man crossed in front of him and walked toward the S train. A couple of kids ran down the tunnel, laughing and chasing each other. He wondered vaguely what it might be like to grow up in the city. He remembered the first time he'd come here as a kid and how overwhelming it had been. The kids ducked in and around people, nearly bumping into a couple of tourists with their heads buried in subway maps. Hands full of shopping bags, an elderly woman turned to avoid the kids. She must have overcompensated, because she fell onto the concrete and the contents of the bags spilled onto the ground.

People continued to pass by and ignore her. He was just about to set his trumpet aside and help when he saw the man—the one he'd been watching before—walk up to her and offer his hand. Galen had assumed the man would keep walking. Instead, he began to gather her items from the concrete floor. The woman blushed charmingly, and they spoke for a few minutes. At one point the man turned toward him as if noticing the music for the first time. Galen watched intently as they exchanged a few more words before the woman hurried off down the tunnel. The man waited until she disappeared from sight, looked over at Galen once more, paused as if considering something, then strode over.

Galen began to play the next piece. *"No one to walk with 'cause I'm happy by myself, ain't misbehavin', I'm saving my love for you…."* The man stopped directly in front of him, canted his head almost imperceptibly, and smiled in recognition of the song. Blue eyes. Galen had noticed them before but hadn't seen them up close and personal. He could get lost in those eyes. Galen's musical training had taught him always to acknowledge his audience when playing close to them, but he worried if he nodded at the man, his attraction would be painfully obvious. Instead he continued to play, focusing even more intently on the way the music echoed around the space. He changed his tone to match the bright acoustics.

The piece ended and Galen did something he'd never done before: he spoke to his audience of one. "I take requests," he said, knowing he sounded like he was flirting. He was, wasn't he?

The man appeared to consider the question before he asked with a charming English accent, "Do you play classical?"

A challenge. One Galen would gladly accept. He nodded and began to play the Rachmaninoff *Vocalise*, a piece originally written as a song without words but transcribed for just about every instrument. Challenging to play, more so for the breath control required than for its technical fireworks. These days Galen had less time to practice, and he had to sneak a few added breaks in the inordinately long melodic line, but the effect still pleased him.

As the piece ended, Galen met the man's gaze. He imagined he could see beyond the alluring blue of those eyes to the soul beneath. He saw understanding there, an acknowledgment of the beauty of the music and of its ephemeral nature. In that instant the din of the subway faded and the music continued to exist on the air for a fleeting moment beyond the playing. Mesmerized by the connection between himself and the stranger, Galen lost track of time.

The sound of a train returned with a roar, snapping Galen out of his brief meditation. Brakes screeched, people spoke, and a crackling, unintelligible announcement over the PA system drowned out the moment. The man with the blue eyes blinked as if he too had felt time stop. He glanced at his watch, dug his wallet from his pocket, and dropped a bill into the trumpet case. He'd made it halfway to the stairs leading to the Lexington Avenue train before Galen managed a soft "Thank you."

Galen took a deep, calming breath and began to play again. *"Moon river, wider than a mile, I'm crossing you in style someday...."*

CHAPTER 3

CAM CLIMBED the stairs of the Spring Street station. The wind had picked up, causing one of his curls to tumble onto his forehead. He sighed as he pushed the hair from his eyes and cursed his mother for her genes. They were too much alike, and not just in appearance. They were both wanderers. Always seeking excitement. Prone to infidelity. But whereas she seemed to revel in her freedom, he'd always sought partners. Not that he'd had any success in keeping them.

He thought of the trumpet player in the subway station. For a moment he'd felt something. He played well. Surprisingly well, really. Had it been more than that? Something beyond the music?

Of course it was more than that. He was attractive. Cam laughed and shook his head to himself. What did it matter? There were plenty of men in New York, and the last thing he needed was a downtrodden fuck.

CAM ARRIVED at the restaurant fifteen minutes late. The place was tiny and the tables so close to each other that Cam had to squeeze between several chairs to make his way to where David Somers and his partner, Alex Bishop, sat. Along the way, a woman at a nearby table stood as Cam was squeezing by, and Cam brushed against a waiter and nearly caused him to spill a tray of food.

"Beer," Cam told their waiter after he'd greeted David and Alex. "Tiger or Halida."

"I'm sorry, sir," the waiter said, "we don't carry those. Would a Saigon be okay?"

"Fine." Cam waived the waiter away and stifled his irritation. What self-respecting Vietnamese restaurant wouldn't carry a decent selection of Vietnamese beer? In New York City, no less?

"So good to see you," David said after the waiter had left. "And happy birthday."

"Happy birthday, Cam," Alex added brightly. "Glad you could join us."

"Thank you." Cam was pleased they had remembered.

They chitchatted about easy topics, catching up on David and Alex's performing schedule—David had three more performances of *Don Giovanni* to conduct, and Alex would be performing the Berg Violin Concerto in Philadelphia over the weekend—and Cam's plans for remaining in New York for a while longer as they ate. Comfortable conversation that had Cam relaxing for the first time that day—until, much to Cam's chagrin, David brought up the topic of Aiden.

"I don't understand why you didn't tell him you were at the opening night performance." David frowned and refilled his glass with more Perrier. "Aiden would have been pleased to know you were there."

At Cam's insistence, David had agreed not to tell Aiden that he'd flown in for and attended Aiden's Metropolitan Opera debut. Cam had hoped to surprise Aiden, but when Aiden hadn't turned up at the opening night party, he'd decided Aiden didn't need to know he'd been there at all. He'd hoped his last conversation about it with David would be the last. Clearly that had been too optimistic. He stifled his irritation and took a long drink of his beer.

Out of the corner of his eye, Cam saw Alex force a smile. No doubt *he* understood why Cam avoided Aiden, even if David didn't. David probably understood Cam's discomfort at seeing Aiden, but he doubted David would ever avoid an ex the way he did. David always seemed so sure of himself.

Cam motioned for the waiter to bring him another drink. "Far be it from me to rain on Aiden's parade," he said as he scooped a noodle from his bowl of pho and contemplated it thoughtfully. "I'm just pleased it was a success. It was good to hear him sing again. It's been a while." Total and utter bollocks.

Perhaps hoping to ease Cam's discomfort, Alex reached into the leather jacket he'd hung on the back of his chair and pulled out a small package. "Happy birthday, Cam," he said. "This is a little something from both of us."

Cam took the package, unwrapped it, and opened the box to find a stunning sterling silver fountain pen. Antique, with raised scrollwork on the barrel and cap. Quite old. "Thank you both. It's lovely." Outrageously expensive, but David could afford it. It wasn't the price tag that impressed Cam, though— David always seemed to take so much care when choosing gifts.

Cam had been nine years old when his father died and left him a small collection of pens. Over the years, he'd added more as he'd traveled. He hadn't bought many recently. He'd spent the last bit of his inheritance on his New York penthouse, several classic cars housed at his family's estate, and financing three stage productions that died slow and ugly deaths off off-Broadway. And although the monthly allowance from his trust fund covered his expenses comfortably, he had little left over for "frivolous" purchases such as pens.

David smiled. "Alex spotted it at our favorite antique market near the villa. We both thought of you."

"It's beautiful. Truly." Cam lifted his half-empty glass in an effort to avoid David's gaze. At least Alex hadn't tried to hug him again. Cam had never been one for public displays of affection, even the strictly friends variety.

"You're welcome." Alex exchanged a quick glance with David, whose expression softened with obvious pleasure.

This sort of interchange always left Cam feeling uncomfortable. Alex and David were so obviously head over heels in love that Cam wondered if falling in love was bound to reduce even the most stalwart of men to sniveling fools. He hadn't been like that with Aiden.

Of course not.

"So how long are you in New York?" Cam asked.

"I leave tomorrow," Alex said. "David leaves next weekend. We'll spend Sunday and Monday in Chicago, and then I'm off to Italy for a week."

"I don't know how you do it." Cam took a sip of water and leaned back in his chair.

David smiled. "The travel's easy. As for being apart... we schedule time together when neither of us is working."

At one time Cam had imagined he might travel with Aiden. Now, if anyone traveled with Aiden, it would be Sam. Cam pushed the thought from his mind. Of course he resented Sam. What sort of idiot wouldn't? Still, he'd have preferred if David hadn't brought Aiden up. It was easier not to think about things.

"I should be going," Cam lied. "Thank you both for the beautiful pen. And thank you for lunch."

"It was our pleasure," David said as he shook Cam's hand.

Alex embraced Cam warmly. Cam patted Alex's back in a pathetic attempt to return the gesture, not wanting to offend him.

"We'd love to have you join us for Thanksgiving at the villa if you happen to find yourself in Italy in November," David said.

"I'll let you know." Cam wouldn't take David up on it. He'd never been one for holidays, especially holidays he hadn't grown up with, and he knew Aiden often attended David's celebrations. An evening watching Aiden and Sam gazing at each other the way David and Alex did would be pure torture.

He left David and Alex with a curt wave, and hurried off. In truth he had nowhere to go, although since he wasn't too far from Barney's New York, he figured he might stop and pick something up for his mother. A necessary evil should he run into her when he returned to London. Gifts went a long way toward placating her, and that, in turn, was usually effective at keeping her out of his hair if they had to share the estate.

CHAPTER

CAM ARRIVED at Riley Weston's Park Avenue apartment a little after ten that night. After leaving David and Alex, he'd spent an hour and a half at the gym, then a blissful few hours getting a massage and a manicure at the apartment. He'd chosen his clothing with care: a new Calvin Klein ultra slim-fit suit in a warm shade of gray wool, with a gray shirt and gray tie to match. The suit had set him back a pretty penny, but as he'd checked himself out in the three-way mirror in his bedroom, he'd smiled with satisfaction. He'd slipped in the single diamond stud he liked to wear for special occasions, then worked his fingers through his loose curls until he was satisfied before he headed out to the impromptu birthday party Riley decided to throw him.

Riley greeted him at the door with kisses on both cheeks. Early thirties, with red hair that was just one shade past natural, she smiled at him with glossed lips that reflected the light of the modern chandelier in the front hallway. "Cameron. Happy birthday, old man!"

He'd forgive her for that, although he guessed it pleased her that she wasn't the only one over thirty anymore. He didn't mind giving her the satisfaction. "You look lovely, Ri." He gestured to her outfit, a fitted trouser suit that hugged her perfect body in all the right places. At her ears, wrists, fingers, and neck, she sparkled with diamonds. Hardly a surprise, since her father owned a national chain of jewelry stores. Not that those stores, most of them located in the shopping malls he guessed Riley would never deign to enter, would carry the quality of stones *she* wore.

They'd met nearly ten years ago at one of his mother's lavish parties at the castle. He'd been home from university; she'd been traveling and bored with sightseeing in London.

"Do you think they'd notice if we disappeared?" she'd asked after they'd spent an hour walking the gardens and visiting the stables.

"Unlikely." He smiled and pulled a set of keys from his pocket and dangled them in front of her face. "How about a little dancing?"

He'd shown her a London she hadn't known existed, including a few clubs he normally wouldn't be caught dead in but where he knew they'd be able to score some poppers along with their overpriced drinks. She'd been openmouthed when they walked into the first club and were greeted by a sea of men in bikinis and thongs. He ran a hand over a particularly sculpted arse and she giggled. "Beach party," he said. "Nothing quite like a man with a tight arse in a tight—"

"You're gay?" She stared at him in surprise.

He just laughed.

"If only straight men had this much fun," she told him as she took his arm and pouted.

Later, he realized spending time with him was her way of getting back at her overprotective parents. He'd called her his little "fruit fly," and she loved him for it. Years later, he still got in touch whenever he came to New York, and they sometimes traveled together when she was in Europe.

"Whiskey?" she asked as she led him into the living room, which was filled wall to wall with people. He'd seen most of them at her parties before, but there were also a few particularly good-looking men he knew she'd invited just for him. "I bought some Knappogue Castle for your birthday."

"Of course." He offered her a charming smile. Several minutes later, a triple shot of whiskey in his glass—it *was* his birthday, after all—he sized up the room and began to make small talk with some of the guests.

As he worked his way across the room toward the large glass doors that led out onto the patio, he glimpsed a very fine-looking man in a very fine-fitting pair of jeans gazing out at the Manhattan skyline. "Nice view," he said as he joined the man a moment later.

The man turned and his eyes widened almost imperceptibly. "Definitely," he answered. He wasn't looking out the window anymore.

Cam felt the familiar flutter in his chest at the knowledge that someone appreciated him, found him attractive and worthy of attention. He couldn't remember when he'd first felt it, but even when things weren't going as well as they were today, it always made him feel special. He deserved it and he needed the approval. He wasn't sure why, but he'd felt a deep-seated need for approval for as long as he could remember. "Cam Sherrington," he said, extending his hand to the man.

"Lawrence Masters."

"Good to meet you, Lawrence." Cam grasped Lawrence's hand. *Good grip.* He smiled at the thought.

"Call me Larry. Please."

"Larry." Cam released Larry's hand and took a sip of his whiskey.

"You're not from here, are you?" Larry asked with a hint of a smile that made it clear he meant the question only half-seriously.

"London."

"Are you an actor?"

"Hardly." Cam chuckled. "Are you?"

"I am."

Cam wasn't the least bit surprised. Riley dabbled in theater, as Cam had until his money had run out. "How lovely." *How boring. Hot body, though.*

"I've got a callback tomorrow for an off-Broadway production. Avant-garde sort of thing. *As You Like It* in modern dress, minimalist sets."

Done a thousand times and about as avant-garde as a 1960s musical with a huge chorus line finale. "Congratulations." Cam didn't give a shit. Maybe they could get the conversation part of the lead-up to fucking done quickly and get the hell out of there.

"What do you do for a living, Cam?"

Damn good question. Cam debated how to respond. British lord who'd spent his inheritance but can't touch the assets of his family's corporation? Sometime impresario who'd financed several productions, all of which were critical failures? Playboy—as much as he hated the term, it was fitting given his penchant for fast cars and faster men.

"I run a company in London," he said, deciding it was simpler than any of the other explanations. Not entirely true, since he wasn't the CEO of his family's business, but close enough for a one-nighter.

"Really?"

This seemed the right answer, since Larry's ears pricked up noticeably. The conversation didn't improve much over the next ten minutes, although his third drink helped his mind wander to what he hoped would be a more interesting entertainment back at his apartment.

He hadn't counted on receiving a call. Flustered and working to hide his discomfort, he excused himself quickly. "I'm sorry. I need to take this," he said to Larry. Without warning, Larry leaned in and worked his way over Cam's neck with a very talented tongue.

"Answer it later," Lawrence whispered before he returned to sucking on Cam's earlobe.

Cam was tempted to do just that. He was already hard. Wanting that pert little arse. But he recognized the number on the display, and he pushed Lawrence away a bit more forcefully than he meant to. "I need to take this," he repeated. Really. What part of that hadn't the man understood?

Lawrence huffed and left the balcony with that wrinkled-up nose that made him look as though he'd smelled something disgusting. *Fuck him.*

"Hello?"

"Happy birthday, Cam," Aiden said in his resonant baritone.

"Thank you." Hearing the longing in his own voice reminded Cam how much he missed Aiden. Not that he needed a reminder. The performance at the Met had brought that one home with acute force.

"How are you?" Aiden asked politely.

Loaded question. If he answered honestly, he'd sound like a maudlin, heartbroken sod. Which he was, but he'd never let on that if Aiden wanted him back, Cam would be on his knees at Aiden's doorstep in a heartbeat. His selfish heart twisted in his chest. "I'm well" was all he could manage in the end. "And you?" Cam wondered vaguely how two people who'd been as close as they had been could have such an awkward conversation.

"I'm great. Everything's great."

Not what Cam wanted to hear. "Congratulations on the *New York Times* review," he said quickly, not wanting to dwell on how wonderful Aiden's personal life might be.

"Thank you." Cam could almost imagine the blush on Aiden's cheeks. He was always so charming that way—understated and humble. Cam envied that.

"Listen, Cam," Aiden said after a prolonged pause. "I need to tell you something. I don't want you to hear it from the press...."

In Cam's experience, it was never a good thing when someone said they wanted to tell you something, then hesitated.

"Sam asked me to marry him, and I said yes."

Cam almost swallowed his tongue as anger and jealousy shot through his veins. "Congratulations. Listen, I need to go. I'm surrounded by people looking expectantly at me. It was terrific speaking with you, Aiden. Congratulations again."

He downed his scotch, deposited his empty glass on a nearby table, and left the party without so much as a wave to Larry. When Riley offered to call him a taxi, he refused. He'd walk. He needed to clear his mind, although he knew the effort would be futile.

CAM CURSED his love for Aiden as he wobbled down the concrete steps to the 42nd Street subway station. Riley had looked at him as if he were mad when he'd told her he was headed home. "Did I do something wrong?" she asked with the same pouty expression she wore on the rare occasion when her father refused to buy her something.

"Nothing," he said as he'd reached for the doorknob. "I'm done. That's all."

"At least let me call my driver to take—"

He'd refused. Seriously, did she think he wasn't *capable* of taking a fucking subway after a few drinks at a party? It wasn't even midnight.

He rubbed an eye with the heel of his hand. The damn telephone conversation replayed in his mind and grated on his nerves like Muzak at a cheap restaurant. He'd tried not to sound eager. Tried to sound nonchalant. He'd gotten good at that over the years. And then the brutal words had come. They'd seared his heart and left him dizzy. *"Listen, Cam.... I need to tell you something. I don't want you to hear it from the press.... Sam asked me to marry him, and I said yes."*

He needed to walk. He needed to clear his head. He needed to shout to the heavens and hit something.

Why in hell had he bothered to look at the phone? Easy: he'd prayed it was Aiden calling to tell him he wanted him back.

You're a fucking loser, Cameron! Nobody wants you!

A memory stirred. Someone holding him. Ruffling his hair. Someone other than his father. Someone had wanted him. Cared for him.

Where the hell had *that* come from? He brushed it off and descended the steps to the Lexington Avenue train.

It was bad enough that Aiden thought he'd tried to sabotage his career. He did everything to make sure Aiden didn't think he wasn't interested anymore. He'd gone to the after-party following Aiden's Met debut—of *course* he'd gone, his company had helped bankroll the production of *Don Giovanni*—and Aiden had been MIA. So he'd decided Aiden didn't need to know he'd been there at all.

And then the phone call. Aiden hadn't beaten around the proverbial bush. He'd said it. Honestly. Simply. Just the way Cam would have expected Aiden to say it. And suddenly Cam didn't care if he fucked that hot little Broadway-bound arse. He no longer cared about the party or its hallowed attendees. He no longer cared about anything except the gaping, jagged hole the conversation had left in his heart. And now, fucking New York pigeons were setting up camp in the hole. Shitting in it.

He walked from the Lexington Avenue train to the S train platform. The achingly mournful sound of a trumpet echoed off the dirty tile walls. He hadn't really noticed them before. The intricate mosaic artwork had probably taken weeks to complete. Decades before, it had probably been stunning, but now it was covered in a film of grayish-black soot and some of the tiles were missing.

How fitting. He looked around for the source of the music, noting the powerful smell of urine. Away from the turnstiles, a mound of blankets and a refuse-filled shopping cart occupied the far corner of the station. He guessed there was a human being under there, although he was hardly going to look. Beyond the automatic ticketing machines, he could just make out the form of a man holding a trumpet. The same man he'd seen playing at lunch. Maybe he lived in the subway. Cam had heard stories of actors and musicians unable to get work in New York living on the street.

"Ain't no sunshine when she's gone...."

Cam walked across the empty space between the train platforms, his feet making soft tapping sounds against the concrete. He paused for a moment to watch the trumpet player standing with his back to the wall. He stared into whatever space musicians liked to stare into—that ethereal place they went when they were so focused on the music that the world around them disappeared. A dusty blond curl fell from the shaggy mop of hair onto the trumpeter's face as he finished another phrase. *"...and she's always gone too long any time she goes away."*

Cam drew a long breath. It was perfect. The angst of it all. The music. The echo of his steps. The blast of cool air as he neared the train tunnels. *Fucking perfect.*

The musician noticed him standing there. The man's eyes were a beautiful hazel, almost green. Why hadn't he noticed before?

What do you care? The man's an unemployed musician.

The guy looked at him and his eyes widened almost imperceptibly, as they had the last time Cam had seen him. Did he recognize Cam? God knew there were enough articles written about him. *Esquire, Elle, Cigars Magazine*, blah, blah, blah. *Glamour*'s "Most Eligible Bachelor" from 2008. *As if!*

The trumpet player finished the song, then stopped for a moment and rested the trumpet against his hip. His lips were swollen and pink from playing. For a split second, Cam imagined tasting them. Then he noticed the torn jeans and white T-shirt with a faded Señor Frog's logo and the words "I got wasted in Cancun" written below it.

Oh, for God's sake, Cameron! He's a loser with a capital L!

Well, that made two of them, didn't it? Even if the guy could play pretty damn well—*very* well, judging by the little Cam had heard—they were both in a stinking, empty subway station on a Friday night at midnight. *Poor sod.*

"Another request?" A smile danced on the man's kissable lips.

Cam shrugged. "Whatever you want to play," he said, not caring how pathetic he sounded.

The trumpeter put his instrument to his lips and began. *"Blue moon, you saw me standing alone, without a dream in my heart...."*

Normally he'd have listened for a moment, left a few dollars, and headed home. But something about the man and the music held him entranced. He felt an odd, otherworldly connection. Was it the morbid, surreal feel to the evening, an evening he'd known would eventually come even though he'd tried to convince himself a thousand times over he wouldn't care when it did? Or was it the momentary feeling that he'd connected with someone, as pathetic as he was? He thought of Aiden and how he'd barely had enough for his next meal when they'd met at a party in London.

"New in town?" he'd asked as he'd taken his full measure of Aiden.

"That obvious?" Aiden's southern twang had been more pronounced back then. Cam remembered thinking how he'd like to wake up to that resonant voice every morning. And when, only a month later, he'd asked Aiden to share his London flat, he'd felt good to know that Aiden wanted him. He'd felt that flutter in his belly. He'd felt wanted. It had felt so fucking *good*.

The song ended. Cam hesitated a moment longer, then reached into his jacket and pulled out his billfold. He'd just used his last twenty for the fare card. He slipped the only remaining bill—a hundred—out of his wallet and walked to the open trumpet case. A few singles, some quarters, and several pennies lay strewn over the faded purple velvet of the interior. He dropped the bill on top, then walked to the turnstiles, slid his fare card through the slot, and entered as the machine beeped. He didn't need to see the musician's reaction to know a hundred was more money than he'd ever seen. He knew the type. Too lazy to bother working a regular job, maybe even addicted. Why else would someone with obvious talent be in a place like this? Surely there was work to be had in an orchestra or even playing the Manhattan Sunday brunch scene.

The last thing he heard when he walked onto the Uptown No. 3 train was the opening phrase of "Stairway to Heaven."

Happy fucking birthday to me.

CHAPTER 5

CAM AWOKE well past noon the next day with a pounding headache and the vague recollection of a dream. Maybe a nightmare—he only remembered the feeling of dread that lingered. Divine retribution for not having drunk more at the party the night before. Not that he wouldn't have had the headache if he'd stayed longer, but at least he'd have enjoyed the party and gotten a little something afterward. Or forgotten, however temporarily, that the man he thought he'd spend his life with was going to spend the rest of his life with someone else.

Fuck. He sat up, rubbed his eyes, and tried not to hear Aiden's voice reverberate in his mind. *"Sam asked me to marry him, and I said yes."* Who could blame Aiden? Sam Ryan wasn't the most fascinating man on the planet, but he obviously loved Aiden and treated him well. And although Cam couldn't fathom why Sam had given up an appointment as a federal judge to travel with Aiden, that fact seemed to be important to Aiden.

He doesn't cheat on Aiden, either, the voice in his head taunted.

Cam fell back onto his pillow and closed his eyes. What the fuck was with the voice in his brain that insisted on reminding him of something he'd tried so hard to forget? His mother had once told him he had no conscience. She was wrong. He not only had a conscience, at that moment he wanted to choke it.

Even now he couldn't explain why he'd done it. Cheated. He hadn't had any serious relationships other than with Aiden. With Aiden he was comfortable. Warm. Happy. The sex had been great. The company even better. But when Jarrod Jameson had shown up at one of Cam's parties at the castle, he'd ended up fucking that pert little swimmer's arse in one of the guest bedrooms while Aiden entertained their friends. Worse, after the party, when Cam had gone back to the room he and Aiden shared, he'd had sex with Aiden.

At first Aiden hadn't suspected anything. Cam told himself he wouldn't do it again, so it didn't matter. But he did it again. And again, and again. Until Aiden caught him in a lie. So he'd begged and pleaded with Aiden not to leave him. He'd promised Aiden he was done with cheating. He'd meant it too. Until Jarrod had flown back into town and Cam had suggested—against his better judgment—that Jarrod come to the party he was holding to celebrate Aiden's Covent Garden debut.

What the fuck were you thinking?

Cam had seen the stricken look on Aiden's face when he'd walked in on Cam fucking Jarrod. Cam had seen it and known that he'd lost Aiden forever, even if he hadn't admitted it to himself for months afterward. The strangest thing of all was that Cam felt *relieved* that Aiden had literally caught him with his pants down. Because he'd known all along that Aiden was too good for him. Too kind and too trusting. Too loving. And if Cam had needed any more proof that Aiden really *was* too good for him, he needed look no further than the threats he'd made when Aiden had left him. That he'd make Aiden pay. That Aiden was nothing without his help and his money. But Aiden had succeeded without him. Cam had known he would.

God, you're disgusting. Stop feeling sorry for yourself!

He dragged himself out of bed. He really should go home to England. What good was it to spend time in New York when David and Alex were leaving and Aiden had Sam? Cam supposed he could call Veronica Landau and see if she'd like to go to the symphony fundraiser on Friday. Or perhaps he could convince Randy Knowles to go in for a friendly game of racquetball at the club. But none of these things, none of these people, interested him in the slightest. In the end, he decided on his old standby, Riley. She knew how to cheer someone up, and she was usually up for last-minute plans.

He picked up his mobile from the bedside table and tapped it a few times. "Riley?" he said as he wandered over to the window and gazed out at the city.

"Cam, sweetness! How's the birthday boy?"

"It's not my birthday today."

"You left the party so quickly," she said, ignoring his comment. "Something come up?"

Nothing he would tell her. "I was just tired," he lied.

"Really?"

"Of course." He took a breath and fought the urge to tell her he was sick. The idea of going out wasn't as enticing as it had been a few minutes before. No. He needed to do something or he'd go mad. "Care to join me at the museum for tea?" he asked, knowing she fancied herself an Anglophile and wouldn't turn him down. He'd overheard her telling a friend that she often took tea with royalty. She used him, but he didn't care.

"I'd love to." Her tone brightened noticeably.

Ten minutes later, he headed out of the apartment for the Metropolitan Museum of Art. He stopped at the nearest cash machine to withdraw some money. He inserted his card, punched in his security code, then waited. The screen flashed blue. *We're sorry, we are unable to process this transaction. Please contact your banking institution for more information.*

He swore under his breath and reinserted the card. The same error message appeared again.

Bloody American banks!

He shoved the card back into his billfold, then slipped his credit card into the ATM and typed in his PIN. Again, the same message on the screen.

Fucking machine.

Five minutes later, he was reading the same message at another machine two blocks over. Much to the chagrin of the people waiting behind him, he tried all of his credit cards this time, including one he used strictly for business—fuck the people tapping their feet behind him—and each time, the machine rejected them.

"Bloody hell," he growled as he walked out of the bank back onto the street. He pulled out his mobile and dialed the number for the credit card company on the back of one of his cards. "We're sorry," the recorded voice on the phone said, "all our representatives are assisting other customers. Please stay on the line and a customer service representative will be with you in approximately five minutes."

Ten minutes later he finally spoke to an employee. "I'm sorry, Mr. Cameron," the woman on the phone said in an oh-so-pleasant-but-there's-no-fucking-way-we-can-help-you voice. "There's been a hold placed on your account."

"It's Sherrington. *Lord* Sherrington." There were times when a title got things accomplished a bit faster.

"I'm so sorry, Lord Sherrington," the credit card company employee told him, "but there's been a hold placed on your account."

"A hold? Why a bloody hold?" he snapped, at his wits' end.

"I'm sorry, but we don't have that information, Mr. Sherrington," the woman said. "The hold originated with your bank. You may want to contact them and see if there's a problem. I don't have the authority to remove the hold."

Cam gritted his teeth and did his best not to shout into the receiver. The end result came out sounding a bit like a growl. He called his London bank. The bank employee who answered the phone said, "I'm sorry, Lord Sherrington, but it appears there's been a hold placed on your account. I don't have any more information about that. I'm afraid you'll need to speak to your personal banker during regular business hours."

As if that helped on a Saturday afternoon. Finally, unwilling to ask Riley to pay for his tea, he headed back to his apartment.

"CAMERON."

Conversations that began with his full name never went well. Cam pressed the ball of his foot against the barstool in the kitchen and fidgeted, causing the counter to vibrate with the movement. "Duncan, what's going on?" he demanded.

"Going on?"

"I tried to withdraw cash today," Cam explained. "I got an error message telling me there was a hold on the account. The bank confirmed this. Said the hold originated in England."

"I see."

Cam waited for an explanation, but when his uncle didn't immediately reply, his anger soared. "What the bloody hell is happening? Has the board decided to toss me out on my arse?" They'd be just the types to do it too. It had been bad enough being dragged in front of them—his own board of directors—and being told they were putting him on a budget.

"Things are a bit more complicated than that, I'm afraid."

"What the fuck is going on, Duncan?" Cam demanded, at the limits of his patience. He abhorred being beholden to the board—what the devil were they up to now?

"Well... it seems the authorities may have found something during the investigation."

"Something?" Cam's gut clenched. *Something to do with me?* There was no other reason to make his life difficult. "What kind of something are we talking about?"

Duncan waited just a second too long to respond. *Something bad.* But what the hell would it be?

"Duncan? Tell me what's happening."

Duncan let out a long, audible breath. "It seems there are a number of questionable transactions they're looking at. Sounds as though they think they've found something interesting."

"Revenue and customs?" Cam laughed. "I thought they'd moved on to bigger and better things." Sherrington Holdings was nothing more than a blip on the radar screen for the big-boy investigators. Surely nothing they'd done warranted anything.... Now Cam felt ill. *Stop this! It's nothing, and you know it.*

"Not HMRC. The Americans."

"The Americans? You mean they're interested in Raice Corp.?" That made a bit more sense. Cam had been the one to convince Sherrington's board to invest in the small green energy company five years before. Duncan had called the deal a "waste of time and money," but he hadn't blocked the stock acquisition either.

"I'm not aware of any other US company we own," Duncan snapped.

Cam ignored the disdain in Duncan's voice. Of course Duncan wouldn't be pleased that one of Cam's "little projects" was the focus of an investigation. "What are the American authorities looking for?"

"If I knew that, I'd have already told you." Duncan sounded tired. Irritated. How bad was this, really? "All I know is that they've issued Raice Corp. subpoenas to turn over banking information."

"Banking?" Not just the company's bank, though. If it were just the company, his personal accounts wouldn't be frozen. *They think I've done something.* "You mean *my* accounts?"

"Your accounts, the company's accounts. All of it."

Shit. Cam realized he was gripping the phone so tightly his fingers had turned white. *Deep breath. There's nothing that interesting in anyone's accounts. Worse comes to worst, we'll restructure my personal accounts to please the authorities and pay whatever back taxes they think we owe.*

"Sherrington's board is acting out of an abundance of caution. The FBI specifically asked about your connection to Raice. Given your history—"

"So the board froze my accounts without speaking to me first?" Cam shouted. "How *dare* they—"

"They have every right. You agreed to abide by their decisions with respect to your allowance."

Duncan was right, of course. Not that Cam had been given much choice in the matter—by the time the board had agreed to give him an allowance, he'd already spent through just about every penny he had. And even though Raice's accounts hadn't been frozen, it wasn't as though Cam could just dip into the company's funds to pay for his personal needs. Especially now that the FBI was poking around in the company's business.

Cam took a deep breath. Angering Duncan wouldn't help. The board would do what Duncan told them. "I need money, Duncan. At least enough to tide me over until this mess is cleared up." He fucking hated having to ask for money! It was *his* company, after all. His father's business, and now his. *And you can't touch a penny of it without the board's approval.*

"I'll see what I can do."

"You do that," Cam snapped.

The pause on the other end of the phone was longer this time. "You may want to speak to Jim Stanton," his uncle said at last.

"Jim? Why? I haven't done anything worth speaking to him about." He didn't need a lawyer.

"I'm only suggesting you speak with him." Duncan's condescending tone had insecurity inching its way up Cam's spine like a snake. He started tapping his foot again.

Something in Cam's brain shouted that this was bad. Really, really bad. "I'll call him. See what you can do about wiring me some money."

"I'll see what I can do." This was the second time Duncan had used that phrasing, and it didn't reassure Cam. But what choice did he have?

"I'll check back with you in an hour."

"Cameron." Again with the full name. *Getting worse at an alarming rate.* "It's nearly midnight here, and I need to get some sleep. I'll speak to you in the morning. With a bit of luck, you'll reach Jim and—"

"Fine." He didn't need a lecture. He needed action, and he bloody well needed it *now.*

He hung up and glared at the phone as if it might stick its tongue out at him, then shoved it back in his pocket. None of this was the least bit amusing. He wondered how long he could last here without money. He had an account at several grocery stores so Luisa could purchase food when he was in town. He doubted whatever hold had been placed on his money extended as far as those accounts. The company paid his rent and Luisa's salary. But could he even purchase a ticket to fly home to England if he had no credit cards?

He returned to the apartment and paced the living room as he gazed out the window. The sun hung low in the sky, barely visible between the high-rises to the west.

He pulled his phone out and scrolled through his contacts. Bailey, Barnes & Stanton would be closed on a Saturday evening. No mobile number. Worse yet, he'd have to wait until Monday to do anything about it.

He told himself Monday would be a better day and flicked on the telly.

CHAPTER

MONDAY MORNING arrived on the heels of a night spent tossing and turning. When Cam awoke, sweaty and shaking, at 4:00 a.m., he knew sleep wouldn't come again. "Jim? It's Cam. Cameron Sherrington." Cam paced the living room once more, this time in his pajama bottoms. He supposed he should get dressed before Luisa arrived, but he'd been too distracted to do anything but wait until the law offices of Bailey, Barnes & Stanton opened.

"Cam, I'm glad you called."

Now that was a first. Jim Stanton had always been cordial on the phone, but he'd never seemed overly thrilled to hear from Cam. "Duncan seemed to think I should speak with you. My accounts are frozen. I need money."

Cam heard the sound of shuffling papers through the receiver.

"That's something you'll have to discuss with Duncan. I received a call from the FBI. An Agent Peterson."

"FBI? I thought they were just interested in Raice's records." This was getting worse by the minute.

"I'm not sure." Jim sounded as uncomfortable as Cam had ever heard him. "But they want to serve a subpoena for your bank records."

"My *personal* records?"

"Yes. All your personal banking records for the past ten years." Jim paused, then asked, "What's this all about, Cam?"

Ten years? Cam ran a hand through his hair and shook his head. "I have no idea. Duncan mentioned subpoenas for Raice, but now…. Shit."

"What do you want me to do? I could move to quash the subpoena, but it's unlikely you'd win. Best we can hope for is to find out why they're poking around."

"What do you recommend?" He had to get this done with quickly so he could move on.

"Do you have anything to hide?"

Cam took a long breath in a futile effort to bite back the nasty words that threatened to fly off his tongue. "What the hell kind of question is that?"

"A question any good lawyer would ask his client," Jim replied, clearly unperturbed. "But I need an honest answer, Cam, or I can't do my job."

"I don't have anything to hide." Cam knew Jim was right, but he sure as hell didn't have to like it.

"Then I recommend you cooperate. Turn the records over."

"Do it." The sooner the better. Then he could move on, go home with his tail between his legs, and try to forget Aiden.

"I'll take care of it. If anything comes up, I'll be in touch."

Cam disconnected the call and tossed the phone onto the couch. *What the hell is going on?*

He shook his head and paced the living room a few times. Outside the floor-to-ceiling windows, it had begun to rain again. He pressed his fingertips against the cool glass. The rain made everything look gray and only served to darken his mood.

He stalked back to the couch, retrieved his phone, and tapped it a few times. "I need to speak to Duncan," he told the secretary when she answered.

"I'm sorry, Lord Sherrington. He's away from his office at the moment. May I have him ring you back?"

"Don't bother. I'll call his mobile." Cam ended the call before the woman could respond. Another tap. Duncan's voice mail played. "The party you are trying to reach is unavailable. Please leave a message after the tone. Thank you."

"I need to speak to you as soon as possible," Cam said. "Call me." He slammed the phone down on the coffee table and paced the room several times. Something niggled at the back of his sleep-deprived brain. In spite of Duncan's obvious disdain for everything Cam stood for, he'd never avoided Cam's calls before. *What the fuck is Duncan up to?*

"Lord Sherrington," Luisa practically squeaked as she opened the door to the apartment, carrying groceries, just as Cam walked by the foyer. "Is everything all right?" she asked tentatively.

"Perfectly all right, Luisa."

She nodded and slipped into the kitchen. Half an hour later, the aroma of bacon and eggs wafted through the apartment. Cam's stomach growled and he remembered he hadn't eaten breakfast. He picked up the cursed mobile and went to change, emerging a few minutes later in a well-worn pair of jeans and a black Royal Opera House T-shirt that Aiden had bought him when he'd gotten his first contract there. The only T-shirt Cam owned. Cam knew wearing it would only remind him of Aiden, but with everything else threatening to come crashing down around him, it seemed morbidly fitting.

He sat at the breakfast counter, opened the *New York Times*, and tried to think about something other than the brewing storm. At least the coffee would improve his pounding head. He leafed through page after page without seeing them.

"Lord Sherrington?"

Cam looked up at Luisa. "Yes?"

"I know it's none of my business," she began, her voice quavering just a bit. "But you look tired. Are you not feeling well today?" She pressed her lips together and glanced away, then back again. "There's been a nasty flu going around."

"I'm fine. Really, Luisa." He forced a smile and sipped his coffee. It tasted heavenly. The woman made the best coffee.

"I've worked for you for a long time," she continued, rallying a bit as she set down a plate filled with food.

Cam schooled his features to avoid showing his growing irritation. His head hurt, his stomach had begun to growl, and he was in no mood for a casual conversation.

She returned his smile, her face lighting up, cheeks dimpling. How old would she be? Thirty-six? Not much older than he. When he looked beyond the basics—hair pulled severely back in a ponytail, the white smock she wore over her clothing, and the horrid plastic shoes she wore indoors—he realized that if she did a little with makeup, she'd be quite an attractive woman. He wondered vaguely why she was single. *Probably because she takes care of two children by herself and works two jobs.*

"You know I'm happy to work for you," she said, her cheeks pinking as she spoke.

"I'm glad." He glanced back down at the paper, feeling uncomfortable. They'd never really had a conversation before. He'd left her generous tips at Christmas and on her birthday, but he knew very little about her aside from the pictures she'd shown him of her children. It was much the same with the servants at the castle. He'd only done what he'd learned from his mother: he treated staff well, but he kept his distance. *"Better service that way,"* his mother had told him.

"You know you can always talk to me... if you need to, I mean." The blush on her cheeks deepened.

"Thank you, Luisa," he said. "I'll try to remember that." He took a piece of the bacon and began to chew. He knew it was terrible for him, but he let her indulge him once in a while.

"I know it's not my place," she continued, "but since you arrived.... This trip.... You seem a little...." She hesitated once again as though doubting herself, then frowned and said, "Lost."

Lost. Was he lost? Worried? Of course. Disappointed? Definitely. But lost?

"Thank you, Luisa," he said curtly. "But really, I'm perfectly fine. Just a bit tired, that's all."

CHAPTER

FOUR DAYS came and went with no word from Duncan, and Friday arrived without fanfare. In spite of the half-dozen messages Cam left on his cell, at home, and at the office, the bastard still hadn't called. Cam puttered around the apartment, trying to focus on anything but what felt like a looming hurricane. He tried to do some work on his computer, reviewing documents for approval at the next meeting of the board of directors, answering e-mail. He tapped his foot against the desk and shifted in his seat. He couldn't focus. Couldn't think.

Luisa went out to do some marketing, and he almost offered to go with her, just to have something to keep busy. He picked up his mobile, debated whether to call Duncan again, nixed that idea, then ended up calling Daniel Bryce in accounting over at Raice.

"Accounting. Ron Welding speaking." Welding was a twentysomething techie and Bryce's second in command at Raice Corp. He'd spent the latter part of two years revamping the outdated accounting software, much to Bryce's chagrin. Cam was quite sure Bryce worried the upstart with the full beard and heavy-framed spectacles was after his job.

"Ron, this is Cam Sherrington."

"Lord Sherrington." Ron sounded nervous. Then again, the few times Cam had had the opportunity to speak with Ron, he'd always sounded a bit nervous. High-strung, geeky type. Cam had hired him. In fact, he'd been thinking of recommending Ron for a technology project at Sherrington Holdings he'd been talking to Duncan about before he'd left London.

"Is Dan around?" Cam asked.

"No, sir. He's on a conference call with your uncle. Can I have him call you back?"

"Tell him to call me on my mobile." What the devil was Duncan doing, meeting with a Raice manager without including him? If he ever got Duncan on the phone, he'd bloody well give him a piece of his mind. Why was Duncan avoiding his calls? *Maybe he thinks he can pin whatever disaster is looming on you.* Cam clenched his jaw and fought a wave of nausea. "Tell him it's urgent."

"Of course. And if there's anything I can help with, please—"

"I'll be in touch." Cam paced the living room as he disconnected the call, then immediately rang Duncan's cell. No answer. Hardly a surprise, since he'd be on the call with Dan. He then left another message with Duncan's office, still furious he hadn't heard back. Finally, at the end of his patience—beyond it, really—he headed to the gym around noon.

The workout did him good—at least it helped him focus on something other than whatever mess was brewing at home.

Two hours later, having barely touched the bowl of soup Luisa had warmed up for him, he got himself a beer from the fridge and stalked into his study. He'd just booted up the computer when his mobile rang. Of course, he'd left it in the other room. He slammed the beer down on the desk, causing some of the contents to fly onto the keyboard—no doubt *that* would help things.

"Yes?" he snapped, not caring if the entire universe knew what a foul mood he was in.

"Cameron, this is Jim Stanton."

He'd expected it to be Duncan. "Jim. What did you hear?"

"I thought you should know," Jim said in a voice that seemed a bit more businesslike than usual.

"What should I know?" Cam tapped his foot against the leg of the table.

"The FBI wants to speak directly with you."

"About what? The same bullshit?" Oh, this was fucking *perfect!*

"They won't say," Jim explained, "except that there are discrepancies in the banking documents. Something about an offshore account?"

"Offshore?" Cam shook his head and rubbed his mouth with his free hand. "You mean Sherrington Holdings accounts?"

"The account isn't in the UK, Cameron."

Why did lawyers always speak to him as though he was stupid?

"This one's in the Caymans."

"The Caymans?" Cam repeated. "Raice doesn't have any accounts in the Caymans." He'd studied Raice's books before he'd recommended purchasing the company.

"I wasn't aware of any either," Jim admitted. "But they seem pretty hot to speak with you. They want you to come in to their office on Monday."

"Monday?"

"I'll go with you, of course."

"That bad?" Cam asked. "That I need representation?"

"Just a precaution." Jim didn't sound all that convincing. *Or convinced.* "I'll contact the British consulate in the meantime. Let them know what's happening."

Cam tapped his foot faster. "And what if I refuse to speak to them?"

"They could take you in for questioning. They might even arrest you if you refuse to cooperate." Jim sighed audibly, then said, "Cameron. Listen, I understand that this is all very uncomfortable. I promise I'll do everything I can to make sure it's as painless as possible."

As painless as possible? And then there was the little question of his uncle's sudden lack of availability. There was more going on here than anyone was telling him, and until he figured it out, he wouldn't be going anywhere.

"No."

"Cameron?" He heard a mixture of exasperation and frustration in Jim's voice.

Twat. He'd always treated Cam like a twelve-year-old in need of constant supervision. Maybe he *was* that, but he wasn't stupid either.

"Fine. Get it arranged." He disconnected the call, stalked over to the window, and gazed out at the darkening sky. The days were growing shorter. The clock was ticking, and his time was running out.

CHAPTER

"THIS SHOULDN'T take long," Richard Johns, one of the FBI agents, had said when he escorted Cam through the building four hours before. Now, emerging from the small windowless conference room, followed by Jim Stanton, Cam had a splitting headache and enough new information that his first order of business was to head to the men's room and vomit.

Another Monday. More bollocks.

"We'd like you to stay in New York for the foreseeable future," another of the men told him as they left. "We may need to bring you back in again." Cam took this to mean that the next thing to happen was that he'd end up in custody, and Jim didn't dismiss the notion out of hand.

"Money laundering? What the fuck gave them that idea?"

"I'm sure it's all a misunderstanding," Jim said before they went their separate ways a few minutes later. "If you ask me, it's just bluster. They've got something, and they're fishing for more."

"What should I do?" Cam asked as he shoved his shaking hands in his jacket pockets.

"Nothing for now. Stay put. I'll make a few phone calls and we'll regroup tomorrow."

Cam watched Jim's taxi speed down the avenue. He'd call Duncan. He needed to get back home—at least there he wouldn't be looking at a jail cell in his immediate future. Not that the Americans couldn't have him extradited, but that would take time.

He still felt sick. Maybe Luisa had been right. Maybe he was coming down with something.

Coming down with a case of being in the wrong place at the wrong time, maybe. This entire situation—the investigation, the allegations, all of it—felt surreal. As though he'd stepped into someone else's life.

Cam's calls to Duncan continued to go unanswered. The niggle had become a full-blown voice screaming in his head. Was Duncan's silence the sign of something more insidious?

No. Duncan has no reason to hang me out to dry. Duncan was paid handsomely for his work as Sherrington's CEO, and he owned nearly a third of the company's stock. But Duncan had never ignored his calls, even though he'd often complained that Cam was interrupting his work.

You're becoming paranoid. Just be patient. It'll all work out.

He spent the rest of the day reviewing Raice's recent financial reports and trying to check some of the business accounts online, with little to show for it. He also tried calling the accounting department at Raice again, but Dan Bryce was nowhere to be found.

"Fuck!" Cam shouted as he slammed the phone down on the table after calling Duncan's home and mobile again. By then he'd given up on contacting the office, since they'd closed hours before. He thought about Duncan again— went over things in his mind—then dismissed the thoughts. He really *was* being paranoid. Things would be fine.

He needed to get out of the apartment. Worrying about what might be happening was wearing a path in the carpet from his pacing. He grabbed the six hundred dollars he had stashed in his dresser drawer and shoved it into his pocket. His *last* six hundred dollars. Next he called Riley, who asked him how he was doing. He did wonderful work lying to her and getting to the point of his call. "I'm trying to reach Larry," he told her. "The actor I met at your little soiree the other night?"

"Is something wrong?" she asked after she'd given him Larry's number. "It's not like you to cancel on me."

"I'm fine," he said dismissively. "Something came up, that's all."

Money and a title clearly went far to smooth ruffled feathers, because Larry was over the moon to hear from Cam. They met at a small bar near Larry's apartment, where Cam made up for what he hadn't had to drink on his birthday. Afterward, Cam wobbled back to Larry's and they spent what was left of the night—morning, really—fucking. Between the alcohol and the sex, Cam managed to forget most everything. They finally fell asleep at the crack of dawn.

Cam awoke with a start, heart racing. A nightmare. He'd dreamed about something. Something chasing him. Something cold. He glanced around the unfamiliar room and tried to slow his breathing. His mind began to clear. *That's right. Larry.* The bedside clock read 1:00 p.m.

Bugger. Afternoon already? He rolled out of bed, showered, and dressed. He was out the door before Larry woke.

He stopped at the nearest coffee shop and downed several cups of coffee at the counter. The fog of the alcohol and the dream lifted, if only momentarily, because the next thing he did was turn on his mobile and listen to the messages.

"Cameron," Jim Stanton said, "call me as soon as you get this message."

The next message was time-stamped about an hour later. "Cameron." Jim again. "I really need to speak to you."

This message was immediately followed by a message from his mother. "Cameron. Your uncle says the American authorities are trying to contact you. He wasn't specific, but he said you might have gotten in a bit over your head. I know it's been difficult for you, but you should turn yourself in. Explain why you did whatever it is—" He deleted the message. *What a lot of fucking bollocks.* Of course she'd assume he'd done something wrong. She'd never minced her words with him when it came to her opinions of his worth as a man or as her son.

Then, around noon, this message: "Cameron, Special Agent Johns from the FBI just called me. They've confirmed they have a warrant for your arrest. I realize this looks bad, but I'm sure we'll be able to get your bail posted."

Fuck! Cam stared down at the omelet the server had just set in front of him, and knew he couldn't eat a bite of it. He struggled to keep down the coffee, knowing he was going to need it.

They've found something. What had he missed? He'd been through Raice's accounting records several times now and had seen nothing. His hand shook as he tried Duncan again at his office. And again on his cellular.

The server handed him back his change. $1.92. He stared at it for a few minutes, then dialed Jim. "What did they find?" he demanded before Jim could do more than answer the phone.

"Cameron. I'm glad you called." The same bollocks as always. Acting as if Cam's world wasn't crashing down around him.

"What did they find?" Cam fought the urge to slam the phone onto the counter.

"A Cayman account with your name on it," Jim said. "All off the books."

"My name on it?" Cam's hands went numb and he began to sweat.

"Your name on it, and twelve million in it."

THE WIND had begun to blow by the time Cam rounded the corner back to his building. The scattered clouds had given way to a gray, overcast sky and the temperature had dropped. He vaguely remembered what he'd heard on the telly at the diner—there was a chance of sleet in the forecast. He pulled his scarf tighter around his neck and raised the collar on his leather jacket. When he looked once more, he saw several large cars parked in the no-parking zone in front of the building. Black. Identical models.

Fuck! He needed to think. Twelve million dollars in an offshore account with his name on it and no record of how he'd come by it except that the transfers had been made from another Cayman account in amounts just under the legal limit for reporting? No wonder the Americans were interested in him! He knew enough about money laundering to know that the shit piling up was now waist deep. And what could he tell the FBI? "I have no idea where the money in that account came from"? Oh, *that* would be helpful! Already he felt the walls of the cell closing in on him.

He thought of trying Duncan again, but this time—for the *first* time—he realized he didn't trust Duncan not to turn him in. Things just didn't add up. The way Duncan had reassured him that nothing was wrong. The accounts in Cam's name linked to the company he'd insisted Duncan purchase. How Duncan fought him tooth and nail against the Raice purchase, then suddenly relented with no good reason. The way Duncan had avoided his calls from the beginning.

It would be easier to get rid of me. And what a fucking splendid way to do it! Who would believe he was innocent? The FBI probably already knew about his empty trust account and the board's scrutiny of his living expenses.

He turned around, his heart beating a steady tattoo against his ribs. He still had four hundred dollars in his wallet. That would get him a hotel room somewhere, wouldn't it? His phone buzzed and he tried to catch his breath. He'd seen movies where they'd tracked people down by their phones. He shut the phone off without answering. He'd keep it off. Even if they couldn't track him with it, he'd save the battery in case he needed it. He walked quickly to the nearest subway station and lost himself amidst the crowd.

CHAPTER

TWO DAYS later Cam had used up nearly all his money and he'd risked a call to David Somers. He'd left the hotel that morning and spent most of the day walking around Central Park, trying to figure out what to do other than call Jim and turn himself in. But he couldn't stop thinking about what might happen—of what *would* happen when he couldn't make bail.

He wasn't sure what he'd even tell David when he reached him, but David was the first person he thought of. David was always calm in the wake of a storm. Maybe he'd know what to do. "I'm sorry I can't take your call," David's recorded voice said. "I'll be traveling in the Far East the next few days. Please leave me a message and I'll return your call as soon as I'm able." Cam didn't leave a message. David was half a world away. What could he possibly do to help?

Cam tapped his phone again. "Riley?"

"Cam, is that you?"

Cam bit back a snappy response. How many men with English accents did Riley know? "Yes, it's me."

"I've been worried sick about you, Cam." Cam doubted that was the case, although the fact that Riley seemed to know something was up was a surprise. "I spoke to Duncan a few days ago. This is terrible. Truly. Why didn't you tell me the other day when you—"

"You spoke to Duncan?" Something about this struck him as odd, since Riley only knew Duncan from the parties at the estate. But he could barely think straight, he hadn't eaten anything since the night before, and he was desperate.

"Oh, I called him, you know, just to see where you were," Riley said quickly. "He told me about the investigation. Said you might need a friend right now."

Cam shifted from one foot to the other and looked out over the park. The bench felt cold and the wind bit at his neck in spite of his cashmere scarf. No matter. He'd stay with Riley, or he'd borrow some money from her and stay at a hotel for a few days.

"Yes. I guess you could say that." Maybe Riley was a better friend than he'd realized. He'd never really given it much thought.

"What can I do to help?" she asked.

HE RODE the subway down to Riley's apartment. Underground, he felt safe. If the FBI was looking for him—and he guessed they were—they'd have a hard time finding him there. Even today, on a Thursday afternoon before rush hour, there were enough people that he could blend in. His MetroCard still had three rides on it, so if he needed to move around, he could.

Every once in a while, his mind would shout things like "What the fuck are you thinking about?" or "How long can you run?" He alternately ignored these thoughts and skipped ahead to "I need to think this through before I end up in a jail cell," before panicking once again.

Time. I need time to figure out what's going on. Figure out who to talk to. He knew he should probably get out of the city and find someplace better to hide, but he only knew Manhattan and the area near Raice's New Jersey offices. Maybe if he had time to think, he could figure out how to make his way to LA or Miami, the only other two American cities he knew well. But he'd need money first, or he wouldn't get anywhere.

He climbed the steps from the subway up to Third Avenue and pulled his scarf over his mouth. Fortunately, Riley's building was only a few blocks away. He turned the corner onto 82nd Street and stopped dead in his tracks. A dark sedan and a police cruiser were parked in front of the building. He headed back to the subway at a brisk pace—nothing that would be too obvious, but fast enough that if the authorities had spotted him, he'd have time to find a place underground to hide. He turned on his mobile and pressed Riley's number as he descended the same steps he'd walked up a minute before.

"Cam?" Riley sounded nervous, tentative.

"You said you would help me." He struggled not to shout at her. "You called them. You told them I was coming."

"Cam, listen. They say you've done things…. And I…. I just wanted to help you…. I mean, you can make it right. You don't have to—"

"You believe them?" This question was met with silence. "Fuck. You do believe them, don't you?" Cam spoke the words through clenched teeth. The signal began to break up as he walked farther into the station.

"Cam," she said, "I'm sure whatever you did, you couldn't help it. Duncan told me about the board cutting back on your allowance and—"

He ended the call and shoved the phone into his pocket, then swiped his MetroCard. Five minutes later he was seated on a Downtown No. 2 express train.

The grinding sound of the train as it hurtled toward lower Manhattan was a perfect complement to his scattered thoughts. He ran a hand through his hair again, ignoring the curls that fell onto his forehead. For a change, he didn't give a shit what he looked like. *Fucking bollocks.* He couldn't go home. The only person in town he thought was a friend had set him up. He only had enough money for some food and maybe a single night at a crappy hotel. Duncan wouldn't return his calls. The only person who'd speak to him was the company's lawyer, but Jim would just tell him to turn himself in. What the bloody hell was he supposed to do?

Turn yourself in. You can explain. Show them that you've done nothing wrong.

He ignored the voice again. From somewhere nearby, he heard an annoying tapping sound. He looked around the subway car, ready to give whoever was making the noise a fucking piece of his mind, then realized it was his own foot to blame. He shot up from his seat, grabbing a hold of one of the slippery stainless steel poles to keep his balance as the car rumbled and rocked on the tracks. He gazed out the window at one of the local stations, the regular patterns of the old metal supports breaking up his view in regular intervals, like bars on a cage.

Bars. He imagined someplace dark with bars on the door. He couldn't get out. He began to sweat as he imagined tugging on the metal and calling out for help. He gasped for air as he drowned in his fear, and a low voice seemed to echo through his mind, familiar. *"My pretty boy."*

"You okay, man?" someone said from behind him, causing him to jump.

Cam blinked and realized the train had stopped and that he was clutching the pole as if his life depended on it. "I'm fine." He waved the kid—long-haired, with a furry beard—away, then stumbled off the train. A few minutes later, he sat on a bench in a small park, then turned on his phone again and tapped one of the presets.

"Mother?" he said after she'd answered.

"Cameron! Where are you?" she demanded.

"That's not important. I really need your hel—"

"Duncan told me," she said as if she hadn't even heard him speak. "I can't believe what you've done. Truly. Duncan says he'll make sure you get the best representation. Surely since you've never been in trouble before—"

He shut the phone off and shoved it into his pocket, then rubbed his eyes. Had he really believed she'd support him? Why had he even bothered? She'd always thought the worst of him. *Probably because you deserved it!* But he wasn't a thief.

He fingered his mobile but didn't pull it out. If he called Jim and told them he'd turn himself in.... If everyone thought he'd done this, what then? Money laundering? That was the stuff of Mafiosi. Movies. And if Duncan had set him up, what chance did he have of convincing the authorities of his innocence? Duncan controlled everything. Duncan controlled *him.*

What will you do?

He was pathetic. He thought of Aiden. Good for Aiden that he'd found someone to take care of him. Love him.

Stop feeling sorry for yourself.

He needed to clear his head. Think. Figure out what the bloody hell he would do now. He stood and waited for the next Downtown train. He'd heard of a place near Times Square where he might be able to get some money. He needed to rest. Eat something. He'd decide what to do after that.

CAM LOOKED up at the flashing neon sign in the window. Blue and red, the light burned letters onto his retinas so that even when he blinked, he could still read the words: *Buy. Sell. Pawn.* The windows were lined in white neon and cast an eerie glow on the sidewalk outside. He shivered. When had the temperature dropped? On his birthday, only a week before, it had been pleasantly warm. Now he could almost smell snow in the air.

He reached into the inside breast pocket of his leather jacket and felt the pen there. The pen David and Alex had given him for his birthday. The pen he was just about to pawn.

Better than calling David and asking him for a handout. He wouldn't do that. This wasn't David's problem, it was his own. Maybe if David and Alex were still in New York, he'd ask for advice, but he wouldn't hit David up for cash....

No. I'll fix this. But first he needed money to pay for a place to stay. Then he could think.

He opened the door to the pawnshop and walked over to the counter. A short, balding man who'd been polishing a piece of silver that looked as though it had seen better days put down his cloth and walked over to him.

"I need money," Cam said. He felt like a petty criminal. The place reeked of cigarettes and fake fruit-scented air freshener. Cam's already queasy stomach protested the odors.

The man's smile faded. No doubt he'd hoped Cam, dressed as he was in his expensive clothes, had come to buy something. "Yeah. Okay. What is it?"

"What?" Cam frowned, uncomprehending.

"Whatcha got to pawn?" the man asked, his eyebrows slightly raised and the edges of his mouth curving upward.

He thought this was funny? Cam fought the urge to turn around and storm out of the pathetic little shop. If he hadn't been so fucking desperate, he'd have done just that. Instead, he clenched his jaw and reached into his pocket.

The little bald man looked down at the pen, then up at Cam. "This is it?"

"This is it." Cam met the man's eyes as he said this. The man didn't blink. "How much can you give me for it?"

The man picked up the pen, pulled open the top, then held it under a magnifying glass. The entire process took far longer than it should, at least in Cam's judgment. *Sharp little bugger. He knows a sucker when he has one.*

"Two hundred," the man said after a moment.

"Two hundred *dollars*?" Cam said, stunned.

"Yeah. Two hundred."

"It's worth thousands."

Little Bald Man narrowed his eyes. "Two hundred. Take it or leave it."

The nausea Cam had been fighting returned with a vengeance. He needed to get out of this place. What if someone had followed him? He glanced over his shoulder where the neon flickered. Was that someone standing outside?

"Take it." Cam shifted from one foot to the other and tapped his finger on the glass case.

Five minutes later—what the fuck took the man so long to do things?—Little Bald Man counted out ten twenty-dollar bills onto the glass. Cam pocketed the money, then turned to leave. He stopped a moment later, looked back at the man, and said, "I'll be back for it."

"Sure you will," Little Bald Man said.

CHAPTER

By the time Galen made it into Manhattan on Friday evening, 8:00 p.m. had come and gone. He'd taught late that afternoon, making up several lessons students had missed the week before when half the high school had come down with the flu. By then, tourists and locals heading out for an evening on the town had replaced the crowds of commuters.

He set up in his favorite alcove, just out of the line of foot traffic but where the sound from his trumpet could dance off dingy concrete walls, floor, and ceiling. He didn't want to be the center of activity; he felt good knowing his music provided a backdrop for it.

He started with a simple piece, something that tickled his lips, to warm up his embouchure—his lips and cheek muscles. Simple, like stretching before exercising, the Brandt étude sounded bright and energetic. He started with the second étude, a piece that reminded him of marching bands and football games in late fall. He'd envied the kids who marched when he was in high school.

As he played, he thought of the man who'd stopped to listen two weeks before, headed home from a party, a bit drunk. He hadn't noticed him the weekend before. Not surprising, since weekends could get hectic and Galen could easily miss spotting someone in the crowds.

By midnight, the crowds of people were gone, although enough still walked the tunnels in a steady trickle and would all night long. The trains never stopped running here, something that always amazed Galen, since he hadn't grown up near the city.

He played some Bach—Partita No. 2—originally for solo violin. He'd adapted it for trumpet himself a few years before. He enjoyed its simple lines and how it pushed him to the limits of his breath control. He loved how the sound echoed through the tunnel, giving him the sense that he wasn't the only one playing.

He almost didn't notice the Brit when he walked down the tunnel toward the No. 4 train platform. Before, the man had seemed a bit down, as though he'd received some bad news but was trying to throw it off. He'd been defiant in his sadness. Now, his entire demeanor had changed. He walked, shoulders hunched, with the collar of his leather jacket pulled up around his face. Unlike before, when his pants had been crisply creased, his clothing appeared rumpled. His hair looked more messy than stylishly mussed, and stubble covered his jaw and upper lip. From where Galen stood playing, he caught only a glimpse of the man's eyes, but they too had changed markedly. Dark circles ringed what had been brilliant blue but was now duller, near gray.

However bad things had been the night they'd spoken, things now appeared far worse. Galen finished the Bach and waited a split second for the echoes of the music to fade. A woman walked by, smiled, then dropped some change into the trumpet case. Galen smiled and nodded. After she disappeared down the tunnel, Galen packed up his trumpet, latched the case, and descended the stairs to the No. 4 platform.

He spotted the man at the end of the platform as a train pulled out of the station. *Not going anywhere.* The man shivered and clutched his collar tighter around his neck. A moment later he shifted, took the scarf from around his neck, and put it over his head. He moved sideways a few inches and lay down for a second, then sat up again. This time he took his jacket off and balled it up. Galen knew the drill well: the city had built the benches with wooden separators that dug into a body when you tried to sleep on them. Experienced subway dwellers got used to the discomfort.

The man sat up again and pulled the jacket back on. He noticed Galen standing there and frowned.

"What are you staring at?" the man demanded as he leaped to his feet and backed away.

Galen hadn't expected the sudden fear or the anger he saw on the other man's face. He never did as well with anger as he did with other emotions. *Breathe. Relax.* He took a deep breath and said, "Sorry. I didn't mean to bother you. You're British, right?" *Wonderful.* He always said amazingly stupid things when faced with anger.

"And?" the man answered after an uncomfortable pause. He glanced around as if expecting to see more people.

Running from something.

"Unusual." Galen had always been better with silences. They helped clear his thoughts and allowed him to think.

"Last I heard there were 63 million of us. Not so unusual." The man closed his eyes, obviously wanting Galen to leave him be.

Galen had meant that it was unusual to meet a Brit sleeping in the subway, but it wasn't worth explaining. He'd been stupid to bring it up—the man appeared very troubled.

"I think you made a mistake," he said as he reached into his jeans and pulled out the hundred-dollar bill the man had left for him two weeks before.

He'd held onto it, knowing he needed to return it although not really understanding why. A hunch. One of those feelings he sometimes got about a person.

The man opened his eyes and was clearly about to tell him to get lost when he saw what Galen held out to him.

"No mistake." The man glanced down.

Galen shrugged and pocketed the bill. "Name's Galen. Galen Rusk."

"Hmm."

Galen waited patiently. He knew it sometimes took people time to warm up to him. He often did things people didn't expect, and this sometimes made for uncomfortable situations. This guy probably didn't trust him either. A good thing, given that the subways weren't always the safest place to sleep.

"Cam," the man said after another pause.

"Good to meet you, Cam." Galen offered Cam his hand. Cam hesitated, then shook it. Cam held Galen's hand a little longer than Galen expected. More signs of desperation, if Galen had needed convincing. "It's not as cold upstairs," he added after nearly a minute passed in silence.

"I'm waiting for someone."

"Sure. No problem." Galen knew it for a lie, but he'd expected that. He wouldn't push any more. "Maybe I'll see you around, Cam. Take care of yourself, okay?"

"You too." Cam appeared unconvinced. Also happy to see Galen go.

Galen offered Cam what he hoped was a reassuring smile. As Cam glanced away, Galen set the hundred-dollar bill on the bench, wadded up so that a passing train wouldn't send it flying. Then, as another train pulled into the station but didn't stop—the MTA did track work after midnight, and the express trains ran on local tracks—he turned and walked back up the platform.

CHAPTER *11*

CAM SETTLED onto the hard wooden bench at the end of the No. 4 platform. Downtown. *How appropriate.* He'd watched the Friday-night commuter exodus, pale-faced businessmen and women eating greasy hot dogs covered in onions and whatever else they dared pile on top as they quickly walked toward the exit for the Long Island Rail Road and Metro-North tracks. He'd never before noticed their tired expressions or how the dim station lights made the circles under their eyes appear darker. He did now.

He'd used his last three dollars to buy himself some soup at Au Bon Pain. It had come with about a quarter of a baguette. He'd finished it in five minutes and he'd felt warm. Now, four hours later, the cold had returned, as well as the empty feeling in his stomach. The expensive calfskin jacket looked great, but he hadn't realized it wasn't meant to keep anyone warm.

The trumpet player finished another piece. Classical. Haunting. It was getting on midnight, and Cam guessed he'd be headed to wherever he went when he wasn't playing. Cam hadn't heard him play on a weeknight. Maybe he played at a different station during the week. Or maybe he had a day job. Cam imagined him as one of those bicycle delivery guys who played chicken with the cabbies on 7th Avenue, hair flying about his face, the bottoms of his jeans held against his ankles with rubber bands or silver tape.

Another train stopped at the station. He moved to the end of the platform where reception was the best and turned on his mobile. He glanced at the screen, cursed under his breath, then shut it off to conserve the dwindling battery. Why the hell hadn't Dan called him back yet? He could hide here for a day, maybe two, but he needed money. He figured he had about seventy-five cents in his pockets. Maybe a dollar. What the hell could that buy in New York City?

He shivered as the train pulled away and the temperature dropped a few degrees. Maybe there was a reason the homeless people slept in the passages that zigzagged under 42nd Street. *It's safer here.* He lay down on the bench and tried to ignore the wood that separated the bench into individual seats. *No doubt meant to keep people like me from sleeping on the goddamned benches.*

He pulled his cashmere scarf out from around his neck and draped it over his head, then scooted up a few inches so one of the wooden separators sat at his waist. Another one cut into his shoulder. He bunched the jacket up and tried to cushion the spot with limited success. His heart pounded. He couldn't sleep like this. What if they found him?

Fuck this. They won't find you here. This wasn't a manhunt. He'd found a discarded newspaper on one of the benches. Nothing about him. Nothing about the investigation. He'd be safe here. Still, he felt anxious enough that he decided to sit up again. He'd sleep upright. Or maybe he wouldn't sleep at all. At the sound of a train in the distance, his gaze strayed to the tracks. That was when he noticed the trumpet player watching him from a few feet away.

"What are you staring at?" Cam demanded, getting to his feet and backing up toward the wall. *And then what? If he's FBI, are you going to frighten him away with your blinding personality?* He took a deep breath. This man wasn't FBI. Cam had seen him before the entire mess of a situation, before the FBI had even been a blip on his radar. The man was irritating but harmless.

"Sorry. I didn't mean to bother you. You're British, right?"

Cam waited for more, but the man just kept looking at him. *Fucking brilliant.* He'd heard of savants who could play but couldn't manage to feed themselves. "And?" he replied at last, after the man said nothing more.

"Unusual."

"Last I heard there were 63 million of us. Not so unusual." Cam closed his eyes. Maybe he'd go away and leave Cam in peace.

"I think you made a mistake," the man said.

Cam opened his eyes again, about to tell the twit to get stuffed, but he stopped. The trumpet player had moved closer to him and was holding something out in his left hand. A bill. A hundred-dollar bill, judging by Ben Franklin's cheery face peering back at him. The hundred-dollar bill Cam had dropped into the trumpet case the week before? He'd kept it? Cam could eat for a week on a hundred dollars, if he was careful.

"No mistake," Cam said. Well, it hadn't been, had it? And if he took the bill, he'd be admitting to this stranger that he was skint.

The man shrugged, then pocketed the bill. "Name's Galen. Galen Rusk."

"Hmm."

Galen didn't respond, clearly waiting for Cam's response.

Fine. "Cam," he said.

"Good to meet you, Cam." Galen offered Cam his hand. Cam hesitated, then shook it. A firm handshake. Confident and warm. In another reality, he'd have wanted to keep holding that hand. Take away the grunge clothing, and Galen would have been someone Cam might have noticed. Cam released Galen's hand.

"It's not as cold upstairs," Galen said after nearly a minute passed in silence.

"I'm waiting for someone."

If Galen knew it for the lie it was, he didn't let on, and for that, Cam was thankful. "Sure. No problem." Galen paused, then added, "Maybe I'll see you around, Cam. Take care of yourself, okay?"

Why did Americans insist on being so informal? As if the guy cared at all what happened to him. "You too." Seemed like the proper response. Bollocks, of course.

Galen smiled to reveal a set of dimples Cam hadn't noticed before, then turned and walked back up the platform and disappeared around the corner. Cam shivered and pulled the collar of his jacket up around his neck.

Another train pulled into the station but only slowed down a bit. An express train on the local track. Cam decided Galen was right: he'd be warmer upstairs. More exposed too, but warmer felt like a higher priority. He got to his feet and wrapped his scarf around his neck. That was when he noticed something on the bench at his side.

A hundred-dollar bill.

CHAPTER 12

"GET UP!" someone shouted in Cam's ear.

Heart pounding, momentarily unsure of where he was, Cam sat bolt upright. *The subway platform. Right.* When his eyes focused, he saw a half-dozen young men standing around the bench where he'd been sleeping.

"What do you want?" Cam demanded angrily. They'd scared the shit out of him. Did they think that was funny?

One of the men—the one standing in front of Cam so he couldn't get up from the bench—looked at his companions and laughed. "Oh, I don't know," he said in a pathetic, mocking attempt at an English accent, "let's start with any credit cards or cash you have."

"Fuck off," Cam hissed. He'd had enough shit, he didn't need any more.

The man hauled Cam to his feet by the collar of his jacket. Cam kneed him in the groin and, in return, got slapped across the face. *Bollocks!* Where the hell was everyone? It was a Saturday afternoon, for God's sake.

"Now are you going to give us what we need, you fucking *queen*"—this drew several sniggers from the man's friends—"or am I going to have to cut you?"

Cam saw the glint of steel out of the corner of his eye. He knew better than to mess with a knife. He pulled his wallet out of his pocket. Not that the credit cards would do them any good, but his wallet had what was left of his money. The hundred-dollar bill and a handful of change. One of the other men pulled the wallet out of his hand.

"Gimme the jacket," the man said after one of his buddies high-fived him. Apparently the gold and platinum credit cards were a good haul.

Cam hesitated, and for that he got a knee to the gut. He bent over and coughed a few times while one of the men pulled the jacket from his shoulders.

Fucking hell. It'd be damn cold without that jacket.

"You got a phone?" one of the other thugs asked as Cam struggled to catch his breath. His gut hurt, and if he'd had anything in his stomach, he might have vomited. *Thank heaven for the little things.*

"Of course he's got a phone," the first man said. "Hand it over."

"No." He couldn't give up his phone. Without his phone, he'd have nothing at all. And if Duncan called—

He won't call. You know that already. Still, he needed to hold on to the hope that Duncan's silence was a huge misunderstanding, or he'd be totally lost.

The second slap hurt more than the first. "Gimme the fuckin' phone, *fag.*" More snorts from the rest of the men.

"No."

One of the other men grabbed Cam by the shoulders and held him upright. And fuck, but his abdomen hurt as they pulled him up! He closed his eyes and waited for the blow he knew was coming, but just at that moment, a train pulled onto the platform. Cam opened his eyes to see the men scatter as some of the riders exited.

He collapsed onto the bench, near tears. He wouldn't fucking cry. He wouldn't. He wrapped his scarf around his neck and took deep breaths until the urge passed. After a few minutes, he slipped one hand into the pocket of his jeans to touch the phone. *Thank God.* He knew it was mad to have worried about the phone more than himself, but at the time, fighting for it had seemed the right thing to do.

He shivered and put a careful hand to his cheek. He guessed there'd be a bruise there by morning. *As if anyone gives a shit.* Perfect. Just perfect.

He hauled himself up and made his way slowly down the platform. He wouldn't stay here. He'd find a busier platform, or maybe he'd just walk around.

FOUR HOURS later Cam stood on the platform of the No. 4 train, listening to the sound of the train from the next station echo down the tunnel. The sharp tang of urine mingled with a smell he imagined was the coating of dust and dirt from the rails as the trains created friction and heat. The floor began to vibrate beneath his feet, and the squeal of metal against metal drowned out the conversations of the few people standing nearby. He looked down at the thick yellow line that ran along the edge of the platform. Some of the paint had been scraped away, and bits of gum and tar covered other parts of it. But it was there. *For your safety, stay behind the yellow line.*

He moved up a few steps until his toes were centered on the line. His eyes burned. He tried to convince himself it was the blast of cold air from the tunnel, or the smells, but his brain kept pulling him back to the black sedans parked outside Riley's apartment building. Waiting to take him into custody. Had Riley even hesitated before she'd called the FBI? Had his uncle called Riley to warn her? How ironic that for a change he'd done nothing wrong. Still, he figured he deserved every fucking bit of shit the universe was sending him, even if his sins hadn't included crossing into the realm of the illegal.

He closed his eyes and tried to block the thoughts and images that replayed in an endless feedback loop in his mind. After spending through his inheritance so quickly, he'd had to beg the board of directors to cover his living expenses. The way they'd looked at each other—judging him, and rightly so. The Broadway-bound productions that had gone nowhere. The fast cars. The clothes. The men. His mother's laughter when he'd asked her to send him some money. The calls his uncle—the fucking CEO of his own fucking company!—wouldn't return.

Fucking.

Fucking Jarrod on the antique sofa. The pain of betrayal in Aiden's eyes. Aiden packing his suitcases, his eyes red from crying. Telling Aiden he'd regret leaving. The fear on Aiden's face when he'd understood the implicit threat. How he'd *meant* that threat.

Fucking.

Fucking some sweet Italian arse aboard his family's yacht the night before Aiden flew to join him. Hinting to some annoying twat of a reporter that Aiden had been unfaithful. Knowing full well how much it would wound Aiden. Faithful Aiden. Aiden who'd loved him.

Fucking pain.

This time his own pain, because Aiden had only told the truth: Cam really didn't know how to live with him, or anyone. Another threat. The feeling that he'd ripped his own heart out of his chest, still beating. Aiden, whom he'd loved.

God, I loved you!

Everything blurred. The guilt, the pain, the anger. All of it. He couldn't think straight. Couldn't see a way out of this. Didn't *want* to see a way out, because if there was a way out, where would he be?

Alone. Pathetic. Locked in a cell no bigger than a box. A dark, damp place. He imagined hands reaching out to hold him down, keep him there. Hurt him. He'd never liked enclosed spaces, although he had no recollection of why. He thought about the cell again and shivered.

He opened his eyes. The toes of his shoes were even with the edge of the platform, his feet now fully *on* the yellow line. The train was close now. *So* close. He watched the lights moving toward him. Felt the air rush past his cheeks. He leaned forward….

A hand grasped his shoulder, sure and steady. He blinked and stepped back as the train whizzed by, inches from his face.

"Are you all right?" The man had to shout the words over the din.

Cam's heart pounded hard against his ribs, racing like the train. "I… ah… yes. I'm quite all right." Total bullshit, and yet he managed to speak these last words with the confidence he lacked.

The man—Cam knew he'd seen him before somewhere—offered him a lopsided smile. Hazel eyes. Dark blond hair. Cam saw he was holding a black fiberglass case.

The trumpet player. The one who'd been playing for tips. What was his name? Galen.

"Can I buy you a cup of coffee?" Galen asked.

THEY SETTLED into one of the booths at the rear of the station's small coffee shop, Cam's back to the wall so he could see people walking to and from the trains. Twentysomethings arriving from Long Island for a night out on the town, laughing, already a little drunk. Parents pushing strollers and struggling with exhausted children after a Saturday spent in the city.

Cam's heart still pounded in his chest. The desperation that had slowly escalated over the past few days seemed to have peaked, but the claw of fear that held his chest in its icy grip remained, making it difficult for him to breathe.

"Coffee okay with you?" Galen asked.

Cam was pleased Galen hadn't assumed he'd prefer tea. With the exception of Americans who had spent time in England, most assumed Brits didn't drink coffee. In fact, Cam preferred coffee.

"I don't have any money." Cam saw no reason to beat about the bush. It embarrassed him that he couldn't even buy himself a fucking cup of coffee. Why? Why did he care what a stranger thought about him? He shouldn't give a shit.

"No problem. I invited you, remember?" Galen glanced down at the place setting and delicately unwrapped the paper napkin from around the flatware, then set his fork and knife quite precisely on either side of the paper placemat, an inch from the edge of the paper.

"Then yes, thank you." Cam's uncomfortably empty stomach made accepting easier. He felt light-headed, although he wondered how much of that was the adrenaline from his near miss with the train.

"Two coffees," Galen told the waitress. She flitted away, tucking her pen behind her ear just like in an old Hollywood movie, leaving them alone once more.

Cam tapped his foot on the floor as he waited for Galen to say something. And waited. And waited, until the silence stretched more than uncomfortably. Throughout the silence, a half smile danced on Galen's lips. Lips still slightly swollen and pink from playing the trumpet. If he hadn't been so wound up, Cam might have admired them.

"I really should be going," Cam said when he couldn't bear it any longer.

He slid on the vinyl bench, ready to stand up, but Galen put his hand on Cam's and said, "Where do you need to be?"

The gesture was anything but sexual, although Galen's hand felt warm and his own felt cold. "I-I...," Cam stammered. What did the man want from him? A fucking confession?

The waitress arrived with two mugs of coffee before Cam could slip away from the table, effectively pinning him there. Galen leaned over to ask her something, his words drowned out by a bunch of teenagers walking by the coffee shop, shouting to each other. By the time the waitress left them alone again, the urge to run had fled Cam's exhausted brain. He slid back to the center of the bench, dislodging Galen's hand, and pressed his palms to the cup. His stomach lurched at the smell of it. How long had it been since he'd eaten anything?

Cam ripped open three sugar packets and dumped them in the coffee, then filled it to the rim with cream. He'd never drunk his coffee anything but black, but he would hardly pass up something approximating food. Galen said nothing as Cam took a sip, then added more cream and finished the cup in a little less than a minute.

The smell of beef on the grill mingled with the scent of the coffee. Cam had never wanted a greasy hamburger more than he did at that moment.

He thought the waitress was coming back to the table to refill their coffee cups, but instead she deposited a plate in front of him—a huge hamburger with a side of fries that occupied nearly two-thirds of the plate. He opened his mouth to tell her she'd made a mistake, but she'd already moved on to another table.

"Eat."

Cam looked up to see Galen smiling at him. "I didn't order this," he snapped. He hadn't meant to sound so irritated, but to have that food in front of him—was this some sort of fucking test?

"I ordered it."

"You?"

That placid smile again. Irritating as hell. What did this man take him for?

Someone who sleeps in the subway. By now, the jolt of the caffeine had hit him hard. The thought of sleeping on the hard bench again, of waking up with every train and every noise, worried that someone might take his phone or, worse, hurt him, made him jumpier than ever.

Cam pushed the plate away from him. "I can't take this."

"My treat. Besides, I'm a vegetarian. Never touch the stuff."

"I don't.... I can't pay you back." The smell of the hamburger was overwhelming now.

"I'm not expecting you to."

The war between Cam's brain and his stomach raged like a Hollywood epic, complete with special effects bombs and mortar fire courtesy of the coffee. Or he imagined his stomach sounded like a special effects soundtrack right about now.

He managed to unclench his jaw long enough to say "Thank you." The curt sort of thank-you one gave when taking punishment for misbehavior in school.

Galen kept smiling. Cam wondered if he was a bit slow, but he was too hungry to care. He took three fries and nearly swallowed them whole in an effort to quiet the growls he was sure Galen and everyone else in the coffee shop could hear. And God, they tasted better than anything he'd ever eaten, even if his belly still hurt where he'd been kneed.

Cam finished the plate clean, then drank another cup of coffee and three glasses of water before leaning back and taking a long breath. Galen was still on his first cup of black coffee. He'd been watching Cam the entire time.

"Thank you," Cam said again, this time with real gratitude. *Time for the other shoe to drop.* Cam waited for Galen to name his price—in Cam's experience, all good deeds came with strings attached—but instead Galen said, "You're welcome," and grew silent once again.

The silence stretched. Cam noticed Galen had straightened his coffee cup so that the handle was parallel to the edge of the table. More time passed. Then Galen pressed his lips together and ran a hand through his hair, as if considering something. "You can't stay in the subway," he said finally.

"What?" Now Cam really *was* irritated. Where the bloody hell was he *supposed* to stay with no money?

"I've got a place in Jersey."

"And?"

Galen looked confused. "You need a place to stay, and I have a place."

Oh, this was just perfect! "I'm not sleeping with you." There, best be up-front with him. He might be desperate, but he'd never be *that* desperate.

Galen shifted in his seat, clearly uncomfortable. Had Cam underestimated him? He looked genuinely embarrassed, as if it hadn't occurred to him until that moment what Cam might be thinking. *Definitely slow.* "I...." His cheeks pinked. "I wasn't expect—"

"I'm fine staying here." The realization that Galen was probably straight would normally have been a disappointment, but Cam was much too far gone to care at this point.

"It's dangerous." Galen frowned and looked at him as though he'd lost his mind. He reached out to touch Cam's cheek. Cam guessed it looked pretty bad now, probably rainbow colored.

"Look," Cam said, pulling away and doing his best not to yell at the man, "I can't even pay you back for the food. Now you're asking me to come home with you? Are you insane?"

Galen opened his mouth to speak, then shut it again, as if thinking better of it.

"Sorry," Cam said. "That was incredibly rude of me, wasn't it?" God, why was he acting like such a prick when the man was just trying to be kind? Misguided kindness, no doubt, but still, he didn't deserve to have someone jump down his throat for it.

Galen shrugged. "You don't need to pay me back. I'm not expecting anything." Galen appeared once again serene. "I realize it might look bad. But it's not like you'd be the first to crash at my place. I've got a few extra bedrooms."

"I don't understand." Cam took a deep breath and did his best to moderate his tone this time. "Why would you offer to take a complete stranger home? You know nothing about me."

Galen's face lit up. "That's where you're wrong, Cam. I know more about you than you realize." Galen rubbed a long finger around the rim of his coffee cup, and for the first time, Cam noticed he wore an odd collection of bracelets on his right wrist, some made of braided yarn and string, others leather, some with sayings carved into them. He'd seen some of the kids in New York wearing similar things. *Friendship bracelets.* "I saw how upset you were the night you left the hundred-dollar bill in my case. I saw how you connected to the music I was playing. You *understood* it. I felt that."

Cam shook his head. "You also thought I'd made a mistake by leaving that much money, didn't you?"

The corners of Galen's mouth edged upward as he shook his head. "I saw you help that woman with her groceries even though I knew you must be in a hurry," he said, ignoring Cam's comment. "You were kind to her. Gentle. Understanding."

"I wasn't—"

"You were the only one who stopped to help her. Everyone walked by, hoping someone else would stop. *You* were the only one, Cam."

Cam stared, unable to form the words to respond.

Galen continued. "You've never needed to ask for help. And now, when you *do* need help, you're not sure how to ask."

"I don't need any help." Cam wished he sounded more convincing. Mostly he didn't think he deserved any help. He half wanted Galen to disappear, half wanted him to stay. Why the hell didn't he know what he wanted?

"Kindness isn't just for other people. It doesn't matter how much money you have. Sometimes you need kindness too."

Cam's eyes burned. He wouldn't cry. He wasn't a child. He was just tired. Stressed. Afraid—not just of getting mugged again but of what he'd be facing if he went back to his apartment. But he'd manage. The memory of the yellow line on the edge of the platform lingered.

I was tired. Nothing more.

"You're welcome to stay with me. No strings. No need to repay me. No quid pro quo. Just a safe place where you can rest." Galen shrugged. "Nothing fancy."

"I still don't understand—"

"I've been where you are," Galen said. "Someone helped me. I'm just paying it forward."

Quid pro quo? So maybe he wasn't as dim as Cam had assumed. Strange. *New age prophet cum beach bum.* But what other options did he really have?

CHAPTER *13*

YOU'RE AN idiot. What the hell was he doing, agreeing to go home with a man he'd met just over two weeks before in a subway station?

Nothing you haven't done before. Well, it wasn't so different from the hookups he'd had in the past, was it? If you ignored the subway part of the equation.

They took the local to 34th Street, then exited near Penn Station. From there they walked about five blocks and then down a side street. At one point Galen offered Cam his jacket, but Cam flatly refused. Bad enough that he needed rescuing like some pathetic animal. He wasn't yet so desperate that he'd take someone else's coat.

"This is mine," Galen said as he pointed to a silver Honda with New Jersey plates and rust that edged the doors and wheel wells. "Not much to look at," he added with his now familiar shrug, "but she gets me where I need to go."

"She?"

Galen laughed, then ran a hand through his hair, appearing a bit uncomfortable. "Yeah. If she sinks, I go down with her." He opened one of the rear doors and set his trumpet case inside. Cam caught a glimpse of a stack of sheet music on the backseat, although it was too dark to make out much. Galen unlocked the passenger side—no automatic locks here—then pressed his lips together and shook his head. Short white hair—fur, no doubt—covered the black vinyl seat.

"Sorry about that," Galen said as he brushed it off. "I usually vacuum the car after Max and I go hiking, but we got back a little late today."

"Max?"

Galen grinned. "My dog."

"Oh." Cam eyed the seat warily, his first thought that his black jeans would pick up the fur like a lint brush. Then he reminded himself that he'd been sleeping in the subway and a bit of fur was hardly the worst of what he might find on his pants. Still, as he settled into the seat, he dusted a few stray hairs off the armrest.

The drive through the Lincoln Tunnel and on into Jersey was an easy one, too late for there to be much traffic. Cam looked out the window, unwilling to engage Galen in conversation. Galen didn't seem to mind. He whistled—a tune Cam recognized but couldn't remember the name of—then tuned the radio to a jazz station that played bebop.

Thirty minutes later Galen exited the freeway, and they drove another ten minutes before turning down a small street lined with cookie-cutter houses. Postwar, Cam guessed, each with the same boxy structure, some with dormers, others with vinyl siding. Galen pulled into a driveway between two of the houses, but to Cam's surprise, the driveway didn't end at either house. It continued on, snaking behind them a few hundred feet to an old farmhouse. Probably the original house on the land that was now cluttered with homes. Built in the 1800s, he guessed.

A single light lit the walkway from the driveway to the front porch. White, with blue shutters, the house was nearly three times as large as its neighbors. A dog barked, although in the semidarkness, Cam couldn't see it. Max, no doubt.

Cam followed Galen up the stairs and through the front door. Galen flipped on the light to reveal high ceilings and wide-planked wooden floors. To the right, in what Cam guessed was supposed to be the dining room, stood two trestles supporting a large piece of wood—a makeshift table stacked high with more than a dozen fiberglass cases and several instruments. On one side, Cam saw a battered french horn and what looked like a tuba; on the other side, a clarinet with some of its keys missing. Between the cases and the instruments were a bevy of tools, neatly arranged by size and shape, most of which Cam didn't recognize. Maybe Galen repaired instruments on the side. Playing in the subway couldn't pay that well.

Galen untied his trainers and set them by the front mat. Perfectly straight, Cam noted, just like the tools on the table. *When in Rome.* Cam slipped his shoes off as well and placed them beside Galen's on the mat.

Galen, who had already made his way past Cam and set his trumpet case down by a steep set of stairs, walked to the back of the house. Cam heard what he guessed was the back door opening; then Galen shouted, "Max!" Seconds later came the sound of claws against wood floors and a blur of white and gray bounded into the hallway. Cam barely saw the dog before it jumped up, its head nearly reaching Cam's shoulders.

Cam gasped and backed up until he hit the wall, heart pounding. Too much caffeine, too little sleep, and the thought that people were out there looking for him, and he was a sniveling mess.

"Max! Down! Sit!"

To Cam's surprise, the dog did as he was told and looked almost apologetically at Galen. Galen, on the other hand, seemed unconcerned with Cam's over-the-top reaction. "We don't get much company," he explained almost casually as he opened a door to a small closet and hung up his jacket.

Cam thought about his own jacket—at least the muggers had good taste—and wondered how bad he must smell to Galen. Pretty bad.

"Get you something to eat?" Galen asked.

"No, thank you." The hamburger he'd inhaled at the coffee shop now sat like a lead weight in the bottom of his stomach. He glanced around, bouncing on his feet—partly to keep himself alert, partly because he was nervous. He didn't know what he was nervous about. The police wouldn't find him here, would they?

Everything seemed so surreal. Then again, the house was warm and clean. Immaculate. The way Cam's apartment looked when Luisa got through with it. In spite of himself, Cam yawned.

"Bed, then."

"That would be lovely." The thought of sleeping somewhere comfortable and relatively quiet was heavenly.

In spite of the mention of a guest bedroom, Cam half expected Galen to invite him into his bed. Instead, Galen showed him to a good-sized room on one side of the house, with its own bath attached. The bed had already been made with perfect hospital corners. Like the rest of the house, the room was spotless and neat. Galen drew the curtains, which appeared a bit worn but were heavy and seemed to block much of the cold air from outside.

"Sometimes I have unexpected houseguests," Galen explained, as if he'd guessed at Cam's unspoken question. He shoved his hands in his pockets and shrugged but didn't elaborate. "There are towels in the bath. A few toothbrushes in the drawer under the sink. Sweats okay?"

"Sweats?" In Cam's exhausted brain, the word didn't register.

"Sweatpants, sweatshirt? To sleep in?"

"Yes. Thank you. Sorry. I'm a bit slow tonight." Cam's brain still felt a bit thick.

"No worries. You'll feel better after a good night's sleep." Galen headed for the door. "Back in a minute."

Cam looked around the room. Much like the curtains, the carpet and bedding were worn. The bed looked old, like it had come with the house. A wooden dresser with a large round mirror took up half of a wall. Opposite stood a bookshelf piled with books. Cam walked over and glanced at some of the titles. Several were in Japanese. He picked up a ragged copy of Goethe's *Faust* and leafed through it to discover it was in the original German. He set it back down. One of the shelves was completely filled with music, neatly stacked.

"I teach high school music," Galen said from behind him, causing Cam to jump. It didn't explain the Goethe, but now the music and the instruments made sense.

"Does teaching pay that poorly?" Cam turned around to find Galen setting some clothing on the bed.

"Oh, you mean the subway gig?" Galen laughed as he turned back the covers and fluffed the pillows. "I do that just for fun." He didn't elaborate further.

"I see." Cam wasn't sure he *did* see, but he was too tired to pursue the topic.

"Feel free to help yourself to whatever you need," Galen said as he headed for the door to the room. "There are towels in the bathroom if you'd like to take a shower."

"I would." The thought of rinsing away the last few days sounded wonderful.

Galen smiled. "We can talk more tomorrow, after you've gotten some rest."

"All right."

"Good night, Cam."

"Good night." Cam hesitated, then added, "Thank you."

CAM SKIPPED down one of the gravel paths past the privet hedges that led from the terrace to the grounds beyond. He whistled a song he'd learned in school a few days before. He felt proud that he'd learned to whistle when Jane Ravenel and Paul Vestry hadn't been able to do more than blow air and spit when they'd tried. He'd said he'd teach them. He, Cameron Sherrington, could do something they couldn't do. He'd be a good teacher and they'd like him for it, wouldn't they?

He reached the edge of the forest a few minutes later. His father had promised to build him a tree house, like in Winnie the Pooh, *but he'd died before they'd had a chance to plan it. He'd asked his mother, but she'd told him he was too old for tree houses. He'd picked out the perfect spot for it too—a huge oak that grew on the edge of one of the fields where the horses often grazed.*

He whistled and ran faster until he reached the pond with the ancient boathouse. He tossed his shoes into the grass and dangled his feet in the water. He didn't notice the dark cloud overhead until everything around him grew black.

Cam shot up in bed, panting. A dream. *It was just a dream.* He looked around the room and tried to remember where he was. Slowly, it came back to him. Sleeping in the subway. The FBI. The music. Galen.

He dry-scrubbed his face, then took a few more deep breaths. He hadn't had a nightmare since he was a kid. He slipped out of bed and padded to the bathroom, relieved himself, then splashed a bit of cool water on his cheeks. The face that greeted him in the mirror looked tired. Older than usual, even. The dark circles under his eyes always looked ten times worse against his pale skin. The bruise on his cheek had blossomed purple. He touched it gingerly and winced. At least the muggers hadn't broken anything.

He stood, just looking at himself, for nearly ten minutes. Days before, he'd been assessing himself in the mirror to make sure his hair was just right. Now he barely noticed the tousled mess. He didn't recognize himself in the reflection. Or maybe he just didn't *want* to see himself looking back. No deep thoughts accompanied this strange, surreal appraisal. Through the haze of sleep and with the slightly edgy memory of the dream still lingering, he saw every line, every imperfection magnified. The small scar on his right cheek from when he'd fallen from a horse jumping far beyond his abilities. The lines at the corners of his mouth and eyes. The tiny birthmark by his nose.

The sensation of something pressing against his leg brought him back to himself. The dog, trying to get his attention. Cam looked down, shook his head, then walked back to bed. Once under the covers, he closed his eyes and tried to fall asleep. But it was nearly light outside when he finally drifted off.

CHAPTER *14*

CAM YAWNED and rolled onto his back. Early Sunday morning, judging by the angle of the sun through the windows of the guest bedroom. He'd slept better than he had in days, but he still felt exhausted.

He nearly jumped when something cold touched his face, and he realized he wasn't alone in the bed. For a split second, he thought it was Galen. Then he realized it was Galen's dog. What was his name? Max. Max, no doubt noticing Cam's eyes were open, decided he was fair game and licked him several times on the cheek before aiming for Cam's slightly parted lips.

Horrid, french-kissing a dog. Not that Cam hadn't kissed men who were equally uninspiring, but really, wasn't the dog supposed to be with his master? Wherever that was?

Cam pushed the animal away—good Lord, he was heavier than he looked. Cam had figured he was mostly fur. *Apparently not.* Clearly Galen fed him well.

He reminded himself he had nothing to complain about. He'd spent the night before in a subway station, after all. Last night he'd eaten a decent meal for the first time in days, even if the grease from the meat and fries still felt heavy in his gut. When Galen had mentioned something about being a vegetarian, Cam hadn't been terribly surprised. It went hand in hand with the California surfer look (Cam had fucked a few of those in his day) and the hound from hell. All right. Perhaps "big sloppy dog" was a better description of Max, who was by now curled against Cam's hip and snoring.

Cam allowed his eyes to close and drifted in and out of semisleep. He awoke to light streaming in the window through the miniblinds. Max was gone, but Cam's eyes itched and his nose had started to run. *Good riddance.* His stomach growled its displeasure. He didn't want to ask Galen to feed him again, but he figured eating Galen's food wasn't any worse than sleeping in his guest bedroom.

"You've never needed to ask for help." Galen was right. He never *had* asked for it, and he hated having to do it now.

He sighed and got out of bed, though he was tempted to stay under the warm duvet. The sheets were nothing like the crisp pressed cotton he was used to. They were a slightly off-white color and well-worn. Still, he liked the softness against his skin. He'd ask Luisa to add a bit more fabric softener the next time she changed his sheets.

The thought made him laugh. Of course she wouldn't be doing anything of the sort. Not for him, at least. Still, she was on the company payroll. *For now.* They'd need someone to keep up the Manhattan apartment until they sold it. He wondered if she'd be able to find another job.

For the first time since the entire mess had blindsided him, he felt something other than sorry for himself. Guilt. He wasn't unfamiliar with the feeling—he'd felt it when he fucked things up and broken Aiden's heart—but somehow this time it felt so much more *real.* He thought of Luisa's kids, the ones she'd proudly showed him pictures of, and wondered how she'd make ends meet.

She'll be fine. He needed to focus on himself right now, or he'd be in far more dire straits.

He ran a hand through his hair and found it soft when he'd been expecting the usual stickiness from the gel he favored. He vaguely remembered having showered before bed. He'd been so tired. He looked around and saw a pile of clothes on the nearby table—Galen must have put them out for him while he slept. Normally someone coming into his room while he slept would have bothered him, but today he didn't have it in him to care.

Cam picked up a pair of jeans from the pile. They were a bit long but otherwise fit well enough, once he'd secured them with a belt. Unlike Galen's jeans, these looked relatively new, with no holes that Cam could see. He'd expected to see a T-shirt but instead found a polo shirt in pale blue. It surprised Cam that Galen had realized he didn't wear T-shirts. He was quite sure it wasn't a coincidence.

He wondered again why Galen had offered him a place to stay. Undoubtedly he expected something in return, and since Cam clearly had nothing to offer other than himself, he guessed Galen probably did want sex, despite what he'd said. Sex with Galen wouldn't be so bad. He might be a bit slow, but he was attractive enough. Cam hadn't been looking for sex, but he wouldn't say no to Galen either.

You don't even know if he's gay. Cam had always been pretty good at guessing. Gay or bi, judging by how comfortable Galen appeared about asking Cam home. Few people wondered about Cam's orientation—only grandmothers and young women seemed to be oblivious. His mother knew and ignored it. Duncan had never asked. No one else seemed to care, if you didn't count the men who came on to him. But he liked that.

He pulled on the shirt, then checked his hair in the mirror. Without product, it was even messier than usual. Well, it wasn't as if Galen cared about how Cam looked—he'd taken him home even though he hadn't bathed since he'd left the cheap motel two days before. Cam yawned and glanced at the clock on the bedside table: 10:00 a.m. Not all that late, really.

After washing his face, he got dressed and walked down the stairs in the pair of athletic socks Galen had left him. They slid over the wood floors, but they were warm. Max met him at the bottom of the stairs, his tail wagging in circles like a furry helicopter. As soon as Cam let go of the railing, Max jumped on him, paws on his shoulders.

Damn animal. Why did people bother with pets?

"Max! Down!"

Cam looked around for Galen. Cam expected to find him in the kitchen, but the voice came from the small sunroom on the side of the house. That was when he noticed two bare feet sticking up in the air behind the couch. He peered around to find Galen in a handstand. And not just any handstand. Galen's hands and forearms rested flat on the floor, his face hovered an inch or two above it, his back was arched, and his legs, bent at the knees, hung over his head.

The thin cotton pants and fitted black tank left little to Cam's imagination. Galen's sculpted body was a revelation after the baggy T-shirt and jeans of the night before, the muscles of his arms and legs tensed as he maintained the pose. Cam watched Galen, noted the steadiness of his body and the relaxation of his face despite the obvious effort. Why hadn't he noticed how beautiful the man was? He'd always preferred men with nicely honed bodies, especially since he himself was far less substantially built.

Max nudged Cam again, bringing him back to himself.

"Max," Galen warned. He wore the same apologetic look as the night before. "Sorry. When he gets used to you, he'll leave you alone."

Cam did his best to force a smile as he wiped the slobber off his cheek. "Not a problem," he lied. He'd manage. There were more important things than having clean cheeks. *Like food or a roof over your head.*

Five minutes later, after Galen had rolled up his yoga mat and put it away, they made their way to the kitchen. "Toast all right with you?" Galen asked, holding up what looked to be a homemade loaf covered in oats, seeds, and nuts.

"That'd be perfect." Any food sounded perfect.

Galen popped several pieces of bread into the toaster, then asked, "Tea or coffee?"

"Tea, if you don't mind." In spite of his penchant for coffee, Cam preferred tea for breakfast, a holdover from his childhood. Some of his best memories were of sipping tea on the veranda with his father in the summer. They hadn't talked much, but Cam had felt close to him.

"Coming up." Galen turned his back to Cam and opened one of the white metal cabinets. "Earl Grey, Irish breakfast, Assam, or Darjeeling?"

"Irish breakfast, please." Another surprise. The man didn't serve Lipton. Or tea in tea bags, Cam now saw. Galen seemed to be brimming with surprises.

"With milk and sugar?"

"Yes, thank you."

Galen whistled and got to work. The tune was vaguely familiar. Not jazz. Classical? Mozart? No, Beethoven.

The table reminded Cam of something from a 1950s sitcom, with its chrome legs and laminate top with silver and gold sparkles baked in. Cam sat in one of the chairs, which wobbled a bit on the uneven tongue-and-groove floor. A few minutes later, Galen set down a large cup of tea and a beaker of milk, followed by the toast, butter, and several jams that looked homemade.

Cam picked up one of the jars, opened and sniffed it, then spread the jam on his toast and took a bite. The taste of fresh strawberries danced on his tongue, reminding him of the jam Cook used to make at the castle when he was little. He'd helped the staff pick them when they ripened, and he'd watched the cook can them afterward.

"Excellent jam," he said as he picked up his tea.

"We've got a great farmer's market not far from here," Galen explained.

"Oh, I see."

"Lots of local produce." Galen spread butter on his toast, then piled several spoonfuls of jam on top of that. "Most people don't realize how much of Jersey is farm country."

"Mmm." Cam, mouth full, figured agreeing with this statement was easiest. He didn't particularly care, although the jam tasted quite good. After he swallowed, he asked, "Was that yoga before?"

Galen nodded and took a sip of his tea. "I've been practicing yoga for about ten years now. Keeps me centered. On the right track."

"I see." Cam didn't, of course, but he'd be polite nonetheless. Riley had been on some hot yoga bender a few years before. Like everything else she'd taken up in what she'd called her "quest for perfection," she'd dropped it after a few months. This thought led him to wonder if he'd been a fad with her too.

"You okay?" Galen frowned, and Cam realized he'd been holding his tea so long his fingers were burning. He set the cup down, spilling a bit of the liquid onto the table.

"Perfectly fine."

"Sleep okay?" Galen stood up, retrieved a sponge from the sink, and wiped up the spill.

"Quite well," Cam lied. "Thank you. The bed is very comfortable," he added, which of course was true.

"Is there anything you'd like to talk about?"

The question took Cam aback. They'd gone from small talk to best mates in the span of twenty-four hours? "What for?" What could he possibly feel the need to tell Galen?

Galen shrugged and offered Cam an understanding smile. "I just wanted you to know I'm a good listener," he said. "If you ever feel you need to talk about things."

Cam schooled his expression and did his best to sound conciliatory. "I appreciate the offer. And I appreciate what you've done for me. But I'm perfectly fine."

"No problem." Galen finished the last bit of his toast, then asked, "More tea?"

"Thank you."

Galen snagged the teapot and strainer from the counter and walked back to the table. "So what would you like to do today?"

"*Do?*" As in a date? *Or maybe a play date.*

"It's Sunday, the weather is beautiful, and I was thinking maybe we could go to the flea market or something." Galen refilled Cam's tea, then his own.

Cam felt the panic return with a jolt to his gut. If he went out, they'd find him, wouldn't they? *Stop it! They're not so interested in you that they'll be knocking on doors in New Jersey.*

"Cam?"

Cam realized he'd been silent for a minute, maybe more. "I... ah.... I probably should be getting back."

"Where do you need to be?" The same words Galen had spoken when he'd bought Cam coffee.

"I've got someone I need to meet. In Manhattan," he added quickly.

Galen wiped down the table, dried it—the man was so bloody neat—then sat back down facing Cam. "I know you don't have anywhere to go. You wouldn't have come here with me if you did."

Cam clenched his jaw. "I should get out of your hair. I'll figure something out."

"You can stay as long as you need. Like I said, Max and I are used to having company."

"What kind of company?" Cam heard himself ask.

Galen laughed, and Cam thought he saw a hint of pink on his cheeks. "Not the kind of company you'd imagine. Usually a stray kid. My brother, when he has business in the city. My folks, when they drive down from Maine."

"Stray kid?"

"I teach high school, remember?" Galen put the top back on the jam jar and turned it so that the label faced toward Cam, perfectly aligned with the edge of the table. "You know, kid gets into a fight with a parent, threatens to run away?"

"I wouldn't know." Cam stood up and walked over to the window. The wind had died down, leaving the yard covered in leaves.

"I'm sorry," Galen said as though he meant it, which just irritated Cam more.

"Don't be. I spent my formative years at a very expensive boarding school in Scotland. After my father died, my mother decided the best way to make a man out of me was to send me to an all-boys' school." Cam didn't add that he'd learned early on that if he was going to survive there, he needed to "help" the older boys out. He'd been quite good at that too. Once, when he'd been caught blowing one of them behind a building, he'd even helped one of the teachers.

"Doesn't sound that great, the way you say it."

"I learned a lot."

Galen's expression didn't waver. "Is your mother still living?" he asked.

Tactfully done change of topic. "I called her before I decided to take a nap in the subway station," Cam said with a laugh he knew sounded bitter. "Shall we just say she wasn't exactly interested in my predicament, and leave it at that?"

This time Cam knew he'd struck a chord. He saw the barely visible shift in Galen's gaze. Good. Maybe Galen wouldn't ask him anything else. Cam didn't want to talk about her.

"I could use a little help with the leaves," Galen said after a pause.

"Leaves?"

"Raking?" Galen prompted. "This time of year, it's all I can do to keep them off the grass."

"What's wrong with leaving them on the grass?" Cam countered.

"Don't know. I guess it's just what I've always done. Rake them, I mean." Galen grinned, then added, "I remember when I was a kid, my dad would gather them into a pile and my brother Ryan and I would jump into them."

Which was how Cam found himself raking leaves in the front of Galen's house an hour and a half later.

"Not so bad, huh?" Galen said as he added to a perfectly rounded pile, pushing some of the leaves over the top of it like a miniature mountain peak.

Cam groaned and looked at his far smaller pile on the other side of the yard. Crooked, with some of the leaves trailing away. What was Galen that he made it look so easy? A bloody lumberjack? Cam, dressed in more of Galen's just-a-bit-too-large sweats, already felt sore.

"You're working too hard at it," Galen said as he stepped behind Cam and adjusted the rake in Cam's hands. "Let the tines of the rake do the work. Like this. See?" He moved the rake in short strokes and the leaves leapt up and began to create a pile.

Cam nodded. Galen's hands on his, even gloved, felt good. He imagined Galen touching his skin, imagined exploring the landscape of Galen's chest.

"You don't need to push down so hard," Galen was saying. "You'll hurt yourself." He worked his fingers into Cam's shoulders and massaged them.

Cam leaned into Galen, closed his eyes, and relaxed. "Feels good," he said in an undertone. Heaven. Just like this. With nothing on his mind but the way the smell of the leaves mingled with the scent of the grass, the sound of a bird chirping, the distant din of the freeway.

He remembered wondering what it would be like to have sex outside. Not now, of course, but when the weather grew warmer. He imagined the feel of the wind on his skin and the way Galen's muscles would ripple with the effort. He moaned....

"Cam?"

Shit. He'd done it again, hadn't he? He'd zoned out. He'd thought about things he shouldn't be thinking about. No. He'd thought about one thing in particular: sex. And didn't sex always complicate things? So why did he want it so badly?

"I'm fine. Thank you." He forced a smile, then got back to work on the leaves.

THEY ATE dinner in relative silence. Cam was too exhausted for chitchat, and Galen seemed to understand. Dizzy Gillespie played in the background—Galen had turned on the same jazz station they'd listened to in the car on the way from the city the day before.

Dinner, Galen's "kitchen sink" chili, which Cam learned meant no meat but every vegetable and bean imaginable, was better than Cam expected. Aiden had cooked chili once when they'd lived together in London years before, but it had been mostly meat.

"How long have you been teaching high school?" Cam asked to break the silence.

"Six years." Galen took a pull on his beer. "I used to teach at two different high schools, but the budget got cut a few years ago, and now I work part-time and teach in the evenings."

"Teach?" Cam felt something brush his ankle and looked down. Max. Of course. He seemed nearly as tired as Cam felt. Cam supposed running all over the yard, chasing birds and squirrels, would wear a dog out.

"Brass and woodwinds, mostly. Trumpet. Trombone. Flute. Clarinet. Oh, and I have one piano student."

"You play all of those?" Aiden had played piano and sung, but playing more than one or two instruments seemed impressive.

Galen nodded. "You pretty much have to play them if you're going to teach high school band and orchestra. When I was a kid, most of my friends took private lessons. Now, most kids learn to play in school."

Cam stifled a yawn.

"How are you feeling?"

"What?"

"I was thinking of a soak in the hot tub." Galen rubbed his right shoulder. "Good for sore muscles."

"That sounds heavenly. Except that I don't have a bathing suit, of course."

Galen's cheeks reddened. "I've got a few extras," he said, then picked his beer up once more and drank the rest of the contents.

Cam had half hoped Galen would suggest skipping bathing suits. Not that Galen had shown one iota of interest in him, but at least he might be able to enjoy the view.

CHAPTER *15*

GALEN SILENTLY handed Cam a bathing suit, then quickly retreated to his own bedroom to change. Good God, had he actually *blushed* when Cam had mentioned he didn't have one?

"I'm an idiot."

Max gazed up at him, pink tongue lolling to one side, tail wagging.

"You're an attention hog, you know that?"

Max wagged his tail in fast circles this time. Galen bent down, scratched his head, and received a sloppy lick in return.

Galen hadn't been a monk for the past ten years, though he wouldn't call the men he sometimes hooked up with dates, either. More like someone to scratch the occasional itch. No real conversation. Nothing to find charming like he found Cam's English accent, or the way Cam liked to nibble his lower lip when he concentrated. Or the tiny moan that had escaped when he'd massaged Cam's shoulders. Or the slightly effeminate way Cam moved.

The last thing you want to do is make him feel like he owes you sex.

He pulled off his sweats and slipped into his bathing suit, then folded the discarded clothing and set it on top of the dresser. One of the books he'd stacked there earlier was just a bit askew, so he pushed it with a finger until it aligned with the other books on the pile. Satisfied, he shut off the light and headed into the hallway with Max at his heels.

Cam was waiting for him wearing the oh-so-slightly-too-large swim trunks Galen had lent him, which hung low on his hips and emphasized Cam's waist. Even in the poor light of the hallway, Galen could see the sleek muscles of Cam's lean body and the pale skin dotted with an occasional birthmark similar to the one on Cam's face.

Breathe. Focus. Relax. Galen repeated the mantra several times over as he offered what he hoped was a pleasant smile. "Shall we?"

Cam smiled back. "Lead the way."

Galen turned and walked down the stairs, relieved not to have to continue to look at Cam. Or stare at him, since he felt pretty confident that was exactly what he'd been doing. He opened the french doors without looking back, then headed to the hot tub as Max zoomed by him into the yard.

"It's a bit chilly out here," Cam said as Galen lifted the cover off.

"It's always colder getting in." Galen pulled out the floating thermometer, checked the temperature, then dropped it back in. "Perfect. You first."

Cam walked past him and climbed the short steps, then paused for a moment, looking back at Galen as if challenging him to take notice. And oh, but Galen had noticed the place where back met perfect ass. Thankfully Cam didn't prolong Galen's discomfort but slipped into the water with an audible sigh. Galen joined him a moment later, sitting next to him.

"Wonderful." Cam leaned against the side of the tub and sighed. "Now I might be able to move tomorrow."

Galen chuckled, happy for the moment of levity. "Thanks for helping today." He'd always enjoyed raking leaves. He relished the satisfaction of seeing the lawn free of leaves at least as much as the physical effort involved.

"I'd say it was my pleasure," Cam said as he massaged the back of his neck, "but I'm feeling decidedly sore at the moment."

"Sorry."

"You don't look particularly sorry." Cam's grin belied his words.

Galen dipped his hand in the water and wet his face. "Nah. I'm *not* particularly sorry. I had fun today."

"I did as well." Cam's cheeks went pink, although Galen figured it probably had more to do with the hot water than anything else. Still, it was charming.

Focus. Breathe. Relax.

Galen leaned his head back on the lip of the tub and looked upward at the sky. The clouds shone silver with the light of the moon. In between them, several stars glittered. He inhaled the familiar scent of the leaves. He could smell autumn on the cool breeze. Their shoulders touched, causing Galen's breath to hitch.

He turned so he could better see Cam. Eyes closed, the curled ends of his hair painted with the water, he looked so peaceful. *What are you running from?* He wondered what had changed so drastically in Cam's life that he'd been driven to hide in the tunnels. Galen knew the look of fear he'd seen in Cam's eyes— he'd seen it on the faces of some of his students, and in his own face, long ago.

Cam pressed his lips together, then opened his eyes and looked down at his hands. "I can't stay here." The sound of the jets as they kicked in nearly swallowed Cam's words. Cam's eyes sparkled momentarily and his Adam's apple bobbed.

However quietly Cam had spoken the words, they hit Galen hard. He'd always had a good sense about people and what they needed. He wasn't sure why, but he knew Cam needed to stay. Best to hit this one straight on in Galen's experience—get it out into the open so Cam could let go of the guilt, or whatever was keeping him from accepting the hand Galen had offered him.

"You have nowhere else to go, do you?"

Breathe. Relax. Focus.

Cam shook his head. Galen saw defeat written on his face. "Then stay. Please. For as long as you need to." Cam was obviously reeling from something, but Galen knew nothing he could say at that moment would help. Cam needed time. Time to trust that Galen didn't expect anything from him. "You're safe here, Cam."

CHAPTER *16*

CAM RAN barefoot down the path that led to the pond near the field where the horses grazed. The warm air and the smell of wildflowers made him smile. On he ran until he reached the boathouse at the edge of the water. He'd dip his toes in— he'd promised his mother he wouldn't swim alone. He opened the door to the boathouse, intending to walk through it to the small dock on the other side. But the door closed behind him and the darkness reached out for him, pulling him away from the door with strong hands and pinning him against the rough wood floor.

"I've been waiting for you," the darkness whispered in his ear. "Why did you keep me waiting?"

He tried to speak, but the darkness pressed a hand to his mouth. He struggled to push the hand away, but it held him tight. He kicked and tried to escape its grasp.

"No, please," he gasped as the darkness finally released his lips. "Please, let me go."

"Relax," the darkness said. "You're safe with me."

He screamed.

"No. Please, no!" Cam batted the hand from his shoulder and scooted away.

"Cam," a voice said. A gentle voice, unlike the rough voice from before. "It's me. Galen."

"Galen?" He opened his eyes and struggled to remember where he was. For a moment he thought he was back in the subway again. But he saw Galen's face, saw his look of concern, and remembered he was in the guest bedroom of Galen's house.

"You were dreaming, Cam," the same voice—Galen—said. "It's okay now."

Cam opened his eyes and realized he'd backed himself up against the headboard, knees drawn to his chest. He couldn't stop shaking. *What the fuck is wrong with me?* He tried to remember the dream, but everything seemed to blur in the darkness.

"I.... I'm f-fine...." He barely got the words out. He clasped his knees tighter as he continued to shake.

"I'm going to put a blanket around you, Cam," Galen said from far away. "May I touch you?"

Cam nodded. Galen helped him scoot down on the bed so he wasn't pressed so hard against the headboard.

Get a grip! He forced his eyes open again as Galen gently laid a blanket over his shoulders. The shaking eased somewhat, more like shivering now, less terror. What had he been so frightened of? The dark? He wasn't afraid of the dark.

"Better?"

Cam nodded again.

"Would you like me to rub your shoulders?" Galen asked.

"Yes." His voice sounded tentative to his ears, but at least he managed to get the word out this time.

Galen rested his hands on Cam's shoulders for a moment. Slowly, he began to work his fingers on the muscles there. Cam was so tense it hurt. "It's all right. Just breathe. Slowly. In...." Cam paused. "And out.... Take your time."

Cam tried to focus on his breathing. It was easier now that he knew where he was. It was also easier as Galen massaged the tension away. The memory of the dream began to fade, and with it, the tension in his body. He sighed and closed his eyes, allowing his mind to drift. And of course it drifted where it always seemed to go. Cam imagined Galen's hands on other parts of his body. Touching him. Stroking him.

"Feels good," Cam said on a voiced sigh.

"I'm glad." Galen continued to knead the muscles of Cam's upper back.

Cam's thoughts wandered again. This time, though, he didn't just imagine what he wanted. He turned and reached for Galen's face, pulling him into a kiss. A gorgeous kiss that had him moaning and tasting Galen's mouth and feeling Galen's slightly rough jaw brush his own skin. Galen knew how to kiss. Galen pressed his tongue around Cam's, then probed Cam's mouth. Cam wrapped his arms around Galen's waist and under his T-shirt—

"Cam," Galen gasped as he pulled away.

Cam heard his panted breaths, saw the slightly glassy look in his eyes, and knew Galen wanted him too. Why was he pushing him away? "But I thought—"

"It's not right, Cam," Galen said as he stood up and brushed his lips with his fingers in obvious shock. The fabric of Galen's sweatpants was tented.

"I don't understand," Cam said, desperate for more. God, he needed more! He wanted Galen and Galen wanted him. How much more "right" did it need to get?

"I'd be a total asshole if I took advantage of you like this," Galen said.

"You wouldn't be tak—"

"Cam," Galen interrupted with a shake of his head, "I'm not going to lie. You're hot as hell and I liked that. Kissing you. But you know it's not right. Not now."

Cam nodded and exhaled slowly. He supposed he could live with that answer. It left open the possibilities and he felt less rejected than he had been a few minutes before.

"You should try to get some sleep. We can talk in the morning, if you want."

Great. More talking.

Max, who'd been sitting at the foot of the bed through all of this, now walked over to Cam and pressed a cold nose against his thigh. Cam rubbed his eyes and sniffed. No doubt noticing this, Galen eyed him warily and handed him a tissue from the table beside the bed.

"Are you sure you're all right?"

"Allergic," Cam said quickly. Did Galen think he'd been crying?

"Let me get you something for that." Galen, with Max following behind, trotted down the hallway and returned with a glass of water and a bottle of pills marked Benadryl. "Should help," he said, and he added, "and it'll help you sleep too. I take a few of those and I sleep like the dead."

Cam took the glass. Galen opened the bottle, shook a single pink pill onto his palm, then offered it to Cam. Cam reached for the pill and brushed Galen's hand as he retrieved it. He ignored the warmth and arousal that brief touch engendered and swallowed the pill without a word.

He'd never been so mortified in his life. Even sleeping on the bench in the subway didn't compare to waking up a complete stranger by screaming in his sleep. How much more pathetic could he get? Waking Galen up in the middle of the night like some stupid child—even worse, with a runny nose. *Coming on to him and getting the cold shoulder….*

"Do you want me to stay a little longer?" Galen asked.

"No, of course not." He wasn't a child. He didn't need coddling. He already resented being indebted to Galen; the last thing he wanted was to owe the man more than he already did. And being rejected hadn't made him any more likely to lean on Galen, either.

"Okay." Galen got up and walked to the door, where he lingered for a few seconds but said nothing.

"I'm fine." Cam yawned. "Tired. Sorry to wake you."

Galen frowned, then shrugged. "Okay. But if you need anything—"

"I'll be fine."

"Okay." Galen pressed his lips together but didn't press the issue any more. "Come, Max!"

The dog didn't budge.

"Max! Come!"

This time Max jumped onto the bed and burrowed his head into Cam's lap, then sighed contentedly.

"It's all right," Cam said, smiling in spite of himself. "He can sleep with me. I've got the allergy thing under control, remember?" It surprised him to realize he actually *wanted* the dog to stay. He didn't want to sleep alone.

"Are you sure?"

"I'm sure. Good night."

"Good night." Galen was gone a moment later.

Max stretched out and pressed his back against Cam's thigh. It took Cam nearly an hour, but he finally fell asleep. And this time, he didn't dream.

CHAPTER

CAM DOZED on and off, waking only when he realized it was well after noon. *Another Monday*. He hoped this one would be better than the last few. He hadn't even thought to ask Galen about his job and whether he'd be around in the morning. The nightmare had been horrible and waking Galen up embarrassing. Cam still couldn't explain it, except that he was under too much stress. Too many things to think about.

"Morning," Galen said with a bright smile as Cam plunked himself down at the kitchen table a short time later. "Or afternoon, I guess."

Cam grunted his response.

"Tea, then?"

"Coffee, if you don't mind." He spoke more coherently this time. Caffeine was too important to be lost in translation. When Galen looked at him with surprise, Cam added, "I prefer coffee after noon."

Ten minutes later, having drunk two cups of surprisingly good European coffee, he felt almost human. "Don't you have to work?" he asked when his head had cleared.

"I need to stop over at the school," Galen said. "But just to drop off a clarinet I fixed. The benefits of part-time teaching. I have a few students coming late this afternoon. Private lessons."

"Anything I can do to help out?" Cam wasn't sure what he was *capable* of doing, but he needed to do something or he'd go mad thinking about all of the shit dogging him.

"You're welcome to come with me, if you'd like. I thought I'd head over there after my lessons." Galen set a pile of scrambled eggs in front of him, along with something he called "facon," which Cam learned was some sort of soy protein shaped to look like bacon. Although he wasn't sure why someone who didn't eat meat would want something to look like bacon, the stuff tasted quite good.

Cam took a few mouthfuls of egg and considered the invitation. "Don't you need to show identification to visit a school?" Cam had heard about some of the security precautions schools were taking in the wake of recent violence.

"Not after hours."

"All right," he said as he picked up a piece of the facon. Nobody knew he'd made his way to New Jersey. Nobody here would know him, especially not high school students.

"We can stop at the grocery store on the way back. Pick up a few things."

Cam stared at his eggs as the realization hit him that he'd been eating Galen's food for nearly two days now. This was ten times worse than the board giving him grief over his spending. He was entirely beholden to Galen, with no means of paying him back.

"Something wrong?" Galen asked when Cam didn't respond.

"No. Just that I'll pay you back for all of this."

"Don't sweat it. If it's the food you're worried about, don't. I've got plenty of money for food." Galen picked up his mug and took a sip of his drink. Cam must not have looked convinced, because Galen added with a chuckle, "Really, Cam. But if you'd be more comfortable paying me back when you're on your feet again, that's fine with me."

"MR. RUSK!" One of the boys in the hallway gave Galen a high-five, then ducked into a classroom.

"Eddie," Galen said to Cam, as though this meant something. "Good kid. Doing better now that he's got a decent foster family."

"Oh." No one had talked much about foster families when Cam had been growing up. He suspected few, if any, kids at Briggston—maybe a few of the scholarship dayers—had been from homes like that. Not that Cam's family hadn't had their own issues. Tylerton High School looked nothing like any school he'd attended either. The brightly painted lockers did little to counteract the dingy yellowing walls. Here and there, signs reminded students of various activities.

"Is it always so quiet?" Cam asked when they'd walked down several hallways without seeing more than a few students.

"School ended at 2:20." Galen motioned Cam to a stairwell, and they began to climb. "Only the kids in clubs and sports are left now, and since the last round of budget cuts, there aren't as many after-school activities as before."

They reached the top of the steps and walked down yet another corridor. "My office is through here," Galen said as he opened a set of double doors onto what Cam guessed was the band room, judging by the instrument cases that littered the steel shelves and the chairs arranged in a semicircle around a podium.

A student sat behind the piano in the corner of the room, playing something familiar. *Rhapsody in Blue*. Surprisingly difficult music for a high school student. More surprisingly still, the boy played beautifully.

"Hey, Mr. Rusk!"

"Jamie," Galen answered as he walked over to the piano. "You're doing a great job with that. I like what you've done with that last section. That's exactly what I was talking about last week."

Jamie grinned from ear to ear, clearly pleased with the praise.

"Cam," Galen said with a quick look in Cam's direction, "meet Jamie. Jamie, Cam."

"Pleased to meet you," Cam said as he shook the boy's hand. Jamie had freckles on his cheeks, pink lips with a lovely Cupid's bow, and sandy blond hair that reminded Cam of Galen.

"Jamie's one of my star pupils. He just scored himself a full scholarship to Juilliard." Galen's face radiated pride as he said this. "Early admission."

"Congratulations." Cam knew the school well—one of the best conservatories in the United States.

"I'd never have gotten in if it hadn't been for Mr. Rusk," Jamie said, his gaze flitting around the room in embarrassment. "He's a great teacher."

"Jamie's been studying with me since he started high school. In fact, he has a lesson tomorrow"—Galen winked at Jamie—"so we should let him practice."

"Good meeting you, Cam," Jamie said as he settled back onto the piano bench.

"You too, Jamie."

Galen pointed to a door at the back of the room. "That's my office," he said.

Galen's office might have measured ten feet by ten feet, although the actual floor space showing was far less. Piles of music, all neatly stacked, lined the walls and covered nearly the entire small desk. Metal mouthpieces and reeds lay on a shelf above the desk.

"Impressive."

Galen laughed. "That's one way to look at it. Fortunately I don't spend much time here. Not really a desk job."

"You obviously enjoy teaching."

"I love it." Galen's face lit up as he said this. Cam had seen that same look in Alex Bishop's eyes when he talked about his own music. He didn't understand it, but it felt palpable and real. "Things are so different now than when I was a kid. For some kids, this is the only exposure they get to classical and jazz."

Galen unlocked one of the desk drawers and pulled a few wooden reeds out, then locked it again. He opened the clarinet case and put the reeds inside, then left the instrument on a shelf with a sticky note that read *Marla*. "She'll pick it up before rehearsal tomorrow," he explained. Cam struggled to keep up with the quick change of subject.

Jamie had moved on to what Cam guessed was Beethoven when they left a few minutes later. "See you tomorrow," Jamie called after them.

"WHY DO you teach?" Cam asked as they wandered the supermarket aisles a short time later.

Galen shrugged. "I'm not sure. I mean, I'm sure I like doing it, but I've never really thought about the why part." He crouched down and pulled a bag of something marked "textured vegetable protein" off a shelf, then handed it to Cam. "Put this in the cart, please?"

Cam held up the box, eyed the bits of dried flaky things, and frowned. "What is this?"

"Fake meat."

"How…?"

"Add boiling water to reconstitute it," Galen explained. "It's used just like ground beef. You can use it in spaghetti sauce or tacos."

"Why would you want fake meat if you're a vegetarian?" Cam didn't understand the facon either.

"No idea. I guess texture's part of it, but it doesn't really explain it, does it?"

Cam shook his head. "Not really."

"You could probably ask a vegan the same question about soy milk too," Galen said as he put a box of crackers in the cart. "I guess vegetarians want familiar things. Most of us grew up with meat and liked the taste of it, so we want a substitute."

"You've lost me." Cam began to read through the ingredients of the protein flakes. "Why bother to be a vegetarian, then?"

Galen's laughter echoed through the aisle. Cam shot him an irritated look. He'd meant the question, after all. "Sorry. I'm not laughing at you, Cam. More laughing at myself, I guess. I can see how silly it must look."

Cam relaxed a bit. "I really did mean the question in all seriousness."

"I know." Galen pulled two boxes of breakfast cereal off a high shelf and added them to the cart. "And you deserve an answer. I personally became a vegetarian when I decided to practice yoga."

"Healthier?" Cam prompted.

"That, yes. But also because it's a practice, just like yoga." Galen leaned against the cart, his eyes bright with excitement. Cam understood how important this was to Galen. He could hear it in his voice.

"I love hamburgers," Galen said with a crooked grin. "The really bad ones. Big Macs. Whoppers. Oh, and the fries...." He sighed wistfully. "I still crave them from time to time when I drive by a fast-food place."

"Then why give them up if you love them?"

"That's just it. It's all about discipline. I drive by the restaurants and my mouth waters. But I've decided not to eat that stuff anymore. And it's a challenge not to give in. A little like a yoga pose. Mind over matter."

Cam considered this. He supposed he understood what Galen meant about discipline. He understood willpower, even if he had next to none when it came to some things. *Things that get you into trouble.* But discipline for the sake of discipline?

"Yeah," Galen said, bringing Cam back to himself, "I know it sounds strange. But yoga and meditation are all about mind over matter, denial and practice to grow the soul, expand the mind."

Cam fought not to roll his eyes. Or imagine Galen surfing a wave. Or riding bareback on the beach wearing nothing but—

"Cam? You okay?"

"Fine." Cam pretended to pay careful attention to a box of something called Count Chocula so Galen wouldn't see his red face. Why did he even care what Galen thought? He'd never been embarrassed to think about another man that way.

"Good stuff," Galen said.

"Huh?"

"The cereal." Galen added, "I used to beg my mother for it when I was little. Not that she let me have it...."

"Then you should buy it," Cam said, happy to have stumbled onto something he could wrap his exhausted brain around. He set it in the cart without waiting for Galen's approval.

Galen pursed his lips, then laughed outright. "Okay. I will. But you'll have to promise to revive me from my sugar coma afterward."

"I can do that," Cam said as they joined the queue at the checkout.

CHAPTER 18

CAM LEANED against the hot tub seat and watched the moonlight dance over Galen's chest. He liked how Galen's hair was fine and so light in color that his skin appeared smooth, almost glowing. He reached out and stroked a finger down from the slight indentation at the base of Galen's throat to the place between Galen's pink nipples. Galen smiled at him and moaned softly.

Cam traced concentric circles around one nipple until he held it between his thumb and forefinger. He pinched, gently at first, then with a bit more pressure, eliciting a gasp from Galen.

"Cam," Galen hissed, his pleasure obvious. "Feels so good."

The scene faded. Now Cam sat on the edge of the pond, toes dipped in the cool water. The sun warmed his shoulders as he splashed and sent droplets up into the air, where they shimmered momentarily, then fell back and made circles on the surface. He whistled a song he'd learned at school the week before. He liked music class. The teacher had said he had a nice voice. He liked her. Nobody had ever told him that before, and it felt good.

Maybe he'd tell his mother. She'd been so angry with him. If he told her the teacher liked him, maybe his mother would like him again. He'd practiced his piano so she wouldn't be angry, but it hadn't made her happy. Maybe only his father made her happy. And now that he was gone, maybe she wouldn't ever be happy again.

He didn't realize the sun had disappeared until he shivered from the cold. When had it turned black outside?

"Galen?" he called, thinking he'd heard something.

No one answered, although the wind sighed through the nearby trees. He supposed he should go back to the house and practice some more. He got to his feet and walked to the boathouse.

He hadn't expected the darkness to wait for him there.

"No, please," he said, his heart beating fast, like the wings of a bird struggling against a strong breeze. "I promised my mother I'd practice. I need to go back inside."

"I missed you," the darkness told him as he wrapped his arms tight around Cam's waist. "I always miss you when I'm gone."

"My mother wants me to practice," he told the darkness. But the darkness didn't understand him.

"Stay with me," the darkness said. "It's been too long. I'm lonely."

Why did the darkness touch him like that? It didn't feel right.

"I need to go."

"Stay with me," the darkness repeated. "You know you want to."

"No, please. Let me go. Let me—"

"—go!" Cam shouted, waking himself up. Max, who'd been sleeping at the foot of the bed, barked loudly enough to make Cam's heart pound.

Bollocks.

"Cam?" Galen poked a sleepy head into his room a minute later. "Everything all right?"

"Everything's fine." Cam struggled to catch his breath. *It was just a dream. It wasn't real.*

"Another nightmare?" Galen asked with a sympathetic frown.

"No. I just forgot where I was when I woke." This dream was even worse than the one the night before, but he'd hardly have told Galen that. He'd now woken Galen up two nights in a row, and Galen's motherly attitude irritated him. When Galen looked unconvinced, Cam added, "I'm fine, Galen. Go back to sleep."

Galen hesitated.

Cam offered what he hoped was a reassuring smile, even though he really wanted to scream.

"Okay. But if you need me, just let me know."

Need him? Did Galen think he was some sort of child who needed someone to look after him? *Pathetic.* Was he that much of a mess that Galen would think such a thing? "Right."

This seemed to placate Galen, because he nodded and disappeared a moment later. Cam realized Galen hadn't offered to take the dog with him, as he'd done the night before. Having the dog might actually make him feel better. Safer.

What the hell? He pushed the thought away as he'd done the other times the dream had stirred. Of course he was safe.

CHAPTER

SIX IN the morning on Tuesday. Cam awoke to the sound of the front door closing and rolled over. Galen had said he'd be at school most of the day. Cam hadn't slept much the night before—maybe a few hours. He considered getting out of bed but decided on more sleep. He had nowhere to go and no one to see.

The sound of barking pulled him right out of a dream. A good dream, this time. Aiden, calling him back and telling him he'd made a mistake, that it was Cam he wanted.

Bloody dog! Cam pulled the extra pillow over his head and imagined the dream, hoping to recapture it. But when he woke two hours later to slightly numb feet, he couldn't remember anything. The numb part? Max, sleeping on top of him. Cam nudged the dog off, but Max, undeterred, just moved up on the bed until he lay pressed against Cam's arm.

Cam tossed the pillow off his head. "You're a stubborn fur ball, aren't you?"

Max lifted his head and nudged Cam's arm. Cam shook his head, then rolled onto his side and scratched Max's head. The soft whap-whap-whap of Max's tail against the covers broke the silence.

The bedside clock read 1:25 p.m. *Time to get up.* Far past that time, but what did it matter?

Cam went through the motions of his normal day. He showered and lingered a bit longer than usual under the warm spray, then dressed in more of Galen's just slightly too big clothes. When he made his way to the kitchen at nearly three o'clock, he found a note from Galen on the counter.

> Cam-
> *I left you something to eat in the fridge. Just pop it in the microwave for a minute. Help yourself to tea. I'll be home around 4:30.*
> -Galen

Cam opened the fridge and found a small stack of pancakes on a plate covered with plastic wrap. He heated the water for tea as he set the plate in the microwave. He leafed through a copy of the *New York Times* as his tea steeped.

Nothing about him or Sherrington Holdings. He wasn't sure whether to be relieved or more worried than before.

He finished his very late breakfast at three thirty, cleaned up his mess—the least he could do to thank Galen for his generosity—then took a seat on the couch. How long had it been since he'd checked his mobile? He pulled the phone from his pocket and fingered the display. He took a deep breath, then powered the phone on. He had nearly a dozen messages and barely enough battery left to listen to them.

"Cameron, it's your mother. This behavior of yours is truly unacceptable. You're acting like a child. It pains me to say it, but I blame myself for this. If I hadn't—"

Cam clenched his jaw and deleted the message. Not that he could blame her for thinking the worst of him. Still, it hurt that she thought him even *capable* of something like laundering money for drug dealers. Not that the next message was much better.

"Cam," Riley said in her breathy voice, *"I'm really sorry about what happened. I mean, I know what you must think of me, but I only wanted to help you. I know whatever you've done, there's probably a good reason for it. Call me. I promise I won't—"*

Cam stabbed the Delete key. Fuck them all. He didn't even bother with the rest; he powered the phone down and threw it onto the coffee table, where it skittered off and landed on the carpet. He made no move to retrieve it.

"You okay?" Galen's voice brought Cam back to himself with a start.

"Fine."

"Sorry, man, but you don't sound fine." Galen chuckled and sat down next to him.

"Bugger off."

"Meant only with the greatest amount of affection, I'm sure." Galen leaned back against the pillows and met Cam's gaze.

"Of course."

"Checking phone messages?" Galen asked.

"Brilliant deduction, Watson."

"Want to talk about it?" Galen wore a patient I'm-here-for-you look that aggravated Cam even more.

"No." Why the fuck did Galen always ask if he wanted to talk about things? He was bloody well sick of talking.

"Okay. That's cool. Anything I can do?"

Cam shrugged. "No idea."

"Okay. That's cool too."

"Thanks for breakfast," Cam said, realizing he'd been sounding like an ungrateful toff. Which he was, of course, but that didn't mean he had to alienate the one human being on the planet who seemed to tolerate him.

"You're welcome."

The next few minutes passed in silence. Galen appeared completely unconcerned as he pulled a leg underneath himself and stretched his arms over his head. Cam wished he was as comfortable with silences as Galen.

"Galen?"

"Hmm?"

"Maybe there is something you can do."

Galen raised an eyebrow. "What's that?"

"Put on the jazz station you listen to sometimes?"

"Sure." Galen got up and turned on the stereo.

Cam closed his eyes and took a few deep breaths. The scent that filled his nostrils was familiar and woodsy. Galen's soap. The same soap Cam had showered with a few hours before. He liked the slightly spicy aroma. Simple, unlike the expensive cologne he himself wore.

"You like jazz?" Galen asked.

Cam nodded. "I discovered it at university. Classic jazz, mostly. Ella, Coltrane, Ellington. My dad loved it too. I found his old record collection. Used to sit for hours and listen."

"You been to any of the clubs in the city?"

"Sure." Cam smiled, remembering how he and Riley had spent weekends hopping from one club to the next. The last time he'd been to a club, he'd gone with Aiden to hear Alex and David perform from their album, *The Lake*.

"When I first moved to Jersey, I'd go into the city almost every weekend to hear music," Galen said.

"Now you play instead?"

Galen nodded. "I like hearing music. But I love playing it more."

"You're very good." Cam remembered the Rachmaninoff Galen played the first time they'd met. Or almost met. "Have you thought about getting a group together and getting some work?"

"Thanks." Galen's expression grew wistful. "I prefer doing my own thing. On my own time. No pressure. Just me and the music."

"In the subway?" Cam didn't understand why someone with such obvious talent would be content to play in a noisy train station. Galen was a bit of an enigma.

"Yeah. I like it there. Watching the people. Playing what I want. It makes me happy, playing there." Galen stood and smiled down at Cam. "So how about some dinner?" he asked. Cam wondered why he'd changed the subject.

"Sure. Need any help?"

"You can set the table, if you'd like." Galen clapped his hands, and Max hopped off the couch and trotted after him to the kitchen. Cam followed a moment later.

CHAPTER 20

CAM RAN along the path, through the rose garden, and back toward the main house. He grinned and began to sing. Miss Marquette had told him he'd played well! He wished his mother could have come to the recital, but when she got back from London, he'd tell her how well he'd played and she'd be proud of him.

"Your father was an excellent pianist," she always told him. "He worked very hard as a boy to play that well."

He wished his father could hear how well he'd played. Maybe wherever he was—if he was in heaven like they'd told him—he had *heard. Maybe he'd be good enough to play with an orchestra someday. His mother had taken him to hear Van Cliburn play a few months before, and he'd imagined that was him on stage with the orchestra. He'd felt the music in his fingers and toes as he'd watched.*

Maybe he'd grow up to be like David Somers, who played piano but was studying to be a conductor at university in the States. Wouldn't it be lovely to tell the orchestra how to play the music? David seemed to enjoy it—at least that was what David said when he'd come to his mother's birthday party. He would be just like David, waving his arms around like a puppeteer pulling the strings to make his puppets move.

"Your mother called," Randall said as Cam skipped into the kitchen for a snack. "She won't be back until tomorrow. Your uncle's in the study. He's staying overnight. You'll have dinner together."

He'd tell Uncle Duncan. Duncan would be proud of him. Maybe he'd even let Cam play a bit of the piece for him. Cam took a few biscuits from a tray, then skipped on through the house until he came to the study at the far side of the eastern wing.

Outside, the sun had just begun to set over the gardens. It would be cold tonight. Another month and it would probably snow. He loved to play in the snow. Loved it when he came back inside and warmed up by the big fireplace in the study and Cook brought him some hot cocoa.

"Uncle!" he shouted happily as he opened the study door. "Miss Marquette says I have talent. She says I might make a fine musician."

Duncan smiled as Cam launched himself into his arms. "My good boy," he said as he stroked Cam's head. "My beautiful, talented boy."

Cam laid his head on his uncle's chest and closed his eyes as Duncan petted his hair, then his cheek.

"Do you think I could be a pianist?" he asked.

Duncan kissed his head. "You have many gifts," Duncan said as he rubbed Cam's back. "Such a gifted boy."

Cam looked up at his uncle, who smiled down at him.

"You please me, Cameron. You make me very happy."

Cam bit his lower lip as his uncle's hand drew circles on his back, then settled low on one of his hips. He liked making his uncle happy. He felt loved.

Lower still, Duncan grasped his buttocks and squeezed. Cam didn't like this part, but he liked that he made Duncan happy. Duncan loved him. Duncan cared about him.

"My lovely, lovely boy," Duncan said as he nuzzled Cam's neck. "My boy. Be my good boy for me. Show me how much you love me."

He liked it when Duncan talked to him like that. But sometimes Duncan called him other things—things that made him feel strange. Bad. He didn't want to feel bad. He wanted Duncan to be happy. He wanted Duncan to love him....

CAM SAT up in bed, wide-awake and struggling to breathe. *No. It was just a dream. Just a—*

He stood, took a step, then grabbed onto the headboard to steady himself. Dreams felt like dreams. This felt... different. He remembered the concert. He remembered how he'd felt when his teacher had praised him—he'd felt like flying. He remembered walking back to the house and how excited he'd been. Why couldn't he remember more?

No. It can't be. He'd never have.... And yet Duncan had abandoned him in the face of the criminal charges, hadn't he? *He's busy. He'll call me back.*

But he hadn't called back. He hadn't. Why hadn't he? *Because he's the one who set you up.*

"Show me how much you love me."

He let go of the headboard and dropped to his knees as the memories came flooding back, along with the shame and disgust. Duncan whispering to him, his voice husky with arousal. Duncan touching him. He knew what Duncan wanted. Knew if he didn't fight it, Duncan wouldn't hurt him, and it might even feel good.

"That's my bad little boy. See how you like it. Look what happens when I touch you like this. Look at how you want me to touch it. Look how hard it gets."

Oh, God! Had he wanted it? Had it turned him on?

He barely made it to the bathroom before he vomited. He coughed and dragged himself over to the sink to rinse his mouth clean. The bitter taste lingered even after.

Duncan? God, no. It wasn't possible. *Duncan would never....* But even as he thought this, more memories surfaced. Not bubbling up this time, but washing over him in a torrent. The boathouse. The study. His bedroom. Duncan's room. He'd woken up in Duncan's bed only to run back to his own and hope his mother wouldn't notice.

"You won't tell anyone, will you? Because if you tell them, they'll know you're filthy and they'll send you away. I'm the only one who can protect you from yourself, Cameron. The only one who understands what you need."

But a few years later, Duncan hadn't wanted him anymore. Duncan didn't love him anymore. And Cam had thought—no, he'd *known*—it was because his body was changing. He was dirty now. Not the boy Duncan loved. Not deserving. No longer special. And now Duncan was trying to get rid of him for good. Lock him away.

Cam leaned against the bath, barely able to catch his breath. His hand—the hand that held the bottle of Benadryl—shook. He vaguely remembered opening the medicine cabinet. *Just do it. Get it done with.* No more nightmares. No more bullshit. No more lies. No more Duncan. No more pain. *No more Cam.*

What had Galen said? *"I take a few of those and I sleep like the dead."* If he took the whole bottle, would he just disappear?

Tears rolled down his cheeks. How long had he been crying, for fuck's sake? He'd woken up from the dream crying. Had that been an hour ago? He considered getting some toilet paper to wipe his nose, but the thought that he might even care if his face was covered in snot when he was about to do this nearly made him laugh.

Shame imbued every fiber of his being, and he shivered again at the memory. How his body had responded. He should have known it was wrong. Why hadn't he said no? *I let him touch me.* Like the boys in school, behind the storage shed. He'd let them touch him then. He'd sucked them off when he hadn't wanted it.

You didn't tell them no. You didn't scream. Had he wanted it?

"Filthy boy," Duncan said as he showed Cam his hand, sticky with semen. *"You like it, don't you?"*

The contents of his stomach—what was left of the dinner Galen had made them that Cam hadn't already vomited—came up without much fanfare. Disgusting. *He* was disgusting.

He wiped his mouth with the back of his hand, then poured a handful of pills out of the bottle. How many would it take?

He turned the bottle around to read the label: 120 pills. Little pink pills. A few swallows and he'd forget everything. He poured the rest into his hand and set the bottle down. Better too many than too few. He turned on the tap and picked up the plastic cup Galen had put there for him, then filled it to the brim with water. One, maybe two swallows and he'd just fall asleep. Easy.

"Cam?"

Startled, Cam dropped all the pills into the sink and the water splashed onto them. Again, that strong hand on his shoulder. Cam pushed Galen's hand off as he spun around. "What the fuck do you think you're doing, walking in on me?" he shouted.

"You sounded like you were sick, so I came to check on you." Galen looked as startled as Cam. He'd clearly figured it out, though. Was the man a fucking mind reader?

"I'm fine," Cam said, knowing the lie was obvious but not giving a shit.

Galen pressed his lips together, eyes wide. "No." He'd always backed down when Cam had bullshitted him before. Not this time. "You're not fine." He walked over to the sink and looked down at the pink gooey mess the pills had become. "You were going to swallow these, weren't you?"

Cam laughed, but it sounded tight and high. Nervous. He didn't know why he was nervous. This was his business, not Galen's. "They spilled," he lied again. Galen kept his gaze fixed on him, making him more nervous still.

Galen's expression flickered with something like anger as he scooped what was left of the pills into his hands and unceremoniously dumped them in the toilet. The sound of the flush made the entire thing seem surreal. Galen returned to the sink and washed his hands, then rinsed the remaining mess down the drain. Through it all, Galen said nothing.

"I'm going back to bed," Cam said. The last thing he wanted was to talk about what he'd just done. Almost done. How pathetic! He couldn't even kill himself without fucking things up.

"No. Not this time." Galen's voice was firm. He planted himself between the sink and the door so Cam couldn't get past him.

"Let me out. I just want to go to sleep." What the hell was the man's problem?

"Not until you admit what you were trying to do." Cam saw no anger on Galen's face, only calm determination. He'd never seen Galen look determined. He'd begun to wonder if the man cared about anything.

"I told you. I spilled the pills." He'd always been a shit liar.

"Stop it, Cam."

"Fuck you." Cam tried to push past Galen. He'd had enough of this. At that moment, he didn't give a shit whether Galen kicked him out on his arse. He wasn't going to stay here and listen to the fucking lecture he knew would come next. He could just hear it.

"You need help. You need to talk to someone."

"Get out of my bloody way." Cam pushed on Galen's shoulder, but Galen didn't budge. He was far stronger than he looked.

"Not until you admit you were trying to kill yourself."

The words hit Cam like a slap in the face. He let go of Galen and stepped back until the small of his back made contact with the sink. The porcelain felt cold through the thin T-shirt he wore. "I wasn't try—"

"The first time, I might have believed it."

Galen sounded so bloody calm, Cam wanted to punch him. "What are you talking about?" he snapped.

"That night in the subway. At the edge of the platform. You almost stepped off the edge."

"I didn't—"

"Stop bullshitting, Cam. We both know you thought about how easy it would be just to step off that platform. How everything would just go away if you did." Galen didn't raise his voice. Didn't even frown at him. *Fucking smug.*

"It's none of your bloody fucking business. None of this is. Now move."

Galen didn't budge. "It's my business if you're trying to kill yourself at my house."

Cam laughed. "And whose idea was it to take me home with you like a stray dog? So you're responsible for me now? Like my mother?"

"No." Galen appeared genuinely mortified. "You're not a stray dog. But I can't ignore—"

"What the fuck do you know about it?" Cam demanded.

Galen took a deep breath, met his gaze unflinchingly, then pushed up the long sleeve of his T-shirt. It took Cam a moment to register the thin white line across the inside of Galen's wrist.

"I know," he said with a sigh. "I know because I've been where you are."

CHAPTER 21

CAM SHIVERED and stared down at the cup of tea Galen had set for him on the coffee table. Chamomile, from the scent of it. Not his favorite, by any means, but strangely comforting. His grandmother had drunk chamomile tea. She'd been a kind woman.

Galen, who had been seated next to him on the couch, now rose and pulled a rainbow crocheted throw from off a nearby chair, then draped it over Cam's shoulders. They'd been sitting for at least a half an hour. Galen hadn't said anything, and Cam was perfectly all right with that. Better than the conversation he might imagine:

"Trying to kill yourself, were you?"

"No, of course not. I just thought a few more pills might help my runny nose."

No. They both knew what he'd been trying to do. Worse, he wasn't sure he wouldn't try it again if given the chance. And what about Galen? What did he think? Cam wondered how old the scars on his wrists were. He supposed he could ask—Galen had opened that door, after all—but he didn't want to. He didn't feel like asking, or listening, or anything right now. He wondered if Galen understood that, because he didn't attempt to engage Cam in conversation.

A few more minutes passed in silence. Max hopped up on the couch where Galen had been sitting, then curled up with his hindquarters pressed against Cam's thigh. Cam made no move to dislodge the dog. He pulled the throw tighter around him and shivered. The wind whistled outside and the farmhouse's old windows rattled.

Galen pulled out the piano bench and opened the cover. It could have been the dim light in the living room playing tricks with his eyes, but Cam imagined panic flashing across Galen's face, then disappearing as he rested his fingers on the keys and closed his eyes.

Chopin Prelude No. 4. Cam had played the piece when he'd been forced to take piano lessons as a child. He'd played it because it had been easy and because he'd never been much of a pianist. He knew now he'd never had the talent Miss Marquette had praised him for. Repeated chords in the left hand, a simple melody in the right. He'd thought it sad and pretty but not much more than that. But in Galen's hands, it was nothing less than stunning. And when he finished, the room seemed to vibrate long after.

"That was beautiful," Cam said after Galen finished. "Did you ever consider playing piano professionally?"

"Not really. I just enjoy playing through music from time to time. Sometimes I fill in as an accompanist for Miss Martin's choir kids at the school."

"You're really good," Cam pressed.

He found it easier to talk about anything but what had just happened. Galen must have known this, because he smiled at him and shrugged. "How are you feeling?"

"I'm fine."

"No, you're not." Galen's expression hadn't changed. "You just tried to kill yourself. Again."

"I told you—"

"When are you going to stop bullshitting yourself?" Galen asked. "When you finally manage to pull it off?"

Cam shot up from the couch, dislodging Max in the process. Max looked up at him, then put his head back down on his paws. "Fuck you."

"Now we're getting somewhere." Galen was far too calm, and Cam was ready to explode because of it.

"We're getting nowhere," Cam snapped, "because you're a pain in the arse."

"Even better."

"Oh, I can bloody well do better than *that*." Cam gritted his teeth. Who the hell was Galen, anyhow? Some sort of new age freak who'd read too many pop psychology books?

"Please do." Galen appeared entirely nonplussed, and the way the corners of his mouth edged oh so slightly upward made Cam wonder if he didn't find the whole sordid affair amusing.

"You think you know?" Cam's voice echoed against the high ceiling.

"I *don't* know," Galen admitted. "Not what you're thinking right now. But I know the general stuff."

Cam hadn't expected that response. Galen had a way of saying things that set him off-balance. He'd figured Galen would just tell him what he should think or feel. The old "been there, done that" sort of condescending shit. Because why would Galen give a damn anyhow? No one else did. Cam ignored the voice in his head that said he was being an arse and feeling sorry for himself. Some people might care what happened to him. A few, at least.

"What are you running from?" Galen asked when Cam didn't answer.

Cam tensed at the words. "What do you mean?"

"You're obviously not used to sleeping in subways."

"No."

Galen shook his head as he said, "I'm not going to turn you in, Cam, if that's what you're worried about. You're safe here."

"You don't even know what I've done. Maybe I killed someone."

"You haven't." Galen got up from the piano and walked over to Cam, then stood between Cam and the window. Forcing Cam to look at him.

"How do you know?" Cam countered as he tried to ignore the concern in Galen's eyes. He knew Galen was trying to be supportive, but he didn't need the man's support. He wouldn't understand anyhow. His universe was so far removed from Galen's.

"The same way I knew you were a good person when I offered to put you up."

"You're naive."

Galen smiled outright this time. "Maybe."

"That's it? Maybe?" The man was exasperating! Beating around the bush, pretending he didn't think Cam should be committed. *Taking me home like a lost puppy.* The fact that his smile was so warm, so genuine, only made the entire situation worse. It made Cam feel *guilty* that he'd imposed on Galen.

"Yep. But I also did my homework."

"Homework?" Cam's exhausted brain couldn't make sense of the word.

"Cameron Allen Sherrington. Only son of Ralph Michael Sherrington and Vanessa Baines Sherrington. Minor British noble. Thirty years old as of about three weeks ago. Chairman of the board of Sherrington Holdings." Galen squeezed Cam's shoulder. "Least that's what Google had to say about you. But that's about all I know."

Cam scowled. He might have expected Galen would put the pieces together. In a way, he figured it was for the best. If he was still here and Galen knew who he was, Galen was probably telling the truth when he said he wouldn't turn him in to the authorities.

"Fine," he said. He'd tell Galen about the investigation, but he didn't need to know anything more than that. "There's a warrant for my arrest. FBI. They think I'm involved in something illegal."

"Are you?"

"No."

"I believe you." Galen's expression of earnest concern hadn't changed.

"You're fucking crazy, you know?"

"I've been told that before. Nothing new." Galen got up from the piano bench and sat down next to Cam. "So if you didn't do anything wrong, why did you run?"

"I don't know." Cam rubbed his forehead with a few fingers and shook his head. "I panicked. I can't explain it very well."

"Try."

"You really are a pain in the arse."

Galen laughed and tucked a leg underneath him. "You aren't the first person to tell me that, although I've never had it said with an English accent."

"I'm not sure. I spoke to the FBI. I had nothing to hide. Then I got a call from our New York attorney telling me about an account in the Cayman Islands with millions of dollars. Turns out the account's in my name, through a company we own here in New Jersey. The FBI thinks I'm laundering money for something. Drugs? Weapons? I honestly don't even know what people launder money *for*." The entire thing seemed so ludicrous when he explained it. Still, he knew *someone* was setting him up. Someone who had access to Raice Corp's finances. And Duncan had more than enough motivation to want him out of the picture. "My uncle runs our family business. I'm just window dressing. He told me to cooperate. But…."

"But you're wondering if you can trust him?" Galen asked.

Cam nodded. He'd really underestimated Galen. He also wasn't sure why he was opening up to him. For all he knew, Galen could call the police and he'd be in jail faster than—

"I'm not going to turn you in, Cam."

Cam eyed Galen warily, then let out a long breath. He hadn't turned him in yet. Why did Cam still doubt Galen was telling the truth?

Because he has no reason to be kind to you.

Galen put a hand on his shoulder. It felt surprisingly good when Galen touched him.

"I like you, Cam." Galen smiled and pressed his lips together.

"Not much to like." Cam's eyes burned as he thought of Aiden. Why the hell was he so fucking emotional all of a sudden?

"That bad?" Galen asked with the hint of a smile.

"Probably worse."

"I burned a few bridges in my day." Galen relaxed against the pillows. Max nudged him with his nose, and Galen tapped the couch. A moment later, Max was happily curled beside him. "Quite spectacularly, in fact."

"The scar on your wrist?"

"Both wrists." Galen sighed and released Cam's shoulder. Cam wished he hadn't. "That was the low point for me."

"What happened?" Easy for him to ask. Not that he'd completely answered the question when Galen had been doing the asking.

"I got in over my head. I wanted to be a success to please everyone else, but I was miserable. I got this half-assed idea it'd be better if I just disappeared. So I tried. To disappear, I mean." He lifted one of his hands and turned it over so the scar there was visible. "I spent a few months in the psych ward at a state hospital. I went back to school a few years later and got my teaching certificate. Started over again."

"Parents?"

"They live in upstate New York. Good people." Galen pulled one leg up onto the couch, reminding Cam of the handstand he'd found Galen in a few days before. "No childhood traumas."

Cam looked away. He didn't expect Galen to take his hand. What a strange man Galen was. Even with everything he'd told Cam, he was still an enigma. "I wanted to disappear," Cam said softly, still unwilling to look Galen in the eyes but glad to feel Galen's reassuring touch. He swallowed hard. "I deserve to disappear. I'm a horrible person."

"No one deserves that, Cam."

Cam looked at Galen. Fucking earnest Galen, who believed that. "I really am horrible."

"Tell me what you've done that's so horrible."

Cam let out a long breath. "I'm a rat bastard and I don't give a shit." He waited for Galen to respond, but he didn't. He kept holding Cam's hand. "I treat people like shit. I lie. I cheat." He dry-scrubbed his face, then added in a low voice, "I hurt people." He wouldn't tell him about Duncan. He *couldn't*. He worried if he spoke the words, he'd just disappear.

"How?" Galen squeezed his hand.

How could he be so fucking supportive? "I take what I want. I don't care what people think." He sighed and said, "I told you, I cheat. I pushed away the only man who really loved me. Poor bugger. He loved *me*. So I fucked someone else on the most important day of his life and he found me doing it." Cam laughed bitterly. "I think I wanted him to find me. He *deserved* to find me... find out who I really was."

"And?"

"And he called me. Before all the other shit happened...." Cam closed his eyes and shook his head. "He's getting married. The little fuckwit is getting married."

"But he's not a fuckwit, is he?"

How the hell did Galen manage to do that every time? Read his mind? Every fucking time? "No," he answered softly. "He's a good man. And he loved me." Cam's eyes burned. He wouldn't cry in front of Galen. He fucking wouldn't cry. But when Galen surprised him once again by taking him in his arms and holding him….

Cam held on to Galen for dear life. Clung to him. And if he hadn't been so buggered, he'd have been able to hold on to the tears. Keep them to himself. But he couldn't.

"Bollocks," he hissed as the tears fell in spite of his resolve. Like a torrent. And damn if Galen didn't hold him tighter and stroke his hair. And Cam kept on crying like a pathetic child. Shaking. Mewling. Pathetic. Lost. Everything blurred, everything combined into a swirling storm of emotion. He thought about his uncle. About Aiden. About the boys who'd used him. Telling himself he'd wanted it, but he hadn't. The FBI. Riley's betrayal. His mother. The loneliness he'd felt—that he *still* felt. The friends who hadn't really been his friends.

"I'm sorry," he whispered as the tears finally abated.

"Don't be." Galen's body felt warm.

Cam shivered. How had he allowed himself to be so vulnerable?

"This stays between us," Galen said, as if he'd read Cam's mind yet again. "No one needs to know."

Cam nodded, unable to speak. He believed Galen. Trusted him with the truth. More importantly, Galen seemed to understand that Cam needed to trust someone.

CHAPTER 22

"I'M HEADING out in about an hour," Galen told Cam from yet another impossible yoga pose. "Wednesdays I'm at the school until around four." This time Galen crossed his legs underneath his body the way he did when he meditated, except that he propped himself up by his arms, seemingly floating above the floor. Without a shirt to cover his upper body, Galen's arms and abdomen revealed the landscape of tensed muscles. As always, Galen's face remained relaxed, the only sign of his exertion a few beads of sweat on his brow and the slightly damp hair at his nape.

They'd both dozed on the couch, never having gone back to bed. Cam hadn't heard Galen get up and change. He wondered if Galen had slept at all. He personally felt like a pile of shit.

How else should you feel the morning after you try to kill yourself?

"I'll call the home phone to check on you. You'll see my name on the caller ID." Galen settled back onto the floor, then inhaled and exhaled audibly.

Cam's first instinct was to ask what Galen would do if he didn't answer, but he held his tongue. For all intents and purposes, Galen had saved his life. He supposed he owed Galen more than an adolescent hissy fit in response to his kindness. "All right," he said evenly. He didn't have to be thrilled with Galen checking up on him.

"Jamie's coming after school today for his lesson," Galen said. "I hope you don't mind."

"I don't mind." He really didn't. Jamie seemed like a good kid.

"If you want to check in with the outside world," Galen said, "feel free to use the computer in the study upstairs."

"I don't want you involved in my mess, Galen," he said. "If they were to trace me to you...."

"I wouldn't care, Cam." Galen slowly moved into another position by leaning on his arms, stretching his legs behind him, and arching his back. "But if you'd be more comfortable, you could use the computer at the library. They have about a dozen workstations set up there."

Cam forced himself to focus on something other than the tight muscles of Galen's arse through the filmy cotton of his yoga pants. "I've never been to a library here. Do I need to join?"

"Not for Internet. Anyone who wants to use it can, even without a library card."

"I'll think about it." He wasn't sure he was ready to face the outside world. Not yet. But he also knew he couldn't stay here forever. Sooner or later he'd have to face Duncan and the authorities.

IN THE end, Cam decided against the library. Or more accurately, the wave of sheer terror he experienced when he got dressed and started to walk out the front door decided for him. He spent the afternoon in the living room, alternately dozing and reading a book about music in ancient Egypt he'd halfheartedly chosen off Galen's shelf the night before.

At some point he stopped reading about the status of musicians in the temples and realized he'd been staring at the words without really seeing them. He shivered and pulled a crocheted throw around his shoulders.

Had he really tried to kill himself last night?

Yes.

What now? Nothing had changed since then. He was still the same person, wasn't he?

He rubbed his eyes and stared out the doors that opened onto the backyard. He thought of raking leaves. Of how it had made him feel good. What the bloody hell was wrong with him that he thought raking leaves was something to be happy about?

In your fucked-up life, it's better than nothing.

Nothing. That was what he felt. Numb. He felt as though he'd been floating in a lifeboat, tossed around by the waves, and then suddenly the water was smooth as glass. But he was still on the water. No land in sight.

The phone rang.

"Hello, Galen."

"I had a few minutes between classes," Galen said. "I wanted to see how you were doing."

"Great."

"Right." Galen's voice sounded warm and reassuring.

"What do you expect me to say?" Cam asked without his usual bile. He felt too tired to find it in him.

"Just that you're hanging in there."

"Yanks." Cam smiled in spite of himself.

"You're just jealous."

Cam chuckled and leaned back on the couch. "Fuck you."

"Glad you're feeling better, Cam."

After that, Galen called him nearly every hour. Cam didn't find it as irritating as he'd thought he would. In fact, he felt good knowing Galen would call again in another hour. Not that Cam had any thought that he'd try to kill himself again, but he felt genuine fear that something might happen to make him *want* to try. He knew that sort of thinking didn't make much sense, but then *nothing* that had happened in the past week or so had make sense to begin with.

Max's bark startled him awake at about four o'clock.

A few minutes later, Galen came into the living room. "Good nap?" he asked as he made his way around the couch, folding the unused throws and placing them in a neat pile, then straightening the pillows.

Cam nodded, not knowing what else to say. Galen bent down and straightened the shoes Cam had kicked onto the carpet. Cam was sorely tempted to move one of the shoes so that it was slightly crooked just so he could watch Galen straighten it again. But he didn't.

"I'll make some tea."

Cam fought the urge to say something about tea not fixing everything. He wondered vaguely if Galen didn't insist on doing things for him because he *knew* Cam felt uncomfortable when he did. Maybe this was like becoming a vegetarian—a test of his willpower.

You're totally mad, you know. It's just tea, for God's sake! Luisa did things for him all the time. *And you pay her for it.*

The doorbell rang a moment later, interrupting his thoughts. Just as well. He was tired of thinking about things. What had thinking about anything gotten him? *A handful of little pink pills and a death wish.*

"Good to see you again, Jamie," Cam said as Galen led Jamie into the living room.

"You too, Cam." Jamie reminded Cam a little of himself, years before. Smaller than most of the other kids. Effeminate. A little shy. Well, *that* had certainly changed when Cam went away to school, and damn quickly.

"I'll take care of the tea," Cam said as Jamie unpacked some music from the backpack slung over his shoulder. "Would you like some too, Jamie?"

"Oh, no, thanks. I'm fine." Jamie set the music on the piano.

"Mind if I listen in?" Cam asked. "If that's all right with your teacher." Cam caught Galen's eye, and Galen nodded his approval.

"Really?" Jamie's face brightened. "You... you'd want to?"

"Really." Cam offered Jamie a smile and added, "I've heard you before, remember? You play very well."

"Thank you. I'd really like that." Jamie rubbed his hands together and began to play some scales as Cam went to the kitchen and put some water on.

Even Jamie's scales and arpeggios sounded lovely as they echoed through the house. By the time Cam walked back into the living room with two cups of tea, Jamie had begun to play the Gershwin. Cam handed Galen his tea, then settled onto the couch. As soon as he'd set his cup on the table, Max hopped up and curled into a ball beside him.

Galen leaned against the piano and listened for a few minutes before interrupting Jamie. "I really like how you're taking more time there." He pointed to a spot in the score. "I think you can do more of that here as well." He indicated another phrase. "And what you're doing, expanding the time between the notes and letting them ring a bit, you can do even more of that. Remember, this is where the piano has the melody. Don't be shy."

Jamie nodded, then played the passage again. This time he did exactly what Galen had suggested. The change made all the difference, turning the broadly written passage from competent and well played into something worthy of a concert hall. Cam marveled at how quickly Jamie adjusted his playing to incorporate Galen's suggestions and how spot-on Galen's suggestions were.

"That's it!" Galen clapped his approval, and Jamie grinned as though he'd just been given a gift. Cam could almost imagine himself in Jamie's place as he remembered his own sense of accomplishment when, years before, his teacher had complimented his playing. Not that he'd ever been as gifted a musician as Jamie, but he understood the pleasure.

The rest of the lesson passed in much the same way, with Jamie playing and Galen encouraging. When Galen suggested Jamie play the entire piece through, Cam found himself listening to see which of Galen's suggestions Jamie remembered. Nearly all, in the final analysis. And when Jamie finished, both Cam and Galen clapped.

"Juilliard will be lucky to have you," Cam told Jamie as he packed up an hour later. "I know you're going to do well there."

"Do you play?" Jamie asked as the three of them walked to the front door.

"Used to, when I was your age. Not that I was anywhere near as talented, but I enjoyed it."

"You should play," Jamie said. "Mr. Rusk always says that music is for the musician first, and the audience second. If the musician doesn't enjoy it, the audience won't."

Cam caught Galen's knowing look from behind Jamie. "Well said." Cam held Galen's gaze for a moment. He'd sensed this in Galen's playing—the sheer joy of creating the music. He'd never thought much about it, but he had to agree with Galen.

"WE'VE GOT about an hour and a half before dark," Galen said after Jamie left. "Mind helping me outside?"

"Leaves?" Cam chuckled. Knowing Galen's need to have everything neat and in its proper place, Cam guessed the piles of leaves had been calling to him the past few days. *Or screaming at him.*

"We could shoot a few hoops instead."

"Hoops? As in basketball?" Cam shook his head. "That's the extent of my basketball ability—knowing that shooting hoops *is* basketball."

"Leaves, then." One side of Galen's mouth quirked upward.

"You never intended to play basketball, did you?" Cam put his hands on his hips in mock indignation.

"Am I that obvious?" Galen grinned outright this time, then motioned to the back door.

"Entirely. And what if I'd said I love to shoot hoops?"

Galen raised his eyebrows and shrugged.

"Lucky bugger," Cam said as he followed Galen out the back door with Max at his heels.

"So what do you do with all these leaves?" Cam asked a few minutes later as they deposited yet another pile on top of the ones at the back of the yard.

"Compost them." Galen pointed to a fenced-off garden on the side of the house, where a few straggly plants remained. "I grow vegetables in the spring. Underneath all these is the good stuff I'll mix into the soil before I plant."

"We had a garden growing up. Mostly herbs, but sometimes Cook would grow tomatoes and peppers. She loved to yell at me when I'd steal them." Cam smiled at the memory. He was pretty sure she'd liked that he'd eaten them. He realized now that she probably felt someone appreciated her hard work.

"I only share my tomatoes with the deer around here," Galen said with a laugh. "But they usually don't clean me out."

Cam raked too hard and several leaves flew into the air. "How do you make your piles so perfectly round?"

"No idea," Galen said. "But I like them that way."

"And what if I were to make them square?" Cam poked at one of Galen's piles. More leaves caught the slight breeze, and one settled onto Galen's head.

"Oh, that's *good*." Galen pulled the leaf off his head and glared at Cam. "Can't make your piles perfect, so you attack me with my own neat pile."

Cam bit his lower lip, put down the rake, then tossed an entire armful of leaves at Galen. "Take that!" he shouted.

Galen leaned his rake against a nearby tree, then scooped up some leaves and deposited them on Cam's head. "Back at you, bro."

By the time Cam had another few handfuls of leaves, Galen too had reloaded. They threw the leaves at each other as Max ran around them and barked. As Cam grabbed more leaves, Galen shoved a handful down his back.

"Not fair!" Cam pulled his shirt from his jeans and shook out the leaves, then ran after Galen before he could reload. "You are *so* going to pay for that!" He chased Galen around the yard. Galen ran faster than Cam, but Max had clearly decided to back the underdog, and between the two of them, Cam was able to back Galen into one of his perfect piles and tackle him.

"You didn't say you played football," Galen said as Cam shoved a handful down Galen's shirt and grinned broadly.

"Maybe I don't play football," Cam said with a laugh, "but I did play rugby."

Galen caught hold of Cam's ankle, and he tumbled into the pile onto Galen. Face to face, both of them panting, Cam met Galen's gaze, and suddenly all Cam could think about was kissing Galen again.

So he did. And Galen kissed him back. Sweetly. Simply. The kind of kiss Cam had thought about since they'd kissed days before. Galen's cold nose pressed against Cam's, and Cam inhaled the warm, earthy scent of the leaves, heard the sound of the wind through the trees. For the first time in far too long, he felt *good*. Glad to be alive. To be here, in this place, with Galen.

When their lips parted, Cam surprised himself by wrapping his arms around Galen and simply holding him. He wanted more, to be sure, but he loved feeling Galen's body against his, feeling Galen's arms encircling his waist. He forgot about the chill in the air and the way his muscles protested the effort of raking. He forgot about Aiden and Duncan and all of the bullshit his life had become. For a few minutes, he felt present in the moment. Happy.

"Thank you," he whispered.

"For what?" Galen asked.

"For this." Cam knew he wasn't making sense. "For now."

But judging by the gentle smile that danced on Galen's face, Cam knew that Galen understood.

CHAPTER 23

CAM WOKE with a stifled moan and a whimper. He pulled his knees against his chest and gave himself over to the shudder that resonated throughout his body. Covered in sweat in spite of the chill from the old windows, he gulped in air until the feeling of terror subsided.

Another nightmare. Another memory recovered. This time, the first time Duncan made him suck on him and how he'd vomited after Duncan forced him to swallow. How many more nights would he dream like this? Since Monday, he had dreamed of Duncan every night. Three more nights of barely sleeping. And it wasn't just that. He *feared* sleep. Feared what he might find when he closed his eyes, what new revelation would shake him to the core.

He'd gotten better at not waking Galen up. He could be strong. He'd get through this by himself. He'd gotten used to the tears now. But he couldn't get used to the rising rage and hatred for the man who'd… who'd….

Fuck! You can't even say it!

"My bad little boy. See how you like it. See how hard it gets when I touch it. My dirty little boy."

He shivered. Sitting here in the dark reminded him of boarding school. He'd told himself he'd never be that shy, frightened boy again. *Then what the fuck are you doing now?*

He'd been fifteen when his mother had decided to send him away to school, far older than the typical boarding school student. She told him he'd get a better education there, but he guessed she'd figured out he was gay, because she also said they'd teach him to be a man. Without a father, he needed that. Or so she said.

The first two weeks of school had been wonderful. Away from the castle, he could be himself. Most of the boys came from backgrounds like his: privilege and wealth. Nobody called him anything but Cam. His bunkmate, Tom, had given him a tour of the grounds, and they'd laughed and joked about things he'd never have had the courage to joke about at his old school.

He didn't tell anyone he liked boys—at least not in that particular way. He knew what he was, and he was fine with it. If they figured it out, he wouldn't deny it. And some did. There were other boys at Briggston who felt the same way. He'd found that out the way he'd always found it out: a sidelong glance, a stray touch, an uncomfortable laugh. These had led to making out with Michael behind the dormitories after an informal game of football on a weekend. Nice, slow, easy touches that Cam loved. He hadn't realized some of the seniors had seen them.

Monday of the third week of school started like any other. He'd finished his homework late Sunday night, slept in his underwear, and skipped breakfast in lieu of another twenty minutes of sleep. After lunch he headed across the quad, then cut behind the humanities building to the dormitories. He'd never seen anyone back there before, but today there were two boys smoking weed. Seniors. Cam had seen them in the cafeteria.

"New student," one of the boys said with a half smirk.

"Pretty one, aren't you?" said the other.

"Want some?" the first boy asked.

Cam hesitated, then stepped forward and took a hit. Nothing new. He'd smoked a few times before with friends. "Good stuff," he said, although he had no idea if it really was. He passed the joint back and inhaled the smoke he'd held in his mouth.

"I'm Stan," the first boy said.

"Cam." Cam smiled.

"Thomas," said the second. "Where you from?"

"Surrey." Cam took the joint again and inhaled. He'd been nervous around the older students, but he felt pretty good now. Relaxed. Even a little bolder than before. "Glad to be out of there," he added, only because he thought it sounded cool.

"Yeah," Stan said.

Thomas draped a casual arm around Cam. Cam liked the way that felt. Like he was part of their little group. "I'm from Bristol," he said. "You ever been there?"

"A few times. I liked it." Cam took another hit. His head grew fuzzy.

"It's all right," Stan said.

"So, Cam," Thomas began with a smirk at Stan, "you like to fool around?"

"What?" Cam wasn't sure he understood.

"You know," Thomas said. "Doing stuff with guys."

"Yeah." Well, Cam did. Although he wasn't sure what it meant in this context. Thomas now had his hand in Cam's hair, working his fingers through it. He pressed against Thomas's hand.

"You like blowing 'em?" Stan moved in front of Cam and rubbed a hand over Cam's crotch. Cam's breath caught and he grew hard.

"Yeah," Cam lied.

Stan squeezed Cam's cock through his trousers. Cam closed his eyes and moaned. "Oh, yeah, you *do* like it, don't you?"

That became the first of many times he spent smoking weed and giving the seniors what they wanted. After the first few times, Thomas and Stan brought some more of their friends. It was all right. Cam belonged somewhere. They liked him. And he knew what they liked.

Now, as he sat in the dark, he wondered why he'd really never felt good about it. Why he felt dirty afterward. Used. But he'd wanted it. At least that was what he'd told himself.

"My bad little boy. See how you want it. Look at how hard it gets when I touch it."

Cam shivered, lay back down, and tried to banish the memories from his thoughts by pulling a book off the shelf.

GALEN KNOCKED on the guest bedroom door. He'd heard the toilet flush. He told himself Cam was doing better, but after a few minutes of internal back and forth, he decided to check on him anyhow.

"Come in." Cam sounded wide-awake.

"Just checking on you." Galen found an irritated-looking Cam sitting up in bed holding a book and Max at his feet. *Zen and the Art of Happiness*. A good choice for early-morning insomnia. Not the most exciting book on his shelf, but something that might help Cam sleep better if he practiced some of the techniques.

"You really don't need to. I'm a big boy."

He'd expected Cam wouldn't appreciate his concern. Not that it would stop him from being concerned. He could be pretty dogged at times. He shrugged and said, "I figured you might need some company."

"You thought maybe I'd try to kill myself again?" Cam snapped.

Galen had expected that too. He remembered his parents walking on eggshells when he'd come home from the hospital. His mother peering in on him when she thought he was sleeping. His father not knowing what to say. "Actually, no. But you don't seem to be sleeping very well." Cam had been sleeping terribly, judging by the dark circles under his eyes and the way he yawned throughout the day.

"Back rub?" A bit dangerous, but it had clearly helped Cam before.

Cam appeared to consider this. After a moment he said, "Yes. Thank you."

Galen climbed onto the bed as Cam set the book next to him. He helped Cam move forward a bit, then pushed the pillows behind him away and settled against the headboard with his hands on Cam's shoulders. Easier to keep his distance if he didn't look Cam directly in the eyes.

I can do this. He took a slow breath and focused on the movement of his hands as he worked. He thought better if he concentrated on sounds. The rhythm of things. The pattern in movement. When his thoughts strayed to things he didn't want to think about, he could pull himself back that way.

Cam's muscles tensed even more at Galen's touch. "Relax," Galen said as he began to work away the tightness.

Cam's sigh caused Galen to shiver in spite of himself. *Focus. Breathe. Relax.* This was no different from the usual distractions in his life. Galen saw each as a challenge to be mastered, like letting go of his own anxiety. He practiced this daily, from the yoga he'd come to love to the meditations that began and ended his day.

Then why do I want to hold him?

He closed his eyes and continued to knead Cam's shoulders. *Focus. Breathe. Relax.* This wasn't about him. He would help Cam through this. This was no different from the kids he'd helped over the years he'd been teaching. Only it had been easier to keep his distance with them.

Cam leaned his head to one side, and the soft curls at his neck brushed Galen's right hand. *Beautiful hair.* Hair he imagined carding his fingers through, maybe even pulling as he bit and nipped at the pale skin of Cam's neck.

Focus. Breathe. Relax.

In an effort to master his body's response, Galen moved to Cam's upper arms and worked the muscles there, then pressed fingers into his right shoulder blade. This time Cam moaned.

Focus. Breathe. Relax.

By the time Galen got up the courage to work on Cam's neck, his mind had wandered once again. He imagined running his tongue under Cam's ear, sucking on the lobe, tasting him—

Focus. Breathe. Relax.

"Better?" he asked. He wasn't sure how much longer he could do this and not give in to the temptation. And why shouldn't he give in?

Because he's not ready came the voice inside his head that always made sense of things. *And because....*

"Much better. Thank you." Cam's voice sounded husky.

Galen swallowed hard, took yet another cleansing breath, and was about to climb out of the bed when Cam pulled him into his arms. They were so close now. Face to face. Too close....

"I know what you said," Cam said under his breath. "About me not being ready."

Focus. Breathe. Relax.

"And you're probably right," Cam continued. "But... would you mind... staying with me? Here? Until I fall asleep?"

Galen saw the need in Cam's face. The fear in his eyes. *I can do this.* "Sure," he said. He knew he sounded relaxed and in control. He wasn't either of those things—not in his mind. He'd gotten so good at the external bullshit. But Cam didn't need to know that. Right now Cam needed him, and that was all that mattered. Galen waited as Cam settled onto the pillow, then lay next to him so their bodies barely touched.

"Thank you." Galen heard relief in Cam's voice, and he smiled. He could do this.

Max, who'd moved while Galen rubbed Cam's back, circled several times, then landed with a plop on top of one of Galen's feet. Cam's soft chuckle reminded Galen of the first strands of sunlight in the morning sky at dawn.

You can do this. Breathe. Relax. Focus.

Cam fell asleep a few minutes later, judging by the slowing of his breaths. Galen watched him for the longest time, partly because he couldn't sleep but partly because he found Cam so beautifully vulnerable like this, he couldn't bear to look away.

CHAPTER 24

CAM GLANCED at the clock: 10:00 a.m. Galen had been gone a while, since on Thursdays the band rehearsed early. Cam had slept so soundly that Galen must have spent the entire night with him. Max still slept at his feet, although he hopped out of bed as soon as Cam did.

Galen. Cam had no idea what to think about him except that he liked Galen. More than liked him. He *wanted* Galen. Wanted to hold him, touch him, have sex with him. The kiss in the leaves…. The way Galen's hands felt on his body…. *The last thing you need!*

As soon as he'd showered and dressed, the phone rang.

"I'm fine, Galen," he said before Galen could get a word in.

Galen's warm laughter came through the receiver and caused Cam to smile. He hadn't smiled this much in a very long time.

"So what are you up to?" Galen asked.

"Going out." He'd decided to make it to the library today. He felt good, having set a goal.

"Library?"

"Yes." Cam half hoped Galen would offer to go with him.

"I'll be home around four," Galen said. "There's leftover chili in the fridge for lunch. Help yourself."

"Thanks." Cam hesitated, then asked, "How's your day been so far?"

"Uh…. Fine."

Of course he's surprised you asked. You've never asked about him before.

"Band getting better?"

"Yes," Galen replied. "They are. I'm beginning to think I wasn't overestimating them."

"Good." An awkward silence settled before Cam said, "I shouldn't keep you. And I should probably get going."

"Right. I'll call again later. If you need me, just call, okay?"

"Sure. Thank you." Cam's face heated as he realized how formal he sounded. They'd slept in the same bed the night before—why was he so damned awkward around Galen?

He knew the answer, but he pushed the thought away. Galen didn't need Cam's mess, and Cam didn't need another complication in his already complicated bloody mess of a life.

CAM SAT down in front of the computer monitor and took a deep breath. How long had it been since he'd been online? He hadn't seen a newspaper in a couple of days, hadn't listened to the radio. He spent the first ten minutes catching up on life in the outside world. The usual wrangling in Washington. More inquiries into phone tapping in the UK. Nothing about him, Raice Corp., or Sherrington Holdings.

But they were still out there, looking for him. That was what the FBI did, wasn't it? Look for fugitives? The only thing he'd proved by not finding a headline about himself was that he wasn't newsworthy.

After a few more minutes of reading through news websites, he decided to search for stories. Something that he might have missed buried under more interesting headlines. Anything that might help him figure out what he should do.

He started by searching for Raice Corp. Not much came up on the screen. Annual reports, a few articles about a new battery technology they'd been working on that held promise. He did the same for Sherrington Holdings and found nothing interesting there either. He'd seen all of this before; he'd made it his business to keep an eye on the Internet, knowing Duncan used it very little.

Next he searched for himself online. He didn't find much. The usual profiles, a few articles from gossip pages. Nothing about an investigation. Nothing about a warrant for his arrest or the FBI. The FBI might have several reasons to keep that news to themselves. Best-case scenario, they weren't sure he was the source of the overseas transactions. Worst case, and probably most likely, they thought he had accomplices and didn't want them fleeing.

Or it's just not interesting enough to report about.

He was overthinking this. It didn't matter why, because he hadn't done anything wrong. He tapped his foot against the table. Forty-five more minutes of searches revealed nothing about the investigation. Nothing at all.

Maybe he should just turn himself in. Get it over and done with and face the charges. He was innocent, after all.

And how are you going to prove that if you're locked away in a cell?

He could check his e-mail. See if anyone had tried to contact him. He'd avoided turning on his mobile because he'd worried the FBI would be able to track him down. He spent a few minutes searching to see whether they could find him if he logged into his e-mail. His answer? Maybe they could.

Not worth the risk. If he was going to tip his hand, he needed a plan. A way to prove his innocence. And he needed more time to think things through.

CHAPTER 25

CAM WANDERED over to the window and looked out over the yard they'd raked the day before, now once again covered with leaves. He'd fallen asleep on the couch and woken to the sound of Max's bark and Galen's car in the driveway. He figured he still needed to catch up on his sleep.

Or maybe you're just depressed. He had nowhere to go—*except jail*—and nothing to do.

"Tea?" Galen asked as he joined Cam at the window with two steaming mugs. "Nice first flush I brought back from Darjeeling last year."

"Darjeeling?" Cam took one of the mugs and inhaled. Floral, quite delicate, with just a hint of spiciness. A lovely tea. He felt relieved that Galen hadn't asked how he'd slept. He was tired of lying.

Galen nodded. "I spent the summer there."

"Why Darjeeling?" The wind blew some of the leaves into the air and scattered them again on the grass.

"Seemed like an interesting place to go, and the school system didn't have money for summer music classes," Galen answered with a shrug.

"Oh." Cam glanced quickly at Galen, then back again at the window.

"Autumn's pretty here." A non sequitur. Cam had gotten used to them with Galen. He'd begun to believe that they really weren't the stream-of-consciousness babble he'd come to expect from his mother over the years. Unlike Cam's mother, Galen didn't seem to need to fill the silences. He simply thought differently from other people. For Galen, it seemed like the world around him was a constant blur of activity, like a melody that floated in and out of the forefront of Galen's thoughts, surfacing from time to time, revealing itself in seemingly out-of-the-blue observations.

"Sisyphus," Cam said with a soft chuckle.

Galen turned and looked at him, lips parted, the edges of his mouth curving upward in obvious amusement. "Raking leaves as punishment? You clean them up only to have them return, just like Zeus's enchanted boulder?"

Cam smiled, surprised and slightly awed by Galen's response. "Something like that." He knew he shouldn't be surprised, but each time he assumed something about Galen, Galen did something entirely unexpected. Cam thought he could read people—he was usually quite good at it—but he'd read Galen spectacularly wrong.

"But you enjoyed raking the leaves," Galen pointed out.

"I did." No use in denying it.

"Then what difference does it make if you have to do the work again?"

Cam considered the question as Galen inhaled the steam from his tea, then sipped it. "I… I guess it doesn't."

"Then it's not the same as pushing that rock up the hill only to have it roll down and start over again." Galen's eyes sparkled with a friendly challenge. "Sometimes pushing the boulder is fun. Sometimes you have to be at the bottom in order to claw your way back up."

More new-age bollocks. Galen seemed full of it today. "I suppose."

Cam stared down at his tea. How many times had he felt as though someone was deliberately pushing that boulder back down just when he'd finally managed to achieve something? His mother laughing as she told one of her friends that he'd taken up a new "hobby" when he'd financed his first off-Broadway production. The way he'd let Duncan convince him that his idea to change the company's focus to include green technology was a child's fantasy and that his time was better spent traveling than working with the board to push the company in new directions. Perhaps he could have succeeded at any of these endeavors, but he'd stopped. He'd let go of the things that mattered to him. He hadn't asked what was happening at Sherrington Holdings. He'd ignored Raice Corp. once the purchase went through.

He'd *let* them push the boulder. He'd given them no resistance. He'd stepped aside, and by doing so, he'd helped them by pretending he didn't care. He'd wasted his time telling himself that it was all about *them*. He'd denied that he had any say. But the truth was that he'd sat back and let other people do things for him. Hell, he'd pushed the damned boulder all by himself.

Fuck. He didn't want to think about that. He wanted to forget about it and go back to the way things had been before his birthday. *Fucking messed-up birthday.* Yes, he was bitter. He had a right to be, didn't he? He set his mug down on a nearby table without drinking, then sat down heavily on the couch and rubbed his face with his hands.

Galen sat down next to him a moment later. "You want to talk about it?" he asked.

Galen sounded like he did when he talked to his students. Cam fought the urge to snap at Galen for treating him like a child, but he stopped himself when he realized that he'd been wrong about this too. Galen wasn't treating him like a child. There was nothing condescending in how he'd asked the question, just as there was nothing fatherly in the way Galen spoke to his students.

Cam ran a hand over his mouth and considered the question. "I'm not great at talking," he said without much thought.

"That's okay. You don't have to be. I'm a pretty good listener." Galen pursed his lips and offered Cam an understanding smile.

"I know." Why did he feel so relaxed sitting here with a man he'd known less than a week? He shifted on the couch, pulling one leg beneath him the way he'd often seen Galen sit. "I just don't know where to start."

"Then just say the first thing that pops into your head."

Shit. He knew what he had to say, but he'd never said it to anyone, not even himself. *Just say it. Just fucking say it.*

"I've been having dreams. Nightmares." He glanced at Galen, then looked down at his hands. He hadn't even realized he'd been twisting them around in his lap. "At least I thought that's what they were." He forced his hands apart and set them on his thighs.

No one will believe you. He wasn't sure he could face that sort of rejection. The feeling of despair came back with a vengeance.

Galen put his arm around Cam's shoulders. "You're doing fine," he said. "Take your time. I'm not going anywhere."

And damn if that didn't nearly make Cam lose it right then and there. He clenched his jaw and forced himself to slow his breathing as he blinked back a wave of powerful emotion. He wouldn't cry again. Not even in front of someone like Galen, who probably wouldn't care. *Cam* cared. That was all that mattered. And he fucking wouldn't cry.

"Something happened to me. Something I think I forgot. Maybe I wanted to forget it. I don't know."

Breathe. Just breathe!

"Something bad. I was nine. It was after my father died. My uncle...." *Fuck. I can fucking do this.* "He came to stay with me and my mother. To help with things. Settle the estate."

Cam stared up at the ceiling. For the first time, he noticed a thin crack that ran from one side of the room to the light fixture at the center. He imagined tracing his finger over it.

Galen gently squeezed his shoulder, pulling him back to himself. Had he understood Cam had needed that? Cam guessed so. Galen always seemed to do that when Cam needed it the most.

"I don't remember much from that time. Things at home were so busy, I rarely saw my mother." He didn't add that he'd guessed much later that his mother hadn't wanted to see him. Not that she'd ever said as much, but she often told him how much he looked like his father, and he knew how devastated she was when he died. "Duncan—my uncle—spent the entire summer with us."

Cam closed his eyes and exhaled slowly. Why was it so difficult to breathe? Fear seemed to have taken up residence in his chest, around his heart, squeezing it so tight it hurt. But Galen's hand was still there, and it felt good. It felt like he was close to someone. That he'd *let* himself get close. And for once, that felt like a good thing.

"You don't have to talk if you don't want to."

"I need to do this," Cam said, his eyes still closed. Inside of himself like this, he could do it. Say it. Admit it. "It's not about wanting or not." *I need someone to know.*

"Okay."

"My dreams... they weren't dreams. They're memories. I think I knew they weren't dreams. They seemed so—" Cam shuddered. "—real. And then the other night.... The night I...." *Fuck!* He could say this too. He needed to say it. Face it. "The night I tried to kill myself... again...." He opened his eyes and realized his hands were back in his lap. He hadn't even been aware of it. He got to his feet. It was either fidget or pace, and pacing seemed good right now. Galen had seen him at his lowest—what difference did it make if he saw him losing it? "The night I tried to kill myself, I remembered. Everything. It all came back to me. And I couldn't.... I didn't think I could handle it. With everything else, I...."

He took a deep breath and glanced at Galen, who watched him with an expression of quiet concern but didn't press him and didn't make any move to stop him. Cam liked that about Galen. No bullshit. Just patience.

"I loved my father. I didn't see a lot of him growing up because he was so busy. But I remember wanting to be like him." Cam smiled in spite of himself. "He seemed so in control. He understood things. I watched him work a few times... just sat in his office, pretending to read a book. But really I was watching him. I tried to talk like him. Move like him. Stand tall like he always did." His father hadn't fidgeted. Hadn't paced. "And when he died, I was so lost. He was so young. He wasn't supposed to die."

"How old was he?" Galen asked.

"Forty-six. Sudden cardiac arrest. I know because I looked it up when the doctors said that. It's a heart attack, but with no symptoms. No pain." Cam laughed. "I told myself I'd grow up to be a doctor so nobody like him would ever have to die again." He shook his head at the memory. "My mother told me that was a nice sentiment, but I knew she knew it'd never happen.

"Duncan was there for me. He was a few years younger than my father. I remember wondering if he and my mother would get married and then he'd be my dad. Take his place. I wanted that. I looked up to him like I looked up to my father. He took me places. The theater. Riding. To the cinema. I remember being really happy. Happier, even, than when my dad was alive." Even now, he felt guilty about that, as if he'd betrayed his father's memory.

"But there were times I couldn't remember from back then. Whole months that disappeared. Later on, when I was older, I wondered about it when I looked at some of the things I'd kept. Souvenirs from places I'd been that I couldn't remember ever going to. That sort of thing. And the photos...." Cam rubbed his lips with his fingers and fought the wave of nausea that always came when he tried to remember. "After a while I just said 'fuck it' and let it go.

"But then the dreams started right around the time we met. The other night... when you found me in the bathroom.... When I realized they weren't dreams, something fell into place. Made me remember everything." He started to shake, and Galen was suddenly there, holding him as he shook like a kid. A fucking kid.

"He.... I.... I liked it. When he touched me the first time. I felt something. Needed? I don't know. Something. I missed my dad so much. It was just a hug. No, more than that, but not... not really *wrong*."

"Cam." No recriminations. No judgment. Just his name. His fucking *name*. And he was losing it. Crying. What the fuck was wrong with him that he'd do that not once but *twice* now?

Galen held him tighter. Galen felt so good. Made *Cam* feel so good.

"It started out like that, and I told myself it was good, because I loved the man. But then it was suddenly more, and he was touching me in other places. And I knew it was wrong, but it felt all right. By the end of that week.... Shit. I don't know if I can even say it. It hurt, but he told me it was all right. It was supposed to hurt the first time. I believed him too. He was the only one who'd ever spent time with me. Cared about me. So I didn't say anything then. I didn't say anything when it happened more and more often. In the gardener's shed. In the boathouse. In my room. Wherever. I didn't stop it."

"You blame yourself for that?" Cam heard no judgment in Galen's voice.

"I should have stopped it."

"You were a kid. He took advantage of you. Hurt you. He's sick, Cam. Twisted kind of sick."

Cam shook his head. "I'm the sick one. If I really hated it, I would have stopped it."

"Would you tell me that if I said the same thing?" Galen asked as he turned Cam's face gently toward him. "Can you honestly say that you'd tell me I was sick?"

Cam looked into Galen's eyes and knew he couldn't. What the hell did that mean?

Galen smiled at him—a smile that revealed depth Galen hid well. Unassuming, quiet Galen. Galen, whose heart was big enough to embrace the world. Cam didn't even care that the thought felt overly romantic and sappy.

"You blame yourself for too much, Cam. Maybe you deserve blame for some things, but what happened to you when you were a boy wasn't your fault."

Cam wiped his eyes on his sleeve. Galen was still holding him gently by the shoulders and watching him. *He's worried about me.* The knowledge that Galen genuinely cared what happened to him made Cam feel uneasy. Other than David and Alex, and maybe Aiden—Lord knew he didn't deserve any of them as friends—there wasn't anyone he was sure genuinely did.

"Sorry," Cam said, incredibly embarrassed. His eyes were undoubtedly red, and his nose was stopped up. He sniffled. Galen reached over to the piano and handed him a tissue. Cam blew his nose.

"Don't apologize." Galen tilted his head to one side, then added, "I know you still don't believe it—that you didn't do anything wrong. But what I said… you get that, right?"

Cam nodded. He did get it, even if he wasn't ready to let go of his self-hatred.

"Let me get you some more tea," Galen said, clearly pleased to have gotten Cam to admit he understood.

"Tea, right." Cam barely registered the offer. "Sorry," he repeated as his face warmed. What a fucking mess he was! He still didn't understand why Galen was being so kind to him.

"Be right back. Why don't you sit on the couch and relax. I'll just be a couple of minutes."

"Right. Thank you." Cam sat down, leaned against the back of the couch, and pulled a multicolored crocheted afghan over himself.

CAM AWOKE to the sound of the piano. He didn't know the piece, but he was pretty sure it was Mozart judging by the sweet melody and the deceptively simple harmonies. He opened his eyes and realized the sun had long since set. How long had he been sleeping? Four hours, maybe five?

"Feeling better?" Galen asked as he continued to play.

"Yes. Thank you." Cam had always marveled at musicians who could play and talk at the same time. He'd barely been able to manage two hands, let alone multitasking like speaking or singing while playing. *Probably why he teaches music and you don't.*

Cam stretched and got up from the couch, then sat down beside Galen as he continued to play. Cam loved being this close to the music; he'd barely played in the past ten years, but he always seemed to seek out musicians, whether as friends or, in Aiden's case, lovers. He'd loved to hear Aiden sing in the old

Edwardian house they'd shared, loved the way his voice soared to the high ceilings and the house resonated as though it were singing along with him.

Galen's long fingers flew over the keys, and he wore an expression of calm focus. The tiny lines around his eyes seemed more pronounced as the corners of his mouth edged upward in a gentle smile. For the first time, Cam noticed the flecks of gold in his eyes.

This thought inevitably led to another. Galen was so fucking attractive. *No.* The last thing he needed now was another relationship to fuck up. He was so wrapped up in his internal dialogue that he didn't realize Galen had stopped playing and was watching him.

"Thinking about something?" Galen asked.

Thinking how much I want to kiss you right now. A few weeks ago, he wouldn't have hesitated. But now he felt distinctly torn. He longed for Galen to hold him again as he'd done before. Something about how he felt in Galen's arms—safe, content—made the memories fade into the background. But in addition to that need and the craving for Galen's touch, he feared that if he gave in to his body, he'd be setting himself up again. He'd fuck things up like he'd done with Aiden. Then he'd lose the warm feeling. And he needed that right now. He needed it so fucking badly.

"Just thinking about how much I owe you for taking me in." Not a lie, but not the entire truth. Better that way.

Galen shook his head. "I enjoy the company. And Max has already adopted you."

Cam laughed when he realized Max had curled up beside him again, his body pressed against Cam's foot.

"Animals always seem to gravitate to the people most allergic to them."

That night Galen slept beside Cam again. This time Cam didn't hesitate— he settled onto Galen's chest and held on to him. Galen leaned in and kissed Cam's head. Cam sighed and closed his eyes. He fell asleep to the steady beat of Galen's heart.

CHAPTER 26

CAM SLEPT so soundly, he barely registered Galen leaving for work the next day. Fridays, Galen only worked mornings at the school. And although Cam had objected, Galen told Cam he was planning on spending the evening with him instead of playing in the subway in Manhattan.

When the library opened at 9:00 a.m. on Friday, Cam was one of the first to arrive. He couldn't stand it anymore. He'd take a chance and check his e-mail. He didn't know what he hoped to find when he did, and he certainly didn't expect the e-mail from Dan Bryce from Raice's accounting department, sent the day before.

> *Cameron—*
>
> *I'm in New York, providing assistance to the FBI on Raice's offshore accounts. I hear they've got a warrant for your arrest. I'm very sorry. I think I have some information that may help you, but I don't want to risk sending it over the Internet.*
>
> *Call me. I'm staying at the Colonial Hotel in Midtown. I'm free tomorrow until about 11:00.*
>
> *-Dan*

Hopeful for the first time in weeks, Cam nearly ran all the way back to Galen's house. Now, as the clock on the mantel chimed the half hour, he powered up his phone.

"Dan?"

"Cameron. I worried you wouldn't call." Dan sounded nervous and exhausted.

"I'm so glad you contacted me," Cam said quickly. "I've been trying to reach you. Duncan wouldn't take my calls, and I knew you'd be able to help."

"This whole thing is crazy. The FBI's saying the accounts are in your name. They've been to the Raice Corp. office twice in the last week, looking through documents. Demanding access to our computer logs. People here are nervous."

"I didn't do anything, Dan," Cam said. "I didn't know anything about the Cayman account before the FBI investigation."

"I know."

Cam relaxed at those words. "But Duncan—"

"Duncan's been tied up with the HMRC and the police every day for the past week. He says they're looking at Sherrington Holdings, trying to decide whether the Cayman accounts are connected in any way."

"What are we talking about here, Dan?" Cam tapped his foot against the wood floor as he spoke, then tried to stop himself and relax. *Breathe in, breathe out.*

"Relatively small transfers, for the most part—all under the reporting limit. Deposited into another Cayman account, then into the account in your name in even smaller amounts."

"And Raice?" Cam pretty much knew what Dan would say next.

"Their records show you've been investing in the company from the Cayman account. Small purchases of stock. It's been going on for about four years, best I can tell. Then it just stopped."

Four years? *Right about the time we purchased the company.*

"Stopped?" Cam asked. "When?"

"Beginning of August of this year. I'm not sure why. Maybe someone got wind of it? The first we heard about an internal audit was around that time."

August? That was when the board had told him they were going to scrutinize his accounts, require approval on his allowance. *Bloody hell.* "I don't know," he told Dan. The last thing he needed was to give Dan any reason to doubt his innocence. Dan wouldn't know about his allowance—Duncan had gotten the board to agree to keep quiet about it. At the time Cam had been relieved. Bad enough that they were treating him like a child and putting him on a budget. But now....

"Can we meet?" Dan asked. "I've got some spreadsheets I'd like to show you."

"WHAT DO you think?" Cam asked Galen after he'd told him about Dan.

Galen frowned and shook his head. "Sounds risky. And very convenient."

Cam had expected that response. He'd thought the same thing himself. "But...," he pressed.

"But if it's on the up-and-up, it's probably worth the risk."

Cam chuckled and shook his head.

"What's so funny?" Galen asked with the hint of a grin.

"You." Cam smiled broadly. "Every time I think I know what to expect from you, you surprise me."

"Good." Galen sat a bit straighter, and Cam understood this pleased him.

"You like surprising people, don't you?"

Galen shrugged. "Maybe. At some point in my life, I decided I would be whatever I wanted to be, not what people expected of me."

"Sounds very Zen."

"You've really been reading that book, haven't you?" Galen asked.

"Maybe." Cam hesitated, then asked, "Would you teach me how to meditate?"

Galen stared at him for a minute, and Cam half expected him to laugh. Galen didn't, and in retrospect, Cam thought he should have known better. "I... I'd love to," Galen said. "Would you like to join me in the morning?"

"Yes." Cam forced a smile. He'd felt so anxious the past week, he'd try anything to learn to relax. He couldn't go on like this much longer, and he knew Galen wouldn't always be there to sleep beside him.

"It'll work out, Cam. You'll get through this." Galen's brilliant smile made Cam's heart feel like bursting. How was it possible that a smile could do that?

It can when it's meant for you and no one else. Nobody had ever smiled at him like that before, as if he were the center of the universe. Not that he thought he was, but Galen made him feel that way, and that was good enough.

He leaned in and kissed Galen. "I like doing that," he said. "Kissing you."

"I like it too."

"But?" There was always a "but," wasn't there?

"But nothing. When you're ready for more than kissing, you'll know."

"You think the fact that we've only kissed is *my* fault," Cam joked as the realization dawned that, at least for the past few days, he *had* been the one to leave things between them at the just-kissing stage. Things inside his head felt so bloody confused right now, between his rediscovered memories, thoughts of boarding school, and Aiden.

"No blame here." Galen's fierce gaze caused Cam's heart to beat faster.

Cam's cheeks heated and he forced himself not to look away. "Thank you," he said after a moment's pause. "For understanding."

"So what will you do?" Galen asked. "About meeting Dan, I mean?" Galen swallowed, his cheeks flushed, and Cam knew he felt embarrassed that Cam might have misunderstood.

"I'll meet him on Monday. See what he has to say. But I'll be careful."

CHAPTER 27

CAM WALKED into Grand Central Station an hour before he'd promised to meet Dan. He leaned against a wall and gazed out at the cavernous room with ticket booths, shops, and Monday morning commuters hustling to their destinations.

At Galen's suggestion, Cam had insisted they meet here, in an open public space, rather than the hotel lobby Dan originally suggested. Still, he knew a risky venture when he saw one. If this worked, if Dan had the evidence he said he did, Cam might be able to go back to his old life. Back to his comfortable existence. Sleep in his own bed. Wake to Luisa's coffee and omelets. Fly home to London and meet friends at the club.

Three weeks before, all of these things would have been wonderful to anticipate. Now, he wasn't so sure. Going back to London meant facing Duncan and his past. He'd need to decide what to do about Duncan and what to say to him. Going home meant facing the empty house where he'd spent so much time with Aiden, and knowing Aiden would never come home to him again. The board would still be holding the purse strings and controlling his life. He'd still be a loser. Someone who'd never amount to anything more than his money and his title.

You're trying to convince yourself it's not worth the risk. He knew the game. He'd played it with himself for years. Stick with the comfortable things you know and life will remain pleasant and predictable. Step out of the box and you'll get trod on. And yet it hadn't worked that way this time, had it? He'd been playing it safe, and here he was, sweaty palms and pounding heart, fearful that he might end up in prison, willing to put it all on the line. *For what?* Why did he even bother?

He shrugged off the maudlin thoughts. Whatever he'd done to deserve the bollocks the universe had decided to dump all over him, he had no intention of sitting back and doing nothing.

He nervously fingered the bracelet Galen had given him the night before. They'd been about to get into bed when Galen had taken it off his wrist and handed it to Cam. "I want you to have this," Galen had said. "It's kind of like a good luck charm—at least it has been for me. A reminder that you're not alone in this, even if I'm not standing next to you."

Cam hadn't known what to say to that. He'd taken the bracelet, a braided leather band with a silver clasp and three silver charms that read *Hope. Healing. Love.* He'd been tempted to tell Galen he couldn't take anything more from him—that Galen had already given him so much—but he managed a mumbled thanks instead. Cam understood that Galen needed him to take the bracelet without question.

"I've collected a few of these over the years," Galen had said, undeterred by Cam's lack of coherent response. "Most of them my students gave me. But this one…. This one is different. This was the first."

Cam had kissed Galen, then put the bracelet on. He hadn't been prepared for the strange sensation of warmth in his chest as he'd settled next to Galen afterward. Like floating in a pool, or the way he felt when he'd dreamed he could fly. He didn't worry about what it meant; he just let himself *feel.* And that night he'd slept better than he had in years, even knowing what might happen the next day.

Now, he half wished Galen was here with him. Not that Galen hadn't offered to come—Cam said no, firmly—but Galen had become his rock. His port in the storm. Not even two weeks, and he'd come to rely on Galen.

Another reason to do this on your own.

He glanced around him again, then shoved a hand in his jeans pocket and pulled out his mobile. Galen had managed to find him a charger, and he figured in a crowd like this, even if the FBI had a way to track him using the device, he could easily hide.

I'm near the southwest corner by the Au Bon Pain, he texted.

On my way read the quick response.

Breathe. Relax. Focus. He'd spent nearly an hour that morning with Galen, working on meditation. He'd begun to think it really *did* help. Not like alcohol, but he needed his wits about him.

Breathe. Relax. Focus.

He spotted Dan coming from the entrance about a hundred feet away from him. Dan, wearing a pair of polyester trousers and a sweater a size too small that hugged his rather large gut, looked nervous and slightly out of breath. He spotted Cam a moment later and shot him a tense smile.

"Good to see you, Lord Sherrington," Dan said as he reached Cam. He breathed heavily and wiped the sweat from his forehead with a handkerchief.

"Cam would be fine, Dan." No point to pretense in a situation such as this.

"Cam."

"I hate to be rude," Cam said, eyeing the closest exit over Dan's shoulder, "but I'm in a bit of a hurry. Can you show me what you found?"

"Oh, right." Dan flushed to his balding scalp and nodded, then pulled some papers from his pocket and handed them to Cam.

"Thank you," Cam said as he began to leaf through the documents—spreadsheets with columns and figures. It took Cam a moment and a few deep breaths to focus on the numbers. He scanned them from right to left, trying to make sense of them. He frowned, then looked up at Dan and said, "I've seen these before."

Dan scratched his head and glanced somewhere over Cam's shoulder. He shifted his weight from one foot to the other, then did something awkward with his left hand, rubbing his neck and simultaneously flicking something nonexistent off like one might get rid of an insect.

A signal.

Cam turned just in time to see several men approaching from behind him. He might have mistaken them for commuters but for the fact that they weren't wearing jackets or coats.

Bollocks.

Cam threw the papers at Dan, who stood there blinking as they fluttered to the ground. Cam pushed Dan toward the men—not hard enough to make him fall, but putting Dan squarely between himself and them.

Cam ran toward the stairs that led to the subway, doing his best to avoid the crowd of commuters who had just emerged from one of the Metro-North tracks. A few people shouted at him to stop running. He ignored them and kept going, reaching the stairs a few seconds later and taking them three at a time. Thank God he'd borrowed a pair of Galen's trainers. If he'd worn his own leather-soled shoes, he'd have slipped and fallen already.

A woman shouted at Cam as he jumped the turnstile and nearly collided with her. He looked up to see three men barreling toward the entrance. *Shit.* He hesitated just a second, until he knew they saw him, then took off down the stairs to the Uptown platform.

As he ran, he mulled over his decision. He'd thought about it before, whether to turn himself in if Dan's offer was really a setup. But he figured if the evidence was so strong that the authorities would bother to lure him in using Dan, he had no bloody way to prove his innocence. And if he was locked in a cell, what could he do to get to the bottom of things?

A train pulled into the station just as he reached the platform. He boarded just as the three agents made it down the stairs. Through the window, he saw them look up and down the platform. Then one of them gestured to the train. Two of them boarded one of the forward cars before the doors closed.

One stop for them to get to the end of the train. Good enough. Cam pushed past a woman with a small wheeled cart filled with grocery bags, and squeezed between one of the floor-to-ceiling poles, several people seated on the slippery orange molded seats, and toward the door between cars. He pulled on the door handle, but nothing happened.

Bloody hell!

With both hands this time, he shoved the handle downward using every bit of his strength. He felt the click of the latch as it opened, and stepped through the door to the place between the cars. The whoosh of the air by his head, the knowledge that the only thing keeping him from falling onto the tracks was the narrow metal platform beneath his feet and the metal chain at waist height—all of this felt exhilarating. He straddled the place where the two cars met, feeling the platforms move against each other like tiny tectonic plates shifting during an earthquake, allowed his body to absorb the vibrations, knowing that if he just leaned forward he might tumble and everything would disappear. No more pain, no more nervous dread, no more memories.

He smiled and placed his foot firmly on the next car. *Not now.* Not ever, he knew. He didn't want to die. Living meant he'd have to face demons, but he could handle that. He'd handle it. Whatever "it" was.

He opened the door to the next car just as the train pulled into the 33rd Street station. He charged up the steps directly in front of him—he knew this station well—and scrambled toward the stairs to the Uptown platform, then descended. He made sure the men following him saw him board the Uptown train, then ducked down low enough that they wouldn't see him exit. He saw them board the train just as he hopped off the front of the platform onto the tracks. He walked a few feet before pressing his body into the indentation in the tunnel.

The train picked up speed as it passed him. He nearly shouted in excitement at the pressure of the air and the slick surface of the cars only a foot away from his nose. He felt like he had when he was young and he'd first ridden the trains. His heart pounded in his ears, barely audible over the squealing of the wheels against the tracks.

He waited a minute after the train left, then peered out of the alcove. One of the men following him paced the platform. Cam quickly returned to his hiding place. He'd wait here as long as he needed, and then he'd head back. The disappointment he'd felt at knowing that Dan had nothing to offer him except a one-way ticket to a jail cell faded with each train that traveled past him down the tunnels.

CHAPTER 28

GALEN PLAYED the last two measures of "Day In, Day Out." He'd tried to focus on the music but with little success. He pulled his cell from his pocket and checked the time. Where the hell was Cam? Nearly 6:00 p.m., and Cam was supposed to have met him at the 42nd Street station two hours before. Something had gone wrong.

"Don't worry. If I get the sense that it's a setup, I'll leave," Cam had said after Galen had quizzed him for the umpteenth time since he'd decided to meet Dan Bryce.

Galen had known the risks, so he'd suggested he go with Cam. But Cam, ever stubborn—and no doubt worried that he'd somehow involve Galen—had insisted on going to the meeting alone.

A little girl walking by with her mother stopped and waved at him. "What would you like me to play?" Galen asked, happy for the distraction.

The girl looked at her mother, who nodded and smiled at Galen. *Former musician.* He knew them well from their wistful expressions and the way they seemed so comfortable speaking to someone playing in the subway.

"Twinkle, Twinkle?" the girl asked.

"I can do that," Galen answered with a grin. He played the melody and the little girl sang along in a sweet voice. Musical, like her mother. He finished the song, then repeated it, this time adding scales and flourishes in his own variation on the theme. At the end, the girl squealed and clapped her hands. The mother gave her a dollar to drop in Galen's case.

"Thank you," the girl said as she left the dollar.

Galen watched as the girl skipped away toward the N trains, holding her mother's hand and asking if she could learn to play trumpet.

Where are you, Cam? He looked around just in time to see a flurry of activity at the end of one of the tunnels. He heard several shouts, then saw someone running. Someone with light brown hair, wearing a blue jacket. Cam.

Shit. Galen pulled out the mouthpiece, then shoved the trumpet into the case and closed the lid without bothering to remove the coins and bills. He threw his backpack over one shoulder and latched the trumpet case as he strode across to where the tunnels converged. He caught Cam's eye as Cam ran toward the S train, then kept walking the way Cam had come.

Several men dressed in dark suits came charging toward him, weaving in and out of the people transferring to different trains. Galen took a long, deep breath and walked directly into their path, trumpet case held in front of him. The collision that resulted sounded far worse than it felt. Galen landed on his butt, staring up at the men.

"Are you all right?" one of them asked. The other nodded at his partner and took off in the direction Cam had been running.

"I… I think so." Galen dry-scrubbed his face and blinked a few times, then tried to get back to his feet. He'd taken the hit on the side of his body to minimize any real damage, but the man who'd run into him didn't need to know that.

"Let me help you." The man offered Galen his hand, and Galen stood slowly, then dusted himself off.

"Thanks," Galen said as the man handed him his trumpet case and backpack. "I'm fine. Really."

"Sure?" the man asked.

"Sure." Galen offered him a reassuring smile, then waved and headed down the passage toward the Lexington Avenue trains.

MORE THAN three hours later, after the tunnels had emptied of most of the evening commuters, Galen stopped playing and packed up his trumpet. He'd seen several uniformed officers walking the tunnels, and the agent who'd quite literally run into him had stopped by to listen as he continued his search for Cam. Each time Galen had seen the authorities walk by, he'd been relieved. When he'd heard one of the police radios notifying the other officers that they'd lost the suspect and to return to their precincts, Galen's heart finally stopped pounding.

He headed back toward the S train platform at nearly 11:00 p.m. He waited until a train pulled away, leaving the platform empty, then walked to the end of the platform and hopped off and into the closest tunnel, taking care to avoid the electrified third rail. He walked about twenty feet down one of the tracks used to take trains out of service, then turned into a small alcove. He pulled a small flashlight from the backpack, opened the door on the left, then stepped inside and closed the door behind him.

"Cam?" Galen shined the light around the small room.

"God, it's good to see you." Cam, who had been sitting on the dusty concrete floor, got to his feet and walked over to Galen.

Galen didn't hesitate. He pulled Cam into his arms and held him for what felt like a long time. *Not long enough.* "I was so worried," Galen said as he regained control of his emotions.

"Your plan worked perfectly. Thanks." In the dim light, Galen saw Cam smile.

"But the evidence Dan told you about?"

"Bollocks, all of it. A trap meant to lure me in." Cam hugged Galen again and sighed. "You were right."

"I'm sorry about that. I really hoped I was wrong."

Cam shrugged. "I'm sure Duncan's paying him. He probably helped with the foreign deposits. He'd have needed someone at Raice to make the scheme work."

"Duncan?"

"I should have realized something was strange when he didn't object to acquiring Raice four years ago. He'd ignored all my suggestions for expanding the business before."

"Then why now?" Galen asked. "Why point the finger at you?"

"Because the jig is up. He didn't count on new software that would allow the FBI to flag smaller transactions. When they started investigating Raice, Dan conveniently provided them with evidence that showed I owned the foreign accounts." Cam laughed bitterly. "I'm sure he hoped the authorities would never figure things out. But just in case, he set me up to take the fall. Perfect timing too, because I'd managed to spend through all my inheritance."

Galen couldn't argue with the logic, even if hearing this made him ache even more for Cam. Duncan had betrayed Cam as a child, and he hadn't thought twice about doing it again. "So what's your plan?"

"I'm not sure. I guess I go back to your place. Regroup. If... if that's all right with you, of course."

The look of desperation on Cam's face made Galen's gut clench. "Goes without saying. I told you, Cam, you can stay as long as you need."

"Thanks." Cam pressed his lips together and shook his head. "I can't tell you how much that means to me. How much I apprec—"

Galen silenced Cam with his lips. The kiss didn't last long, but Galen felt a hell of lot better afterward.

"Oh... wow," Cam croaked. "That was...." Cam's cheeks pinked.

"Here's the clothing." Galen handed Cam the backpack, which he'd completely forgotten about. "Once you get changed, we can head back to my car. You can tell me all about Dan on the drive."

Cam nodded, then opened the backpack. "Camouflage?" he asked as he pulled the pants out and studied them. Then he dug through the rest of the clothing and pulled out the beanie cap from the bottom of the pile.

Galen laughed and shook his head. "Don't worry. They're my brother's. He forgot them the last time he came to visit."

"I take it *he's* not a vegetarian."

"Not in the least." Galen looked away as Cam changed into the pants and dark T-shirt. He knew it was silly—they'd slept pressed against each other for several nights now, after all—but he still felt uncomfortable. He'd begun to realize that part of the reason he hadn't been more tempted to do more than just kiss Cam was that he didn't want Cam to feel taken advantage of. If they were going to do more than sleep in the same bed, Galen needed to know that Cam wanted it and that he was ready.

CHAPTER 29

CAM STIRRED the curry and grinned. It tasted damn good. Even better, he'd made it himself with what he'd found in Galen's cupboards and some of the butternut squash Galen had brought back from the farmers' market. He inhaled the fragrant basmati rice as it cooked, and leaned back into the bend in the counter.

In spite of the excitement of the day before—the chase through the subway, the adrenaline that had coursed through his body in anticipation—he'd slept like a rock next to Galen. He'd *wanted* Galen so badly it had taken every bit of his willpower not to beg him for sex. But he'd struggled to stay awake, and he knew that whatever might happen between them, as exhausted and ragged as he felt after they'd made it back from the city, it wouldn't be the first time he wanted.

He laughed to himself to realize that he could think about sex that way, as something to be savored. Something that needed a proper time and place and, even more surprising, a proper state of mind.

Max, who'd been sleeping under the kitchen table, barked several times and trotted off to the front door.

"Cam?"

"In the kitchen," he answered.

"Sorry I'm later than I said I'd be," Galen said as he walked into the kitchen. "I got stuck in a meeting...." He saw the table and stopped speaking. Cam had set it with a tablecloth he'd found and ironed (he had the burn on his thumb to prove it), china he'd found in a high cabinet, a couple of wineglasses (he couldn't find two that matched), and a tiny bud vase he'd snagged from the mantel that he filled with a few straggler roses from the climbing bush on the side of the house.

"Thought I'd make dinner for you for a change," Cam said, feeling keenly uncomfortable and worried Galen wouldn't appreciate him digging in the cabinets and refrigerator.

"Wow." Galen smiled. The kind of smile that made Cam surprisingly weak-kneed. Cam brushed the thought away.

"I hope you don't mind."

Galen leaned over the stove and sniffed the curry. "Mind? It smells amazing, Cam. I didn't know you could cook."

"I asked our cook to teach me, when I was a kid. I'd forgotten how much I enjoyed it." Cam lifted the lid on the rice. "Almost done." He reached for one of the knobs to turn the temperature down on the curry and brushed Galen's hand by accident.

"Cam, I…."

Galen turned and gazed at Cam. Neither of them moved, but somehow they stood closer than they had before, faces inches away from each other. Cam heard Galen's stuttered breath. Then Cam leaned in without really thinking anything but that he wanted to be close to Galen. Galen didn't pull away as Cam kissed him the way he'd imagined kissing Galen all day, hard and deep and full of hunger.

The hissing sound of water brought Cam back to himself with a start. "Bugger!" The rice had begun to boil over. Cam wrenched himself away from Galen and pulled the pot off the heat, then set it down in the center of the stove.

"Everything okay?" Galen looked stunned, and his slightly swollen lips made Cam want to kiss him again.

"Just a little more mess to clean," Cam said as he turned back to the stove in an effort to hide the blush he was sure stained his cheeks. He stirred the curry for good measure.

"Should I open a bottle of wine?" Galen asked from behind him.

"Sure."

"White?"

Cam nodded. "Sounds perfect. Oh, and there's a bottle of chutney I found in the cupboard. Maybe you can open that and put it on the table, please?"

"Sure."

A few minutes later, they were seated at the table discussing Galen's day at school. "They're making progress on the selections for the statewide competition," Galen said as he poured their wine.

"Do you think they'll be ready in three weeks?" Cam set some rice on Galen's plate, then spooned curry over the top.

"I think so," Galen said as he inhaled the fragrant rice and curry. "But even if they're not, I think they'll enjoy the trip to Princeton."

"I don't remember doing much traveling when I was in school. A few archeological sites near Edinburgh, that sort of thing. Old churches, mostly just ruins. I only played piano, so I wasn't in orchestra or band. I skied in Switzerland a few times, but we never did much there but ski. When I got control of my trust fund, I finally got to see some of the places I'd dreamed about."

"Do you have a favorite place to travel?" Galen asked.

Cam shrugged. "Not really." He'd once loved Rome, but after Aiden left, the city had lost its appeal. Everywhere he'd looked, he'd seen Aiden and remembered the week they'd spent there. Their first holiday together. "You?"

"Don't have a favorite place," Galen said. "I never go to the same place twice."

"Never?" Cam found this rather odd, although he wasn't sure why.

"Never. I'm not one to put down roots."

"But you've been living here a while," Cam pointed out.

"Three years." Galen speared a piece of squash and brought it to his lips. "It's about time to move on, I guess."

Cam didn't know how to respond. He'd owned his New York condo longer than that, and if the world hadn't come crashing down around him, he'd have been happy to keep it until he was old and gray. He'd often thought about giving up the London rental he'd shared with Aiden and taking up residence permanently in the US. He supposed that wouldn't happen now.

Galen finished chewing and went for another bite. "Wow, this curry is amazing, Cam."

Cam hadn't even realized he'd been tense, waiting for Galen's opinion of the food. "Thank you. It's one of my favorites. Got the recipe off the net a few years ago. Not too spicy, I hope?"

"No, it's perfect." Galen grinned. "I love things with a bit of a bite."

"Good. I was missing a few ingredients and I tend to go a bit heavy on the green curry."

They chatted comfortably, and for once the silences between didn't bother Cam. Like the food, conversations also needed to be savored. The wine gave him a nice warm buzz. He spent more time looking at Galen, and Galen looked back. Cam guessed Galen understood what would happen later, and from the way Galen met his gaze, he knew Galen wanted it as well.

After nearly an hour, Galen got up and began to clear the table.

"I can help," Cam offered as he gathered some of the condiments and put them in the refrigerator.

Galen had just started to put the dishes in the dishwasher when the doorbell rang. Cam nearly jumped out of his skin. Had they found him? Could they find him if his mobile was turned off?

"Expecting someone?" Cam's heart raced and his hands felt suddenly cold.

"No." Galen frowned. "I'll answer it. Wait here. If you need to, you can go down to the basement and hide," Galen said, clearly sensing Cam's fear.

Cam nodded and Galen was gone a moment later, closing the door to the kitchen behind him. Cam tried to look out of the kitchen window, but the bushes were too high, and he couldn't see to the front of the house.

What's the worst that can happen? The thought of being locked in a cell made him shiver. He'd always been a bit claustrophobic, but since the dreams had begun, it had only gotten worse. What if they wouldn't grant him bail? What if—?

"It's okay, Cam," Galen said from the other side of the door. "You can come out."

Cam drew a long breath and, after a moment's hesitation, peered out of the kitchen. The kid seated at the dining room table was barely recognizable—the only giveaway the curly red hair that peered out from under his hoodie. "Jamie?"

Jamie turned his head and Cam's heart leapt into his throat. The boy was beaten and bloodied, his lower lip split, his left eye nearly swollen shut. Several cuts bled from his forehead, and a gash ran from his cheekbone halfway to his nose. His very bloodied nose.

"Cam," Galen said in an impossibly calm voice, "can you please bring me the first-aid kit from under the bathroom sink in the front hall?"

Cam nodded dumbly, biting back the urge to demand to know who had done this to the boy. Thank God for Galen, whose reassuring smile when Cam reentered the room with the first-aid kit set the tone for Cam's more muted response. "How can I help?"

"Can you please get me a bowl of warm water and a washcloth from upstairs?"

When Cam returned a moment later, Galen had an arm around Jamie's shoulder. Jamie's eyes were red, no doubt from crying. "Please don't call Child Protection," he whispered as Galen dipped the washcloth in the warm water and began to dab at Jamie's face. "I don't want to go back to foster care."

"I'm not calling anyone right now," Galen said, his voice gentle. "Let's get you cleaned up first. We can talk about that later, okay?"

Jamie nodded.

"Will you tell me about it?" Galen asked as he dabbed Jamie's face. He rinsed the washcloth in the bowl of water and dabbed again.

"You promise you won't call Child Protection?" Jamie asked. "Because I've only got seven months, and then I'm outta here and he can't touch me again."

Galen nodded. "Your stepfather?"

Jamie pressed his lips together and looked away.

"It's okay, Jamie. Deep breath." Galen continued to clean Jamie's cuts.

"Are you going to call them?" Jamie asked Cam. He looked far more frightened than angry, and Cam knew he hadn't meant it as an insult.

"I'm the last one who would call the authorities," Cam said. "Believe me."

This seemed to placate Jamie, because he turned back to Galen and said, "Yeah. My stepdad. We don't get along very well. Never have. We had a few... run-ins." Jamie shrugged and stared at his hands.

Cam immediately understood this wasn't the first time something like this had happened.

"Is it all right if I explain?" Galen asked Jamie.

Jamie nodded.

"When Jamie's stepfather lost his job about a year ago, things got worse at home. Then Jamie came out to his parents six months ago, at the end of his junior year. His stepfather gave him a black eye and kicked him out of the house. He spent a few months in foster care, but the social services folks returned him to his parents," Galen said.

"My stepdad took anger management classes." Jamie winced as Galen dabbed at the gash on his right cheek. "Not that it helped. My being gay just gives him a new excuse."

Galen frowned. "This one's going to need stitches."

"If I go to the hospital, they'll put me back in foster care."

"Okay," Galen said as he shook his head. "We can try some Krazy Glue. But it'll hurt. And it may scar."

"I don't give a shit."

"Krazy Glue?" Cam stared at Galen as if he'd lost his mind.

"Great for paper cuts," Galen explained. "Holds the skin together."

"Oh." One of these days, Cam would ask Galen how he knew all these things. For now, though, he focused his attention once more on Jamie.

"You hurt anywhere other than your face?" Galen asked. The water in the bowl had turned a brownish red from blood.

"Nah. He threatened to break my fingers, but he knows I'll lose my scholarship if I can't play. Then he'd be stuck with me longer."

"What set him off this time?" Galen opened the first-aid kit and pulled out a tube of ointment.

"I told him I was taking Rich to the winter dance." Jamie spoke the words defensively, as if challenging Cam and Galen to tell him what a mistake that had been. Neither of them would, of course. "He said something obnoxious, like he usually does when it's about me. My mom told him to lay off of me, but that just pissed him off more."

"Your mom okay?" Galen's brow furrowed, and Cam guessed the stepdad didn't always stop at hitting Jamie.

"Yeah. One of the neighbors heard the shouting and my stepdad took off. I figured I didn't want to be around when he got back." Jamie clenched his jaw and hopped off the chair.

"Dude." Galen raised his eyebrows and pointed to the chair. "I'm not done with you yet."

"Sorry." Jamie sat back down and nibbled on a fingernail. "It's just that he makes me want to punch him back. That's all."

"I know." Galen went back to work on Jamie's chin. Jamie flinched once, then sighed and relaxed. "But if you hit him back, you'd give him cred."

Cam knew he'd have hit the bastard and enjoyed it.

"You can't go back there," Galen said after he'd finished cleaning the cuts. "Your sister still living around here?"

Jamie stared at the floor. "I don't want to make things hard for her."

"She told you last time she'd be there if things didn't work out at home." Galen pulled a small tube from the first-aid kit, then eyed Jamie's cheek. The cut had stopped bleeding, but it looked terrible.

"I know, but that was before Carlos was born. Things are pretty crowded at her place." Jamie inhaled sharply as Galen applied the glue and brought the edges of the cut together.

"You doing okay?" Galen asked. Jamie nodded. "I know you're worried you'll make things difficult for them," he continued. "But Kathy will be more worried about you if you *don't* stay with them. We've talked about this. The only other option is foster ca—"

"I *won't* go back to that!" Jamie shouted as he sprung up once more.

"Whoa. It's okay. I'm just trying to level with you, man," Galen said.

"I know." Jamie sighed and sat down again.

"We'll call Kathy. Explain what happened." Galen took the small Band-Aid Cam offered him, then covered the cut.

Cam only half listened as Galen and Jamie discussed longer-term options for Jamie's last year of high school. Cam's mind wandered, revisiting some of his rediscovered memories. As Galen put his arm around Jamie's shoulders and comforted him, Galen's words echoed in Cam's mind. *"You were a kid. He took advantage of you. Hurt you. He's sick, Cam. Twisted kind of sick."*

He'd warred with those words since the day he'd told Galen about the abuse. He'd understood he wasn't to blame for what Duncan had done to him. But he hadn't truly believed it. He'd told himself if he'd hated it, he'd have done something to stop Duncan.

Cam tried to imagine himself as a child, this time from the outside looking in. Jamie hadn't wanted the bruises. But he hadn't been able to stop them either. Was it really so different?

He knew the answer. He and Jamie were the same.

He imagined himself running through the gardens at the castle, the wind in his hair and the sun on his face. He'd been so happy. The way a child was supposed to be. He hadn't asked to be hurt. He hadn't asked to be betrayed. He'd just wanted to be loved.

A flicker of something kindled within his heart and caught fire. Something born to protect and keep his newfound hope for the future. A reason to be strong. For the first time since he'd remembered, he recognized it for what it was: anger.

CHAPTER  30

GALEN PULLED into the driveway at nearly 1:00 a.m. He'd driven Jamie to his sister's place in Hackensack, a small two-bedroom apartment she shared with her husband and eighteen-month-old son. Decent people who'd keep Jamie safe.

He killed the engine and just sat in the car. He needed to clear his thoughts. When he'd seen Jamie, his face a bloodied mess, he'd nearly lost it and gone after the stepfather.

Not the first kid beaten up by a parent. Not the last. These thoughts intruded as he struggled to focus on his breathing and relax. He'd held on to the steering wheel so tight on the return trip, his fingers ached. His chest tightened uncomfortably as his anxiety grew.

Breathe. Focus.

Failing to report child abuse. He could lose his job for that. He knew the drill all too well. But calling social services meant breaking his promise to Jamie.

Breathe. Focus.

And then there was Cam. Making dinner. Looking so good. Looking *happy* for a change. Relaxed, even. And no matter what he told himself, Galen couldn't deny he wanted Cam. Hell, he'd wanted Cam since the moment he'd seen him shed that prickly exterior. The day he'd tried to kill himself. Again. He'd wanted to help Cam. But he also wanted more. He guessed Cam sensed it too.

Breathe. Focus.

Cam would be leaving soon. A good thing. He was building his strength, getting ready to take his life back. As he should.

Breathe. Focus.

Galen imagined the sound of waves crashing on the sand. Imagined the blue and white of the surf.

Breathe. Just breathe.

His breath like the waves, retreating, then returning. Softly.

Inhale. Exhale.

No mantra. Just the music of the world around him. Sound. Vibration. Filling his heart and mind. Cleansing it. A single note, joined with others. Colors of sound wending their way around his mind, chasing his blood to his heart and limbs.

Cam.

CAM LAY asleep on the couch. Galen smiled to see Max curled up against him. Max could always sense kindness—and although Cam tried to deny it or even hide it from the rest of the world, dogs *knew*. And Galen knew too.

"Hey," Galen said in a low voice.

Cam opened his eyes slowly. "You're back?"

"You waited up for me."

Cam looked away, then met Galen's gaze. "Yes."

Galen knew how hard the truth was for Cam. He wouldn't let on how much it mattered that Cam had started to level with him—that would make Cam uncomfortable. But he could appreciate it even so.

"How's Jamie?"

"He's okay. His sister'll watch out for him." Galen sat down next to Cam and scratched Max's head. Max pressed into his hand and stretched. "I called a friend of mine who works with runaways in Trenton. Jamie's probably old enough to live on his own now. His sister will take care of him until we get that part straightened out."

"What about school?"

"Got it covered. I'll pick him up at the train station on my way to school and his sister will take him on the days I don't work." Galen took Cam's hand and held it. "He'll be all right, Cam. Promise."

Cam said nothing. Galen guessed he was thinking about something in his past. Ghosts lingered, no matter how ancient.

"This isn't about him, though, is it?" Galen asked after a few minutes passed in silence.

"I'm worried about you," Cam said in a half whisper. "If they find me—"

"I'll tell them you took advantage of me," Galen joked, hoping to put Cam at ease.

"Galen…," Cam warned. "I'm serious. I need to think about turning myself in."

"I know." Galen made sure Cam saw his face and knew it was okay, that he'd support Cam any way he could. "And then what?"

"Then I'll end up in jail." Cam's voice quavered slightly.

He's afraid. Much as Cam might not see it, Galen figured it was a good thing. It meant Cam wanted to survive. Galen could let Cam go knowing that. "No, you won't. You'll figure out how to prove you're innocent."

"Maybe." Cam appeared to mull the idea over. "But I can't stay here forever. You've got a life. I've got—"

"Do you want to leave?" Galen asked, knowing Cam wanted him to ask him to stay.

Cam stood and pulled his hand free of Galen's, then walked across the room, past the piano, and over to the french doors he loved to gaze out of. Sometimes Galen wondered if Cam saw something out there that he couldn't. Maybe it was like music was for him: a place where he could let his thoughts coalesce.

"Cam?"

"The school will find out about what happened with Jamie. And then what? They'll find me here and it'll be a hundred times worse for you."

More excuses, Galen knew. At their heart, more fear. "What are you running from?"

Cam laughed and shook his head. "You already know what I'm—"

"This is something different, isn't it?"

"I don't know what you mean." But of course it was different, and they both knew it. This wasn't black and white, right or wrong. This was *them*. One subject they hadn't yet broached.

Galen walked over to Cam and rested a hand on his shoulder. "Cam. Talk to me. Please." He wouldn't take the first step. Cam had to do that, for so many reasons. The next step in their relationship needed to be more than just a way to quiet the noise in Cam's brain.

"There's nothing to say."

"You're running." Galen waited until Cam turned to look at him, then tenderly touched Cam's face. Cam tried to look away.

"I'm a shit, Galen. Haven't you figured that out?"

"You're complicated. That doesn't make you a shit." Galen rubbed his thumbs over Cam's cheek.

"Don't do that."

Galen stopped and let his hands rest at his sides. "Why not?"

"Because it makes me want to do things." Cam hadn't moved away from him. Galen sensed the conflict beneath the surface—he knew it well. There had been a time when he'd felt worthless too.

"What things?" Cam's lips were so close to his, all Galen had to do was breathe and they'd be kissing. "Like kissing me?"

"Among other things."

"Then do it, Cam. Kiss me."

"But you know this time's different. This time...." Cam leaned back and rubbed his eyes. "You were right to push me away back then. I can't. I don't want.... I can't do that to someone again."

Galen understood Cam's hesitation only too well. The last time—maybe the *only* time—Cam had let himself love someone, he'd fucked things up. Galen knew loss, even if it had only been part of the story. He knew the self-recrimination and the guilt. He knew the emptiness.

He could make this easier for Cam too, simply by speaking the truth. "I don't do permanent, Cam. I'm here for as long as you need, and then we move on. You go back to your life."

Cam stared at him, assessing him, no doubt trying to make certain of the truth of Galen's words. Galen saw the moment Cam decided. Cam's lips parted as if he were about to speak, but then he closed them again. Those beautiful lips Galen loved to kiss.

Galen felt Cam's need. He understood it. There was a time when he'd felt worthless too.

Cam swallowed visibly, then licked his lips. Galen guessed Cam rarely hesitated. Cam had changed. His brash exterior felt muted. Not surprising, given the enormity of what Cam had learned in the past two weeks. Betrayal did that to a person. Betrayal on a level like Cam had experienced.... Galen would never understand that.

Cam reached out with a trembling hand and stroked Galen's cheek. Gently. Tentatively. A question: *Do you want me?* He didn't blame Cam for needing to ask—Galen had pushed Cam away, given him mixed signals because, God, he'd wanted Cam all along.

Galen put his hand on Cam's wrist in answer. A gentle, reassuring touch he hoped would communicate how much he wanted Cam. Cam leaned forward once more, and this time he met Galen's lips. Just lips at first, brushing against his own. Did Cam have any idea how beautiful he was, vulnerable like this? Sure, Cam must have known men wanted him—physically. Seeing Cam without his armor—the distant, slightly haughty, overconfident demeanor—made Galen realize how much Cam held back from the world. He wondered if anyone else had seen the man beneath the bullshit and the pain.

"Bedroom?" Galen prompted. Not that he wouldn't make love to Cam here in the living room, but he wanted Cam to understand that this time was different. Cam's expression told Galen he'd made the correct choice.

Cam nodded, and they walked in silence to the guest bedroom. Galen had come to think of it as their room, and given how few nights he'd slept in his own bed since Cam had come to stay with him, it just felt right.

Galen closed the door behind them. Max could wait outside—Galen wanted nothing to distract them tonight. He wanted to focus on Cam, on pleasuring him, on giving him the affection he needed and that Galen wanted Cam to feel.

Cam stood at the edge of the bed, clearly unsure of what to do. Galen knew enough about abused children and about Cam's past that he guessed Cam had never been in a situation quite like this, where he wasn't the person instigating the sex. It didn't surprise him that Cam had taken comfort in sex or that Cam had destroyed the one relationship he'd cherished by cheating. A child who learned to associate sex with love would naturally seek sex as an adult for the very same reason.

As Cam watched, Galen pulled off his shirt, then his pants and boxers. Cam's lips parted and his cheeks flushed almost imperceptibly in response. "I've wanted to see your body," Cam said after a moment's silence. "Wanted to touch it."

"I've wanted you to touch me." Galen spoke the truth, because no matter what of Cam's past still held him captive, Galen felt powerfully attracted to him.

Cam closed the gap between them and touched Galen's chest with his soft fingers. Galen closed his eyes and gave himself over to the sensation. He leaned his head back as Cam ghosted his hands over his shoulders and neck before resting them just beneath his jaw.

"May I undress you?"

"Yes." Cam's voice sounded low and throaty. Aroused.

Galen gently lifted the pale yellow polo over Cam's head, then paused to touch Cam's chest. Unlike his own more muscled body, Cam's body was lean and smooth, with just a hint of definition at his abdomen and on his arms. Galen felt a wave of anger and possessiveness to think what Duncan had done to mar the soul beneath the body. A beautiful body, perfect in every way, with a dusting of hair that made his skin feel silkier to the touch. A soul in need of affection and approval.

But Galen didn't linger long. He wanted Cam naked, just as he was. He wanted to take in the whole of him. He carefully undid the top button of Cam's jeans, then the zipper, then slid the jeans down with his underwear and waited until Cam stepped out of them.

Cam's pale skin seemed to glow in the low light of the single lamp. Galen followed the line from the indentation of Cam's waist over his hips and thighs, then calves. Cam's cock was long and pink tipped, the same color as Cam's lips, jutting out from his body. But Galen didn't move to touch Cam there, although he wanted to. Instead he drew Cam close and kissed him, a gentle kiss that grew into something demanding and hungry.

"Please," Cam whispered as their lips parted. "Touch me."

Galen heard the unspoken words: "I need to know you want me."

CHAPTER 31

"PLEASE. TOUCH me." Cam had never asked anyone for anything sexual before, except to demand someone blow him, and there'd been nothing vulnerable about that particular request. Now, he felt as though he'd opened his soul to Galen and let him peer inside, knowing Galen could step on what little remained.

Galen brushed his lips with his fingers, then kissed him sweetly, tenderly. The sigh that escaped Cam's control sounded at least as needy as his words of a moment before.

"You're beautiful, Cam," Galen whispered against his ear as he kissed his way over Cam's neck and shoulder.

Cam didn't feel beautiful. He didn't feel anything but broken inside, although a spark of hope still burned somewhere amidst the pain and hurt. But the way Galen said it, Cam almost believed him.

"How do you like it?" Galen asked.

"I like it any way you like it." He didn't know how to respond. He liked fucking. Wasn't that good enough? He liked the way he felt when someone told him his body felt good.

"That wasn't my question, Cam." Galen found one of his nipples and rolled it gently between his fingers until Cam gasped. "I want to know how you like it. Whether you like it when I suck on you—" Galen licked around the hard bud until Cam moaned. "—or whether you like it when I take it in my teeth."

"Yes. Like that." Cam's heart beat faster. "Harder."

Galen bit gently, just to the point of pain.

"Fuck, yes." Cam leaned against Galen to steady himself as Galen released his nipple and gave the other his full attention. Tongue, teeth, lips combined in a blur of sensation. Galen pressed his thigh against Cam's hard cock, a tacit acknowledgement that he knew what he was doing to Cam and was enjoying every bit of it.

"What do you want?" Galen said a few minutes later.

The thought came into Cam's head and took him by surprise. Normally, at this point, he'd have been fucking. But instead he said, "I want to taste you."

Galen looked up with eyes full of pleasure and surprise, as if he understood what a departure this was for Cam to ask. "Where do you want me?"

"Right where you are." Cam grinned as he got to his knees. Delicately veined, thick and long, Galen's hard cock seemed to beg for his lips. He took it slowly into his mouth, tasting the slight ridge where it had been cut. He loved a cut cock, even though his own was not. He loved the look and feel of an unsheathed tip and the smooth underside.

He couldn't remember the last time he'd sucked someone else off. Now, having faced the truth of his past, he guessed he'd avoided it. But now.... God, how he loved the way Galen tasted—sweet and a little spicy, like the earthy soaps he favored.

Galen trembled as Cam took him deep in his mouth. Cam clasped Galen's muscled arse and pressed his fingers between the globes of it, separating them and kneading as he sucked. He'd never have imagined yoga could sculpt a man's body like this, but he couldn't remember ever having felt anything quite so wonderful as Galen's arse. Jarrod's athletic body had been bloody amazing. But the way Galen's buttocks tensed and relaxed beneath his probing fingers was pure inspiration.

"Fuck! Cam."

Cam smiled around Galen's cock, then released it from his mouth and used his mouth to press it against Galen's abdomen, skating his wet lips over the smooth tip until he felt Galen keen in a silent plea for more.

This time Cam wet his fingers and felt between Galen's legs, behind his sac, to find the tight opening beyond. Galen's buttocks clenched as Cam swallowed him down again. He rubbed a finger against Galen's hole, teasing in a rhythm to match his mouth's, around and around until Galen whimpered and begged for more. He wet his fingers again as Galen hissed at the lack of contact. Then he made each circle smaller until he'd set his forefinger at the entrance. Slowly, he pressed the tip inward just as he increased the suction again.

Galen cried out and begged, "More. God, please, more."

Cam pushed inward to his knuckle and paused, leaving Galen's cock at the back of his throat, then launching in once again, rubbing his teeth on the underside of Galen's cock and moving his finger back and forth.

"I'm going to come," Galen warned. As if Cam would stop now! He wanted to taste Galen, to feel him shoot down his throat, to swallow every bit of what he offered.

Cam looked up at Galen and nodded reassuringly. *Come for me, Galen!*

"Oh, fuck!" Galen shouted as he climaxed into Cam's hungry mouth. Galen trembled and shook, his groans and satisfied grunts making Cam want it all the more. Cam greedily took every drop. He reveled in the pulsing release and the way Galen's hips thrust as he came.

As Cam released Galen's softening cock, Galen drew him up and into a bruising kiss that made Cam's cock ache with need. Their tongues tangled, Galen's slightly bitter taste mingling with the sweetness of his mouth. Cam gasped for breath as the kiss broke.

"What do you want?" Galen asked in an undertone.

"You know what I want," Cam countered.

"I want you to say it, Cam. Tell me. You don't know how fucking hot it is when you tell me what you want." Cam saw the truth in Galen's eyes, heard it in his voice.

"I want to fuck you. I want to come inside of you and I want to make you come again when I do." Saying the words. Speaking his need.

Galen kissed him again. "I'll be right back," he said.

Galen walked over to the door, Cam admiring the firm contours of his thighs and arse as he moved. He returned a moment later with a condom and lube, which he set on the bed.

"How do you want me?"

"How do you like it?" Cam countered with a smile. Another first, that he'd ask. He hadn't even considered that it might please him to know his partner's preference.

"I want to see your face," Galen said.

Cam nodded.

Galen ran a hand through his disheveled hair. *He's nervous.* Galen, always calm and in control, was nervous. That made two of them. The thought made Cam feel better, somehow. Less vulnerable. Cam touched Galen's cheek, met his intense gaze, and touched him reassuringly.

Galen lay back on the bed and Cam straddled his hips, then leaned over to kiss his Adam's apple, tease it with his tongue, and nip and lick his way around Galen's jaw and feel the stubble there. With his fingers, he explored Galen's chest and the downy, almost translucent hair. He flicked his tongue around Galen's ear and nibbled on his lobe as he tweaked Galen's nipples. Galen's soft sigh caused Cam's softening cock to fill once again.

Cam reached for the bottle of lube, slicked his fingers, and parted Galen's thighs. All the while, Galen watched him with his singular gaze. Cam had known many a man to avoid his eyes in such an intensely personal situation.

Galen sighed again, visibly relaxing as Cam pushed a single finger inside and began to gently pull and stretch the muscles.

"Mmm," Galen murmured as Cam took his cock in his hand and continued to work him open. Galen grew harder and moaned again as Cam pressed a second finger into him. Galen's breath stuttered as Cam continued to work Galen's cock and opened Galen enough to fit another finger inside.

Cam leaned down and took Galen's cock in his mouth. "Cam!" Galen shouted, no doubt still hypersensitive from his orgasm. Cam gently released him, slipped his fingers slowly out, then rolled the condom onto himself. Enough denial. He wanted Galen *now*.

He pushed Galen's impossibly flexible legs back so they touched Galen's shoulders. Another benefit of yoga, Cam thought with a barely repressed grin. He wondered what other positions Galen might be able to manage that he'd never considered himself. *Another time.* He hoped there would be another time.

He paused with his tip at Galen's hole. He wanted to take his time and feel all of this. He pushed inside, savoring the sensation of Galen's muscles resisting the intrusion, watching himself as he entered Galen slowly, fully, glancing up from time to time to see the expression of pain and pleasure on Galen's gorgeous face. Their gazes locked as Cam seated himself inside, then began to move.

Cam saw Galen struggle to keep his eyes open. With any other man, even Aiden, Cam might have looked away, afraid to open himself and risk rejection. But with Galen, he felt nothing but acceptance.

Cam moved faster now, his own moans joining Galen's. Galen smiled and clenched around him, pushing him to his limits before releasing the tension.

"Bloody hell, Galen," Cam laughed as he responded by varying his speed to pull himself back from the edge.

Galen's eyes sparkled with pleasure and he bit his lower lip in a playful, impish grin. Until Cam squeezed his cock harder and ran his slicked palm up and down. Two could play at that game.

"Oh, fuck!" Galen shouted.

"Like that?" Cam asked, almost giddy at eliciting that response.

"You're going to make me come again." Galen seemed to lose the battle for control, his eyes fluttering and closing of their own accord.

Cam picked up the pace, knowing his own orgasm was imminent but wanting to make Galen come again before he gave himself over to his own pleasure. He rocked on his knees to change the angle, watching Galen carefully to see when he'd found the perfect spot. The subtle tilt of Galen's head and the way he moved to meet Cam's thrusts told Cam what he wanted to know. Over and over again, he aimed for that spot until Galen convulsed beneath him and spilled into his hand.

Cam let himself over to his body's need. He felt the tingle at the base of his spine, felt it build until he cried out and came with such intensity that flickers of silver clouded his vision. "Galen!" he shouted as he collapsed onto Galen's chest. Galen wrapped his legs around him as he shook.

Their gasped breaths settled into an even rhythm, Galen breathing out as Cam breathed in, sharing the space between their bodies. After a few minutes, Galen released Cam from his legs and rolled onto his side, taking a boneless Cam with him.

"You really are beautiful, Cam," Galen whispered as Cam struggled to understand why sex felt so different this time. Then Galen kissed him again and Cam forgot he wanted to know.

CHAPTER 32

CAM RESTED his head on Galen's chest. They'd washed up more than an hour before, but he couldn't sleep. He'd wanted to tell Galen over dinner what he'd learned at the library, but with Jamie showing up, he hadn't had the chance. Now he didn't know how to tell him.

Lord Sherrington, I really need to speak with you. I heard about what happened with Dan. Call me at home. Please.

Cam had spent the better part of the day replaying the e-mail message in his head. A message from Ron in accounting on Cam's personal account. The same account Dan had e-mailed before he'd set Cam up. Was it another trap? Either way, the FBI would know about the e-mail, since they were probably monitoring the account.

"Something up?" Galen asked as he stroked Cam's hair.

"It can wait." *At least until I can figure out how to tell you.*

"Cam, just say it." Galen kissed Cam's head. "I'm sure it'll be fine."

"You have an uncanny knack of knowing what I'm thinking, you know?" he said with a chuckle. "Must be all the meditation."

"Process of elimination," Galen replied. "We just had amazing sex, it's really late, and I know you're tired, but you can't sleep. So whatever you have to say must have something to do with us, or it wouldn't be keeping you up."

Cam wasn't quite sure he followed the logic, but he wouldn't question the end result. "I went to the library again today. There was a message from Dan's underling, a kid I hired a few years ago. Techie working in accounting. Said he had something for me. Wants me to call him."

"Are you sure that's safe?" Galen tensed just enough for Cam to notice. Strange, how he'd become more attuned to that sort of thing having spent some time around Galen.

He's worried about me.

"No." Cam laughed. "It's probably not safe. But I called him back. Call it a hunch."

"You? A hunch?" Galen leaned in and kissed Cam's cheek.

"I can be spontaneous," Cam protested, knowing Galen wouldn't buy it for a minute.

"All right." Galen pressed his lips together and grinned.

"In any event," Cam continued, enjoying Galen's gentle teasing, "he didn't ask to meet. He e-mailed it to a new account I created."

"And?"

"And there's a spreadsheet in cyberspace the authorities haven't seen yet." Cam had spent most of the afternoon reviewing the document and thanking his mother for having pushed him to study accounting at university. "A spreadsheet that shows someone *else* made the transfers the FBI is looking at."

"So what's wrong with that? It's what you've been hoping for, right?"

Cam nodded. "But—"

"But nothing, Cam. This is great news, and why you're not jumping up and down because of it...." Galen looked at Cam and frowned. "You're worried about me, aren't you?"

"Yes." He knew he should be thrilled at the prospect of returning to his former life. But leaving Galen now, when they'd finally gotten together—*No. He made it clear he isn't interested in that, and you're the last person who needs a relationship right now.*

"What does it show?" Galen held him almost imperceptibly tighter. Almost. But Cam felt it, and it made him feel safe. He could do this with Galen's support.

"It's a second set of figures for the wire transfers the FBI is looking at. These are the *real* numbers. And one more thing. There are approval codes associated with these transfers listed on the document. Only certain people within the company have access to those codes. I'm not one of them." Cam closed his eyes and drew a long breath, then released it slowly.

"But you know who *does* have access." Galen kissed him again, and Cam nearly sighed in response.

"Yes. And my uncle's at the top of the list." It wasn't proof that Duncan had done anything, just that Duncan had the means at his disposal to wire the money.

"But you think he did it."

"Yes." Cam whispered the word, as if by speaking it, he might cause something to happen: the world might shift, and he wouldn't be able to maintain his precarious balance. But things had already changed, hadn't they? They'd changed the moment he'd realized that Duncan had more than one reason to want him out of the picture. "I think he's trying to set me up. By changing the access codes, he pointed the finger at me, while all along he's been pocketing the money he's made illegally."

"And if he makes you out to be the criminal...."

"He undermines my credibility if I ever bring charges against him for abusing me," Cam finished. Saying the words wasn't as difficult as he'd expected it to be. He still felt the demons dance around his mind—whispers of thoughts, questions. Why hadn't he pushed Duncan away? Why hadn't he told anyone? Why had his body responded to Duncan's touch when he knew it was wrong?

"Will you tell them?" Galen asked after a long silence.

"I don't know." He really didn't. "If I can prove he was the one who made the transfers, he'll probably rot in jail the rest of his life."

"But that's not the question, is it?" Galen pressed, his voice gentle, his body warm, welcoming, and reassuring.

"No."

Galen stroked Cam's cheek. "You'll do what you need to. Whatever that is, you'll figure it out. Sometimes it just takes time to see the right path."

CHAPTER 33

THAT NIGHT, Galen awoke to Max's protective barking and someone pounding on the front door. Cam grabbed Galen's waist and shivered.

Galen kissed Cam's cheek, then slipped out of bed and pulled on a pair of sweatpants and a T-shirt. "Someone's at the front door. Stay here, okay?" He schooled his expression and breathed deeply—Cam didn't need to know his heart was pounding and his chest suddenly felt tight.

Breathe. Relax. Focus.

Cam nodded, although Galen saw fear on his face.

"Don't worry. I'm pretty sure I know what this is about. I'll be back in a few minutes. You stay put, all right?"

Cam nodded and pulled the covers over his shoulders.

Barefoot, Galen padded down the stairs and over to the door, followed by Max, who stood sentry and barked. Galen drew a long, slow breath, then opened the door. Before he had it open more than a few inches, someone pushed hard on the other side, nearly causing it to hit him in the face.

"You fucking piece of shit!" Charles Thompson shouted as he punched Galen in the jaw.

Knocked backward from the impact of the blow, Galen managed to regain his balance in time to catch Charles's fist as he swung again. *Damn.* He'd been an idiot not to realize the man would come in fist-first. And drunk. Galen smelled the liquor on him.

Breathe. Focus. Relax. He'd become stronger. He could handle Charles.

"You the fag who called the cops on me?" he demanded, undaunted by Galen's grip on his fist. "Told them I beat that little shit?"

"Are you all right, Galen?" Cam asked from the landing.

Galen nodded, not taking his eyes from Charles. He ignored the throbbing in his jaw. His racing heart had slowed a bit, and he was once again clear-headed.

"Mr. Thompson is Jamie's stepfather," he said, hoping Cam would stay where he was if he understood the danger. He doubted Charles had a weapon, but he wouldn't bet Cam's safety on it.

"I asked if you're the one who called the cops," Charles hissed.

"Would it matter if I told you I didn't call them, Mr. Thompson?" Galen spoke calmly. He knew it wouldn't help to escalate the situation. He guessed Jamie's sister had reported the beating to the police.

Charles ignored his response. "Where's Jamie?" he demanded.

"Somewhere safe." Of course, Jamie would be safer if Charles hadn't made bail so quickly, but maybe Galen could make sure Charles stayed longer the next time.

"Fucking fag. You're the one who encouraged him, aren't you?"

"This isn't about Jamie's being gay, though, is it, Mr. Thompson?" Galen kept his tone even, controlled. "You're jealous of him. Of his talent. It's easier to deal with your own bullshit if you drag everyone around you down with you. Your wife, your step—"

"Don't *fucking* mess with me!" Charles punched Galen again, this time in the eye, then pushed him up against the wall. One of the photographs on a nearby table crashed to the floor, breaking the glass.

"Leave him the hell alone!" Cam grabbed the man by the shoulder and pulled him off Galen.

"Cam, get back!" Galen shouted. "I've got this under control." *Shit.* He'd handled this badly. The last thing he wanted was Cam in the middle of this fight. Cam had probably never fought in his life.

"Oh." Charles grabbed Cam by the wrist and twisted his arm behind his back. "I see you have company. Another piece of shit."

Cam winced and tried to extricate himself from the man's grasp, but to no avail. Galen doubted Charles could break Cam's arm, but he didn't want to risk it.

"Let him go, Charles," Galen warned. Charles ignored him. Galen caught Cam's eye and gave him a reassuring smile. Cam stared at Galen as if he'd lost his mind. This *so* wasn't going the way Galen had intended. He should have realized Cam would try to help.

Charles laughed and pulled Cam's arm farther back. Galen gritted his teeth. He'd hoped to get Charles away from Cam, but that clearly wasn't going to happen. Time to do something.

Galen darted behind Charles, wrapped his arm around Charles's neck, squeezed. "Let him go, Charles. This is between the two of us."

Charles gasped and released Cam, who stepped forward in shock.

"Stay back, Cam. I can handle him," Galen said, hoping his voice conveyed the strength he wanted Cam to hear.

Cam didn't move away, but he also didn't move closer. He rubbed his arm and looked up at Galen.

"You okay?" Galen asked.

"Fine," Cam said, looking shell-shocked.

"I'm going to ask you to leave now, Mr. Thompson," Galen said. "Do you think you can do that?"

Charles nodded as he struggled against Galen's grip.

"Okay." Galen released Charles, who staggered a foot or so toward the door, then dropped to the floor and grabbed one of the glass shards from the picture frame. Cam was too close—far closer than Galen.

Galen didn't hesitate: he stepped between Cam and Charles. He grabbed the shard, ignoring the sting as it sliced into his palm, then kicked Charles in the face. Charles fell backward. The glass skittered across the floor and splintered into smaller pieces.

Cam stared at the unconscious Charles, then back at Galen again. His eyes widened in what Galen guessed was recognition, his lips parting. "You... you.... You *let* him attack you?"

"Yep."

"And during all of that, you let me think he'd beat you and tear you to pieces?"

"That wasn't exactly my intention." Galen rubbed his jaw absentmindedly. His eye had already begun to swell.

Cam narrowed his eyes. "You knew if he hit you a few times, they'd lock him up."

"That's the plan."

"You're a bloody idiot, you know?" Cam said.

Galen smiled. He'd expected Cam would be angry. He hadn't expected he'd care. "Sometimes," he said. "In this case, I think particularly so."

Cam crossed his arms over his chest and frowned back at him.

"But I fucked up. I didn't think it through. Now you're a witness to this. I'm sorry." He *hadn't* thought it through. He'd done what he'd told himself he wouldn't do anymore: he'd acted without thinking first. He'd acted out of emotion.

"*That's* what you're worried about?" Cam said with a laugh. "Me? You really *are* an idiot. What about your job?"

Galen shrugged. That was nothing new. He'd been lucky this far, but he always knew there'd come a day when he'd have to face the proverbial music, that what he did for students would eventually become an issue. "They'll figure out who you are, Cam."

Cam smiled. He glanced down at the broken glass on the floor and Charles sprawled across the rug. "So they will," he said. He walked over, took Galen's right hand, and turned it over. The cut was deeper than Galen had realized. "Krazy Glue?" Cam asked, the edges of his mouth turning upward ever so slightly.

"You're getting good at this."

Cam shook his head. "You're still a bloody idiot, you know."

Galen just smiled.

CHAPTER 34

WHEN THE police took Charles away in a squad car, he was still shouting curses at Galen. The two uniformed officers who'd stayed behind to take statements from Cam and Galen left at 5:00 a.m. After that, Galen and Cam cleaned up the front entrance.

"Yoga and karate?" Cam smiled and shook his head as he swept the rest of the glass shards from the wood floor.

"I got beaten up a bunch in middle school. My mom thought I should learn to defend myself. I don't use it much, but I've never forgotten it either." Galen dumped the contents of the dustpan into the garbage, then took the broom from Cam and proceeded to sweep the area Cam had just finished. He didn't add that he'd been bullied in middle school and that some days, he'd pretended he was sick just to avoid having to go to class.

"Not up to par?" Cam said with a raised eyebrow.

"I'm a little—" Galen hesitated. "—picky."

"You could say that."

Galen hoped Cam would drop the topic. He was too tired and he didn't want to talk about it.

"You're obsessively neat."

"And you're blunt," Galen countered with a measured smile. Generalized anxiety disorder. That was what the doctors had called it. But what difference did it make if someone gave it a name? He knew what he was. Cleaning helped him relax. With each shard of glass he found, the tightness in his chest faded.

"Order is a false construct," his therapist had once told him. *"Someday you'll see that you don't need to put everything in its place. You'll just let it go. Just be."*

"Does anything ever bother you?" Cam asked. "Even with that bastard, you were calm."

"Other than having a messy house?" Galen shrugged. He wouldn't tell Cam that his outward calm was just an act. He supposed Cam would see through the bullshit eventually, when he wasn't as focused on his own issues. By then, it wouldn't matter anymore because Cam would have moved on. Which was exactly the way it should be. "What are you going to do now?" he asked, knowing full well Cam would know he'd deliberately changed the topic.

"You mean now that they know where to find me?"

"Yes." Galen saw Cam struggling to maintain his composure. He rested the broom against the wall and put his arm around Cam, who leaned against him. "I'm sorry," he said as he stroked Cam's hair.

"Don't be. I'm bloody well done with sorry. Time to be a man. Get my shit in order. Turn myself in and hope that the truth is good enough." Cam laughed, but Galen couldn't miss the fear in his eyes.

"And then?"

"And then...? I have no bloody clue."

Galen leaned in and kissed Cam. "You'll be fine. And I'll be there with you, if you'd like."

"Really? You'd do that for me?"

"Yep. Not that I'm a lawyer, but I can give you moral support." Cam would need it. It would take the FBI time to sort through the electronic records and confirm what Cam suspected: that his uncle had been the one to set up the wire transfers and make it look as though Cam had done it himself.

"Thanks." Cam sighed against Galen's neck, then pulled away. "Time to make a few calls, then." He grinned at Galen and added, "Since you're not a lawyer."

BY THE time Cam had finished his calls, Galen had fallen asleep. For a few minutes, Cam watched the slow rise and fall of Galen's bare chest. The past week—since he'd told Galen the truth—had been nice. Better than nice—it had been lovely. He'd almost forgotten about Duncan. The dreams had lingered since he'd remembered, but they were now less frequent. He knew sleeping with Galen at his side had been the cause. Next to Galen, he felt safe, warm. And if his life weren't in such a total shambles at the moment, Cam might even have felt loved. But now wasn't the time for more than comfort, especially since Galen had made it clear he wasn't in it for the long-term. Still, Cam wouldn't pass up the opportunity—the last one, perhaps—to feel Galen's body beneath his.

He leaned down and claimed Galen's lips in a slow, sweet kiss. Galen, sleepy-eyed, awoke at the touch and sighed. "I was hoping you'd wake me up when you came to bed," he said as he pulled Cam close. "Got everything taken care of?"

"We have until four this afternoon." Cam kissed Galen again. No tongue, just his lips sensually brushing against Cam's. "Enough time for sleep and maybe something more."

"Something more?" Cam loved how Galen's eyes seemed to change color when he smiled and how the tiny lines at the corners of his mouth nearly met the dimples on his cheeks. "I'm not sure I know what that means."

"It means this," Cam said as he nipped at Galen's lower lip, then feathered kisses over Galen's neck and shoulders until Galen shivered.

"I'm still not sure I understand what you mean, Lord Sherrington."

Cam winced.

"Sorry. You really hate the title, don't you?" Galen asked.

"I'm not sure 'hate' is the correct word. 'Dislike,' certainly."

"Why?" Galen pulled Cam against him and kissed him soundly on the lips.

Cam shrugged. "I'm not sure. I wonder that myself sometimes. Maybe it's that I've done nothing to deserve it except being born. Or maybe it's that people expect me to be something more than I am because of it."

"It's part of you," Galen said before kissing Cam again. "Like your hair—" He kissed Cam's hair. "—or your baby blues—" He kissed the bridge of Cam's nose. "—or the birthmark right here." He kissed the spot next to Cam's nose, then hugged Cam again. "There's nothing to live up to unless you let yourself believe you need to live up to something."

Cam hadn't thought of it that way. How many things did he look at differently because of Galen? Too many to count. "Thank you," he said as he sighed against Galen's cheek.

"For what?"

"For making me think about things. For making me realize I do a bloody good job of creating my own angst."

Galen chuckled. "I'd never thought of you as having angst. But I know a little about what it's like to create my own mess."

Cam was just about to ask Galen what he meant, ask him what had driven him to want to kill himself, when Galen claimed his lips. It could wait. Maybe after he'd faced his own music and stopped running away from his problems, he'd sit down and ask Galen flat out. But for now….

"Make love to me, Galen," Cam said as the kiss broke. *Give me something to hold on to.*

GALEN SWALLOWED hard and forced himself to tamp down the emotions that welled up when he heard the unspoken need in Cam's words. Why did Cam scare him so much? He'd been honest with Cam all along. He didn't do long-term. And yet each time he and Cam shared their bodies, Galen felt a wave of emotion lapping at the supports holding up his fragile house, eroding the foundation.

Breathe. Relax. You want this. You want him.

He wanted to show Cam how beautiful he was. That his strength and vulnerability were things to be treasured. But first Galen needed to remind himself that when the time came, he could let Cam go.

Breathe. Relax.

Galen met Cam's intense gaze and his fear fled as he let his body guide him. He pulled the pale blue polo over Cam's head. He loved it when Cam wore that shirt—his eyes seemed even bluer, brighter. He kissed Cam's neck, eliciting a soft sigh and sending a shudder through his own body.

"Cam," he whispered as he trailed his lips over Cam's shoulder, his reward a barely audible gasp. He worked his way back to Cam's face and they kissed again. He lingered this time, tasting Cam, teasing his tongue, moaning.

"Does it hurt?" Cam asked after their lips parted. He gently touched Galen's jaw. Galen saw the concern in his eyes.

"A little," he admitted.

Cam leaned in and kissed the place he'd just touched. Galen closed his eyes—well, his left eye, since his right was still pretty swollen. He'd seen Cam's heart weeks before. He hoped Cam would eventually come to see that heart for what it truly was: kind and loving.

"Feels so good," Galen said.

"I'm sorry I got in the way."

Galen opened his eyes to see Cam clench his jaw. "Got in the way? You mean with Jamie's stepdad?"

Cam nodded.

"It made me feel good," Galen said as he brushed a thumb over the tiny scar on Cam's cheek. "You cared about me enough to come to my rescue." He kissed Cam's nose. "Now stop worrying about me and let me worry about you a little. Okay?" Cam's shy smile called to mind the young boy Cam must have been. *Before Duncan.* Before his childhood had ended abruptly at Duncan's hands. "Please?" he added when Cam didn't answer.

"All right."

It would take Cam time to realize he deserved to be treated well. "Good. So how about you take off those jeans?"

Cam stood and shed his boxers and jeans. "Better?"

"Much." Galen opened his arms. "Now come here and let me make sure you feel as good as you look."

Cam's smile broadened as he moved toward Galen and Galen wrapped his arms around his waist. Galen kissed Cam's abdomen, taking time to explore the feel of Cam's skin with his tongue. He pulled Cam closer and worked his hands around the perfect globes of Cam's ass as he licked a circle around Cam's belly button.

"Hmm," he said as he looked up at Cam. "I think I have a better idea."

Cam pursed his lips and eyed Galen warily. Galen grinned and stood up, shed his sweatpants so he was comfortably naked, then settled onto the floor in front of Cam. "Much better idea," he said before taking Cam's hard cock in his hand and pushing back the foreskin.

"Bugger," Cam said as Galen took him in his mouth and playfully flicked his tongue across his slit.

Galen looked up to catch Cam's eye but didn't take his mouth off Cam. Cam had closed his eyes, his face serene, his lips, pink from being kissed, now slightly parted. Galen went back to work, listening to Cam's soft moans and panted breaths and relishing each for the gift it was. He loved the feel of Cam's cock in his mouth, loved the way his smooth skin felt against his palms, loved the way Cam tasted.

He released one hand and reached between Cam's legs to brush the sensitive skin behind his balls and work his fingers slowly forward until he held Cam's sac. He tightened his suction on Cam as he rolled Cam's balls and squeezed his ass. Throughout it all, Cam remained quiet, eyes closed, the only indication of his pleasure the pink cast of his cheeks and his ragged breathing.

Time to come back to the present, Cam. He wanted Cam to enjoy this, but he also wanted him to know that he *deserved* it. Galen released Cam's cock.

"Cam," he said, pausing to lick his lips and glance upward, "look at me."

Cam opened his eyes, slowly, almost as if he was afraid to look. When their eyes finally met, Galen swallowed Cam's cock.

"God, Galen!" Cam shouted. "Fuck!"

Galen hummed his approval as he worked his lips up and down, using just a bit of his teeth to up the pressure and lazily circling Cam's opening with a single finger. This proved too much for Cam, who moaned and shot into Galen's mouth, shuddering and gasping. He grabbed Galen's head as if to steady himself as he rode the wave of his orgasm.

Galen stood and took a slightly shaky Cam into his arms. "Better?" he asked as Cam laid his head on his shoulder, his breath stuttering in Galen's ear.

"Bugger," Cam said with a soft laugh that made Galen shiver. "You do know how to take my mind off of all the shit in my life."

"We aim to please."

Cam laughed outright, then pulled Galen so that they both tumbled onto the bed. They lay there for a minute or so, Galen stroking Cam's soft curls, noting the slowing of Cam's breath and the calming of his heartbeat.

"I...," Cam began. "I want to be inside of you. I need to feel you. I want to remember how it feels when I'm locked...."

"Shhh." Galen brushed his fingers over Cam's lips. "You're going to be fine." He knew Cam was terrified. "You know what to do if it gets to be too much. And we'll get you out of there as soon as we can."

Cam nodded. Galen hoped Cam would use the meditation techniques they'd practiced together. Cam had admitted only a few days before that Duncan had locked him in one of the buildings at his family's estate.

"I remember," he'd told Galen as he'd shivered in Galen's arms. "I tried to get away. He'd hurt me the day before. I guess he'd lost control and I...." Cam's tears were silent. "It still hurt, and I tried to run away from him." Between gulped breaths, Cam had added in an almost inaudible voice, "He locked me in the boathouse. I stayed there until after dark, when he finally came back for me. He said he was sorry... that he didn't mean to... but...."

Now, as Cam clearly struggled for control, Galen kissed him again. He took his time as he kissed Cam's cheeks and chin, then brushed his lips against Cam's. Cam sighed and visibly relaxed.

Cam curled into Galen's embrace and his breathing slowed even more, until Galen knew he had fallen asleep. Galen smiled and inhaled the sweet scent of the shampoo that lingered in his curls, feeling the warmth of Cam's breath against his chest. For some time, Galen held Cam, fighting the need to rest. He didn't expect the strong wave of emotion that nearly overwhelmed him. Something warm, comforting. Something that made his heart swell. A feeling he had successfully avoided for more than ten years.

Chapter 35

"Lord Sherrington? I'm Marc Silver," said the lanky man who met Cam and Galen outside the FBI field offices in Lower Manhattan the next day. They'd spoken earlier that morning after Cam had reached David Somers in London.

Cam hadn't expected David to worry about him. "You should have left a message, Cam," he'd said. "I'd have been happy to give you Marc's name sooner. He's a good lawyer. A good man too. He's handled a few criminal matters for Somers Industries over the years."

Cam had apologized, but David would have none of it. "No apology needed. What you forget is that I *enjoy* helping friends. Truly." Two hours later, through Marc, David had set up a special account with more than enough money to cover Cam's expenses until Cam's accounts got sorted out. Cam had reassured David he would repay him, but David clearly didn't care if he ever did.

You can do this, Cam reminded himself as he met Marc's gaze and shook his hand. "Good to meet you, Marc. And please, call me Cam."

"Cam." Marc smiled and turned to Galen.

"This is my good friend, Galen Rusk."

"Pleased to meet you, Mr. Silver." Galen put his hand on Cam's shoulder, and Cam felt a bit less nervous.

"You can speak freely in front of Galen," Cam said when Marc shot him a questioning look. "He knows everything."

"Good." Marc nodded. "So let me give you the quick update, then. I've spoken to the supervisor assigned to your case, Cam, and let her know you intend to turn yourself in. I've explained that you've retained me as private counsel and that I have no outside affiliation with Sherrington Holdings or Raice Corp."

"And the files I sent you?" Cam asked.

"I've forwarded copies to the FBI. They promised not to share them with your uncle or anyone else for now. Ron Welding came in for questioning over the weekend."

"He's not under arrest, is he?" Cam asked with growing alarm. The last thing he wanted was to cause any distress to Ron, his only true ally at the company.

Marc shook his head. "No. Of course not. The supervisor indicated he seemed happy to help in any way he could, and he told them he believed you were innocent."

Cam took a deep breath and relaxed a bit more. "So what's the plan?"

"They'll take you into custody today," Marc explained. "Fingerprint you, that sort of thing. You'll stay in their custody while they review the evidence Ron provided. Once they're satisfied you aren't involved in the transfers, they'll probably release you pretty quickly, but it may take a few days before that happens."

"I won't go to a regular jail?" Cam had worried about this in particular, although the thought of being locked up anywhere wasn't exactly comforting.

"You'll stay here for the time being."

Cam clenched his jaw and mumbled his thanks. He suddenly felt dizzy. Weak.

"Why don't I give you two a few minutes," Marc said. "I'll get things going and you can come inside when you're ready, okay?"

"All right. Thank you." Cam's voice shook. For a moment he thought he might pass out, but then Galen put his arm around him, steadying him. Without really thinking, Cam touched the bracelet Galen had given him. He found one of the charms and began to rub it between his fingers. *Healing. Hope. Love.*

"It'll be fine, Cam," Marc said. "They'll treat you well. I'll make sure of it. We'll get you out of custody as soon as we can."

"Thanks." Galen spoke for Cam.

When they were alone a moment later, Galen gathered Cam into his arms. "I know I'm acting like a child," Cam said against Galen's shoulder.

"You're not." Galen kissed Cam's head. "And for someone who's claustrophobic, the idea of being locked in a cell isn't exactly pleasant."

Cam stared at Galen, dumbfounded. "How did you know?" He'd barely admitted it to himself, although he'd begun to understand it was part of the reason he'd run when Jim had told him the FBI planned to take him into custody.

Galen shrugged. "The way you told me about Duncan and what happened to you, it made sense when I put the pieces together."

Panic zinged through Cam's body as he imagined them locking him in a cell or a room. "I don't know if I can do this."

"You'll be fine." Galen pulled him close again. "Just breathe, remember. If you ever feel like you can't handle it, just breathe. In... and out...."

Cam focused on Galen's words, slowing his breathing. *Breathe in. Relax. Breathe out. Relax.* Slowly, the panic ebbed, then subsided.

I can do this. I can do this.

"Better?" Galen asked after a few minutes.

"Yes. Thanks." He took another deep breath. "I can't thank you enough. For everything."

"Ready, then?"

"I'm ready." Cam opened the glass doors and walked into the office.

CHAPTER 36

London, England
One week later

CAM GLANCED out the window of the plane as the outskirts of London came into view as they dipped below the thick layer of clouds. Four hours late, thanks to a mechanical problem that ended up turning into a change of aircraft. Not that it mattered much. He had no plans—he'd cancelled them all when he'd flown to the States. He'd hoped he wouldn't be coming back here for a while.

He absentmindedly fingered the friendship bracelet Galen had given him. *Healing. Hope. Love.* How many times had he looked to that bracelet for strength? He wished Galen had been there to meet him when the FBI released him. But they hadn't discussed what would happen after he turned himself in. He'd had too much on his mind. He'd been too frightened to think that far into the future. But he'd thought about Galen a lot when he was in the cell. Each time he'd thought the fear would overwhelm him, he thought about Galen and pulled himself back from the brink. Thinking about Galen gave him something to focus on other than the bars.

He knew he'd done well. He'd been strong. He'd survived being locked up for nearly a week. The knowledge left him feeling empowered. He was ready to move forward. Ready to face his past and his future. Dan Bryce had confessed to helping Duncan set up the Cayman accounts after the FBI confronted him with Ron Welding's evidence of tampering with the authorization codes.

"It's just a matter of time," Marc had told him when he'd given Cam the news that he would be released that morning. "They've contacted the UK authorities about Duncan's involvement."

The flight attendant handed him his jacket and scarf when they landed. He pulled them on, then turned on his mobile and waited for it to connect to the network. He scrolled down the list of missed calls. There were none from Galen. Not that he'd expected any, but again, he'd hoped.

He'd missed a call from his New York number. Luisa, no doubt checking to make sure he'd arrived. He'd check the message and call her back later—it was far too late to bother her.

He emerged from immigration and customs about forty minutes later and headed toward the door to find his driver. He'd just managed to get past the crowd of people waiting to meet their friends and relatives when he heard the sound of crashing luggage behind him. He turned around to see a woman trying to right several bags a dozen feet behind him as four children chased each other around. Cam smiled and walked over to help.

"I'm so sorry," the exhausted-looking mother was telling a few irritated passengers around her. "My husband went to find a porter and—" One of the children ran directly into Cam, colliding with his legs.

Cam laughed, took the child's hand, and brought her back to her mother amidst the child's giggles. "I think this one belongs to you," he said as he set the child down and kneeled to assist.

"Thank you." The mother smiled at him as he began to gather up the contents of what he guessed was a diaper bag.

"My pleasure." Cam handed her back the bag, then noticed the teddy bear a few feet away. The child he'd just returned began to cry and point to it. "I'll get it. Don't you worry." He reached for the stuffed animal, but before he could grab it, someone else stooped down to pick it up before it got stepped on.

"Thank you," he said as he looked up. "You saved—" He stopped speaking when he took in the familiar face.

Galen smiled back at him, his hazel eyes bright with pleasure as he handed Cam the bear.

Cam swallowed hard, then stood and absentmindedly rubbed a thumb against the soft fur, unsure of what to say. "Galen," he managed after a moment. "Why? How?" Something—someone—tugged at his pants leg. The little girl he'd rescued before had her hand out. "Oh," he said. "This is yours, I imagine."

The girl nodded, solemnly took the bear from him, and hugged it tight. A moment later she jumped into her mother's arms. The woman smiled back at him. Her husband had rejoined her, and they were helping a porter load bags onto a cart.

"I heard the FBI released you," Galen said. "But by the time I called your apartment, your housekeeper said you'd already left for London. I caught the next flight I could book a seat on."

"But… I don't understand. Why did you come?" Cam still couldn't quite comprehend seeing Galen here.

"Thought you might need some moral support." Galen embraced Cam. Cam felt a slight shudder pass through Galen's body at the contact.

"You shouldn't have. It's too expens—"

"Shhh." Galen kissed Cam's cheek. "Don't worry about me. I've got enough to cover it. And I figured you could use a friend right about now."

Galen made it sound so simple. *And he's right too.*

"I.... Thank you." He wanted Galen here. Galen obviously wanted to be here. Why was he hesitating to accept Galen's gift? Because that was what it was: a gift.

Because you don't deserve his friendship, the voice in the back of his brain whispered. Cam ignored the voice and all the memories it recalled. "But what about your job?" he asked.

Galen shrugged. "The school system suspended me," he said.

"What? For not reporting Jamie's stepfather?"

"No biggie."

"The hell it isn't," Cam snapped. "You love that job." Galen wasn't telling him everything. He probably didn't want to worry him. And even though Cam wanted to hear the entire story, now wasn't the time to press Galen on it.

"Yes. I do." Galen smiled at him reassuringly. "But there's no telling if I'll lose it anyhow. The board is supposed to meet soon."

"And what about the competition? Who's going to do that?"

Galen shrugged again. "We'll cross that bridge when we get to it. For the time being, the choral teacher will work with the students."

Cam wasn't convinced, but he dropped the subject. He sensed Galen's discomfort with the topic. If he'd learned anything in his time with Galen, it was that he didn't have to know the answers to all his questions all the time. He'd become more patient. He'd wait to ask again when he sensed Galen was ready.

"Do you have a place to stay?" he asked Galen as they headed toward the elevators.

"Nah. I figured I'd find a hotel once I caught up with you."

"You're staying with me," Cam said fiercely. He rationalized this by telling himself he didn't want Galen to spend any more money on his account, but the truth was that he wanted Galen with him. *Needed* his support.

Galen appeared surprised. "Well, if you put it that way...." He leaned in and kissed Cam again.

"So what will you do now?" Galen asked as they stepped into the limousine a few minutes later.

"Now?" Cam gazed out the window as they rounded the corner into London traffic. "Now I pretend that nothing has changed." Easier said than done, since the thought of getting out and about scared him more than he cared to admit. But he felt better about the prospect of showing his face again knowing Galen was at his side.

"And what does that mean?" Galen asked.

Cam grinned. "We paint the town red."

"WELL, DO I look like I'm ready for the town?" Galen asked as he walked down the steep stairs of Cam's Edwardian house four hours later. Too tired for anything but rest after having been awake for nearly twenty-four hours, Cam had fallen asleep in Galen's arms in the large antique bed he'd purchased a year before, not wanting to keep the bed he and Aiden had shared.

Even though he loved the old house, Cam hadn't spent much time here since Aiden left. Too many memories. There had been a time when he'd thought about purchasing the home from his landlord, but after Aiden left, he'd given up that idea. Continuing to pay the rent was easier than coming to terms with the loss of Aiden. With Galen, though, he felt strangely comfortable. When they'd awoken, Cam had showered and dressed first, telling Galen he'd wait for him downstairs. In truth, he needed the time to gather his courage. He'd been hiding too long. Tonight he would remind London who Lord Cameron Sherrington was, and in the process he'd send a message to Duncan that he would not be intimidated or frightened.

He'd been sitting by the fire, sipping whiskey and watching the flames dance, when Galen came downstairs. When Cam turned to look, he nearly spit a mouthful of expensive spirits. "I... you.... Shit, Galen, you look fabulous." An understatement, really. Galen looked good enough to eat.

Dressed in a pair of well-tailored wool pants and a green sweater that picked up the color in his eyes, Galen looked so different that Cam guessed he wouldn't have recognized him if he'd passed him in the street. Galen's hair, normally an impossible mess, now framed his face in waves the color of wheat. Smooth and shiny. He'd shaved his usual stubble and wore a single silver cuff on his right ear.

"Didn't think I owned anything other than T-shirts and jeans, did you?" Galen joked. Cam guessed Galen felt uncomfortable with the compliment. He'd rarely seen Galen uncomfortable about anything, and this realization came as a surprise.

Cam stood and slipped his arms around Galen's waist. "Maybe we should just order in tonight."

Galen offered him a crooked smile. "You need to do this, Lord Sherrington," he said as he kissed his way up Cam's neck, causing Cam to shudder with pleasure.

Cam sighed theatrically. "I know. But it was a lovely thought."

Galen took Cam's earlobe into his mouth. "Something to look forward to, then," he whispered a moment later.

CHAPTER 37

GALEN WAS still smiling as they hailed a cab outside the Edwardian a few minutes later. He hadn't asked Cam where they were headed. He didn't care. He'd have been perfectly happy if Cam had suggested they stay in bed instead of going out, but he knew Cam needed this.

"I'm glad you came," Cam said as the taxi sped down the street toward the heart of London. Cam fingered something on his wrist.

"You kept the bracelet?"

The corners of Cam's mouth quirked upward into a half smile as he pushed his sleeve up to reveal the friendship bracelet. "I've come to rely on it."

"Really? I'm glad." In fact, it made Galen's heart beat a little faster to know that Cam had held on to it all this time. But Cam didn't need to know that.

"This all feels so strange." Cam ran a hand through his hair. "Surreal."

Galen saw that Cam no longer used the sticky gel in his hair that he'd favored when they'd met. Once, in passing, he'd mentioned that Cam's hair looked different, and Cam had teased him about the dearth of hair products in the house. But when Galen had offered to buy more, Cam had told him he'd come to like the natural look. Galen loved Cam's soft curls, so he didn't argue.

"Are you nervous?" Galen asked, clasping Cam's hand and giving it a reassuring squeeze.

"Yes." Cam held Galen's hand a bit tighter. "A few weeks ago, I wouldn't have admitted it." He laughed and added, "Then again, a few weeks ago, there'd have been nothing to be nervous about."

When Cam stepped out of the elevator and into Zyng a half hour later, any trace of nerves had vanished. The bar took up an entire floor of the trendy London hotel. The textured glass dividers that wove in and around mirrors and modern seating in shades of red, silver, and gold reminded Galen of the ocean at sunset. The effect was quite beautiful, even if the clientele—men and women dressed in outrageously expensive designer clothing with perfect bodies, perfect skin, and perfect hair—left Galen feeling cold.

Cam's entrance to the pounding techno beat had heads—both male and female—turning. He looked beautiful in the perfectly fitted black suit that skimmed the topography of his lean frame. The white shirt and just barely darker white tie reminded Galen of an angel, but the diamond stud in Cam's ear and the look in his eyes were anything but angelic. Galen had never seen him as focused.

"Cam? Cameron Sherrington?" The tall blonde with a French accent and a very short skirt swept over to them and kissed Cam on both cheeks. "Je me suis inquiété pour toi. Comment vas-tu?"

"Tout va bien, Caroline," Cam answered easily. "I'm well. Truly. Just a bit of trouble with my visa. Nothing to worry about."

"But we heard—"

"Caroline, I'd like you to meet Galen Rusk. Galen, this is Caroline Bernard. A friend of mine from uni."

"Pleased to meet you." Galen leaned in and kissed Caroline on each cheek.

"And I you." Caroline smiled knowingly. "At least now we know why Cam has stayed so long in New York."

Cam laughed but did nothing to dispel her assumption.

"Why don't I get us drinks?" Galen asked. "Caroline?"

"Gin and tonic." She laced her arm through Cam's and began to lead him over to a table on the far end of the bar.

"Whiskey. Knappogue Castle, if they have it," Cam said over his shoulder with a look meant just for Galen that said *sorry to trouble you.*

Galen didn't mind. This was Cam's moment to shine, and he was happy to be the window dressing. He walked over to the bar and ordered their drinks, then watched as Cam greeted the men and women at the table.

"He is quite lovely, isn't he?" a man said from behind Galen.

"What?" Galen turned to face the speaker, an attractive man in his late twenties. Tall, dressed in dark jeans and a button-down shirt opened just enough to reveal his smooth skin, he wore the same expression Galen had seen on Caroline's face.

"I'm Leslie Gartner."

Galen shook Leslie's hand. "Galen Rusk. Good to meet you."

"American," Leslie purred. "How quaint. He does seem to like himself a good Yank."

Galen decided he'd best play dumb. "He?"

"Lord Sherrington. Used to bring his last Yank here too. Big-name opera singer. Arden, or something like that."

"Aiden," Galen corrected.

"Of course." Leslie clearly didn't care what Aiden's name was. "Then there was the swimmer. Nice body, not much else to offer. Other than the singer, none of them lasted long."

Galen didn't appreciate the not-so-subtle warning in Leslie's words. He clenched his jaw and took a slow breath. *Breathe. Relax. Focus.* He'd avoided this sort of place for years, preferring the more intimate bars in the West Village to the trendier clubs in SoHo. But he could do this for Cam. He would do it. "I don't think I need to—"

"Mind you, he's a good fuck. Although he prefers to do the fucking, if you know what I mean."

"Excuse me," Galen said, his urge to throttle the little shit surprisingly powerful.

Leslie waved, made a point of looking Galen up and down, and then went back to his drink. At least he and Leslie agreed on something: Cam really *was* quite lovely. *Jealous son of a bitch.*

Galen snagged two of the drinks—he couldn't manage to carry his own, especially if it meant navigating the sea of people who had gathered around Cam—then made his way across the room. Caroline greeted him at the edge of the crowd, thanked him and took her drink and Cam's, then worked her way back through the throng of people to the center, where Cam stood.

Cam chatted with several men, one of whom was standing so close that Cam was forced to back up to avoid being touched. If this bothered Cam, however, he didn't show it.

"Hardly," Cam said, then laughed his silvery laugh. "But there was an FBI agent who thought when I said 'blow me' after he told me I'd need to wear an orange jumpsuit while in custody, I was asking for sexual favors."

Total bullshit, Galen knew, but the crowd ate it up. He grinned and headed back to the bar for his beer. Thankfully, Leslie had moved on to smaller and shallower things, annoying another man at the bar. Galen picked up his beer, this time lingering near the bar, where he had a better view of Cam.

Drink firmly ensconced in his hand, Cam said something that made the group laugh. Galen couldn't hear above the sound of the thumping bass, but Cam's friends were clearly enthralled. Cam took a sip of the alcohol—Galen saw that he barely drank any—then listened intently to the man beside him who'd once again gotten too close to Cam.

Galen held his beer so tightly his fingers hurt. He hadn't even taken a swig yet. Good thing too, given he'd been clenching his jaw again. What the hell was wrong with him? This entire evening was an act for Cam and he knew it.

You're jealous.

The realization took him by surprise. He hated the way everyone looked at Cam. Clever, charming Cam. Poised, confident, carefree Cam. Complete and utter bullshit. And with the realization came clarity of thought: not one of them knew Cam. Really *knew* him. They didn't know the big heart underneath the cool exterior. They didn't see the vulnerability, didn't know of the grief and the heartache. They didn't know that even now, Cam still hated himself for what he'd done to Aiden. Hated himself for what he was. For what he'd been.

You've fallen for him. Again, a jolt to his system.

Galen took a long pull on his drink, swallowed deeply, and then drank again. He barely tasted it—he was too busy watching Cam. Wanting Cam. Wishing he and Cam were together somewhere quiet. Wishing he could rake leaves with Cam again so he could see the *real* Cam smile. *His* Cam.

Breathe.

He remembered how it had felt to hold Cam as he'd cried. How his own heart had broken for Cam. How he'd wanted to tear Duncan limb from limb for hurting Cam. *His* Cam.

Relax.

He remembered how he'd watched Cam sleep, knowing how precious that sleep was. Knowing that he'd help keep the dreams at bay, at least for a short time. He'd felt so good knowing he could do something for Cam, since Cam had given him happiness. Little pieces of happiness. Falling into a pile of leaves. Laughing. Making dinner. Keeping him company. Listening to him play. *His* Cam.

Focus.

He finished the rest of his beer, but it did nothing to quell the strange feeling in his gut.

You're leaving in a few days. You'll say your good-byes and you'll both move on.

He closed his eyes, inhaled deeply, then exhaled slowly, releasing the tension that had suddenly taken hold of his body. When he opened his eyes again, he looked to where Cam still held court. This time their eyes met. There was no mistaking the way Cam's face lit in that instant. Whatever he might tell himself, Galen knew his presence had made a difference tonight. Cam didn't need him, even if Cam hadn't realized it himself yet, but Cam was stronger because he wasn't alone.

The last thing Galen realized before the moment of clarity vanished into the noise and distractions of colors and light was that he'd seen something in Cam's face. Something beautiful and frightening all at once. Something Galen had never seen directed at him. Cam's blue eyes shone with an intensity that made them appear almost turquoise. The hardness around Cam's mouth—armor, Galen now knew—gave way to the slightest hint of a smile, noticeable only for the tiny lines that framed Cam's eyes and mouth.

He loves me.

GALEN HAD just made it inside the door when he turned and pulled Cam against him. He held Cam's face in his hands and drew him close for a blistering kiss. God, he'd wanted to do that all night! Every time Cam had flirted with someone, every clever joke Cam had cracked, Galen had imagined storming over and kissing him until there was no doubt at all who Cam was *really* with.

"Galen," Cam gasped as their lips parted. "What was *that* for?"

"Do I need a reason?" A lame excuse of an answer, but he wasn't going to tell Cam he'd been jealous. Or that he'd realized something had changed and he didn't know what the fuck to do about it except drink in as much of Cam as he possibly could.

CHAPTER 38

THEY SLEPT late the next morning, Cam spooned against Galen's back. Breakfast turned into a late lunch. They didn't make love again—Cam was content just feeling Galen's body against his own. The night before had become something far more than he'd expected. Cam had felt powerful and strangely detached, as if he were observing himself from a distance. The Cam who'd strutted his stuff at the club had been as fake as the too-perky breasts and Botox foreheads of the women who'd hung on his arms, or the smiles plastered on his erstwhile friends' faces. But he'd been fine with that because Galen had been there and he'd seen himself—the *real* Cameron Sherrington—reflected in Galen's expression.

Tonight would be less of a chore. Cam looked forward to seeing David and Alex again. And although some of the guests would no doubt gossip about rumors of his brush with the US authorities, most were people Cam genuinely liked.

"Ready?" Cam asked as he and Galen sat in front of the fire sipping brandy. He leaned against Galen and kissed his cheek.

"Ready." Galen spoke in a bright tone, but Cam thought he'd seen something flicker across Galen's face. Galen was always quiet, but he'd been even quieter since their lunch.

"Everything all right?"

Galen smiled at him. "Perfectly all right." He pulled Cam toward him and brushed his lips against Cam's. "I'm just a little jet-lagged, I guess."

"You'll like David." Cam kissed Galen and sighed. "And he'll like you."

Galen turned and watched the fire for a moment, then said, "I'm sure I will."

THEY HAD barely handed their coats to one of the servants when Alex Bishop strode down the hallway. "Cam," he said as he pulled Cam into a bear hug, "you had us worried."

Cam smiled. He'd never been very comfortable with Alex's affectionate greetings, but this time he didn't pull away as quickly as he might have before. "Everything's fine. Bit of a rough patch, but nothing to be concerned about."

Alex frowned as if he didn't believe that, then glanced at Galen expectantly. Cam forced his wandering thoughts back to the here and now as he realized he hadn't introduced them. "Sorry. I'm being quite rude. Alex Bishop, this is Galen Rusk. Galen, Alex."

Alex shook Galen's hand. "Good to meet you, Galen."

"It's a pleasure and an honor. I heard your Dvorak a few months ago. Brilliant. Took a few of my students with me." Galen chuckled, then added, "They wanted to know why you weren't playing any Rolling Stones. I had to explain that the New York Phil wasn't exactly the venue for that."

"You're a teacher?" Alex asked as he motioned them down the hallway toward the ballroom.

"High school band," Galen replied. "We're trying to raise enough money to start an orchestra too, but with the economy in the dumps, it's slow going."

"Sorry to hear that. If there's anything I can do to help, let me know, okay?" Alex's interest appeared genuine, and Cam guessed he was remembering his own difficult childhood.

The ease and comfort with which Galen handled the conversation with Alex took Cam aback. Galen had always been a man of few words, but he chatted comfortably with Alex as though the two had been friends for years. By the time Alex had left to greet another guest, he'd arranged to meet with Galen the next time he was in New York.

If he still has a job.

"Cam?" A tall woman wearing an extremely short dress nearly knocked Cam off his feet when she grabbed him by the arm and pulled him into her embrace. "I heard about things in the US. I can't believe they even thought you might have done something like that."

"Good to see you, Ceci." Cam kissed her cheek after extricating himself from her grasp. "Galen, this is Cecilia Troy. She and my mother play a mean game of poker." He winked at Cecilia and added, "And she usually takes my mother for all she's got."

"Good to meet you," Galen said, taking her hand and kissing it. "And good to know."

"You play poker?" Ceci pursed her lips and gave Galen a thorough once-over.

"A bit." Galen smiled and winked at Cam.

"Then you must join us sometime." Cecilia looked ready to devour Galen.

"I'm guessing the stakes are a bit too high for me," Galen said as he shook his head. "But I'm happy for any pointers."

Cam watched, incredulous, as Cecilia and Galen spoke for nearly ten minutes about betting strategy like a couple of high-stakes players. Galen appeared completely comfortable. By the end of their conversation, he had a standing invitation to one of the most sought-after poker games in the city.

"Did I do something wrong?" Galen asked as they waited for the bartender to make their drinks. "You're staring at me like I grew a second head or something."

"Nothing wrong." Cam struggled to put into words what had been swirling about his brain as he'd watched Galen and Ceci. "You just…. I mean, Ceci isn't exactly the type to invite someone into her little circle."

Galen laughed and waved his hand dismissively. "She just thinks I'm cute, that's all."

Cam wouldn't argue with that, but he was quite sure it wasn't just Galen's looks that had sold Ceci.

They stopped several more times as Cam led Galen across the large living room toward where David Somers was conversing with several people. Each time, Galen chatted comfortably with not even a hint of his usual awkwardness. By the time they reached David, Cam could only conclude that either Galen was a very quick study or he'd suffered through nearly as many parties as Cam had over the years. Which, of course, made no sense at all.

"Cameron." David Somers smiled broadly as he shook Cam's hand and clasped it between his own.

"Thank you for inviting me." Cam met David's gaze and smiled. Of all the people in the room, David was the only one other than Galen who knew the full extent of what he'd been through in the past few weeks. Did David know how much that meant to him? Probably. When it came to his friends, little escaped David's attention. The thought that David really *was* a friend made Cam smile. He'd been stupid not to appreciate that friendship before. Stupid to wait so long to reach out and ask David for help. "Good to see you."

Eager to avoid any questions, Cam turned to Galen and said, "David Somers, I'd like you to meet Galen—"

"Arendale," David finished, his eyes wide.

Cam was just about to correct David when Galen smiled and shook David's hand. "Maestro."

Arendale? Who the bloody hell was Galen Arendale? The scene played out like in a movie, with Cam the only actor who didn't seem to know his lines.

"It's been a long time."

Galen nodded. "About ten years. Although I've been to more than a few of your concerts since then."

"Arendale?" Cam finally managed to choke out.

Galen shifted from one foot to the other—the first time the entire evening that he'd looked the least bit uncomfortable. "It's my father's name," he said. "It was my stage name."

"Stage name?" Cam looked at David, but David looked nearly as confused as he felt. "You know each other?"

"I'm very sorry, Galen," David said after an awkward pause.

Cam saw Galen inhale before he said, "It's all right, David. I have nothing to hide."

David nodded, then looked back at Cam and said, "Galen made his debut with the Chicago Symphony the first year I was there. Brilliant performance."

Cam tried to understand what David had just said, but couldn't process this new information. "Debut?"

Galen shifted on his feet and took a slow breath that reminded Cam of when he'd found Galen seated on the couch, legs twisted like a pretzel, meditating. "Yes," Galen said after a slightly uncomfortable pause. "I used to perform a little back then."

David was frowning now, and Cam realized David had assumed he knew about this. "I apologize, Galen," he said. "I didn't realize you hadn't spoken about it."

"No apology needed." Cam forced a smile. Out of the corner of his eye, he saw Galen chew his lower lip.

"YOU LIED to me," Cam snapped as soon as they got inside the house. Galen had watched Cam seethe at the party. How they'd gotten through two hours of schmoozing at David's, he still wasn't sure. And during the cab ride back, Cam had barely looked at him.

"I didn't—" Why had Cam needed to know any of it? Ancient history. Something to forget about and leave languishing in the past.

"Galen Arendale?"

"Arendale is my father's name," he said, knowing he'd already said that and that repeating the fact would do little to placate Cam.

"So you've said. And Rusk?"

"My mother's name. The name I use now." He'd used her name for so long, he hadn't really thought about it.

"Now?" Cam's pale cheeks flushed with anger.

Galen knew Cam had a right to be angry, even if the past was done and gone. Even if the past had nothing to do with now. With *them*. He'd lied to Cam—a lie of omission, certainly, but a lie nonetheless. His guilt threatened to overwhelm him, and he gritted his teeth against a sudden wave of dizziness. He teetered on the edge of his fear, his Zen failing him, everything he'd worked so hard to attain fleeing him as he struggled for an explanation. Why did it feel as though his control was taking a stand against the man he... *loved*?

"After I stopped performing," he said, hoping the explanation would suffice but knowing Cam had every right not to let it go at that.

"Chicago Symphony *debut*? That's more than just a hobby, Galen. How old were you?"

Galen schooled his expression. "I was eighteen."

"Eighteen?" Cam shook his head and clenched his fists at his side, looking as though he'd explode. Galen couldn't avoid the hurt in Cam's face, along with the anger. Pain that Galen had inflicted. Trust that *he'd* breached, even though he knew how important that trust was to Cam.

"Trumpet." He didn't want to talk about this. Not now. Not ever, really. Bad enough that David had brought it up with all the memories. And the fear. God, he didn't want to do that again. He'd spent *years* just getting past the fear that he'd relapse. But he owed Cam the truth.

"You were eighteen when you played with the Chicago Symphony? When the *hell* were you going to tell me?" Cam demanded.

Galen swallowed hard. "It doesn't matter now. That was a lifetime ago. I was a different person." Easy to say, even as the memories flooded back in a torrent.

"How did you end up in a psych ward? That had something to do with this, didn't it?"

Breathe. Relax. Inhale. Exhale. "Yes. But what difference does that make? It was more than ten years ago." Ten years that felt like yesterday. Ten years of learning to survive without the drugs. Ten years of practicing yoga. Of trying to let it go and stay on his path. And it had worked. He'd been fine. He hadn't had to go back to the hospital. He hadn't needed the meds.

I want to tell you, Cam, but I'm afraid if I do, the dam will break and I'll be back there again. Wanting to die. Lost. Locked up. He shoved his trembling hands into his pockets in an effort to hide his fear.

Cam stared at Galen, clearly at a loss for words. He shook his head, then walked to the couch and tossed his jacket there. "It makes a difference because you know everything about me. I've told you everything. Every horrid thing I've done, all the things that I'd never thought to tell another person. And all along, you knew that I'd want to know, and you didn't say a word!"

"You never asked why I tried to commit suicide." No, not outright. But he'd known Cam *wanted* to know. Cam was too polite to ask, and Galen had taken advantage of that.

"Bollocks! I shouldn't have had to ask. There were so many times you could have told me, but you didn't. I figured I'd wait. You'd never pushed me about difficult topics, and I didn't want to push you. But you knew I wanted to know."

Of course he did. Galen tried to swallow, but his throat felt dry. Tight.

Breathe. Relax.

"Galen?"

Inhale. Exhale.

"Why don't we just let this go?" he said, knowing Cam wouldn't. That he *shouldn't* let it go. That Cam deserved *all* of the truth.

"Why? Because you're afraid to tell me?" Cam demanded.

Breathe. Relax.

"Because it's ancient history and it makes no difference. Especially to you. You have an entirely new future to look forward to, to live for. Possibilities you hadn't even imagined two months ago." The words helped him regain his center. He always did better when he was helping others. His students, his friends. Cam. He was so fucking proud of Cam for taking his life back. And when Cam moved on, he'd make damn sure Cam moved on without the excess baggage of someone else's past. Cam would remember him the way he was now and not the way he was ten years ago.

Cam blinked and clenched his jaw. Galen hadn't been prepared for this—the feelings, the depth of the emotion the chance encounter with David had stirred in Cam.

Inhale. Exhale. He forced his shoulders to release their tension, then moved on to the muscles in his neck. Methodical, familiar relaxation. He fought the urge to straighten Cam's tie, which was slightly askew.

"Galen...." Cam shook his head. His voice sounded tentative this time.

The anger still simmered, but Galen noticed that Cam had slowed his breathing and recovered his focus. *So proud of you, Cam.* Even as he thought this, his guilt surged again, like a tide rising around his heart.

"Remember when we first met?" Cam asked. "And how you told me I was kind?"

Galen nodded.

"I didn't believe you then." Cam inhaled audibly, then exhaled. "Sometimes I still don't believe you." The tension in Cam's shoulders began to fade.

So proud of you.

"But sometime along the way, I began to understand that I could be kind. That I could *be*."

"Be?"

"Yes, *be*. I could be whatever I wanted, because I'd lost everything. Lost myself. Maybe even a part of my soul." Cam paused as if gathering his thoughts, and he inhaled and exhaled once more. "I didn't know what was left except to disappear. Die.

"But you showed me that there was so much more.... That I could have faith in myself. I could create something. Hope. Kindness." Another pause. "Love. You helped me find the confidence I'd never really had."

Cam ran a hand through his hair. Those defiant curls Galen loved to wrap around his fingers. He'd come to think of them as a visible extension of Cam's soul. Those curls had never cooperated, never behaved the way Cam wanted them to. Cam had spent his entire life trying to behave, trying to be something he thought he should be, and in the end he'd denied his heart and so much more. Denying his heart, he'd become the antithesis of what had been expected of him.

"I'm glad." What else could he say? He felt truly happy for Cam.

"Galen. I want to understand you."

Galen forced a smile. "Nothing much to understand. I'm a what-you-see-is-what-you-get kind of guy. Not all that interesting."

"More bollocks." Cam shook his head and sighed.

"It doesn't matter, Cam. What matters is that you're doing fine. Me? I'm just a guy you met along the way. And if you think I helped, then I'm happy."

"Is that all you feel?" Cam met his gaze with those piercing blue eyes, and Galen knew in that instant he'd miscalculated. He'd always been good about toeing the line between teacher and student. Not this time.

"My feelings are irrelevant." A half-truth, but the best he could manage under the circumstances. Speaking was hard enough—the dizziness and the cold sweat on the back of his neck made it difficult to focus.

"Irrelevant?" Cam laughed. "This from the new-age guru who guides his students to enlightenment?"

Galen should have known Cam was too smart to continue to play the role of student. Too smart not to want more. Worse, he knew he loved Cam, even though he'd denied it all along. Even though he had no place for Cam in his life.

"I am who I am," Galen said at last. He struggled against the feeling that he was drowning. The pain in his chest made it difficult to breathe, and the mantra that had gotten him through so many other challenges now seemed powerless to help. *Breathe. Just breathe.* "No commitments. No long term. I made myself a promise when I was in the hospital, doped up on meds. I'd be the stone. Immovable. Immutable. I'd just *be*."

Cam frowned, his lips parting in obvious surprise. "That's it, isn't it?" he said. "I'm the slow one here."

"I don't know what you mean."

"The hospital. I don't know what else happened to you back then, but there was someone, wasn't there? Someone you cared about? Someone you loved?"

Inhale. Exhale. He didn't want to go there. Didn't want to remember. He gripped the chair and willed the room to stop spinning.

"That's it, isn't it, Galen? Someone hurt you. Maybe even left you after you'd pulled yourself back together."

Breathe. Relax. Galen forced an image from his mind. Brian kissing him. Telling Brian he loved him. Telling Brian he wanted a relationship. *Inhale. Exhale.*

"I can't, Cam." His voice cracked. *Breathe. Relax.* "My life works because I'm past that."

"Past it the same way I denied that I wanted to kill myself? Twice?"

Was Cam right? Was he doing exactly what he'd called Cam on?

No. That was different. We're different people.

He closed his eyes and saw himself watching the blood pool on the floor of the bathroom. He remembered the feeling of peace, of falling into the warmth of nothingness. He heard music and allowed himself to be enveloped in it. The music that comforted him. The music that he'd tried to share. But when he'd shared it, he'd lost it somehow. *I can't lose it again.* He needed to guard it and keep it safe.

"Galen." Cam's voice brought him back to himself.

"I can't, Cam."

Then Cam did something that took Galen by surprise. Something beautiful and frightening. Cam walked over and took him in his arms. Just held him close without speaking.

I can't do this. The fear made his blood pound in his ears. What if this time he couldn't fight his way back? What if when Cam left him—and he *would* leave, because all things ended eventually—he lost himself so completely that he could never escape the confines of his mind?

"Please, Cam." He gently pushed Cam away. "I told you. I don't do long term. It's here and now. That's all I can do."

"I want more than that." Cam pressed his lips together. "I love you, Galen. I want you for more than here and now."

You can do this. Just breathe. Relax. Inhale. Exhale.

The mantra wasn't working. Every muscle in his body screamed at him. His heart hurt. "I'm sorry, Cam," he said in an undertone. "I don't love you."

He'd never lied to Cam before.

CHAPTER *39*

MUSIC BLARED from a set of speakers near where Cam danced with Bill. He'd taken off his jacket and unbuttoned his shirt. Bill traced his fingers over Cam's skin as they moved in time to the music, their bodies pressed together. All around them, men danced, some shirtless, sweaty, aroused. Cam had been to the club before he'd met Aiden. A great place to find a quick fuck or a blow job in the toilets. Cam had met Bill here a few years before, and they'd ended up in bed on a few occasions since. Bill had suggested it when Cam had called an hour before.

"I don't love you."

The loud music did nothing to erase Galen's words from his mind. *No!* Galen had lied to him. Cam could feel it. *I know he cares about me.* Still, he'd left Galen alone at the house a few minutes later, unwilling to challenge him but unable to face him after confessing his love. And fuck, Galen's rejection hurt more than he'd expected.

Fuck him.

"I thought you were with the singer," Bill said when Cam called to ask him if they could meet.

"There was someone," Cam told him. "But it was a mistake."

He'd been wrong about so much. He'd misread Galen. He'd been so desperate that he'd let himself fall in love.

That's not right, and you know it.

He'd seen the fear in Galen's eyes. He wanted to challenge Galen, force him to answer truthfully. A month ago he'd have done exactly that. But now he saw things differently. He knew challenging Galen wouldn't help. Instead, he'd frightened himself by doing something he'd never have done before. He'd taken Galen in his arms. Just held him close without speaking.

And it didn't work. Galen had lied to him just when he'd come to trust him. Cam felt angry. Angrier than he had in a long time. Hurt, too. But he wasn't willing to let Galen go.

You've already lost him, the insistent little voice at the back of his mind whispered gleefully.

He and Bill ordered a few more drinks from the bar, Bill some fruity drink that made Cam queasy just looking at it, Cam a double shot of an outrageously expensive single malt that he barely tasted as he downed it in one swallow. Heat from the alcohol radiated to his fingers and cheeks. Aiden had always said he was cute when his pale skin flushed pink from whiskey.

Bill hooked a finger through one of Cam's belt loops and his thumb brushed the skin of Cam's ass beneath the material. The suit he'd worn to David and Alex's party, the one Galen had told him looked really good. Why had he bothered to tell him that? *Because you're a player and he knew you wanted to hear it. He knew it'd make you feel good.*

Galen hadn't led him on. He'd been up-front from the start, and Cam had been fine with that.

"FUCK, CAM," Bill said as he pushed Cam against the door and ground against him. Cam felt Bill's cock through the fabric of his jeans, hard and waiting. "I'm so glad you called me." He slipped a hand around to grab Cam's arse, and Cam's cock responded.

Bill pressed his lips against Cam's and sought his tongue. Not a kiss—there was nothing tender about it. He didn't care. That made things easier. Fucking was good. He could bloody well live without the other bullshit. He'd focus on the company. He'd already decided he would run it. He'd do a damn good job with it too, not because he gave a rat's arse what his mother or anyone else thought, but because *he* wanted to do it and do it well.

Bill pulled off his jacket and threw it onto the floor, then began to unbutton the shirt Cam had rebuttoned before they'd left the club. Cam drew Bill's jumper over his head. Bill had a nice body. Toned, muscled—a bit broader in the chest than Galen, but well looked after.

A minute later Bill had unfastened Cam's belt and unzipped the front of his trousers. He reached into Cam's boxer briefs and cupped his arse with his big hands, squeezing and working the muscles until it hurt.

"I want to fuck that pretty little arse," Cam said by Bill's ear. "Feel my cock in that tight hole." As always, his mind followed in quick succession. He imagined seeing Bill bending over, hearing Bill's pleasure as he fucked him over and over. Wanting Bill to tell him how good it felt. Wanting someone to make him feel wanted. Wanting....

Wanting what? What did he want? He remembered Galen's words the first time they'd made love. *"How do you like it?"*

"I like it any way you like it," he'd answered.

"That wasn't my question, Cam. I want to know how you *like it. Whether you like it when I suck on you or whether you like it when I take it in my teeth."*

Galen had wanted to know because he cared about him. He'd wanted to know... *because he loves me.* This time, Cam ignored the devil on his shoulder who said otherwise.

If you believe he loves you.... He needed to stop sulking. Stop feeling sorry for himself. Stop being a pathetic little boy and be a fucking *man* for a change. Stop telling himself that things just *happened* to him. Stop being a victim. Ask for what he fucking *wanted* for a change.

"Stop."

Bill looked at him as though he were mad.

"I can't do this." How had he let himself be taken in so fucking easily? Galen had *lied.* He'd lied, but Cam didn't understand why. Something about what happened. About his life working because he was past something? Past loving? Past the pain? The fear?

"I don't understand," Bill said as Cam refastened his belt and buttoned his shirt.

"I'm sorry, Bill. I like you. You've got a great body. But I don't want this. Not now." *Not ever again. I want more.* He wouldn't tell himself he was worthy of more. Not yet. Maybe someday. But he knew what he wanted, and that was good enough for now.

Bill blinked, clearly not understanding. Cam took his hand and squeezed. Why did everything he did—every gesture of kindness—remind him of Galen? Maybe because Galen had been an excellent teacher.

CHAPTER 40

CAM GLANCED at his watch as he unlocked the front door: 3:00 a.m. Why did it seem that revelations and epiphanies always happened in the middle of the night? And why the hell had he left Galen alone when the thing he wanted—he *needed*—the most right now was Galen?

History repeats itself, and you have no one to blame but yourself.

He climbed the stairs and found Galen asleep in the four-poster, thankful that he was the only idiot who thought cruising was a good way to deal with conflict in a relationship. The thing that had taken him by surprise about all of this was that he'd realized he wasn't the only one who was afraid.

Cam struggled to put the pieces together as he took off his clothes. In spite of his yoga, in spite of his outwardly calm appearance, Galen was afraid. Terrified. The way he'd spoken about the mental hospital had made clear his desperation and fear of his time there.

He's afraid he'll have to go back. That he'll become the person he was then.

Was that why Galen had taken him on? Because Cam didn't doubt Galen had seen him as someone needing his help. Paying it forward. He wondered if there had been others like him or if Galen usually just helped his students. Did he think this was about hero worship? Because he bloody well wasn't the type.

No. For once this really isn't about you.

He'd been selfish not to see the truth behind Galen's words.

He slipped under the covers, naked, and wrapped his arms around Galen.

"Cam?"

"Expecting someone else?" he said before kissing Galen's back.

"Have a good time?" Galen turned to face him.

"No. I missed you." He leaned in and caught Galen's lips for a brief kiss.

"Listen… Cam…. I—"

"Shhh. We'll talk about it later. Right now, I want to make love to you." He kissed Galen again, this time pressing his tongue into Galen's sweet mouth and tasting him. Galen responded with a moan. "I know what you said, and I get it. So why don't we forget about what happens after tonight? Because no matter what, I want this."

No matter how long you need, I'll give it to you.

He pulled Galen's shirt over his head and pushed back the covers to better see his body. He studied Galen's chest for a moment, then ghosted his fingers over Galen's skin and watched as the gooseflesh rose and Galen's dusky pink nipples peaked of their own accord. He rubbed each with his thumb, brushing until Galen arched his back to meet his touch, then grasping them between thumb and forefinger and rolling them to Galen's stuttered breaths.

"Cam...."

Hearing Galen speak his name made Cam ache to have Galen inside of him. That it had been years since he'd last bottomed made the whole experience with Bill—of realizing that he didn't want to be with anyone but Galen—take on extra meaning. But he'd take his time. He'd show Galen that he meant what he'd said before. Show him he loved him. Help him to move past his fear the same way Galen had taught him.

Cam leaned over and flicked his tongue over Galen's left nipple, his skin pressed against Galen's, creating warmth. He reveled in the slightly salty taste, reveled in the soft down of the pale hair that covered his body, nearly invisible except to the touch. Felt Galen's heart accelerate and loved that he was the cause of it. He pulled on the nipple, sucking it as he gently bit the sensitive flesh, then releasing it and latching onto it again.

"Oh fuck!" Galen cried.

"That's better," Cam said as he reached down and pushed off Galen's sweatpants so that he, too, was naked. "I was worried you might still be sleeping."

Galen laughed and pushed Cam onto his back. "No way in hell I could sleep through *that*."

"Good." Cam drew Galen's face to his own and kissed him. Galen responded by running his tongue over Cam's teeth, pressing inward and sweeping around Cam's tongue, then tangling with it. He sucked Galen's lower lip and nibbled at it.

"You feel so good like this," Cam said as he reveled in the feel of Galen's warm skin against his own. He pulled the covers over his head and kissed Galen's chest, glancing up from time to time to see the pleasure on Galen's face.

He kissed his way down to take Galen's cock in his mouth and licked around the crown, feeling it harden, feeling Galen's pulse race as he ghosted his fingers over Galen's chest while he sucked. Galen canted his hips to meet Cam's mouth and moaned. When Cam released Galen's erection, he saw the disappointment on Galen's face. Not that Galen would ever complain, but Cam knew he'd wanted more.

"I don't want you to come yet," Cam said as he pushed the covers off and rose up on his haunches. "I want you to come inside of me."

Galen's eyes widened. "You...?"

"I want you inside of me."

CHAPTER 41

GALEN WASN'T sure he'd heard correctly. "You want me to top?" he asked.

"Yes." Cam smiled back at him, serene, confident. "But it's been a while, so you'll need to be gentle with me."

As if he'd be anything *but* gentle. Galen knew this was about more than the physical. Cam hadn't told him much about Duncan's abuse, but he'd made it clear his uncle had repeatedly raped him, even if Cam still didn't call it that. Someday Galen hoped Cam would take that piece of himself back from the bastard. Galen guessed that at some point in his life, Cam had decided to take control by always being on top. He hadn't minded; he enjoyed both aspects of sex, and he'd been happy to take Cam's lead.

Galen wondered if when Cam and whomever he'd gone home with earlier in the evening had had sex that had changed something in Cam's mind. He brushed away his jealousy. He had no right to expect Cam's fidelity when they'd both agreed they'd go their separate ways. He knew Cam needed reassurance. Who was he to deny Cam that?

"Are you sure about this?" Galen asked as he brushed Cam's cheek with his thumb.

"I'm sure." Cam retrieved the bottle of lube from the nightstand and slicked his hands. But instead of touching Galen's cock, Cam began to work himself open. Perhaps Cam wasn't ready to let someone else touch him that way. Perhaps someday he would be. It was still the sexiest thing he could imagine, watching Cam lick his lower lip with his pink tongue, hearing his stuttered breaths and soft moans.

"Do you know how incredible you look when you do that?" Galen asked.

Cam was pleased to hear that, judging from the slightly deeper flush of his already flushed cheeks.

"May I touch you?" Galen asked.

Cam nodded, then groaned when Galen took his half-erect cock in his hand and slipped his other hand down to cup Cam's balls. Cam continued to stretch himself, pausing only to catch his breath when he teetered too close to losing control, judging by the change in his breathing.

Galen poured lube into his hand, then rubbed his hands together to warm it. Cam gasped when Galen began to work his cock in earnest, pulling and squeezing as he rolled his sac. Cam was without doubt the most beautiful man he'd ever been with. Galen loved his pale skin and pink lips. He loved the way Cam's face expressed his joy, even his fear. He wondered if Cam knew how much of his emotion shone through his eyes. Probably not, given how Cam had fiercely defended his vulnerability when they'd first met.

"Galen."

Galen loved the way Cam said his name, not only because of the charming accent but also for the way Cam's breath permeated the sound of it, like the sound of a bow pulled across a violin string. From a distance, you might never hear the buzz of the horsehair across the string, but up close, Galen treasured that earthbound sound. It reminded him of his own breath combining with the warm vibrations of his trumpet, and that the only people who could hear that surprisingly personal, *human* sound were the orchestra members who sat nearby or the people who walked by him in the subway tunnel, if they were paying attention.

By now Cam's hisses and groans had become music of their own. With each sound, Galen imagined Cam grew closer to freeing himself from his past and from the chains that bound his heart and prevented the kind, loving man from fleeing his protective cell.

"That's it," Galen said in encouragement. "Open yourself to me."

Cam answered with a radiant smile.

Galen put on the condom, then slicked it with lube. Cam positioned himself over Galen's cock and lowered himself onto it. Cam didn't look away. He showed Galen every thought, every sensation, every fear, every pleasure as he took Galen into himself.

Cam didn't speak. He didn't need to. With each stuttered breath, each gasp, Galen understood how much this meant.

"Beautiful," Galen said as Cam began to move up and down. Galen clasped Cam's cock again and moved his slick hand up and down, mimicking Cam's movements. Each time he reached the tip of Cam's cock, he swiped his thumb over it, causing Cam to shudder.

"Galen," Cam repeated. "Feels incredible. Hot. Hard."

Galen thrust upward, carried away by the emotion of hearing this. Cam cried out and spilled hot and thick over Galen's hand. Galen came a moment later, unable to hold back, shouting Cam's name as his orgasm blossomed red-hot and shot through his limbs so that he shook with the overwhelming pleasure of it.

"Cam. Beautiful, wonderful Cam," he whispered against Cam's ear as they held each other. *I will never forget you.*

"Galen, I—"

"Shhh," Galen interrupted. He knew what Cam had meant to say, and he knew he couldn't let him say it. He couldn't hear it, or he might not be able to do what he needed to do. "Rest now and let me hold you."

CAM SMILED and listened as Galen's breaths deepened as he fell asleep. He didn't need Galen to tell him he loved him. He could wait for that as long as Galen needed.

CHAPTER 42

CAM ROLLED over and felt for Galen but found only a pillow. Last night he'd nearly made the biggest mistake of his life. He'd come so close to losing Galen because he'd been too stupid to realize Galen simply wasn't ready to admit his feelings. He reminded himself that he could wait. He *would* wait, regardless of his insecurities. He smiled at the thought.

He slipped out of bed, pulled on a pair of pajama bottoms, then began to look for Galen. *Probably still jet-lagged.* He descended the steps to the ground floor. He saw Galen's suitcase next to the door and his gut clenched. *No. He's just leaving because he needs to get back to work.* He drew a long breath, then another. His racing heart calmed.

He smiled and walked through the living room, dining room, and into the kitchen, where he found Galen seated at the table, sipping tea. He leaned over and kissed Galen's head, then wrapped his arms around Galen and kissed the side of his neck.

"Morning," he said next to Galen's ear.

"Good morning." Galen stood and asked, "Tea? Or would you prefer coffee?"

"Tea would be lovely, thank you." Cam followed Galen to the counter, where Cam refilled the electric kettle and turned it on. He slipped his hands through Galen's arms and encircled his waist. "Although I'd prefer a repeat of last night."

"Cam, I need to go."

Cam smiled and pressed his head against Galen's shoulder. "I know. I'm sure by now the school's realized they need you back and—"

"I heard from the disciplinary board the Thursday before you were released. Looks like I don't have a job to go back to." Galen scooped some tea leaves into the teapot.

"Wait a minute," Cam said as the impact of Galen's words hit him. "You *knew* almost a week ago that the disciplinary board recommended firing you, and you didn't tell me?" Cam frowned and tried to remember if Galen had even given him a clue, then decided he hadn't.

"I didn't want to worry you," Galen said as the kettle clicked off. He poured the water over the tea. The rich scent of English breakfast rose on the steam. Cam had always loved that smell.

"Didn't want to…. Galen, you know how worried I was about that. I'd want to know that. I'm capable of thinking about something other than myself."

Galen shrugged but didn't turn around. "I didn't mean to imply that you aren't. I just didn't want you to worry about it when you have so many other more important things to worry about."

"You're going back to appeal the decision, then," Cam said as he struggled to understand. Why the hell hadn't Galen said anything? Did he think Cam wouldn't care?

"No." Galen replaced the top on the teapot and it made a soft, clinking sound.

"No? Then why are you…?" Cam's sleepy brain finally sorted things out. Galen still hadn't turned around, hadn't even looked at him, not from the first moment he'd come into the room.

"Cam…." Galen spoke in a soft, low tone, but the silence cut Cam deep.

"I thought…," Cam began. His voice sounded steady enough, but fear crept over him like an icy rain. He repressed a shiver and wished he'd had the presence of mind to pull on a T-shirt before coming downstairs.

He waited for Galen to say something, but when the next minute passed in silence, he pulled Galen around to face him. "You're leaving me, aren't you?" he asked.

"I need to get home."

"That's a lie, and you know it."

"Cam, it's time for me to go home." The edges of Galen's mouth curved faintly downward and he pressed his lips together. His eyes looked sad.

"No. You don't need to go home," Cam insisted.

"Cam, I—"

"If this is about last night when I left and went to the club," Cam said, knowing he sounded desperate but not giving a damn, "nothing happened." When Galen didn't immediately respond, Cam continued, "I mean, I wanted it to happen, but I—"

"It doesn't matter." Galen turned back to the tea.

"Doesn't matter? *Doesn't matter?*" Cam didn't even know how to process that.

"I don't care if you cheated on me," Galen explained. "This isn't about that."

"You don't care?" For once, Cam *wanted* someone to care. Again. Like Aiden had cared for him once upon a time. He wanted Galen to know, to understand that he'd chosen to be faithful to Galen. He wanted Galen to tell him he was proud of him. He wanted Galen to know why he'd stopped. Because he cared about Galen. Loved him.

"I told you when we first started sleeping together that I didn't do long-term," Galen said.

"Yes, but—"

"You said you understood that. You said you wanted that too." Galen leaned on the counter, his back still to Cam.

"I said…. Yes, I said that. At the time, I was fine with it too. But now…." Cam took another deep breath. "Last night…. Leaving you here and going to the club…. That was a mistake. I never should have left, and I never should have gone home with someone." Cam put a hand on Galen's shoulder and squeezed gently. How many times had Galen reached out to him that same way? But this time it did nothing. Galen didn't respond, and he still didn't face Cam.

Why won't he look at me?

"It's okay, Cam. Really. I don't care what you did last night."

"But I didn't—"

The doorbell rang. "That's my taxi. I need to go."

"Then let me come with you," Cam said. "We can talk and I can show you that I really have changed. That *you* changed me. That I—"

The doorbell sounded again.

"Fuck!" Cam slammed his hand on the counter, causing the teapot to ring as the counter shook.

Galen turned around and looked at Cam with his beautiful eyes, now filled with tears. "You'll be okay, Cam," he said. "You're strong. You're taking back your life. You don't need me anymore."

"I *do* need—"

Galen pressed a single finger to Cam's lips. "That's what you don't understand. You don't need anyone to be strong. You don't need me."

"I want you, Galen. Maybe you're right. Maybe I don't need you. But I love you."

Galen bit his lip in an obvious effort to maintain his composure. He leaned in and kissed Cam on the cheek before saying in a husky voice, "I need to go."

Cam watched as Galen left the kitchen, picked up his suitcase, and walked out the door. He wanted to scream. He wanted to grab Galen and hold him so he couldn't go. But he didn't do any of those things—partly because Galen was right: he thought he needed Galen. That having Galen by his side to do what he needed to do would make it easier. And partly because he knew at that moment there was nothing he could say or do that would make Galen stay.

"You can take your life back," Galen said as he stepped into the cab. "If that's what you want."

CHAPTER 43

A LITTLE over twenty-four hours later, Cam stood in the doorway to Duncan's study, willing his feet to move. The way his stomach was doing somersaults, he was glad he hadn't drunk anything but water before going to see Duncan. He fought the urge to vomit. He shoved his hands in his pants pockets when he realized they were shaking. He'd thought he was ready, but he wasn't. He'd never be ready for this. *Shit. I can't do this.*

He'd gotten the call Sunday, a few hours after Galen left. The British authorities would likely arrest Duncan the next evening. Cam had known then what he had to do. Now, when he and Duncan were on the same footing. It would have been easier to wait until Duncan was in jail. But he knew it needed to be this way. He didn't want to look back at this in fear. The fear would end today.

Galen's words echoed in his mind. *"You can take your life back, if that's what you want."*

Galen. He'd known Galen would head back to the US. He'd never expected Galen would show up here at all. So why, in his mind's eye, had he always seen Galen by his side when he confronted Duncan?

Because Galen helped you find your confidence. The very confidence Duncan had systematically and brutally torn away from him. Galen's belief in him had given him a new foundation, a new perspective, a chance to be what he always could have been. Galen had helped him grow stronger, and though he wanted Galen with him, for the first time in his life, he knew he didn't *need* Galen or anyone else there. He could do this. He *would* do this. Alone.

"He'll be with you in just a moment, Lord Sherrington," the servant who had let him inside said from behind him.

"Thank you." He offered the woman a pleasant smile and a nod. As he'd often done over the past few weeks, he found himself rubbing one of the charms on the bracelet Galen had given him. Like a talisman, it seemed to give him strength.

Galen knew I had to do this by myself. There might be a future for them, but even if Galen had stayed, Cam would still be standing here alone. In some distant part of his mind, maybe Cam had known that all along.

He imagined himself as the little boy he'd been before... before Duncan, before *everything.* Naïve. Hopeful. Even a little talented.

I should have stopped him, the voice in his head repeated for the thousandth time.

He heard Galen's voice again. *"You were a kid. He took advantage of you. Hurt you. He's sick, Cam."*

Of course Galen was right. He'd been a child. Duncan was a man. An adult. An adult who knew what he did was wrong.

Knowing that didn't make any of this easier, because no matter whose fault it had been—and he really *did* know it hadn't been his fault, in spite of the self-recrimination—this confrontation was something only he could do. And if he didn't confront the monster now, he would never move on.

Cam closed his eyes and rubbed them with thumb and forefinger as he allowed the memories to crash in on him. The fear, the shame, the humiliation, the profound sense of loss for the childhood stolen from him. The anger, the betrayal. The isolation.

Cam remembered when Duncan hadn't wanted him anymore: the year he'd gone away to school. He guessed that his mother's choice of schools hadn't been accidental. Duncan would have counseled her to send him far enough away that he and Duncan wouldn't cross paths often. And sometime between then and the end of school that year, he'd simply repressed the memories. Shut the pain, humiliation, and shame away in a place in his brain where it wouldn't haunt him.

The feelings cascaded faster now, the memories a macabre daisy chain in his mind. Duncan had controlled him. Killed every bit of his self-worth to do it. Duncan had raped him—Cam hated that word, such an ugly word—and each time he'd done it, he'd left less of Cam behind. Less trust. Less of his heart.

Cam gritted his teeth as everything came into stark focus. The parties, the alcohol, the anonymous fucks... everything and anything to dull the pain. One-night stands, failed relationships. And worst of all, he'd lost Aiden, the only man he'd ever loved.

Until Galen.

He'd lived *down* to the reputation he'd earned. He'd played right into Duncan's hands. And now, years later, Duncan was trying to destroy him for good. Lock him away and take the tidbits of Cam's soul he'd left behind. And what for?

All so you could control my company. My *company.* Cam's rage swelled into a red-hot leviathan. He needed the rage. He needed the strength for this.

Cam fought for emotional purchase as he realized Duncan almost certainly didn't know he'd suppressed the memories. Duncan believed Cam had lived with them day in and day out all these years.

Breathe. Relax.

No more. He wouldn't allow Duncan to control him again. He breathed deeply and fought to reclaim every lost and scarred part of himself.

Damn you to hell, Duncan.

"Lord Sherrington? He'll see you now."

Cam opened his eyes and stepped into the study. By the window sat a collection of photographs. He walked over to them slowly, as if by taking his time he might somehow lessen the weight of what he saw. *Silly thought.* Those photographs were his past and present. He picked up a faded color photograph in a silver frame. A photo of him and his dad playing football on the lawn at the castle. A photo of Duncan and his father. He guessed they'd been younger than he was now when it had been taken. A photo of him and Duncan when he'd graduated from Brixton.

"You always did get into trouble." Duncan's voice startled Cam, and he nearly dropped the frame. He set it down and willed his hands to stop trembling. It surprised Cam to realize that it was not fear that caused his hands to shake. They shook from rage.

Cam inhaled deeply, remembering what Galen had taught him as he turned to face the man he'd come to hate. "Uncle." He didn't move to shake Duncan's hand.

"Angry with me?" Duncan's smile appeared forced.

"For not returning my calls?" Cam shook his head. "No." Cam forced himself to meet Duncan's eyes—really *look* at him and see him for what he was. *An old man on a precipice he doesn't even realize he's standing on.*

"I heard the authorities released you," Duncan said after an uncomfortable silence. "I'm pleased to hear it."

"Are you?"

"Well, of course I—"

Cam shook his head. "I can't imagine why you would be, dear Uncle." His body felt hot, his anger ready to erupt.

Duncan scowled at him. "I do not appreciate the interruption, nor do I appreciate the condescension in your tone."

Cam laughed softly, his voice full of sarcasm. "Oh, I'm certain you don't."

"If you insist on speaking to me with such disrespect—"

"Disrespect?" Cam forced himself to close the gap between them so that they stood only a few paces apart. "You know *nothing* about respect."

"Given the foul mood you seem to be in, I think you should leave, Cameron."

A year ago, the look on Duncan's face would have sent Cam storming from the room to cover his terror. *Not this time. No more.* This time he took a step closer, in spite of the old fear roiling in his belly like a snake. "I'm not leaving."

"Then I will leave *you.*"

Cam blocked Duncan's path. "You'll leave when I say what I've come to say. It's time for you to admit your many wrongs."

"I don't appreciate the inference that I'm somehow in the wrong here." Duncan lifted his chin and pressed his lips together as if daring Cam to stay.

"But aren't you in the wrong, dear Uncle?"

Duncan glared at Cam. "Just what the bloody hell are you inferring?

"I know the truth about the Cayman accounts," Cam said. "I imagine by now the FBI knows as well."

Duncan stepped back, his face set in a scowl, his eyes reflecting anger and something Cam guessed was the leading edge of fear. "I have no idea what you're talking about."

"Of course you do," Cam said softly. "You set the accounts up. And if I'm correct, you did it four years ago, when we purchased Raice. For four years, you thought you'd gotten away with it. Then a computer program found the transfers." Cam shook his head. "You set me up four *years* ago, Uncle. You pocketed the money, and you made sure that if any of your scheme came to light, you'd have a scapegoat. I was a perfect chump. The one thing I don't understand is *why.* Why risk your freedom when you already have more money than you can possibly spend?"

"I could ask you the same."

Cam had expected this. "Touché. You never did pull your punches, did you?" Cam stepped closer to Duncan—uncomfortably close, so that Duncan tried to step backward but had to stop when the backs of his legs met one of the chairs. "Fair enough. I deserve that. I had enough money to live comfortably and never work another day in my life. And I spent every penny and then some.

"But that's where the similarities end. I may be everything they say about me. Vain. Self-centered. Willing to fuck anything that moves. But I am not a criminal. I might beg the board for money. I might come crawling to you to ask for it. But I'd never sell my soul for it."

"I don't—"

"You wanted me out of the picture, *dear* Uncle. You saw your chance when I suggested purchasing Raice. You were greedy. And if your little scheme failed, you'd get rid of me and end up with Sherrington Holdings to yourself."

Duncan's derisive laughter felt worse than a slap to the face. Cam faltered, struggling to maintain his calm exterior as he fought the need to beg for Duncan's forgiveness. One second and Cam felt like a child again. Pathetic and weak. Scared too, although now he couldn't figure out what he had ever been afraid of.

"I've always wanted the company, boy," Duncan hissed. "Why do you think your father put me in control of it? Because he knew how you'd turn out. If you'd been in charge, there would *be* no company left now. Now run along, pretty boy. Have your fun. I'll hold down the fort so you have a home to come to when you're done." Duncan waved dismissively, then turned once more to leave.

"Don't you *dare* call me that!" The anger that roiled in Cam's gut exploded, chasing away the fear once again.

Duncan looked at Cam as though he'd lost his mind. "Who do you think the authorities will believe? Me or you? Now, leave. You'll get nowhere with me like this, Cameron."

"I'm not leaving," Cam said with more authority this time. "You're going to listen to me if it's the last thing you do."

Duncan narrowed his eyes, causing him to look every bit of his nearly sixty years.

Cam swallowed hard and slowed his breathing. "I remember when you touched me in the boathouse the first time," he said, finding that once he had started to speak his piece, he couldn't stop. "I remember how I told you to stop, and how you told me I liked it."

"You always were a worthless piece of dirt. Talented in nothing. Wanting everything. Taking. But for me you would have nothing. If you think you can come here and take my company from me—"

"*My* company, you sick bastard." Cam drew so close to Duncan he could hear Duncan's raspy breaths. They were about the same height, but in that moment, Cam felt larger. Stronger. "And if you think this has *anything* to do with the company, you're sorely mistaken, old man."

"Don't you call me—"

"You took advantage of me. You told me I was dirty. But *you* were the dirty cocksucker. You took my fucking childhood from me, you bastard!" He hadn't meant to shout again, but he couldn't contain the anger any longer. No, anger wasn't the right word for it. He felt rage.

"You worthless son of a bitch," Duncan hissed.

"I am not worthless! *You* raped me. And when I said I didn't like it... when I said you were hurting me... you didn't stop! Over and over! You *enjoyed* hurting me!" Cam was yelling now, and damn if the tears didn't stream down his face. Tears of anger, hurt, pain. "I trusted you! Looked up to you! I fucking *loved* you! And you *raped* me! I was nine fucking years old. I didn't know what sex was. I didn't understand what you wanted."

"You wanted it." Duncan's face had turned an ugly shade of red.

"I wanted a father, for God's sake!" Cam yelled and slapped Duncan hard across the cheek.

"You were a little piece of shit then, and a bigger one now," Duncan growled.

Duncan had once been handsome, much like Cam's father, but age had taken its toll. Cam now saw him for exactly what he was: a pathetic old man and a pedophile.

"You don't get it, do you? You can't control me any longer because I don't give a damn what you think anymore, Uncle. And you will never take my companies from me."

He walked past Duncan and out into the foyer, where he found a half-dozen uniformed officers waiting. *Good.* With the evidence Ron had given the FBI, Duncan would probably be spending the rest of his days in a US prison. It might take a while to extradite him, but Cam didn't doubt it would happen.

"What will you do after you confront him?" Galen had asked him. Cam hadn't known the answer to that. He still wasn't sure. But as he walked out the front door and down the steps, past the police cars, and headed onto the wet London street, he knew Galen had been right. He'd taken the first step toward taking his life back.

CHAPTER 44

CAM ARRIVED back in Chelsea in the early evening, having taken the Underground and then walked the rest of the way home. He stopped at the local grocery for a few things for dinner. He didn't want to eat out, and the thought of cooking made him smile. He couldn't remember the last time he'd cooked dinner here. Probably before Aiden had left. He'd never cooked dinner for himself.

While he cooked a lamb chop and sautéed the vegetables he'd cut, he glanced at the small flat-screen TV hanging under one of the cabinets. He considered turning on the news, then thought better of it. He didn't need to see Duncan paraded in front of the press. The thought surprised him. Even a week ago, seeing the media circus with Duncan at the center would have made him smile. Now, as much as he despised Duncan, it gave him no joy to know he'd probably die in prison.

He finished cooking the lamb chop, added a drizzle of balsamic condiment in an artistic zigzag pattern over the top of it, added the vegetables to his plate, then retreated to the dining room. The music he'd chosen reminded him of Galen: Ella Fitzgerald's 1963 album *These are the Blues*.

The table seemed far too big for one person. The entire place did. The lease would be up soon. *Probably time to move on.* Maybe a modern apartment near the Sherrington Holdings Canary Wharf offices? If he was going to take over running the company, that might make sense.

Do you want to run it? Another question he couldn't answer. Everything felt so unfinished. He smiled to remember Galen telling him, *"Life is about unfinished projects. When I die, I want my in-box to be full."* Like with many things Galen said, Cam hadn't understood that right away.

After dinner he turned off the music and sat down at the grand piano in the main sitting room. He'd taken it with him when he'd moved out of the castle, and he'd had it tuned religiously, but he hadn't touched it. Aiden had sometimes used it to practice, although he'd never been much of a pianist.

Cam opened the cover and settled his fingers on the keys. For a minute, maybe two, he did nothing but feel the keys beneath his fingertips. *Nothing to prove.* He'd never be a professional musician, but he didn't need to be. He just wanted to enjoy the pleasure of creating music again. This thought led him to think of Galen, of course, and why he played in the subway after he'd played some of the greatest venues in the world. With this thought, Cam began to play scales and arpeggios from memory. He missed plenty of notes, but he was fine with that. Up and down he moved his fingers over the keys, faster with each pass as his fingers remembered what they'd learned so long ago.

After fifteen minutes he stopped playing and lifted the hinged cover of the piano bench and pulled out a dog-eared book of Beethoven sonatas, then leafed through them. He'd played many of these before he'd given up his lessons. The book fell open to the second movement of the *Pathétique*. His favorite, and one of the best known.

Breathe. Relax.

He played the opening phrases of the piece, slow and measured in the left hand, the sweet, simple melody in the right. By the time he got to the second page, he realized he didn't need the music. He remembered this too. The feel of the music resonating through his body, the satisfaction that *he* had created it. Better than a meditation, the music became his body, and the tense muscles of his neck and shoulders eased with each passing measure. His heart rate slowed, and the tiny part of him that clung to the heat of his confrontation with Duncan let go. Just let go, like a wicked light going out.

An hour later, having played the entire sonata, he pulled his mobile out and tapped one of the presets.

"David, it's Cam."

"Cam. I just heard about Duncan. I'm sorry." David sounded worried.

"Don't be," Cam told him. "I'd expected it."

"I see."

Cam knew he'd need to explain the details, but he wasn't ready to do that over the phone. "Listen, David. I know you're probably busy, but I was hoping I might speak to you at some point. In person."

"I've got the entire evening free," David said. "Alex just left for rehearsals in Barcelona, and I've got nothing planned. Why don't you stop by?"

"BRANDY?" DAVID said as he held the cut crystal carafe over two snifters.

"Thank you."

David smiled and motioned Cam to take a seat on the couch, then handed him a glass and sat facing him. "I'm glad you called me when you were back in New York. Alex and I were worried when we heard you'd disappeared."

"My mother?"

David nodded. "I know things are strained between you, but she genuinely does care what happens to you."

"I know. What's the saying? 'You can choose your friends'?" Cam knew well that David's relationship with his grandfather—the only father he'd ever truly known—hadn't been the best.

"If you don't mind my asking," David said after a slight pause, "do you believe the charges against Duncan are true?"

"Another reason to choose friends over family." Cam forced himself to breathe through the tension in his body. "Seems he thought I'd make a good scapegoat. And I did what everyone expected I would do. I went and got myself into more trouble."

"I truly am sorry, Cam."

Cam wouldn't tell David about the rest of it. Perhaps someday he'd have the courage, but for now.... Cam took a gulp of his cognac to steady his nerves. It was all still too close. Too raw. Too unsettling.

"But there's something on your mind, isn't there?" David raised his glass and took a sip.

"I want—no, I *need* to know more about Galen," Cam blurted. "He went back to the US and I'm about to lose my mind."

"I thought that might be why you called." When Cam opened his lips to protest, David shook his head. "You should never be embarrassed to ask for what you want. Especially in matters of the heart."

David's formal language made Cam smile just a little. "Thank you. I'm not sure where to turn or what to think right now."

David chuckled. "Sorry," he said quickly. "I find it amusing that you'd tell me that when at one time, *I* was the cause of the same sort of turmoil for Alex."

"Really?" This surprised Cam. David and Alex had seemed to fit together perfectly from the first time he'd seen them together.

"Let's just say that I caused Alex a great deal of grief when we first met. Fortunately, he's long forgiven me, even if I still regret it." Pain glittered in David's eyes. "But you didn't come here to ask me about my relationship. How can I help you with Galen?"

"Tell me about him? I know so little. I know it's only my fault, since I never asked him, but I want to understand." Cam hoped he was making sense, because he wasn't sure he even knew *what* he needed to understand. He took a sip of his brandy and leaned back against the pillows. "You said he played with the Chicago Symphony."

"Galen was a prodigy. I'd heard him play in Indianapolis about a year before, and I knew I had to bring him to Chicago. By then he'd played all over the country, although he'd not yet played with any of the larger orchestras. He'd appeared on several late-night talk shows on the West Coast, and he'd made the rounds of some of the jazz circuits.

"The CSO began a series for rising young artists under John Fuchs's tenure. Galen was one of the first young musicians I brought in when I took over from him. He played the Haydn Trumpet Concerto, and I remember being floored by the performance." David's expression made Cam wonder if he could still hear the echoes more than ten years later.

"I met him in the subway," Cam said with a smile as he recalled the first time he'd noticed Galen. "I still don't understand why he played there."

"Being anonymous has its advantages. Fame is a burden to most."

"How do *you* handle it?" Cam asked, genuinely curious now.

David laughed. "Most people don't recognize me when I'm not dressed in tails and waving my hands in front of an orchestra."

"Fair enough." Cam had never thought David seemed uncomfortable with his success. "Then how does Alex handle it?"

"I wish I knew." David smiled. "I'm not sure handling it is the key. There's something in how he's wired. Something in his personality. He's comfortable in his own skin, and he doesn't need anyone to tell him if his performance is adequate. In my experience, the artists who are successful over time are like that."

"Do you know anything about Galen's family?"

"He hasn't told you?" David asked, appearing confused.

"I'm beginning to realize he didn't tell me much of anything." Why was Galen so bloody exasperating? "The first I heard about his solo career was when we came to your party."

"His parents were friends of my parents," David said. "Country club friends. A few years younger than my parents, but they spent a great deal of time together before my parents died."

Cam stared at David. Of course he'd guessed Galen's family had money. The way Galen acted around people with means, the way he'd comfortably mingled at David's party. How he'd said he didn't worry much about money after the school system suspended him. "I had no idea."

"Old family out of Boston. Our fathers played polo together."

"Polo?"

David nodded. "The Arendales raised their own horses for the sport."

"And Galen?"

"He never seemed very comfortable with his family's wealth." David ran a hand through his hair. "I know the feeling well."

Cam frowned in growing recognition. Why had he never noticed that about David, even after knowing him so long? The small voice in his head that had gotten louder over the past few weeks said, *You never took the time to understand.*

David's lips parted and his brow knitted. Then, just as quickly, his expression changed to one of recognition, and the corners of his mouth edged upward. "You're in love with him, aren't you?"

"I know," Cam said with a self-deprecating laugh. "Not the best choice for him." *Or anyone, for that matter.*

"You sell yourself short. You always have. I—" David hesitated for just a moment. "—know the type."

"You're nothing like me. You know what I've do—"

"People change. *You've* changed. Sometimes it takes losing something important to make changes happen."

Aiden. Cam supposed David was right. "I don't want to lose Galen like I lost Aiden. But I'm not sure what to do."

"You know I can't tell you what to do." David smiled openly this time. "But I can tell you that nothing happens by itself."

CHAPTER *45*

New York, New York
Three weeks later

CAM'S FLIGHT from London had arrived late Thursday morning, and there'd been a limo waiting to take him into the city. For once he hadn't pulled out his phone to make the obligatory calls arranging evening plans. Instead he'd just watched the Manhattan skyline from the window.

"Lord Sherrington," Luisa exclaimed as he walked into the apartment. "I was so worried about you." She burst into tears. "When they came... the police.... I...," she said between gasps.

He smiled, then stopped fighting the urge to hug her and just did it. "Hush," he said as he patted her back. "I'm fine. I really am."

He napped while she made him dinner; then he showered and dressed in jeans and a New York Yankees T-shirt he'd picked up at the airport. He couldn't deny he'd bought the shirt because it reminded him of one Galen had worn. Maybe that made him a sap, but he didn't give a damn.

"Join me?" he asked Luisa when he walked into the kitchen to find a single lonely place setting.

"My lord?" She stared at him as though she hadn't heard him correctly.

"For dinner." He offered her a reassuring smile. "I don't want to eat alone."

As often happened when he spoke to her, her cheeks pinked in response. She didn't argue, though, instead setting a second place at the counter. Five minutes later, they sat side by side and ate the wonderful spinach pie she'd baked.

"This is one of my favorites," he said after savoring a bite or two.

Her blush deepened. "I know."

"Thank you," he said. "For welcoming me home."

"Do you think of this as home?" she asked.

He hadn't even realized he'd called it that. If someone had asked him point-blank whether he thought of New York as home, he'd have said no. But this last trip to London, even the house hadn't felt like home.

"Yes," he said. "I suppose I do."

Her smile was radiant. "I'm glad. I'd hoped you'd say that."

THE NEXT morning dawned bright and cool over Manhattan. For the first time in days, Cam didn't sleep in late. He went for a walk in Central Park, then stopped for coffee and a pastry at a small restaurant near his apartment.

As he'd done the day before, he tried calling Galen at home and on his cell. Galen hadn't answered either, and Cam had left a brief message asking Galen to call him back. He doubted Galen would. He spent the rest of the morning working from his computer. The board of directors had agreed to appoint him as interim CEO during Duncan's absence, which looked increasingly as though it would be permanent. The board members, no doubt nervous over the allegations of money laundering against Duncan, were eager for someone to lead the company through the crisis.

"Lunch was wonderful, Luisa," Cam said as she retrieved his empty plate from his desk.

Luisa beamed. "Will you be back for dinner tonight?"

He pressed his lips together and released a soft breath. "I'm afraid I'm headed back to London this evening."

"London? But you just arrived here three days ago."

"I was hoping to stay a bit longer," he said wistfully, "but I have a few things there I need to see to. I plan on returning in a few weeks, though."

"I'm glad to hear that, my lord."

"Call me Cam. Please."

"I.... I don't know if I can do that, my lord," she said.

"I'd like you to, Luisa."

Her cheeks pinked as she nodded.

"Good. I'm glad that's settled." He got up from the table, hesitated a moment, then hugged her. "Thank you," he whispered. "For taking such good care of me."

A moment later, she scurried out of the room. He knew he'd embarrassed her, but he also knew she was pleased. He'd told her the truth: he had work he needed to take care of in London. And in spite of Galen's brush-off—he knew one when he saw one—he intended to return as soon as he could. He might not know what he'd be doing a month or two in the future, but whatever it was, he knew he'd be spending more time in New York.

He glanced at his watch. Noon. *Plenty of time.* He took a cab, though, just to be safe. He handed the driver a twenty, then opened the door and looked up to see the familiar neon sign: *Buy. Sell. Pawn.* The sign flashed, an echo of the brightness he remembered.

The empty store seemed smaller than before. The same bald man who'd given him next to nothing for the silver pen stood behind the counter. "May I help you, sir?" he asked.

Cam repressed a smile to realize the man didn't recognize him. Whether because he had many people come through the store or because down-on-his-luck, disheveled Cam had been unremarkable, he wasn't sure. It didn't matter. He hadn't come here to prove anything.

"I pawned a pen," he told the man, whose eyes widened in obvious recognition when he heard Cam speak. The accent, no doubt. "I'd like to buy it back."

"I…. Of course," the clerk said. He scurried off, then returned a few minutes later with a small box, which he handed to Cam.

Cam opened the top and took the pen out. The silver warmed to his touch, and he knew this pen would never sit in the display case along with the others. He would use this pen. And each time he used it, he'd remember David and Alex and the true friendship they'd offered him.

"Two hundred," the clerk said.

Cam smiled and pulled out his wallet and handed the man two hundred-dollar bills. The clerk pulled out what looked like a felt-tipped pen and touched it to each of the bills. A month before, Cam might have enjoyed commenting about the authenticity of the bills, but instead he took the pen from the box and slipped it into his jacket without a word. When he stepped out of the shop and into the street, he pressed his hand to his heart and felt the pen there.

He remembered Galen's words: *"Sometimes it just takes time to see the right path."* He smiled.

Outside, the snow had finally begun to stick to the sidewalk. The city was beautiful like this. He'd just never noticed.

BY THE time Cam headed down the steps to the 42nd Street station an hour later, it was a little after two o'clock. The snow now fell faster, clinging to his hair and jacket. Just a month before, he'd have run for cover. Today he looked up and opened his mouth to capture a bit on his tongue. And he laughed when he did.

He heard the music before he'd made it down the steps. Galen, in his usual spot, facing away from him. Cam paused and leaned against the concrete wall.

Watching. Listening. A few girls exited the turnstiles, giggling, oblivious to the music. A mother coaxed her young son underneath the turnstile as he cried that he wanted to ride the train again. An old woman pulled a metal basket on wheels through the handicapped exit, then paused to listen. He watched as she closed her eyes and listened to Galen play "Summertime," from *Porgy and Bess*. When the music finished, she fished around in her purse and pulled a dollar out, then set it carefully in the trumpet case. She smiled, and Cam knew Galen had smiled at her in thanks even though he couldn't see Galen's face. She was gone a moment later.

"In the subway, I can love the music without all the bullshit," he could hear Galen say. He hadn't understood it then. He wasn't sure he understood it now. But he was trying to understand.

He walked past the ticket booth and into Galen's line of sight. His heart beat faster when Galen's eyes grew wide. If he hadn't had the mouthpiece pressed to his lips, he'd have been smiling, judging by the way the lines around his eyes deepened and his cheeks moved upward.

Galen finished the piece he'd been playing—"Blue Moon"—but he didn't speak. Instead, he took a slow breath and began to play again. It took Cam a minute to realize what piece he played: the Rachmaninoff *Vocalise*. Cam swallowed hard and forced a smile. One of the first pieces Galen had ever played for him.

The music ended and Galen let the trumpet come to rest at his side in his right hand. *Concert's over.* A train pulled into the station, causing the floor to vibrate. Why did Cam barely hear it? *"Silence is a conversation too,"* Galen had once said. He'd been right, only this time the silence made Cam ache.

"I've done a shitty job at asking for what I want," Cam said when he couldn't stand it anymore. "Everything I've gotten has come to me, good and bad. I never looked for any of it." He pressed his lips together for a moment. "You taught me that if I wanted my life to be different, I had to go after what I wanted."

"Cam, I—"

"Don't say it. Because it's bullshit." Cam shifted his weight and shoved his hands into his pockets. "You taught me well. The problem is that I'm too good a student. I learned about more than just me. I learned about you too."

The sound of brakes screeching from one of the platforms made Cam wince. This time he heard every bit of it. He waited until it left. No—he waited until the silence returned. It was different somehow. He'd needed a moment to think. Galen had taught him that too: sometimes you need to take a minute and process what life throws at you.

"You lied when you said it didn't matter if I slept with Bill." Cam inhaled slowly and his shoulders relaxed. "I *wanted* you to care, Galen. I figured if I fucked him, I wouldn't have to make the decision about letting you go. You'd make it for me, like every other person I've cared about. So I went back to his place.

"But I realized that fucking him was my choice. I didn't have to. Even though you said you didn't want a long-term relationship, I had a choice. I could sleep with him and give you the excuse you needed. I could go on telling myself I was a worthless, damaged piece of shit who nobody wanted. Or I could turn around and choose you. Convince you that you want to be with me." Cam smiled and glanced down at the trumpet case, then back up at Galen to meet his gaze.

"You're a good teacher," he continued, "but you've got one little secret you don't tell your students. You're scared. You're afraid of hurting again because you're scared you won't survive it this time. I know what that feels like."

Galen's lips parted, but he said nothing. Cam knew he was right about this. He knew that fear. He'd tried to kill himself twice, even though he'd pretended the first time had been something else. He'd been desperate to end the pain. But he'd survived it. He knew he could survive it again—even if it was the pain of Galen's rejection. For everything he understood, Galen had never taken a chance. He'd lived his life helping others but never really putting himself out there to be hurt. Admitting that he cared about someone—that he *loved* them—meant risking pain again.

The silence stretched, punctuated by another train arriving and the sound of passengers coming through the turnstiles.

"I care about you, Cam," Galen said after the silence returned.

"I know." Cam pulled a hand out of his pocket, palming the leather bracelet he'd been fingering the past few minutes. The silver charms warmed to his touch.

Hope. Healing. Love.

"You've given me each of these," he said as he set the bracelet in the trumpet case alongside the coins and bills. "I want to give them back to you." He backed away, took a few steps, then stopped and turned around. Saying it wouldn't make Galen's rejection hurt more. He knew that now. He'd hurt a long time, but he'd survive.

He took a moment to let his emotions wash over him like a wave buffeting a stone on the sand. Galen had taught him how to appreciate his feelings without being ruled by them. The knowledge that he'd learned this empowered him. Gave him strength to say what he knew he had to say. "I love you, Galen. But it's *your* turn to answer the question you asked me weeks ago: Where do you need to be?"

He saw surprise flash bright in Galen's eyes, in spite of Galen's silence. "When you're ready, Galen, I'll be waiting." He turned and walked toward the tunnels and the Lexington Avenue trains.

The sound of screeching brakes echoed off the concrete walls. The scent of dust and people and worse mingled with the cold air from outside. Cam smiled. He loved the subway.

CHAPTER 46

GALEN DIDN'T care that several people were waiting for him to start playing again, and had seen all of what had just transpired. Still holding his trumpet, he bent down and retrieved the bracelet from the case. He fingered the charms. *Hope. Healing. Love.*

He swallowed hard as he realized why Cam had given the bracelet back to him: Cam didn't need it anymore. Didn't need the shoulder. Didn't need the sympathy. Didn't need a reason to wake up in the morning except that he wanted to wake up.

He hesitated just a moment, then shouted, "I'll be back!" as he sprinted toward the tunnel where Cam had disappeared. He held his trumpet in one hand, the bracelet in the other.

He got to the top of the first steps, ignored the burn of his lungs from the exertion, then looked around, desperate to find Cam. He finally spotted him headed toward the longer tunnel leading to the Lexington Avenue platforms. Galen ran, darting around the pedestrians, nearly colliding with several before reaching the stairs.

Uptown or Downtown? Uptown. Cam lived Uptown, near Central Park, didn't he? Galen kicked himself for never having asked. He took the steps to the platform two at a time and arrived just in time to see a train pull away from the station.

Fuck! His own stubborn, stupid fault! He struggled to catch his breath, then turned to head back upstairs when he noticed someone seated on the bench at the end of the platform. Cam.

"Cam!" he shouted over the sound of a downtown train. "Cam!"

Cam turned the second time Galen called his name. His lips parted and he looked momentarily confused, his eyes widening as he saw Galen running toward him.

"I... I'm... I'm sorry...." Galen gasped as he leaned over and tried to catch his breath. He'd forgotten he was still carrying the trumpet in his left hand. The metal charms on the leather bracelet pressed into his skin. A reminder of what he needed to say.

"What?"

"I'm sorry." Beads of sweat ran down Galen's spine. He pushed away the hair that had fallen into his eyes.

"You have nothing to be sorry for." Cam pressed his lips together the way he did when he was trying to hide his emotions.

"Yes. I do. And I need to explain."

"Explain? Explain what?" Cam frowned and eyed him warily.

"Oh, fuck," Galen growled under his breath. "I'm screwing this all up." He glanced down at his feet, back at Cam, shifted his weight a few times, then shook his head. "This whole thing got away from me," Galen began after another pause. When Cam met his gaze with obvious confusion, Galen repeated, "I'm screwing this all up."

Cam grinned. "Deep breath. Focus. Have a seat?" Cam combed his fingers through his hair. His beautiful, soft, curly hair. Different from the controlled way he'd worn it before.

Galen smiled and nodded, taking a seat next to Cam on the bench. "It was a cop-out for me to blame you for not asking about me," he said. "And I lied. I wouldn't have told you if you'd asked. I didn't want anyone to know. *I* didn't want to remember some of it."

"Fair enough."

Galen drew a long breath, then haltingly told Cam about his last days as a professional musician. About the times he'd wanted to hide in his dressing room, and the way the panic began to eat away at the joy of performing.

"Music was everything to me." Galen clenched his jaw, then released the tension there. "But somewhere along the way, it all got to me. Performing. The pressure to be perfect." He laughed bitterly and shook his head. "I did that part to myself. I know that now." He paused and met Cam's eyes, finding the courage to continue in the sympathetic, loving look he found there.

"I lost my love of music. I knew I was letting everyone down. I was convinced of it. So I decided if I just went away... if I ended it...."

Cam put his hand on Galen's thigh. Galen fought the urge to close his eyes. Every night since he'd left London, he'd dreamed of Cam holding him. He'd missed Cam more than he thought he would. How had he thought he could just go back to his old life after Cam?

"My parents were there for me. They'd always supported me. I knew people gossiped about me. Bad enough that I'd always been a bit of a joke, but now I was committed to a psychiatric facility. I felt guilty. I wanted to get the hell out of there, because I knew how hard it must be for them." Galen watched a train pull out of the station, speeding up until he couldn't focus on the windows of the cars anymore.

"I pretended I was fine." He laughed softly and shook his head. "And I convinced the doctors I was ready to go home. I think I even convinced myself. But really, I was still a mess."

Cam squeezed Galen's thigh reassuringly. "You told me you took me home because you wanted to pay forward something someone else did for you years ago."

"It's true. Well, mostly." Galen pushed his hair from his eyes again. *Breathe. Focus. Relax.* "There was someone... but it was a long time ago. His name was Brian. He was older. Late twenties. I met him through a program when I was at the hospital. A mentor sort of thing. Once I could go on supervised visits outside—after they figured I'd had enough of trying to hurt myself—he took me. We had so much fun going to the movies, hanging out at the mall.... It didn't really matter, because everything we did together was so much better than being at the hospital.

"And one day I did something stupid." *Breathe. Focus. Relax.* He could do this. He *had* to do this. "I kissed him. And he kissed me back. I think he liked it too. But after that, he stopped coming. I didn't understand then, but I know now he couldn't come anymore, that we'd crossed a line and that I'd lost him. I thought I loved him, and when he disappeared....

"A few years later, I looked him up," Galen continued. "But he was in a relationship. He was very kind about it all, but he told me that I'd fixated on him because he'd been the one to show me how to live again." Galen leaned back in his seat and slipped one leg underneath him, as he'd done so many times before when they'd sat like this, just talking. "I told him he was wrong. That I still loved him and that I needed him. But he sent me on my way. He was kind but firm."

Galen took another steadying breath. He'd never spoken about this to anyone before. Even now, years later, it frightened him to face the truth of how close he'd come to throwing his life away. "That night I tried to kill myself again. I took some pills. No one ever knew. I went to sleep thinking that was it. I *knew* that was it. And I remember thinking that I wasn't sure I really wanted to die. I was scared. Alone...." Galen blinked back the tears that threatened. "You were right," he said in an undertone. "I'm scared. Terrified, really."

"Somehow that doesn't make me feel any better."

Galen laughed and met Cam's gaze. "You were right about a lot of things."

"I was?" Cam put his arm around Galen.

"I've gotten good at lying. Mostly to myself." *Breathe. Focus. Relax.* Why had it become so difficult for him to hold things together? He'd been doing fine for so long.

No. You haven't been doing anything. You've been hiding. "I lie to myself every day I avoid feeling things, you know, the kinds of things that led me to lose it back then. I thought if I kept everything in its place, the feeling like I'm drowning would go away. And it did. I could breathe again when I stayed in control. It was the same with the emotions. I thought if I could control them, I'd be all right. But that was a lie." Galen met Cam's gaze again and forced himself to look into Cam's eyes. "I lied to you, Cam."

"Oh." Cam looked as though he were steeling himself.

"I told you I didn't love you."

"I see."

"Fuck, I've done it again, haven't I?" Galen said. "Screwed things up with you." Galen hoped Cam couldn't see that his hands trembled.

"You haven't screwed things up," Cam said. "And I'm glad to hear that. It makes me happy. But I still don't see where this leaves us."

Galen found this part the most frightening of all. He knew what he wanted to say, but gathering his courage to speak the words, he felt as though he was about to jump off a cliff attached only to a bungee cord. "It leaves me asking whether, knowing all about me, knowing that I'm a total mess of a person, you want to be with me."

Cam answered by kissing Galen. Cam's kiss wasn't tentative, and it didn't judge. Galen wrapped his arms around Cam, trumpet and all.

"Oh," Galen said after he'd caught his breath. "I forgot. I want you to keep this." He opened his hand and showed Cam the bracelet he'd been holding. "I know why you gave it back. I know you don't need the reminder anymore. But I'd like you to keep it. For me."

"For you?"

"Yeah." Galen nodded. "Because I'm going to need all of these things. And I'm hoping you'll be able to give them to me."

Cam's face lit in a big smile as he took the bracelet and fastened it around his left wrist. "I'll do my best." He leaned in and kissed Galen again. "But there's something I don't understand."

"Yes?"

"What changed your mind about us?"

"The bracelet," Galen said. "It reminded me of why I've done everything I've done in my life. Why I started to practice yoga. Why I decided to play in the subway. Why I decided to teach. All of it.

"I did all those things to become stronger. But somewhere along the line, I started to use them as crutches. Something to protect me and my heart. Like a good luck charm someone wears around their neck to ward off evil. I used them to push away things that might hurt me, and I forgot that I'd gotten stronger."

"I might hurt you," Cam said, his expression serious.

"Yes. That's true. But I'm strong enough to handle it."

"Hope, healing, and love?" Cam sighed as he rubbed the charms.

"Something like that."

CHAPTER 47

Surrey, England
Eight months later

CAM ARRIVED at the castle in late afternoon, exhausted. He hadn't slept on the plane—he'd had too much work to take care of ahead of Monday's board meeting.

In late May the gardens leading up to the main house were in full bloom, and the trees and grass were a deep green. The air here smelled good, crisp and fresh, with none of the metallic overtones of the city. Still, he missed New York already. Missed the walks through Central Park at sunset and the familiar noise of cars and people.

Buck up. You're only here a week.

He'd given up the house in London a few months before. Too many memories. Some good ones, but the past was just that: past. The castle would do for visits to England. The castle wasn't his home anymore—New York City was—but he'd made his uneasy peace with it. He'd applied for a green card and only flew back to England when he needed to for his work. Soon, he hoped, he'd find a replacement for Duncan at Sherrington Holdings, and he'd be able to focus completely on his plans for Raice.

Roger, the Sherringtons' longtime butler, took his bag from the taxi. "Thank you," Cam said as he ran a hand through his hair. "I'm sorry to come on such short notice."

"Hardly a problem, my lord," he said with a smile. "We're pleased to have you back. Shall I have Cook make you some lunch?"

"Soup and a sandwich would be wonderful, thank you. I'll take lunch in my office."

"Of course, my lord." Roger nodded and headed up the large staircase as Cam carried his laptop to his office at the back of the building.

"Lord Sherrington!"

Cam turned to see Luisa running toward him, cheeks flushed. He smiled and embraced her. "We've missed you."

"I'll be home in a week," she said. "This was your idea, remember?"

"And it seems you're doing a wonderful job of working with the staff. Roger actually smiled at me this morning."

"Far be it from me to speak ill of someone," Luisa said, "but you were right when you said your mother hadn't exactly been kind to them."

"If it were up to me," he told her, "I'd have you coordinate the staff. But I doubt Roger would appreciate that."

"It's better this way," she agreed. "When I first got here, I thought I'd gotten a case of frostbite, as happy as he was to see me." She laughed, then added, "But when he realized I was only here to coordinate the corporate retreat you've planned for summer, he warmed up a bit."

"Good. But don't get any ideas of staying here longer. We can't manage things at home without you." He saw the pleasure in her eyes at hearing this.

He'd sent Luisa to facilitate the retreat with staff from Raice and Sherrington Holdings, but he'd also hoped she'd put the castle's staff at ease with the transition between his mother's oversight and his own. Not that his mother had been thrilled, but she'd get used to him taking charge.

"Carlos and Claudio are so excited about spending the summer here." She blushed, then added, "You really shouldn't have arranged for the riding lessons. It's too much."

"It's the least I can do since their mother will be working here. While you're making sure the corporate retreat goes off without a hitch, they'll be bored out of their minds if we don't give them something to do."

"But paying someone to take care of them for me. That's far too generous—"

"We've had this discussion before, Luisa," he told her gently. "I don't want you running yourself ragged or worrying about them getting into trouble. Vivian will make sure they get to explore London when you can't be with them."

She blinked back tears, then leaned in and gave him a peck on the cheek. His turn to blush. He knew she struggled to juggle her work and her children in the summertime. "I'd better be getting back to work, then. Will we see you for dinner tonight?"

"You will. I hear you and Cook have been trading recipes. Leek soup, perhaps?"

"Of course. She's been so excited to have you try her version of it," Luisa said.

"I'm sure it will be wonderful. But it will never be as good as yours."

"Thank you." Her cheeks reddened again; then she waved as she trotted off toward the kitchen.

A few minutes later, settled behind his desk, Cam opened his e-mail and started to make his way through the messages. With the exception of a few, most of the e-mails from board members were supportive of his leadership. The few holdouts were Duncan's old friends, who, no doubt, had decided to weather the storm and see where their fortunes deposited them after the deluge. Not that things looked very bright for Duncan, who'd been formally charged and remained in custody pending extradition. The board had fired Duncan, of course, then reluctantly asked Cam to take over for him. They'd recently asked Cam to stay on and run the company on a permanent basis. Flattering, but not an option. It was time to move on. Time for Cam to take a chance on something *he* wanted. Some of the green energy projects at Raice looked promising too, and for the first time, Cam felt excitement at the prospect of long hours of work.

Cam still wasn't sure he'd press charges for the years of abuse. He needed more time to think things through and make his peace with it. He wouldn't see Duncan prosecuted to exact vengeance, only to see justice satisfied.

By the time he looked up from the computer, the first reds and oranges of sunset had begun to streak the darkening sky. He leaned back in his chair and watched the colors change, reminded of the evenings he'd spent with Galen watching the leaves dance on the grass and listening to Galen play piano.

He smiled at the memory, then shut the laptop and made his way down the hallway to the end of the east wing of the house and the music room. He flipped on the lights and looked around. As with everything else in the castle, the room appeared spotless, the only sign of disuse the lack of the freshly cut flowers his mother preferred. His mother never played, although she used to tell her friends she was a fair pianist in her youth. Still, she'd complained when he'd moved the piano to his house.

He sat down on the piano bench and ran his fingers over the wood. How many days had he spent here as a child, imagining his father playing this very same piano? He'd only heard his father play a few times here, but he could still imagine him, fingers flying over the keys, the brooding chords of a Tchaikovsky sonata echoing off the walls.

Cam walked over to the cabinet at the far end of the room, which was filled with sheet music. He remembered how he'd taken it all out and laid it across the Persian rug, imagining he might someday play all of the pieces he'd discovered. Some of the scores were crumbling, ancient books from his great-grandfather's time; others were newer pieces his father had played. Cam had added his own music to the collection, and from that stack he pulled a book of Bach dance suites and set it on the piano stand.

As a child, Cam hadn't enjoyed the Bach much, but his teacher had insisted he play it. He played, not really concentrating at first. He remembered the pieces, but he'd had no emotional connection to them. He began to play the next dance, a lovely bourrée. This time he allowed his mind to take his fingers as he had done playing the more familiar Beethoven a week before. He imagined Galen playing the piece, imagined his quiet concentration and the way his face appeared so peaceful. One with the music, as though the light of his musical heart shone through each phrase.

He ended the piece and closed his eyes. He'd been practicing at the house, and he was getting better.

"Beautiful. You must have an excellent teacher."

Cam spun around on the bench to see a very rumpled Galen standing in the doorway. He got up and took Galen in his arms. "How did you—?"

"Thank Jamie. He insisted on spending his summer helping out at the music school settlement. I told him he should relax a little before he starts at Juilliard, but he wouldn't listen. Said he owed it to you since you're paying for his apartment." Galen leaned in and kissed him. Cam wondered if he'd ever get tired of kissing Galen. Probably not. Something in how Galen communicated everything in a kiss—love, sex, need—made Cam wonder how he'd ever lived without those kisses.

"He's teaching the introduction to music theory class I was supposed to be teaching today." Galen grinned and shook his head. "Gave me a lecture about how I should delegate and spend more time with you. So I brought Max over to his place and hopped a late flight from JFK."

"Smart boy. If he doesn't end up as a concert pianist," Cam said, only half jokingly, "I'll hire him myself." The way David Somers had spoken of Jamie's playing, Cam guessed it was just a matter of time before they were sitting in the audience, hearing him perform with an orchestra. The least Cam could do was make sure Jamie had a safe place to live and didn't have to worry about juggling a full-time job while he went to school.

"Not if I have anything to say about it. He's single-handedly raised $20,000 for the music settlement since we opened. $20,000 in four months, can you believe it? He's been hitting up some of the patrons David introduced him to for donations. My parents said they'd match whatever he raised, and I think he's enjoying making my father sweat. Not that he can't afford it."

"You're enjoying the change of scenery, aren't you?" Cam knew how difficult the past eight months had been for Galen and how difficult it had been for him to decide not to appeal his dismissal from the high school. The Bronx Music School Settlement's board had fallen all over themselves to hire Galen as the school's director.

"I guess I never considered what I could do outside of teaching. You were right." He leaned in and brushed Cam's lips with his own. "About a lot of things."

"So you'll admit you aren't perfect?"

"Let's just say I think you are"—he winked at Cam, who blew him a kiss in return—"and leave it at that."

"So, my perfect partner," Cam said as he took Galen's hand in his own, "I was thinking we might spend an hour or two practicing our yoga technique."

"Yoga?" Galen laughed. "I thought you were about to shoot me last week when I showed you the tree pose."

"I never said I had very good balance, just that I'm naturally flexible." Cam repressed a smirk. "But I had a thought about yoga."

"Oh you did, did you?" Galen's eyes sparkled with mischief.

"Naked yoga," Cam deadpanned.

"Naked...?"

"Downward dog and all that? I could watch. And maybe—"

Galen pulled Cam toward him and claimed his lips with a happy sigh. "Only if you join me, my lord."

Cam smirked and pretended to consider this. "All right," he said after a moment. "I'll join you."

"God, I love your little toff arse," Galen said in a fair approximation of an English accent. He slipped a hand down Cam's pants and squeezed a bare cheek.

"I'll forgive you that." He leaned into Galen. "Uncouth Yank that you are."

"I'm a quick study." Galen began to nibble a line up Cam's neck.

Cam closed his eyes and shivered. "Yes," he whispered. "That you are."

SHIRA ANTHONY was a professional opera singer in her last incarnation, performing roles in such operas as *Tosca*, *Pagliacci*, and *La Traviata*, among others. She's given up TV for evenings spent with her laptop, and she never goes anywhere without a pile of unread M/M romance on her Kindle.

Shira is married with two children and two insane dogs, and when she's not writing, she is usually in a courtroom trying to make the world safer for children. When she's not working, she can be found aboard a 35' catamaran at the Carolina coast with her favorite sexy captain at the wheel.

Shira's Blue Notes Series of classical music themed gay romances was named one of Scattered Thoughts and Rogue Word's "Best Series of 2012," and *The Melody Thief* was named one of the "Best Novels in a Series of 2012." *The Melody Thief* also received an honorable mention, "One Perfect Score" at the 2012 Rainbow Awards.

Shira can be found on:

Facebook: https://www.facebook.com/shira.anthony

Goodreads: http://www.goodreads.com/author/show/4641776.Shira_Anthony

Twitter: @WriterShira

Website: http://www.shiraanthony.com

BLUE
NOTES

SHIRA ANTHONY

A BLUE
NOTES
NOVEL

http://www.dreamspinnerpress.com

THE MELODY THIEF

SHIRA ANTHONY

A BLUE NOTES NOVEL

http://www.dreamspinnerpress.com

ARIA

SHIRA ANTHONY

A BLUE NOTES NOVEL

http://www.dreamspinnerpress.com

PRELUDE

SHIRA ANTHONY
VENONA KEYES

A BLUE NOTES NOVEL

ENCORE

SHIRA ANTHONY

A BLUE NOTES NOVEL

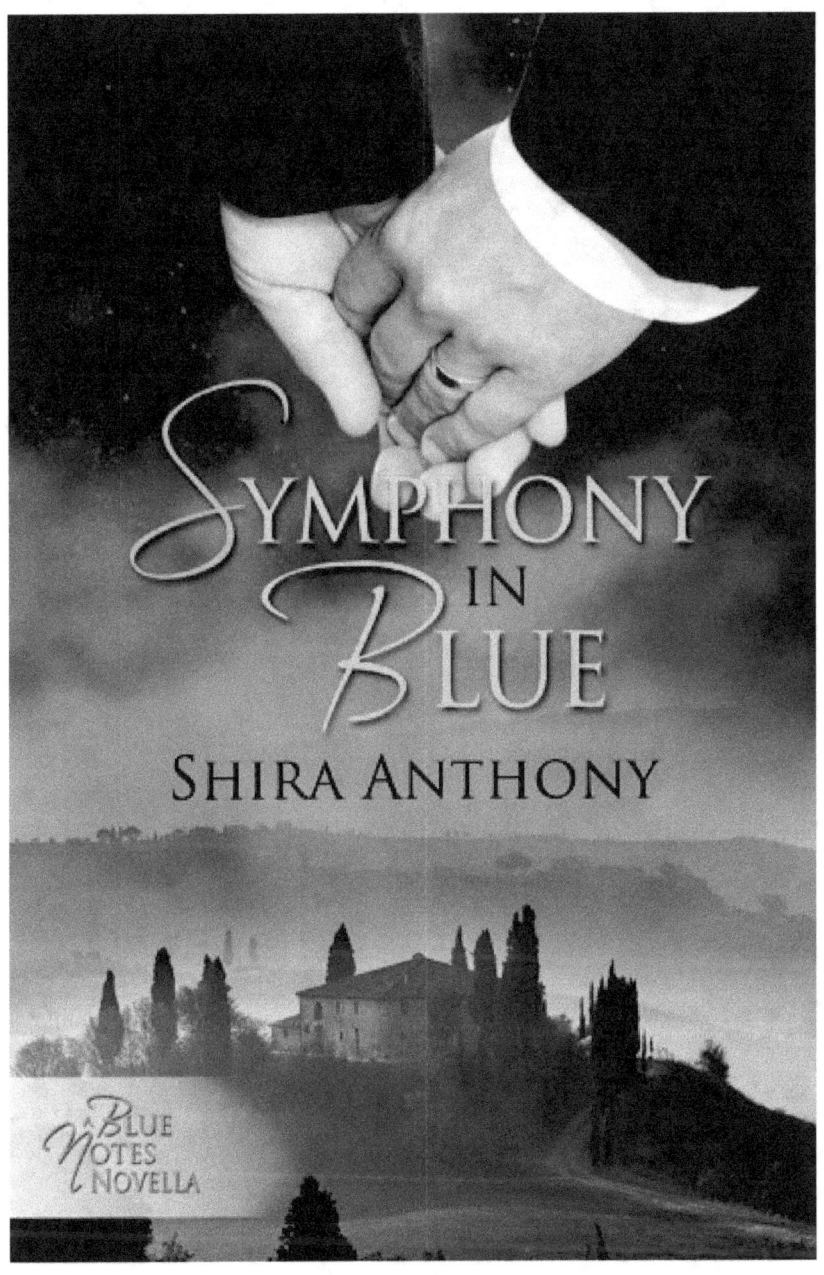

SYMPHONY
IN
BLUE

SHIRA ANTHONY

A BLUE
NOTES
NOVELLA

http://www.dreamspinnerpress.com

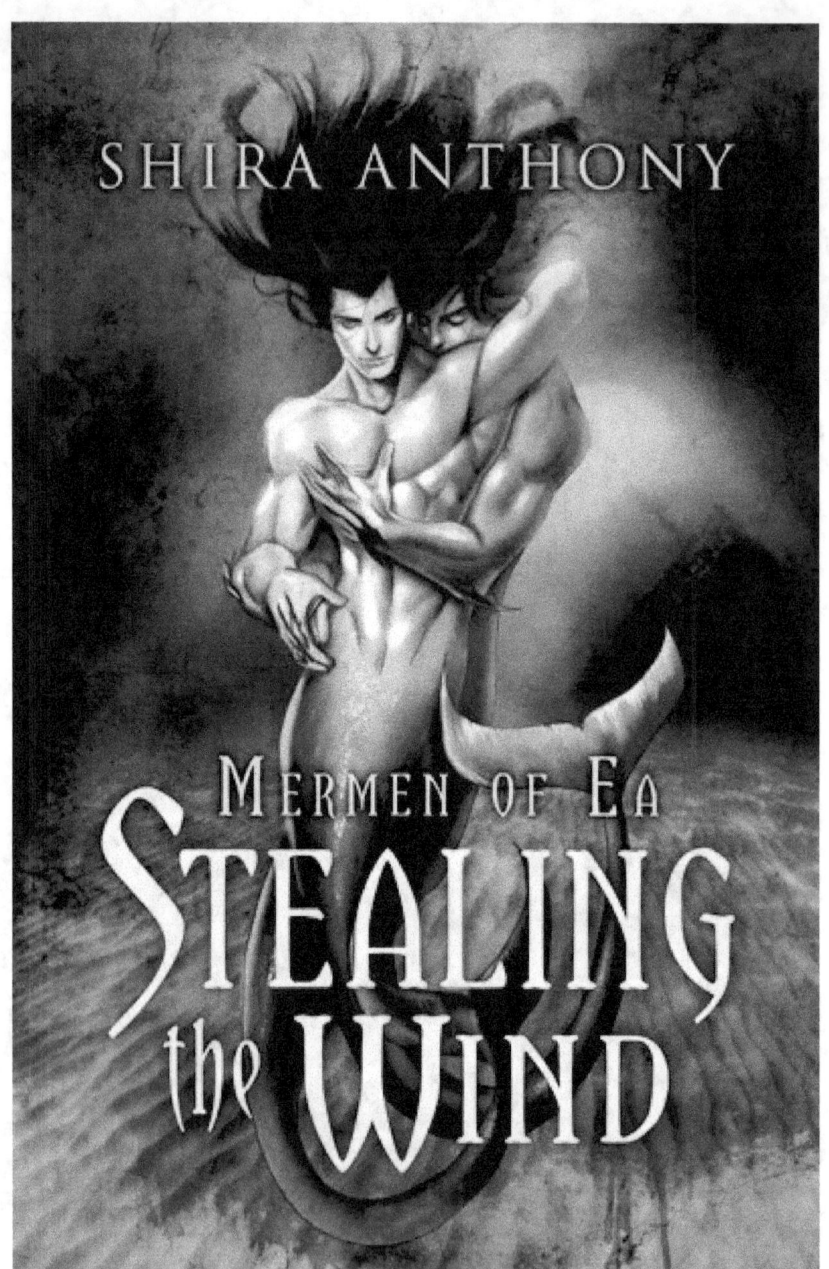

SHIRA ANTHONY

MERMEN OF EA
STEALING
the WIND

http://www.dreamspinnerpress.com

SHIRA ANTHONY

MERMEN OF EA

INTO the
WIND

http://www.dreamspinnerpress.com

the trust

Shira Anthony
Venona Keyes

http://www.dreamspinnerpress.com

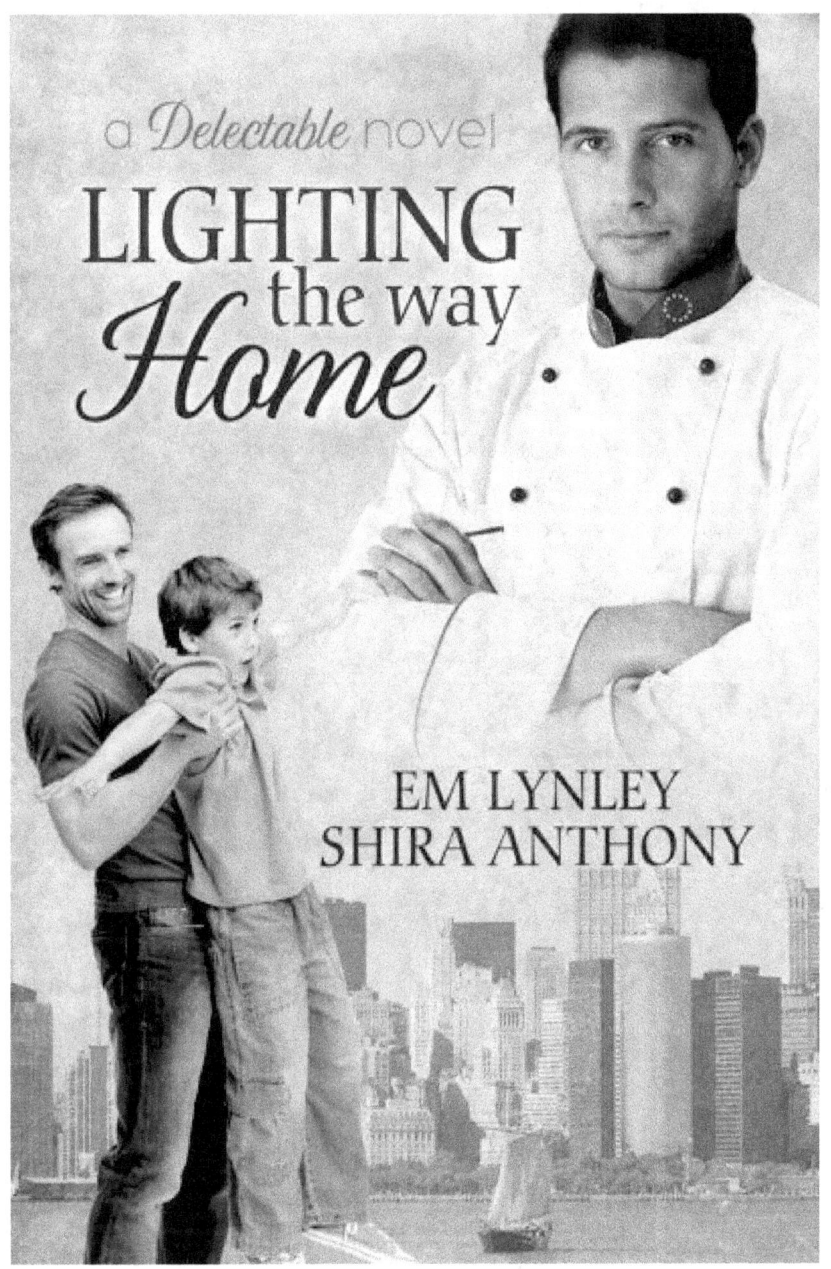

a *Delectable* novel

LIGHTING
the way
Home

EM LYNLEY
SHIRA ANTHONY

http://www.dreamspinnerpress.com

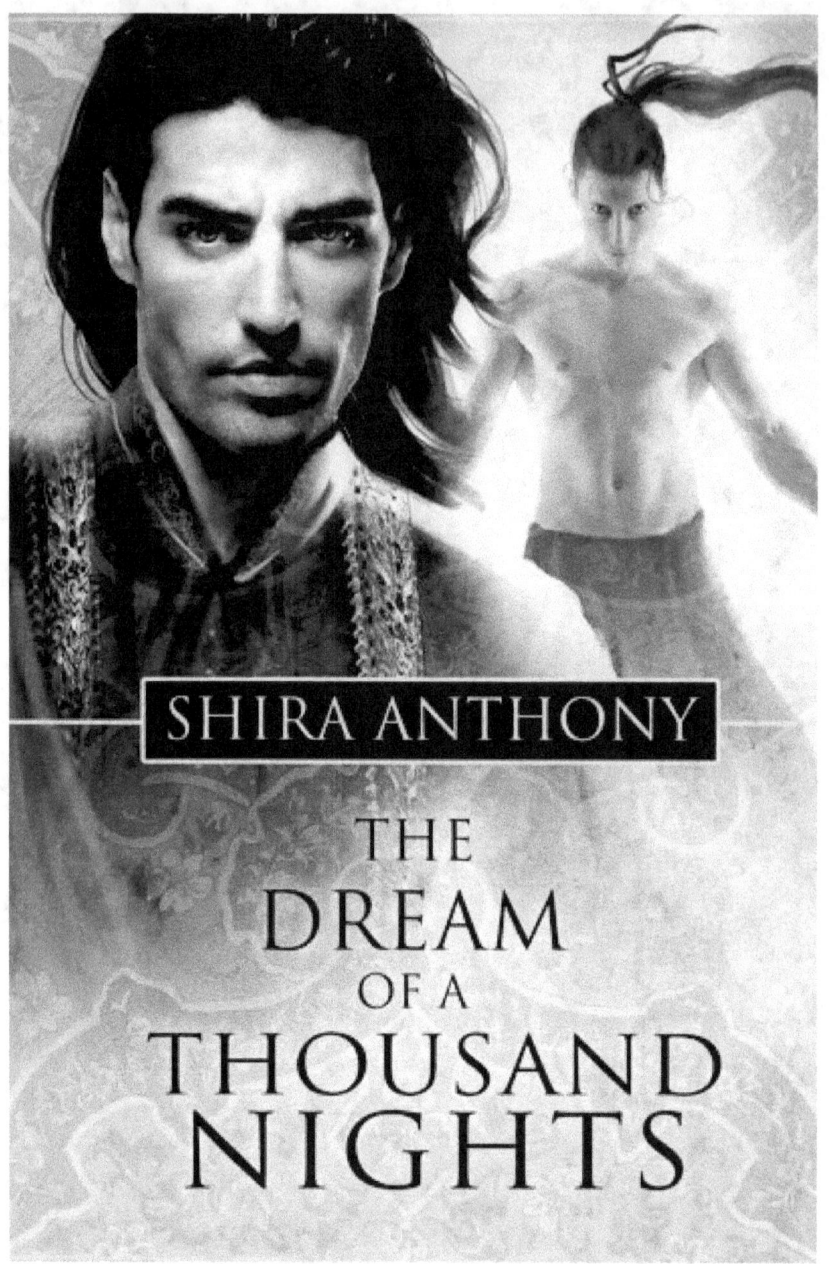

SHIRA ANTHONY

THE
DREAM
OF A
THOUSAND
NIGHTS

http://www.dreamspinnerpress.com

The Art of Breathing
of
Breathing

TJ Klune

http://www.dreamspinnerpress.com

The
ONLY GUY

SKYLAR M. CATES

http://www.dreamspinnerpress.com

On
ARCHIMEDES
STREET

Jefferson Parrish

http://www.dreamspinnerpress.com

www.ingramcontent.com/pod-product-compliance
Lightning Source LLC
Chambersburg PA
CBHW070100260626
47160CB00004B/1269

* 9 7 8 1 6 3 2 1 6 1 8 1 9 *

Also by Eva McCall

Edge of Heaven

Children of the Mountain

Lucy's Recipes for Mountain Living

Murder on Haint Branch

Button
Box

Eva McCall

Moonshine Press • Franklin, North Carolina

Published by:
Moonshine Press
522 Allison-Watts Rd.
Franklin, NC 28734

International Standard Book Number : 978-0-9889431-5-5

Thanks to all my friends that helped with the editing. Thanks to Barbara McRae for the formatting template. Thanks to Tyler Cook for formatting and being my PR/Promotional manager. And a special thanks to my friend, Henry Fichner, for the cover.

*In memory of my Aunt Hattie Southard,
who always wanted to write a book called
Button Box*

❧ 1 ❧

New Orleans: New Years Eve, 1858

"Hey, come back here you little thief. Thief! Stop that urchin!" The bakery owner's shrill voice split the chilly evening air.

Abigail elbowed her way through the crowded New Orleans street. She ducked behind a woman wearing a full skirt then dove around a fat man's trouser legs to escape. The bread she'd snatched warmed her hands, but the sweet smell caused her insides to gnaw.

No one's going to take this loaf away!

She tucked it under her arm, then pulled a thin shawl tighter over her shabby cotton dress, and wished for some of the warmth that radiated from the gas street lamps. It was New Year's Eve and as cold a night as it had been this winter. Hopefully, 1859 would bring her better luck. She'd find a quiet spot to enjoy every crumb, even though it was smashed flat as the noodles her mama used to make back in Georgia. She aimed on celebrating the new year with a full belly.

She found an alleyway and crawled through a maze of rubbish as she held her nose to block out the rank odor. Finally, she crouched behind a pile of boxes and bit into a chunk of the ill-gotten bread. The taste had barely reached her tongue when a hand gripped her shoulder. Fear formed a tight ball in her throat. She stuffed in another bite, determined to die on a full stomach. She glanced about. There wasn't anyone to help, only drunks staggering about. Slowly, she turned and looked up at her assailant.

To her surprise it wasn't a back alley drunk but a nice looking gentleman. Maybe he was some kind of lawman—one the bakery owner had sent to look for her. No, if he were a policeman he'd be wearing one of those crescent badges. And for sure, he wasn't a merchant. He was too refined. He wouldn't be taking her food. She took a deep breath and let it seep out. At least she wouldn't be going to jail.

The stranger eased his grasp. "What's your name?"

The girl swallowed so fast she nearly choked, then stood, drew herself up to her full four feet, ten inches, and pushed back dark, matted curls. "Abigail Sloan, sir."

"Why are you out here alone this time of evening? Don't you have a home?"

"I've been takin' care of myself fer quite awhile now. I'm doing alright at it." She shifted from one foot to the other.

"It's freezing. Don't you know you'll catch your death of cold?"

Abigail's pulse quickened. Why didn't he yell for the law and be done with it? "I only took a loaf of bread, Mister."

"Bread, what're you talking about?" He dragged her over to a street light, lifted a lock of curls, and peered at her face. "How old are you?"

"Was sixteen my last bir . . . but that ain't none of your business." Abigail jerked from his strong grip. If he was like the men at the brothel, he was up to no good.

With that thought, the shadows moved in and danced about; pulling everything she didn't want to remember into the present. She blinked and pushed at them, but they swallowed her.

* * *

Cobwebs clouded Abigail's mind. Her lips moved, but no words came. She had to get away! Run while there was still time. No telling what would happen if she stayed here.

Slowly, her senses returned. The softness of a feather tick mattress and the warmth of a coverlet soothed her. She heard the gentle murmur of voices. This wasn't the alley. There was a sweet smell in the air like the perfume the women at the brothel wore. Something was wrong. Had she died? Had the stranger been an angel sent to bring her to heaven?

With all the strength she could muster, she forced open her eyes. The man who'd found her stood at the foot of the bed, his arm around a lady with hair as yellow as butter and skin as white as wild lilies in the fields of her home back in Georgia. From what she remembered of her stepdaddy's preaching this had to be paradise.

The door opened and a large black woman entered, carrying a tray.

No, this wasn't heaven! There'd be no niggers there.

The servant closed the drapes, filled the washbasin, and laid out clean towels as though she followed silent orders, or did she read minds? Abigail had heard these folk sometimes had supernatural powers. Shuddering, she huddled further under the covers. The last thing she needed was voodoo. Wasn't it time for a little heaven?

Another sweet, sick odor drifted through the room as steam rose from the kettle that the maid held. She'd smelled this scent before. The memory of the horrible medicine her stepdaddy shoved down her throat sent chills over her. He'd said it was spring tonic, but only the Lord knew what it was. These people were up to no good, just like he'd been. But this time she was trapped with nowhere to go, even if she could get away. She scooted deeper under the covers as the man stepped closer to the bed.

The black woman placed a cup to her lips. "A few sips of mah special brew shore to work wonders. I ain't ever knowed it to fail."

"I can always count on you, Stella." The man said.

Abigail's mouth tightened in a hard, straight line. She wasn't about to drink any strange tea, and they couldn't make her. The feather mattress sagged as the man sat next to her and lifted the pillow. She squeezed her eyes tight.

"Come, sit up and take a sip. Stella's herbs will have you on your feet in no time."

As the cup touched her lips again, a shudder shot through her body. Hot liquid dribbled down her chin. She gritted her teeth and swore as long as she had an ounce of strength, the tea wouldn't hit her stomach. No telling what'd happen if it knocked her out.

"Keep trying, Stella. Tomorrow she'll have lots of questions."

Peeking from beneath lowered eyelids, Abigail watched the couple leave the room. Yes, he was right. She could think of a million things to ask. Where was she? And who was this man? Why had he taken such an interest in her?

Fear rose like a knotted fist. Why had she fainted? What had happened to her in the alley? She'd gone without food for much longer and been fine. Memories of the rotten smelling garbage drifted back, but she fought them. She didn't want to think any more—remember any more. All remaining strength left her in a rush. She snuggled under the quilts and fell asleep.

* * *

From furrowed eyebrows, David Cranshaw studied his wife. He loved her slim figure and the way she wore her hair, pulled back and tied loosely with light green ribbons that matched her dress. But the paleness of her thin face worried him. Would she ever regain her healthy color? A year had passed since they'd buried their week old daughter, and Mariah hadn't made much progress.

He waited until she sat before he spoke. "The girl . . . upstairs. She doesn't have to stay if you don't want her to. I only brought her home because she fainted. I didn't want to leave her lying in that filthy alley. Besides, it's a new year. Can't we start it by opening our hearts and home to the less fortunate?"

His wife leaned her elbows on the table and met his gaze. He felt the tension grow but kept his silence until the servants set an assortment of fresh fruit, beignets, and lots of cream, country ham and biscuits in front of them. After they left, he reached across and took her hand. "Well, do you understand?"

The question hung heavy between them. He knew his work with the orphans was not a topic that she was eager to discuss since they'd lost their child.

Mariah dipped two large spoonfuls of sugar into her coffee, stirred it, and then shrugged. Tears threatened to spill from her blue-green eyes. "I haven't said anything, but I can barely stand the sight of the poor waifs you bring home."

"My dear, you don't get into the city much. If you did, you'd understand. Orphanages are so overcrowded, and they won't take the bigger children."

"I don't want to hear about them or see them. They remind me too much of what we've lost."

David squeezed her hand. "The one upstairs . . . she's older, but I can find a home for her. Mother needs a companion since . . .." He let the subject drop. This wasn't the time to talk about his mother's problems. Not when his wife needed his full attention.

By now her eyes were red-rimmed. "No matter how many children you bring into this house, none of them will ever take our baby's place!"

"I'm not trying to replace Rosemary. Can't you find it in your heart . . .?" He stopped as tears streamed down her cheeks.

"No! Don't ask anymore of me. There's no use. I can't . . .." She tossed her napkin on the table and ran from the room.

He massaged the deep wrinkles in his forehead. He'd made a mistake bringing the urchin home. He'd go upstairs, and if the girl was up to it, he'd take her anywhere she wanted to go.

* * *

Abigail stirred from a deep sleep. She had to get out of here. That nigger woman would try and force that horrible smelling brew down her throat. There was probably something in it to kill her.

A breakfast tray sat on the nightstand. Lord, she was hungry. She picked up a muffin. Had they put something in this, too? Hunger overcame her fear. Gobbling it down, she then grabbed a few and stuck them under her pillow. At least, she'd be able to eat. As her fingers closed around the last roll, a hand caught her wrist. She looked up, startled. It was the man who'd brought her here. His dark brown eyes twinkled. She dropped the pastry back onto the tray. "I was jest gonna keep it, in case . . ."

"In case you get hungry later? I understand. I'll have a box of food packed for you to take."

Abigail's fears vanished. Whatever happened last night, this dark-headed stranger with the bright smile didn't mean her any harm.

He picked up the shawl that hung across the back of a chair. "We'll have to see what we can do to replace your wrap. You can't weather the winter in this. My wife might have some clothes that'll fit you."

Abigail cringed as he dropped it in the fireplace. This man aimed on sending her back on the streets. He must've brought her here just because she'd fainted. Who'd she think she was, anyway? If she wanted to stay alive, she'd best remember to make it on her own. "Sir, I thank you fer what you've done fer me. I'm sorry if I put you out. I wish I could do somethin' to repay you."

"My name is David, and you're at the Cranshaw Plantation. Get up and see how you feel. I'd hate to send you away if you're going to keep fainting. After dinner, if you're all right, I'll take you wherever you want to go."

Her hope died as he walked toward the door. "Forgive me, sir. I didn't mean to be no bother. I'll go back to the Wellington Brothel. They're like my family. I only run away because . . . well, that ain't your problem." She threw back the quilt and jumped up. "I'll get dressed and get outta here right away." But the room spun, and she groped for something to cling onto. Strong arms caught her. Voices echoed in the room. Feet rushed about. She gave herself to the shadows that once more hovered close.

* * *

Abigail opened her eyes and looked up at the long nosed man bending over her bed. Lord, what was happening? Why'd she keep fainting, and who was this? She rolled away. Surely he wouldn't bother her here, but after what had happened at the brothel, she didn't trust anyone.

The man patted her on the arm. "I'm Dr. Daniels. David sent

for me because you've been fainting."

"I ain't sick. Got dizzy 'cause I ain't had much to eat." She threw back the covers and stood. "See I'm good as new. Now, I've got to go."

"We need to talk."

"I ain't got nothin' to say to no doctor."

"But I've something to tell you."

"Well, hurry up. I've got to get out of here before Mr. Cranshaw comes back."

"Did you know you're having a baby?"

As hard as she tried not to think about the man who'd stuffed her into that broom closet and took what he wanted, the memory rushed back. No, this couldn't happen. She wouldn't let it. She stomped her foot. "You're crazy if you think I'm gonna be a mama! I'll fix it when I get back to the brothel."

"You're in no condition to go anywhere."

She walked toward the door. "My condition ain't your concern." A sickening feeling churned in her stomach. Bile filled her mouth as her legs turned to mush. She had to get out of here before . . . slowly the shadows crept in and once again she surrendered to them.

* * *

David paced the library. What was taking so long? He probably shouldn't have sent for the doctor. Another day's rest and a few more meals and the girl would be strong enough to leave. But in case . . .

"I'd say you've gotten yourself in quite a fix this time."

He wheeled to face Dr. Daniels. "What do you mean? If you'd found *that* girl, wouldn't you have done the same thing?"

"My circumstances are different from yours. Anyway, your guest is going to be a mother in a few months."

"So that's the reason for the fainting. Did you tell her?"

"Yes. She stomped her foot and said she wasn't going to be a mama right before she fainted again. Your wife doesn't need that girl here. Find her a place and soon!"

"I'll get to work on it this afternoon."

The doctor left, and David began looking through his files for a list of services available for girls like Abigail.

"Come quick, Massa! Please hurry! It Missus. Sump'n awfully bad wrong."

David dropped the folder and made a dash toward the stairs. Mariah had been extremely tired since the baby died, and he'd let her rest as much as possible. "What's the matter?"

Stella's black face wrinkled with worry as she pointed down the hall. "I wish I know what's a-happenin' to Missus, but I not know."

"What do you mean?"

"I not know. Ain't ever seen nothin' like it. She settin' in dere rockin' back and forth and talkin' outta her head."

He rushed by the maid. Mariah sat in a rocker near the window. Her blond hair fell over half closed eyes, and she gazed down into cradled arms. Bare toes peeped from beneath the hem of her nightgown. The chair, creaking back and forth across the wood floor, sent shivers through him. "Dear, it's afternoon, and you're not dressed. You should change. The Wilsons are coming for tea later."

"Sh-h-h, you'll wake Rosemary. I've been up all night. Now that she's sleeping, I want to sit here and hold her for awhile."

He eased onto the bed. Good Lord! She was out of her mind. Why hadn't he seen what was happening? He forced his voice to sound calm. "Why don't you let Stella take the baby to the nursery?"

Mariah's arms tightened. "No, I'll take care of my own baby!"

"She's my baby, too. Can I hold her for a while?"

A slow smile found its way to the corners of her lips, and she reached out empty arms. "You're a good father, but be careful not to wake her, or we'll be here the rest of the day."

He sat on the edge of the bed, cradling his arms and humming a soft lullaby. He glanced over at the crib. He should have removed it when the baby died, but she'd insisted it stay. He couldn't pretend all day. What now? Doctor Daniels wasn't good for more than the grippe or bringing babies into the world, but maybe he could get him back out here. Hopefully, he'd know of something or someone who could help.

"I want to hold my baby now. She's my responsibility." Her face flamed with an unnatural flush and her blue-green eyes glazed over.

He placed the imaginary child in her outstretched arms. "Here, you're better at singing, and I have something important to tend to."

For a moment, her eyes cleared. "Isn't it time to plant the sugar cane?" Then her eyes grew vacant once more.

David squeezed her shoulders. "No, Dear. It's still the middle of winter. Soon, the sun will shine and the earth will warm. Then, we'll plant." She'd remembered the growing season. Yes, his sweet, lovely wife would be fine. Their love would make her well again. He motioned for Stella to follow him. Outside the room, he asked, "Did anything happen this morning to upset the mistress?"

"Nothin' I knows of, Massa."

He glanced down the hall. "That girl, has she been down here?"

"No, she shore ain't. She still too weak to get across ta room."

He walked toward the stairs. He'd have to find a place for the girl right away.

"One minute Missus fine and ta next she mumblin' 'bout ta baby." Stella's eyebrows furrowed as she looked back at Mariah's door.

David rubbed his forehead. *Think!* There had to be a reason for this. "Has the mistress mentioned our house guest?"

"No. She not say nothin'."

"I've got to get help. Stay with her, you hear." He rushed downstairs then hesitated in the foyer. *Today is January first, the day our baby died!* A sudden chill rippled across his shoulders. *A year!* It seemed like yesterday that he'd held his infant daughter in his arms. She'd been a beautiful, perfectly formed baby, except for the hole in her back. They'd baptized her Rosemary Mariah Cranshaw. A week later, they buried her in the Dawson crypt with Mariah's mother and father. Doctor Daniels had warned him that another baby might have the same problem. Of all the times he could have chosen to bring home a street child, this was the worst. But right now, he had to get the doctor back out here and there wasn't a minute to lose.

* * *

Abigail woke to urgent voices and hurrying feet. This house was usually quiet, not like life on the New Orleans streets where there was always a mass of stomping, moving, rushing feet . . . feet that never went anywhere. Her's would soon take her back to the same streets. Then what . . . slowly, the doctors words seeped through her foggy mind. A baby! She was having a young'un. She had to get out of here. Get back to the brothel where she could get help. She snatched the pillowcase off the pillow, dug under the covers, and gathered the few muffins she'd stored there. She dropped them in her makeshift bag and pulled the faded gingham dress over her nightgown.

She went to the door and eased out. The slave woman, Stella, vanished down the hall with her behind rolling back and forth under her green striped dress like two ripe melons. Stopping every few feet to rest, Abigail finally reached the stairway and peered over the banister to a huge foyer. Her head spun, and she clung to the railing. Slowly, she looked in the direction the servant had disappeared. Where did the hall lead? Maybe there were back steps.

The third door down was halfway open. The pretty lady, with the yellow hair who'd been in her room last night when she came here, sat on the bed with her eyes fixed on an empty cradle. Her hair was as tangled as the sheets on the bed, and she was still in her nightclothes. What could be wrong with a lady who had everything? Had she barged in on something private? She'd heard that many of these rich folks were Catholic and prayed a lot. Praying hadn't helped her. It had never stopped her stepdaddy's beating, never put food in her stomach, and never found her a home off the streets.

When the woman looked in Abigail's direction, her face twisted with rage. "You can't have my baby. She's mine!" Then she glanced toward the cradle, suddenly calm. "See, she's sleeping good now." A shadow crossed her face. The rage in her eyes was back. "They said you'd come! You can't have my baby. Hear me?" She stood and tiptoed closer to the cradle, the calmness returning. "We had a rough night. New babies often have colic. Are you a new neighbor?"

Before she could answer, the woman rushed on. "It was so good of you to make a call, but under the circumstances, you understand, don't you? Maybe you'll come again, and we can have a nice long visit."

Abigail backed toward the door.

Mariah took a step forward. A sick smile tugged at her lips. "I said get out. You can't have my Rosemary!"

Abigail fled through the door and down the hall. She had to get out of this house right now. Even if she wasn't having a baby, she didn't want to stay here any longer. That woman oughta be locked up.

Outside, she gazed at all the plowed fields. She'd been pushed and shoved just like that dirt until there was no place to go. She touched her stomach. Yes, she could go back to the brothel and get the help she needed.

* * *

Fear twisted like a knife in the bottom of David's stomach. He'd been lucky to get Dr. Daniels out here again today, especially this late.

What was taking him so long? Things must be very serious. The crypt and the child that was buried there filled his thoughts. His eyes blurred, and he dabbed at them with his handkerchief. There had to be someway, somehow, to make their world right again.

"David?"

He wheeled to find the doctor standing in the doorway. "My wife . . . what's wrong? Tell me, please."

The doctor held up his hand. "Slow down. Let's take this one step at a time. First, your wife is in good physical condition."

"But she looks so pale and drawn. If she's all right physically then it has to be . . ."

"In her mind. There isn't much I can do. I warned you this morning. She didn't see that girl, did she?

"Stella said she hadn't."

"Well, another baby might help, but the same thing could happen again."

David jammed his hands in his pocket and walked to the window. "The girl . . ."

"Don't say what you're thinking. It won't work."

David ran his hand over his furrowed brow. Somehow, he had to find a way. "If it were possible . . .

The doctor held up his hand. "I don't want to be any part of any of your hair-brained schemes."

David couldn't tell if the ticking in the room was the clock on the mantle or the pounding of his heart. The weight of the situation settled over him. An ill wife and now a girl who was having a baby.

He bowed his head. *Oh, Lord, what am I going to do?* Suddenly Stella's voice brought David's head up, and he rushed toward the door.

"Massa Crenshaw, she gone. Not be a trace of her. I not see how she make it. She wobbly as a newborn calf."

"Who's gone? Tell me it's not my wife." He faced the doctor. "Did you give her any medication?"

"I gave . . ."

"I not talkin' 'bout Missus. It be dat young'un yo brung home."

David's legs went weak. Thank the Lord, it wasn't Mariah. Abigail had made her choice. She'd have to live with the results. He had his own troubles. But what would happen to the baby?

The doctor handed him a small bottle. "Well, I'd say you're rid of one of your problems. Give Mariah two drops of this laudanum in warm milk three times a day. It'll make her sleep. The rest will help. I'll be back soon." He closed his bag, pushed his glasses up on his long nose, and stepped toward the door. "You're lucky that girl's gone. She'll probably try to find someone to fish that baby out of her. Girls like that often do. It's dangerous. Whatever you do, don't bring any more of those homeless children here. It's too much for your wife."

The doctor left David alone with the ghost of his lost child and the insanity that consumed his beloved wife. He had to save her! If that meant giving up his work with the street urchins, so be it. As for the girl, he was better off without her. They all were. But the baby . . . he'd have to think. There had to be a way to save it.

❧ 2 ❧

Elizabeth Cranshaw's Home: January 2, 1859

David stood at the garden gate watching his mother pick dead leaves from her rose bushes. He marveled at this tiny woman. She'd been the one who'd managed the family business after his father's death, closed the door on his sister's memories, gave him the strength to go on when his baby died. Her faith was unwavering. She'd understand his concern for Abigail and the unborn child.

Thoughts of the urchin held his heartstrings. Why? He'd taken in many children and found them homes in the past few years, but never one who was going to have a baby; one who'd run away. Had she gone back to the brothel? If so, there'd be no baby. He'd heard about the alley behind Canal Street. But keeping her at the plantation wasn't an option. His mother's place was perfect.

Elizabeth Cranshaw straightened and smiled at her son.

He strolled toward her with outstretched arms. "Let the gardener take care of your garden."

She removed a glove and squeezed her son's hand. "I was just checking the rose cutting he started for me last fall. Remember how you and your sister used to help me?" She pulled the basket stick from the ground and hooked her arm through the handle.

"Remembering isn't always good. Sometimes it's better to forget."

A shadow crossed her face. "You're right. What brings you here this time of day? Mariah isn't sick again, is she?"

"Yes, she's in a bad way."

"She's not withdrawn like she was after the baby died, is she?"

"Worse than that. Yesterday, Stella found her sitting in her room with arms cradled and rocking. She believes the baby's still alive. I had the doctor out last night, and he gave her medicine to make her sleep. Said it was mental and about all we can do is pray."

Elizabeth touched the crucifix around her neck. "I've been praying constantly, son. Lord knows we've had our share of sorrow. I hope you've decided not to bring home any more of those street urchins. I've been against it all along. I'm telling you, one of these days, you're going to get more trouble than you can handle."

David took his mother's arm and guided her toward the veranda. "I know what you've been saying, and if it makes you feel any better, you're right. Last night the doctor warned me about the same thing. He said my wife didn't need to be upset. I should've known, but she didn't say much until this last one."

Elizabeth's brow furrowed. "What's so different about this one?"

"She's older. I stumbled across her in an alley off Bourbon Street. The only reason I brought her home is because she fainted. I couldn't leave her there with all those drunks. I didn't plan on her staying, but . . ."

"Oh, David, it's always a 'but' with you. Don't you know by now that you're too caring for your own good? Does she have anything to do with Mariah's sickness?"

David helped his mother up the steps and sat beside her in the swing. "I wondered the same thing. Anyway, it doesn't matter now. The girl's gone."

"Did you find her a home?"

"No, didn't have a chance. She ran away."

"That's just as well. Mariah needs you. You don't have time to chase around trying to find a place for another waif."

"That's what the doctor said. Yet, I feel bad. She's going to have a baby. Can't help but wonder what will happen to them."

Elizabeth stopped the motion of the swing with one foot and turned to face him. "You brought a girl into your home that was with child? No wonder Mariah is having trouble. You should've known better."

David cupped her hand in his. "Calm yourself, Mother. I didn't know at first, and Mariah doesn't know. The doctor said that she'd be a mother in a few months–that when he told her, she said she'd never be a mama. I have my suspicions that she's out looking for one of those back-alley butchers who take care of such 'problems'. It's my bet she won't have a hard time finding one."

Elizabeth's small body shuddered. "I tried to tell you, didn't I? Poor girl, poor baby. Both lost and there's nothing we can do about it."

"Yes, there is. This girl needs a home, some place to give birth to the baby. I can't provide that, but you can."

"Me! I'm an old lady. It's all I can do to take care of myself."

"Just my point, you can help her, and she'll help you if you're willing to take the risk. That is if we can find her before it's too late."

Mrs. Cranshaw resumed rocking and let out a long sigh. "I know what you're trying to do, but it won't work. I don't want a stranger in my home, especially one with child. Besides, how would you find her?

"I believe I know where she is. She mentioned the Wellington Brothel. That's probably where she went to find the kind of help she needs. I'm not asking you to make any long term commitment, but if I find her, will you keep her long enough to give her time to decide what she's going to do? Time for me to see if I can find her another place?"

Elizabeth turned tear-filled eyes toward her son. "I can't deny you anything. I'll give it a try, but I can't promise it'll work."

The silence hung between them like a thick veil of pain that they both knew too well–sorrow that couldn't be wrapped in tissue and tucked away inside some old trunk in the attic. It grew roots deep in one's soul and was watered by everyday living. Each day's watering tightened the vine around the heart a little more. Would it some day choke out the breath of life?

∂ 3 ∽

New Orleans Cemetery: January 3, 1859

Abigail clutched the carriage seat as it jolted over the rough road. Where was David Cranshaw taking her? If he wanted her gone, why'd he come to the brothel looking for her? He'd begged her to come with him. Said there was something he needed for her to see. Then maybe she'd understand why it was so important to save her unborn baby. She cradled her arms under her stomach. *What am I going to do? Living on the streets with a young'un won't be easy. The girls at the brothel know how to get rid of it.* She shivered.

"If you're cold, there's a blanket in the back."

"No, I ain't cold, and I don't need your pity." She hugged herself tighter. Fingers of cold fear wrapped around her heart as the carriage came to a stop at a cemetery.

David stepped down, tied the horse to a gatepost, and reached his hand up to her.

She hesitated. "Why are you bringin' me to a graveyard?"

"Come, I want to show you something."

Abigail followed him between rows of crypts. Finally, he knelt in front of one. Slowly, painstakingly, she read over his shoulder the words carved on a marble slab: Rosemary Mariah Cranshaw. Born: December 25, 1857 . . . Died: January 1, 1858. She stepped back. This sure was strange.

David looked up at her. "I hoped bringing you here might make it easier for you to understand why I don't want you to get rid of your baby. They're so special. Not everyone can have children. I'd say you're lucky. Even if you don't want to be a mother, someone will take the baby. Mariah and I have lost so much. I don't want you to get rid of your baby." Tears gathered and streamed down his cheeks.

Abigail felt her own eyes grow moist. This man was hurting, and all she could do was stand here.

"When the doctor told me you were going to have a baby, I wished it were Mariah, but that can't be. If she had another child, it'd wind up here with this one." David buried his face in his hands.

She stepped closer and touched him on the shoulder. "You and your wife can have my baby."

He slowly raised his face. "No, I can't bring home any more children. The doctor says that's what's bothering my wife. She'd never take your baby." He stared at the name on the marble for sometime. "I shouldn't have come looking for you, but I couldn't live with myself if I didn't try."

Abigail squatted beside him. "Let's say I have this young'un. How am I gonna earn my keep 'til it's born? I can't scrub floors at the brothel in my shape, and I don't have nowhere else to go."

David's eyebrow shot up. "Scrub floors—what do you mean? When you said you worked there I thought . . .?"

Abigail rubbed her calloused hands up and down her chilled arms. For sure, this man had to be crazy. "You believe I bedded with them men. There's not enough money to get me to do somethin' like that."

Alarm showed in David's eyes. "Then how . . .?"

"It wasn't my choice."

Horror replaced the surprise in his eyes. "You mean you were . . ."

Abigail felt hot tears roll down her face, and she began to shake. "Wasn't any way to stop him. Believe me, I tried."

David stood. "Well, there's nothing left for us to talk about. We have to go to the sheriff."

"Won't do no good, and it'll only make life hard fer Miss Wellington. I can't do that. She's been too good to me. When I got here from Georgia, I was living out of garbage cans. She found me and took me to the brothel. I only ran away because I didn't want to cause her no trouble."

David's shoulders sagged. He cleared his throat as he reached out and took her hand. "I've given your problem a lot of thought. When Stella said you were gone, at first I believed it was a good thing. I have my share of problems. Even the doctor said I should be glad you were gone, but I kept seeing the girl I found in the alley wandering around with no one to care for her."

"You shouldn't worry. I learned early to take care of myself."

"You probably can, but it won't be the same now. I told my mother about your problem. She wants to help. She's alone and needs someone to fuss over. Company will be good for her, also, this will give you a safe place to stay until you decide about the baby."

"In my condition, I'd jest be a bother to her."

"We'll see how it goes, and if you two get along, I'll pay you to be her companion. You can save enough to start your life over."

Abigail touched her belly. She'd never wanted to be a mama. This young'un would only be here because... because... she'd been used . . . not because she'd loved the pa. She shuddered. The image of the crazy lady back at the big house haunted her. Life in the streets of New Orleans replaced the picture. A baby . . . she couldn't make it with a young'un. Wasn't but two choices, give it away or get rid of it. Looking at the crypt, she said, "I ain't thought 'bout much except how I'm gonna make it on my own."

David's eyes softened until they looked like brown velvet. "If you don't want to say anymore right now, we can talk on the way back into town."

Mr. Cranshaw had promised her money for a new beginning. Starting over was what she'd planned on when she left her mother and stepdaddy in Georgia. She'd hoped to find her father and the grandmother who had let her play with her button box when she was small, but that hadn't happened. Would money make her a lady? No, it'd take more than wealth. It'd take grooming and finding the right husband. Besides, Dr. Daniels knew about the baby and no telling what others knew by now. She wiped at tears streaming down her cheeks. "It'll never work, Mister Cranshaw." She shook her head. "I'm afraid I'm doomed to a life on the streets, and the bab . . . ."

"Stop, girl. I don't want to hear anymore. I'm going to take you to my mother's. Let you see how you like it there and how she likes you. I'll come back in a few days. If you decide to have the baby, I'll find someone to adopt it, but if you're determined to get rid of it, I won't stop you. At least I've done all I can."

Back in the carriage, Abigail wrapped the blanket David had offered her earlier around her shoulders. She didn't know if it was the chill in the air that made her shake or the decision she had to make.

❧ 4 ❧

Elizabeth Cranshaw's Home: January 3, 1859

David veered to the right and turned down a lane lined with massive oak trees. At the end, a Negro swung open a tall iron gate and motioned them through. On each side of the gate ran a hedge. A brick archway shaded the front of the house and a wrought iron stairway led to the second floor balcony. To the rear sat a carriage house.

Abigail gasped at the size. Only plantation homes were supposed to be big, but this one was just as large and stood alone surrounded by trees instead of fields. A small silver-haired lady, round as she was tall, appeared on the porch.

The carriage stopped. David hopped down and extended a hand up to her. As her feet touched the ground, the little woman rushed forward and crushed her son to her full bosom. Finally, she quit hugging and looked in her direction. "Let me have a good look at my company."

Uneasiness gnawed at Abigail's insides. *What will this woman think of me?* She wished for the witching spirit of the people back in Georgia so she could read minds.

"Well, it looks like this child needs something to eat. Come on in."

As Abigail entered, she took stock of all the lavish furnishings. Large flowered rugs covered the floors. She pictured herself trying to beat one of them. It'd probably take her all day. This house put David's to shame.

"Come, have a beignet and of course, you need milk."

Mrs. Cranshaw pulled a chair near the table, ushered her toward it, then fluttered about like a mother hen getting ready to nest.

Abigail, now, understood David's concern. The servants were here, but there was no one to talk to, no one to fuss over. And this woman was definitely the fussing kind. It had been so long since anyone had spoiled her.

David came in and sat. "Well, what do you think, Mother?"

"She's not much bigger than a mite."

"She's taller than you," David teased. Then his face turned sober. "Abigail hasn't decided what she's going to do about the baby. She needs some time. If she decides against having it, she'll be leaving."

"To where?"

"Her old place of employment."

Mrs. Cranshaw's eyes narrowed. "And the baby?"

"That's her decision, not ours."

Abigail hugged herself tighter and set her lips in a hard line. She hated it when people talked about her as if she were not there. It looked to her like they'd do anything to save a baby. Well, she'd do what she had to.

"Finish your milk, then we'll go upstairs and get you settled. I'm giving you David's old rooms. You'll be comfortable there. There's a nice sitting room with lots of windows.

Abigail listened to Mrs. Cranshaw's chatter, half aware of what she said. This woman struck a chord somewhere deep within her about someone who had cared and loved her a long time ago. After a good night's sleep, maybe she'd be able to remember.

"Abigail, I hope you understand the arrangement I've made

with Mother. It's far too risky for you to stay at the plantation with my wife so sick."

"You don't have to explain. I done told you I'd think about this, and that's all I'm promising. I don't want to cause you no trouble." Abigail took a deep breath and stood up. "I'm ready to take a look at my room."

David touched the small of her back and guided her toward the staircase. A warm shiver ran through her. If she decided to stay, this was definitely a good place to give birth to her young'un. No, not hers . . . she didn't want to be called Mama. She shuddered again, but this time it was from the memory of her own mother being with child.

Upstairs, Mrs. Cranshaw stepped past her into the living room. Abigail saw a pleasant sitting room, furnished with a divan and a couple of chairs. A desk, in perfect order, stood on the far wall.

David went into another room and Abigail and Mrs. Cranshaw followed.

"Mattie, bring that lamp over here closer to the bed," ordered Mrs. Cranshaw.

A servant slipped across the floor as silent as the shadows that lurked in the corners. As she moved, the flame from the oil lamp bathed the center of the room in a circle of soft light. The flickering caused eerie, dancing movements on the ceiling.

"I had Mattie put one of my best feather ticks on David's old bed. And this cover is one of my favorites. Over here is a washbasin and fresh towels. Mattie will see that you have plenty of hot water for bathing," said Mrs. Cranshaw.

Abigail touched the double wedding ring quilt with the tips of her fingers. The ring was in the wrong place. If the ring were on her finger, then she wouldn't have to make a decision about the baby. She traced the delicate design. Every patch fit perfectly, the way a woman's life should be when she was getting ready to give birth. Someone had told her about making quilts. Someone from the past had shown her how they were put together to make a pattern. Someone had also told her never to throw away anything. Even when a dress was worn out cut off the buttons and put them in a box, and save the good fabric.

The glow from the lamp faded into the soft flicker of firelight. A little girl sat on the hearth playing with a colored box. Abigail squeezed her eyes tight. Oh, she remembered, a button box filled with all kinds and shapes of buttons.

" . . . And this window faces the south. You will get plenty of sunshine and fresh air."

At the sound of Mrs. Cranshaw's voice, Abigail opened her eyes. Mrs. Cranshaw stood near one of the windows and smiled as though she were offering her a room in a palace.

Tears surfaced, and Abigail blinked. This woman was just like the plump grandmother she'd been torn away from years ago. Slow warmth spread through her body as she wiped her eyes.

"Well, I'll go so Mother can help you get settled."

Abigail sighed with relief as David closed the door. He'd been good to her, but he had a sick wife to tend. Slipping her gingham dress over her head, she pulled on the flannel gown Mattie gave her. "You must be proud of your son, Mrs. Cranshaw. Must be somethin' to have someone love you like he loves his wife."

"They've both suffered a great loss. I don't know what's going to happen to my daughter-in-law, poor soul. All I can do is pray." She picked up a mirror and handed it to Abigail. "Take a look. You're an attractive young girl. I hope you decide to do right by your child. David can find a good home for it, and some day you'll find a man who'll love you. Now, rest. Tomorrow we'll get acquainted. Come, Mattie."

After Mrs. Cranshaw left, Abigail studied her reflection for a few minutes then laid the mirror down and moved about the rooms touching the carved furniture. She didn't know much about such things, but they must have cost a fortune. The scent of fresh lemon polish filled her nostrils. She took a deep breath, letting this room become part of her. She laid her hand against the fireplace and felt the warmth. Would David hate her if she got rid of the baby? If she had it, would he find it a home like he'd promised? If he saw her on the arm of another man, would he wish she belonged to him? Where'd that come from? He had a wife who needed him. One he loved more than life itself. If she wanted to survive, she couldn't start getting no fool ideas.

She paused at the window and pushed back the curtain. A full moon lit the yard, casting a glow to the skyline of the city she knew all too well. It'd be pleasant to sit here and watch life on the streets instead of being part of it. A faint quiver rippled through her stomach. She shouldn't have eaten that cabbage last night. A movement outside caught her eye. A shadow lengthened up the street. Soon the figure came into full view. *A man!* He paused and looked up. She dropped the curtain and stepped back. Uneasiness replaced her feeling of contentment. What if someone found her? Like her attacker? No, she'd be safe here. She blew out the lamp then went back to the window. No one was there. She groped her way back to the bedroom and crawled into bed. Tucking the quilt under her chin, she let the memories of her grandmother's button box chase away her fears.

☙ 5 ☜

David Cranshaw Plantation: 1859

David sat up in bed. He felt like something wasn't right. He was clammy. What had awakened him? A bad dream? As he lay back against the pillows, troubles lurked in every corner of his mind. A heavy sigh escaped his lips. Good Lord, his whole life was a living nightmare. Abigail, Mariah, and to add to his worries, in town he'd heard more rumors about unrest between the North and South. His slaves were content, but if there was a war, that could change. Hopefully, the girl wouldn't get rid of the baby. He was sure Mrs. Wilson would take it. They already had six and two of them were not theirs. His eyelids drooped, but uneasiness remained. He slipped on a wrap. He'd check on Mariah. Maybe then he'd be able to settle down.

From the first time they met, there'd been a special connection. Even in her present condition, was it possible her spirit inter-mingled with his? When he reached her door, dread washed over him as if he'd been dipped in a cold bath. Gooseflesh ran the length of his body. He breathed a silent prayer and pushed open the door. From the four-poster bed, he saw the slow rise and fall of her breast. Inside this body lived the remnants of the woman he'd fallen in love with.

A trace of a smile lingered on her lips as her hand caressed her stomach. David stepped closer, bent down, and took her in his arms. "Oh Mariah, I love you so. Please, come back to me. We'll make it all right. I'll never bring home any more street children." He had a sudden inspiration. "I know! We'll go on a trip. How about Paris? We can buy you a whole new wardrobe. I need some new clothes, too." No response, only shallow breathing and fitful cries. He settled her on the pillows. As he left the bed, he heard a faint whisper. He leaned close enough to hear her words.

"Your name's Rosemary, my darling child."

Gently, he smoothed the blanket and brushed a kiss across the hand that rested on her stomach, crossed the room, and closed the door behind him. The uneasy feeling still lingered. He'd go downstairs and smoke a cheroot before retiring.

* * *

In the library, David paced back and forth. Pausing at the window, he gazed out. The heavy mist twisted and twirled, fighting to float away, but the ghostly shapes were bound to earth to haunt the night. The mist had struggled the same way when Rosemary was born. A bad omen, no . . . a bad case of nerves. Would his mother like Abigail? He'd been so worried about her since his sister . . . he'd not think about Candy right now. He rang a small bell. Monroe appeared almost instantly.

"Massa, whatcha doin' up so late? It well after ta 'witchin' hour. How yo gwine work so hard and stay up all night?"

The wrinkles that caressed old Monroe's face had been there for as long as David could remember. Most of the slaves on the Cranshaw Plantation were passed down from his grandfather. He'd only bought a few and that was to save them from torture of another owner. "Thank you for your concern. Something woke me from a deep sleep. I came down here to think."

"I make yo a cup of tea?"

"No, I called you in to ask if there's any unrest amongst the slaves."

David sat on the corner of his desk and picked up a crucifix-shaped paperweight. Gently, he wiped away the dust. "Please, sit down." He pushed a stool toward the old man.

"I not set in yo' presence, Massa. It not right."

"It's the middle of the night. None of the other servants are going to see you, and besides, I asked you to."

Monroe eased himself onto the seat. "Hab I done sump'n wrong?"

"No, you've done everything just right. You're a good man, Monroe." David gave him a reassuring smile.

"I not like to talk 'bout dis war thing." He glanced toward the door. "Dere not much to tell, anyway. Ain't I always tell yo ta truth?"

"You're the most honest person I know." David studied the crucifix. "There's a lot of turmoil in our country. There are folk from up north called abolitionists. They say they're out to free their brothers."

"I heared all 'bout dem, but yo ain't gotta worry none. Ta slaves here know dis home and yo be family."

"I try to be fair. Lord knows it's not easy with so much to do. And my personal life has been bad since the bab . . ." He looked away.

"Yo not hab to say nothin' else, Massah. We is all awful worried 'bout yo and Missus. And dere ain't gwine be none of dem dere folks from up north causin' no trouble 'round here. Yo count on dat."

David placed the paperweight on the desk. "We've all been bought. Black or white, there's been a price paid. I've always tried to see that everyone is taken care of properly, and I want this to be your home." He turned to the window again. "See how the mist tries to pull free? A person's spirit needs to be the same no matter

36

where he is."

"I knows what yo be sayin'. Now, why don't yo get yerself to bed and get some rest?"

"I will. I feel much better now. You may go."

The old man rose slowly and hobbled toward the door.

David watched him leave. It wouldn't be too long until Monroe's spirit broke free of its physical bonds and floated home. And his lovely Mariah lying upstairs, would that happen to her, also?

❧ 6 ❧

Elizabeth Cranshaw's home: January, 1859

Abigail stretched, opened her eyes, and yawned. Bright rays of sunshine danced on the polished pine floorboards. Folding back the covers, she sat up. Two weeks today. Two weeks in heaven! There were servants to scrub the floors, a cook in the kitchen fixing food that she liked, and a personal maid to see to her needs.

Her hand slipped across her stomach. The baby continued to grow. What should she do? Life at the brothel was hard work, but the cot in the back room was comfortable. Calloused hands and knees were a small price to pay for food and shelter. She could always go back. But to live there meant getting rid of the baby.

The quiver in her belly returned. It gripped her insides and grew stronger. She caught her breath. The baby. . . no . . . it couldn't be. Another flutter rippled through her abdomen. Lord, she'd have to decide right away. Be indebted to the Cranshaws or face the man the girls at the brothel called "the butcher". If she lived here awhile in comfort, David would find the baby a home.

A light tap sounded at the door. "Come," she said.

Mattie peeked her curly head in and then entered. "Missus send me to hep yo get ready fer breakfast." She laid a freshly laundered dress of blue cotton across the foot of the four-poster bed. At the dainty, white-skirted table, she picked up a gold plated brush and comb. "Dis belong to another young missus. She like purty things."

Abigail wondered who the maid was talking about, but held her tongue. In time she'd find out why this family would go to any means to save an unborn. "Mattie, you spoil me comin' in here

38

every mornin' helpin' me like I'm a young'un. I ain't gonna die or nothin'. Women have babies all the time, and I ain't sure I'm . . .." She swung her legs over the edge of the feather tick and slid onto the oval, rag rug beside the bed.

Mattie raised an eyebrow. "Yo a spirited one, Missy. Dat jest be ta reason yo not get rid of ta baby." She poured water into a washbowl and dipped in a cloth.

"I'll wash myself." Abigail slipped off the flannel nightgown.

"That gown be too hot 'fore long. I tell Missus yo need some light weight ones."

Abigail held up her hand. "Wait a minute 'fore you go askin' fer things I can manage without. Mr. Cranshaw already bought me four dresses. That's more than I've ever owned."

"Yo be askin' yo'self in a few more days. It's gonna get hot as blue blazes soon."

Pulling the dress over her head, Abigail emerged with a smile. "Go ahead then, ask. Wouldn't want to melt and leave a mess fer you to clean up."

"Talkin' 'bout messes, dat hair need a good brushin'. I fix dem curls outta yo face."

As Mattie struggled with the thick mass of hair, Abigail thought about her life now.. Here she ate in the dining room and spent evenings in the parlor listening to Mrs. Cranshaw read or tell stories.

Mattie finished arranging her hair and left.

Minutes later, Abigail sauntered down the stairs, following the delicious smell of frying bacon. Her fingertips brushed the tops of tables and backs of chairs. With the toe of her black shoe, she nudged the fringe on a large oval rug. She traced the gold rim of a vase. If she broke one of these, she'd have to scrub forever to pay for it. In her condition, scrubbing might cause her to lose the baby, and that wouldn't be good. She was beginning to see that this young'un was her ticket to a better life

"There you are, child."

Abigail whirled to face Mrs. Cranshaw who sat in front of the French doors, that led to a wraparound veranda, leisurely sipping a cup of tea.

"You look very pretty. That color matches your eyes, and your hair has begun to take on a healthy glow. Yes, you're a good looking girl. Sort of frail, but stronger than you look." She stood and set her cup down. "Now, let's see you walk over here and sit down."

Abigail knew her usual tomboyish stride would be unacceptable, so with some effort, she glided across the room, slid out a chair, and eased onto it rather than plopping.

Mrs. Cranshaw gave thanks, then unfolded a napkin and laid it across her lap. "You remembered to wait for the breakfast prayer. You're learning."

Her heart pounded with the complement. Mrs. Cranshaw seemed to be warming toward her. If she were going to stay on here, she needed a friend. As for right now, she had to figure out this bunch of silverware. Her stepdaddy would use his fingers; said they were made before forks. The lace trimmed napkin slipped to the floor. She eased her hand down and picked it up, then reached for a biscuit. The fluffy texture broke apart easier this morning. At least her hands didn't shake when she smeared on the butter. After taking a bite, she sipped the amber breakfast tea. Her lips puckered. She dabbed her chin, then folded the napkin and laid it by her plate as though it were something she'd always done. "I have a question. I thought I'd have to stay upstairs while I was here. I did at Da . . . I mean, Mr. Cranshaw's house."

Elizabeth smiled. "It's all right if you call my son by his name. It's difficult for me to think of him as mister. To me his father was Mr. Cranshaw." A shadow crossed her face.

Curious, Abigail wanted to ask about her husband, but felt it would be too personal. "I felt the baby move this morning. I can't put off my decision any longer. I want to talk to your son."

Elizabeth leaned forward. "I will send someone to get him. I hope you've made the right choice." She touched the crucifix around her neck. "God doesn't look approvingly on the willful act of taking another's life."

"That's what my stepdaddy would say, but there's other ways to kill. A person with a broke spirit might as well be dead, and he done and broke mine when I was a little young'un."

A gush of tears filled Elizabeth's eyes, and she gripped Abigail's hand. "Oh, child, I know you've suffered, but remember you're not alone."

"I ain't gonna be a mama no matter what."

Mrs. Cranshaw released Abigail's hand and dabbed at her eyes. "We'll see. Where there's life there's hope, and time does change a lot of things. Before I agreed to take you in, I had my mind made up that I didn't need or want anyone here, but in this short time, I'm beginning to see how wrong I was."

"But there ain't nothin' I can do fer you. You've already got someone to scrub your floors. No, all I can see is bein' a bother."

41

"Why we could be quite a team. I can teach you how to walk and talk properly. You can keep me company and show me how to laugh again. I don't get many visitors, only the church ladies. They'll be here this afternoon."

Abigail stood and backed away. "I'll stay in my room while they're here. I don't wanna see anyone."

"That's all right. I understand. That'll be a good time for you to take a nap."

"I might look like a young'un, but I'm past sixteen and that's way too old for naps."

"Anyway, as your baby grows you'll need more rest. Anytime I have company, and you don't want to be present, you can take the back stairs off the kitchen to your room. I don't have visitors that often, since . . .."

Mrs. Cranshaw looked away but not before Abigail saw sorrow cloud her blue eyes.

Good Lord! Was there a ghost living here with David's mother, also? Wasn't there any place to get away from them, anywhere to find peace? She touched her stomach. For now the baby was safe, but what would happen once he lived in this crazy mixed-up world? Well, thank the Lord that wouldn't be her problem.

* * *

The church ladies gathered in the dining room as a servant poured tea, then served cookies. Elizabeth Cranshaw played the role of perfect hostess, asking each of the ten women how their families were. When she finally had everyone settled, she said, "Today we need to decide how we're going to raise money for our mission project."

Lily Roland drained her cup and set it on the table. "We should collect furniture and give it to the needy right here in the city. Your David's been gone for a long time, just like my John has. Why, we can clean out their bedrooms."

Mrs. Cranshaw patted her mouth with a napkin. "You've got a good point. I bet if we went through our homes, there'd be enough to furnish quite a few houses. I have a lot of items I can donate, but nothing from David's room. He still uses it from time to time."

Lily put an arm around Mrs. Cranshaw. "It's too bad about David's wife. My husband said she's as . . ."

Mrs. Cranshaw shrugged away her friend's arm. "You don't have to repeat what he said." She didn't plan on sitting here listening to what was being said about her family. "None of us are without problems, but we're not here to discuss them. We're here to help the less fortunate. At least we have money to take care of our own."

Lily folded her hands in her lap and her lower lip dropped. "I didn't mean any harm. We all know what his poor wife's been through. I pray for her daily. David, too."

"Thank you, Lily. Most people think they need to know all the details in order to pray, but God sees the heart and knows what's best."

The women nodded their heads in agreement.

"Good afternoon, ladies."

Elizabeth turned to find David standing in the door. She got up and rushed to him. "Thank God, you're here," she whispered. "Lily Roland tried to talk about Mariah, but I shut her up in a hurry." She turned to her friends. "See, I told you he dropped by to use his old room." She faced David again. "You go on, and I'll send Mattie up with a pitcher of lemonade. We'll visit later. The girls and I have to discuss spring cleaning to raise money for our mission project."

David looked at his briefcase. "I do have some legal papers to fill out." He gave his mother a reassuring grin. "You always know what I need. Ladies, I apologize for the intrusion and if you want to spring clean, come on out. I can find plenty for you to do."

Elizabeth went back to the group, grateful to David for keeping Abigail a secret for now. She didn't care if her friends knew about the girl upstairs, but Abigail had made it clear that she wasn't ready to be sociable. Anything could send her scurrying like a scared doe.

David felt his heart pounding as he mounted the stairs. Had Abigail decided to have the baby? If she did, would she stay on here? He paused at the door that used to be his private sitting room. In this room, he'd dreamed about his future as the owner of his grandfather's plantation. His own father had wanted to run it, but his father-in-law didn't have a son to take over his banking business so he became a banker instead. Grandfather Cranshaw had taught him to love the smell of freshly plowed earth, promising when the day came, he'd take over. David tapped on the door.

"Come on in, Mattie. I need my dress unbuttoned."

What was he going to do? Maybe he should just take the back stairs and leave. No, the maid hadn't arrived, so she'd still be dressed. He stepped inside. "I'm sorry I'm not Mattie, but I'm pretty good with buttons."

Abigail whirled. "Mr. Cranshaw, I'm glad you came so soon. I've decided what to do."

David set his briefcase on the floor near the door. "I hope you've made the right choice."

"For who?"

"For you *and* the baby."

"Choices, as you call them, is somethin' people like me don't have many of, but yes, I think I'm gonna have this baby. Ain't the baby's fault."

David took a step forward. "Oh, I'm so glad. I'll find it a home and take care of all the legal matters."

"I guess I should thank you for all you're doing, but can that wait?"

David smiled, pulled two chairs near the window, and motioned for her to sit.

She took the seat. "Your mother said she'd help me learn to talk proper and learn good manners. I was thinking by the time I'm through having this baby I might be on my way to being a lady like your mama. She acts so sad sometimes. Did your father pass away?"

"Yes, but that's not what broke her heart."

"The loss of love ones will do it."

"There are worse things than death." David took a deep breath and slowly let it out. "It's my sister."

"Is she dead, too?"

"As far as my mother and I are concerned, she is." David stared out into the street for awhile then his gaze returned. "You might as well know, my sister ran away with . . .." He lowered his eyes. "The wrong class."

"You mean somebody like me?"

"No, I mean the wrong color, and that's worse than being dead!"

Abigail sat in stunned silence.

45

David touched her hand. "I know you're puzzled. I try not to make a difference, and I don't believe I do. We're all the same in God's eyes, but in man's eyes, we see color." He glanced out the window. "I see Mother's company's leaving. I have to go. Could I come again? I'd really like to get to know you."

"That'd be nice."

"Is there anything you need?"

"I'll need some bigger dresses 'fore long."

For the first time since he'd entered the room, his eyes came to rest on her stomach. He felt the heat rise to his face. How he wished this baby could belong to him.

* * *

After a few weeks, Abigail settled into a routine. Mattie helped her style her hair and dress. She ate breakfast with Mrs. Cranshaw, and once they finished, they went into the library. Like a thirsty sponge, she soaked up the math, history, and social studies, but reading was her favorite subject. This morning Mrs. Cranshaw read Psalms. As she listened, she wondered if David was named for the David in the Bible. That one had also lost a baby, but he also had stolen another man's wife. David Cranshaw was too good a man to do something like that. Her mind was so occupied she hadn't noticed Mrs. Cranshaw had stopped reading.

"The ladies from church will be here again this afternoon. As soon as we have dinner, you go to your room and practice reading the rest of the Psalms. We'll work on your speech tomorrow." Mrs. Cranshaw handed her the Bible. "You look tired, child. Would you like for Mattie to bring up your food?"

"Yes, that'd be nice. I didn't rest very well last night. I dreamed the whole time."

"Do you dream often?"

"Sometimes."

"I'll have my cook fix you a cup of my special herbal tea tonight. It always helps me get a good night's sleep."

Abigail wrinkled her nose.

"Don't worry. It's just catnip tea. A small amount of sugar makes it tasty. It won't hurt you or the baby; just let you get some rest. Now, you run on, and I'll have Mattie bring up a tray."

Upstairs, Abigail laid the Bible on the nightstand and sank down in a chair near the window. The reading had caused her to think too much. She just wanted to show the world she was through being used, abused, and accused. As she cleared her mind, sleep took over, and she slipped into a frightening dream.

"See what you've done? Now he'll scream all night. Get yerself out to the barn. The Lord wants me to punish you."

"Please, Pa! Please don't. I didn't mean to make noise."

His massive hand closed around her thin arm and shoved her toward the door. She had to get away, run—find help. Her bare toe caught on the doorstop, and she landed, hard, on the floor. Darkness swallowed her.

"Come on, Miz Abigail. Wake up. I brung yo dinner. Yo not want it to get cold."

Relieved that her dream was gone, Abigail straightened. "Put it over there. Would you come back later? I'd like to change before supper. This dress feels tight."

Mattie stepped back and eyed her mistress. "I *say* yo be needin' some bigger clothes any day now."

"Guess you're right. I told Mr. Cranshaw last week I was going to need some. Hope he doesn't mind."

"He see how happy his mama be since yo be here. He be happy to get yo a bigger dress."

"Thank you. Your mistress is a fine lady." Abigail had already made up her mind once this baby came she'd find her a rich husband. One who was handsome and caring. One who'd love her like David loved his wife.

* * *

As the child grew inside Abigail, so did her desire for a life like the Cranshaws. Her baby would have a good family and why shouldn't she have the same thing. She didn't want to return to the streets. She smiled and closed her eyes. Although this baby hadn't been wanted, she talked to him like he was a real person. Her feelings were changing, not only about the baby, but also about lots of other things. She'd seen how David treated his mother and the lengths he'd gone to for Mariah. His servants also loved him. If she could have the love of a man like him, that would be enough for her. Sleep crowded out thoughts of her future and dreams took their place.

She was propped up in bed at the Cranshaw mansion. A nanny bustled through the door with a blue bundle.

"It be time fer yo' son to et." She placed the baby next to Abigail. "Yo awfully tired, Missus. Ta Massa wanna send fer a wet nurse."

Abigail folded back the quilt and gazed into the baby's face. He had black wavy hair like David, and that button nose was like hers. "No, I'll feed my son."

The door squeaked as the nanny left.

Abigail jumped, her pulse pounding.

"I didn't mean to startle you. Mother said you were resting. I brought you some larger clothes." David set a package down.

Abigail smoothed her dress. "You're not bothering me. I was just thinking about you." But she said nothing of the dream. "How's your wife?"

David pulled a chair near the window. "She's about the same. The medicine makes her sleep a lot. When she's awake, sometimes she sits and cradles her arms, rocking an imaginary baby. Other times she roams about the house like a ghost."

"I'm so sorry. I wish there was some sort of help fer her."

"Thank you. We've done an awful lot of talking about my family and the problems we have. Why don't you tell me about yourself? How'd you get to New Orleans?"

"I walked, rode on a train, and on a wagon. I even rode a few miles on a cow."

"A cow?"

"Yeah, she was headed my way. Didn't think it'd hurt her none to give me a lift."

David smiled. "The word's *any* not *none*."

"I know, but you'd say *none* too if you'd rode her. Boniest back I've ever sat on."

"Do you have family here?"

"I used to. I lived here until I was five. My mama left Papa fer a traveling preacher man. They settled in Georgia near his family. My stepdaddy was strong on discipline. The last time he sent me to the barn to wait 'til he could beat the tar out of me, I decided to keep right on walking."

David leaned forward. "And just how old were you when you embarked on this journey?"

Abigail looked confused. "I didn't bark. I stayed real quiet. I got here the best way I could fer a twelve year old. Guess I thought I'd get back here and find my grandmother and Papa waiting fer me. Your mother reminds me of my grandmother."

"And you help fill the spot in her heart that my sister left. She's becoming attached to you."

"I owe you'uns. Me and the baby . . . I mean the baby and I . . . we'd be doomed to a life on the streets if it weren't fer you."

"Can I help you find your family?"

She wanted to make him understand how she felt. "I might have took . . .taken . . . you up on that six months ago, but now I'm putting everything behind me. I'm going to build a new life. Maybe after I have this baby, I can find myself a fine gentlemen and live like you."

"And you'll be a wonderful wife and mother. Any one who can put her child first is all right in my book. I must go. Is there anything else I can bring you?"

"No, I have all I need."

The word *anything* resounded in her heart as the door closed behind him. Yes, there was something she wanted from him, but it wasn't anything she was likely to get or had any right to ask for.

❧ 7 ❧

Elizabeth Cranshaw's: Spring, 1859

Abigail watched Spring blossom from her window. She was not yet accustomed to the long shadows that stretched around a building before the owner stepped into view. Would the law still be looking for her or worse yet–the man who'd misused her at the brothel. She'd have to get over being afraid. Ladies were composed, refined, and in control. She glanced over at Mrs. Cranshaw, a perfect example of a southern lady.

"Looks like someone's day dreaming," said Mrs. Cranshaw as she smiled.

"I was just thinking about how much I want to be like you."

Elizabeth placed her plump hand over Abigail's delicate one. "Oh, my dear, you don't know what you're wishing for." Sadness once again clouded her eyes.

Was her hostess remembering her daughter? Thoughts of her own grandmother crept into her mind. She was glad she'd told David that she was putting her past behind her. She pinched at her dress, stretched over her growing belly. Even if he found her grandmother, she was in no condition to see her. More than likely she'd be an outcast.

"Don't look so worried, dear. Once the baby's born and you're back into regular clothes, you won't recognize yourself."

"I'm not concerned about my looks. I was just remembering my own grandmother."

"You've never said much about your family. Where do they live?"

"My mother and stepdaddy live in Georgia. My papa and his mother used to live here. I lived with them until I was five. Then Mama took me away."

Mrs. Cranshaw shook her head of white curls and squeezed Abigail's hand. "And you miss them?"

"Yes, she was so much like you. One of my best memories is playing with her button box. I spent hours sorting buttons and listening to her stories."

As the sun faded from the sitting room, the church bells pealed out their lonesome melodies across the city. Abigail held onto the older woman's hand, wishing she could ease the pain each of them bore.

"I have a button box. Why don't I get it? We can pretend I'm your grandmother. You can pick out buttons, and I'll tell you their story."

The sparkle returned to Elizabeth's eyes as Abigail felt the baby give a hard kick. Yes, she'd love to imagine this was her grandmother. The Cranshaws were becoming like family. "I'd love to."

"I'll be right back."

There were only six weeks left until Abigail's confinement was over. What would happen then? Would Mrs. Cranshaw want her to stay on as a companion. The thoughts of leaving this house left a heavy feeling in her heart. She'd learned how to wade through that bunch of silverware. For the most part, all her ain'ts and gonnas had been replaced by proper English. She'd grown accustomed to Mattie keeping her mass of curls neat. As soon as the baby was born, the maid would lace her up in a tight corset, and she'd be as slim as always. Wouldn't be a man in town who'd turn her down, except . . .

"Here they are. It's been years since I've looked at these. My little girl . . .." She shoved the box toward Abigail. "Here, you look at them."

Abigail hugged the box close. The gold leafed lid even resembled the one her grandmother owned. She shook the box. It was difficult to tell much without seeing them, but the soft rattle was so welcome. Memories of long ago crowded in. Maybe there'd be some of the same kind of buttons. She opened the box and picked up a square, white one. Where would something like this come from?

"There are eleven more like it in there somewhere. They're from the dresses my best friend, Annie, and I wore to our coming-out party right here in New Orleans."

"What happened to her?"

"She married a wealthy tobacco farmer in North Carolina. She was so in love, I don't think it would have mattered if he'd been some backwoodsman." Elizabeth smiled. "I don't guess that's too good a thing to say. Lots of people have pulled themselves up by their own bootstraps. Why, there's a young man up in Illinois I've heard that splits rails. Yet some folks believe that he's destined to be the President of the United States." The expression on her face was the same as when she spoke about her loss.

Abigail understood wanting to keep certain thoughts to yourself.

"As I was saying," Elizabeth continued. "We grew up here in New Orleans."

"Did she have a son like yours?"

"Yes, she had her son right away. His name is Seth. I had David much later in life. I can't say Seth is half as good looking as mine, but he's nice. He married quite young and had a daughter. Her name is Sophie. She married a trapper at the age of fourteen, and he took her to the wilds of the North Carolina Mountains. Annie was so distraught she took ill and died."

"I didn't know a broken heart could kill a person."

"Yes . . ." Elizabeth looked away and blinked.

"Death is final. Mama used to say God don't allow no wrinkles. That was her way of saying everything happens for a reason," Abigail said as she dug through the box.

"Well, God must have mine pressed out real good by now." Mrs. Cranshaw laughed.

"Oh look, here's a bundle of little pearl buttons. They're so tiny. Looks like they're from a baby's dress." She slipped her forefinger across the packet.

Mrs. Cranshaw took the buttons and held them close. "The wearer of these was the one to break *my* heart." She wiped at her eyes, then resolutely handed the buttons back. "That's enough story telling for now. We'll do it again soon."

"Can I keep these?"

"For your baby?"

"If it's not asking too much . . ."

"They'd look real pretty on a christening dress." David could take them with the baby to its new home." Elizabeth's voice broke.

"The baby needs to start life being buttoned in real tight to its new parents." She touched the place where she thought the baby's heart beat.

"What a sweet thing to do. You're an angel. You may have them. Now, I'll send Mattie up to help you get ready for bed."

The door closed and she was alone. No—not alone. There was always the baby. He'd get hiccups when she ate sausage, kick like mad when she drank tea or coffee, and sometimes he'd let a little hand or foot poke up on her belly, like he wanted her to shake hands. Would there be an angel watching over him when he went to his new home?

* * *

A few days later, Abigail woke with a strange uneasiness. Her lower back ached. She stood and stretched. The growing child was demanding more space, but there was little to give. She eased onto the bed to rest until breakfast. Her eyelids drooped, and as they closed, the dream came.

David paced the floor with a frown. Mariah floated across the room and vanished like a ghost into the wall. He reached out his arms. She ran into them. He nestled his chin in her hair. "My love, my darling, Abigail. How long I've waited for this moment. I'll always take care of you." He cupped her face and placed a gentle kiss on her forehead. She'd never experienced such love and tenderness. A sweet ache filled her soul, an ache so deep she couldn't keep from calling out.

Someone touched her shoulder and called her name. She fought to stay behind the mist that screened her from lonely reality, but when her eyelids finally opened, Mrs. Cranshaw bent over her.

"Are you all right?"

She pushed herself up on one elbow and looked at Mrs. Cranshaw. The dream had seemed so real. "Yes. I'm just fine . . . a little tired. It's hard to get a good night's sleep."

"I understand, my dear. I heard you up. If you need anything, no matter how late it is, just ring your bell. As your time grows closer, it might be wise for Mattie to stay in the sitting room."

A sudden chill swept over Abigail's body. *My time.* The idea of the child actually being a separate person was beyond her. A baby she'd never know. But her life would go on. If her plan went well, she'd be a southern lady. She imagined herself walking tall and proud down the street instead of darting in and out of the crowds to find a safe haven to eat stolen food. To survive the ordeal ahead, she must plan for the future. She shook her head to clear it of her dream. Did she really want another woman's husband and her own baby? No, she'd have to remember her vow to have a better life.

* * *

Heavy with child, Abigail moved her body restlessly in the chair. David would be here any minute. Unexpected warmth crept to her cheeks. She'd be signing papers today that would settle the future for all of them

A gentle knock sounded. "May I come in?"

"Yes, come."

The door opened, and David stepped into the setting room. Heat spread like a raging fire throughout her body.

"Are you sick? You look flushed"

"I'm all right." Just then the baby gave a hard kick and a multitude of needle-like pains shot up from her groin. It still wasn't time for the baby. If it came early would it live?

"You don't look well. Why don't I have the doctor come by and check you?"

Abigail clenched her teeth as pain ripped across the bottom of her stomach. Sweat beads collected on her nose, and she wiped them away with her sleeve. "I'm fine. It's just warm in here." She shifted, hoping a change in position would ease the discomfort. "Raise the window a little higher, would you please?" The heat in her body raged as David pushed up the window. Lord, what would she do without him or his mother? She had to calm herself. Nerves weren't good for the baby.

He turned.

Abigail slipped trembling hands under her legs so he wouldn't see how they shook.

"When I go downstairs, I'll have Mattie bring you a cold pitcher of lemonade." He pulled papers from his pocket. "I need you to sign these in order to place your child in a home."

She cleared her throat and shoved her hands further under her legs. "There's something I want to talk about."

His eyebrows shot up in a questioning arch.

Was she doing what was best? Once the paper was signed, the baby wouldn't be hers. She had to know what would be in store for her child. "You'll make sure that whoever gets my baby will take good care of him?"

"I can assure you that the people who get your baby will give it everything it needs to grow up and be a good person."

She stood and pulled the small package from her pocket. She pressed them into David's hand as shivers ran up her arm. "These came from your mother's button box. Will you ask the new parents to use them?"

He looked at the buttons, tenderness in his eyes. "I will. I'll ask if they can be sewn on the christening dress." He squeezed her shoulder. "You're doing the right thing."

The warmth of tears gave little relief to the hurt as she sat at the sitting room desk and signed away the rights to her baby. She'd never see him take his first step or say his first word, never see him run and play, never see him grow into an adult. The pain of signing was just as bad as the day she'd made the choice to walk away from her own mother. But she had to do what was best for the child and for her. This was the kindest man she'd ever known.

David looked over the papers then said in a gentle tone, "I have one more question. The baby's father. Can you tell me anything about him?"

Even in this heat, Abigail's insides turned to ice. In that instant, contempt for the stepdaddy who'd beat her on a regular basis, and for the man who'd pinned her down in a broom closet in the brothel overwhelmed her. Folding her hands in her lap, she raised angry eyes to meet his. "No! I want to be alone, now." Deliberately, she stood and walked to the window. Behind her the door closed. Her clenched hands shook. Men! Did they all want something?

As the flood of hate washed from her, warm water gushed and formed a puddle on the floor. What was happening? She didn't need to relieve herself. Did this have anything to do with having the baby? There was the bell on the table. Should she call someone? Was David gone? She didn't want *him* coming back!

As she shuffled into the bedroom, the wet clothes clung to her legs. After slipping on her nightgown, she returned to the sitting room and mopped up the puddle with the dress. She pulled a chair near the window and waited. When the carriage left, she might ring the bell. Had the baby pushed the pee out of her? She smiled at the thought. This child wouldn't have to push and fight to survive like she had.

What had come over her the day she'd left her mother standing there in the kitchen? Once she was around the bend in the road, she'd glanced over her shoulder at a trail of dust. It spelled freedom from her stepdaddy, but she didn't think about what the future would hold. If she'd realized . . .

The rattle of carriage wheels below jarred her back to the present. Cradling her stomach in her arms, she waddled to the bedroom. Another sharp pain rippled through her abdomen. As it eased, a certain satisfaction settled over her. There'd soon be a baby a part of her who'd always be out there, somewhere, in the world.

* * *

Later that night Abigail's labor came hard and fast, waking her from a sound sleep. Why hadn't she called someone earlier when all that water had spilled out? Her time was here. She groped for the bell. It was a little early, but May was a beautiful time to be born. The clank of the brass bell echoed in the room. Almost immediately, footsteps sounded on the stairs. It seemed from the start this young'un had a mind of its own. She was glad. He'd need to be strong to make his way. Only her headstrong and stubborn ways had gotten her this far.

A pain cut a path across the bottom of her belly and into her back. She gripped the bedpost until her knuckles turned white. She'd never felt anything like this. Even when that man . . . a cramp caught her off guard. A sharp cry escaped her lips.

The door burst open. The maid took one look and retreated

from the room, yelling for help.

Abigail called after her, "Help!" Where was God when she needed him? She was probably being punished for running away. Running . . . running . . . running . . . her thoughts were going crazy. She had to regain control, and then she'd be in charge of the pain. *Think of something else! Think about when this is over, I'll be slim again. There'll be parties and dancing—young men wooing me.* Men—weren't they the reason for this suffering. There had to be something to take her mind off of what was happening. Desperately, she looked around. A baby quilt lay on the dresser. *It'll keep the baby safe and warm until he arrives at his new home. And the buttons—David promised they'll be used on the christening dress.* The warm glow that filled her helped ease the pain.

Rushing steps and loud voices drifted in the open door. She sank back onto the pillows. Help was coming. She smiled. Before long there'd be a new life. No, not a new one—this one had been here with her these many months. He'd listened to her in the middle of the night when she'd been alone, but she wouldn't be there to listen to his cries or kiss away his tears.

"Is your time here, child?"

She looked at Mrs. Cranshaw. "I think so. He's ready 'cause he peed all over me earlier tonight. I guess that was his way of telling me he needed more room."

Mrs. Cranshaw turned to the doorway where the maid waited, half-hiding behind the door jamb. "Send for the doctor. And don't forget David." The servant's footsteps moved quickly away and down the steps.

Another contraction tightened across the lower part of her

stomach. She gasped.

"I'm going to tie this knotted sheet to the foot of your bed. When the labor is hard, pull on it, and as soon as it eases, try and relax. Save your strength."

She filled her lungs with air. No one had told her birthing would be like this. A pain hit her hard and her body went rigid. The gentle touch of Mrs. Cranshaw's fingers wiped the sweat from her forehead. Her soothing voice cut through her foggy mind, urging her to pull on the sheet rope.

Across the years of her forgotten childhood came another voice. Much like this one, it had soothed many a tear. Then shadows of a worse time crowded in. A large form overpowered the good memories. Slowly, it took on the features of the man who'd used her at the brothel. His hands ripped at her clothes, and that animal scent. . . no, she wouldn't remember. The man bent and whispered into her ear. "You little devil. Finally, you're gonna get what you deserve. I'll fix you fer good. Never again will you witch a good man." The man hovered over her a minute before totally consuming her. The hurt he inflicted ripped her apart over and over. As he withdrew, leaving her for dead, she heard a faint whimper in the distance.

Abigail groped, hoping to find someone or something. As hard as she tried, there was no help. Then as gentle as the patter of raindrops on a tin roof, a faint sound came, growing until its song soothed her soul. Each little cry increased her awareness; then finally, a loud wail up-rooted her from the horrible darkness. Tears slid down her cheeks. The baby was here! It was going to live! And as for her, it didn't matter. It would be so easy to let go and just drift away forever, where no memories could ever hurt her again.

The cries of the infant ceased and Abigail slipped into a peaceful sleep. Her dreams were of another life–another time another place.

A tall dark skinned man, wearing a uniform, strolled along the levy, holding the hand of a curly-haired little girl. The child stepped in front of the man. "Swing me up, Papa. Way up high in the sky!"

He picked her up and tossed her in the air. She squealed as he caught her and swung her high, and then hugged her tight.

The child pulled loose and grinned down at her father. "I love you so much. Why don't you come home more?"

He pointed at the great Mississippi River that curled and twisted like a giant snake. It reached as far north as the eye could see, and to the south, it rushed into the ocean. "See those ships out there? They belong to me."

"You must be awfully rich. But if you're so rich, why does Mama cry so much?"

He set her down. "Money doesn't make happiness, Honey. I'm learning that the hard way."

The child was quiet for a long time. When she finally spoke, it was with a tone more mature than her five years. "The other day me and Mama were in the city. She was talking to a man. He said money was the root of all evil. I didn't know it had roots, did you Papa?"

A loud chuckle escaped his lips. "I wish it did, Abigail. If it did, we'd all plant our plantations with it, instead of planting cotton and sugar cane. Wouldn't that be great? Except there would be one problem."

The girl lifted her eager face toward her father's. "What?"

"Well, there'd be so much it wouldn't be any good. But you know there will never be too much love for little girls like you." They walked

in silence for a long time then the man asked, "Was this the only time you've seen your mother talking to the man in the city?"

"No, they talk a lot. Sometimes he gives me a penny and sends me off to the candy store. One time I came back and found Mama crying. She cries an awful lot, Papa."

"I know, Honey, but don't you worry. Everything will be all right. Look! Your grandmother is waving."

The child pulled her hand free and ran ahead. As she reached the bottom step, her toe caught on a root, and she stumbled forward. Warm arms held her and cradled her close. She was loved . . .

"Abigail, wake up and try to eat something. You need to get your strength back."

She opened her eyes. Mrs. Cranshaw held her and wiped her face with a damp washcloth. Where was the baby she'd heard crying? She tried to sit up, but fell back like a limp rag doll against the pillows. "The baby . . ."

Elizabeth's arms tightened. "The baby's fine. You had a beautiful child. A little early, but healthy. David was here with Stella. They've already taken it to a new home. He thought it was better that way, and I agreed. You've been through a difficult birth. We didn't believe you were going to live, but you're strong. Still, it'll take a while to get on your feet."

Abigail let out a sigh and turned her back. There wasn't anything left to live for. "The baby, was it a girl or boy?"

"A sweet little girl. She's beautiful. Dark hair like yours, but fairer skin. David said to tell you he'd see that she had a good home. He'll return later."

After a time, she faced Mrs. Cranshaw. "Could I have a drink of water?"

"I'll have Mattie bring a fresh pitcher."

As Abigail waited, she thought about signing away the baby without ever looking into its eyes or touching the tiny fingers. What had she done? It didn't matter, what was done was done. Maybe her new life would ease her loss. She studied the room that had been her home for the last few months. These four walls had shielded her from the world, the first home she'd had since childhood where she felt safe. She slid her hand over her stomach. The bulge that used to rest on her lap was no longer there. Closing her eyes, she prayed, *Dear Jesus, please keep my little one safe and let it know real love. And help me live with what I've done. Amen*

A cold glass was pressed in her hand. She sipped the water and watched Mrs. Cranshaw over the rim. "Do you think I've done what's best for my baby?"

"Yes. You're going to have a whole new life before long. Now, try to get some rest. I'll be downstairs. If you need anything, just ring your bell."

Abigail rolled toward the wall. She'd done what she must, but she'd take the memories of her baby with her no matter where she went.

❧ 8 ❧

Cranshaw Plantation: May, 1859

The horror of Abigail's cries still filled David's ears as he guided the carriage along the lane to the plantation house. With his left hand, he shaded his eyes against the blazing ball of fire that peaked over the eastern horizon, and then glanced toward Stella who sat in the back, cuddling the newborn to her full bosom.

"Massa, what yo gonna do with dis here young'un? Yo knows what ta doctor says 'bout bringin' chill'uns home. Missus ain't strong enough."

"I know what he said, but I don't have a choice. The baby wasn't due for another few weeks, and I haven't found a home for her yet. I figure you can go up the back stairs and keep her in your room for now. I'll talk to the Wilsons about taking the baby. Maybe they'll even want to adopt her."

"I do mah best, but ain't nothin' I do to keep her from cryin'."

David's eyes rested on the bundle in her arms. He should have left Abigail at the brothel. Who was he to play God? Would he ever learn not to interfere in other people's lives?

Mariah still had spells. Dr. Daniels drops weren't curing her, but some days she was almost like her old self. The child they'd lost was never mentioned. But when her hallucinations resumed, she'd rock with cradled arms. The least little thing triggered a spell.

"I've only heard a few whimpers. You sure she's breathing?"

"Jest like a baby bird. Her mouth be all puckered up. She gonna wanna et soon."

"When we get to the house, I'll have Monroe find a wet nurse. A good meal will keep her quiet. Hopefully, Mariah will sleep late."

"I not count on dat, Massa. She be up at ta crack of dawn lately. Some days she be fine. Others, well . . ." Her voice trailed off on a lonesome note.

He tried not to dwell on the old servant's tone. He'd rather think about his wife and all the good times—times they'd gone riding together—times they'd made love. When the bad times were gone, he'd have her back.

* * *

Outside Mariah's door, David hesitated. She hadn't had a wild look in her eyes for over a month. If she were in a normal frame of mind, he'd invite her to ride over to the Wilsons. She could visit with Mrs. Wilson while he made arrangements with her husband. Stella could take the baby over later. If she were in one of her states, she'd never know the baby was here.

Inside her room, David found Mariah rocking and singing to empty arms. Guilt tightened in his chest. My Lord, what had he been thinking? His first duty was at home. His mother could have handled the birth. This was the sort of behavior that always got him into trouble. He searched his pockets. Where'd he leave the drops? His other jacket—he'd had it on yesterday when he had given her the medicine. "Hannah, come here?"

The large boned servant materialized like a ghost. "Yo need sump'n?"

"You left your mistress unattended? Haven't I told you to stay with her when she's not well?"

"I jest be down ta hall fer clean sheets. Her bed be a mess. I not go fer, Massa."

"Give them to me and run down to my room. In my jacket pocket, you'll find a bottle. Bring it, and hurry." David grabbed the linens and threw them on the bed, then extended a hand. "Come on, dear, let's go have breakfast." No response– just the creaking of the rocker and a soft lullaby. The doctor had warned him that this might happen.

He had to do something, anything, to save his beloved wife. The baby! Couldn't it be hers for just a little while? In her condition, she'd never know the difference. He pushed Dr. Daniels warning from his mind and wheeled, bumping into Hannah. "Don't leave her. I'll be right back."

He returned with the baby and Stella in tow.

"Massa, what yo do?" A distraught Stella said in a whisper. "Has yo lost yo' senses? Missus can't know 'bout dis . . ."

David ignored Stella's pleadings. *Please, dear God, let this work. I need Mariah, and she needs a baby . . .* gently, he placed the infant in her arms. The creakings and moanings of the rocker grew faster. The little bundle wiggled and squirmed, then settled close. Her singing rose a notch. He held his breath, waiting, praying for a miracle to happen. He leaned forward. "Look, Stella! I think she knows she's holding a baby, don't you?"

"Yo seein' what yo wanna. I sees a missus dat not know nothin'."

"Don't say that. She's going to get better. You saw it didn't you, Hannah?"

Hannah glanced toward Stella, worry marring her dark eyes. "Looks like she move a little, but I not be sure."

The three waited like cats watching for a mouse to make its get-a-way.

Mariah's mouth twitched then came a flutter of her eyelids. The tiny bundle of flesh cuddled even closer.

Finally, Stella spoke softly in wonder. "If dat littl'un hab its way, ta Missus be its new Mama."

Wearily, David sank onto the bed. The full impact of his impulsive action beginning to seep in. "What good is a crazy mother? Children need more than rocking and cradling." Memories of his own mother kissing a bruised knee or wiping away tears flooded his mind.

"What we do now, Massa?"

"I guess I'll have to go on over to the Wilsons and make arrangements for the baby, Stella. I was hoping it would . . ." His shoulders slumped as he stood.

"Massa, look. She hugging ta baby."

David whirled; hope filled his heart. "I told you something was happening. See, right in the corner of her mouth, there's a slight smile. You two get back to your chores. I'll sit and talk to her. Hannah bring up some warm milk, and I'll try and get her to take the medicine."

Sitting on the floor he talked in a soothing monotone. "Mariah, please come back to us. Your baby needs you, and I need you. You've been awfully sick, my love, but you're getting better; you and I are going to give our daughter a wonderful life. Please, come back. I don't know anything about raising a little girl." He paused, rubbing her hands that clutched the child. "See, how beautiful she is. I think she looks like me. Dark curls, but fair skin like you."

Mariah's eyes looked more like a frightened animal than human. Suddenly, she glanced around the room with her gaze coming to rest on David. He dared not move. It wouldn't take much to plunge her into the depths of darkness. With a whimper, the baby yawned and stretched out a tiny hand. Ever so slowly, he clasped it.

"Rosemary, your mama isn't feeling too well. We'll make her better, won't we? There's nothing love can't do." He lifted his eyes toward her. The blankness was fading and a glimmer of light flickered deep within them. "Come on, my love. I know you're in there and that you need us as much as we need you."

"Massa, here ta milk."

He took the cup. Dropping in the medicine, he placed the glass to her lips. She drank without being encouraged. He reached for the baby. Her arms tightened possessively. He'd just sit here quietly on the floor and see what happened. Gradually her voice grew softer and a glimmer of light shown in her eyes. A smile spread across her face.

She stopped singing and looked down. "What are you doing down there, David? Rosemary can't see you."

David clutched her hands. "Oh, my darling, are you all right?"

"Don't be silly. I only had a baby. Women have been giving birth from the beginning of time. Have Hannah take her to the nursery. I'm tired and want to lie down for a little while."

David stood and held out his arms. "Can I take her? I haven't gotten to hold her much."

She placed the child in his arms. "I didn't mean to be selfish." She stood and stretched. "She must have colic. She's been so fussy. She's got her days and nights mixed up. My throat is sore from all that singing."

"I'll be right back as soon as I give the baby to Stella. Hannah, help your mistress get settled in bed and then bring our breakfast up. Would you like that?"

"Yes. For some reason, I'm awfully hungry. And sleepy too."

David paused at the door then looked back at her clear eyes. It had only taken a brief moment to make them a family. He hadn't planned on keeping the child, but now it appeared that he had no choice.

* * *

In the nursery, the new baby slept peacefully. Gently, David tucked a blanket over her. The dark curls and the button nose were unmistakable her mother's. He didn't want to think about Abigail or remember her screams in the night. Yet he had to face her. Once the baby had a Christian name, he'd feel better about things. But Abigail's softness and sweet smile intruded on his repressed need for a woman. It'd been months since he'd been with his wife.

Immediately, guilt filled him. This beautiful child had saved Mariah from a life of insanity, and he was thinking about his own physical needs. Hadn't his prayers been answered? She would be his again and as soon as this christening was over, he'd check on Abigail.

Stella held out the six, seed pearl buttons. "Massa Cranshaw, what I do with dese."

He picked one up. They reminded him of Abigail, small and delicate, but yet so durable. He returned the button. "I want you to sew them down the front of Rosemary's christening dress."

"Dat what I think yo want. I get right to it." She started for the door then stopped. "Missus want breakfast dis mornin'. Hannah say it ta first she say since comin' outta ta spell ta other day. She thin as a rail. Ain't et nuff to keep a bird alive since she be sick."

He took a step forward. "Has she mentioned the baby?"

"No. Ain't said nothin' much."

David turned and gazed at the sleeping child. "When the baby wakes, I want to be called. I'm going to talk to Monroe about some things. Remember, the christening is at four."

"It be Missus' birthday too, Massa."

"I know. That is why I chose to have it this afternoon. The priest will be coming to the house. I know I can trust you to get the baby ready." He walked to the door. "Call me when the baby is through nursing. I want her to be calm when I take her to her mother." As David descended the stairs, he breathed a silent prayer that everything would go smoothly.

Inside the library, he rang the bell, and Monroe appeared. "There are some things I need to talk to you about. I want you to get the stone-cutter to blot out our baby's name on the crypt. The new baby will be christened Rosemary later today. I want you to see that there's no evidence that there ever was another baby."

The old Negro hesitated then started toward the door.

"If you have any questions, now is the time to ask. I'll be busy later."

"No, Massa, dere ain't nothin' wrong. Least ways not yet, but my ole bones tell me dere be trouble a-brewin' at ta Cranshaw Plantation like it ain't never seen b'fore."

"Are the slaves restless? Tension over states' rights is running high. If there's not some give and take, there'll be war."

"What I see ain't got nothin' to do with ta servants. Mah pa told me a story 'bout a man who hab a milk cow and her calf died. Well, he not want to have to milk her so he bought a newborn calf fer her. Ta next day, he sell bof of 'em. Two days later, ta man come back and told him dat ta cow not let ta calf suck. He say, 'It not her calf'. Ta man say, 'I know it hern cause I give it to her'. Yo see, Massa, if ta animals know their own, how yo think yo gwine trick Missus into takin' another woman's baby?"

David wiped his brow, considering the old man's words. He wasn't meddling. He'd lived long enough to know much about human nature. "I can't bear the thought of having to keep Mariah locked up for the rest of her life. All we can do is pray that my plan works."

"I be doin' plenty of dat. Yo jest let me know if dere sump'n I do 'sides pray. I not long fer dis world, but ain't nothin' I not do fer yo and Missus."

"I appreciate your support and concern, Monroe. You found a good wet nurse for the baby, and I don't think there'll be a problem. Now, if you'd send in the housekeeper."

As Monroe hobbled toward the door, David heard him mumble something under his breath about curses. He put so much stock in stories his people handed down, and maybe for black folk, there was some truth in them. But as an educated man, he knew better.

"Massa Cranshaw, ta baby woke up. She jest 'bout done nursin'."

He followed Stella up the stairs and into the nursery. He took the baby from the wet nurse and went to Mariah's room. He marveled at how his life had changed in such a short time. Only a few days ago, he'd had no hope.

She sat near the window, staring into the courtyard.

He pulled up a rocking chair. He hummed a soft lullaby. The baby whimpered, and he cuddled her closer. The soft sounds developed into a loud wail. He rocked her, but she still fussed.

Finally, his wife looked at him and the baby. Slowly, she reached out her arms. Carefully, he gave her the child. Without emotion, she placed the baby on her shoulder and patted her back. A burp erupted, and the crying ceased. Silently, she handed the baby back.

He took her and rose. He'd have Mariah brought downstairs when the time was right. At the door, he paused and waited. He could sense her watching him. Her whisper barely carried across the room. "I have to go to the cemetery. Will you take me?"

For a moment, David's heart filled with joy. She'd spoken again. She must be getting better. But then he realized what she'd said. "I'd be glad to take you, but it'll have to wait until tomorrow. The priest will be here at four to christen the baby."

She looked past him as though he were invisible. "I have a feeling that my baby is there."

He wanted to hold her in his arms—tell her this was their child that a trip to the cemetery wasn't necessary. He'd have to take her, but he needed to give Monroe time to have the name removed. He must have been a little crazy to slip another woman's baby into her arms. "Mariah, I hope you don't mind. I've tried to see that you weren't bothered with any household problems since you've had the baby. I went ahead and took the liberty to plan the christening for this afternoon." He saw her flinch. "I'm so sorry. I should have consulted you."

She turned toward the window. "You did what was necessary. That's an important matter. What time is the service?"

"Four. I've only invited a few neighbors and my mother."

"You did right. The cemetery can wait until tomorrow."

David watched her for a few moments then said, "I'll send

Hannah in to help you get ready." He left her staring out at the courtyard and took the baby back to Stella. Would this child ever find a place in her heart?

* * *

That afternoon the Cranshaw house buzzed with preparations for the christening. David stepped into the nursery and picked up the dress. The pearl buttons glistened in the bright May sunshine that streamed in. He found himself thinking about Abigail. She'd be the kind of woman he'd want if there were no Mariah.

The baby whimpered, and he realized he'd have a part of her for as long as he lived. Could he deal with what he'd done? He had no choice. He'd live with his guilt and pray that his wife never learned the truth.

"Massa, ta priest be downstairs. I tell him I send yo down, but yo might wanna look in on Missus."

David's heart pounded. "She's not sick is she, Stella?"

"No. She jest act kinda sad like. Not say much. Make me feel uneasy, somehow."

"She asked me to take her to the cemetery. She said she thought her baby was buried there. I promised to take her."

"But she see ta name."

"No, she won't. Monroe is out there right now having it removed. The christening is going to make us a family, and that's what we both need."

Stella picked up the dress and smoothed it. "I jest hope dat so."

David paused at the door, watching her work. He was so blessed. He had a child who was about to take the Cranshaw name and a wife who was recovering from a serious illness. He would show her there was no baby in the crypt. His prayers had been answered. As for Abigail, he'd blot any thoughts of her from the corners of his mind.

* * *

David hitched the horse to the gatepost of the cemetery and helped Mariah down. "Now that we're here, where would you like to go?"

"To the family crypt," she mumbled uncertain.

He followed her through a maze of tombs. His heart beat with an increasing thud. "Don't you think the flowers are beautiful?"

Without answering, she looked at each crypt with anticipation. At the family tomb, she ran a finger over the granite and read aloud: "Rosemary S. Dawson. Born 1795, died 1845. Loving wife of Charles M. Dawson." With tears streaming down her face, she said, "Fifty short years on this earth, but Mother left something of herself behind. I wish I could do the same." Her hand slid across the letters that read: Charles M. Dawson, Beloved Husband and Father. "My parents loved each other so much."

David drew her into his arms. "We have a beautiful daughter. There's nothing here for you. Let's go home." He wiped the tears from her cheeks with his forefinger. An overwhelming urge swept over him, but he hesitated. She needed time. He steered her toward the waiting buggy and helped her up. For now, he'd try to dream away his need. The trouble with his dreams was that desire for the baby's real mother was beginning to take over. Mariah's hand on his arm drew him from his thoughts.

"Do you think my final resting place will read Beloved Wife of David Cranshaw?"

Her voice, so lost and forlorn, shocked him. "Why would you ask such a thing? Don't you know you're the love of my life?" He dabbed her eyes with his handkerchief.

"I ask that sort of question because I know men have certain *desires*, and it's been a long time since I've been a *real* wife. I also know there are always women who are . . . "

David hugged her close. "You have nothing to worry about. I can assure you that you alone own my love." Almost as soon as the words were out of his mouth, he felt guilty. He picked up the reins and flicked them, promising himself that Abigail would never hold the key to his heart. The silence between them grew; wrapping itself around the carriage like the shroud of fog that crept in from the river and hovered over the plantation. Not even a bird sang.

Then she spoke. "Hurry, Let's get home! I want to hold our child. Another rush of tears gathered in her eyes.

He stopped the buggy and pulled her into his arms. Joy filled his heart. She had said our child. She was on the road to recovery.

❧ 9 ❧

David Breaks Ties With Abigail: May, 1859

David flipped the reins as excitement trickled through his veins. "Get up, Flossie. I don't have all day." He had so much to be thankful for. They'd christened their new daughter Rosemary Mariah Cranshaw. The legal papers were filed, and now he had to see about Abigail. He was eager to settle things with her. It'd probably take all summer for her to recover. Mariah had been in bed for a couple of weeks when their baby was born, but then there'd been no problems with the birth.

As he neared the graveyard, he remembered Mariah's obsession with visiting here. Had there been some foggy memory of the day they'd buried their baby? If she brought it up again, he'd convince her it'd been a bad dream.

At the gate, he drew the horse to a halt and made a vow to leave the memories of his dead child here on the land Mariah's Grandfather Dawson had given. The old man had thought it high enough for burial underground, but the first grave filled with water before it was half opened. That was over fifty years ago. Now, row on row of crypts covered the landscape.

David knew that some day he'd rest here with his beloved. He prayed his new daughter would tend their crypt.

Far in the distance tiny specks of barges made their way up the mighty Mississippi. He took a deep breath and slowly let it escape. If he could only send away his desire and guilt over Abigail, let it be carried off on the boats out there and dumped in some foreign port, then he'd be free to live. But that wouldn't happen. Dwelling on the *truth* would hinder him from living his lies. Starting today, he'd live as though there was no past. He flicked the reins and drove toward the city. He'd make his peace with Abigail and then hopefully his life would come together.

* * *

David paused at the half-open door. Abigail lay on her bed staring toward the window, no more than a child herself. He still remembered her cries while she was in labor. He'd heard Mariah yell out during birth, but she didn't have the same forlorn sound as Abigail. Had Abigail's come from old wounds? Why did he sense her hurt?

He knocked. "May I come in?"

When there was no answer, he pushed open the door. Abigail sat up in a trance-like motion. The trace of a smile crossed her lips, momentarily; then the lines of sadness returned, but not for an instant did her beauty fade.

"We don't have anything to say to each other. Why don't you just leave me alone with what I have . . .?" Her face paled, and slowly she sank onto her pillow.

David rushed forward. Dipping a washcloth in cold water, he wiped her face. "Abigail, come on. Open your eyes. Tell me you're all right."

Her eyelids fluttered, and he offered her a drink.

She pushed away the cup. "You don't have to act so worried, Mr. Cranshaw. I'm not going to die."

He gripped her firmly by the shoulders. "Now, you listen! I never had anything but your best interest at heart, and you know it. If you'd got rid of the baby, you could've died. And living on the streets or even at the brothel wasn't an option."

Abigail turned her head away.

"We christened your baby yesterday. We named her Rosemary for our dead one."

"You what? I offered my baby to you. No, you didn't want her then; said your wife wouldn't want it. And I was glad. I don't want some insane woman raising my baby! You promised to find her a good home and make sure she grew up safe. You're as crazy as your wife! I want my daughter back!"

"Calm yourself. It can't be too good for you to get so upset after having such hard labor."

"How can I be calm when the only child I'll ever have is in danger? Who's with her?"

"Stella, you don't have to worry. Mariah's fine. Why, when I placed that baby in her arms, she snapped out of her spell and thought she'd given birth to Rosemary. And what do you mean, the only one you'll ever have?"

"Didn't the doctor tell you, Mr. Cranshaw? The birthing left me in no condition to have another baby. But you needn't think for one minute that I'm going to give up on life. No, sir, there are other things, and I aim on having them. And now, about my baby . . ."

David stiffened. "There's nothing to discuss. You signed a paper giving her to me. Yes, I said I'd find her a home, but that was before . . ."

"Before you decided to let that crazy woman raise her!"

"Don't call my wife crazy! She's as sane as either of us."

"Speak for yourself . . . . No, you're right, I must've been crazy to sign my baby over to you. But you're right, she's yours, and I've got a promise to keep to myself. Now, leave me alone!"

David reached out to console her, but she pulled away.

"And I have one to keep as well." David wiped his brow. "Mother has grown quite fond of you. I'd like for you to stay on with her, at least for awhile. I'll pay you, but under no conditions are you to try and see the baby. And believe it or not, I *do* know how you feel." He looked toward the window so she couldn't look into his eyes. Eyes were windows to the soul and his couldn't bear examining. If there were only some way to comfort her. His mother would know what to do. He reached for the bell, but her arm swung out and knocked it to the floor. He bent and picked it up. "Abigail, please . . .."

Her small fists clenched and unclenched. "Don't you 'please' me! Just go. Do you hear? Leave me alone! If you hadn't found me at the brothel, I wouldn't have suffered so much!" Her face turned purple with rage.

"I'll only go when you've calmed down. You have no right to blame me for what went wrong during the birth. You might have died at the hands of some back-alley butcher. I wish I could do something to help you now. I only wish . . .." He stopped. He wasn't sure what this girl stirred in him. It wasn't the same feeling he had for his wife. Was it pity, or could it be . . .? No, he loved Mariah. He'd always loved her and always would. Besides, this girl was not much more than a child . . one he felt sorry for.

"I've seen people like you before . . .."

She was speaking. He had to listen.

" . . . always wanting something. Well, you got my daughter for your trouble."

He got up and walked to the door. She couldn't have been more deliberate if she'd been trying. She'd driven another nail in his coffin of guilt. There was no use in talking. She was right. There wasn't anything left to say. All he could do was go and be the best father he could to the child he'd taken. He paused. "I *do* care." He hurried down the stairs. Caring was what had caused his problems, he tried to convince himself

Abigail heard the echo of his words—*I do care—I do care—* resounding from the depths of her heart. She dropped back against her pillow. Sobs shook her tiny frame. He cared, all right; cared enough to take away her baby; cared enough to have another woman be its mother. Well, she'd show him! She'd show the world she was a survivor! And she'd do a good job. She'd never be used, abused, or accused again.

Mariah Cranshaw: Early Summer, 1859

Mariah Cranshaw stood in front of the oval mirror in her bedroom, brushing her long blond hair. As hard as she tried, she couldn't remember much about the last year. There were moments she thought she remembered. Or were they fevered dreams brought on by her illness? Slowly, a crypt replaced her image. The inscription read: Rosemary Mariah Cranshaw. With a cry, she threw the hairbrush, and the mirror cracked.

"Dere sump'n wrong, Missus?"

She wheeled at the sound of the maid's voice. "No, Hannah. The mirror broke."

Hannah's eyes fixed on the crack. Her hand flew to her mouth as her body began to shake. "Ta mirror be fixed, Missus, but not ta curse of bad luck yo hab fer ta next seven years."

"What in the world are you talking about?"

Hannah ran from the room, mumbling, "Poor soul . . . poor Missus. Ain't she hab 'nuff bad luck?"

Mariah gathered her toilet items and dropped them in a drawer. She'd forget the past. No matter what had happened, it was over and done with. A beautiful baby girl slept down the hall, and her wonderful husband would protect them from curses. Anyway, that was just Negro superstition. How could a broken glass bring bad luck? Didn't people make their own luck? And she was going to start making her's tonight. She'd greet David with a kiss and have supper served here in the bedroom. Afterwards, well, nature would take over. It was time she became a *real* wife again. She didn't care what that long-nosed doctor said. Men had needs, and she wasn't letting David find another woman to take care of his.

"Hannah said you had a little accident."

Mariah looked up to find David standing in the doorway. "Oh, darling, you're home. Yes, I lost my grip on my hairbrush, and it hit the mirror. My maid said I'll have seven years of bad luck. You don't believe her, do you?" She went to him and put her arms around his neck.

He kissed her on the forehead. A warm blush rippled over her.

"How could someone as beautiful as you have bad luck? The only luck we're having is good."

She stepped from his embrace. "That's right. Now, you sit over here by the window, and I'll be back." She hurried out the door and down the stairs. Yes, she'd be back and serve her husband more than supper.

Mariah's head of golden hair swept through the door and disappeared out of sight. David reached out and traced the line in the mirror. It only took moments for thoughts of Abigail to take Mariah's place. He knew how it felt to be broken in two. He couldn't bear anymore. And his wife . . . .. She was the reason he'd done what he had. She'd have been lost to him forever if he hadn't tried giving the baby to her. He'd live the rest of his life in this box of guilt, unless . . . no, the only option he had was to see that she focused on the good.

"Hannah's getting our meal. I hope you don't mind. It's cozier in here."

He looked up at the sound of Mariah's voice. "I think everything is perfect, including you."

"Oh, David, you've always been able to say just what I want to hear and at the right time."

Again thoughts of Abigail filled his mind. He hadn't said the words she'd wanted to hear. But no matter what kind of misgivings he'd had, he'd never feel for anyone like he did for Mariah. How could he have doubted his love for her?

"Supper's served," said Mariah.

David moved away from the mirror as Hannah set down a tray. He hadn't realized how hungry he was until she lifted the cover from two plates of steaming roast beef and mashed potatoes, plus generous helpings of green peas, and bread pudding for dessert.

"The food looks good." said Mariah.

The servant girl's eyes darted toward the broken mirror. "I hope yo like supper. I make sure myself dat it fixed jest ta way yo like."

"Don't be such a worry wart. It's fine." She pointed at the broken glass. "I don't believe in those old superstitions. See that we have a pot of fresh coffee in time for dessert."

"Yes'um, it be here. Anythin' else?"

"No. You may go."

The servant girl backed out the door, her head still bobbing in answer to her mistress's orders. David remembered Monroe's cow story and feeling like there was trouble brewing at the plantation. Was there something to their superstitions?

"Wouldn't it be awful to live with that sort of fear?" asked Mariah.

"Come eat, Dear. Forget the servants. We don't know how we'd feel if we'd lived their life."

She sat down, spread her linen napkin on her lap, and picked up her fork.

Later, Hannah returned with the coffee and left without a word, but not before David saw her steal another worried glance at the mirror. Uneasiness tugged at his insides. Surely, he was right . . . just black superstition . . . nothing else. He drank, watching his lovely wife over the rim of his cup. He'd done everything in his power to protect her from harm. If the North attacked, he'd send her and Rosemary overseas until it was safe to return. He pushed away ugly thoughts of war. Hadn't he decided just this afternoon to live for now?

Without warning, Mariah said, "Stay here tonight. I've been in that big old bed by myself long enough ."

He choked on his coffee then wiped the bitter brew from his mouth with a napkin. He'd forgotten that she was so forthright. She'd always been that way. That was one of the things that he loved about her. "The doctor. What did he say?"

"I don't see what he said has anything to do with where you sleep. I'm lonely, and you're my husband."

He pulled her to her feet. He wanted nothing more than to spend the night in her bed. He ran his fingers through her hair as desire filled every fiber of his being. He'd have to be careful not to spill his seed within her. If that happened, maybe Hannah's predictions would come true. And as for the mirror, well, it could be replaced.

* * *

Mariah walked toward the nursery. She'd vowed to make an effort to try and be more of a mother to the child they'd christened Rosemary. Despite her doubts, she couldn't remember giving birth, and David sure acted like the baby belonged to him. There wasn't a day passed that she didn't see him head this way.

Inside, she stood watching her sleep. Why didn't she feel for the child? Wouldn't any woman love such a perfectly beautiful baby even if it didn't belong to her? She scooped her up and went to the rocking chair and slowly began to undress her. Ten toes and fingers, a button nose, two ears, one mouth and two eyes, everything was here even to the wrinkles in the tiny arms and legs. She was so busy with her inspection that she didn't hear Stella come in.

"What yo doin', Missus?"

"Don't all mothers inspect their babies? I can't remember if I did or not."

The maid placed a pan of water on the table and reached for the baby. "Here. I bathe her then put her back together fer yo."

Mariah clutched the baby tight. "No, I'll do it. If I'm going to be a mother, I need to learn to . . . .."

"You not hab to do nothin', Missus. Dat what I be here fer."

"You can't love her for me. I'll have to do that myself."

"Why, dat not be a hard job. Ever mother love her baby."

She shoved the baby toward Stella. "They do if it's theirs. Somehow, I don't feel like she's mine. Would you know why that's so?"

Stella took the baby and began to wash it. "Yo be with child so I guess dis be her."

Mariah felt the water. As little circles rippled out from her finger tips, so did the image of the crypt. Lord, what was happening to her? Here she had a healthy baby and signs of death were robbing her of all her happiness. Could it mean she was going to die? If that were so, she need not get too attached to anyone else, including this baby. She dried her hand and rushed from the room.

❧ 11 ❧

Elizabeth Cranshaw's Home: Early Summer, 1859

The front door bell clanged. Abigail moved from the table toward the back stairs. This was the first time someone, other than the church ladies, had called on Mrs. Cranshaw since she'd been here. Automatically, her hand touched her stomach. Now that the baby was born, there wasn't any reason to rush upstairs. Sooner or later people would know that she was here. Now was as good a time as any. She stepped toward the door leading to the hall. A loud angry voice stopped her. Who would Mrs. Cranshaw be arguing with? Maybe it was news of Elizabeth's daughter. She pressed her ear to the door.

"I tell yo ta baby ain't gonna make it without it gets some lovin.'"

"I tell you, Monroe, she can't have anything to do with that child. If she ever sees it, all my son's plans will be finished, and what's going to happen to his wife? No. You run along and get the doctor to take a look at the baby."

"She not growin' ta way a baby oughta. If she die, Missus be crazier than before. She ain't well yet."

"That's a risk we'll have to take. Now, go. And not a word of any of this to David. Do you hear me?"

"I hears yo, Miz Crenshaw."

Abigail moved in a daze up the back stairs. She bet a dime to a dollar that crazy woman wasn't mothering Rosemary. Well, she'd find out what was happening at the plantation. She wasn't a prisoner here. She'd healed from the birthing and could leave anytime. Elizabeth had said she could use the buggy if she wanted to get some fresh air. That's what she'd do. She closed her bedroom door and sat on the bed. Yes, she'd find a way to go see about the baby. A soft knock interrupted her planning.

"May I come in?"

"Yes, Mrs. Cranshaw. I'm getting caught up on my reading." She picked up a book.

Elizabeth came in holding the button box. "I've got some time, so I brought the buttons. Can I tell you another story?"

She lay down the book and smiled. Mrs. Cranshaw was already busy fishing out a handful of big, white ones. The soothing tone of Mrs. Cranshaw's voice always carried her into a world where there'd never been a stepdaddy; where there'd never been a life on the streets or at the Wellington's brothel; where there'd never been a David Cranshaw or a baby. But this afternoon she didn't have time for fantasies. She had to figure out how to deal with reality!

"I'm not up to a story. Can we do it later?"

Mrs. Cranshaw set the box on the nightstand and felt her head. "Aren't you feeling well? You know it's only been two months. When I had my babies my feet weren't to touch the floor for nine days, and then I could only sit up for a few hours at a time. You're doing too much."

"Doing too much! With so many servants, how can I?" she had to fight back a smile. "I want to finish this book and maybe later take the carriage out for a while. I could use some fresh air."

"Very well, my dear. I am a little tired." She walked toward the door.

"I thought I heard the doorbell. Did you have company?"

"No one important. Just a servant from the plantation who

stopped by to say he was on his way to bring the doctor to check Mariah."

"Is she still ill?"

"Nothing like before. David's away at the Capitol on business, so the servants are overly cautious."

Abigail picked up the book and pretended to read again. David was away. Surely that crazy woman wouldn't do anything to hurt her baby. This was her chance to see her child. Mr. Cranshaw wouldn't have to know.

❧ 12 ❧

Cranshaw Plantation: Early Summer, 1859

Mariah clutched her stomach and bent over. She didn't feel well. And the baby had been fussy for the last few days. It must be the July heat. She couldn't remember a summer this hot. As much as she tried to be a doting mother, she had more and more doubts. David must never know. He was so proud of his new daughter. She eased down on the bed, mopping her brow with the back of her hand. "Hannah, come here a minute."

"Yes'um, yo need me?"

"Yes. Tell Monroe to go for the doctor. I'm not feeling well, and I also want the baby checked. She's been so fussy. David's gone, and he'd never forgive me if something happens to her."

"Stella already send Monroe fer him, Missus. And ta baby not be good fer some time now. I not think she growin' ta way babies oughta."

Mariah threw back the covers and swung her feet over the edge of the bed. "There's nothing wrong with my baby. Tell Stella to bring her to me!"

"Yo shore yo oughta be 'round her 'til ta doctor see yo? What if yo hab a fever?"

Mariah felt her lips quiver. "I'm tired of everybody else knowing what's best for me. I'm your mistress. Tell Stella to bring the child!"

"I knows yo be ta mistress. I not hab to be told. Yo lay back 'ginst dem pillers, and I get Stella to bring ta baby."

Mariah settled back in bed. No servant was going to run her family. Anyway, Rosemary was *her* baby, or at least that's what everyone said. Starting right now, she'd take over.

As she waited, loud voices drifted through the door. It sounded like some of the servants were arguing. Crawling out of bed and holding onto the furniture and the wall, she edged her way to the stairs. Below, she saw Monroe and Hannah in the large foyer. Hannah's voice was too soft to hear, but Monroe's was elevated in an irritated tone.

"I done what I hab to. I done and tell Massa dere gwine be big trouble. Not listen to ole Monroe. Now, ta doctor be right along." He moved away, stumbled, and slowly sank to the floor. Hannah rushed to him and then ran from the room, screaming.

Mariah stood for a few moments, watching, and then eased back into her room. Why on earth was Monroe so angry? What kind of trouble was he trying to warn David about? Was there a problem with the servants? Or is it something else? As soon as she felt better, she'd have a talk with the old servant. He couldn't look her in the eye and not tell the truth. She'd find out if her memories were real or just dreams. He would know about the baby down the hall.

"Missus, Hannah say yo ask fer yo' baby."

She held out her arms and Stella placed the tiny bundle in them. "Yes. It's time I start being a mother." Mariah saw streaks of tears as they made trails down the nurse's face.

"What's wrong, Stella?"

"I fear ole Monroe not gwine be with us much longer. Doc jest got here, and he be with him right now. Doc say he gwine die."

Mariah cringed. *Monroe dying.* Without him the truth would be lost. She looked down at the child who everyone said favored

David. Maybe she should thank God she'd never know.

She cuddled the baby to her and rocked back and forth. No matter what sort of dreams she'd had about the cemetery, this child was very much alive and in need of a mother. Unfamiliar warmth stirred deep inside her, and she held the baby even closer. "I've got so much to make up to you, Rosemary." She began to hum a lullaby.

The baby breathed softly against her neck. And maybe, they could have another baby. A son this time, to carry on the Cranshaw name. Yes, another child was what they needed to be a complete family.

Stella touched Mariah's shoulder. "Yo and ta baby is both sleepin'. Let me take her to ta nursery."

"I'm not sleeping. I'm just enjoying holding my baby. And I've been thinking Rosemary needs a little brother."

Stella took the baby. "Missus, yo not hab no more babies."

Her hopes dashed as though Stella had drowned them. *No more babies?* Why hadn't the doctor told her? Surely if this were so, he'd have said something. She brushed at tear-filled eyes. The desire for another child rekindled in the depths of her womanhood. She longed for David's return. She'd convince him to be as excited about her plan as she was. But with her excitement came a new wave of nausea. Her body retched, and she felt like she was going to faint.

"See what I means, Missus? Yo ain't strong 'nuff to hab 'nother baby. I sure ta doc will tell yo ta same thing. Here he be now. Ask him."

"Ask me what?"

Mariah lifted her head to find Doctor Daniels standing in the doorway. "I was telling Stella I'd like to have a brother for

Rosemary. She says it's too soon. What do you think?"

"The most important question is what David thinks. He will be responsible for the welfare of another one."

"We haven't talked about it yet, but as soon as he gets home, I'm going to ask him." Her eyes traveled to the sleeping infant in Stella's arms. "Isn't she the most darling child you've ever seen, Doctor Daniels? She deserves a brother to grow up with."

"Yes, I guess every child needs to have siblings, but sometimes it's not the right thing for the parents. Mariah, you should be thankful for *one* healthy baby. You've been an awfully sick woman, and another one so soon could cause problems." The doctor turned to Stella. "Take the baby back to the nursery. I'll come by and check on her, too. You might want to go see Monroe. He's not long for this world."

"I gwine miss him."

"We'll all miss him, especially Mr. Cranshaw. He's been with the family for three generations." said Doctor Daniels as he gave Mariah his attention. After his examination he said, "You're in good health, Mariah. You have a simple case of the grippe. How have you been, emotionally?"

She closed her eyes. The visions of the crypt plagued her. Fear clutched at her heart. Was Hannah right? Could this be the beginning of trouble? No. She wouldn't believe in any old superstitions. David would be home soon, and he'd take care of everything. But there'd be no Monroe to . . .. She felt a chill run down her back.

"Are you cold? You shivered."

"No. I was thinking of David coming home to the loss of Monroe. My problems seem small."

"He's strong. He can handle it. He's a man with deep faith. And I might say you've given him a lot to live for. Now, why don't you tell me what's bothering you besides the flu?"

"Are you a superstitious man?"

"You haven't been listening to old servant's tales, have you?"

Tears spilled down her face as she nodded. "I keep having this vision of the family crypt. Right after Rosemary's christening I had David drive me out there. I felt so foolish. On the way home, he assured me everything was fine."

"He's a good man. He wants to make life easier for you because he loves you so much."

Mariah wiped at her eyes. "I realize that. I'd like to get rid of the feeling that the baby down the hall isn't mine. You'd think the trip to the cemetery would have eased my mind, but that horrible vision won't go away." She pointed to the mirror. "I was brushing my hair and the crypt appeared. I got so upset I threw my hairbrush and broke it. Hannah thinks I'm going to have seven years of bad luck. I keep telling myself there's nothing to an old superstition, but here I am flat on my back. Then the other day I saw the crypt in the baby's bath water."

"You have nothing more than a case of the grippe and an over-active imagination. We've all had dreams we can't forget. As far as the superstition goes, you're looking for signs to connect with it. We make our own luck, Mariah. That's why I'm encouraging you to forget the idea of another child, at least for now."

"But my husband deserves a son."

"Let's have this conversation in about a year. I'm going to check on your lovely daughter. I'll leave instructions for you with

Hannah. Get some rest, my dear, and think about what a lucky young woman you are." The doctor patted her shoulder, picked up his bag, and left.

Mariah pondered his advice. She'd concentrate on the baby in the nursery for now, but David was too good a man not to have a son to carry on his family name. She planned on changing that.

* * *

The edge of dark gathered and hung heavy over the Cranshaw Plantation as Abigail tied the horse to a limb. Low mournful singing filled the air, sounds she had never heard before. It was the sort of song that carried on the wind and into the night, reaching to the depths of every soul it touched. She shuddered and hugged herself. She couldn't make out the words, but the tune spoke clearly of death. Maybe she was too late and the baby had already died.

A few minutes later she tapped on the kitchen door. A large servant woman with tears streaming down her face, greeted her. "I so glad yo come, Miz Abigail. Ta baby cry fer most of ta day. Missus, she ain't no help even when she ain't feelin' poorly. Monroe say right 'fore he die he go fer yo. Say Miz Cranshaw not let yo come, but I be praying. I jest know yo come."

A surge of relief washed over Abigail, as great as the waves that lapped at the shoreline of New Orleans. A slave had died, not her baby. No, the Cranshaw baby. She must remember or else lose sight of her promise to take care of herself.

"Come on, I sneak yo up ta back stairs to mah room. I bring ta baby in dere fer yo to hold."

The servant turned and waddled away, her watermelon hips rolling back and forth the same way they had the first time Abigail had seen her. Surely this woman knew what was right for the baby. Well, it was too late to back out now. Before she could think anymore, Stella opened a door and called, "Come on up and be quiet."

Only the flicker of the oil lamp relieved the darkness. The shadows reminded Abigail of the night the child was born. As she eased her feet up the stairs, the boards creaked and her heart hammered. What would she find waiting for her? Would she regret coming? Pulling a rocking chair near the door, she sat down. The room was very plain, but exceptionally clean. The door opened and Stella was there, holding her precious daughter.

"She quiet right down when I says, 'Yo' mama be here'. She ain't growed much since she born. She two months ole and ain't no bigger'n a mite."

Abigail reached out for the baby. Folding back the blanket, she saw a face that looked just like hers. "I ain't never seen my own baby." She immediately noticed her lapse in grammar. Did surroundings make that much difference? Tenderly, she cuddled the baby to her bosom as tears of joy ran down her cheeks. Yes, she was thankful she'd gotten the chance to see her baby. Thankful she'd come to set her on the road to a healthy and wonderful life. But more than that, thankful that David Cranshaw had a living memory of the woman who had given him a daughter.

❧ 13 ❧

Elizabeth Cranshaw's Home: July, 1859

It was after nine when Abigail got home from visiting her baby. As she paused at the parlor door, she heard a murmur of voices. Who was here? Mrs. Cranshaw never stayed up this late. Maybe David was here. What would he do if he knew she'd just come from his plantation house? Tapping on the door, she waited.

Mrs. Carnshaw answered and ushered her in. "Remember I told you about the friend of mine who married and moved to North Carolina? This is her son, Seth. He is in New Orleans on business. I've been telling him all about you."

She stepped from the shadows and extended her small hand. The man who pressed it to his lips was a far cry from the one she'd given her baby to. His frame was slim while David was muscular. His wispy, blond hair was slicked back. Yet, he was attractive. He was dressed neatly, but that wasn't it. Something about the narrow nose and deep set blue-violet eyes was quite appealing. "So pleased to make your acquaintance. Mrs. Cranshaw has spoken highly of you, Mr. Seth."

"The pleasure is all mine, Miss Abigail. You're as lovely a young lady as Elizabeth described."

With a gentle tug, she removed her hand. "If you'll excuse me, I've had a long evening. I think I'll retire for the night and leave you two to visit."

Mrs. Cranshaw looked at the clock. "Oh, my goodness, it's after nine. I never stay up this late. Seth is spending the night. There will be plenty of time for you to get acquainted tomorrow. Did you have a nice evening?"

"Yes, it was very enjoyable. I took the carriage and went for a long ride. We'll have to go out more. It's not good for you to stay shut up here in this house."

Mrs. Cranshaw raised an eyebrow in Seth's direction. "Didn't I tell you she was a thoughtful young woman? I suppose, any day now, there's going to be a string of men wanting to call on her. I might give her sort of a coming out party and introduce her to the eligible men in New Orleans."

She felt her cheeks grow warm and her pulse race. Who was she to deserve a party? Where'd that thought come from. She'd given her baby to the Cranshaws. Why not let them do something nice for her?

"Are you going to stand there all night gazing into the fire, Abigail? Come, let's go upstairs, and we'll talk about the ball another time."

She shook her head to clear away the thoughts and followed Mrs. Cranshaw and Seth upstairs. Yes, she'd be happy to talk about a party. Her spirits lifted. Why not enjoy all the things that were being offered? Hadn't she vowed never to be used, abused or accused again? Now, was a good time to start living that vow.

"Good night, Miss Abigail. I'll be looking forward to getting to know you better." Seth picked up her hand and pressed it to his lips, then opened the door across from hers and went inside.

Mrs. Cranshaw patted her on the shoulder. "Isn't he sweet, my dear? A little older, but then there's something to be said about maturity. See you in the morning."

Once in her room, Abigail relived the events of the day. She'd love her baby into growing. With the use of the carriage, she'd go see her at least once a week. It would be nice if she could talk to David about the baby, but he'd never allow her to visit and the baby's welfare did come first. But as much as she loved the child, she didn't want to remove it from the Cranshaw house. And the man across the hall. Did he have intentions, or was she reading something into the way he'd held her hand? Crawling into bed, Abigail tucked the blanket under her chin. It was so warm and safe here, but it wouldn't last forever. Nothing in her life ever had.

❧ 14 ❧

Cranshaw Plantation: September, 1859

David paced the library as the clock on the mantle tolled the bewitching hour. He stopped at his desk to check the calendar. Already September. How had his life gotten so complicated? Immediately, he knew the answer. Who said, "When first you practice to deceive?" He couldn't remember, but the lies started when he placed Abigail's baby in Mariah's arms. He had done only thing he knew, and he wasn't sorry. He opened the drapes and looked out into the night. Down by the servants' quarters smoke boiled into the air. Their lives were so simple. He raised the window a little bit more in order to listen to the singing as it drifted on the wind. The slaves were always so happy.

The melodious voices were interrupted by a loud piercing scream. *Mariah*! Rushing up the stairs and into her room, he found his wife drenched in sweat and tangled in the sheet. Kneeling, he wiped her face. "Dear, open your eyes. You're having a bad dream." He straightened the cover. "Come on. Wake up. Talk to me."

Her eyelids fluttered and her face relaxed in a gentle smile. "I love you so much."

He held her. "I love you, too. Now tell me why you're so frightened. You almost scared me out of my wits."

Mariah slipped her arms around his neck and pulled his face close.

"Were you dreaming?" He kissed her on the forehead.

"Yes, there were lots of babies crying. Did you hear them? Is Rosemary all right?"

"All I heard was your scream. The baby's fine. Stella takes good care of her. Want me to go check?"

"No, please don't leave me. I'm afraid." Her arms tightened.

He stretched out on the bed beside her. "I'm here. Now get some rest."

"I don't want to rest. I want to talk."

"We'll talk all night if it'll help. What do you want to talk about?"

"Babies."

He closed his eyes and tried to shut out that single word. Hadn't that *word* brought them enough suffering . . . but now the one in the nursery was making them a family.

"Let's have one. It's not fair for Rosemary to grow up alone. I want to have it right away."

He took a deep breath. "You don't know what you're asking. It could kill you. We can't take the risk. The answer is *no*. I can't be that selfish."

"You wouldn't be. It's *me*. I'm the one. There's a void in my heart that needs to be filled."

"Let's not plan anything now. I want to enjoy you and the baby we have." He gathered her into his arms and buried his face in her long silky hair. "We'll talk again after I've had an opportunity to ask the doctor, and you're feeling better."

David felt her tension ease, as she cuddled into the curvature of his body. Her softness and willingness to please was more than he could resist. He kissed her tenderly on the cheek.

She turned her mouth up to his.

At the touch of her lips, fire leaped in his groin and a moan rose from deep inside as she slid soft hands over his chest. He slipped her nightgown off and cradled a breast in his hand. Its silky whiteness gleamed in the lamplight. For a moment, he imagined it belonged to the baby's real mother. He felt only lust for Abigail. He was safe now; no more temptation. He'd do everything in his power to keep his wife happy even if it meant giving . . . no, he couldn't let her have another child.

The steady rhythm of their bodies echoed in unison until he could no longer contain himself. He withdrew just before spilling his seed, then continued to fondle her as she wilted in a shivering heap next to him. He smoothed her sweat-drenched hair and kissed her forehead.

"I love you, David Cranshaw."

"I love you, too, Mariah Cranshaw. Now do you think you can sleep?"

She answered by closing her eyes and snuggling closer. Before long her easy breathing assured him that she was asleep. Maybe the bad dreams were banished for this evening, but what about tomorrow, and the night after that? Would her doubts and fears ever cease?

* * *

David sat at his desk going over his bookkeeping. His head hurt. Life at the plantation wasn't the same without Monroe. He'd picked a young field hand by the name of Arnell to replace him. A boy would be easier to teach. He should've had Monroe train someone to take over. Well, he had until harvesting time to set things right in the house. He'd also spend lots of time with Mariah and the baby. Their lovemaking filled him with guilt. He'd have to be careful. Her desire for another child would only cause worry and heartache.

A tap on the library door caused him to flinch. Now, what? "Come in."

The door opened and the round face of Arnell appeared. "Massa, ta doctor be here."

"Take his coat and send him in. And don't forget the tea."

"Yes'suh, I hab it right here."

David smiled as the boy left. What a change for the boy. Hopefully, for the better. He pulled two chairs in front of the fireplace and greeted Dr. Daniels, motioning him to sit. "Tell me what brings you out here today. As far as I know, everyone's well."

"You have been gone a lot, and we haven't had a chance to talk." He crossed his legs. "I came out in late July when your wife was sick. I'm concerned. She has some fool notion about having another baby. You know what that would mean."

David held up his hand. "I know all about what she wants, and I understand what it'd do to her. But I'm also worried about what will happen if she doesn't have one." He rested his head in his hands. When he looked up, he said, "Doc, what am I going to do?"

The doctor hooked his thumbs in his suspenders. "Mariah's still sick, physically and mentally. Her mental state is responsible for some of her physical problems. Do you know about the mirror?"

"Yes, I saw it after it happened. That first night I stayed in her room."

"I warned you about sleeping with her. There's plenty of young wenches right here who can take care of your desires."

David picked up the cross-shaped paperweight and studied it. Finally he spoke. "I've been taught that marriage is holy. There are masters who use their slaves that way, but I can't . . .. " His feelings for Abigail caused him to flush. "Even if something happens to my wife, without love, another woman is out of the question."

"I understand. What about Mariah?"

He sat on the corner of his desk, looking the doctor straight in the eye. "She's not already . . .?"

"I don't think so. The last time I saw her there was evidence of her monthly sickness. But you can answer that better than I."

The memory of last night's love making quickened his pulse. His lovely, sweet wife . . . how he loved her. Never to touch her again. How could he bear such a burden? Unless he stayed away.

The governor's invitation to help with the state's orphans would keep him away more. "This mental problem. Do you think as Rosemary gets older Mariah will improve?"

"To be truthful it can go either way. The responsibility of being a parent can make her worse. You're needed here. I can't express that enough."

Arnell came in with the tea. David took the tray and dismissed the boy. Somehow he'd find a way to make the love of his life completely better. He'd come too far to give up now.

* * *

David didn't have long to contemplate his dilemma. The next day, as he went upstairs, Mariah came out of the nursery, wringing her hands.

"Rosemary! She's gone!"

He shook her shoulders. "What do you mean, gone?"

She collapsed in his arms, sobbing. "I've been trying to tell you that she's in the graveyard."

He heard a door open and close and looked up as the nurse stepped out into the hall holding the infant.

"Look, Stella has her. She's fine. I took you out to the cemetery, remember? You're going to have to forget this foolishness. Come, sit and rock the baby. She really needs her mother." He led her back to her room and the maid followed, placing the baby in her arms.

She began to rock and sing a lullaby. The baby snuggled close.

"I want to be alone with my baby."

He motioned for the maid to follow him. "Stay near by. I think she's fine, but just in case . . .." He couldn't finish, couldn't say he might have to lock her up somewhere to keep Rosemary safe.

Mariah unbundled the baby and inspected fingers and toes. *Perfect, not a blemish anywhere. David was right. She's not in the graveyard but here, and this is where she's going to stay.*

The child smiled and her heart warmed. She tucked the blanket tight and rocked her to sleep. There'd be plenty of times like this. She put the baby in the cradle that was still there then stood in front of the beveled mirror, looking deep into her eyes. "You're crazy for thinking your baby's dead. Now, pull yourself together. You have a husband to keep happy." She touched the blush on her cheeks then went to the window. "A son could be growing inside me. After another baby, the nightmares will stop." The words were barely out of her mouth when she caught a glimpse of the crypt in the pane. With both hands clenched into tight fists, she hit the glass full force. Several cracks ran in different directions from the point of impact.

"Missus, yo be alright? Do yo want me to fetch Massa?"

She looked down to see blood dripping from her hands then

faced Hannah.

Her servant's eyes grew big and her mouth dropped open as she backed away shaking her head. "I not know what Massa say when he see dat." She pointed toward the broken glass. "I brin' ta conjure woman. Maybe she break ta spell."

Mariah immersed her bleeding hands in a basin of water. "Don't be silly. I don't need any old witchcraft. Get someone up here to fix the window right away, hear me?."

"Yes'um. But yo need hep bad, Missus."

"I'll be the one to say what I need. Now, get some of that salve over there and put on my scratches. As Hannah helped, Mariah swore not to let this happen again. She'd ask the doctor for some sort of medicine to make the nightmares go away. No, she couldn't have a baby if she was medicated. Nor could she be a mother to Rosemary. She'd beat this obsession on her own!

The maid left, shaking her head.

She crawled into bed, blew out the lamp, and slid under the blankets, praying for God to free her from the grip of Satan. Maybe she'd ask her servant to bring the conjure woman. If it was all superstition, what harm could it do, anyway?

❧ 15 ❧

Elizabeth Cranshaw's Home: Late Summer, 1859

Abigail sat in the sitting room with the button box on her lap. She couldn't quench her uneasiness. All summer she'd been sneaking weekly visits to the plantation. The slave hadn't let her know about a visit this week. Was the baby all right? Had Mariah found out? Or worse yet, David? She sighed. There was no way to find out. She'd have to wait until the maid sent word.

She opened the box and began sorting them. Her eyes were drawn to the ones that came on the dress worn by Seth's mother. She picked them up, smiling. The time spent with Seth this summer had been fun. He was from an old family steeped in history and money. Nice, as men went, but much older.

The buttons sifted through her fingers and dropped into the box. She needed to do something about her life before it slipped away.

Seth didn't regard her as a child. In fact, she couldn't quite figure him out. Did he treat her nicely because she lived here with his friend, or did he really see her as a *woman*? Placing the lid on the box, she set it aside. It had been nice to have someone else in the house. Her problem was lack of companionship. Once she had a party, some young people would replace the likes of an old man like Seth.

"You're so lost in thought. Is anything wrong?" said Mrs. Cranshaw.

"No, I'm thinking about the ball."

"Who's having a soiree?" David entered with his coat hanging loosely on one arm.

Abigail looked up.

"We've been discussing a small social gathering for our girl," said Elizabeth, stepping forward to kiss him on the cheek. "Something to let the young men know she's available. It will be a busy time until after harvest, so late October should be good. When you have some spare time, we'll sit down and make out a guest list. You must have some friends you'd like for her to meet." She put her arm around the girl. "I admit I'm not particularly anxious to marry her off."

A gush of sympathy replaced Abigail's excitement. They had both lost daughters. Could it be possible that Elizabeth Cranshaw would miss her when she was gone?

❧ 16 ❦

Cranshaw Plantation: Fall, 1859

As David adjusted the harness on his favorite riding mare, he thought about all the changes in his life. Autumn had arrived in splendid color, and along with it came Mariah's brilliant smile. Rosemary had also changed. She no longer cried all the time, and her little arms and legs were creased with wrinkles. Her cheeks blossomed, and she laughed a lot. Life was truly becoming what he'd dreamed it to be. Spending more time here was paying off. He looked up to see Mariah coming toward the stable.

"David, are you going somewhere?"

"Yes, for a ride. Would you like to come along?"

A wistful look crossed her face. "It's been so long . . . not before—"

"You run to the house and put on your riding habit. I'll have another horse saddled." David watched until she disappeared. What had she started to say? Did she remember anything? No, she'd been her old self of late. It was good to have her back. He wouldn't spoil his thoughts with ghosts from the past.

* * *

Upstairs, Mariah raised the trunk lid and rummaged through the contents. The riding habit had to be here. She found a bundle of old letters from David. They'd had a whirlwind courtship and a simple wedding. The corner of a picture caught her eye, and she pulled it free. She and David-they both looked so happy. Looking closer, she saw that her belly protruded. *This picture isn't that old. How had it gotten buried here?* She turned it over—*no date. I'll keep it out and ask David.* Picking up the riding habit, she stood

109

and laid the picture on the dressing table. "Why can't I remember? But today's not the time for wondering. David was waiting."

Her nimble fingers soon had the jacket buttoned. Slipping on the skirt, she fastened it down to where the split started. As she slipped the last pearl button through the hole, the image of the crypt filled the tiny surface No . . . this wasn't happening, not now when every thing was so perfect. She'd not think about the visions. She was going riding with her husband. Grabbing her belt, she ran from the room.

* * *

David's heart quickened at the sight of Mariah in her riding habit with her long, blond hair blowing free. Maybe this wasn't such a good idea. Spending the afternoon in her room sounded better, but he'd promised. She swung into the saddle before he had a chance to help her.

"Race you to the end of the lane," she called.

"Wait until I'm ready."

She spurred the horse in the side. It didn't take but seconds for her to push ahead. He enjoyed the picture she made, riding in the wind. She'd always been a good horsewoman, and it was so nice seeing her enjoy it again. He slowed to a fast trot. He was winning the race that *really* mattered.

At the end of the lane, she stopped "David Cranshaw, you let me win. You didn't even try."

"Why should I when you're so good?" He raised an eyebrow and grinned mischievously. "I'll try at other things. And I'll win." The warmth in his groin grew as she reached out and took his hand.

"Did anyone ever tell you that you're a big flirt?"

"Oh, I've had a few women in my day that thought I'd be quite the catch."

He forced away the picture of another woman, vowing she'd survive without the likes of him. He had to forget about the baby's mother. His life didn't need anything to complicate it. He was a lucky man. Even Monroe had been wrong. His wife had accepted the baby. He shifted in the saddle, and as he did, he realized the direction they were headed. It was too late to change, but it'd be a true test of her recovery. They'd ride right by the graveyard, and she wouldn't say a word. He wished Monroe were here to see for himself. He missed the old fellow.

Mariah sped up, leaving him behind in a trail of dust. As it settled, he saw her standing at the cemetery gate. He slid from his horse and caught her hands in his. "Why did you stop? Today is too lovely to be visiting *this* place." The sweetness in her upturned face almost took his breath away.

"It's serene here. Come. Let's visit the Dalton crypt. I miss my mother so much."

He dropped one of her hands, and they walked down the path. He was going to have to stop being so jittery or she'd become suspicious. Why wouldn't she want to stop? They had done it many times before. He smiled at her then said, "Must be the difference between us. This is the last place I'd want to come for a little peace. Mother used to drive out here and visit often. She said it made her feel closer to my father."

"How did he feel about visiting here?"

"As I remember, about like I do. I guess it's harder for men to face mortality than women. Do you think it has something to do with a woman's ability to give birth? "

"She's your daughter too. We'll live on in her and her children, but our soul will go to be with God. Only our bodies will be buried."

A chill gripped him. For the first time since he'd taken Abigail's baby, he wanted to pour out his heart. To tell her that he wouldn't live on in his children. It'd ease his conscience, but more than likely, it would destroy her. "I agree with you, my dear, but let's change the subject. It's too nice a day to be so serious." He squeezed her hand and continued down the path, wondering if deceiving her would keep his spirit from returning to God. Everything had been for love, even a special kind for Abigail.

Mariah knelt and began weeding around the tomb. With every weed pulled, David felt his heart tear. She finished and patted the soil back into place. He needed to go to confession. God would mend his soul in the same way as Mariah tended the soil. He reached down his hand, "Come, let's go home. I need some of the same gentle loving care you've given this tomb."

At the gate, Mariah looked back. This was the last time she was coming here. She didn't like it here any more than David did, but she'd never let him know, any more than she'd let him know that the crypt still haunted her. For whatever reason, it was her cross to bear, and she would until . . . until what? Until either the child in the nursery, or the next one, finally caused the vision to stop.

* * *

Abigail cringed at the sound of voices. The Cranshaws were supposed to be out all afternoon, but they were home and she was stuck here with Rosemary! *Where was Stella?* A door opened and closed. Giggles and whispering seeped through the walls. Would she be forced to listen to them make love? It was quiet for a few minutes. Were they undressing? Should she leave the baby lying on Stella's bed? No, too dangerous. She might roll off and get *hurt.* How about the floor? No, the only safe place is her crib, and then get out of here. She peeked into the hall.

She picked up the baby and made a dash for the nursery. Inside, she put Rosemary in the cradle, and reached for a quilt as the door opened. *Good,* Stella *was back.* The door closed and heavy footsteps approached. That wasn't Stella's steps. What should she do? There's no place to hide. By now the intruder had her by the shoulders and whirled her toward him. David Cranshaw's face was twisted with rage. She'd never seen a look like this before, not even her stepdaddy's. Would he kill her? From his grip, he could easily do it.

"I might have known you'd come snooping! It's lucky we came back early from our ride. Thought you'd waltz right in here and take the baby? Well, I've caught you red-handed."

"What's taking so long?" called Mariah.

He shoved her toward the closet.

Her heart raced. Would he stuff her in there?

"Get in and be quiet. I'm not through with you yet. I'll be back."

He slammed the door, and she was alone. Now she'd done it. The last thing she wanted was to have David angry with her. Maybe when he returned, he'd listen to her. How would he feel when he discovered how she'd helped the baby, that she was responsible for the baby's thriving? Would that change his feelings?

Abigail tried the door. It was locked and the house was quiet. She heard the baby cooing. Its cries would bring Stella. There was nothing to do but wait.

As she sank to the floor, the swish of a furry tail brushed against her leg. For a second, she stiffened in horror, then realized that rats didn't have hairy tails. As she relaxed, the soft meow of a cat came out of the dark.

"Kitty, come here," she whispered

The animal wrapped itself around her legs, purring like a steamboat. She patted it. "How in the world did you get in here?"

The cat moved away and meowed again. Abigail followed. She bumped into a wall. Hope ebbed away. Where had the cat gone? It wouldn't take much of a hole for it to climb through. She sat and waited. It wasn't long and the cat came back, rubbing against her legs. This time when the cat moved away, she never let it out of her reach. At the wall, it disappeared. She felt around, and her hand slid through a space underneath the wall. It was about two feet off the floor. Lying flat, she wiggled under. The faint light from under a door revealed the cat perched on a large box. As she stood, soft laughter flowed under the door. This had to be Mariah's room!

The cat jumped from the box and landed with a thud. She ducked behind some boxes as the door swung open. David stood only inches away, chest bare and hair ruffled. He reached down and scooped up the cat.

"I'm going to have to find out how you keep getting in here." He shut the door, leaving Abigail alone.

This time there was no cat to lead the way. She eased herself past the door. There was the wall. Bending down, she felt. Once again, she crawled through and on the other side found a door that stood open. She stepped into a bedroom. Massive, mahogany furniture filled the room. The faint smell of a man's cologne clung in the air. The bed was covered with a maroon velvet spread, and the windows were draped in matching fabric. It was definitely a man's room. David obviously slept here when he wasn't in Mariah's bed. She briefly thought about what would happen if she removed her clothes, crawled under the covers, and waited for him. Wouldn't he be surprised to find the closet empty? And more shocked to find her in his bed? What more could he do to her than he'd already done? She shook her head to clear her thoughts and looked around for a way to escape.

A warm breeze drifted through the partially opened window. This was her way out! Tucking her skirt into her waistband, she hiked her leg and pulled herself through onto the roof. To get to the back of the house, she'd have to pass Mariah's window or go down the other side. Peeking, she saw them on the bed. They were far too busy to notice her. With a long leap, she crossed to the other side. As her feet hit the slate shingle a loud crack filled the air. It had split in two. Hovering behind the gable, she waited with baited breath.

David opened the window. "What was that noise?"

"It must have been the cat, dear. Come back to bed," said Mariah.

Abigail heard a thud, let out a deep sigh, and sat for a moment with her face buried in her hands. Then realizing someone might see her, she crawled toward the rear of the house. At the porch roof, she slid down the post and onto the ground.

On the main road, she didn't slow down until she was back in town. David would come after her when he discovered she'd escaped. Heaviness settled in her heart. She'd lost all hope of having the man she'd grown to love. Nothing would ever fill the void inside her. She'd never forget the look of rage on his face. What was she thinking? She should've stayed and told him the truth.

As she neared home, the vow to care for herself burned fresh in her memory. On Seth Turner's visits this summer, he'd been more than attentive. Elizabeth had told her about his family. It didn't matter that she couldn't have children. Why not pursue Seth. North Carolina was a long way from here. And as for the baby, she'd miss her, but after today she wouldn't be allowed to see her any more. Yes, she'd be the next mistress of Seth Turner's plantation. Seems she remembered him calling it Greenwillow. The name didn't matter as long as she was in control!

* * *

At long last, Mariah slept. David smoothed strands of loose hair from her face and covered her with a sheet as he recalled the events of the day. They'd had so much fun. Why couldn't every day be this way? Old Monroe's voice whispered as though he was right here beside him. "Wuz'n fer ta bad, we'd not know ta good." He'd almost lost his daughter today. Thank God he'd gone to the nursery. By now, the mother could have been halfway to Lord knew where, but instead he'd safely locked her up. He'd better get in there and send her packing. This wouldn't happen again, even if he had to post guards.

At the nursery door, he hesitated. All his feelings for Abigail pushed their way back into his thoughts. He took a deep breath and went in. He loved Mariah, and he had to remember that. It was only normal he'd feel something for the woman who had given them a child but with her actions today.. .. He unlocked the door. "Get yourself out here and let's settle this once and for all. You signed a paper giving away your baby. I might turn you over to the law."

His voice echoed. Not a movement or a sound came from within. Nothing. Was he going crazy, also? Did he dream the whole thing? He went to the crib and looked down at the sleeping baby. *Thank God, she was all right, but how I n the world did her mother escape from a locked closet, unless she was a witch. The though struck h*im funny, and he chuckled to himself. W*itches, of all things.*

"Massa, what yo doin' in here?" Everythin' be alright?"

David faced Stella. "Can't a father visit his daughter when he wants?"

She fumbled with a stack of diapers. "Yes'suh, of course, suh."

"Have you seen this child's mother snooping about here?" He studied her face as she placed the clothes on a nearby table.

"I ain't seen no sno-o-pers no w'eres. All I see ta last little while is dese here clothes."

"I could've sworn I came in here earlier and found her bending over the baby. I locked her in the closet, but you know what? She's gone."

Shock registered in Stella's eyes as she took a few steps back. "I swear I ain't let no girl outta no closet. Yo think she one of dem conjure women? I think all along she hab a funny look in her eye." She moved closer to the baby. "If dat be so, dis baby might hab powers, too." She squinted and peered at the sleeping child. "I hab noticed sump'n different 'bout her."

David realized how insane this conversation was. Abigail wasn't a witch, and he'd never seen a more normal-looking baby. She'd found a way out. Wait! This room connected to Mariah's. And if he remembered right, there was also an opening into his room. That was how she'd escaped, and if he was a betting man, that was how the cat kept getting in. Well, there'd be no more cat or Abigail. He'd see to that!

* * *

Mariah woke with a start. Where was David? He'd been here when she'd gone to sleep. Raising herself on one elbow, she saw that night hovered close. She'd have to hurry and freshen up before supper. As she stood, a long shadow moved from the foot of the bed.

"I be waitin' fer yo to wake up."

"Hannah, what in the world are you doing lurking in the shadows? How long have you been here?"

"I hab sump'n fer you. And I wanna make shore I gib it to yo. I hab ta Conjure Woman fix yo dis potion. Keep it with yo or sump'n awful happen."

Mariah took the handkerchief and sniffed it. At least it didn't smell bad. Then she laughed at herself. What difference did it make how it smelled? There wasn't anything to all those old superstitions, but it had been kind of Hannah. She'd keep it in case . . ... "Thank you for your concern, but everyone here is safe."

"I hab ta pane fix, Missus."

Mariah rubbed her forehead. "What was wrong with it?"

"Yo not remember. Yo hit with fist. Blood get all over. Yo say fer me to get fix 'fore Massa see. I hab Mr. Wilson fix it. Dat what he do 'fore buyin' plantation. I hope yo not break nothin' else. "

Mariah touched the bulge in the lace-edged cloth. She'd have to keep her visions a secret. "You're going to have to be more careful when you clean my room. The mirror and the window can be replaced, but what if you'd gotten hurt real bad? I don't want another servant. You've been with me since I came here. Let's see, it's been almost four years now, hasn't it?"

"But, Missus . . . "

"I understand. Accidents do happen. But watch out from now on, please."

Hannah backed from the room, shaking her head. After she disappeared, Mariah picked up the handkerchief and pinned it to her petticoat. She didn't believe it would help, but it couldn't hurt either.

ꙮ 17 ꙮ

Elizabeth Cranshaw's Home: Fall, 1859

Ominous black clouds roiled over New Orleans. As the first clap of thunder shook the windows and lightening lit the streets, David burst through the back door into his mother's kitchen where he found her putting roses into a vase.

She glanced up. "What brings you out in this storm? How are Mariah and the baby?"

Without as much as a word, he threw his raincoat on a chair and strode toward the back stairs.

"Answer me! Something's wrong. Abigail is lying down, but I don't think she's asleep, so keep your voice down."

He wheeled and came back to the table. "The girl that you're becoming so fond of is the problem. Do you know where she was late yesterday evening?" "If you remember *that* girl was your idea. Are you jealous? I haven't seen you display symptoms of such jealousy since your sister . . ."

"This has nothing to do with sibling rivalry! This has to do with that little tramp upstairs."

"Don't you call her that! I've done a fine job with that young lady. She's even been taking me out for carriage rides. It feels so good to get out of this house with all its memories."

"I'm happy for you. As for my wife, she's fine. And the baby's growing like a weed." He glanced, uneasily, toward the stairs. "And it's because Abigail has been visiting her. I haven't said anything to you, but Mariah hasn't taken to the baby like I'd hoped. The servants told me she hardly noticed her when I was away."

"You should spend more time at home."

He wiped his forehead. "I stayed away to protect her."

Elizabeth touched his arm. "Looks like you'd want to be home to do that."

"It's so hard to live in the same house with the woman you love and be afraid to touch her, to . . . ." He saw a flush creep into his mother's cheeks. "I shouldn't be talking to you about such private feelings."

"Son, you can talk to me about anything, anytime you want. I only wish . . ." She looked down.

"Wish what."

"That your father was still alive for you to talk to."

"I'm sorry. I forget you've suffered as much loss as I have. Anyway, I caught her, red-handed, bent over the crib. I locked her up until I could figure out what to do. When I went back, she was gone. I forgot the closet wall didn't reach the floor. The window gable sets in, leaving a space between the rooms."

"Come sit, and let's talk abut this before we do anything rash. Abigail's upstairs and your baby's safe. I know how this happened. Before Monroe died, he came to see me. He said he was afraid the baby wasn't going to live. Said Mariah wasn't mothering her. I told him to forget it and to go get the doctor. I'll bet she overheard our conservation and took it upon herself to do something. It wasn't too long after that until she started taking the carriage out. It never dawned on me not to let her go. She's not a prisoner. She could leave any time and there'd be nothing we could do."

"Well, let her walk. But she's not having our baby."

"I don't think she wants to go, nor do I think she wants the baby. She wants to be the kind of person I am." Mrs. Cranshaw sat in silence for a few minutes. "Can you imagine anyone wanting my life?"

"Yes, I can, Mother. You're a wonderful woman. You've got to quit blaming yourself for what happened to Candy. Besides, we've got more important worries."

"You're right. There's no use crying over spilled milk. We've got to get busy and plan a 'coming out ball' for Abigail and get her married. "

"I'm going upstairs to confront her. When I return, we'll talk about this party thing. Maybe if she has something other than the baby to think of, it will keep her away." He stormed up the stairs. He'd keep his child safe even if it meant . . ... No, he wouldn't decide on what to do until he'd had a show-down with Abigail.

* * *

Elizabeth pulled a rose from the vase. She loved fresh cut flowers, especially roses. Her peach rose bush was looking sickly. She'd have the gardener sprout a new one in case it died. Fond memories of days spent in the garden brought a smile. David and Candy had followed like puppies, asking endless questions as she clipped sprouts, cut their stems at an angle, dug holes under an overgrown lilac bush, and put in the cutting. With small chubby hands, David pressed the rich soil around the stem. Candy poured water from a watering can and, in her baby voice, encouraged the bush to grow.

When the children had done their part, she'd take a canning jar and cap it over the plant and bury the top in the soil. This created a hot house for the rose. In the spring when the jar was removed, tender young sprouts grew from the stem.

Now, she wasn't good at growing much of anything. Old age had set in and there were many mornings it was a chore to get out of bed. As much as she'd like to blame age, it wasn't all the problem. Her reason had walked away on the arm of a nigger. Love, Candy called it. Well, in her book, love didn't hurt. Love nourished, like the way she'd cared for the roses. Guess she wasn't good for much now except . . . she glanced toward the stairs. No, that was wrong. Every day Abigail's cheeks blossomed with more vitality. It'd be fun to give her a coming out party. She'd already introduced her to her church friends, telling them a good friend had died, and she'd taken her in. Their eyes had filled with sorrow.

The way Seth had eyed Abigail when he visited stirred the making of a plan. She'd hate to lose her companion. After all, people weren't beating a path to her door, but she had to think of the welfare of David and his family. And for them, having the mother as far away as possible would be best. She'd also seen the way her son looked at her. And he'd just admitted his fear of being with Mariah. Yes, it'd be better for all to have her in North Carolina.

* * *

David hesitated then knocked. He'd bring in the law if need be. There must be plenty in her past that she didn't want uncovered. He'd find out, if she didn't cooperate.

"Come in, Mrs. Cranshaw."

He pushed open the door. "It's not my mother, young lady. It's me. You didn't think I'd just go away after what I saw yesterday, did you?"

Abigail jumped to her feet and rushed at him. "And what did

you expect me to do!? Monroe was right. She'd have died without getting some love! You'd have let her die!" She beat at his chest with clenched fists.

Finally, he caught them and held tight.

"Let me go, you . . . you . . . you baby stealer! I wanted you to take her from the first. Remember at the cemetery? No, you couldn't take anything from a girl from the streets!"

He dropped her wrists and turned toward the window.

"What happened, Mr. Cranshaw? A sane woman wouldn't forget to mother her child?"

"Your baby saved my wife from having to be locked up somewhere. She's tried, but she can't help it if she doesn't feel motherly. If you think I'm going to say I'm sorry for what I've done, then you're crazy too."

"I'm the only one that's loved *that* baby."

He wheeled to face her. "When I put the baby in my wife's empty arms she thought it was ours. Please don't take away the only hope Mariah has!" He watched her rage ebb away to be replaced with a calmness. No, more of a sadness.

"You don't have to worry, Mr. Cranshaw. I signed the paper giving her away. You did what you could for me and for your wife." Sadly, she backed toward the bed. "Leave, now. I'm tired."

With sagging shoulders, David left. He was also exhuasted. Would this thing ever end?

Downstairs, he pulled out a chair and sat across the table from his mother. "I went up there ready to kill her and left feeling like I'm the criminal. It's my fault. Even Candy. If I'd been a better brother and watched out for her more . . ."

"I can't believe you. You've got a heart as big as all outdoors. You take other people's problems too personally. Come on, let's not have anymore of that sort of talk. I have a way to fix Abigail up with a nice husband. Do you remember Seth Turner?"

"Yes, he's the son of your best friend who lived in North Carolina."

"That's right. He's been here some this summer. I could tell that he took a liking to her."

"Isn't he married?"

"He was, but his wife died."

David sat straight. "That's a long way from here." He jumped up and hugged his mother. "You're on to something. Is he coming again? We can plan the party during that time."

"He'll be here next weekend."

"Can you get a party together that quick"

"That's all I've got to do. I'll get the invitations out this week, and then I'll take her shopping for a dress. Now, you run on home to your family. I've got work to do."

David strolled toward the door. As for the girl, well, he hoped that Mr. Turner would see to it that she had other interests.

❧ 18 ❧

Elizabeth Cranshaw's Home: Late October, 1859

Abigail fluttered about the kitchen, flushed with excitement, as the servants made preparations for the ball. Fall was a perfect time. She'd heard about cotillions and coming out parties for young ladies, but she never dreamed anything like this would be held in her honor. The white trash of Georgia would call this *putting on airs*. Well, she didn't care. It was all for her. She dipped fingers into the chocolate pudding destined to fill tiny pastry shells.

The cook swatted at her with a big cooking spoon loaded with hot sauce. "Scat! I hab work to do."

Abigail wandered about the dining room, marveling at the polished silver trays, saltcellars, and toothpick holders lined up on the table. Large boxes of candles waited to be placed in the gleaming chandeliers and wall sconces. As she made her way through the maze of preparations, her fingertips brushed the rose and teakwood furniture . . . not a trace of dust anywhere. Even the scarlet carpets had been beaten and fluffed. The brass fixtures shined to perfection, and it was all in honor of her.

On the porch, she wrapped her arms around her shoulders and smiled.

Moments later the door slammed and Seth Turner joined her. "I hear there's going to be a ball for a certain young lady, and she seems very pleased."

"Y-e-s-s, I am. The ball is nice, but it makes me happier to know Mrs. Cranshaw cares enough to give me such a grand party."

"Elizabeth is a lady of culture. She comes from a fine old family

126

who settled here straight from France, same as my mother's." Seth brushed at a spot on his coat then looked off into the distance, as though he were living in another world.

"Are you worried about something?"

"I'm really concerned that fine old families like ours are going to have lots of struggles ahead. Life is changing, and it won't be for the better. There are numerous accounts of insurrections. There have been some reports of slaves poisoning their owners. It's getting dangerous. We can't survive without workers."

Such murders had never entered Abigail's mind. From what she'd seen, they had a good life. Besides, if they didn't have the plantation and their work, where would they go and what would they do? The way she saw it, everybody needed somebody. "I wouldn't worry, Mr. Turner. It won't take them long to find out freedom's not as great as it sounds."

"You sound as though you know something of being on your own."

"Far more than most girls my age. But tell me about your family. Mrs. Cranshaw seems to be extra fond of you."

The spark returned to his eyes. "That story goes way back to our families . . ."

Mattie interrupted. "Miz Abigail, time fer you to come get ready."

"I'll be looking forward to dancing with you tonight, Mr. Turner." She curtsied and went into the house. Yes, he definitely could help her with her plans.

Seth watched her go, but his unfinished thoughts were not of the history between families. They were about the freshness and youth of the girl he planned to take to his tobacco plantation in

North Carolina.

* * *

Young people arrived long before Abigail was ready to make her grand entrance, but Mrs. Cranshaw had told her it was proper that most of the guests be present before she came downstairs.

Mattie tightened the corset strings and then helped her into a slip of white crinoline, which draped over three wide hoops. Next, she slipped a dress of light rose taffeta and lace over her mistress's head. As Mattie buttoned the row of covered buttons up the back, Abigail saw herself in the full-length mirror. The reflection was not that of a child who'd been abused by a stepdaddy; nor of a girl who'd been used in a brothel; nor was it the girl who'd been accused of trying to steal her own baby. It was of a woman who planned on making her future better. She drew a few dark curls near her face. The color of the dress gave her skin a faint glow. Taking a deep breath, she vowed again not to forget the promise she made when she gave her child away.

* * *

And that was exactly what she kept in mind as she entered the courtyard where gentlemen bowed and young ladies stood in small groups, whispering. For a moment, she had the urge to rush back inside. No, this was the first step to her new life. Fear would not win out. She reached for a glass of punch a servant offered and took a few sips. Maybe once the party got underway she'd feel more relaxed.

The party started and soon she was light-headed and giddy from all the dancing. A certain young man kept cutting in. He was clumsy and insisted on holding her too tight. Seth Turner tapped him on the shoulder, and taking his place he whirled and dipped her across the yard.

When the music stopped, the group cheered and called for more. Once again, they glided in circles. She glanced up at the man who moved about with so much ease. There was something about him. Was it his experience with women or his social graces? Whatever, she liked it. When the dance was over, she sat down on a lawn settee and began to fan.

"Would you like some punch?" asked Seth.

She looked for a servant. "Where is all the help?"

"Never mind. I'll get it."

She nodded, glad to have a few minutes alone. She wanted to look over the selection of prospective husbands that Mrs. Cranshaw had gathered in. It was all she could do to keep from smiling about the situation. Who would have thought she'd be in this position a year ago? Had praying worked after all? As she inspected the group of young men, she saw David and Mariah Cranshaw step out onto the veranda. She was going to have some intervention of a different kind.

He waved and guided his wife toward the settee. Thank goodness, Seth would be back soon.

"Good evening, Abigail. I'd like for you to meet my wife, Mariah. One of mother's church friends stopped by and was telling her about the young woman my mother had taken in. Mariah hasn't been out much since our daughter was born. I thought this would be a good chance for her to meet you and have some fun also."

David turned to Mariah. "Why don't you two get acquainted, and I'll get us some punch."

Abigail felt her whole body tense. He must be awfully sure that

Mariah didn't remember the past. "Would you like to sit?"

"Thanks, and please call me Mariah."

"So, tell me about your little girl."

Mariah took a deep breath and looked in the direction her husband had disappeared. "Every one says she looks like her father."

"And do you think so?"

Mariah shrugged her shoulders. "Babies have their own look, but there's something different about her eyes. Not the color so much but the way . . .."

She shifted as Mariah's gaze bore into her, but she never took her eyes away.

Finally Mariah looked away. "Here comes David and there's someone with him."

"Oh, that's Seth, a friend of Mrs.Cranshaw's. He's from North Carolina. He went to get me some punch."

As David handed Mariah the punch, he said, "I'd like for you to meet Seth Turner. His mother and mine were best friends." He turned toward Abigail. "Seth says you're quite a dancer."

"Thanks to your mother, seeing to it that I had some lessons." Dancing was the furthest thing from her mind. What had Mariah started to say? Did she have some sort of doubts? And why was she looking down into her glass so oddly? Before she could ask what was wrong, Mariah threw the liquid onto the ground.

David looked at her. "Is something the matter, dear?"

"No, there was just a bug in my drink. I'd like to go home. It's been a long day, and I'm not comfortable leaving the baby yet."

"But Dear, Stella will take good care of her."

Abigail reached out. "Here, take mine. I haven't drunk any and

Seth can bring more." She saw fear fill Mariah's eyes as she knocked the glass from her hand.

"I said, we have to go." She ran toward the porch.

David smiled. "I'm sorry, but new mothers often suffer anxiety attacks when they leave their babies. Excuse me, but I'd better get her home."

As he turned and followed Mariah, Seth said, "Would you like more punch?"

"That would be nice. I'm quite thirsty from all that dancing."

As she waited, she wondered about the outburst. She'd heard about this type of behavior, but she'd bet there was more going on than fear of leaving her baby alone.

* * *

The last carriage pulled away. Abigail dropped onto a chair and wiped her face with the back of her hand. *What a party.* There'd be plenty more times like this. She'd received two invitations tonight.

"Is the princess dreaming of a handsome prince?"

She slowly let her eyes meet Seth's. "This whole night has been a dream." She let out a long sigh. "But tomorrow reality will be back."

"Is that so bad?"

"No, I guess not. Except . . ."

"Except what, my dear?

"Oh nothing, just the every day routine."

"That's one thing about plantation life. It's never dull."

"I've not spent much time on a real one. Just a short time, but from what I've seen, it's not a bad life."

Seth reached down and took her hand. "You're quite a lovely woman, my dear. You'd make a beautiful bride."

Abigail felt her cheeks grow warm. She'd already decided to be the next mistress of his Greenwillow. She'd have to make him believe her act. Slowly, her bottom lip protruded, and she let her eyelids drop. "Yes, I suppose you're right, but I doubt that anyone will ever ask me."

Seth drew her hand to his lips and kissed it. "Why would you say such a thing?"

A few tears escaped and rolled down her cheeks. "Who'd want a wife without a dowry? My poor parents didn't expect to leave me penniless, but Papa's illness took every dime. The stress of losing my father and the embarrassment of being left poverty-stricken killed my mother. If it weren't for Aunt Elizabeth, I'd be a homeless waif. Thank God, she took me in." Fresh tears surfaced and made trails down her face.

Seth took a handkerchief from his pocket and blotted at them. "There, my dear, let's not have a pity party. You've had a wonderful night, and there's a whole line of young men waiting to sweep you off your feet. But I'm not going to let that happen. I plan on asking for your hand in marriage. I don't need a dowry. I have plenty of *things*, but I don't have a wife. And that's what I need most."

Abigail hadn't been prepared for such a quick proposal, but this had been her goal, and here was the opportunity right under her nose. "Why, Mr. Turner, I'm so honored that you'd think a little orphan like me worthy of being mistress of your plantation. Of course, you'll have to ask Mr. Cranshaw, seeing he's the head of the family."

"I know about southern customs, but first, would you like to become my wife?"

"I'd consider it a great privilege to be Mrs. Seth Turner." She reached up and touched his cheek. She'd miss her life here with Mrs. Cranshaw, but a whole new world awaited, and she was ready to start a new life.

❧ 19 ❧

Wedding at Elizabeth Cranshaw's: Late November, 1859

Exactly a month later, Abigail smiled at herself in the mirror. She'd soon be Mrs. Seth Turner and the mistress of a large tobacco plantation. The sooner she was married and in North Carolina the better off she'd be.

Mattie lifted her hair and secured it on top of her head. "Dere dat show off yo' nice skin. Dat dress yellow from age, but it look good with yo' dark hair. It shore pleasin' Missus Cranshaw dat yo be wearin' her weddin' gown and a-marrying her best friend's son. I guess we needs to go. It 'bout time to start. Mr. Seth said y'awl has to hurry or yo miss ta train, and dere ain't another fer three days. Said he hab to git back to make sure ta backer is curin' on time. Did you knows day hab to worm it in ta summer? I jest see dem worms a chewin' and a spittin', cain't you?"

Abigail stared at the maid. Lord, this woman could talk the socks off the devil, but she was right. She hadn't thought much about life at Greenwillow. The image the servant painted brought a smile to her lips.

"Ain't no use in a-primpin' too much," she continued. Yo ain't gwine wear dis fer long. Yo hab to change and get right to ta train station."

Mrs. Cranshaw came in. Abigail took the older woman's hands in hers. "I was hoping we'd get to talk before the ceremony. I want you to know I've grown to love you. And this house has come to feel like home."

"I'm happy you've found someone like Seth to take care of

you. I'll miss you, but hopefully, I'll be able to come for a visit."

"You've become like my grandmother and that means so much to me. You'll always be welcome in our home."

"I've packed the button box in your trunk. I want you to have it to remember our good times together."

A lump rose in Abigail's throat. No one had given her anything special since her fifth birthday when her father had presented her with a small gold locket. She went to the window as her hand slipped around her neck. What ever happened to it?

"Are you all right?"

"Yes, I'm fine. Just remembering."

Mrs. Cranshaw placed an arm over her shoulder. "We've only had a short time together, but it's healed a lot of hurts for me."

Abigail dabbed at her eyes with a lace-edged handkerchief that Mrs. Cranshaw had slipped into her hand. "I'll never forget my time here with you, and I want you to be sure and come visit me in North Carolina."

"Horses can't keep me away, but I'll give you time to adjust to your new life."

"Will you keep a watch over my baby? I'm sure David will take care of her, but if something were to happen . . .."

"My dear, you have nothing to worry about. That child will never want for anything. You've made the right decision, and you have my undying love for what you've done for my son and daughter-in-law."

"I did what I had to and that's all there is to it. Now, there's a man waiting downstairs who's going to give me the kind of life I want. Let's go." As Abigail descended the stairs, she couldn't help but feel a little sad about leaving the place that had become home.

* * *

When Abigail entered the parlor, David took her arm. "You're so lovely, I wish . . ." He glanced over at his wife who was talking to the priest.

Abigail gritted her teeth. "You wish what?"

"I wish you the best."

She wanted to scream that he had her best, a gift that looked like it had made his wife well again.

The priest came forward and greeted them. "Mariah has been telling me how you've helped David's mother get a new lease on life. Sounds like this family has your best interest at heart. And the Turners are a fine old family, also."

Abigail looked David straight in the eye as she answered. "And I can tell you about fine old families, but time won't permit. If you're ever in North Carolina come visit. We can talk then."

"I'll remember your invitation. Who knows where any of us will be if our country goes to war?"

"You're right, but we all have our own personal battles to fight every day. And hopefully we're winning."

Seth walked toward her with outstretched hands. The priest smiled at him. "I think you're not only getting a beautiful wife but a wise one, too.

Abigail stepped forward and placed her hands in his.

"I agree whole heartily. Now, we don't have much time," said Seth. "Let's get started."

Abigail repeated her vows without much thought as to what she was saying, but she couldn't ignore the look in Seth's eyes. He looked as eager to take a bride as she was to leave this place.

"I pronounce you man and wife."

Seth kissed her.

She knew he now had the right to touch her anywhere he wanted. What had she done? She'd have to bed this man. Her eyes were drawn to David. She could give herself to David--but then there was his wife. Her feelings for him could go nowhere. She'd done the only thing left to do. She'd have to make the best of it.

❧ 20 ❦

Cranshaw Plantation: November, 1859

On the way back to the plantation after the wedding, David couldn't get Abigail off his mind even though Mariah held tight to his arm. He'd never imagined her married to anyone, but why not? She was an attractive young woman, one any man would be proud to make his wife, and now his family was safe. He squeezed his wife's hand. "I'll have to check on Mother more often now that she's alone. Maybe I can find someone else to keep her company."

"Or she can come live with us. I'm sure she'd love being with her granddaughter."

"Mariah, that is so thoughtful of you, but you know she'll never leave her home."

"I guess you're right, but I wanted you to know she's always welcome."

David patted her hand. "I know, but I'm a little selfish. I want my family all to myself." He gave her hand another squeeze. Yes, life would be good now that the baby's mother was gone. But the thoughts of Abigail wouldn't go away. There was no doubt in his mind that he'd been attracted to her as a man is to a woman. The feelings were there even though he hadn't done anything about them. Did he yet harbor some secret wish that someday she'd be his? *Of course not*, he consoled himself. Mariah was the only one he'd ever love.

Admittedly, Abigail had made a tremendous sacrifice. And he'd repaid her by locking her in the closet. Guilt was part of what he was feeling.

As they neared the lane leading to the house Mariah said, "I want to walk."

David called to the driver. The carriage stopped, and he jumped down and helped her to the ground. "I'll walk with you. I need a little exercise, too."

"No, I want to be alone. You go ahead and check on the baby. I'll be on soon."

"Are you sure?"

"Yes. I don't get much time to myself."

David kissed her on the cheek and climbed back into the carriage. "If you don't come along soon, I'll be back to walk with you."

She smiled and waved. David watched until he was out of sight. He was sure she'd be fine. The wedding had been a nice outing for her. There'd been no evidence of the behavior exhibited at Abigail's party. He'd check on Rosemary and then walk to meet her.

The maid greeted him outside the library door, wringing her hands. "What's wrong, Stella?"

"It Missus I worried sick 'bout."

"Stella, she's never been better. We had a good time at the wedding, and she just asked to walk home from the main road. Said she needed some time alone. What makes you think something's wrong?"

"It Hannah, Massah. She say Missus keep breakin' things, but blames her fer it."

"That's strange. The time she broke her mirror, she said it was an accident. I can assure you my wife is fine. I'll talk to Hannah. Maybe it's all a misunderstanding. I'll clear it up. Now bring my daughter to me."

David went into the library and sat down at his desk. Hannah had things mixed up. After all, she was getting on in years. Could her memory be going? His Mariah was better, and he planned to keep her that way.

❧ 21 ❧

Abigail Leaves for Greenwillow: November, 1859

Abigail settled in for the long train trip. For quite a while, she watched the countryside rush by. Occasionally, she glanced at her new husband. He seemed more concerned about the possibility of war than the Cranshaws. War! Even the word sounded bad. But then hadn't her whole life been like a battle? If she could have had the man she really loved—but even then, there would have been problems. The landscape became a blur as she thought about the child she'd left behind. If war came, would David keep Rosemary safe? Maybe she should've taken her when she had the chance? No, she'd done the right thing. He'd take good care of her.

Seth leaned over and kissed her on the cheek. "I tried to get us a berth, but there's not one available. There's a convention going on in Washington. You can curl up in your seat and sleep quite comfortably."

"I'll do fine. You try and rest. You'll have lots of work to do when you get home."

"Yes, even though the harvesting is done, it's a job curing the tobacco. I have to keep a tight rein on them niggers. I think I've got the laziest bunch in the whole south."

"Don't you have an overseer?"

"You could call him that, but he's not much better than the slaves. He's from a family of white trash. I can't expect much from his kind. A good nigger is a lot better than white trash. You're going to be surprised. If I didn't run the plantation with such a firm hand, we'd all be eating potato soup."

Seth's voice droned on, but Abigail's thoughts were in her own little world. She was glad he hadn't been able to get a berth. Bedding on the train with him wasn't something she wanted to do. It'd be bad enough when she had her own room. She breathed a sigh of relief and snuggled deep into the seat. There'd be no more shadows, for she'd left them all in New Orleans. The hum of the wheels and the sound of Seth's voice soon lulled her to sleep, and being Mistress of Greenwillow filled her dreams.

❧ 22 ❧

Greenwillow Plantation: Early December, 1859

The day Abigail Sloan Turner arrived at Greenwillow Plantation there wasn't a cloud in the sky. The only shadows were the ones cast by the shanties that lined the dusty lane. She'd dreamed of this day, but never a dream this big. Here on this land she'd become a fine southern lady, one that would make David Cranshaw green with envy. She'd show him how to survive!

Someone stood on the porch, waving arms and yelling, "It ta Masta, and he be bringin' home a lady!"

Little faces framed with pigtails, peered from behind doorjambs while others were brave enough to saunter toward the carriage. The woman descended the steps, using her apron to wave away the children as if they were a swarm of black flies. "Now you'uns get on back to yo' chores. Be plenty of time to meet ta new lady."

Abigail tilted her parasol to shade her face in time to see the pickaninnies disappearing as quickly as they'd appeared. The face of the slave drew closer, her smile radiating as bright as the sun beating down on the vacant fields.

Seth drew the carriage to a stop and handed the reins to another servant who materialized beside the buggy. "Corrie, I've brought home a new mistress for Greenwillow."

She rushed up to the buggy. "I shore was a thinkin' a pretty young thing be why you mak'n 'em trips down to New Orleans! Business, my eye, I tell ta others. It shore be eye business. Ain't been ta same here since yo' girl married dat mountain man and moved on up in ta hills and first misses died. Be nice if she bring 'em three littl'

143

boys and live here."

Seth stepped down and reached up a hand to his new mistress. "Now, you know that's not about to happen. That husband of hers won't live on a plantation. Time waits for no man. I'm getting on with my life, going to start over, have me a new family. This is Abigail. Show her to her room."

A trail of children followed them toward the porch. Corrie turned once again and waved her apron, and they scattered like a flock of chickens. Abigail was amused at their curiosity. Would a new mistress make that much difference in their lives?

As they mounted the veranda steps heads popped up and peered through the banisters. It was evident that these children didn't miss too much of what went on in the big house.

"Are any of these yours?" asked Abigail

"No 'am. But got me a son, he all growed up. His name be Sullus for his great-granddady. He be younger than Sophie.

"How long have you been at Greenwillow?"

"Twenty years or so. Mastah Turner bought me after his wife hab Sophie. She be feeble, not able fer much." Corrie shook her head. "Poor thing, she die of a broke heart not long after Sophie marry dat mountain man."

Abigail knew all about broken hearts. That's what had brought her to this place, but from now on her main goal was to mend it.

"I be lucky. I a house nigger, and I hab a room off ta kitchen. If yo be needing sump'n, jest send fer me. But right now come on upstairs, and I get yo settled in. Be time to see ta house later."

"Looks like there's a lot to see. I'd like to do some exploring on my own."

Corrie called to a young boy who lurked in the shadows. "Abe, fetch some hot water up ta ole missy's room." She wiped at her face with the tail of her white apron. "I fix a bath and yo freshen up while I make yo' bed."

Abigail followed Corrie up the winding stairs and into a large sitting room. Before she seated herself on one of the flowered settees, Abe appeared with a bucket of water.

Corrie filled a basin and laid out towels. "There, yo clean up. It be a hard trip." She disappeared into the next room.

Abigail eased down on the settee, picturing the first mistress of Greenwillow sitting here prim and proper. Would she be able to fill her shoes? As time passed, would she be sorry for the choice she'd made? Seth's words resounded in her mind. He was so right. Time didn't wait. What was done was done. All she could do now was use her days wisely.

* * *

Abigail stepped into the room where Corrie smoothed the sheets on a sleigh looking bed. "Where does your husband stay?"

Corrie blinked and reached for a pillow. "I not hab a man. Hab one once, but Masta trade him to ole Masta Jackson. He try to see me at church, but his masta find out and beat ta tar outta him." She swiped a tear as she finished the bed. "If yo married, some of ta mastas fix it so your man can visit."

"Why didn't you marry your man?"

"Masta Seth not allow that. I be his. We'se be getting on downstairs now. Masta be waitin' on ta veranda fer yo."

As they descended the stairs, Abigail wondered what the maid meant about belonging to Seth. Didn't all the slaves belong to him?

145

At the door, she heard voices on the porch and stopped to listen.

Seth barked out an order. "Boy, go spread the word that there'll be a gathering on the front lawn after supper to introduce the new mistress."

Abigail smiled and stepped out beside her new husband. She was about to take her place as mistress at one of the biggest plantations in eastern North Carolina.

* * *

Later that evening, Seth took Abigail's arm and guided her onto the veranda. As she looked over the front lawn, a sea of black upturned faces stared back. Surely, all the slaves in the South must be gathered here.

Seth stepped up to the railing and raised his hands. Immediately, a hush fell over the group. "I have called this meeting tonight for several reasons. First, I want to introduce to you the new mistress of Greenwillow." He drew Aigail close. "She's just what this plantation needs. I expect all of you to abide by her wishes. If I hear of any disrespect, I will personally deal with the offender."

A low rumble moved through the crowd. Again, Seth held up his hands. He gave them a few moments and then spoke. "Second, I suppose all of you know about the abolitionists from up North who are trying to stop slavery in the South. I've heard of one in particular by the name of John Brown. Rumor has it he's headed this way. I want to tell you now, anyone making contact with such people will be dealt with harshly."

Abigail moved aside as Corrie stepped up and handed him a book. *Seth, a Bible reading man?* She'd never suspected, but then there was a lot she didn't know about the man she'd married.

Seth opened the Bible. "I'm going to read from the scriptures tonight, the way my dear mother used to do. Hopefully, we can all find comfort in Paul's writing." He cleared his throat and read.

"*Servants obey in all things your masters according to the flesh: not with eye service as men pleasers; but in singleness of heart, fearing God: and whatsoever ye do, do it heartily as to the Lord, and not unto men; Knowing that of the Lord ye shall receive the reward of the inheritance; for ye serve the Lord Christ. But he that doeth wrong shall receive for the wrong which he hath done: and there is no respect of persons.*"

"You're to look at me as your Lord, and any one disobeying will be made an example of for others to see. Now the mistress and I are retiring for the night. I plan to spend quite a bit of my time showing her about, so don't plan on any Christmas this year." He hugged Abigail close. "But don't think you can slouch off. McRoy will keep me informed."

As they turned toward the door, an uneasy murmur swept through the crowd. Abigail glanced nervously over her shoulder. Was there a possibility of a slave uprising? From the tone of Seth's voice, perhaps he wasn't the kindest of masters. She stole a look at him as they mounted the stairs. Would he be the best of husbands? Well, she'd soon find out.

In her room, she faced her new husband. "Don't you think you were a little too forceful? Seems to me, contented slaves would be better workers."

Seth's eyes narrowed. "Let's get something straight right now! *I'm* the master, and I don't intend to let anyone, including you, tell me how to run my plantation! My mother, God rest her soul, tried that nice stuff and all it got her was a hard way to go. I'm successful, and it's because I'm stern." His eyes softened, and he pulled her to him. "Now let's forget business. We've some things of our own to take care of."

He kissed her tenderly and let his hands slide down over her hips. Abigail returned his kiss. After all, she was his wife, and he had certain rights. And as for the slaves, she'd have to keep her opinions to herself. The hardness of his body pressed against hers as his hands wandered feverishly. She slipped from his embrace. "If you'll give me a few minutes, I'll change."

A slow blush ebbed its way over his face. "I'm sorry. Of course, I'll go downstairs and have a drink. I'll send Corrie in to help you, and when you're ready, she'll come for me."

As the door closed, Abigail sank down on the bed. What would it be like to bed Seth Turner? Just the thoughts of warm arms holding her and soft kisses stirred an unfamiliar yearning. All her life, except for the few short months with David's mother, she'd not had any love, any soft touches. The maid's entrance interrupted her daydreams.

"Masta says I to hep yo into yo' night clothes. Where is day?"

"All my things are in the trunk over there by the fireplace. Mrs. Cranshaw bought me a new trousseau. You'll find my nightgown on top."

Corrie lifted the lid and took out the white dressing gown.

Abigail choked back an unexpected moan. White, of all colors! But then, she'd be expected to wear white.

'This shore ta purtiest thing I ever laid eyes on. Day hab nice stuff in New Orleans."

Corrie babbled on as she helped her out of her dress and into the gown, but Abigail's thoughts were back in Louisiana. She closed her eyes and immediately David's face appeared. The look of rage that she'd seen the day he'd caught her with the baby was now replaced by adoration.

"I go. Masta be right up."

Abigail sank back onto the bed pillows and shut her eyes. Seth might be the man she'd married, but her dream was of David. *His face appeared. He laid her down and placed a soft kiss on her cheek.*

"I got myself a pretty young thing this time."

Abigail opened her eyes and found Seth, stark naked, stretched out beside her. She gave him a weak smile and moved away, her mind still on David. Maybe pretending would get her through the night.

Seth's touch was gentle at first, but soon became more demanding. "You might as well learn early on that I'm an impatient man. It will save us both a lot of grief if we're honest from the start."

Abigail stifled back a giggle. Honesty. Well, if that was what he really wanted, she could give him a good dose. But then, he was the one who wanted it, not her. Let him unburden his soul just like he'd bared his body. She closed her eyes as he slipped the gown over her shoulders. His lips moved down her throat and took one of her nipples in his mouth. She felt him press his knee between her legs and shift his body on top of hers. The cry of agony that escaped her lips only served to stimulate him. The shadows that had crowded in the night of the baby's birth, once again found her. Soon a large specter blotted out the small ones. "You little witch. I'll teach you to tease a good man." She squirmed to escape, but the shadow kept her pinned. When at last it began to fade, the form of Seth loomed over her.

"I can assume from all the wiggling, I have satisfied my bride. Don't worry, my pet. There'll be plenty more where that came from before this night is over." Seth rose and slipped on his smoking robe. Pulling a cheroot from the pocket, he lit it and then sat down on the bed. "I think now would be a good time for us to talk about your duties."

Abigail pushed up in bed as rings of smoke rose into the air. This man had spoken of honesty, and he was laying all the cards on the table. Could be when he was through, she'd tell him a thing or two. "Duties? Should I consider being your wife a duty?"

"Of course not, my dear, but there are certain expectations."

"Such as?"

"Such as giving me a son. As you know, I only have a daughter, and she lives in the mountains with her trapper husband and three sons. My first wife was sickly all her life. After the birth of Sophie, she ceased her wifely duties." He rose and went to the window. "You'll give me a son, and while we're waiting, you will do the entertaining here at the plantation. We'll start with a party in your honor. That way, you can meet most of the neighbors. You'll be in charge of all the house servants. Pearl runs the kitchen. She's married to Asa. He's not worth much, but he makes her happy, and I do like good food. Corrie is my personal servant. She can help with your daily routine." He came back to the bed. "Let's work on getting that son."

Abigail now knew what the gleam in his eye at the wedding meant. He needed her so she could give him an heir. He'd had a motive all along. All men had a purpose when it came to women. She'd give herself, but she'd never give him an heir!

↶ 23 ↷

Greenwillow: September, 1860

Abigail didn't have time to be remorseful about her decision to become mistress of Greenwillow. Time had flown by. It would soon be a year since she'd come here. The spring and summer of 1860 had been ball after ball, one tea and one party after the other. Now it was early September and the activities were dying down.

On one of these dreamy afternoons, she found herself alone on the veranda. She took a deep breath and smiled, thankful Seth had gone into town. It felt good to have some leisure time. Gazing over the plantation, she saw slaves bending over the long tobacco rows. They had already begun to strip the bottom leaves. This was only the beginning. It would be picked in about three stages. It was different from cotton. When cotton was ready it was ready. For a moment, she saw herself as a small child, dragging a long sack through a dusty field. Her fingers ached from the jabs of the burs. She closed and opened her hands. Thank God, she no longer had to work like that.

The workers had her sympathy. How their poor backs must hurt, not only from the bending, but also from the lashes the overseer gave when they weren't picking fast enough. Over the summer, she'd begun to understand why slaves were unhappy. It didn't seem right the way Seth treated his. David never spoke to his that way. But after *that* awful confrontation when she first came, she had refrained from making any comment.

Thoughts of life in New Orleans brought memories of her child. Rosemary was probably walking by now. She counted on her fingers, sixteen months old. Abigail touched her stomach. It felt like a lifetime since she'd given birth. Her husband expected her to announce any day now that she was going to have a baby. Smiling, she rose and walked down the steps. At the corner of the house, she saw McRoy leaving one of the slave huts. He waved and came toward her.

"Seems I've misplaced a slave. You haven't seen that no good Asa, have you? For the life of me, I don't know why Pearl keeps him. She works all day in that hot kitchen then goes home and pleasures him the rest of the night. He ain't worth the salt that goes in his bread. Don't understand why Mr. Seth don't sell him."

Chills crept down Abigail's arms. Sell Asa! Surely, he wouldn't do that to Pearl. He was firm, no, down right harsh sometimes, but sell Asa? That would mean splitting up a family. The man she'd married couldn't be that cruel. "No, McRoy. I haven't seen him, but maybe if you were a little bit kinder, he wouldn't give you so much trouble."

"You don't know nothin' about these here niggers. Give them an inch, and they'll take a mile."

Pearl rushed out, waving her arms in the air. "Sally Mae, get yo' black self in dis here kitchen right now."

Abigail and McRoy looked in Pearl's direction.

A sheepish grin etched its way across the overseer's face. I bet if I find Asa I'll find Sally Mae." He moved closer with the smile still on his face. "You talking about that girl that carries water fer the kitchen?" I can't find your man, either. Do you think they run away together?"

Pearl's dark eyes narrowed as she snarled at McRoy. "My Asa

ain't run away with no nigger gal. *I* his woman. He know who feed him and warm his bed. He never leave his woman fer dat scrawny gal. More than likely if yo look out yonder behind dat old apple tree, yo find him sound asleep."

McRoy started toward the tree. "I'm gonna find Asa and put his lazy butt to work. You get me one of Sally Mae's aprons and meet me back here. I'll bring the dogs and some men. We'll have your help back before dark."

Abigail looked helplessly at the cook. "He won't let the dogs hurt her, will he?"

"It not ta dogs dat gwine hurt her. McRoy wanna be ta one a do dat." Pearl went back to the kitchen wringing her large, black hands.

Abigail no longer felt happy, but sick at her stomach. Was there some way to help the girl? Would talking to Seth do any good? She gazed nervously down the road. "Seth, you'd better get back here tonight or there's going to be real trouble."

Inside, she paced the library floor. Dark crept in and still no Seth. Surely, he'd be home soon.

Finally, she went up to bed, and when she woke the morning sun streamed through the window. The house was quiet. Throwing on a wrap, she rushed down to the dining room and called, but no one came. Turning, she made her way to the veranda. Out in the side yard, she found Sally Mae tied to stakes, spread eagle, on the ground. The yard slaves idled about, looking like they wanted to run. A few children peeked around the corner of the house. Out in the tobacco rows, the field hands picked away as though nothing were different.

Abigail broke into a run and then squatted by Sally Mae who

had passed out. As she reached for one of the ropes, the crack of a whip filled the air. She looked up into the face of a guard.

"What do you think you're doing? Get away from *that* girl and back where you belong. What's gonna happen here ain't meant fer a lady's eyes."

Abigail placed herself in front of the girl. "You'll have to beat me before you get to her. Then see what Mr. Turner says."

The man turned to the yard boy. "Get the fire started and then bring me the branding iron." The whip hummed overhead. "Mr. Turner knows. This happens every time a slave tries to run away. She won't be going very far with a great big T stamped on her forehead. If you don't want to watch, you'd better get back in the house."

"I'm finding my husband. If I ask him, he'll put a stop to this. She stomped her foot. "And don't you dare lay a hand on her."

"No sense wasting time looking. He rode out early yesterday for town and won't be back until tomorrow."

Abigail fled toward the kitchen. Why hadn't Seth said he'd be gone for three days? Didn't she have the right to know? She found Pearl stirring a pot on the stove. Gasping for breath, she dropped on a chair. "Do you know what they're fixing to do to that girl you called a scrawny gal. That guard is heating an iron. He said they're going to brand a T on her forehead."

Pearl never missed a beat, nor did she show any emotion. "Go in ta dinin; room, Missy, and I bring yo' breakfast."

"You expect me to go in there and sit down and eat while that man treats a young girl like some animal."

"It ain't ta first time, and I expects it not be ta last. Yo jest gwine hab ta get used ta life on ta plantation."

"I've *been* on a plantation, but I've never seen anything like this. And you stand there doing your work like you don't care!"

Pearl whirled and placed her hands on her hips. "Carin' ain't got me nothin' but heartache. I not tell her ta run away. I be doin' my job, and I ain't gwine cause no trouble. And Missy, yo hab to do ta same thin'. Ain't nothin' we do fer ta girl now. Later, I take care of her ta best I can, but fer now, yo jest run along and let me do what I hab ta."

Abigail ran from the kitchen and up the stairs. She threw herself across the bed and sobbed. When the girl's screams rose from the yard, she plugged her ears. She'd tell Seth a thing or two when he got home.

* * *

Pearl waited until the yard was deserted then went out and untied Sally Mae from the stakes. She shaded her eyes, looking down the rows of tobacco for help.

Asa sauntered into the yard from behind the big house, scratching his mustache and craning his long neck in all directions. "Get yerself over here now. McRoy gone and done his dirty work fer today. I see'm ride off ta river. Guess he spend ta rest of his day fishin' since Masta be gone."

With Asa's help, Pearl got the slave girl inside. She pressed cold clothes to her face. "Go fetch ta old granny woman. I knows she is fer gettin' babies born, but she hab some good healing salve."

Asa didn't have to be told twice. He left in as fast of a trot as his short legs would allow.

Pearl tried to sooth the hurting gal. "This ain't half as bad as some. I done and see one who git it on ta jaw. Yo ain't never see sech a ugly scar it leave. I see 'em on ta arm, too. Dis be a little mark. I say, if we gits some of granny's secret salve on it right away, yo ain't gwine have a bad scar. Yo' hair cover most of it."

Pearl tried to hold Sally Mae's arms as she rolled in agony, all the time muttering under her breath. Soon the babbling gave way to real threats. "Day pay. Every last one of dem gwine get what's day gone and give me. Fire! Yes, I burn ta sons of bitches, all of dem."

Pearl gathered her into her arms. "You gwine do what yo oughta in ta first place. Yo get better and come back to ta kitchen. Yo do yo' job and not cause no more trouble. Dat what yo do."

Releasing her grip, Pearl turned to Granny, who had arrived with her jug of magic cure.

Granny lifted the cold cloth that covered the burn. "Hum, yo be a lucky nigger. I see worse in my time."

Pearl grabbed Sally Mae's flailing fists and held them, but she couldn't shut her mouth.

"I be in no mood to hears yo tell me what yo seen. Pearl already done dat. Jest fix me so I can get dem dirty . . ."

Pearl held tighter as the girl winced; Granny cleaned the wound and filled it with salve. "Save yo strength, gal. Yo need it 'fore yo through."

Pearl cut strips from old sheets and made a bandage. The healing process would be painful. But the healing inside was going to take more than medicine and bandages. It'd take a lot of talking and a lot of working to take this gal's mind off what the white man had done. If it were even possible.

* * *

Abigail sat in the library, waiting for Seth to return from

town. She had her speech ready. The minute he stepped through that door she'd let him have it. He could throw her out on her ear. She wasn't staying where slaves were treated like animals. She stood and paced back and forth. She'd take a train back to New Orleans. Mrs. Cranshaw had written several times and talked about coming for a visit, but with the way things were, she didn't want her here.

"Miz Abigail, ta mail be here. I leave it on ta desk fer ta Mastah." Corrie laid down a bundle of letters. "Is der sump'n I git fer yo while yo waitin'?

Abigail eyed the pile of mail. "No, I'm fine. Or as fine as anyone can be after what happened in the yard."

"Missy, yo has ta ferget what yo done and see. Dis be our lot. I done and learned my place at a young age. We all has ta learn. Some of us jest has ta do it our own way, Dat's all." She straightened her little white apron. "Now, I knows yo wants to hep, but believe me, yo cain't change ta way it be fer a long time. Yo gwine only make things worser fer you." She went to the window and pulled back the curtain. "Do yo wanna wait fer you husband ta hab supper?"

"Yes. We'll let you know when we're ready to eat."

Corrie left the room.

Abigail picked up the letters and thumbed through them. There was one addressed to her. The postmark was from New Orleans. Her heart raced. Could it be from David? Wouldn't it be something if he were begging her to return to the Cranshaw Plantation? She ripped open the letter and began to read.

Dear Abigail,

I hope you're happy and everything is going the way you hoped. I'd like to come for a visit if it's all right. I can't stand to spend another holiday in this tomb of a house. If I don't hear from you, I'll be there two days before Christmas.

Lovingly,

Elizabeth Cranshaw

Abigail folded the letter and slipped it into her pocket, suddenly changing her mind. Yes, she'd let her come. At least it'd give the servants a reprieve from Seth's cruelty. As for what had happened in the yard, it'd be better not to mention it. Corrie and Pearl had said it would only make things worse if she confronted Seth. She'd act normal. In other words, keep the peace until . . . .. Heavy steps moved steadily down the hall

"Corrie said you were waiting in here for me. Did you get my message that I would be gone for a day or so?" Seth kissed her lightly on the cheek.

Abigail purposely smoothed her dress over her stomach and returned his kiss. "Yes. It was thoughtful of you to let me know. You're a busy man, and I don't expect you to account to me every time you leave."

Seth picked up the mail and thumbed through it. "There's nothing here that can't wait until later."

Abigail slipped her hand into her pocket and grasped the letter. "I got a note from Mrs. Cranshaw, and she's coming for a visit at Christmas. I'm looking forward to seeing her. Do you mind?"

Seth lay down the mail and pulled her into his arms. "Why,

no. Mother asked her many times to visit, and I've tried. You are special to her. And she's not the only one who's fond of you." He kissed her hard on the mouth.

Swallowing a lump that rose in her throat, she tolerated his kiss. With every nerve in her body, she wanted to pull away; wanted to scream about what had happened to Sally Mae; wanted to tell him she'd never give him an heir. But the timing wasn't right. She'd play the waiting game. The day would come, and when it did, she'd be ready.

❧ 24 ❧

Greenwillow: December, 1860

Harvest time was over. Abigail had watched the servants gather in the tobacco and hang it in huge barns to cure. She'd personally overseen the filling of large crocks with hominy and sauerkraut. The larder shelves were filled with jars of blackberry, wild plumb, and crab apple jelly. She'd seen a portion of food passed through the window into hands waiting outside, but hadn't stopped it. After all, the Turner family had plenty.

Corrie had assured her that most of her people knew how to gather fruit and berries from the nearby woods, and how to mix them with brown sugar or sorghum to make their favored wine or beer. When the frost turned the leaves, they'd collect a winter's supply of black walnuts, hickory nuts, and hazelnuts. These goodies were wrapped in rags and stored for the long nights ahead.

The Negro men could barely wait until cold weather to start hunting possum and coon. This would be the extent of their meat except for the chitterlings, liver, lights, and sometimes feet and heads they were given at hog killing time.

The big house would have plenty of pheasant, wild turkey, and duck. Occasionally, a big buck would wander out of the woods, and then they would have venison roast and steaks.

Tonight, Abigail let her fingertips walk across the leather bound books that lined the library shelves. If someone had been watching, they'd have thought she was counting them. From the bookshelves, she went to the window, pulled back the drape, and looked out into the night. Her resentment grew over the way the slaves were treated.

She turned to face Seth who sat in front of the fire reading. "Christmas is coming. We have so much more than we need, do you think we could have some sort of feast for the slaves?"

The muscle in his jaw worked up and down as Abigail waited for him to close his book. She was not prepared for the hard cold look on his face when he finally slammed the book and looked up.

"I do believe you think too much. Since you're doing so much of it, why don't you think about giving me the son I want? That way we'd have someone who has our blood running in his veins to help eat the food instead of feeding it to them niggers."

Abigail's temper reached the boiling point. She wanted to scream that she'd never give him an heir, and even if she could, she wouldn't want to. Who'd want a child with Seth Turner's blood in his veins?

"Well, what do you have to say for yourself?" He demanded. "We've been married long enough for you to give me a son."

"I can't control such things! Besides, how do you know it's my fault?"

The color slowly ebbed from Seth's face. His mouth moved, but no words came. For a moment, she wished she hadn't said anything, but then he hadn't been the kindest.

Seth's eyes narrowed, and he jumped up in front of her. "If you don't know it, girl, it's always the woman's fault. If you haven't conceived by spring, I intend to make sure you see a doctor."

"And I'm telling you right now, Mr. Turner, I'm not one of your servants you can order around and treat like . . . ." She had to stop before she said too much. Mrs. Cranshaw would be here week after next, and she wanted everything to be perfect. She reached out and touched him on the shoulder. "Aren't we getting a little ahead of ourselves? Babies take time, and we still have lots. Let's not fight over something that is out of our control, anyway."

The lines in his face softened.

He pulled her close. "You're right, my dear. They do take time. By Spring we could have twins on the way." He tilted her face and kissed her gently. "They run in the family. My dad's grandmother was a twin, and I've heard they skip a generation. We'd be next in line . . . and you, my love, have too big a heart. Don't you know we can't just go giving out food like there's no tomorrow? If there's a war, next year might not be as good. I don't know about you, but I don't plan on being hungry. Besides, the niggers wouldn't like our kind of food. They'd rather have their chitterlings and poke salad than what they call white-folk food. Don't worry. Come Christmas morning, you'll see that *I do* have a heart. I didn't do much last year for them; seeing it was your first Christmas I didn't want a big celebration, but this year will be different. I've sent for Sophie and the boys. We'll put a big dent in our store of food with three growing boys and Mrs. Cranshaw here." He picked up his book and sat back down. "Why don't you run on to bed?" he said without looking up. "I want to finish these few pages."

* * *

Upstairs, Abigail placed her nightclothes on the bed as Corrie came into the room.

"I figure yo need some hep gettin' outta yo' clothes. Must be a hundred buttons down ta back of dat dress."

"Tell me about the first mistress of Greenwillow."

"I sure if dese walls could talk, we both know things we not wanna. I come here right after Sophie born. Masta Seth bought me at a auction down in Fayetteville, so I not know 'bout her early life here. She not as purty as you, and not half as alive. I thinks she jest finally will herself to die after Sophie marry." She lifted the dress and petticoats over Abigail's head and began to unlace the corset.

"She wasn't happy?"

"She be a gentle lady. Too soft fer plantation life ta way it be here."

"I see. In other words, the way Seth treats his slaves was too hard on her."

"That 'mong certain other things."

"What other things?"

"I not say nothin'. I already say ta much." She slipped the nightgown over Abigail's head. "Dere, ain't yo a sight fer sore eyes. I jest hang yer dress here b'hind ta door."

"Tell me about Sullus?"

Corrie's eyes brightened. "He a good boy. Jest two years younger than Sophie. They play together when they be little. He a field slave. I worry sump'n fierce ta Masta sell him, but so fer, I be a lucky nigger. Guess it cause I . . .." She tilted her head toward the door. "I hear ta Masta callin'." The door opened and closed, and she was gone.

Abigail crawled into bed, pulled the covers under her chin. Corrie hadn't wanted to talk about the first mistress. Was it out of loyalty to her memory, or was there something else? Something like her being Seth's mistress. If she were a betting woman, she'd place her money on Corrie being the mistress. If that were so, then more than likely, Sullus was Seth's son.

* * *

Two weeks later Abigail welcomed Mrs. Cranshaw to her new home. The next day Sophie and her boys arrived. Abigail was taken with the little boys. Adam, the oldest, looked just like Seth. Allen must look like his father with all that red hair. And John. He wasn't but six months, and it was hard to tell who he favored. As she surveyed the small gathering, her heart warmed with joy. This was going to be a good holiday season.

The next morning she woke to the sound of cheers.

"Christmas gift, Masta? Christmas gift!"

Abigail jumped out of bed. There had to be a whole army out there to make that much noise. Pulling on a dressing gown, she ran down the stairs.

Seth stepped out of the library.

"That hollering. What is it?" asked Abigail,

"That's all the field hands, my dear. They're wishing us a Merry Christmas. Go upstairs and bring down our company. You're about to find out this master does have a heart."

Abigail ran up the stairs, calling for everyone as she went. The loud cheer outside continued. She met Mrs. Cranshaw coming out of her room.

"What's that noise? Sounds like a riot of some kind." She wrung her hands and looked nervously toward the stairs. "I shouldn't have come with all the unrest and war talk. I should've known something like this would happen."

Abigail put a reassuring arm around Mrs. Cranshaw's shoulders. "I'm sure it's nothing like that. Seth sent me up to get everyone. Apparently, this is some sort of tradition."

Sophie came into the hall, her eyes shining. "I'd forgotten what Christmas morning on the plantation was like. I'll get the boys and be right down."

"Corrie will bring them. Let's hurry, Seth's waiting," said Abigail

Downstairs, Seth took Abigail's hand, opened the door, and stepped out on the veranda. The loud cheers and smiling faces indicated that the slaves had feelings for him. Or was it the Christmas Spirit? Seth dropped her hand and raised his arms and almost immediately the roar ceased.

"It's become a tradition that I give a Christmas speech, and there will be gifts for everyone, but not until I've finished. We've had a good year. The tobacco yielded a good crop because of all the field hands hard work. It's good to have my daughter and grandsons here, and also Mrs. Cranshaw, a friend from New Orleans."

Abigail wondered at his sincerity as another cheer rose from the crowd.

Seth cleared his throat. "When I was a boy, my dear mother, God rest her soul, saw to it that you all received something for Christmas. Even in lean years, I've tried to keep that practice alive. For every child, there's a sack with an orange and some hard candy. For the women, there's enough calico for a new dress, and for the men who've worked so hard in the fields, there are new pipes. And of course, there's the traditional keg. Just watch and don't get too happy down there at your meeting place. I know you all have been soaking that Yule log for half the year just like your parents did. But wood can only get so wet no matter how much it soaks, and it'll only burn so long. As soon as the last ember dies, I expect everyone back to work. Now, we all know the meaning of the season. I could stand up here all day and talk about it, and still not say what those old carols do. I'm going to ask you all to sing, now, and when you're finished, you can file by the veranda and pick up your gifts."

The slaves huddled together and lifted their voices in beautiful music.

"*Dere's a baby in a manger, Rise up shepherds and foller ta star. It will lead to a place where ta Savior be born. Rise up shepherds and foller.*"

Abigail marveled at their spirit. They seemed so happy, yet they had so little and were treated so badly. A sick feeling gnawed at her stomach as she contemplated their gifts. These gifts were a measly pittance for a man with so much. He'd expected her to appreciate what he called, *his heart.* Well, it was going to take more than a few sticks of candy and nice words at the holiday season to prove he had a heart. When a person had a heart, he didn't allow his slaves to be burned with hot irons. He didn't let overseers beat them with whips. Or take a servant woman as his own.

Abigail looked at the rest of her family. All the adults had tears in their eyes, and Sophie's little boys were tugging on her skirt complaining they were hungry. With the song still lingering in the air, she went inside. Somehow to listen to the slaves pour out their hearts in song felt wrong.

The others followed. Soon they were enjoying a hearty breakfast of pancakes, sausage, and various kinds of jellies and jams. The aroma of steaming black coffee rose from an urn on a nearby serving table, but Abigail didn't have an appetite. Pictures of the slaves clustered together with rags wrapped around them wouldn't go away.

167

"Abigail, you look pale. Aren't you feeling well?"

"No, I'm not. Guess it's all the excitement. I think I'll go back upstairs and lie down."

"Of course, my dear. Don't want you getting too worn out. Who knows, by this time next year we could have another reason to celebrate." Seth winked at her.

Bile bubbled up from her stomach as she left the room. No, there'd never be a reason to celebrate in *this* house!

* * *

Pearl pulled out her lip and filled it with a dip of snuff. "Ain't it sump'n ta way Masta Seth carry out his mama's wishes after all dese years?" She added a little more snuff and waited for Asa's reply. When he didn't answer, she continued. "I can't wait to get to sewin' my new dress, but guess I hab to 'til all ta Christmas doin's over at ta big house."

"Yo sew all yo like, but I ain't gwine give up mah corncob pipe fer some old store-bought clay one." Asa hobbled over to ta table and sat down. "Ta way I sees it, all dat man is a-doin' is tryin' to show off. Yo is crazy as a bed bug if yo thinks he care 'bout us. He only care 'bout his own skin."

"I not know, Asa. Sometimes, I thinks he not got a heart, then he go and do sump'n nice fer us. Did yo ever think 'bout what happen if we not hab a life here at ta plantation?"

"All ta time. Some dese days, I gwine be a free man."

"Well, that sound mighty good, but yo knows yo shore hab to work then."

Asa stood and pulled Pearl to her feet. "Come on, dere a party waitin' fer us. Hear that banjo music? Make my feet itch to dance."

"Oh, Asa, if yo be on yo' feet all day, ta way I has, yo not wanna dance. All yo wanna do is flop. But, come on. I wanna hear ta gossip." She took his hand, and they went outside."

Pearl's body swayed to the fiddle and banjo music as she and Asa edged their way through the crowd until they could see the Yule log spitting and smoldering. "Good evenin' to yaw'l," said Pearl.

"Here come Pearl," called one of the half-stewed field hands. "She gib us ta talk from ta big house. And Asa, where yo' brand new pipe ta masta done and bought fer us?"

Asa dumped tobacco into his homemade corncob pipe and lit it. "I ain't smokin' nothin' but *mah* pipe. Be smokin' it fer some time now, and ain't no white man gwine replace it with some store-bought one."

"That ta spirit, Asa," yelled someone from the outer edge of the group. "We need to take a stronger stand. Dere be lots more of us than dere be of ta Masta. I tells yo, if we jest all stick together, we get sump'n more than cheap clay pipes!"

Pearl took a step backwards when the man threw his pipe in the fire. The music stopped and the children, who had been dancing in their own little circle, clung to their mothers' skirt tails. Something was about to happen.

Sally Mae pushed Pearl aside and stepped into the firelight, lifted her hair, and pointed to the T branded on her forehead. The edges had rolled in an ugly scar that even her hair couldn't hide. "Yaw'l think dis ta price I oughta pay fer a old piece of calico?"

Pearl shuddered as a loud chorus rose and filled the night air and soon turned into a mournful chant. Immediately, a line formed and moved by the fire, and the men threw in their pipes. By the time they finished, the women had returned with their cloth and made a line.

Pearl was the last one to drop hers into the fire. She sure hated to burn it. There hadn't been a new dress in so long, but if she didn't add it to the fire, she'd be an outcast.

At the last stench of burning cotton, Sullus stepped in front of Pearl and raised his hands. "I thinks ya'wl shore know I be in town with ta masta right 'fore Christmas. I hears him talkin' to some man who been up north. He say that Lincoln man dat's President want slaves free. From all ta talk, I say dere be hep a comin'. Let's jest try and be peaceful at least 'til Spring, den we see." He turned to Pearl. "Yo work up at ta big house. What yo say."

"I say if us want to eat fer ta winter we'se keep our noses clean. Jest do yer jobs and not cause no trouble."

"Course, she say that, wouldn't doubt she ain't warmin' Masta's bed."

Pearl caught Asa by the shirttail as he made a mad dash toward the speaker. "Come on, Asa. We gwine. All we needs be fer a fight to break out down here tonight."

Asa muttered all the way home, but Pearl wasn't worried about him. He'd be as calm as a lamb in the morning. She shuddered and spit a stream of tobacco juice onto the ground. But she *was* worried about the mood back at the fire. It'd only take a few drunken niggers to start big trouble.

* * *

By suppertime Abigail felt like joining the family. By now the boys had captured her heart. Playing with the baby brought back fond memories of the time she'd spent with her child. She was sure the Cranshaw house was a happy one this Christmas. She wasn't sorry for her choice. Her baby had a good home and life here was bearable. After all, wasn't something better than nothing? Maybe that was the way the slaves felt. It was better to have a home and a roof over their heads than living in the swamps and being on the run. A dog howled in the distance. She looked up from where she played with the baby on the library floor. No one else had seemed to notice the lonesome sound.

"I don't want to alarm anyone," said Seth, "but you all are going to know soon enough. South Carolina left the Union last week. I'm afraid we're in for rough times. I suppose a lot of the other southern states will follow. Don't see how we're going to avoid a war, but everyone knows the South will win. We're going to have to make some sacrifices."

Abigail sat quietly absorbing what he'd said. How would her husband handle a war? Worse yet, how would he react if the slaves *were* freed? Would he expect her to–no, she'd not scrub his clothes! And he could just . . . .. The sound of Adam's voice broke into her thoughts.

"Why didn't Papa wanna come here to Grandfather's? Sure is a nice place. I wish *we* had a house like this and some niggers to do the cooking."

Abigail patted Adam on the head. "I'm sure your mama is a wonderful cook."

"Yes, but I sure wish Papa'd come."

"Your papa had to take care of his traps," said Sophie. "Besides, if he'd come, you wouldn't have any reason to want to go home!"

Abigail rose as Corrie bustled through the door. "I thinks it be time fer some young men to go to bed."

"Mama puts us to bed," piped up the second boy.

Abigail handed the baby to Corrie. "Come on, give your mama a rest."

As the boys followed Corrie out of the room, Abigail studied their mother. There was a remarkable resemblance between her and Seth, the same blond hair, the set of the eyes and nose, but she was much sturdier. It probably was a good thing since she'd become a mountain woman. It would require a lot of physical as well as internal strength to homestead.

Mrs. Cranshaw reached out and took Abigail's hand. "Are you feeling better, my dear? I sure hope it's nothing serious. Seth has been telling me about his future plans."

Did Mrs. Cranshaw know she couldn't have another baby? Even if she did, she'd never tell Seth. She'd do anything to save her son and his family. Abigail stole a sideways glance at Seth. He was busy talking to Sophie and from the look on his face it must be serious. "Seth would like an heir, Mrs. Cranshaw, but life seems so unstable right now." She watched Elizabeth Cranshaw's face for some sort of reaction, but if she knew that she couldn't have another child it didn't show in her eyes.

"I know what you mean, dear. There's so much unrest. We've got a new President, and he's for the slaves being free. That could cause a whole uprising against plantation owners. It wouldn't take a *war* to free them if they got riled enough."

Abigail lowered her voice. "From what I've seen, I can't say as I'd blame them. Their life is hard."

Mrs. Cranshaw nodded in agreement. "Seth's mother owned

servants," she whispered, "but she was very kind to them. Seth's father, well, that's another story."

Corrie came back into the library. "The boys be all bedded down," she announced. "They like fer their mama and Missy to tuck dem in. I get some fresh coffee and dessert."

"Those children sure have taken to you, Abigail. Are you coming?" said Sophie as she got up.

"Tell them I'll be up in a few minutes."

Abigail went to the window and pulled back the drape. Soft moonlight bathed the lawn. Down by the servant quarters, smoke billowed from their fire. Slowly, dark shadows emerged at the edge of the lawn, growing in length as they closed the space between them and the house. What was happening? Then it dawned on her that they were probably headed for the kitchen to help themselves to some of the goodies left over from supper. The first figure moved toward the window, and Abigail stepped back. As it moved closer, she could almost trace the burnt T with her forefinger. .

As the shadows merged with those of the house, a dog howled and immediately another followed. Abigail pulled her shawl tighter. Sure was a spooky night, even with the moon shining. As she was about to drop the curtain, the flicker of a small flame caught her eye. Backing away, she screamed, "Fire!"

Seth ran to her side. "What?"

Abigail pointed. "Fire! At the corner of the house!"

Seth dashed for the door, yelling for the house servants as he went. Abigail and Mrs. Cranshaw followed as Sophie ran up the stairs toward the boys' room. By the time they got outside, Seth was beating at the blaze with his coat. As the fire leaped toward the house boards, a multitude of slaves appeared with buckets of water.

Soon a smoldering patch of grass near the foundation was all that was left. Abigail breathed a sigh of relief and sat down on the porch swing. Fire, here at the big house! Seth deserved what he got, but Sophie and those little boys hadn't done anything. And Mrs. Cranshaw, she couldn't let something happen to her. This truly had been a day to remember. And if it was any indication of things to come, no one would be safe.

❧ 25 ❧

Shady Junction, North Carolina: Winter, 1861

Sophie Miller shifted the baby from one hip to the other, stirring a batch of cornbread with her free hand. How she wished she could have brought Corrie back to the mountains! Ned didn't think slavery was right. He said mountain people had no need of them and didn't take kindly to those who did. But Corrie was like a member of the family. At Christmas when Adam had asked why his father hadn't come to the plantation, she should've said that his pa didn't believe owning another human was right. But the boy was too young to understand.

Sophie set the baby on the floor. A wail of protest filled the room. She ignored the crying and dumped the cornbread into the heated skillet.

"Mama, Mama! Adam won't give me my ball."

Sophie pulled free of Allen's tug on her shirt and tried to shut out the baby's cries. She thumped the empty bowl down on the table, placed her hands on her well-rounded hips, and glared at the scene. Tears stung her eyes, and she blinked them away. Why had she married Ned Miller and moved to the mountains? But young men hadn't exactly been knocking down the door at the plantation. If she'd been little and pretty, but life hadn't been that kind. She was lucky to have a husband, even if he was a mountain man. "If you want your ball, take it. That's what your pa'd do." She wiped her hands on the apron that covered her protruding stomach.

Allen eyed Adam who stood in the doorway clutching a ball in his hand.

"Mama, make him give it to me."

Sophie looked into the gray eyes of her three-year-old son, the same gray eyes as his father. She felt Ned's eyes stripping away her clothes. *Give it to me—to me*—beat like a drum in her ears. And she'd given herself completely to satisfy his needs. Now look where it had gotten her. Three babies, another one on the way, and a man who demanded supper when he walked through the door. What was she going to do?

"I said if you want your ball, take it."

He gave her a startled look and made a dive for his brother. Adam flew out the door like a quick March breeze.

Sophie reached for the plates. Her mother had told the servants that if a meal was going to be late at least have the table set. That would pacify any man. He'd know his meal was coming along soon. Thoughts of Mama and Corrie filled her mind as she finished. Mama had known all the tricks when it came to telling the servants how to run the big house. She wished she'd been more observant.

The door opened, and she looked up to find Ned watching her.

"When are you gonna ever get the knack of homemaking? My mama would never let Papa come home to a mess like this." Ned glared at the disarray like he could wish it away.

Why was he always comparing her to his mama? Before she could answer, the wails of Allen filled the room.

"Give it to me! Give it to me!"

She wanted to say, *Listen to yourself, Ned. Listen! It's that kind of demanding that makes it hard for me. Give! Give! Give! It's all I ever do.* Instead, she picked up the baby and said, "Wash up. Your super'll be ready soon."

Black smoke rolled from the oven.

"Sump'n burnin'," said Ned without moving.

She handed him the baby and rushed toward the stove. She pulled the cornbread from the oven just in time, but before she set it down, the scent of scorched potatoes filled the air Frantically, she dropped the bread pan and shoved the skillet of fried potatoes to the back of the stove. "If Corrie were here . . ."

Ned held the baby out to her. "Take this squallin' young'un. I ain't the only hungry man. Yer son wants his supper. And seein' his ain't burnt, I suggest you give it to him. And as fer Corrie being here, fergit it. Six months from now she'll be a free woman. I heared there's been shooting at Fort Sumter. There'll be a war, and it's gonna change the South."

Sophie took John and sat down in her cane-bottomed rocker, unbuttoned her dress, and cuddled the baby to her bosom. "Humph! Papa said at Christmas that he'd heard South Carolina had left the Union. We both know who'll win."

Ned filled the wash pan with hot water and soaped his hands. "Lincoln won't stand for his army to be treated that way. He'll see this war through, and the slaves'll be freed."

Sophie's chair groaned and creaked on the hard plank floor. "There'll be a lot of moaning across the nation if there's war. You'll see. There's no backwoods rail-splitter going to keep us down. Besides, my family's slaves are like family, and we'll stick together. It'd be cruel to turn them out. What'd they do?"

Ned dried his hands. "Mark my words. Lincoln is gonna go down in the history books as a great President."

She shifted the baby to the other side.

"Ain't you gonna get my supper?"

She sighed and pulled John from her breast. He screamed.

Ned slammed the table with his fist. "Feed the young'un! I'll eat at Mama's. At least she'll have a decent supper, and my pa ain't sired a bunch of little niggers like yours."

* * *

Sophie fed the boys, put them to bed, and then sat down to write a letter.

Dear Papa and all,

I'm so homesick. I should have listened to you, Papa. Ned is a good man, as mountain men go, but they expect so much from their women. I sit here and look at my surroundings, and I wonder how I'm ever going to survive without my Corrie. I did enjoy the help she gave at Christmas. She always took care of my needs. If she could see my table now, she'd have a fit. It's covered with dirty dishes. If it weren't for Ned's hound dogs, the floor would be littered with bits of food from the children. There's not a tablecloth. Doesn't make much difference. The two older ones would use it for a napkin. Papa, I can't imagine you sitting down to eat without a cloth. Of course, Ned didn't eat at this table tonight, but it wasn't because it didn't have a cover. He went to his Mama's to eat because I burned his supper. The kitchen still smells of scorched potatoes. It never occurred to him to help. Cooking is woman's work and so is raising kids. His mama did both without any help, and he wants a wife that can be as good a woman as his mama. He says there's going to be a war, and there won't be any more slaves. I hope not. I'd hate to think of them without a home.

Tell Corrie that I miss her. I can still feel the warm sudsy water as she washed my back. And I can smell the scent of fresh clean sheets or a freshly ironed blouse. These are all luxuries that I gave up to come here and homestead with a trapper. It sounded so exciting and romantic. Well, there's excitement if you like snakes, bears, and wilderness. And as for romance, well, if you can shut your eyes and imagine sleeping on a nice feather tick in a spacious plantation home with a southern gentleman by your side, instead of being on a straw tick in a rustic cabin with the smell of bear grease clogging your nostrils, then you can have romance—

"You mean you ain't got the dishes done? When I left Ma's, she already had hers done and was washing Pa's feet. I guess gettin' my feet washed would be too much to expect."

Sophie looked up to find Ned's huge body filling the doorway. Again, she felt tears swell in her eyes. She blinked and with her finger wiped her cheek. Carefully, she folded her letter, put it into her apron pocket, and moved toward the table to scrape cold food from the plates. She gasped as Ned's hand touched her waist and slid down over her hips. She drew a sharp breath, and it stuck in her throat as his hand caressed her thigh. The air seeped from her in a long heavy sigh. With some effort, she wiped at a plate. His hand slid down her leg and rough fingers massaged the bare skin beneath her dress. As he worked his way upward, she filled the pan with the last of the dirty dishes. *They won't get washed, but at least they can soak.*

* * *

Ned unbuttoned his britches and the moon wrapped his nude

body with rays of soft light. Sophie remembered how embarrassed she'd been on their wedding night. She'd never seen a man in undershorts much less one naked. She assumed all men wore underwear. The maid even ironed her papa's. If her mama were alive, she'd be mortified to know that Ned didn't wear any. Even in the winter, when he wore long-johns, he always removed them before going to bed. Well, that was one less thing she had to iron. She rolled over on her side as the bed sagged from the weight of his body.

Ned curled himself around her and let his hand slide over the fullness of her stomach. His breathing grew heavy as he began to work up her flannel nightgown. "I don't know why you wanna wear this thing."

Sophie flipped onto her back. "And how'd it look when I had to go to the children in the middle of the night? Now, if I had Corrie here, she'd take care of them. Then maybe I'd have time to wash your feet."

"If you ever think I'm gonna allow a slave in this house, you're out of yer cotton picking mind."

"What if Corrie came for a visit? Would she be welcome?"

"Anybody is welcome here, but not as a servant. If your Corrie comes, she will be treated like anybody else."

Sophie folded her hands behind her head. "I'm not going to be in any shape to treat anyone any way in a few months."

"Why? What's gonna happen to you?"

"Shows how much you really look at me. Can't you see I'm putting on weight?"

"Are you gonna have another baby?" He placed his hand over the bulge in her stomach. "I'm gonna have myself another son. Pa had five boys and I'm gonna outdo him."

"And what if it's a girl?"

"Don't worry. I know how to place a boy order, and I ain't about to have no girls, not at least until I have me six sons."

Sophie heard the echo, six sons–son–sons. Sons had to fight. At least daughters–her heart leaped. She shook Ned hard. "Will you have to go?"

"Hush, woman. You're gonna wake the young'uns with your hollerin' and then you'll be too tired to even burn my supper."

Sophie swung her legs over the edge of the bed and stood. "You want me to be quiet when at any minute my husband, and the father of my children, could go to war that makes no sense–a war that would ruin my family! Just how can you free somebody who doesn't want to be free?"

"Calm yourself. I ain't gonna go nowhere. I'd never fight fer slavery. It jest ain't right. One man ownin' another."

Sophie glared at him. "And you want my stepmama to wash and scrub like I do?"

"That's not what I'm sayin', and you know it."

Sophie sat down on the bed. "And how do you plan on getting out of fighting? Probaby people with money won't have to go, but . . .."

The same nude body that only a short while ago had flamed with desire now got up and paced the floor. "Money ain't got nothin' to do with how I feel about this war. Your pa has money, wonder if he'll buy his way out? No, I ain't fightin'."

Sophie lay down. "Then, pray tell, what do you plan on doing?"

"Thinkin'. That's what I'm gonna do, woman. Got me some

thinkin' to do. Now, be quiet."

As a cloud slid over the moon and the room grew dark, Sophie vowed that tomorrow she'd add a postscript and tell her papa he was going to be a grandpa again and ask if Corrie could come for a visit. Then she'd go to the post office and mail it.

❧ 26 ❧

Greenwillow Plantation: Early Spring, 1861

Corrie stood at the library door and knocked tentatively. "Masta Turner, is yo in der?"

"Yes. I'm going through the morning mail. Come on in. What do you want?"

"I gwine dust and clean off yer desk. I be back later if yo wants me to." Corrie watched him lay down the mail and go to the window. After a few minutes, he came back to the desk and picked up a letter.

"That won't be necessary. Look, mail from Sophie. You might as well stay and find out what news she has. I'm sure she'll have something to tell you. She thinks of you as her second mother." He looked down at the letter again. "I've always wanted a son. I love Sophie." He gestured toward the window. "Everything I have will be theirs someday. Reckon she'd let one of her boys come here to live? I've missed them so much since Christmas."

"I not think so, Masta. Yo knows Sophie always loved chile'uns . . . no matter who day is."

Sadness settled over the room as Seth sat down at his desk.

Corrie fanned her apron. "Oh, I miss dat young'un so much. It be so good to have dem here fer Christmas. Not see why she wanna marry dat mountain man and leave all dis behind."

"She has the right to live her life the way she wants."

Corrie nodded and walked to the window. A lump formed in her chest and worked its way up into her throat. She gazed into space. She saw herself as a young girl of fifteen being lead onto an auction block.

The auctioneer examined her. "I ain't even gonna take bids on this scrawny looking nigger. She might be a good chambermaid. Anybody here got any use fer her?"

A gentleman from the crowd stepped forward. She squinted her eyes against the bright sunlight. When she opened them, the man looked down at her with a self-satisfying grin. "Been needing myself a young wench. You're kind of on the skinny side, but I like mine a little thin." He cupped his hands on her cheeks, forcing her mouth open. "Good looking teeth." He took a step backward. "Drop those rags so I can get a better look at what I'm buying."

"She's the worst of the lot, Mr. Turner," said the auctioneer.

Corrie stood motionless, glaring at the auctioneer.

"Did you hear me, girl? I said undress."

When she made no move to obey, he tore the ragged dress from her shoulders. It dropped in a heap at her feet. . Mr. Turner touched one of her breasts. "Not much there." His hand slid down over her buttocks. "I'll give you thirty-five dollars for her."

The auctioneer snatched the money. "She's yourn. Get her outta here so we can get on with our auction."

That's how it had all begun some twenty years ago. She had lived in this big house, sleeping in a little room off the kitchen, tending to the Missy's needs, and pleasuring Masta Turner. She had her boy, food for her stomach, and a roof over her head. She was a lucky nigger. She gave a sigh and turned from the window as Seth lay down the letter and smoothed back his wispy blond hair.

"Guess what? Sophie wants you to come for a visit."

"When, Masta Turner?"

Once again Corrie waited for him to speak, but he picked up the rest of the mail and thumbed through it. Pulling out a long envelope, he ripped it open. She couldn't read, but she stared at the paper covered with large black print as Seth studied it for a little while and then laid it down.

"Life's changing. Makes me sad. I'm getting old, and nothing is working the way I'd planned. I need a son. Who's going to run this place when I'm gone? Got a new wife that doesn't know the first thing about plantation life. Thought *she'd* give me a son, but that hasn't happened yet."

Corrie lowered her head. She wanted to say, "*Yo hab a son. His mamma come from good Mandingo people. Did Masta know he be Sullus' daddy? Surely he know. But again der not be no mention of sellin' him, and usually a master get rid of such a chile.*

"And now my daughter is asking me to give you up." He looked back at the paper on his desk. "There's a big auction next fall. I expect there won't be many more of those for a while with this war business, so I'm going to sell part of my slaves."

Corrie felt an ache in her heart and tears well up in her eyes. She reached a shaky hand out toward her master. "Yo ain't gwine sell mah boy is yo, Masta Turner? Not mah boy!" *Our boy,* she wanted to say. "Please, not sell him. He all I got."

The lines in Seth's face hardened. "Remember your place. I was the one who saved you that day at the auction." His face softened again. "But don't worry about 'the boy'. I have other plans for him.

* * *

Later that evening Seth went to Abigail's room. He sat down and pulled a cheroot from his vest pocket and snipped off the end as he studied his wife's face. She was a spunky little thing. When he'd gone to New Orleans on business, he hadn't planned to come home with a wife, but every plantation needed a mistress, someone to oversee the house and the servants and fill the social aspects of life. As for his bed, Corrie had done a good job, but some spice, especially one so pretty, helped satisfy his hunger. He'd needed her to give him an heir, but that hadn't happened yet. With the war, well he'd see. He held out the letter. "I got a note from Sophie today. She is expecting again. Don't see why it couldn't be you." He stared at her for a long minute then switched the subject. "I wish you two would have had the time to get to know each other better. You seemed to get along good at Christmas."

"Yes, I admire her for what she's doing. I don't have what it takes to start a homestead."

"No, I don't think you do, since you don't have what it takes to give me a son."

"Since that mountain man is supplying you with grandchildren, and you want a son so bad, why don't you adopt one of their boys? The oldest one looks like you, and he really liked it here."

"Ned Miller would never agree, but that's why I'm sending you so you can find out if there's a chance. You have a way with the boys." Seth took a match from his pocket and lit the cigar. "Sophie wants Corrie to come for a visit. I think it's a good idea. She could use the help right now. Maybe if Ned got to know and like you at least he'd let them come more often."

Abigail set her jaw and tossed her head. "If you think I'm going to go visit up there in those mountains, you're crazy! Don't forget I was raised in New Orleans. This plantation is as backwoods as I plan to get! Why don't *you* go? McRoy is capable of running Greenwillow."

Seth took a long draw of his cigar and slowly let out the smoke.

Abigail waved her hand in front of her. "I wish you wouldn't do that in the bedroom. I've never known a man who smoked in front of his wife."

"It's this thing *that* keeps you living in the style you're accustomed to. Besides, it's my house, and I'll smoke where I please. And as for who goes to visit Sophie, it will be you! Mountain people don't like slaves, so I wouldn't want to send Corrie off up there alone."

"But Seth dear," she said in a voice as smooth as freshly gathered honey, "there is really no reason you can't go. I'll be fine here."

Seth threw the cigar in the fireplace. "It's settled! If she thought she was going to sweet talk him, she could think again. "You *are* going! For your own protection. Haven't you heard? We're going to have a war."

"We're already having it. They're shooting."

"That's just why I want you somewhere safe!"

"Why, Seth darling, how sweet of you. I didn't know you cared so much. I've gotten the impression I was only brought here as a– could you say–show piece."

Seth watched her for a few minutes. She was a bright young woman, not easily fooled. "You're partly right, Abigail, but not totally. I'm still a man with certain needs." He raised a knowing eyebrow at her. "This will be a sacrifice on my part. Hopefully, if you can't get me one of my grandsons, you can convince them all to move back to the plantation. There's plenty of room in this big old house. I'm getting older, and I'll need someone to take over someday."

Seth stood and moved toward the door, scowling at her. Somehow she knew he was going to tell her things that she'd just as soon not know. But she'd not let him see how she felt.

"My first wife was sort of sickly all her life. After the birth of Sophie, she ceased her wifely duties. That's why I bought Corrie. A man needs someone to warm his bed. Nigger women are good at pleasuring their men. See, why this arrangement is a sacrifice for me." Seth reached for the doorknob. "That's the way of life on plantations."

Abigail gave him a cold stare.

"Don't tell me you're going to be like my mother. My father left us because she wouldn't allow–no sense talking about that. One of the reasons I want you to go to the mountains is to find out what it will take for Miller to let me have one of his sons. The way I see it every man has a price." He eyed her stomach. "Seems you're not giving me an heir."

"What about me! Do I have a price?"

He opened the door as he peered at her through narrowed eyes. "Oh, you have one. The question is, have I already paid it?"

Abigail listened to Seth's steps, fading down the hall. So that's what Corrie had meant when she'd said, 'I be his', the first day she'd come to Greenwillow. And the night back before Christmas when Corrie had talked about Sullus, she had wondered then if she might be his mistress. The whole ugly picture of plantation life closed in. There were all sorts of children running about, and many were a lot lighter than their parents. Yes, it was possible that Seth already had an heir? She slipped from the bed and bolted her door. As she passed the dresser, she looked into the mirror and brushed up several loose strands of dark hair. She smiled at her reflection and whispered, "Yes, Seth dear. I have a price. I've paid it once, and I won't be paying it again."

Settling in bed, she closed her eyes. Actually, she'd like nothing better than to go to the mountains. At least there she wouldn't have to put up with his repulsive mauling. But if he thought she *wanted* to go, he might not allow it.

❧ 27 ❧

Laural Grove Trading Post In Virginia: May, 1861

Ned Miller slung his load of hides onto a bench outside the Laurel Grove Trading Post in Virginia and rubbed his shoulder. This made the second run he'd made over here since late winter, but he loved making the trip in the spring because of all the mountain flowers. His pack mule was a big help, but there still was a lot of heavy lifting and pulling. Besides, he had other worries. A war had started and as sure as these hides would be turned into leather, his hide would have to fight in a war that he didn't believe in. Somehow, he had to find a way to stay out of it. So far, North Carolina hadn't left the Union, or at least he hadn't heard about it, and until they did, he'd try and not worry too much. No sense in wasting good energy over something he had no control over. Ned looked up to find Chester Kimsey standing in the door. Chester owned the trading post, and Ned considered him to be one of his closest friends.

As Ned stomped his feet to remove the red clay, he saw a frown mar Chester's forehead. "From what I hear, you'll get your chance to fight in the army."

Ned followed Chester inside. "What'd you mean? Have you heared anymore war news?" Little beads of sweat formed on his upper lip as he waited for Chester to sit down and lean his chair against the wall the way he always did when he had news. Could he talk better in this position?

"Fellow through here yesterday said North Carolina left the Union. Think he said it was the twentieth of May. Let's see. Today is May the twenty-eighth. Suppose any day now, you'll all have to go."

Ned took another chair and joined Chester. "How's it that you've not gone yet, Chester.? You livin' here in Virginia and all. Seems like you would have already left. Let's see. Virginia left the Union a while back, didn't it?"

Chester scratched his head. "If my memory serves me right, it was the twenty-seventh of April. They could be here anytime to get me. You know that's what happens when you don't go. They come and get you. They're even takin' all the young boys. I mean like thirteen and fourteen. Guess they use them fer drummer or bugler boys, or that's what they say until they get them in there. They'll carry a gun before it's over with. Can't protect yourself with a drum."

Ned thought about his three little boys at home. He sure was glad they were too little. "What happens if they can't find you when they come?"

Chester shrugged his shoulders. "Guess they can't get what they can't find, can they?"

Ned's thoughts ran wild. He knew of a perfect place to hide. And he could be close to home. He could even continue his trapping. "You gonna go when they come fer you, Chester?" Ned jumped at the thud the chair made when it dropped to the floor. It sounded a lot like gunshot.

"Guess I'll have to. But they'll have to come get me. Ain't gonna join on my own. The man that said North Carolina had left the Union said they probably wouldn't take me because they need the trading post fer supplies."

"Seems like they would. What else did this fellow have to say?"

"Not much. He did say it looked like the state of Virginia would be divided. You know how mountain people are about slaves. Very few of them own them."

"Would your trading post be in West Virginia?"

Chester went behind the counter and began to count out Ned's money. "No. I'd still be in Virginia. Guess I'm glad. Don't wanna fight, but if I do, I'd feel like a traitor fighting fer the North. I hear slavery ain't the main issue. They're sayin' it's all started over states' rights."

"I know and that's what I told my friend, Zeb, but you and me know different. It's the slavery that is tearin' our country apart. I can't see what gives a man the right to own another, no matter what color his skin."

Chester wrote something down in a book. "Seems to me like you should be fightin' fer the North, Ned."

Ned turned to leave. "Ain't fightin' fer nobody if I don't have to."

Chester followed him to the door. "What's wrong, Ned? You a coward?"

Ned turned with his fists doubled up.

Chester grinned. "Guess I know how to get your dander up, don't I?"

Ned smiled. "You know better than that. Ain't a man in these mountains I'd be afraid to take on. But war jest ain't my way. We'll be payin' fer years to come no matter who wins. I gotta be goin', Chester. Hope you're still around the next trip I make."

Chester stuck out his hand to Ned. "I'll try and be. But if sump'n happens that I'm not, good luck, Ned. A man has to live by what he believes. I know that."

"And the same to you, Chester. We've been friends a long time and no matter what, I can assure you that I won't be fightin' against or with you or any of my other friends." With that promise still ringing between them, Ned left to make his plans.

* * *

The sun dropped behind the mountains. Ned knew that dusk would not linger. Before long, he found a spot off the trail to build a campfire. He tied the mule and his horse to a low branch. When his bedroll was spread out, he put coffee in a pot and hung it over the flames then poured beans in a tin bucket and hung them to warm. He settled back against a tree to wait.

Around the bend in the road came a rider at a fast gallop. The man reined to a stop in front of Ned's campfire. Jumping from the horse, he extended a hand. "Name's John Simmons. Been following you from the trading post. For a minute there, I thought I'd lost you. That coffee smells awful good. Can you spare a cup?"

Ned nodded and took two cups and poured the steaming coffee, handing one to his visitor. "Now suppose you tell me why you've been followin' me. I ain't done nothin' wrong, unless you think I got my hides wrongfully, and I can prove I didn't do that."

John chuckled and placed a hand on Ned's shoulder. "Relax, my friend. I'm here to be of service to you."

Ned was puzzled. He didn't need any help. Trapping was a one-man job. "Guess you could be hungry seein' it's nigh on to supper time. Would you care to share my beans?"

John rubbed his stomach. "Beans sound fine. Haven't eat since this morning. Could take a little nourishment."

Ned filled two plates with beans and refilled their coffee cups. When they were settled he said, "Now, suppose you tell me why you've been followin' me."

Ned's eyes never left John's face as he took a couple of bites of beans then wiped his mouth on his sleeve. "Was a hanging round Chester's trading post. Overheard you tell him that you wasn't too crazy about fighting in a war."

Ned looked at the man who had just eaten most of his beans and was now enjoying another cup of coffee. "What business did you have eavesdroppin'. You some sort of spy?"

"Never thought of myself as a spy, but I guess, in a funny kind of way, you could say I am. I listen. Have to so I can learn who I can count on. From what I heard at the trading post, I'd say you and me have a lot in common."

Darkness settled in. Ned watched the dying flicker of the campfire hiss and sputter. Could the fire tell how he was thinking? Somehow it seemed to know—one minute willing to reach out and trust this stranger, and the next drawing back, not sure. A flame leaped high in the air and for an instant lit the stranger's face. Ned leaned back against his tree. "I'll buy that. Let's hear what you have to say, then I'll decide fer myself."

John filled his cup again. "First off, I admire a fellow who knows what he believes and lives by it. That's why I'm doing what I'm doing. Living by what I believe."

Ned rubbed his chin then filled his cup again. "Well, if a man don't, the way I see it, he ain't much of a man."

John nodded. "That's the reason I think you will be willing to help me. You won't have to worry about going to war right away. There's plenty of volunteers right now. Now, say, if this war last for long, I'm sure they'll be drafting anybody who can carry a gun."

Ned felt relief sweep over him. For now, he didn't have to worry. "I can't believe men would actually go fight on their own free will." He watched his visitor make himself comfortable as he leaned against another tree and stretched out his legs.

"Yep! Young men from all over the state have rushed off to training camps. Going in the spirit of a holiday outing. Taking all the comforts of home. They're gonna be in for a big surprise. Colonel Hill has already left with the first state troops for Richmond. Guess when word gets back about the real war, boys won't be so eager to volunteer. That, my friend, will be when you'll have to start worrying."

Ned studied his new friend for awhile. He seemed to know an awful lot. "Suppose you jest out and tell me who you are. Then maybe, we can get down to business."

John set up and stretched out his hand again toward Ned. "John Simmons, abolitionist, at your service."

Ned was shocked. He'd heard about these people. Men who had set out to make a wrong, right, but in their own way had brought on lots of trouble. He eyed the man cautiously. "You any kin to that man, John Brown? From what I hear, he caused a whole bunch of trouble. Also, got hisself hung."

"Never knew John. Like you, just heard about him. I go about my job a little different than he did. I work as much undercover as possible. Can help more people that way."

Ned threw another log on the almost dead fire. Looked like they'd be here awhile. "Tell me how you think I fit into your plans."

"From what I heard at the Post, you also don't believe in slavery. That's my main reason for thinking you'd help me. Your job is perfect for what I need. And most of all, by helping me, they'd have a hard time catching up with you when they start the draft."

Ned poured more coffee. This man sure had given him a lot to think about, but he wasn't sure. Trapping was the only thing he'd ever done. And for the life of him, he couldn't see how he could help. "Tell me. Jest what would you want me to do?"

"I'd want you to smuggle slaves from your part of the country into Western Virginia. You know these mountains like the back of your hand. When you get them to Western Virginia, there'll be someone there to take over. By then, I suspect that part of the country will be broke from Virginia, and they'll more than likely fight for the North.

"And how will they get to Shady Junction?"

"That's where I come in. I'm going on down to the eastern part of the state and bring back a bunch of slaves."

"You can start at my father-in-law's tobacco plantation about two hours north of Fayetteville. It's called Greenwillow. I'd love to see his slaves free."

"Sounds as good a place as any to start. By that, I take it you're willing to help?"

Ned stretched out his hand to the stranger. "I'd love to see my father-in-law squirm. Been using them nigger wenches fer years. Probably a lot of those little pickaninnies belong to him."

"From what I hear, that's a common practice. How will I contact you when I get to Shady Junction?"

"There's a old man there by the name of Zeb Watts. Jest ask him. He'll know where to find me."

"You'll be hearing from me. It might not be right away, but you'll hear. I'm sure you won't be sorry for your decision."

John was gone before Ned could think of anything else to say. He shook himself. Had he been dreaming? What had he gotten himself into? He hadn't planned on helping John. It had sort of just happened. The thought of Seth Turner had clouded his thinking. He stretched out on his bedroll. Well, whatever happened wasn't going to happen right now. He'd have some time to mull it over, and thank God, he didn't have to worry about war right now either.

❧ 28 ❧

Shady Junction: May 30, 1861

"I done and told you what would happen when we started accepting *furiners* in these here parts. I tell you, I could see it as plain as the nose on my face when that Ned Miller went off down yonder to the low country and come back with that woman Sophie." Zeb Watts stomped his foot as though that would help pound his message into his friends' heads. "Let one in and it won't be long 'til there'll be more traipsing in. Ain't nothin' here fer a nigger." Zeb pointed at Amos Ledbetter with the stick he was whittling on. "You men think I'm just flapping my jaws to hear myself talk, but I tell you, I know. I've been out in this world, and I know what goes on." Zeb filled his jaw with a plug of home-cured chewing tobacco and spit into the blacksmith's fire. He listened to it crackle and pop then continued. "You'uns don't believe me, do you?"

"We've heared all about yore travels, Zeb. What we can't figure out is why you come back here seein' how you made it so big out there in the world," said Amos.

Zeb folded his knife and put it in his pocket then stood and brushed the shavings from his overalls. He pulled on his gray beard and spit out his wad of tobacco, then walked to where the blacksmith was forging a horseshoe. "Well, if I'd been as big and burly as Grimes here, I'd probably still be out there. Take a little drawed-up-stump of a man like me, ain't safe out there. How's a-body like me gonna protect hisself? Did I ever tell you about the time I got me a job on one of them big plantations as a guard?"

"Can't say as you have, Zeb. But fer the life of me, I don't see how you fergot that one," said Will Grimes.

Zeb paced the length of the blacksmith's shop. "Could be 'cause it was the shortest job of my life. Didn't stay but a week. Them there niggers are jest plain loony. Have all kinds of superstitions."

The sound of a wagon rattling into Shady Junction brought Zeb to the door. "It's the supply wagon from Asheville."

"It's the wagon alright," said Amos. "But looks to me like, it's hauling more than supplies. Looks like two women and one of them is a nigger."

Zeb wagged his finger at his friends. "I've been trying to tell you'uns, but you'uns wouldn't listen. Now we're gettin' invaded with them *furiners*. Jest you wait! Won't be none of us safe."

Zeb peered out the door as a wagon jolted to a stop in front of the general store and every window and door in Shady Junction filled with curious spectators. He knew mountain folk didn't cotton to owning slaves but how would they be with living with them? As the mysterious visitors stepped down from the wagon, he felt an uneasy chill sweep through the air.

* * *

Abigail viewed her welcoming committee with unease. What did she know about mountain people? How would they react to Corrie. Well, she'd show them she was in control and maybe that would ease any tension. "Girl, get the trunks unloaded."

"Yes'um, Missy. I git dem right away."

The last trunk had just landed on the ground when Abigail's hat blew off and went dancing down the street. She called, "There goes my new hat. Catch it, girl. Hurry! It will be ruined."

"Yes'um,Missy. Sorry, Missy!"

Abigail placed the retrieved hat back on her head as she stared out at the mob. *There that will show them who's in charge.* She saw a little man in overalls working his way toward her. As he shuffled toward the wagon, a woman pushed in front of him.

"Where you'd get sump'n like that? Wonder if they're sold through a catalogue." She stepped a little closer to Corrie then jumped back. "You think maybe a-body could go down to the post office and check on this. The Federal Government must know sump'n 'bout them. Think I'll run on down there and see what I can find out."

Abigail walked up the store steps and called to Corrie, "Fetch my fan over here and fan me." As she sat down she heard

a woman near the porch say, "There should be a man to handle this situation. Where's that man of mine when he's needed?"

Abigail watched her scan the crowd then turn to the woman by her side. "Helen, maybe one of us should go up and find out who they are and what they want. Could be some of our relatives. I have some cousins who live down in New Orleans. Maybe with all this war talk, they've decided to come fer a visit."

"Could be, Sissy. I also have some plantation family down in South Calina. Wouldn't it be sump'n if they'd decided to pay me a visit? Come on. Let's go together."

The man in overalls stepped toward the porch. "Wait! I'll take care of this. Who knows? They could be sent here from the Union Army to spy on us.'

"Think we best do as he says. You know Zeb's been out and about, and he knows what goes on more'n we do," said Sissy.

Abigail heard a hush fall over the crowd as the man in overalls sauntered up the steps.

"Howdy, ladies. Name's Zeb. Can I be of service? If you need a place to stay, there's the Ledbetter boarding house, but as I recall, they're all filled up. Maybe you folks have some family in these here parts? Be glad to help you locate them."

The woman extended her hand and looked directly into Zeb's eyes. "Why, thank you, Mr. Zeb. My name's Abigail Turner and this is my servant girl, Corrie. I do have family here, the Miller family. Do you know them?"

Zeb took a step back, pulled on his beard, and cleared his throat. "They live out a little ways. Ned's probably off in the mountains a trappin', but if you'd rent a wagon to haul you and all this stuff..." he gestured toward the pile of trunks, boxes, and bags on the porch. "I'd be glad to drive you out there."

Abigail turned to Corrie. "You heard the man, girl. Go find us a wagon."

"Yes'um. I be right back, Missy."

Scratching his head, Zeb stared after the girl who scurried off down the street "Jest like I told the boys at the blacksmith shop. Won't be long 'til it won't be safe around here fer nobody."

Abigail didn't answer, after all he was right. If this war continued, even the mountains wouldn't be spared.

* * *

"Lawdy, Mercy. Ain't yo a site fer sore eyes? And dis here baby, he's growed a whole bushel since Christmas! Where be ta other boys?"

"They're off in the woods some place, Corrie." Sophie straightened her apron over her stomach and said to Abigail, "Well, what do you think of where I live? I know it's nothing like Greenwillow. We're just getting started."

Abigail examined the cabin Sophie had described at Christmas time as "charming". It was built from roughly hewed logs, and the cracks were filled with mud. There had only been enough trees cleared to build the cabin, which sat into the side of a mountain. A well-worn path led from the front door to the right side of the house and off into the bushes. To the left stood a makeshift dog pen. Inside the cobbled-up fence, six flea-ridden hounds lay scratching themselves. Beyond the dog pen, a shed covered with furs shaded the yard. Before Abigail could speak, a blood-curdling scream came from the roof of the house.

"Mama, Adam won't give me my snake!"

Abigail looked up. Adam stood at the front of the roof, dangling a long black snake over the edge. Right behind him was three-year old Allen.

Sophie shoved the baby toward Corrie. "Here, take him until I tend to those boys."

The servant woman's eyes grew to the size of saucers. She shook her head and at the same time backed toward the woods. "Miz Sophie, Corrie not stay where der be snakes."

"Here, Abigail. Take the baby and go inside with Corrie. I'll be right there when I take care of the boys."

Abigail took the baby, holding him away from her dress so as not to get wet from the soggy diaper. He wasn't the same clean baby that she'd played with at Christmas. "Make sure those boys don't bring that snake in the house, or Corrie and I will both be leaving!" she called after Sophie.

Before Abigail could move, Sophie grabbed up a hoe and pulled the snake from Adam's hands. She chopped off its head and threw it over the fence to the hounds. "You boys get yourselves down here! Your Grandmother Abigail and Corrie are here to see you."

Adam backed up a few steps. "Promise not to switch me, Mama. I was teasing Allen. Can't I ever have any fun?"

"We'll talk about it later. Right now I want you to get down from there and wash your face and hands then come in the house and see your grandmother!"

Inside, Abigail found Corrie huddled in the corner of the room. She handed the baby to her. "He needs his diaper changed."

Corrie closed her eyes and scooted deeper into the corner.

"Corrie, the snake is dead. Now, this baby needs changing." She reached for a diaper hanging on the back of a chair.

Sophie came in and took the baby. "I'll change him. You all must be worn out from that long trip."

Abigail folded the diaper. "And you must be tired from living like this. Children running all over the roof, playing with snakes and God knows what else."

Sophie finished diapering the baby and set him on the floor. "What's wrong with Corrie?" She asked Abigail.

"She's afraid of snakes, and I can't say I'm fond of them."

Sophie held out her hand toward Corrie. "I took care of the snake. Come, tell me about Papa."

Slowly, Corrie emerged from the corner, but her eyes never left the door. "I wanna go back home. Miz Abigail stay and help."

"I promise you, the boys won't be playing with any more snakes after Ned tans their hides."

"Dat what ta Missy say when I be a little young'un. She promise not to send us to ta snake pit if we do our work."

Abigail's skin crawled. "What do you mean, Corrie?"

"I be running all day on ta plantation in South Georgia. Fetchin' dis or dat fer Cook or back and forth to check on ta chilluns playin' in ta yard. When I not runnin' fer somethin', I be washin' cannin' jars. I jest finish ta last batch of jars when Big Missy yell. I run upstairs. 'Fore I catch mah breath, she cap a chamber pot over mah head. Said, 'Take dat, yo lazy nigger. I've said time and again ta first thing yo do in ta mornin' be empty mah pot.'"

Abigail had an image of Corrie standing there with the pot over her head, arms hanging helpless at her side, urine dripping from the edges, soaking her ragged dress. "How old were you, Corrie?"

"My mama say I be twelve. But I try extra hard to please since ta day I ferget to dust under her bed. Ta missy yell fer ta houseboy. He come a-runnin'. She send him fer ta overseer and he drag me outside, tie a rope around mah waist and drop me down in a pit." She looked down at her hands. "I still feel dem der snakes crawlin' over mah fingers."

Abigail looked away to hide the tears that gathered in her eyes. She pushed the thoughts of the snake pit from her mind. Yet, the present offered just as much danger to a slave. Look what had happened to Sally Mae.

Two little boys sheepishly slipped through the door and stood behind their mother. Abigail saw the love for the boys in Sophie's eyes. Maybe this wasn't the life Sophie had on the plantation, but she had something Seth wanted, and that was a son. *Would he be concerned for my safety if he knew I'd never give him an heir?*

"Come here, boys. Remember Grandmother Abigail? She's

married to your Grandfather Turner. He owns the big house we went to at Christmas."

The little boys stood behind their mother's skirt and peeped out.

Abigail reached out her hand. They hadn't acted this shy at Christmas. Had she lost her touch?

Adam looked up. "I wish Pa'd get home."

The air filled with the wails of the flea-ridden bunch of hounds.

"Sounds like someone's coming. Probably your pa. Said he'd be home tonight. Ned doesn't believe in servants like my father does. He's different, but he's just like all other mountain men, good at heart."

"By now, Sophie, I think I can get used to almost anything."

The door opened and Abigail faced the roughest looking man she'd ever seen. With determination, Abigail extended her hand as Sophie spoke.

"Ned, I'd like for you to meet my stepmother, Abigail, and of course, you know Corrie. She's still a little shook over the snake the boys dropped over the edge of the roof." Sophie glanced toward Corrie, who took a few steps back.

Without delay the boys stepped from their mother's skirt and stood in front of their father. "Pa, I was jest teasing Allen. I swear, Pa! I didn't know there was anyone in the yard." He faced Allen. "Ain't that right?"

Allen bobbed his head up and down.

"Outside! Both of you. We have some business in the shed."

Soon father and sons returned. The boys went straight to their bed in the loft and Ned sat down. "Where's my supper? I bet our company's starved, too."

"I get yo' supper, Masta Miller. Miz Sophie not be doing too much work in her condition."

"What condition? She's gonna have a young'un. Most natural thing in the world. Now, Corrie, you come sit down."

Corrie backed away. "I not set with ta white folk, Masta Miller. I take my plate outside and eat."

"You'll do no such thing. We're all gonna sit down here and eat, and we'll talk later."

Abigail set the table while Corrie and Sophie dished up a supper of dried beans and cold cornbread. Corrie pulled her chair to one end of the table and sat down.

Ned ate without saying anything. When he was through, he pushed away and leaned his chair back on two legs. "Chester, who runs the Laural Grove Trading Post, said my hides would be in demand now that there's a war going on. They'll need leather."

Sophie sighed. "As long as they just need animal hides and not yours. But I'm afraid before this is over . . .."

"We don't have to worry yet, Sophie. Chester said he thought North Carolina left the Union May the twentieth, but they're gonna take the young boys first. They're telling them they're gonna be drummer boys, but you know they'll be carrying a gun before it's over."

Abigail took her plate and scraped it into a bucket by the stove. "What about Virginia? Have they left?"

"Yeah, Chester said they left the twenty-seventh of April. He won't have to worry about going because they need him to run the trading post. The mountain part of Virginia is siding with the

North. Don't know who Chester'd fight fer. Think he feels like me."

Abigail dropped the plate in the dishpan. "Who would you fight for?"

"Don't believe in slavery, so I couldn't fight fer the South."

"You can't fight for any side and leave me and the children out here in these mountains! I'll take them and go home to Greenwillow."

Abigail drew a long breath. Maybe she wouldn't have to ask them to move back.

"Sophie Miller, it'll snow in July before I let you take my young'uns back to that plantation to live. And fer your information, I'm not going to fight. Know that cave that's right at the back of our house? I'm gonna hide out in there. I can watch fer the law from the roof. If I'm out tending my traps and there's trouble, you can hang a sheet in the trees on the hill in the back. One more thing, I met a man on the way home by the name of John Simmons. He's an abolitionist, like that John Brown who got hisself hung."

Sohpie picked up her plate. "You're not going to get involved with any of them radical groups, are you?"

"No, I jest sent him on down to Greenwillow to see if he can help some of your pa's servants find freedom." He turned to Abigail. "That's enough war talk. Mrs. Turner and Corrie, I want you both to know you are welcome in my home. Corrie, you're to think of yourself as one of us. Do you hear?"

Corrie scraped the last of the food from her plate. "Yes'suh, if you says so, Masta Miller."

"I'm not your master. My name's Ned, and that's what I expect to be called."

"Yessuh, Mista Ned Miller. I means Miller. I means Ned."

The tension eased as everyone laughed.

"What brought on this visit?" asked Ned.

"Miz Sophie write and ast me to come," said Corrie.

"And Seth sent me because of the war," said Abigail.

"Seems to me like a man that's not been married any longer than he has would want his wife at home," said Ned.

Abigail hadn't expected this sort of questioning. How much could she say without upsetting Sophie? "I think I've disappointed him. He wants an heir, and I've failed to give him one. He'd like for you to move to the plantation with your family."

Ned chuckled. "As fer as my living on a plantation, I'm a mountain man, and I guess I'll die as one. As fer heirs, I dare say Seth has plenty, the only thing is they're not all white."

Abigail felt the heat rise to her face, but Sophie had not even flinched. *Does she know about her father sleeping with the slave women?*

"Ned thinks Papa has fathered half his plantation."

"That ain't so Mast . . . Ned. He only father Sullus. He not sleep 'round with a bunch of wenches."

This obviously caught Sophie by surprise. "You mean your boy that I played with is really my half-brother?"

"He shore is, Miz Sophie."

"Does he know?"

"No, I not ever tell him, and I shore he not find out or he'd a-say so."

"This war's gonna bring a lot of changes," said Ned. "We're gonna live here together the best we can. I'll sleep out'n the shed tonight, and tomorrow we'll make some sleepin' arrangements."

As Ned stepped out into the night, Abigail started unfastening her dress. A button dropped off, and she pulled the loose threads from it. There'd sure be lots of cleaning up to do after the war. But for now, it sure looked like they'd be like all the buttons in her box, living together in this tiny house. And Seth. Well, maybe if he weren't such a harsh man she'd feel sorry about not giving him a son.

≈ 29 ≈

Shady Junction: June, 1861

Abigail read the sign tacked to the Post Office door: POSTMASTER GENERAL ORDERS ALL POSTAL SERVICE CEASE AS OF MAY THE THIRTY-FIRST. She should've written the note to Seth and mailed it the day they got to the Junction, but then she wouldn't have been able to tell him there was no hope of getting his daughter back to the plantation because Ned Miller was his own man. Now, what was she going to do? Maybe the store owner knew of some way to send it. As she walked in that direction, a lady stepped out on the porch.

"Haven't seen you since the day you got here, Mrs. Turner. Are you doing some shopping?"

Abigail wiped her dark hair from her face. "I came to mail a letter to my husband, but I see the post office is closed."

"It's the work of that President Lincoln."

"When will that delivery wagon be back this way? Maybe he'd take it for me."

"Don't come on a regular basis. Can't depend on them. Always a different driver. Your mail would probably wind up in Timbuktu."

"How could it, when we are already there?"

The lady gave a chuckle. "You have a sense of humor. My pa always said you didn't have anything to worry about if you could joke. Why don't you come on over to the boarding house and have a cup of tea? My name's Sissy Ledbetter."

Abigail was taken by surprise. She'd never been the visiting kind. Back on the plantation, she only saw neighbors at parties. The woman was already halfway down the steps. "Tea sounds wonderful. Thanks."

As they neared the house, she was astonished to see how well-kept it was. Flowers lined the walkways and off to the side the earth had been turned and planted in a small vegetable garden. Inside the floorboards shined. The rose patterned, gray carpet looked as though it had just been beaten. It brought back memories of Mrs. Cranshaw's home. For a moment, she felt like crying.

Sissy touched her on the arm. "You all right?"

"I'm fine. This makes me remember . . ."

"Of your plantation down East?"

"No, it reminds me of a house in New Orleans."

Sissy's face brightened. "New Orleans? I have cousins who live there. Ain't this something, you and me both having folk there? Have a seat. I'll bring us some tea, and we can talk about it."

Abigail seated herself on the small settee in the parlor. As she gazed about, her attention was drawn to a gold framed picture on the wall. She got up to take a closer look. It was of Mrs. Wellington, and one of the four girls that stood near her looked just like Sissy Ledbetter. It couldn't be! The brothel was a thousand miles away. What was the picture doing here? Her knees grew weak. She had to sit down before she fainted, or get out of here. She backed away as Sissy came in.

"You can sit over there. I'll pull this chair over near the table. That way I can pour, and we can talk."

"Don't you think it's a little warm for tea? Maybe a glass of lemonade would be better," she said weakly.

"Oh, I'm sorry. I'm so used to having tea myself. It helps me unwind. You sit right there, and I'll get you some lemonade."

Abigail went back to the photo and studied it. Would her past always haunt her?

"Here we are, my dear, your lemonade. I see you've found my picture."

"Is this some of your family?"

"I call them my cousins. And the woman in the back, she was like a mother to me. Took me in when I had nowhere else to go." She poured herself a cup of tea. When she had taken a couple of swallows, she set her cup down. "Sometimes outsiders can be more like family than the real ones. Somehow, I believe you understand."

Abigail sipped her lemonade and studied Sissy's face. What did she see? Concern or curiosity? Was this woman trying to pick her brain, and if so, why? She traced the rim of her glass with her forefinger. "Family is responsibility, and that sometimes hinders the development of a relationship."

"You're right. Never had any children of my own, but I can imagine what a worry they can be."

"Yes. Take Sophie. A girl that had everything her heart desired, and she chose to marry a mountain man and moved to the middle of nowhere. That takes courage. I couldn't do it."

"It's different, I must say. The mountain men, they wanna be the boss, but a woman can handle them if she wants to." She winked at Abigail. "You know what I mean. To hear my husband talk you'd think he was the king."

Abigail drained the last of the lemonade from her glass and glanced out the window. "I'd better go. Once the sun goes down it's not long 'til dark." She rose and extended her small thin hand. "It has been most pleasant, ah . . . ah . . ."

"Why don't you call me Sissy? I hope we can become friends."

Abigail gave a nod. She had to get out of here before she was caught in some kind of web. She'd decide later if she wanted Sissy Ledbetter for a friend.

Outside, she followed the setting sun toward the Miller cabin. As darkness crept in so did the horror of her past. The night of the baby's birth returned as a shadow darted across the path. The trail took a sudden turn, and the dirt beneath her feet gave away. She landed against a tree trunk. Were the shadows out to destroy her? Brushing the loose debris from her dress, she pulled up. She'd always managed to take care of herself, and this time would be no different. But she might need a friend, and Sissy seemed willing. *Since living conditions are so crowded at Ned's, tomorrow, I'll go rent a room at the boarding house.*

* * *

The next day the sun had already started its journey toward the western sky when Abigail knocked on the boarding house door. Finally a man answered. "I'm sorry to bother you, Mr. ah--"

The man wiped his hand on his pants, then stuck it out. "I'm Amos Ledbetter, Sissy's Husband. I was a washin' and polishin' the floor. You're that new lady who come to town with the slave, ain't you? The one that's visitin' out to Miller's place."

"That's right. I came into the Junction yesterday to mail a letter, and the post office was closed. Your wife asked me over for tea. It's awfully crowded out at the Millers. I left the slave to help out, but I came to see if I could rent a room." She set a suitcase down by her feet.

Sissy moved from the last step leading upstairs toward the front door. "Why, Abigail? You're back so soon. What a pleasant surprise. Won't you come in? Amos why don't you go and find Zeb and shoot the breeze for a while? Abigail and me would like to visit a spell."

"I'll do that, and you'uns have a nice visit. Be home for supper." Amos disappeared toward the back of the house.

Sissy gave a chuckle. "He's relieved that you showed up. He helps with the heavy cleaning, and he's happy for an excuse to get away."

Abigail smiled apologetically. "I'm sorry to be a bother. As I was saying to your husband, do you have any rooms for rent? It's a little crowded out at the Millers."

"I have plenty. Not much business in a place like this. Just a salesman once in a while. I have two boarders, nice young ladies. One's Margaret, the schoolteacher, and the other one, Alice, has a corner in the general store where she makes hats. They've been here so long they're like family. I know you'll enjoy them. Come on upstairs, and I'll show you to a room."

Abigail followed her up the stairs. "Tell me, how'd you get to know the woman in the picture?"

"Well, believe it or not, in my younger days, I wasn't bad looking." She brushed at a strand of graying hair over one ear. "Anyway, when I was about fourteen, Pa traded me for a milk cow."

"A milk cow! That's horrible."

"Oh, I don't blame him too much. If you had a young girl you'd drug all over the country, and she was getting older, and you knew that she'd probably find somebody and get married before too long, wouldn't it make sense to get something for all the trouble she'd been to you?"

"Did he trade you to that lady in the picture?"

"No. I wasn't that lucky."

"I didn't think so. She doesn't look like the type that would be in the milk cow business."

"The man my pa traded me to had a whole herd of them. His wife was sickly, and he needed help with the cooking and housework."

"And you were that someone."

"Right. At first it was fun. Having a real home to live in, and knowing that when you woke up in the morning, you'd still be there when night came. My pa was always on the move. I never had time in one place to make friends or even get any schooling." At the head of the stairs, Sissy opened the first door to the left and went in.

Abigail sat down her belongings. "I can imagine how you felt. How'd you get to know the lady in the picture?"

"That came a little later. My new home wasn't nice for long."

"What happened?"

"I woke in the middle of the night to find the woman's husband in my bed. I tried to scream, but he capped his hand over my mouth. He said, 'You didn't think I was goin' to give away one of my prized cows without gettin' more than my floors scrubbed and my meals cooked, did you?'"

"What did you do?"

"I didn't have much choice that night, but I can tell you one thing. If he thought I was going to stand for him to use me that way, he got a surprise. The next morning, when he went to the field, I packed my things and got out of there."

"Did you tell his wife?"

"Oh, I told her all right. She didn't act surprised. I'd say it wasn't the first time. I left, and that's when I met Mama Wellington. She was young then. I'd say early twenties. She'd had a hard way to go in life. Her mother let men friends use her for a drink of booze. The way I see it, I hadn't had half the bad time she'd had. She got the home place. By that time, there was quite a string of men coming so she had a ready-made business. She found her some young women and started a whorehouse. At first I was the cook-cleaning girl, anything that needed to be done. When I got a little older and Mama saw how the men cottoned to me, she put me to work and got more help for the kitchen."

"Did she always find ones who needed a home to help in the kitchen?"

"As long as I was there, which was quite a few years, that's what she done."

Abigail wondered if she got much pay at Mama Wellingtons'. She touched her arm. "I have money for my room. My husband is a rich tobacco grower in the low country. But if this turns into a long stay and the fighting gets bad, I may not have enough to outlast the war."

"Don't worry, my dear. I don't think this war business is gonna last very long. But if it does money won't be worth the paper it's printed on. If you want to freshen up, I'll call you when supper's ready."

When Abigail was alone she spent the first few minutes admiring the beautiful furnishings. A high poster bed sat in the middle of the room. A chest to match the bed and a washbasin stood on the outside wall. The room was filled with all the little touches that said 'woman'. She fluffed her pillow and stretched out on the bed, letting her body sink into the soft feather bed. It sure beat the straw tick she'd slept on at Sophie's, but she'd miss the boys. As the aroma of supper drifted up the stairs, she closed her eyes and thought about David Cranshaw. She hadn't had much time, lately, to think about how much she loved him. And Rosemary. She sure hoped this war wouldn't change her life, but it looked like everyone was going to be affected before it was over. Night sounds filled her ears as peace flowed over her. She sensed this place held many good times. Good times without the likes of Seth Turner.

* * *

A week later Abigail woke to the smell of coffee brewing and bacon frying. The sun peeked through the morning fog. She stretched and wiggled her way deeper into the feather bed. She hadn't enjoyed this sort of comfort since she'd left the plantation. *Yes, this will be my home until I return to Greenwillow. Let Seth pay. He's the one who has money.* A loud banging at the front door jarred her from her soft nest of eathers. Who would be calling this early in the morning? She slipped from bed and went to the window and pushed back the curtain. Ned Miller, what did he want?

The front door cracked. The sound of Ned's voice alarmed her. Throwing a wrap over her shoulders, she hurried down the stairs. By the time she'd reached the hall, Ned was inside.

"Come quick. Sophie's havin' the baby. It's not time. There's no doctor. My mama is the granny woman, but she's birthin' another young'un."

She gave a heavy sigh. "I don't know anything about birthing babies. But maybe I can comfort her. Give me just a minute to get dressed."

As soon as they got to the cabin, she jumped down from the horse and rushed inside. Corrie mopped at Sophie's face with a damp cloth. "Thank the Lord, you be back. This here baby ain't a wantin' to come, and I not know what to do."

"My mama is gone to birth another young'un so I brought Abigail to help. I'll go bile the water."

Corrie rushed toward the kitchen door. "I bile water. I bile good water."

"Hel . . . p! I think the baby is coming." screamed Sophie. Abigail grabbed a sheet and tied knots in it, tied one end to the bedpost, and gave the other to Sophie. "Pull as hard as you can and push that baby out. I'll catch it." She positioned herself at the foot of the bed. This couldn't be too hard. All she had to do was take the baby and wrap it in a blanket.

"Here be ta biling water. I bring some scissors and a twine to tie ta cord. Mr. Ned, I hopes yo be good at tiein'. I ain't never done dis."

He patted Corrie's shoulder. "I think I can manage. How's she doin', Abigail?"

"One more push, and I think it'll be here. I can see red hair."

Sophie's stomach hardened in a contraction.

"Push . . . push!" Abigail encouraged.

The head cleared the birth canal, but the shoulders didn't come. Another contraction, and she took the baby's head in her hands. "Push harder! It's coming."

Sophie pushed but nothing happened.

Abigail realized the baby was lodged. "It won't come out. It's stuck. What do we do?"

"You're gonna have to un-stick him, Abigail. You have the smallest hands."

She looked desperately, at Ned. He expected her to free this baby? She wasn't a doctor. The only thing she'd done was have a baby, and she didn't remember it.

He held out a jar. "Don't panic. Here, rub some of this bear grease on your hands then just slide them around its shoulders and free it. Mama's done it many a time. You'll do just fine."

Abigail greased her hands and did exactly what he said. "There, I have a grip." She looked up. "Tell her to push. I think I can pull it out"

She pulled as Ned encouraged Sophie to push. To her amazement, the baby slid into her hands. She felt tears running down her face. "It's a boy. You have another son."

"You did good. Now you go wash up and me and Corrie will finish here."

Abigail was too weak to argue. She went into the kitchen and washed her hands, then poured a strong cup of coffee and sat down at the table. Maybe mountain life wasn't so bad after all. There was a certain satisfaction that came from making it on your own.

❧ 30 ❧

Greenwillow: July, 1861

In the library, Seth stared out the window, watching his slaves worming and weeding the tobacco. With every breath came a new surge of energy. As soon as the harvesting was over, he'd sell all slaves that were dead weight. True, it would reduce his work force considerably, but he'd still manage if the slaves left were pushed. He already had some gold put away. It would be good no matter what, and he'd save more after the harvest and the auction. A wisp of dust caught his eye. The speck grew to a steady stream. The rider was in a hurry. Seth took his drink and went out onto the veranda and waited for the visitor, his foot on the railing. It was Billy Jackson from Five Oaks Plantation. What did old man Jackson want now?

The boy stopped, dismounted, and rushed up the steps. "My pa sent me over here. He just got word that Gregg's Confederate Calavry ambushed a Union troop train in Vienna, Virginia. We're going to win."

Seth straightened. "I can't say that I'm surprised. Knew we could lick their butts. You fighting, boy?"

"Me and my friend, Rubin, we've been thinking about volunteering. Thought it might be a good way to see the country. We heard you could go for three months. That wouldn't be too bad. Long as it's on a volunteer basis, we can leave when our time's up."

Seth squinted. "You think this is some kind of party or something, boy? War is killing; plantations being burnt; people being hungry; losing all they've worked for all their lives. You'll see. This war business is not fun and games."

"Maybe not, but are people like you and Pa gonna fight?"

Seth patted Billy on the shoulder. "We'll see, son. We'll see. Tell your pa I have myself a good nigger for breeding. If he needs his services, let me know."

Billy went down the steps. "I'll tell him. And when I go off to war, I'll shoot two of those Yankees. One for you and one for me."

Seth stomped back into the house as the boy rode away. War! *Them young boys are thinking of getting away from home. Time will show it's not play. I'll prepare for the future the best way I know. Corrie's gone. It's time I put my plan for* Sullus *into action.* He called through the open door. "McRoy! Where are you? Get in here right now." Every time he needed his overseer he was nowhere to be found.

In the library, he shuffled through a pile of papers, looking for the auction handbill.

"You yelling fer me, boss?"

Seth glared at him. "Yes. The Jackson boy was just here, and he said the Confederates won a battle up in Virginia. You know what that means, don't you?"

"That we're gonna keep our slaves. Anyway, I was over at Asa's cabin. You know that no good lazy nigger who's married to Pearl? I found him curled up under the shade of an apple tree, sleeping. Don't know why you don't sell him."

"And eat rotten food the rest of my life? No thank you. I enjoy my meals. After all, eating is about all I have left. You about got the breeding cabin ready?"

McRoy opened the door. "Come take a look."

Seth followed McRoy across the veranda. As they neared the servant quarters, Asa moved down a row of tobacco. Seth looked back toward the big house. Pearl was leaving the kitchen. Seth knew that Asa would drag himself back and complain about what a hard day he'd put in. She'd rub his back and wash his feet before they ate. What he wouldn't give for a little of the same kind of care. He'd have to see what he could do to fix his situation.

McRoy kicked at a male slave who sat near the door of the new quarters. "Why ain't you workin' you no good, lazy niggar?"

The servant sneaked behind the cabin and was gone.

"See, boss? You have to stay on them every minute, or you never get anything done."

Seth walked up the steps. "That's your job. If you can't do it, let me know, and I'll find somebody who can."

"That's not what I mean, boss. I can do the job, but it's hard."

Seth pushed open the door and went in. "I understand. That's why I need somebody like you . . . someone who can handle the slaves. This looks good. Is it ready to move *the boy* into?"

"Anytime you say the word, boss"

"Well, get him up to the big house, I'll meet you there." Seth felt satisfied with the plans he had made. No matter how the war went, he'd never go hungry.

* * *

McRoy shoved Sullus into the library. "Here he is, boss. Found him with one of the slave girls out in the tobacco field."

Seth smiled. "Seems you're good for something. Is it the blood that pulsates through your veins that gives you a craving for wenches?"

"I ain't shore I knows what yo mean, Masta."

"Forget it. We have more important things to think about. Heard today that the Confederates whipped the Union up in Virginia. Know what that means?"

Sullus shook his head. "I not know what a Union be."

McRoy jabbed him in the ribs with his fist. "See, I told you they're all dumb. Can't teach them a thing."

Seth pulled up a chair and sat down at his desk. "That doesn't matter much. Figure with a war, slaves'll get killed off like flies." He turned toward Sullus. "And since you're so good at pleasuring your wenches, that's going to be your job from now on. No more working in the fields, boy. I've fixed you some special quarters. From now on, all you have to do is pleasure all the young girls that are brought to you.

"Do what, Masta? I not know what yo mean."

McRoy shoved him against the desk. "Make babies, dummy. You're gonna be a baby maker! Now do you understand?" He smiled at Seth. "Why do you think the boy will be good for this job?"

"I hire you to work my slaves. Now, get out of here and do it. And don't let me catch you fooling with any of the girls. Remember, that's the boy's job now."

As McRoy left the house, Seth suspected he'd been with the wenches, but it hadn't stopped him from being a good overseer. After all, everybody deserved a little pleasuring. He hadn't had any since Corrie left. He'd never been like lots of the other plantation owners, sleeping with whomever, whenever. She'd been the only one. But now things were different. There was a lot of young blood out in those cabins. Maybe the boy needed help!

～ 31 ～

Greenwillow: September, 1861

By late September the young girls of Greenwillow were being ushered one by one to Sullus's quarters. Seth watched, envisioning the action inside. His body grew warm. This sort of urge had not bothered him since Abigail and Corrie left for the mountains. In the past, when he felt the need to be with a woman, he'd sent for Corrie. Seth shifted uncomfortably. The mountains were too far away to send for either of them. He'd have to forget his need. He picked up a book and tried to read. His lips said the words, but the message never made its way past the part of the brain that controlled physical urges. Soon, he threw it down and returned to the window. McRoy was taking a girl to the quarters. He called to the houseboy.

Abe appeared as though Seth had rubbed a magic lantern and he'd popped out. "Yes'suh, Masta. Yo want sump'n?"

Seth's first impulse was to laugh. Of course, he wanted something, but what he wanted this lad could not provide. "Yes, boy. Run down and tell McRoy I want to see him."

"Yes suh, Masta. Right away."

The boy disappeared and soon Seth saw him talking to the overseer. McRoy looked up at the window.

Seth motioned for him.

Before he could seat himself, McRoy said, "You want me fer sump'n boss? I'm awful busy with the breedin'. If it could wait til morning, I'd be appreciative."

"If it could wait until morning, I wouldn't have sent for you! I know you're busy. But some things just can't wait."

"You ain't sick or somethin', are you, boss?"

"Nothing one of those young wenches can't cure."

McRoy rubbed the back of his neck and turned away, muttering.

"You got a problem with my request?"

"No, boss, jest wonderin'"

"And don't you go making light of my situation. Get yourself out of here, and bring me back a few of the best looking ones. I'll choose. Don't take all evening. I want one tonight, not tomorrow morning!"

"I'll be right back with what you want." He was gone before Seth could reply.

Seth kicked at a footstool. "Should send him packing, that's what I should do." He walked to the mirror that hung above his dressing table and brushed a strand of wispy blond hair into place. "We'll see," he whispered to the mirror. "I'm still as good a man as McRoy thinks he is. I'll show him. Wonder what he'll say when my wench has a baby before Sullus's? We'll see. Besides, why should Sullus have all the fun?"

"Here they are, boss." McRoy stood in the door.

"Well, get them in here. I can't see them out there."

McRoy pushed the girls into Seth's room. "You want me to wait?"

"Yes, this won't take long." He reached out, and tilted one of the girl's faces, stroked another on the butt, cupped his hand over the breast of the third. "I must say you did bring some mighty fine wenches. Maybe I'll keep all three." He stood back and admired the girls. "Who's the youngest?"

McRoy pushed the third girl forward. "She is, boss. Just turned sixteen. And she's not been with Sullus yet."

"You can take the other two back, but see to it that they have a turn with Sullus."

"I will, boss."

Seth watched the young girl who stood alone in the middle of the bedroom floor, her eyes darting about the room. She looked like a bird that faced a snake–a trap that had no escape. Even if the war did do away with slavery, this girl would be branded forever with his mark.

* * *

Last night McRoy had left the youngest wench with Seth and had been the best night he'd had since Corrie and Abigail went to the mountains. This morning she stood near the door, sullen and distant. Seth slipped out of bed and reached for his wrap. He went to the window and looked out over Greenwillow. Rows and rows of tobacco as far as his eye could see, and a couple hundred slaves, picking the bottom leaves were enough to fill a man's chest with pride.

Yes, life was great, and he planned to make sure it stayed that way. Folks were saying this was a rich man's war, and a poor man's fight. He'd earned every dime he had, and he didn't have to apologize to any of that white trash for what was his.

When he dressed, he said to Tasha, "You'll be living in the big house now. You can help Pearl in the kitchen, but your job will be to pleasure me."

Tasha looked at the floor as big tears slid down her cheeks. "I needs to . . ."

"You need to do what you're told. There's a small room off the kitchen. Was Corrie's. It's yours now. Go get your things and then find the cook and tell her to put you to work. Seems to me, you'd know what a lucky nigger you are."

He'd stormed out the door and down the stairs. As he stepped onto the porch, McRoy came around the corner of the house with a lanky youth at his side.

"Have a good night, boss?"

"I wouldn't be surprised if it went better than yours. Saw you out late. Suppose you were up pestering my wenches. Who's the boy with you?"

"This here's Paul, the younger Jackson boy. He came by this morning to see if his pa could rent Sullus come spring. Figures he needs some new blood. Said Billy told him about Sullus, figured he'd be a good investment."

"Yes, I'd say he's worth his weight in gold. Glad he doesn't want him 'til spring. I'm keeping him busy right now. Seems I'm not going to have any trouble renting him."

Seth studied the lad for a few minutes. "Children grow up faster than they did when I was a boy. Only seems like yesterday that you were running about in diapers. Have you heard anything from your brother since he went off to Virginia to fight in the war?"

"Pa was in Goldsboro yesterday. Said he heard General McDowell attacked our troops at Manassas back in July."

"Is that where Billy's at?"

"We're all praying he wasn't there. He's with Captain Evan's patrol. All we can do is hope and wait for some news."

Seth smoothed back his wispy hair. "Yes, news does travel slow. I haven't heard from Abigail and Corrie since they went to the mountains where they're safe. I think the Yankees will try to work their way toward Goldsboro and the railroad."

"That's not very far from here, Sir. You think they'll bother our plantations?"

Seth looked back at his fields of tobacco. "Could be, son. War is war. Those Yankees don't give a damn about our plantations except what they can take. Then there are the criminals running wild, that's what they are. Hiding behind the real army to do their meanness." Seth's gaze came back to the boy. "Enough of this war talk. Tell your pa I'll have McRoy talk with his overseer, and they can work out a time to bring Sullus over. And also tell him, I charge for each one serviced whether or not it takes." He looked up in time to see Asa slip from a row of tobacco and head for his cabin. "Wait a minute. I've been thinking about Pearl. She's about thirty-five and not producing any off spring. I think it's about time she went to visit Sullus."

McRoy stopped short. "You know what you're saying. Asa will be furious when he finds out, and besides she's your cook."

"I don't know if Asa has enough energy to get mad. I'd like to find out. And since when does having a baby affect cooking?"

"I'll be happy to see that Pearl is with a real man, boss."

As McRoy and the boy disappeared into the barn, Seth stretched and looked back at his fields. It was indeed a good day. His potential for income was getting better all the time. He swung back toward the porch, then remembered the war. The possibility of it being fought right here on this very soil hit him. His precious Greenwillow, destroyed.

He'd have to make sure no one found out about his gold. Gold that guaranteed his future.

* * *

Momentarily, Pearl felt faint and reached for the cooktable to support herself as she wiped the sweat. "This heat. Every harvest season it get harder to take."

"What you mumblin' about?"

She faced McRoy who stood slouched against the doorjamb leading to the kitchen. "What yo doin' sneakin' up on a-body like that? Don't yo know it ain't a-good thin' to do? Could scare a person to death. Yo need sump'n?"

He straightened his shoulders and ambled toward her. A smile flickered across his lips. "Well, it ain't food I'm after today. The boss told me the other day to come fer you, but I've been awfully busy with the breedin'."

She mopped at her forehead again. "If it somethin' special he be a-needin' yo sho' ain't been in no hurry."

He stepped closer and caught her by the wrist. "Ain't food the boss needs either."

She tried to pull away. "Den what is he a-wantin'?"

"He wants you to give him another little slave."

The other Negroes stopped their work and waited. The hot kitchen grew silent. A kettle boiled over and bubbled onto the stove.

Pearl's eyes darted from McRoy to the pot. Was someone going to clean up that mess, or were they waiting for her to answer? "Cain't yo see I has work to take care of?" She tried to free her arm.

He yanked her toward the door. "You got work to do, but it ain't here. The boss has done give the word. I'm to take you to see Sullus." He shoved her outside.

She heard the pot bubble over again and a murmur swept through the slaves. *Trouble's a-brewin' and der ain't nothin' I kin do to stop it.*

* * *

As McRoy drug Pearl away, Tasha pushed the pot from the heat, then looked at the others. "Seems this here ain't none our business. We got work to see to."

A cook stepped forward. "My, whatta we hab here? A new boss?"

The rest pressed closer. "What's a field hand doin' in our kitchen, anyway?" Someone asked.

A half-white girl pulled at her braid, "Listen here, we is worked hard to be house niggers, and der ain't no field hand gwine come in here and tell us what to do."

Her eyes darted from face to face then to the door. What had she gotten into? She knew how house niggers felt about field hands. She took a couple of steps backward. "The Masta, he done and told me to help Pearl."

Finally one said, "You jest go help carry out ta slop jars. Dis here kitchen run jest fine without yo. Pearl be back any minute. She ain't gwine bed with dat Sullus. She luvs Asa. Yo jest wait and see. She not do it."

Tasha ran from the room. *Asa! Where he be. He take care of McRoy.* When she reached Pearl's cabin, she stood on tiptoe and peered into the one room in time to see McRoy shove Pearl onto the bed.

"Can't see why I can't do jest a good a job as Sullus. Boss'll thank me when he sees your young'un."

She tried to stand.

He pushed her and she fell in the same spot.

Tasha knew she had to get help. She ran for the tobacco field. "Asa, where is yo? Come quick! Pearl need yo. Now!" Row after row of heads popped up as she ran through the field, calling.

"I be over here, Tasha. Why is yo so all worked up? It be too hot to get in such a dither."

She grabbed him by the arm. "Come quick! Please!"

"What be wrong with yo, gal?"

She glanced side-ways then pulled him down and whispered into his ear. He took off so fast that she couldn't keep up with him. As she came through the door of Pearl's shack, Asa had the overseer by the nape of the neck and was slamming him, face first, into the wall. Pearl sat huddled in the middle of the bed with a sheet clutched to her. She looked up like a wounded animal. Tasha put her arms around her as Asa continued to bash McRoy's head.

"Beg, yo white trash, or I is gwine make mush outta dat dere brain of yorn. Shore kill yo wile I at it, but yo ain't gettin' off dat good. I keep yo 'round and make yo pay fer what yo do to my Pearl."

"Please, let me go. Please!"

"Louder. I not hear good."

"Please!"

Tasha looked toward the door. If his screams brought the masta, they'd be in big trouble.

He shoved McRoy toward the door. "Get yo' white butt far away from dis cabin as yo can, and not let me catch yo lookin' at mah woman again, or yo be buzzard bait."

He came to the bed and pulled Pearl into his arms.

231

Tasha wondered if she would ever know this kind of love. She doubted it. She'd helped out of loyalty. Her place at the big house would be easy now. Pearl would make sure of that.

❧ 32 ❦

Auction Preparations: Late October, 1861

Pearl hung her apron on the peg behind the door. She had used this same peg since she'd come to work in the big house when she was sixteen. For the past fourteen years, she'd worked in the kitchen. She'd started by washing dishes, and now she was the head cook. Tonight, she wasted no time getting to her hut. Since the attack, she'd been feeling awfully tired. Bursting in the door, she yelled, "Asa! Yo here? No good lazy nigger. Loll-a-gaggin' 'round here all day while I works mah butt off at ta big house."

Asa stuck his head around the sheet that divided the bed from the rest of the room. "I in here tryin' to get a little rest. Cain't a-body have no peace and quiet?" He ran his fingers through his mass of black curls. "Lord knows it hot in here. Get dat fan over der and fan me."

The bed sagged as she sat on it. "Fan yerself, and fer all I care, yo can pleasure yerself. If what I heared at ta big house today be true, all yo men hab to pleasure yerself, anyway."

Asa hitched up his pants and rubbed his nose on his sleeve, then dropped down beside her. He slid his arm around her waist. "Now come on. Yo knows yo likes ta way I make yo feel. Tell me what yo done and heared."

She settled into the corn shuck mattress. "They is sayin' up at ta big house dat Masta Seth is gwine take a bunch of us to ta auction. And if I wuz yo, I not let him catch me loafin' in ta middle of ta day."

Asa leaned back and let his hand slide down her leg. "Don't

worry. Yo knows what I heared today? Ta North done whipped ta pants off ta Confederates up in Virginia. We gwine be free, but while we wait, let's see if we start our own little fire right here."

She sat up. "Der's sump'n to ta rumors 'bout why Masta done and sent Miz Abigail and Corrie off to the mountains. And I heared der be a big auction in Fayetteville. Shore as I settin' here, der sump'n up."

"Der be sump'n up fer shore, and we's gonna have us some fun." He pulled her back down beside him.

The rustling of corn shucks and an occasional moan were the only noise in the cabin.

At the sound of loud voices, they bolted upright. "What's all ta hellabaloo out there?" Cain't a man ever get a . . .." He jerked his pants on and headed for the door.

She followed. It was unusual for the slaves to raise a ruckus this time of evening. Most of them were in their shacks. If they were lucky, they'd just finished a supper of collard greens and maybe a little fatback meat. She'd seen some of them lounging about earlier. And there were always the ones who took their pallets and headed for the fields for some privacy. But now several groups stood on the lawn of the big house.

She grabbed the arm of a girl that rushed by. "What's happenin'? Why yawl rushin' 'round like chickens with their heads cut off?"

The child stopped and looked up at Pearl. "Masta Seth, he done and called a-meetin' on ta front yard. I hab to go. Mama be a-waitin' fer me." She pulled free and was soon lost in the crowd.

She turned to Asa. "I done told you, ain't I? Der be big trouble a brewin' at Greenwillow, and all ta burnin' and fightin' in Virginina ain't gwine help us niggers."

* * *

Seth took the handbill he'd received last spring from the desk drawer and read: "AUCTION TO BE HELD IN FAYETTEVILLE, NORTH CAROLINA ON NOVEMBER 1." He knew what he had to do. First, he'd hire some guards, then he'd pick the slaves to send to market. The South would win, but many slaves would be lost so he'd might as well get something for them. He sat down and began to write down names.

More gold was what he needed to add to what he already had. He hadn't worked himself nearly to death since he'd taken the plantation over from his ailing mother just to be broke because of some people's moral convictions. If things got tight, he wasn't going to spend good money to feed niggers who'd run away the first chance they got.

He went to the window and looked out into the gathering dusk. He could barely make out the forms of the servants as they gathered around the front porch. He'd told Corrie he wouldn't sell Sullus. The way he was using him would be very profitable. He scratched his head. Feeding and clothing a bunch of lazy slaves could soon use up his gold. That would make any plantation owner desperate enough to sell.

McRoy opened the door and stepped in. "You ready, boss?"

"Yes, I'll do this alone. I want you to hire some extra gaurds. They'll be needed."

"I've already taken care of that." He nodded toward the edge of the yard. "I'll be right over there in the shadows if you need me."

"Sometimes you are worth the salt in your bread. I'll raise my arm over my head if you're needed."

As he stepped out onto the veranda an immediate hush settled over the crowd.

Children scrunched closer to their mothers. Men's eyes darted from their families to the porch. Women clung to the little ones and waited with bowed heads.

Seth cleared his throat. "I've received word that the Confederates, lead by Nathan Evans, have won a victory for the South in Leesburg, Virginia. Our way of life will be preserved, but until that time, there's going to be some changes for us all."

Asa stepped from the crowd and worked his way to the front of the veranda. "What is yo' talkin' 'bout, Masta Seth?"

He walked the length of the porch then faced the group. "To be truthful, I really don't know. There's several things I can do. My main purpose is to make sure my slaves are provided for. I've only sold a few. My dear Mother, God rest her soul, never sold one. Said a happy slave made a better worker. I have to agree. With the war, there's going to be a shortage. I'd hate to see any of you go hungry. I want all of you to understand I'm only thinking of your best interests."

A murmur swept through the crowd, and Seth took a step back as they pushed closer to the porch.

Asa put one foot on the veranda railing. "Masta, some a-sayin' yo be plannin' on sellin' a bunch of us."

Seth felt uneasy. Maybe he should take more precautions tonight. Have McRoy post a guard or two. He glanced around, then raised his hand for quiet again, and slowly, the murmuring ceased. "Now, don't y'all go getting all worked up. I'm going to carefully consider my choices for a few days. I'm not saying selling isn't an option. There's also a possibility I might be able to work out something with the neighboring plantations." He stepped back inside before the crowd had a chance to respond.

The overseer followed him into the library and pulled the heavy drapes. "Boss, I guess you know tonight is going to be bad. If I were you, I wouldn't sleep too much. Never can tell what them niggers might decide to do. I'll post guards, but I can't promise there won't be a riot."

Seth picked up a paper from his desk. "I'm not worried. This is the list of servants to go to the auction." He handed it to McRoy. "I want you to have the drivers ready to go at daybreak. It'll take a couple of days to get to Fayetteville. Don't want to give them time to think."

"Fifty-seven, that will take a big bunch. You sure you wanna do this, boss? And you don't have that no-good Asa on here. Why not?"

Seth walked around his desk. "I've thought about it since we talked. Seeing how Pearl is such a good cook, it might make a difference in my meals. If he doesn't shape up, I'll work out something later."

"All the neighbor plantations are wantin' to use Sullus."

He gave the overseer a cold smile. "I told you! That nigger is gonna make me some money."

McRoy gave him a knowing grin and left the room.

Seth sat down. The soft call of a whippoorwill drifted through the open window. He remembered what his mother used to say: 'Talk has feet and can walk'. If he was a betting man, he'd bet there was plenty of talk in the servant quarters. "But Mama," he said to the empty room, "gossip has wings and can fly. And it'll be flying, when tomorrow comes."

* * *

Pearl held tight to Asa's hand as pitch dark settled over the plantation. She felt the unrest that hung heavy in the night air. She heard the rustling of twigs and smelled the smoke as they were lit. The fire caught and someone piled on more wood. As the flame leaped high, Pearl saw the crowd that had begun to gather and knew they were here to talk about what the master said earlier this evening. She looked over at Asa. *I not hab to worry 'bout no chilluns being sold, but I hab to worry 'bout mah man. I like to kick his lazy butt sometimes, but he be true to me. His laziness be why he be sent to ta auction. Mah cookin' keep me at ta big house. But if Asa go, der be no reason to live. It be easy to slip sump'n into Masta food, and McRoy's also fer what he done to me.*

Asa dropped her hand and stepped into the light of the fire. "As I sees it, Pearl be ta only hope any of us hab."

She was so shocked to hear him voice her thoughts that she backed into the shadows.

Someone else said, "Dat be right, Pearl. Yo ta only one of us dat hab a way of gettin' to him. We be shot if we try."

Asa reached out and pulled her into the middle of the circle. "How 'bout it, Pearl Baby? Yo like to be a hero amongst our people?"

She quivered inside as the angry mob cheered and pressed closer. The cheer turned into a chant.

"Pearl, save us—save us—save us."

Their dark eyes bore down on her. If she said no, the results could be as bad as poisoning the Masta. *This be a desperate bunch a niggers. Day not be marched off to no auction block without a fight.* Her eyes darted from Asa to the crowd. "Now listen, yawl. Ta Masta ain't said he gwine take nobody to ta market yet. Ain't yawl gettin' all stirred up over nothin'? I say we wait fer a few days and keep our ears and eyes open to see what happen. I expects to see Miss Abigail and Corrie show up any day now. Dat fix Masta Turner."

A boy yelled. "Pearl's a liver-bellied chicken. She protectin' Masta. Not surprise me none if she pleasurin' him."

Asa doubled up his fists and started through the crowd.

She pulled him back. "We not need a fight down here tonight."

She felt no emotion about the plan, only numbness at having to do such a horrible deed. "If some yawl fix up ta pisen, I make sure he get it in his breakfast, and before noon Masta Turner be no more." She wrapped her arms protectively around herself as another cheer went up.

* * *

Near the back, a tall skinny woman slipped away. As she saw it, she didn't have a choice. If the crowd's plan was a success, they'd all be left to survive on their own. If they failed, her children would be taken, and she'd never see them again. Back in her cabin, she went about her work in a matter-of-fact way. Her long black shadow followed, mocking her every step. When everything was ready, she went to the door and called to her children. She'd sealed their fate. When they'd eaten, she, also, would take her last meal.

* * *

Later that night at the far corner of the plantation, Willy Pope made plans for his family's future too. Carefully he placed burlap sacks over part of a load of manure, and then glanced around to where they waited in the shadows and motioned for them.

Nervously, they approached. Gwen, the biggest girl, looked up at her father. "Is we gwine hab to ride up there, Papa?"

The man ignored his daughter's question and turned to Elijah, the oldest boy, and placed his cap and coat on him. "Now, I want y'awl to drive right down ta road toward ta main gate."

Elijah shuffled from one foot to the other. "Won't ta guards stop me, Papa?"

Willy adjusted the team's harness. "No, I done and told Mr. McRoy I be gettin' out a load early. He'll hab told ta guards to let yo through."

Elijah grinned at his father. "Yo be a smart man, Papa. I hope I grow up to be jest half as smart as yo be."

Willy patted his son's shoulder. "Yo will be. Dat why I gotta try and get y'awl to free country. I want mah family to hab a better life."

Namoi, his wife, slung her arms around her husband. "It not be much of a life without mah man. How yo 'spect us to last out dere alone?"

Willy reached in his pocket and handed Elijah a piece of paper. "I done and took dis from ta big house. It be directions to Miz Sophie's in ta mountains. I learned yo to read so yo can make out what dis here map say. When she find out what her pa has went and done, she'll wanna help. I heared her man don't believe in slaves. He'll help y'awl." He took a handful of reeds from a sack and passed them out. "Make sure y'awl keep up with dese. They be your life line to ta outside world."

The smallest girl, Opal, blew threw her reed. "Can we hab soap too, Papa?"

Her pa set her on the wagon. "Dese ain't fer blowin' bubbles, chile. Yo is gwine use dem to breathe through." He placed the other two girls up with their sister, and then turned to his other son.

"I wanna ride with Elijah. Papa, please?"

Willy ruffled his son's hair. "Seein' how yo' brother will need some hep once yo be on ta road, I guess yo can, but stay under ta seat 'til yo be past ta front gate." He said to his woman. "Yo ready? I gwine finish loadin' ta wagon before it get too late." He took his wife in his arms and held her close for a moment, then without a word helped her climb up. He picked up some more sacks. "Lay down and put ta reeds in yo' mouths."

Opal wrinkled up her nose. "Do us hab to, Papa? It be awfully smelly."

"Yo rather go to ta auction?"

The girl shook her head and lay down. Willy covered them with sacks and another layer of manure. When they were well hidden, he slapped the horses on the rear, and sent them galloping toward the main gate. If his plan worked, they'd soon have a new life. They'd never again have to worry about an auction.

* * *

Pearl woke at daybreak to the horrible wails and moans from the servant quarters. She didn't have to go outside to know what had happened. Why hadn't she slipped back last night and poisoned the Master? But everyone had believed him when he said it'd be a few days. Besides she hadn't had time to fix the poison.

Asa rolled his eyes at her. "Masta Seth gwine get his comin' up's one of these days, and I hopes I be ta one dat heps give it to him. Pearl Baby, if sump'n happen to me, I swear I find a way fer us to get back together."

Outside, someone screamed for Masta Seth. Then above the commotion, she heard the overseer.

"They're dead. Every last one of them. Can you believe it? A whole family of twelve. Wonder how they done it and when. Thought we had everything tight."

There was some more banging, and then Masta Seth yelled. Pearl and Asa edged their way to their door and peeped out in time to see Masta Seth and the overseer going into the hut next to theirs.

Before long the door opened and they came out. Seth said, "Looks like poison. Probably the mother did it after they came back from the meeting."

McRoy threw up his hands. "I don't see how. While you was havin' the meetin' at the big house, I had all the cabins searched, and the guards found nothin'."

"McRoy, if I've told you once, I've told you a thousand times. Some of these niggers will go to all lengths to protect their own."

"Even to killin' them, boss?"

"Even that. I've seen it before. They have deep religious beliefs that when they're dead, they'll all be together in some wonderful promised land. Some had rather be dead than be separated."

"How'd you think she did it, boss?"

"Probably had poison stashed away on her. After their little pow-wow by the fire last night, she fixed it and fed it to them before bed."

Down the lane one of the guards yelled. "McRoy, come

here. We can't find Johnson's family anywhere."

Pearl and Asa slipped outside and followed. A guard pushed Willy out of his cabin, twisting his arms behind him. The overseer cuffed him up the side of the head.

"Where are they?" demanded Seth.

"I swears I not know. When I get in from haulin' manure, dey is all gone. All six of dem. I not know nothin'."

"Was this slave hauling this morning, McRoy?"

"I suppose so. He told me last night that he'd be gettin' it out. With the smell, we move it early. I'll check to see if there is a wagon missin'."

One of the guards stepped up. "He's right, Mr. Turner. I waved him through about three-thirty."

Seth looked at the man holding Willy. "Lock him up and get the blood hounds on their trail. I'll post a reward. When we find them, they'll pay."

He whirled back to the overseer. "See that the dead are buried before you leave."

Pearl squeezed Asa's hand as they watched Willy being led back into his cabin. She knew they could look all they wanted, but his family was safe by now.

243

☙ 33 ❧

Shady Junction: November, 1861

When Ned Miller arrived at Shady Junction, the street was filled with people. Were they planning some sort of celebration for the holidays? As he neared the center of town, he saw they were crowded around a wagon with about half a dozen Negroes on it.

A woman from the back of the crowd ran toward him. "Lawd-a-mercy. I didn't mean fer it to happen, Ned, I'll swear. That's our government fer you."

He reined his mare to a stop and dismounted. "Now calm yourself, Sadie. Gettin' all worked up ain't gonna help none. Take a deep breath, and tell me what all the commotion is about."

She gulped a mouthful of air and then said, "You know, when your company come, I was jest a wondering where a-body would find one of them niggers, so I went on down to the post office and made some inquires. And what'd you know, this afternoon, a whole bunch of them shows up."

He jumped down. "You didn't have anything to do with them coming. Anybody talked to them?"

She twisted on a chunk of hair. "Zeb's talking to them. You know him. Ain't never seen a stranger. Think he should be spokesman fer Shady Junction?"

He led his mare over to a hitching rail and tied her up.

Sadie followed, still twisting her hair, obviously having more to say. "You wait and see, Ned Miller, there's about to be a black cloud settling over our town. If you hadn't a went off down to the flat country and brought back that woman of yourn, this wouldn't be a happenin.'"

Ned wheeled. "I'll have you know *that woman*, as you call her, is my wife. And if you ain't heared, there's a war goin' on to free the slaves. Get ready. There's gonna be a lot more of them comin' our way."

She pulled on the piece of hair that she had twisted as tight as it would go. "And you might as well know, Mr. Ned Miller, folks here in Shady Junction ain't gonna stand fer a bunch of niggers takin' over. We don't use them, and we're not livin' by them either."

Ned started toward the crowd. "Don't get your bowels in a uproar. I think we'll find a way to cope, when and if the time comes, we have to."

"Ain't what folks is sayin'. You jest wait and see."

Ned wheeled to face her. "What are they sayin'?"

"Can't say, but you'll find out. You jest wait and see."

The crowd parted, and they walked toward the wagon. Huddled on top of the load of manure were a woman and three little girls, watching the mountain folk with mutual curiosity. A bigger boy and a smaller one sat on the front seat. A rank odor filled Ned's nostrils. He'd never seen a more pitiful sight.

Zeb took his foot off the wheel and reached out his hand. They shook. "How you been, Zeb?" asked Ned. "Ain't seen you since my company come a while back."

"Been fine. It looks like you have yerself some more vistors. They're askin' where Miss Sophie and her man lives. When the others came, I told you there'd be more along soon. I was right. Women and children today, men tomorrow. Ain't nobody gonna be safe 'fore long."

"So it's you that's gettin' everybody all worked up. Niggers ain't any worse than some white trash I know. Now get on 'bout your business, if you have any, and I'll take care of these folks." Ned heard Zeb muttering as he wandered through the crowd. "You jest wait and see. Even our animals won't be safe."

Ned knew Zeb could cause more trouble than the Negroes, but for now, he had a much bigger problem. As he neared the wagon, the boy handed him a note. He unfolded the paper and read it. "You'uns can relax. This is my company. I'll take them home with me, and I can promise you, they won't be seen in town no more."

Zeb sauntered back up. "You take them niggers out to your place, and we ain't gonna be responsible fer yore family when sump'n happens to you. Mark my word. I've been around, and I know what I'm talkin' about."

"I'm not takin' your word fer nothin'. These are just harmless people, who need a helpin' hand to freedom. Don't you go stirrin' up things. I'll take care of them." He untied his horse. "Has there been a man by the name of John Simmons askin' fer me?"

"No, ain't seen nobody but these here niggers. Trouble. That's what they are." Zeb stomped off toward the blacksmith shop, mumbling as he went.

Ned knew there wasn't time to wait for Simmons to get these people to freedom. Probably slave hunters were already out looking for them. Besides, with Corrie at his place and a new baby, he couldn't keep them for long. Tomorrow he'd talk to Abigail and let her know they were here. He had a load of pelts to take to the trading post. If Simmons didn't show up soon, he'd take them as far as the post.

* * *

A week later, Ned pulled in at Chester's. A head of black curls popped from under the furs. "Can us get out now? It mighty hot under this here mess a skins."

A mouthful of white teeth gleamed up in the evening sun. "Keep down and stay quiet. I have to find out if you'uns are welcome here before you come crawlin' out fer the whole settlement to see."

The head disappeared. Ned heard a ripple of mumbling beneath the furs, then all was silent. He'd better hurry and find his friend. This trip had been hard on the children. He couldn't expect them to stay put much longer. He stuck his head through the door.

"Chester, you there?"

The store owner's legs appeared on the ladder from the attic. "Hope you have a good load of furs this time. With the war, there's gonna be a great demand fer 'em."

Ned glanced back outside. How was he going to explain his cargo? Could he trust his friend to help? Well, he was here and it was a long way to Ohio. He'd need some help. "I have you some furs, but I also brought sump'n else." Ned took a deep breath and plunged ahead. "I have a nigger woman and her young'uns hid under my furs. I need your help. If you can give them a night's lodging and a meal, we'll be on our way tomorrow."

Chester glanced toward the back door. "Ain't nobody seen them, have they?"

"No, I've kept them covered, but the little'uns are mighty restless." He followed Chester outside and looked around. He was getting ready to unload the family when they heard the faint sound of hoof beats. The two men glanced at each other and then back at the wagon. There was no time to debate the issue. What had to be done, now, was to unload the woman and children and find them a safe place to hide. He threw back the pelts. "Out, and make it fast."

Chester set down the smallest girl. "In the store and up the ladder. There's plenty of cover in the attic. Hide and be still as a mouse."

The last child disappeared through the door as the riders rode into sight. As they halted in front of the wagon, Ned took his foot off the wheel and walked over to where his friend inspected the furs. "You won't find a better lot of fox hides in these here parts."

The men dismounted and congregated around them. Ned counted under his breath. There were ten, big and ugly. He wouldn't want to meet them alone.

A man with hair halfway down his back and a beard to match picked up a handful of furs and threw them down. "I want the niggers you've been hauling under them furs, Mister."

Ned took his time picking up the hides and putting them back as he eyed the man with all the hair. He must be the ring leader. "You're welcome to look, but please don't damage my goods. I need all I can get out of them."

The man gestured toward his men. "Search here and then the store."

An unspoken question hung between Chester and Ned. What would these slave hunters do to them and the Negroes if they were found?

"As I was saying, Mr. Miller, furs are gonna be in demand with this war. You could be a rich man."

A man with a hair lip muttered. "Or a dead one, if we find any of those black hides."

Ned fingered the knife in his pocket. These men were out for blood. And he'd gotten his friend involved. After this, if they lived through it, Chester probably wouldn't even buy his furs.

* * *

Inside, Elijah ushered the family up the ladder to the loft. He stuffed the small ones into empty boxes and closed the lids and then looked around for a place to hide his mother. A huge tin tub stood in the corner. He flipped it over and motioned for her to get under.

She shook her head and backed away.

The boy picked up an old saw that lay near the opening and, leaning down as far as he could reach, weakened a rung part way down the ladder. The woman smiled and crawled under the tub. Her son grabbed a piece of timber and stationed himself a few feet away. If someone stuck his head through that hole, he would be dead.

* * *

Outside, Ned watched the men search the underbrush and then gather back at the wagon.

A man with a long nose spoke. "Not a sign of anything, boss."

The hairy man slung the last fur to the ground.

Ned wanted to sling him down the same way.

The man called, "Search the inside, boys, and don't go easy."

This post was Chester's livelihood. If they got too mad, they'd burn the place down. Ned laid a hand on his friend's shoulder. "Come on. Let's go see if we can help."

They followed the group. The store was quiet. The gathering dusk cast eerie shadows across the floor. The men ripped through stacks of yard goods, overturned kegs of beans, and threw down piles of hardware. They dug under the counter and ransacked the back room. Someone went for the stairs.

"Ain't nothing up there but rats. Don't use it except fer empty cartons. And that ladder ain't too good," said Chester.

The hairy man they all called Boss took Chester by the collar. "I think they're here." He kicked at his man's rear. "Up there, now! And don't leave a box unturned."

Ned shuddered. Should they ease outside and make a run for it?

A rat peered through a large crack and hissed. The man stepped down. "Boss, you can search this time."

The boss man pushed his friend aside. "Coward! It's just a rat." He grabbed his gun from his holster and fired. The rat disappeared.

Ned listened for screams, but nothing happened. The boss started up the ladder. The room grew darker. A dog howled somewhere outside. The group of men stood at the bottom like a bunch of hounds waiting for their master to shake a possum from a tree. The man took a few more steps. The fourth one brought a loud crash, and he stared up from the floor and swore.

The hair lipped man said, "He tried to tell you, boss."

The man got up. "Shut up, you no good scum! Let's get outta here. At the door, he looked back at the broken ladder. "Guess we could burn the place. That would take care of all the varmints."

As the last man left, Ned saw dust sift through the cracks overhead.

* * *

The slave hunters gathered at a campfire a short distance from the post. The boss watched as rings of smoke swirled and twisted toward a starless sky. He was disappointed. Greenwillow offered a handsome reward for the Negroes. They'd ridden hard from Shady Junction to catch up with Miller, and now, not to find the slaves aggravated him. He kicked at a smoldering log. It sparked and then leaped into a flame. As it reached out and licked up the moist November air, he swore under his breath. "Damn it! I planned on taking them in."

The log broke in the middle and sank down into the glowing coals. Another gush filled the air. The wheels in the ring leader's mind turned. *Ain't nothing more in the world than a good dose of smoke to scare a nigger out of his wits. That's what I need--a smoke bomb. I don't have to burn the post. I'll make a bomb and stick it in the window. If they're inside, they'll waste no time getting out.*

* * *

The next morning the man called boss and the hair-lipped man squatted in the fog outside the front of the trading post. The boss held a long pole. The other man dampened a piece of old blanket with kerosene and wrapped it around the pole. He then lit the rag and smothered out the flame. When a good stream of smoke rose into the air, the boss rammed it through the window.

As the shattering of glass covered the floor, they waited for the room to fill. "How long do you think it'll take, boss?"

"I'll bet you any minute now we'll see a bunch of niggers scrambling down that rickety ladder. They're up there."

"Could be they got away last night. Can't see them staying here after we searched. I'll bet they're halfway across Virginia now."

The boss waved at a swirl of smoke that curled back in their direction. "No, they're in there. I know it. They stayed. Miller ain't no dummy. That's what he thought we'd think, so he figured they'd be safe here. Bet he thinks we're riding north. Won't he be surprised?"

The men watched in silence as smoke boiled and rolled through the room and then seeped toward the ceiling. "See, the smoke has found the cracks overhead. If they were up there, boss, they'd be coming down."

"Damn! I can't believe it. I was sure they were still up there. Stomp out that rag and let's get going. You're right. They're probably halfway to Ohio by now."

* * *

At the sound of the shattering glass, the boy, who'd sawed the rung, lowered a rope out the upstairs and into the thicket below. As silent as the morning fog, the Negroes slipped down and into the heavy undergrowth. Ned had told him to expect this and had removed the board last night. He'd instructed the family on where to find the wagon loaded with supplies. They were to hide until the posse left. Ned said it would be better to have the slave hunters in front of them.

* * *

A soldier on a pallet groaned and lifted his head. He tilted it to one side. Did he hear the rattle of wagon wheels? He put his ear to the ground and listened. Yes, someone was coming. Every nerve in his body tightened as he waited. Soon the sound grew louder. He watched another of his comrades moan and try to rise, but he fell back with a thud; his hand gave one last twitch, and he lay as still as the stones.

"Help! Help! We're over here." He paused for a moment and

gasped for air. "Please, somebody. Help!" After a while, his hand moved, groping for anything he could use to get attention. His fingers touched something cold. He stopped, then as if commanded by some outside force, he gripped the barrel of a gun and pulled it toward him. With this new strength, he found the trigger, raised the gun, and fired. As soon as the shot rang out, the gun dropped. The rattle drew closer, but he never heard it.

* * *

Ned halted the team and listened. That was a gun, and it came from his left. He glanced around. The slave hunters were probably on his trail by now. Chester said he'd find troops in this area, and they'd need supplies. The only thing he hadn't said was who to give them to. Well, it didn't matter. He'd feed whoever needed it. He slapped the team with the reins and headed toward the sound.

As Ned rounded the curve, he felt his stomach go weak. Soldiers covered the ground. There were a few Confederate uniforms, but most were Yankees. Occasionally, a head lifted and then dropped.

Ned worked the wagon through the maze of bodies and into a grove of laurel bushes. He instructed the slaves to unload, then crawl back under the tarp and wait for his return. At the edge of the camp, he stopped and looked about. A charred rabbit hung on a stick above a dying campfire. He rolled over a couple of dead soldiers. *They won't be using supplies. What should I do? Most are beyond my help. I've been on the road three days. The Ohio River is so near, and that means freedom for the Negroes. I'll get them to safety, then do what I can here.*

An hour later, he pulled up to the spot where Chester had told him he'd find help. Out in the water sat a small boat with an old man fishing.

When the wagon stopped, heads began to pop from under the tarp, and he helped the children down. The mother refused his offer. "Mister Ned, you be too good to us. We owe you. But us can't swim. How we gwine get cross that there big ole river?"

Ned pointed. "The man in the boat is gonna help you across. He can't take you all at once." He looked back. Where was the posse? Hopefully, they'd been here and gone, but he'd better find a place for the Negroes to hide until they crossed.

Elijah was already down at the bank helping the man tie up the boat. The old man met Ned halfway up the trail. "I'm shore proud to see yawl. Got word dere be some people along. I be fishin' almost two days now." He wiped at his face then stuck out his hand. "Name's Dan."

Ned shook his hand. Who'd told him they'd be here? He didn't have time to ask questions. There'd be time when this family was safely on the other side. "How many can you take at once, Dan?"

"Two and be safe. I'll take the mother and the little one."

The woman stepped back. "No, I ain't gwine 'til my young'uns be safe." She hugged the smallest to her.

Dan smiled. "That be alright. We take ta chile'uns first." He turned to the oldest. "I'm gonna take your brother and sister, and dat one yo' momma be holding, now. Ta rest of yo take cover."

Ned helped the old man push the boat out, then came back to the others. "Do you still have the reeds you used when you were under the manure?"

The mother pulled them from her pocket. "Here day be."

"You might need them, so keep them handy. He searched the

water's edge and found a spot where a large tree with long roots grew over the bank. "I know it's going to be cold, but I want you to stay right here, and if you hear anyone coming slip into the river. Use the reeds to breath through."

"You ain't 'spectin' trouble, is yo, Mister Ned?"

"I don't know. Let's hope you'uns will be safe on the other shore if they do come." As Dan unloaded, Ned heard the pounding of hooves. He motioned for the woman to get in the water. "Hang on to the roots and you'll be fine," he ordered. "Right over here where the branches hang low will be a good place. Nobody will notice your reeds. Goodbye, and God Bless." As he picked up the reins and drove away, he saw a few bubbles float down stream. The sound grew louder. He'd done his best; staying wouldn't help. It'd only risk his life, and he had a family who needed him. .

* * *

The stench from the battlefield drifted on the wind and filled Ned's nostrils as he rode along. The edge of dark slipped over the forest and long shadows crept across his path. He glanced uncertainly behind him. If that was the bounty hunters they would soon find the wagon he had abandoned. Every minute was precious. He remembered the sight he'd seen yesterday. His heart ached for all the wounded men. Maybe some of them could use the supplies he'd left. He needed to find a place to make camp, but he wanted to be well beyond the smell of death.

The sound of hoof beats grew closer. Ned slid from his horse, untied the mare he led behind, and slapped both on the rear. "Don't go too far. Hopefully, I'll need you later." He crawled through the undergrowth toward the stench. It wouldn't be hard to hide in a field of dead men. At the edge of the battlefield, he picked up a blanket and lay down close to a corpse, then covered up and waited.

A man called. "Maybe he's in here."

He'd heard that voice at Chester's trading post. Crunching closer to the dead man, he pulled the cover over his head.

"Why'd you think he'd be here, boss? Ain't nothin' here but dead soldiers. Looks like the Confederates got them a bunch of Yankees."

Ned held his nose and barely breathed. He heard one of the men coming in his direction.

"All that's over here is dead men, boss."

Ned felt the weight of legs as the man rolled the dead solider over onto him. He flinched and stuffed down a cry of pain.

"He's been here. See, over there are supplies. That's how he got them out." The man walked away.

"Yeah, but where is he now?" grumbled someone.

"Don't guess it matters much. He ain't got them now. I'll bet that old man in the fishin' boat knows."

"We're gonna find Miller. We'll follow him back to Shady Junction and keep an eye on him. I have a feeling there'll be more coming that way, and we're gettin' in on some of that bounty money."

Ned shuddered as he heard them ride away. What had he gotten himself into? What would he do when that Simmons man showed up and expected help? Well, he'd worry about that when the time came. At least this family had made it to freedom. He crept out.

"Please, Mister. Help me!"

Ned hesitated. He wanted to call his horse and ride away from the terrible stench. He looked about. Some of the supplies were gone. There were probably survivors lurking in the brush or the many caves that nestled in the bosom of the mountains. Whatever had happened here the Yankees had taken a licking, but many in gray uniforms were strewn across the battlefield, also. These were his people. The question of why they were fighting didn't seem too important at this moment. Again, he heard the cry. The voice came from his right where a trail descended down the side of a mountain into a little ravine.

As he passed a huge boulder, someone grabbed his pant leg. "In here, Mister. I'm the one that called to you. I seen them men looking for you. What kinda trouble you in?"

Ned studied his assailant's face, a mere boy, too young to be out here amongst a graveyard of soldiers. "Looks like I ain't in any more trouble than you, son. Are you hurt?"

The soldier stood and steadied himself against a rock. "My leg. Ain't nothin' but a flesh wound. It's healing right nice. I jest can't move about too good."

"Anyone else with you?"

The boy scouted his surroundings then his eyes met Ned's. "Some, can't say how many. I have a buddy that's hurt worse than me back here behind the rock." He stepped aside and a boy, even younger, looked up. "You gonna help us, mister?"

Ned took a step forward. "I'll try. Let's see how bad you're hurt." He ripped away the shirt soaked with dry blood and dirt. Without help, this one wouldn't be here too long. "What's your name?"

"Billy Jackson."

Ned's eyebrow shot up. "My wife's family had some neighbors by that name."

Billy moaned with pain as Ned began to peel away the shreds

of fabric. "Your wife, where's she from?"

"The Greenwillow Plantation down in the tobacco section of North Carolina."

"Your wife wouldn't happen to be Sophie Turner would she, Mister?"

"Sure is."

The boy tried to sit up, but fell back.

Ned leaned him up against a large boulder. "Think you can stay like that fer a few minutes?"

He nodded and took a deep breath. "I joined this here fight to see the country. Told Mr. Turner I'd kill a Yankee for him, and one for me."

"You did?"

Suddenly, Billy gasped, his face paled as he tried to speak, but could only point.

Ned whirled. Jackson's buddy had his riffle aimed at something. A blast filled the air, and Billy's friend dropped. Ned hit the ground. Another shot exploded, then all was quiet. Ned looked up. The Jackson boy held his gun with his good arm as smoke boiled from the barrel.

"You can let Mr. Turner know I just killed him a Yankee. Got mine back in Manassas."

❧ 34 ❧

Shaddy Junction: December, 1861

A week before Christmas, Abigail stepped out onto the boarding house porch as Ned rode into town, leading a horse with someone lying across it. She rushed down the steps.

"Sissy got a extra room?" asked Ned

"There are rooms, but looks like that man needs more than a room."

By now, Ned had the boy on his shoulder. "If we don't get this soldier's wound cleaned up soon, he'll need a grave."

Abigail held the door open. "Take him inside. There's an empty room at the head of the stairs to your left. Should I find help?" She followed him.

"You can send someone fer my mother, and then go bile some water. I'll need plenty of clean bandages, some liquor, and any kinda disinfectant you can find. Plain old hard lye soap will help. Bring anything you think I might need."

In the kitchen, she set the kettle on the stove as Mrs. Ledbetter came in the back door. "Where's Amos?"

"Down at the blacksmith shop, why?"

"Ned's here with a wounded soldier. I have to heat water. Would you send Amos for Mrs. Miller?" For a moment, Abigail thought Sissy would faint.

"You mean a real live soldier? One who's fighting in the war?"

"That's the only kind there is, but without our help he won't be alive long. Now, tell me where I can find something for bandages, and you go send for Ned's mother."

259

"There's some old sheets in the drawer of the dresser in my room." She called over her shoulder as she went out the door. "In the bottom one."

Gathering all the supplies, Abigail headed for the stairs. She might be able to bring a baby into the world, but putting a soldier back together wasn't anything she wanted to undertake. The foul odor that met her at the bedroom door sent her stomach into spasms. Ned had ripped away the tattered uniform to expose the rotting flesh.

"Hurry, drop them scissors in the hot water. You'll have to help me. Don't think we'll have to worry about someone holding him. He's unconscious. Looks like there's going to be a lot of digging to find the bullet in his shoulder."

Abigail heard the splash of the scissors, or was it her stomach growling? She didn't know which. The only thing she knew was that Ned expected her help. He was too busy to notice her. The scent of alcohol replaced the odor of rotting flesh. Could this boy still be alive?

Without looking up, Ned ordered the scissors.

She fished them out with a large spoon. He began to snip away damaged tissue.

"Should you do that?"

"It has to go. Can you think of a better way?"

"No, I can't. It's all I can do to keep breathing." Abigail looked away as he laid a chunk of dead skin in a pan.

"Here's some blood. Must be getting to raw skin. Grab that cotton and press against this spot."

She pressed and prayed. Help should be here soon, and she'd

be able to get out. The roar of hooves came through the window, and she almost dropped the swab. Could it be someone looking for this soldier? And if it were, would it be enemy or friend? She watched Ned wipe the last of the decay away, so absorbed in what he was doing he hadn't heard anything.

The door burst open and Sissy came in. "Amos should be back any minute with your mother, Ned, but I'm afraid we have trouble a-brewin' outside."

For the first time since he'd started working on the soldier, Abigail saw his head come up.

"Can't you see I have my hands full here? Get Zeb or some of the other men to take care of it."

"They're asking fer you, Mr. Miller."

Ned dropped the scissors into the hot water. "Who are they?"

"Didn't say, but I've never seen such a rough looking bunch of men."

Ned straighted. "It's the bounty hunters. They're after me." He looked back at the soldier. "And I've got to finish here."

"Sissy, you help Ned, and I'll take care of them." Abigail removed her hand and stepped toward the door.

Ned reached out to stop her. "You can't deal with that bunch of men. They're out fer blood."

She glanced back at the boy and saw that the cotton was beginning to turn red. "Seems like I've proven my ability to handle gore. Sissy, you'll need to put pressure on that wound." She was out the door and down the stairs before Ned could stop her.

Outside, she took a deep breath and struggled to compose herself. She'd have to appear calm and interested in the men and try to forget what she'd left upstairs. She could take these men's minds off their hunt, especially if they'd been out of the company of a lady for a while. She smoothed back her hair and stepped off the porch. With her head held high, and the look of a woman with a mission, she deliberately walked toward the general store where they gathered.

As she neared, their heads turned. A man with lots of hair let out a long whistle, and the other men chimed in. Hopefully, she could divert their attention long enough for Ned to finish and leave. "Hello, Gentlemen. I haven't seen you here before. Are you lost? If you're looking for someone, maybe I can help you." The odor, as the men pressed close, was almost as rank as what she'd left upstairs. Trying not to react, she moved to one side.

"Boss, this woman looks lots better than Miller."

She stomped her foot. "I dare you to mention that man's name in my presence. Some southerner he was!"

The man called boss held out his arms in front of the others and took a step forward. "What do you mean, *was*, lady?"

Abigail placed her hands on her hips and stared into the man's face. She had to be convincing, not only for Ned's safety, but also for her own. "What Miller did makes my blood boil, and if you men are good southerners, you'll feel the same way. That man! He's run out on his wife and a house full of young'uns and went north to join up with them there Yankees. If I was a man, I'd go get him and string him up right here in this store yard!"

Boss wheeled. "I told you that Ned Miller was trouble. I bet he crossed that river with that bunch of slaves. Can't waste no more of my time on him. Come on, let's go. There's plenty of others to look fer."

"But we ain't seen no good lookin' woman in a while."

The ring leader looked at the man and shook his fist. "This hunt ain't about women. This is about run-away niggers. Let's get goin'"

Abigail didn't breathe easy until the men rode out of sight. Brushing her hands together as if to say a job well done, she went back to the boarding house with a feeling of satisfaction. She might not be able to fight in a war, but she was more than able to do her part here.

❧ 35 ❧

Five Oaks Plantation: Late February, 1862

Sullus stood, stark naked, in the Five Oaks slave quarters, his black eyes darting about. He didn't know what to expect next. All he'd been told was to strip.

The door opened and Jackson and McRoy came toward him. "Well, on first glance, I'd say I'm getting what I need. Spring is here, and by winter, I want to have a new batch of little Pickaninnies. Let me get a good look at you."

Sullus shuddered at the tone of the white man's voice.

"Open your mouth," ordered Jackson.

Hate boiled inside him. He'd breed the wenches, but he wasn't an animal. He'd kill Seth Turner for what he was doing to him.

"You heard me, boy. Snap to it," demanded McRoy.

He felt the sting of a whip on his ankles and jumped to avoid the next lash.

"Open," demanded McRoy. The whip snapped again.

He bared his gums.

Jackson grasped his jaw with his left hand. "They look good and sound. Should make babies with the same kind."

Sullus snapped his teeth and growled. Jackson jumped back.

McRoy cracked the whip across Sullus's back. "Mind your manners, boy."

Jackson poked at his private parts with his cane. "Looks good."

Sullus whirled and at the same time his right arm came up. Before he could finish his swing, the overseer's whip came down hard. He gritted his teeth, determined not to show his pain.

Jackson stepped toward the door. "I've seen enough. I'll send my overseer in, and he can put him to work. Tell Turner I'll send him home when he's through."

Sullus watched the man leave. Hate brewed like a volcano deep inside him. *Day would pay, all of dem.*

* * *

A week had passed since Sullus was brought to the Jackson plantation. There'd been a steady flow of slave girls going in and out of his quarters. He'd do his job over and over. Tonight he was alone, thinking about how he was going to repay his torturers.

A tapping sound drew his attention. He glanced toward a small hole that served as a window. The large brown eyes of an old Negro man peered through the bars. A white beard rested on the old man's chest. His head jerked back and forth. Sullus stepped to the makeshift opening.

The man's face lit with a smile. "I hab to talk to yo. I not wanna get yo in trouble, but I hab to know 'bout yo' Mama."

Sullus' mama hadn't been on his mind much lately. At Greenwillow her lot was better than most, or so it looked to him. "What 'bout mah mama? How yo know her?"

The man brushed away a tear. "It kinda like this. Yo' mama and me, we be in luv fer a long time."

In love! Mah mama in love? Sullus had never thought of her in that way. To him, she had always been Masta Turner's woman. *Does mama love dis nigger man?* He peered at the old man. "Tell me, how long yo knowed mah mama?"

The man grinned, showing toothless gums. "I knowed her since I be a young man. Use to be one of Masta Turner's slaves 'til he sold me to Masta Jackson. Yo' Mama, she wash a mighty lot of blood off me after one a mah beatin's from Masta Jackson."

"How yo see mah mama after yo come to live here?"

"Yo' mama and me, we go to ta same church. Masta Jackson not know dat. He stop me from gwine if he a-knowed it. One Sunday when I go, I be beat so bad I pass out. Yo' mama, she take good care of me."

The sound of the key in the lock halted the men's talk. The old Negro ducked out of sight. The door creaked open and a plate of food was shoved across the floor. Just as quickly, the door shut. Sullus took his supper and sat it on the table, then went back to the window. He gave a low whistle and the white head reappeared. "Yo see somebody out dere?" asked Sullus.

The old man's head shook. "Day be gone. It wuz ole Tom, and he not say he seen nothin'."

"Mister, jest who is yo, anyhow? I ain't never heared my mama talk 'bout bein' in luv with no nigger man."

"No, son. Don't guess yo hab. I shore dat why Masta Turner sell me to Masta Jackson. He not like it cause yo' mama luvs me instead a him. He wuz her duty. I wuz her luv. Mah name be Jeffro. If yo hear from yo' mama, tell her I still luv her."

The man vanished in the gathering dusk. An empty spot formed in the pit of Sullus' stomach. He took a few bites of his supper, but the food didn't take away the feeling. There was so much he didn't know about his own mama, things that he wanted to know. If the old man came back, he'd try to find out.

When the tray was taken, a young girl was shoved into the room. The door slammed and the lock clicked. Sullus faced the girl standing in the middle of the floor, her hands shaking. Two large tears rolled down her cheeks. With his forefinger, he reached out and brushed them away. The girl backed toward the wall.

"How ole is yo, gal?"

The girl bit her lower lip and fumbled with the button on the blue striped housedress. "Thirteen, or at least there 'bouts. Mama ain't right sure."

Sullus motioned for her to sit down. "Yo know why yo be here, don you?

"Yas'uh. Masta says I gonna be a mama."

"That's his plan, and quit twisting dem buttons 'fore they pop off and have to live in yo' mama's button box."

The girl's head bobbed up and down. "That ta only box Mama hab. Her Mama gib it to her. She done and said it be mine someday." Her hand shook harder. "I not want to be a mama. I seen how it hurt mah mama when she hab a baby. And dat ain't all, Mama still cries 'bout ta chile'un Masta Jackson sell."

Sullus studied the young girl's face for a while. He wanted to spare her the heartache of motherhood. "I ain't gonna hurt yo. I not like what I do, but if I not do it, day jest find 'nother nigger to do it. At least I be easy, honey. I try not to hurt."

The girl's hands paused on the buttons. Her eyes brightened. She rose from her chair and paced the room.

Sullus wanted her to relax and understand that he wasn't going to harm her. He needed contact with the outside world, and this might be the girl to give him the information he needed. She was young enough to blend in, and no one would suspect she was listening to what was being said. "Come here."

The girl stopped her pacing and stepped closer to Sullus.

"I fix it so ta overseer believe I be with yo. I jest gwine muss yo up some, and den yo go out a-cryin'. I even smear a little blood on yo. Dat make it look real good."

The girl twisted harder on her buttons. "What day say when I not be a mama?"

"Day probably think yo wuz too young."

Instantly, the muscles in the girl's face relaxed, and she began her steady twist of the buttons. Outside, the Negroes' chant rose and fell in a sweet melody. The girl glanced up at him. "I guess I owes yo."

Sullus took both the girl's hands in his. "Yo know a old nigger man named Jeffro?"

The girl's face lit up. Her head bobbed, but this time with excitement. "He be a good story teller. He tell us big tales. Ain't too well, though. Mama say he not be 'round long. What yo want with him?"

"I want yo to hab him come here tomorrow night. And keep yo' ears open 'bout any war news. Now, let me make yo look a little mussed up." He ripped the buttons from her dress. "Take dese fer yo' box. Now, let me see . . .." He took his knife from his pocket and opened it, carefully selected a vein on the inside of his arm, and stuck the point into it.

The girl flinched as the blade sank into his flesh. When the blood gushed, she looked away.

Sullus smeared some on her skirt. "Dere, look like yo hab a bad time of it. Day bring yo several times, but dis be ta only time I need to do dis." He lifted his head and listened. The night air was too still. As quickly as the song had stopped, it began again. This time there was no sweet melody, no rise and fall of song, only the long drawn out sound of the death chant. Keening–wailing–on and on into the Carolina dusk.

* * *

Sullus waited. There hadn't been any women all day. He paced the floor. Someone had died. Who? The old darkie had not returned. Could it be him? If it were, he'd never know the truth about his mother.

The chain on the door rattled. The young girl from yesterday was shoved in. "Day be done with yo. I jest heared ta Masta tell ta overseer to take yo home in ta mornin.'"

The word *home* raced through Sullus' mind. Was Greenwillow home? He'd been born and lived all his life there, but *home?* No, he'd never know home until he had his freedom. The kind of life his mama had at the plantation clouded his thinking. Did she consider Greenwillow home. No, it was just a roof over her head. And her man, how could you have a home without the one you loved? He touched the girl's arm. "Tell me. Who die?"

"It be old nigger, Jeffro. Yo know ta one yo want me to find out 'bout. Ain't none of us surprised. He been a ailin' fer some time."

Sullus' hopes of finding out about his mama and her lover vanished as quickly as they'd come. The eyes of the old man danced before him. Could this man be his daddy? He'd never given much thought about having a daddy. He'd have to ask his mother. "Did he talk 'bout his past?"

"No, he jest tell awful good stories." She pulled a bundle from under her coat. "While ta women wash him and get him ready to

269

lay out, I find dis. Yo want it? Could hep yo."

He took the package. "Hab yo heared any war news?"

"No, but I fine out 'bout a meetin' down in ta swamp."

Sullus dropped the package on the bed and grabbed her arm. "What kinda gatherin'. Tell me!"

The girl grinned as she twisted on a button. "Day say it gwine be with a man named Simmons. First name's John. That's what I done and heared. Day say he a abolitionist. Whatever dat means."

"I think dat be one of dem white folk dat tryin' to help us get free. I heared day be smugglin' niggers north by ta bunches. I like to hear what he hab to say. When is it?"

"Tomorrow evenin', out in ta swamp where dat travelin' preacher hab his tent meetin'. Mista Sullus, if yo find out 'bout a bunch leavin' will yo please see dat I get to go? Ain't nothin' in ta world I like better than be free. Not wanna spend mah life like mah mama. Habin' one baby after 'nother."

He glanced at the package on the bed then back at the girl. "I find a way to get to ta meetin'. If I kin, I promise yo be in ta next group dat go north."

The girl impulsively kissed him on the cheek. "Day be comin' fer me soon, but I wants yo to know yo ta best friend I ever hab."

Sullus squeezed her hand. "Tomorrow day take me back to Greenwillow. I find a way to go to ta meetin'. Hopefully freedom jest around ta corner, and we not hab to wait fer ta war to free us."

* * *

The swamp was as dark as the blacks that swarmed through the undergrowth. Sullus' eyes darted from side to side. He didn't see a white man anywhere. An uneasy feeling stirred in the pit of his stomach. Maybe this was some sort of trick.

A man stepped into the midst of the circle and lifted his arms. The crowd grew silent. "To this group I'll be called Reverend Simmons. I'm here to offer you all freedom from a life of slavery. I'll help you get to a land where men are treated as equals. Jobs, homes, a place where you can walk the streets any time of night or day. No more being beat like animals."

Someone mumbled, "Sound like heaven."

Another asked, "And how much this freedom gwine cost us? Yo know us ain't got no money."

"We're not in this for pay, brother. Those of us who are trying to help our Negro brothers believe slavery is wrong. And we want to see you free."

A man asked, "When we go?"

"Meet me here the same time tomorrow night."

Someone asked, "Who get to go?"

"Anyone that can take care of hisself."

Sullus remembered the stubborn set of the jaw of the girl back at the plantation; the way her black eyes snapped when she was determined to have her way. Yes, she could survive. There was no doubt in his mind. As for him, he still had unfinished business at Greenwillow. He'd find freedom, but it'd be in his own time and own way. Until then, he had things to do. He worked his way through the crowd of murmuring slaves and headed toward Five Oaks. He'd tell the girl to be ready to leave tomorrow night.

When he reached the clearing, he heard the dogs. They were on a hunt, but he knew it wasn't for raccoon. Or at least not the four legged kind. He'd take a look. Might be that Sally Mae had decided to run away again. In that case, he'd send her with Simmons.

* * *

Later that same night, Seth moved through the swamp as silent as a black panther looking for prey. He'd find the right spot. A place where no one would ever think of searching for gold. He'd already put some away at the house. This gold would insure his future. If things got too bad, he'd take the money and go west. A smile tugged at the corners of his lips. He'd leave Abigail in the mountains with Miller. Seems she wasn't going to give him an heir and she'd only slow him down.

Cautiously he moved a large stone and then glanced about. What was that sound? He peered through the undergrowth. He didn't think he had been followed. He parted the bushes with his hands. A flock of pheasant flew up, startled. He never saw the dark shadow of a man that watched him from a clump of bushes. He stepped back and began to dig. The smell of damp earth and rotting leaves filled his nostrils.

The scent reminded him of the poverty after his father left him and his mother when he was ten years old. If his plan worked, he wouldn't ever suffer again. He'd always been a survivor. The whispering wind stirred memories of bits and pieces of conversation he'd heard long in the night when his parents thought he was asleep. His mother's voice had been soft, but stern. "I won't have it—I know—I know—but—we'll see. My son—school—no half-breeds."

Then his father answered, strong and determined. "Accept it—That's life—can't live this way."

Then, Seth hadn't understood the meaning of what he'd heard, but now he knew all too well why his father left. A man needed a woman. If she was at all like his first wife, he didn't blame his father.

His mother showed no signs of emotion as she looked at him. "Your father won't be here anymore. We are going to have to work hard, but this place will feed us. We have slaves and some money. We'll make it on our own."

From that day forth, she never mentioned his father again. They had survived and so had the plantation. He was proud of his Greenwillow. Maybe the war would destroy a way of life, but one thing for sure, he'd have plenty gold to start over. He put the bag of gold in the hole, rolled the stone in place, and then raked dead leaves and moss over it. Off in the distance he heard the dogs. He knew the sound well. Let them hunt. His future was secure. He muttered to himself, "Let the damn Yankees come. They won't feed their bellies with food from *my* table."

❧ 36 ❧

Greenwillow: Late February, 1862

Tasha had grown accustomed to spending her nights in Seth's bedroom. That was her job, but she lived for the times she could slip away to Corrie's old room off the kitchen and be with Abe, the houseboy. Most of the help in the big house still shunned her, but Pearl and Sally Mae treated her well. She tolerated the others. She touched the bulge of her stomach. Her breasts, round and tender, filled her faded housedress. No one needed to tell her that by early summer, she'd be a mama. She wasn't the only woman who was expecting. Pearl's belly also swelled and her dress pulled tight across her bosom.

She pushed open the door to Seth's room. "Yo send fer me?"

He laid down a magazine and gave her a wicked grin. "A man needs his bed warmed when he gets in." He patted the roundness of her stomach. "Seems to me like you're pooching out in the front. It wouldn't be you're having a baby, now would it?"

Tasha cupped her hands under her stomach. "Yo knows, Masta Seth. It yo who done and put it dere."

Seth's eyes grew hard. He took her by the shoulders and shook her. "Everybody here knows you've been bedding with my houseboy. And you know as well as I, you'll have a nigger baby, don't you?"

Tasha bowed her head. In her heart, she wished it were Abe's child.

"Don't just stand there. Get those rags off. I need a little pleasuring."

Tears started down her face. "Please, Masta. Not again. Don't pump me up tonight."

"Speak up, girl. I can't hear your muttering."

"Nothin', jest clearin' mah throat."

Seth let his satin smoking jacket slip to the floor. "Get over here. I'm not in any mood to listen to the mumbling of a nigger. Got more important things to do."

* * *

Asa watched Pearl's stomach without a word, but as it grew, hatred for McRoy filled his heart. When the time came, he wanted to be the one to cut off his balls. He'd dig them out and leave him to die a slow agonizing death. This way McRoy would know his pain.

Asa's love-making grew in passion as he tried to blot out the one time the overseer had taken his woman; as if he loved her hard and long enough, the baby would be his, a son he'd always wanted, a son to carry on his name, a son to see the freedom he'd probably never see. He looked up as Pearl came in.

"What mah man a-thinkin' 'bout?"

Asa tilted his head toward her. For a moment, he stared at her belly and then touched it. His eyes grew large. "I feels it. Ta baby, it movin'."

"Yes, it be stirrin' fer a while now."

Asa took her in his arms. "Why yo not tell me?" He felt her snuggle closer. Poor Pearl, it was hard for her to pretend everything was normal; pretend she was having his son; pretend McRoy hadn't taken her. That's why he planned on making this baby his.

"Pearl baby, talk to me."

She kissed him on the cheek. "I jest thinkin' what a good daddy yo be. Ta baby need someone while I up at ta big house all day. Yo knows I not be worth much up dere if I hab to worry 'bout mah chile all day."

Asa tugged at her apron. "Come on, gib yo' ole man a little luvin'. Even if yo carryin' a young'un, it not matter none."

Pearl let her faded dress slip over her shoulders.

Asa knew she had to be tired, but he needed to love her; needed to know she belonged to him. At first he touched her gently. He didn't want to hurt the baby. He moaned with pleasure. This woman made his life bearable. His thoughts were swept away as passion carried him on a tidal wave of emotion. This love would help him overcome the troubles that lay ahead.

The quietness that followed their love-making was a welcome change. After some time he said, "What new at ta big house? Any more war talk?"

Pearl traced the outline of his mustache with the tip of her finger. "Dere be a man up from ta coast today. Heared him tell Masta Seth dat Fort Macon be took by ta Union a while back. Didn't say nothin' 'bout killin' though."

Asa pulled her close. There didn't have to be war to be killing. All his waking time was filled with hatred for McRoy. But he'd have to wait for the right time, and he was sure it'd come.

Pearl stirred in his arms and looked up. "Penny fer your thoughts."

Asa smiled. "Ain't worth a penny."

"I heared sump'n else at ta big house today."

Asa stared out the window; his mind still on McRoy.

"Sullus back from Five Oaks. He go to a-meetin' in ta swamp last night. Said a white man there called hisself John Simmons. Said he one of dem dere abolitionist. Wants to hep us niggers to freedom. Bet if us get to ta mountains, Miz Abigail help us." She pushed herself up on her elbow. "If yo is a-wantin' to go, day a meetin' tonight." She wiped at her eyes. "I think yo oughta go. If yo stay here dere ain't gwine be nothin' but trouble. And dat ain't sump'n I be a-needin' right now."

Asa hugged her tighter. "I ain't gwine. Yo know dat. And ta baby, I wanna be here when my son be born."

"Yo knows I can't travel now. Ain't nothin' in dis world I'd like more dan fer ta baby to be born free. But I jest cain't take ta risk."

Asa touched her stomach. "I ain't gwine no wheres without yo. Us wait dis out together. When ta baby come, dere be a way. Or maybe ta war be over and we be free." He felt her give a heavy sigh. Freedom. What difference would it make? What if Pearl's baby was more white than black? He wanted to choke McRoy, but then he'd be strung up. How would Pearl make it alone with a baby? No, he'd not do that even if it was what the overseer deserved.

*　*　*

The next morning Asa had a fire in the stove and coffee made when Pearl got up. She looked at him with concern. "Asa is yo feelin' alright. Yo not get up 'fore I leaves."

Asa poured two cups of coffee and pulled out a chair.

Pearl sat down. "What got yo up so early?."

Asa grinned and took a swallow of the strong brew. "I ain't slept much all night. I be thinkin' 'bout dat abolitionist."

Hope rose in her heart. "Yo gwine with him!. After ta baby come I find a way to get to yo."

Asa pushed back his chair. "No, I ain't gwine, but I plan to help dat man get a bunch of our people rounded up and get dem outta here."

Pearl drained her cup and set it down. "And how yo gwine do that?"

"Well, fer starters, I'm gwine to Willy's house and tell him what happenin'. Yo know how sad he be since he ship his family off under that load a-manure. He jest be waitin' fer a chance to find 'em."

Love filled Pearl's heart. "Ain't yo sump'n? Please be careful. Remember, I need yo. Ta baby need yo."

"Trust me. I watch out. Yo try to find some others on ta plantation that like to get to freedom and send dem to ta swamp."

Pearl watched him leave. A strange feeling stirred inside her. He now had something to take the place of his anger, and this purpose would change all their lives.

* * *

That same night Simmons looked out at the group who gathered with their few belongings. A quiet whispering rippled across the clearing as he stepped into view. He raised his arms and immediately a hush fell over the crowd.

"Sullus and Asa will help us through the swamps, then we'll head due west. We'll hide out during the day and travel at night. Any signs of war, and we change directions. Do as you're told, and don't ask questions. Farther west, I hope to be able to get you onto a freight train that goes into Morganton. From there, we'll head north to a place where I've made arrangements for a man to get you to the Ohio River. When we get there a boat will take you across. All of you have family and friends who probably would like to go, but fifteen to twenty is about all I dare take at one time. I'll be back as soon as I get this group to safety. Hopefully, before long, there won't be any need for my help. If the Yankees proceed the way they've started, you will *all* be free. We just don't know when. Now say your goodbyes, and let's get going."

The night air shook with sobs as the long trek to freedom began.

❧ 37 ❧

Shady Junction: Early March, 1862

Two weeks later, Ned Miller awoke to a noise. He slipped from bed and dressed. He didn't want to rouse Sophie. She was having another baby and this time she had been awfully sick. He was glad Corrie had been here to help with the boys, especially the baby. Maybe four sons was enough. In his heart, he hoped she'd have the little girl she wanted so bad.

Ned picked up his shotgun and went outside, looking for some signs of life. The noise could spell danger. From the left side of the house came a low whistle, Ned wheeled, holding his gun in position to fire. "Who's there?"

"It's me, Simmons. Don't shoot." He stepped into view. "Remember me? We talked when the war started. You said you'd help me." He reached out his hand.

Ned lowered his gun. "I thought you had probably got yerself killed."

"No, this is just the first chance I've had to come this way. Are you still willing to help me?"

Ned motioned for Simmons to follow him into the shed. He set down his gun. "I've already took a woman and her young'uns north and helped them get across the Ohio River. They were runaways from my father-in-law's plantation. I was hoping you'd be along to help, but when you didn't show up, I took them myself. We went to Chester's trading post and he hid them, but there was a band of slave hunters on our butts all the way. I had a load of supplies for the troops in the western part of Virginia, and the darkies hid in the wagon. When I got there, you've never seen so much slaughter in your life. I left the food, and on the way back, I hid among the dead until the bounty hunters gave up and left. I found Billy Jackson from the plantation near Greenwillow. He was hurt bad, and I brought him back."

Simmons sat down on a chunk of wood. "I've got the husband with me. He'll be glad to hear his family is safe."

"Well, I done what I could. I'm afraid all I can do fer you now is give you a place to rest before you head on north."

Simmons stood. "I was hoping you'd take them on, and I could go back for more."

"I'll do what I can, but these mountains are swarming with troops looking fer men like me. I don't go along with slavery or the governor's idea to use the last man and dollar to win a war. Besides, I have a wife who's expecting, and I need to be home."

"I understand. If you'll just give us a place to rest and a hot meal, we'll be on our way."

"There's a cave right behind our house. You'll have to go through the front room to reach it. That's where I hide when the patrol comes looking fer me. When I'm hunting, my boys play up on the rocks that overlook the valley. If they see troops, my wife hangs a white sheet on a tree limb. I high-tail it home and go into the cave and stay until they're tired of looking. You go get the darkies." He'd do all he could for Corrie's people. She had done an awful lot for him and Sophie since she'd come, but staying out of the army was his main purpose in life right now.

* * *

Later that same night, Abigail sat up in bed. She felt that

something was wrong. Sophie was due in three more months. If the baby was born now, it wouldn't live. At the window, she looked out into the darkness. The low-hanging clouds blocked out any light from the moon. Opening the shutter, she stuck her hand out. It was snow! She'd come to love waking to a world draped in white. There were no words to describe the way it made her feel. With the snow always came a certain hush. The tree limbs were laden, causing their boughs to sag. The only disturbance was the occasional tracks of a rabbit or some other animal. She wished that somehow there would be a way to freeze time and keep it this way. She crawled back into bed and snuggled under the covers. She was being foolish. Tomorrow would be a beautiful day in spite of all her feelings.

It didn't take sleep long to pull her into the land of dreams, but it wasn't into a snow covered world that she was taken. *She was back at the Cranshaw Plantation suspended in the room where a dark-haired little girl played at the feet of a blonde-headed woman who sat in front of the fire, sewing. Abigail felt their happiness.*

The library door opened and David watched his wife and child for some time. The love, plainly visible on his face, made Abigail flinch, but she saw something else. Was it concern that caused his brow to furrow? The child glanced up, saw her father, and ran to him with open arms. He picked her up and hugged her. "Why don't you run on out to the kitchen and have the cook give you some milk and cookies?"

The child looked back at her mother as though asking permission.

"Cookies sound like a good idea to me. Maybe your papa and I will join you in a little while," said Mariah.

David put her down, and she was gone in a flash. Abigail wanted to follow, but somehow she couldn't move. She watched him kneel in front of his wife and take her hands in his. "I've been drafted. The war is getting worse and there is no way for me to stay out of it. I'll be stationed at the Capitol. I hate to leave you and Rosemary, but—"

Abigail's spirit screamed. No, this can't happen! Not David, he can't be taken! She tried to reach out to him, but there was only thin air. She felt hands on her shoulders.

"Wake up, Abigail. You're having a nightmare."

She opened her eyes to find Mrs. Ledbetter leaning over her.

"You were calling for David. I thought your husband's name was Seth."

Abigail felt her body trembling and the little beads of sweat trickle down her face. "Seth is, but David is the man—"

"Who you love?"

Abigail felt chilled and drew the cover tighter about her. "It's not what it seems."

The older woman pulled her close. "You poor thing. You're shaking. I've had a feeling that you'd like someone to talk to. Anything you tell me won't be repeated. I'd never betray a confidence."

Abigail knew she could trust her. "It's not what you think. I do love him, but he is in love with his wife. And that's not all, they're raising my baby."

"And he is the father?"

"No, I don't know who the father is. Like you, Miss Wellington took me in when I was about thirteen, and I worked for her. One of her customers decided I looked better than what she offered."

Sissy hugged her tighter. "I remember men like him."

"I ran away and Mr. Cranshaw, that's David, found me in an alley and took me home. When the doctor said I was going to have a baby, he fixed it so I could stay with his mother and have the baby. His wife was losing her mind from the loss of her own child. I wanted them to take it, but he said Mariah wouldn't. When the baby was born early, he took it home before taking it to the adoptive parents. His wife was in a real bad way. He placed it in her arms and left it there until she came out of her spell. She thought it was the baby she'd given birth to, so they're raising her. The sad part is, while I waited for the baby, I gave him my heart."

"And I suppose you married Seth to get away. That's an old but familiar tune."

"Yes, but I still dream about David. Tonight I dreamed he had to go to war. Do you believe when you love as much as I love him that somehow you know what's happening?"

"There's no doubt in my mind that a person's spirit can transcend time and be in tune with another. It's natural you'd dream of someone you love, especially with so much trouble in our country. Can I get you anything before I go back to bed?"

"No, but you can say a prayer that if David has gone to war, he'll be safe, and that nothing happens to my little girl."

"You can count on my prayers." At the door she stopped. "I forgot to tell you earlier about Margaret and the Jackson boy."

Abigail gave her a warm smile. "You don't have to tell me. They're in love. Talk about wearing your heart on your sleeve! If Billy wore his any plainer, he'd have to get a shield for it."

"You're right. They are planning to be married in the summer. He owes her an awful lot. You know none of us thought he'd live when Ned brought him here, but she wouldn't give up hope."

The door closed and Abigail was alone. Once again she snuggled under the quilts. *Yes, love can do anything. I'll will my love to keep David and Rosemary safe.*

❧ 38 ❧

Birthing at Greenwillow: 1862

Tasha clutched her stomach and bent over. The first pains of labor worked their way across her middle, rippling like a washboard as it traveled. She held on to the cooktable as she thought about what was happening. *I ain't never knowed dis kinda pain, not even when I be beat with ta whip. Dere must be sump'n terrible wrong! I gotta get hep.* Her mind whirled in the midst of the pain. She fought to regain control. *Sally Mae be near. I jest heared her in ta larder a minute ago.*

"Sally Mae, come quick. Hep! Ta baby. I think it a-comin'!"

Before Tasha could move, Sally Mae rushed in. "Baby! Did yo say baby?"

Tasha mopped at the sweat on her forehead. "Can't yo see, it be time fer this ba . . ." another pain stabbed her. "It be time."

Sally Mae took a step toward her. "Birthing babies ain't my job."

Another pain racked Tasha's body. She clutched at the end of the table in a mad frenzy. Only her eyes spoke to Sally Mae.

"Come, lay down in yo' room, den I fetch ta granny woman."

Seth stuck his head in the kitchen door. "What in the world is all that screaming out here?"

"Tasha think her chile a comin'," said Sally Mae.

"From the looks of things, I'd say so. Well, just don't stand there. Get her down to one of the servant cabins. I don't want a nigger baby born in my house."

"But, Masta, she not hab a cabin. She sleep in Corrie's old room."

"I don't give a damn where she sleeps. She's not to have her baby in my house."

Another scream filled the kitchen.

"And I'd say you shouldn't wait too long. Out of here, the both of you."

Sally Mae placed a hand on Tasha's shoulder. "Come, we gwine to mah cabin." She half-led and half-pushed Tasha toward the door. She had to do something, and her cabin and Pearl's was the only place that wasn't already crammed full of children.

* * *

Time dragged. Sally Mae mopped at Tasha's face and tried to comfort her. Once in a while she'd look out the window. She'd sent for the granny woman. *What was taking her so long?* She looked back at Tasha.

"Am I gwine die?"

"Women hab babies all ta time and live. Yo be alright."

If I can get her to walk, it help ta baby be born. "Come on. We gwine fer a little stroll 'round ta room." As she lifted her in a sitting position, another pain tore through Tasha's stomach, and she slumped onto the corn shuck mattress. Sally Mae wiped her face with a wet washcloth. *Water! It take hot water to hab babies.*

She patted Tasha's face again and rushed to fill every container she owned from the well, then raised the stove lid and filled it with wood.

"Sa-l-l-y Ma-e, come quick!"

She dropped a stick of wood and ran to the bed. "What wrong, hone-child. Is ta baby comin'? Do yo knows what to do?"

Tasha tried to sit up. "Ta bed be wet."

Sally Mae looked down. Blood and water soaked the sheet. She gasped in horror. Never in a million years had she expected something like this to happen. She looked up at Tasha. "Ta baby. Where it be? With all dis here mess dere hab ta be a baby."

Tasha lifted her head and tried to sit up again, but flopped like a rag doll. "My water, it break. I think dat mean ta baby be here soon."

Sally Mae took a few steps back. "And jest whatta yo want me to do when it get here?"

Tasha gasped again. "I seen my mama birth a baby. Yo need some twine and scissors. Cut yo'self a good length . . ." a pain cut off the rest of her sentence.

"I hope yo say what to do with dis here string. Never know yo has to tie up a chile when it be born." Sally Mae cut a couple of feet of twine

Tasha pushed herself up on her elbow. "When ta baby come it be hung to me with a long cord. Take ta yarn and tie ta cord real tight . . . oh, my Lord," She gasped and her face turned purple. Finally, the color ebbed away. "Tie another spot a inch from ta first place yo tie and cut between."

Sally Mae wondered if the pain was getting to Tasha. "Yo shore yo wants me to . . ."

Tasha screamed.

Sally Mae tried to push on the hard lump. "Somehow, someway, I hab to get dis baby outta yo. Can yo walk some?"

The only response from Tasha was a groan.

Sally Mae prayed. "Good Lord up above, please not let my friend die. Please send hep!" She looked toward the window as though she expected an angel to appear. "Ta bed. I hab to clean up ta mess."

She folded a sheet and worked it beneath Tasha's hips. "Dere, dat be nice and clean fer ta baby if it ever get here."

Tasha's pulse hammered beneath Sally Mae's fingers. She looked like she was sleeping, and there had been no pain for about five minutes. "Yes, she still alive." She glanced back at the window. Still no angel, but the shadows were growing longer and that meant evening was near. *What if ta baby not come right away? I've heared ta grannies say dat dry births be real bad.*

Granny stepped through the door. "I be here sooner, but Pearl, she done and decide to have her chile, too. She be a while. How Tasha doin'?"

"She done and made a mess of my bed."

Granny felt Tasha's stomach and shook her head.

Sally Mae took a step forward, thankful that help was here. *Sump'n wrong. I know it. Granny make every thing right.*

"Hep set her up," said Granny.

Tasha let out a sharp cry as her stomach rose and fell in another contraction.

"I brung mah birthin' chair. It jest outside ta door. Get it."

When Sally Mae returned with ta chair, Granny said, "Hep me lift her on it."

Once they had Tasha on her feet, Granny grabbed the chair and shoved it beneath her.

Blood gushed onto the dirt floor. Sally Mae screamed. "She gonna bleed to death?"

Granny placed pillows beneath the chair and began to push on Tasha's stomach. "Take a look and see if dere be a baby comin'."

"I see a spot of wet hair. "It comin'. It really comin'."

Another hard pain swept across Tasha's stomach. Granny pressed down.

The baby slid into Sally Mae's waiting arms. "It be blue," she screamed.

Granny grabbed the baby and unwound the cord from its neck then ran her finger down its throat, pulling out a wad of phlegm. With a sharp smack, she hit the baby on the backside.

The baby turned from a dark shade of blue to red. Then it coughed and sputtered and gave a faint cry. Granny slapped him again, and the room filled with wails.

After cutting the cord and tying it, Granny gave him to Sally Mae. "Yo clean him up. I think dere be another one. Put ta baby over dere on dat blanket and hep me lay her down. Dis gonna take time."

As soon as they had Tasha back on the bed, Sally Mae washed the baby, wrapped him in a quilt, then sat down by the door. She rocked and hummed a soft lullaby. The old clock in the corner ticked away, but she wasn't aware of time. She was only aware of what would happen if the other child didn't come soon.

The last of the dying embers had turned to white ash in the stove. Tasha no longer moaned and Granny went about her work tight-lipped and grim. When she did speak it was to tell Sally Mae to go to the big house and bring Masta Seth. Sally Mae laid the baby down by the mother and left in a run.

Out of breath, she rushed into the library. "Masta Seth, Granny say fer yo to come to mah cabin and come right away. I think dere be sump'n awfully wrong with Tasha."

Seth threw down his magazine. "Don't get so worked up. Nigger women squat in the tobacco field and have their babies. Tasha's

290

probably putting on a show so the niggers will feel sorry for her."

"I not think so, Masta Seth. She not say nothin'. Jest lay dere like she dead. Maybe, yo' send fer a real doctor."

"I'm not going to waste my hard earned money on a doctor for some nigger gal. I'll come down and have a look for myself. You get on back and tell that Granny woman that I'll be down in a little while."

Sally Mae couldn't have gotten back to the cabin faster if she'd had wings. She stumbled into the cabin. "Ta Ma-s-ta, he said he be down soon. How she doin'?"

Granny stood near the bed cuddling the baby in her arms. "She ain't doin'. She done and died on us. Died with one baby out and ta other in." She handed the sleeping baby to Sally Mae. "I gwine to see how Pearl be a-doin'. I guess she gwine hab two babies to feed now."

Sally Mae took her chair and placed it just outside the door. She didn't want to sit in the room with the body. Before she could sit down, Seth came into the yard.

"Well, take me to her. I don't have all night,"

"She in dere dead, Masta Seth. If yo' wanna say yo' good-byes, go on. I ain't gwine in with no dead person."

Seth kicked at the hard red clay. "I'll be damn. If you niggers can't get at a person one way, you'll take another." He lifted the quilt and looked at the baby.

"I'd say dis baby hab a white daddy, wouldn't yo', Masta?"

"Keep your mouth shut. Find some of your people to get her ready for burying, and when they're done, I want to see this baby in the coffin with her."

"Yo can't bury a live baby, Masta. Dat ain't right!"

"Only you, me and Granny knows it was alive. I expect it to stay that way. If you want your rear branded just like your face, you just tell somebody, girl." He grabbed her and with his knee booted her in the behind. "When she's prepared for burying, I want to see so I can make sure the baby is there too." Seth stomped back toward the big house.

Sally Mae held the baby close, rocking back and forth as she sang.

"Poor little nigger baby,

Ain't got no Ma.

Poor little nigger baby,

he ain't got no Pa.

Poor little nigger baby,

not see ta mornin.'"

The sultry July night closed in around the cabin. Sally Mae still sang her haunting song, but all the time she schemed. Morning would come, and with it, she'd still rock this child. She was not going to let it be buried with its ma.

* * *

Tasha was laid out in her night clothes and placed in a rough homemade coffin with the baby by her side. Granny said to Sally Mae, "We be ready fer Masta Seth. Yo run on up to ta big house and bring him down."

Sally Mae found Seth pacing the veranda. He stopped when he saw her coming. She wondered if he was nervous about the burying. If she were in his shoes, she would be. As she mounted the steps, she said quietly, "Masta, Granny says yo come on down and see Tasha and ta baby any time yo like."

Seth grabbed his hat and jammed it on. "I'm coming right now. I won't be able to sleep until that wench and her child are in the ground."

When they entered the cabin, Seth only glanced toward the woman and child he'd had killed.

"Don't yo think yo ought a-feel ta baby?" said Sally Mae. "Ta last time yo see it, it be warm. We . . ."

"I don't care how you did it. Only that it's done." He stepped closer. Finally, he reached out and touched the baby with one finger then shuddered. "Get them buried so you can get back to work." He stalked out of the shack.

"It worked, Granny," said Sally Mae. He never guess we be buryin' ta baby dat was left in her. Now let's get dem in ta ground 'fore he ast any questions. While ta buryin' gwine on, I be over at Pearl's rockin' ta livin' chile."

All the way to Pearl's cabin Sally Mae sang.

"Poor little nigger baby,

Ain't got no Ma.

Poor little nigger baby,

him ain't got no Pa.

Poor little nigger baby

gwine cry in ta morning."

* * *

Pearl's door was open and Sally Mae stepped inside. Asa peeked his head around the sheet that divided the cabin and motioned for her. She found Pearl sound asleep with a baby cuddled in each arm. Light brown fuzz covered the babies' heads and neither one looked very dark. "Seems ta babies hab a white daddy, don't it, Asa?"

"I reckon so, but day be Pearl's babies. I luv her so I luv her babies."

"Asa, yo might be a lazy nigger, but yo be a good one. Wish I hab me a good man, but ain't no man gwine hab me with dis ugly scar."

"I not say dat. Yo still good lookin'. Why, yo hab a shape no man not like."

"I not worried 'bout no man right now. I wanna hep Pearl with ta chile'uns. She done and took good care of me when I needs her. Two babies gwine be lots of work."

"Who would hab ever thought Pearl birth twins? I hab me two sons."

One of the babies yawned and puckered up his little mouth as though he wanted to speak. Sally Mae picked him up and walked outside. Off in the distance, she saw the funeral possession winding its way toward the servants' graveyard. She rocked the baby back and forth and sang.

"Lucky little nigger baby, yo has a Ma.
Lucky little nigger baby, yo has a Pa.
Lucky little nigger baby, yo gwine grow
up strong."

❧ 39 ❧

Greenwillow: Emancipation of Slaves, 1863

Sullus stood in the doorway of his quarters, watching the winter snow birds peck in the dirt. In sixty-two, he'd helped Simmons round up a group of slaves and get them out. There had been a few trips since, but with all that was going on with the war, no telling what had happened to him. He wished for Simmons return. He might just go this time.

Off in the distance, Sullus spotted a fast approaching cloud of dust. The rider was obviously in a hurry. Maybe he had some war news. As the rider neared, he walked up toward the big house and hid behind some bushes below the veranda.

Seth met the man as he came up the steps. "Mr. Jackson, have you come to rent Sullus again?"

"Don't know what for, Turner. Haven't you heard? Lincoln signed something they call the Emancipation Proclamation. They tell me the niggers are free now. Guess that means they'll have to fight in the war. And I don't have to tell you whose side they'll fight on.

"I say as long as we're fighting a war, they're not free. Besides, I sold a lot of mine back in the fall of sixty one. I've had some runaways, and death has claimed a few. Lost a good nigger wench last summer in childbirth. Her and the baby both. Rotten luck, wouldn't you say?"

"I'd say you're better off than most of us. Don't know how I'm going to run my plantation with no more help than I have."

"So far, the plantation owners haven't been drafted. We're needed to grow food, but the way the soldiers are deserting the army, we may have to fight."

Sullus had heard all he needed to hear. The President had said they were free! He'd have to find Asa and tell him. They could all walk away in broad daylight, and there would be nothing Turner could say. He wanted to see Seth's face when he found out his slaves were going to have to be paid, *if* they chose to stay.

Back in his cabin, he gathered some of his belongings. As he sorted through what he wanted to take, he found a bundle tied with heavy cord. He sat on the bed and untied it, remembering the girl who had given him the package. It belonged to his mother's lover, old Jeffro. He'd brought it home, put it away, and forgotten all about it.

It looked like a bundle of old clothes. He unfolded some shirts, long johns, and socks, none of which were any good. He picked up a pair of pants, and when he shook them, a letter fell from the pocket. He recognized his mother's name. Pearl had some learnin'. Maybe she'd tell him what it said.

Sullus stood outside Pearl's cabin for a few minutes watching through a window as she played with the boys. It sure would have been good if these chile'uns could have been born free. Seeing they were half white, they were going to have a hard time. He guessed freedom wouldn't do them much good. He would look for Asa. He couldn't wait to tell him he was a free man. He stepped inside the door. "Where be Asa, Pearl?"

She looked up. "Oh, it yo, Sullus. Come on in. Asa, be out huntin."

"What he huntin' dis time a year?"

"What he huntin' ain't walkin' on four legs. It white and walkin' on two legs."

"I know he hate McRoy's guts, but he not hab to worry 'bout him no more. Asa be a free man. He can pack yo'uns up and walk away and dere ain't nothin' ta Masta do."

Pearl's face wrinkled in a worried frown. "What yo sayin'? We starve without ta plantation to feed us."

"Dat President Linclon say we be free."

Pearl jumped up and clapped her hands. "Praise, ta Lord! Ta war is done and over. I guess Miz Abigail and Corrie be comin' home soon. Ain't dat sump'n? Things gwine be like day used to be. Hallelujah and Praise ta Lord!"

Sullus didn't try to quiet her. Let her enjoy herself. There would be plenty of time to tell her that the war wasn't really over and that things would never be the same. When she understood, he was sure her and Asa would take their family and leave.

Suddenly, she stopped. "Sullus, McRoy try to bother me again. Asa took off after him like a hound dog after a rabbit. If he find McRoy, I sure he kill him. Den his freedom not be worth a red cent."

"Yo's right. Ta whites'll string him up and yo hab to raise dese chile'uns on yo' own. Yo not even hab ta plantation to live on." Sullus looked at the room. All of a sudden, it didn't look so bad. It was warm and there were beds and a table, plus food to eat. He wasn't worried about himself. He'd kill enough wildlife to survive, but what were people like Pearl and Asa going to do? Could it be this freedom the people up North had fought for wasn't such a good thing? Especially for families.

"Sullus, yo hab to find Asa. Please! I not go on without him. And ta boys, day luv him so much."

297

Pulling the letter from his pocket, Sullus handed it to Pearl. "I know yo hab a little learnin'. I go look fer Asa while yo figure out what dis say. Which way he go?"

"He headed fer ta swamp. It be bad out dere! Yo be keerful! I not need two dead men."

* * *

Sullus combed the swamp looking for Asa. Once in a while he saw tracks, but then lost them in the marsh. Asa knew this swamp well from helping smuggle slaves. *I doubts if McRoy know anythin' 'bout it. Be all sorts of dangers lurkin' in dere. If ta snakes don't get a-body, ta quicksand will. Asa not hab to kill McRoy. Ta swamp do it fer him.* He shook his head and sat on a log. *After what he do to Pearl, he deserve what he git, as long as it ain't Asa who gib it to him.*

A sound from his left caused him to jump. A large fox darted across the path. A little farther away a flock of wild turkey flew up. He stood as a deer bounded up in front of him, stopped and stared, then turned and dashed back the way it'd come. What had disturbed them all? *Asa be in here. I feel it in mah bones.* He had only taken a few steps when he heard the cry for help. Before long the call echoed across the swamp in a steady wail. It was McRoy.

Let it happen. I take mah time. I be dere in time to see him go under. The cry became weaker and sounded muffled. *If I gwine fer ta buryin', I best hurry.* He stepped from the undergrowth to find Asa sitting on a stump, whittling. McRoy was about two feet away in the quicksand. He'd been pulled under until only his head showed.

Asa moved over on his stump. "Good day fer watchin' a buryin', yo think?"

"Never a finer day. Especially, when all yo hab to do is watch."

The cry for help became a gurgle. Suddenly, a big bubble rose where McRoy's head had been. The sand gave a big belch and settled down to rest.

"Guess ta sand jest hab supper. Now I need to hab mine." Asa stood and took a few steps toward the path. "Wanna eat with us tonight? We is gwine celebrate."

"I always in favor of celebratin'. 'Specially when dere be sump'n to celebrate!"

"I happy McRoy gone."

"Ain't only McRoy's demise we gwine celebrate. We be free! Sullus got up and followed Asa. "As free as ta deer and fox. Ain't dat sump'n?" Sullus watched his friend's eyes grow until they almost filled his face.

"Where yo hear dat?"

"I hid under ta porch when Masta Jackson come tell Masta Seth."

"Free, like in we can go where we want? Free, like in we not hab to work ta plantation no more?"

"Free, like in, he hab to pay us if we do." Sullus said.

The swamp echoed with Asa's hallelujah chorus. "Come on, let's git home! Ain't Pearl gwine be happy?"

"She already happy. She know Lincoln done signed fer our freedom."

Asa stopped. "You mean ta war ain't over?"

"No, day still fightin', and I guess we hab to fight now dat we be free."

"I ain't gwine fight fer what I already got. Dem white folk, North or South, hab some crazy notions. Don't yo reckon?"

"Day all purty loony. We ta only sane people."

Sullus and Asa traded punches and laughed as they danced in circles.

"Maybe we get Masta Seth to take a walk in ta swamp, too!" said Asa.

"Yo run McRoy into ta swamp a-purpose, din yo?"

At that instant the quicksand gave one last burp, then settled to wait for its next victim. Sullus looked back. It would be nice if Masta disappeared to. That way they'd be free to stay at the only home they'd ever known.

Sullus and Asa walked home in silence, but as soon as they entered the hut, Asa grabbed Pearl and hugged her. "We be free. Praise ta Lord! We not only free, Pearl, you not hab to worry 'bout McRoy no more."

Pearl stepped back. "Yo ain't done and killed him, hab you? Yo know if yo hab, dem white folk string yo up to ta nearest tree."

"I not hab to kill him. Ta swamp et him. People is jest gwine think he took off on his own."

Pearl breathed a deep sigh of relief. "Do ta others know we free?"

"Yo'uns is the first ones I tell. When we see ta campfire, we go down and tell'em. Day can dance all night, but 'fore yo take off, could yo make out what ta letter 'bout?"

Pearl picked up the wrinkled paper. She reached out and gently touched his hand. "I sorry, it hard to read 'cause it so ole. Lots of ta words 'bout faded. All I make out be dat Jeffro luv yo mama, and dat Masta be yo daddy."

Sullus dropped to the dirt floor in front of the fire as a hush settled over the room. "I think I gonna be free. Wherever I go, I know d*at* man be my daddy." He beat the dirt floor with his fists. "My soul never be free. Not now! I oughta pick him up by ta nape of ta neck and take him down to ta swamp and bury him with McRoy." He sat up on his knees and rocked back and forth. "No, I not do dat. But I hab to see ta man who be mah daddy." After a moment, the anger dissipated. He took a deep breath. "I gwine up to ta big house."

Pearl grabbed Sullus by the shirttail. "Now, don't yo go runnin' off up dere and doin' sump'n crazy. Yo mama, she gwine be home any day now, and she gonna want ta see her boy. Fer shore, day hang yo up if yo hurt Masta, 'sides we ain't et."

"I ain't gwine kill him. I jest gwine make him do a little beggin'. And 'sides food ain't what I need now."

"Why not take yo belongin's and head on out to Ned Miller's? See yo mama. She be right proud to see yo," said Pearl.

"First things first." Sullus slammed the door. *My mama be glad to see me. But daddy, dat be another story.*

* * *

At the big house, Sullus took the stairs two at a time. He found his daddy lying on the bed, reading. Seth stood up, anger flashing in his eyes. "What're you doing up here, boy? Get out before I call McRoy!"

Sullus felt a new sort of power surge through his body. "I be free now. I go where I want, when I want. And dere ain't nothin' yo do 'bout it."

"McRoy!"

"Yo yell fer him all yo want, but he ain't a-comin'. He jest went fer a swim in ta quicksand. Yo oughta try it, Masta." He stepped closer. "Think yo find it coolin' fer a man like yo."

Seth backed toward the window and held up his hands. "Now, boy, haven't I always looked out for you? I could have sent you off to the auction block. You'd have brought a good price, but instead, I gave you a job I knew you'd like. You can't tell me you haven't enjoyed pleasuring all those wenches."

"We be talkin' 'bout yo, Masta. No, yo is not mah Masta anymore. Let's see. What I call you. How *Daddy* sound?"

"Boy, I don't know what you've been smoking, but you're crazy as a bed bug."

Sullus held up the letter. "See this? This wrote to a ole man named Jeffro. Yo heared dat name, Daddy?"

"Seems I had a servant called that. Sold him to Mr. Jackson. Couldn't get too much work out of him because he was always pleasuring your mama. He's the man you should call Daddy."

"I think we know yo be my daddy. It not matter now. Jeffro be dead, and Mama, she won' come back when she find out she free. Yo ain't gwine get much pleasurin' now."

Seth waved his arms toward the door. "So, you're free. Go. See how you like it. Don't come crawling back when you're starving. I don't need any of you. I've got enough gold hid away to do me for the rest of my life."

"Blood money, I say."

"You're just a nigger. A stupid, stupid nigger like all the rest."

"I show yo how smart I be." Sullus took a step into the room. "Take off dem fancy duds. I needs to take a good look at ta man who done and brought a half-breed into ta world."

Seth untied his smoking jacket and let it fall open. "Well, look and get out of here."

Sullus took another step. "Dat not do. Day tell me at ta Jackson plantation to strip. Dat what I tellin' yo. Strip! And if yo not do it, I do it fer yo."

Seth turned his back to Sullus and let his clothes fall to the floor. "You've got what you wanted, now, get out of here and don't come back."

"I ain't got all I want. I wanna see ta thing that poke at my mama all dem years. Turn around so I can get a good look." He heard steps in the hallway and glanced toward the door as Sally Mae stepped into the room.

"Let me see what yo see, Sullus." She glared. "Well, if dat ain't ta thing dat killed Tasha. If I hab a knife I cut it off, but maybe it be good dat yo burn jest like yo hab me burned." She picked up the oil lamp and threw it. The glass crashed on the floor and a trail of flames licked up the spilled oil. Almost immediately, a wall of fire rose between dem. Seth stumbled forward into the flames with his hands out.

Sullus grabbed Sally Mae by the arm. "Come on. Let's go."

Once they were outside, they heard the slaves screaming. "Fire in ta big house. Hurry! Fire!

Sullus turned to Sally Mae. "We is gwine leave. Meet me in ta swamp. One more thin' I hab to do."

Sally Mae didn't ask any questions, but headed straight for the swamp. Sullus stood for a moment watching the fire reach out the window for air. People had already formed a line and were passing water buckets the way they had been trained. *Well, I ain't gonna pass no water. Let ta son-of-a-bitch burn to death. He hab it comin'.* As he walked by the end of the line, he heard someone say, "I knowed Masta Seth gwine catch hisself on fire one day from smokin' in ta bed."

Asa spoke from behind Sullus. "I know yo be a-leavin'. I wanna come with yo, but dere be Pearl and ta boys."

"I know, Asa. Yo take care of dem. I say hello to my mama from yawl."

Asa nodded, and Sullus slipped into the shadows. *I find dat stash of gold den go see mama. I be a free man with money.*

Not too far into the swamp, he stopped at a large rock. He had seen Masta Seth roll this stone into a hole the night he had gone to the swamp to hear Simmons. Now he pushed it out of the way. At the bottom of the deep hole lay a tow sack. He knelt down and untied it. Inside he felt the hard gold coins he had expected to find. He closed the sack and picked it up. It was heavy, but when he found Sally Mae, he knew she'd be more than glad to help him carry his treasure. Come to think of it, Sally Mae might be good for more than carrying gold. She might be good for carrying babies.

❧ 40 ❧

Shady Junction: March, 1863

Abigail held Sophie's beautiful little redheaded girl on her knee and bounced her up and down. This baby's birth had been easy. Ned acted happy about having a daughter, but Sophie had told her that he'd have liked another son.

Corrie came into the room. "Yo' shore good with chile'uns, Missy. It too bad yo' not have some of yo' own. Maybe when this war be done with, yo' hab ta boy Masta Seth want."

Abigail grimaced at the thought. She didn't want a child with Seth even if it were possible. Now if it were David, yes, there would be nothing she'd like more. Thoughts of her own child filled her head as she played with the baby. She breathed a silent prayer that the war hadn't upset her life.

Someone knocked. Abigail held the baby close and stood. Corrie's eyes darted toward the door. "Yo' think it dem soldiers come fer Sophie's man?"

Abigail moved toward the bedroom door. "I don't think so. I'd think they'd have better things to do than be out hunting in this cold. I'm not afraid of our soldiers, but what if it's the Yankees? Or worse yet,Seth come to take us home."

"I think I 'bout as soon see a Yankee. Yo take ta baby in ta other room. I find out."

Abigail had just stepped into the bedroom when she heard Corrie scream. "Lord bless my soul, it be mah boy!"

By the time Abigail got back into the room, Corrie had her arms wrapped around the son she loved so much. She watched mother and son with tears running down her face. There were so many questions, but she needed to give them some time. She turned and went into the bedroom and put the baby in the cradle, covering her with a quilt. Soon the baby was asleep, and she went back to the front room.

When Abigail came in Corrie and Sullus were still laughing, crying, and hugging. Sullus stepped toward her and said, "Miz Abigail, I like to thank yo fer being so good to mah mama. She done and tole me how yo treat her like family."

"Sullus, your mama has been good to me, also. Here in the mountains everyone is treated the same. I think I'm becoming a mountain woman." Then the thought struck her that maybe Seth had sent Sullus to bring her and Corrie home, and all the joy she'd felt earlier vanished. "Sullus, what are you doing so far from the plantation? Did Seth send you to bring us home?"

"No, Miz Abigail. I not come to fetch yo home. I ain't never gwine back to ta plantation. I guess yo not heared way up here, dat Lincoln man done set us free. Our people free to go where day want, when day want."

Corrie was sobbing by now. "We be free. Ain't dat good? What yo gwine do, son?"

"Thought I head on up North and see what kinda jobs day hab fer us. Day say now dat we be free we hab to fight, but dat not make no sense to me. I not wanna fight."

Corrie shook her head. "Yo like Mr. Ned. He not wanna fight either. Yo be careful. Day lookin' fer Mr. Ned to make him fight."

"I be careful, Mama. Could I get a night's lodgin' and a good meal 'fore I head on out."

"Yo shore can, boy. Dat gib yo a chance to see Sophie and her family."

"I hab Sally Mae waitin' out in ta shed. Can she come in?"

"Of course. Yo stay right here and talk to Missy, and I fetch her."

As soon as the door slammed, Abigail said, "Sullus, what's happening at the plantation?"

"Ta war ain't hurt it, yet. I suppose it will. Ta night Sally Mae and me run away dere be a little fire at ta big house, but ta servants had it 'bout out when we left. I not think yo hab to worry 'bout Masta Seth sendin' fer yo fer some time."

Abigail wiped at her eyes. "Are you going to take your mama with you now that she is free?"

"I take her if she want to go, but I not think she want to, do you?"

"No, Sullus. She is needed and loved right here. I think this is where she'll be the happiest. I'm going back to the boarding house where I live and give you and your mama some time to visit. Good luck and God bless you." She wrapped her scarf tightly around her head and slipped on her coat.

As she started toward home, she was thankful that Seth hadn't sent for them. It seemed she was going to be here for a while. If this war continued, money would be hard to come by. She'd see if Alice would give her a job making hats.

❧ 41 ❧

New Orleans: David Cranshaw, 1864

Captain David Cranshaw looked out over his desolate fields, thinking of all that had happened since the war started. Even though New Orleans had been virtually untouched, the iron fist of the Yankees had ruled it since they'd taken over in the spring of sixty-two. Plantation life had mostly been ruined, but because of the loyalty of his slaves, his family had been able to maintain a descent lifestyle.

He had been stationed at Shreveport, but now his regiment was on the run, hiding out to avoid capture, but still doing what they could to make the Union army's job harder. He'd been gone two years. Surprisingly, he found his household in good order. Mariah had taken over like a trooper, and with the help of the servants, who had stayed for lack of anywhere else to go, there hadn't been much change, except in the fields.

Tomorrow was Saturday, May the fourth, Rosemary's fifth birthday. The house buzzed with preparation for a birthday celebration. He was amazed at how happy and strong Mariah appeared, over any traces of her illness. It didn't seem to bother her that the countryside was overrun with Yankees. When the war started, he'd wanted to send her to Paris, but she had flatly refused.

A rosy-faced little girl bounded down the stairs. "Papa, Papa! Can we go riding? Please? Mama said she had too much to do, but it would be all right if you took me."

David picked up the child and twirled her. "I'll give you a piggy back ride in the house. How's that?"

"That would be fun, but not half as much as horses. I bet if we raced I could win."

"I wouldn't doubt that a bit, Shrimp."

He placed her on a chair and went back to the window and gazed at the open fields. Would he dare go out, even if he didn't have on his uniform? There were all sorts of dangers. He'd practically begged on hands and knees for this little bit of time with his family, and it had been a risk getting here. Somehow, he'd have to pacify Rosemary without alarming her. Turning, he lifted her into his arms. "You know, Shrimp, Papa hasn't been home in a long time. I've missed you so much."

"Why do you call me Shrimp, Papa?"

"Because you're little like . . .." He bit his tongue. He'd almost said, *little like your mother*. He'd have to watch himself because this child was the spitting image of Abigail, except for some of her mannerisms. He could see ways in which she imitated Mariah, like standing in front of her mirror and brushing her hair. She was forever folding her hands and twirling her thumbs. Where had that trait come from, maybe her father.

"Little like what, Papa?"

"A shrimp. And you know what else I've missed?"

"What's that, Papa?"

"I've missed all you've learned in the past two years. I'll bet it will take all morning for you to bring me up to date. And then guess what? I want to play hide-and-seek with you. Won't that be fun?"

"You'll play hide-and-seek with me? Mama never has time to play games."

"You have to remember, honey, with your papa being gone,

Mama has a lot more to do. I think she would if she had time." He hugged her tight. Yes, if life was like it used to be, he was sure Mariah would spend every second of her day with this beautiful little girl. He envisioned the three of them riding off across the plantation, the wind caressing their faces, Rosemary laughing as she raced ahead. But the way things were now it was a dream.

"Papa, you're squeezing me too hard."

"I'm sorry, Shrimp. It's just that I've missed you so much."

"Why'd you have to go away, Papa? Why can't you stay here with me and Mama?"

"Hopefully, someday soon I'll be home for good. Let's go up to your room where it's quiet. Your Mama said you know your ABC's." He carried her toward the stairs.

"I can write them, too. I'll show you."

They spent most of the morning in Rosemary's room. She wrote her ABC's and numbers to a hundred. She told him two stories, and they'd built a castle out of her blocks.

"This is fun, Papa. Can I play with you this afternoon instead of taking a nap?"

"What do you think your mama would say about that?"

"Mama wouldn't say much, but Stella wouldn't like it. She says I'm so little that I need to get a good rest."

"Well, who am I to argue with Stella? I'll tell you what, after we've had dinner, and you've slept for a little while, we'll play that game of hide-and-seek I promised you. Now, let's go downstairs. I'll bet dinner is ready."

As they passed the library door, David said, "Tell your mama I'll be there in a few minutes." It was as though the ghost of yesterday beckoned him into the room. He went inside, and sat down at his desk. How many times had he sat here and talked to Monroe? He could almost see the old man hobbling toward the door. Well, Monroe might have known a lot about human nature, but he'd been wrong about Mariah. She'd taken to Rosemary like she was her own. It had taken a little time, but after she realized there wasn't going to be another child, she'd doted on this one.

David couldn't help but wonder about what had happened to Abigail. From all he'd heard, the war was worse in the east. Back in December of sixty his mother had gone to North Carolina for Christmas. She'd reported that Abigial was happy. But later she'd gotten word from Seth that he'd sent Abigail and Corrie to the mountains of North Carolina for their safety. He hit the desk with his fist. He should have made Mariah take Rosemary and go to Paris. There, life would have been a lot easier, but Mariah wasn't the type you could force into anything.

"Papa, Mama says dinner's ready."

David got up and took his daughter's hand. As they left he gently closed the door on all the memories. Things were the way they were, and he had so much to be thankful for.

* * *

David watched the birthday guests trickle in. Most were women with children. All the young boys and men were off to war. Mr. and Mrs. Wilson came with their brood. By mid-afternoon the front lawn swarmed with boys and girls. The parents sat on the veranda, fanning themselves and talking about the war.

Mr. Wilson lit a cheroot and held it between his fingers for a moment. "Guess this is one luxury I'll have to give up if this war continues. Yankees are making it hard on us. Yet here it is eighteen sixty-four and we're still holding on. I believe we can win if we hang on long enough."

Mrs. Wilson waved away the smoke that drifted her way. "I can't say I'd be sorry to see those awful cigars go. They're about as bad as the Yankees. Stink to high heaven."

Everyone laughed.

Mariah placed a tray of cookies on a table. "What's so funny out here?"

David moved over in the swing and patted the seat. "Come sit, my dear. Mrs. Wilson was just telling us how bad the Yankees stink."

Mariah sat and sipped her lemonade. Mr. Wilson put out his cigar and stuck the remains in his shirt pocket. "Guess I'll save a bit for later. What sort of war news have you heard, David? Or are you free to talk about it?"

David drew Mariah close. She stiffened and moved away slightly. Was there something wrong? They'd have a long talk after the party was over. He looked at Mr. Wilson. "I can tell you Sherman is moving down into Georgia. He's probing about, searching for weaknesses in the Confederate entrenchments. I think he's going to have to be reckoned with."

Mariah stood and when she spoke it was in an icy tone. "I'd say the Yankees aren't the only stink around here, and Sherman isn't the only one to be reckoned with." She moved toward the porch railing and watched the children playing for a moment, then went into the house.

Suddenly, David felt a chill even in all the heat. It wasn't like Mariah to be so negative, especially in the presence of company. She had always been out-spoken but never in front of so many people. As soon as he could excuse himself, he'd go check on her.

"Papa, come play hide-and-seek with us. We never got to play yesterday," called Rosemary.

"That's right we didn't, did we? You all hide while I go in the house for a minute, and then I'll find you. He started toward the door. "But don't hide anywhere but the front yard, hear?"

He found Mariah in the library looking at an old photograph. "Mariah, what's wrong? We have guests. And what you just said on the veranda. That is so unlike you."

She held up the picture. "I found this in my trunk a long time ago. It's of me when I was pregnant with Rosemary. I found it the day you and I first started riding again. I can remember as well as if it were today. I put it on my dressing table. I was going to ask you about it later. But when we came back that evening, I guess it had been moved. Anyway, I forgot about it."

David was taken by surprise. Rosemary hadn't been a year old when he'd hid it in his Bible, thinking she'd never look for it there. "How should I know anything about it?"

"All the time I was preparing for Rosemary's party, I kept thinking I needed to check the family Bible to see if we had recorded her birth. I was so busy yesterday, I forgot. Just this afternoon, when I was getting the cookies ready I thought about it, again. I looked, but the record page was blank. I remembered that you'd taken care of the christening and might have put the record in your bible. It was there along with this picture." She laid the picture down and covered her face with her hands and sank into a chair.

David felt not only were the Yankees going to ruin the South, but his own private domain was about to crumble. He'd have to think of something good to cover this. "Come, we have guests, and I have a yard full of children waiting for me to find them. I'll try to solve this mystery when everyone leaves."

"I don't want to go out there and make pleasant talk."

David took her arm. "Come on, honey. You worked so hard to make this a special day. I promise you, we'll figure this out. We'll gather the help and ask them. Probably someone picked it up while they were cleaning and stuck it in the Bible, that's all."

"Even if that's so, David, there's something about the picture that bothers me. I can't quite put my finger on it. Do you see anything different in it?"

He glanced at the picture. "All I see is my beautiful wife. Now, come. Let's not keep our guests or the children waiting." As Mariah went out the door, David looked at the picture once again. Surely there wasn't anything in it that would give away his secret. He'd have to ask Stella to say she'd been the one to put the photograph away. He shivered again. Was it yet possible that the lies of long ago would ruin his life?

* * *

The last of their company had left and David carried a very tired little girl up to bed, tucked her in, and kissed her good night. She begged for a story, and he wanted to stay and tell her one, but he knew Mariah was waiting downstairs. And with the mood she'd been in after the picture incident, he didn't want to keep her waiting. The sooner he eased her mind the more fun they'd have while he was home. Monday would be May the sixth, and he'd have to get back to his unit. As he stepped into the hallway, he met Stella. "Rosemary is already tucked in and probably sound asleep. It has been so much fun being here for her birthday. Stella, you and I have been through a lot, haven't we?"

"Yo right, Massa. And yo knows dere ain't nothin' I not do fer yawl."

"You're a free woman, Stella, but there's just one more thing I need you to do, concerning Rosemary."

"All yo hab to do is ast, Massa."

"Well, I don't have time to explain now, but in a little while there's going to be a meeting downstairs with all the house help. I'm going to ask who picked up a picture in Mariah's room five years ago and put it in my Bible. I want you to step forward and say you did it."

Stella chuckled. "With mah memory, Massa, I probably did. I not remember what I et dis morning. Now, yo go spend time with Missus and don't worry none."

He'd barely touched the downstairs floor when Mariah handed him the picture. He reached out and took it. Without looking up he said, "Why don't you give me some time to look this over? Maybe, I can find what there is about it that bothers you. While I'm looking, how about gathering all the help into the library? Some of them will know something about how this got from your room to my Bible. He heard the rustle of her skirt as she left the room. Taking the picture over to a lamp, he studied it for some trace of evidence that might give his secret away. He flipped it over–good, no date. He turned it back. What was there about it that bothered her? He couldn't see anything. As he laid it down, he saw a little patch of cotton in the far corner. Cotton wouldn't have been ready for harvest when Abigail's child was born, but it would before their baby was born. What was he going to do? Maybe, he could accidentally knock over the lamp and ruin the picture. No, he couldn't do that. He'd pray she didn't notice, and as soon as she went up to bed, he'd destroy it.

He went into the library and sat down behind his desk.

Mariah followed with all the household help. When they were all inside, she said, "The question I'm going to ask is about something that happened a long time ago. I won't be surprised if none of you remember. All I expect is an honest answer." She took the picture from David and held it up. "I left this on my dressing table, upstairs, planning to talk to David about it later. When I came in, it was gone and I forgot about it. Just this afternoon, I found it in the family Bible down here in the parlor. What I'd like to know is how did it get there?" She looked at David. "There isn't a problem with it being moved. Mr. Cranshaw and I would just like to know how it got there."

Stella stepped forward and took the picture and studied it, then handed it back to David. "I take it, Missus. I 'member jest as clear as if it be dis morning. I goes into yo' room to fetch some of yo' things to be washed. I sees it dere and thinks I put it were it be safe. Yo not hab many pictures, and I not want it to get lost."

"Are you sure, Stella? It's been five years."

"I remember, Missus. I not know what I et fer breakfast, but I can tells yo 'bout when I was little."

David slipped the picture in his pocket. "I can understand what you're saying, Stella. Sometimes I'm the same way. We've all had a busy day. Let's get some rest."

Mariah stopped at the door. "Are you coming, David?"

"I'll be along in just a minute. I have a few things I need to take care of."

"Don't be long, will you? I'll be waiting for you."

David felt relieved. His old Mariah was back. He could tell by the twinkle in her eyes, and the teasing in her voice. He touched the picture in his pocket. Apparently, she'd forgotten about it, or she was going to bring it up later. What should he do? Destroy it or risk her seeing what was wrong? For now he'd just take it with him. If she questioned why, he'd tell her he'd wanted a picture of her while he was away. He picked up the paperweight that had been on his desk for so many years. Looking down at the cross, he knew just a little of the pain that the man who had died on it had suffered. Surely God, in all his mercy, wouldn't take away all he'd worked so hard for.

A terrorizing scream cut a clear and vivid path throughout the sleeping house. David shot from his chair and up the stairs. He came face to face with Hannah and Stella in the upstairs hall.

"It come from the Missus room, I shore," said Stella.

David pushed open Mariah's door. She lay in a crumpled heap in front of her dressing table face down. Glass was strewn over the floor and the mirror frame was draped over Mariah's head. David grabbed her and turned her over. A sharp shard of glass had pierced her heart and blood gushed out of the wound. David gathered her to his bosom and rocked back and forth. His Mariah—the love of his life—gone, because he hadn't seen her need. Hadn't listened to the different times Hannah had told him about the mirror being broke. He hadn't loved her enough to make her well.

Stella tilted her head toward the door. "I thinks I hear, Rosemary. I

317

go to her. I not needed here no more."

Hannah slipped a little closer, wringing her hands. "I done and gib her a potion to keep away bad spirits. I knows she wore it cause I pin it on her ever mornin.'"

David didn't hear anything. All he could hear was the pounding of his heart. He knew he had lost this war.

❧ 42 ❧

New Orleans: David Cranshaw, 1865

The war was over. David went home, or at least, he went to a place. For him, it wasn't *home* anymore; only a house filled with haunting memories of dreams that would never be. It didn't make much difference who had won the war. Life didn't matter without Mariah, even Rosemary was only a reminder of his loss.

He spent his days wandering from room to room, hoping to find a clue to her final breakdown? He found nothing. All her belongings were neatly in order. There were no notes, no letters, to or from family.

Today, he sat in her room with her dressing gown in his arms. At least here, he smelled her presence. The night before Rosemary's party he'd held her. She'd worn this very wrap. Absent-mindedly, he raised the trunk lid. On top lay a book. He hadn't remembered ever seeing this. Picking it up, he opened it. The words, "Dear Dairy" leaped out. He didn't want to invade the private thoughts of his dead wife, but he had to know. As he read page after page, he began to catch a glimpse of how she'd suffered. The dead baby was always with her. A vision in the mirror—in window panes—shiny buttons a glass of water. He wiped tears from his eyes. How could he have missed the signs? Had his own pain kept him from seeing hers? In the back was a recent picture of Mariah and Rosemary. They both wore riding habits. They were standing right here in front of her dressing table. From the looks of their wind-blown hair, they'd just returned from an outing. The looking glass! It had a crack down the middle. That was odd. It had been broken a couple of times before, but Mariah had said it was Hannah who'd broken it the last time.

He slipped the picture in his pocket and went downstairs to the dining room where he found Hannah polishing silver.

She looked up as he entered the room. "Is dere sump'n yo want, Massa?"

"I want you to stop working your fool self to death. You're getting too old to work so hard. Besides, don't you know you're a free woman? I don't own you anymore. I'd pay you, but since the war . . ."

"Shush, such talk. Besides where else is I gwine live? And as fer ta work, I go crazy without it. I get me a cold drink, and I bring yo one."

"Thanks, I'll be in the library. There's something I want to ask you."

Soon Hannah returned with a pitcher of cold lemonade, moisture beads dripping down the sides.

"Come sit. We haven't talked since . . ."

"Since ta night in Missus's room. Yo ain't heared nothin' nobody say to yo. Yo got a-start livin'. Yo hab a little girl. She lose her mama, too."

David filled his glass again. "I know, but I can't bring myself to face . . ." He held out the picture. "I found this in her diary. Do you remember when she had it made?"

Hannah took it. A big smile spread across her face. "Yo mean, Missus not gib dis to yo? She hab it made not long 'fore yo visit last year. Say she want yo to hab it to take back with yo."

"Do you see anything about it that would connect with her death?"

Hannah studied the picture.

"The mirror. "Did she break it?"

"At first, Massa. When I come to yo long time ago 'bout it, it happen some, but as time pass, and she wear . . ." Her eyes darted toward the door. She looked as though she wanted to run.

"She wore what?"

"Her potion ta conjure woman fix. It really hep when she wear it." She shifted uneasily in her chair. "I pin it on her, but she change clothes to go riding."

David waved as though to brush away such garbage. "You and I both know potions don't work. The mind just thinks they do. Now, did the mirror get broken before she went riding?"

"It must have. I go in soon as she leave and it broke." Hannah rung her hands. "I sorry . . . I . . ."

"It's not your fault." He drained the lemonade from his glass and stood. "There's something I have to do. Ask Arnell to go into town and bring the stone-cutter out to the cemetery."

"I do dat, but don't yo go off and do sump'n crazy. Remember yo hab a chile to raise."

David didn't answer. He was already to the front door when the demanding voice of Rosemary stopped him.

"You're *not* going to leave me again! I won't *let* you!"

A tiny figure in a riding habit stood on the stairs with clenched fists. It was as though he were standing in the presence of Abigail six years ago. He closed his eyes and shook his head to clear away the vision. When he opened them, his daughter replaced Abigail. He held out his arms. "Come here, Shrimp. Give your papa a big hug. I have something to do, but I'll be back."

"Could we go riding then?"

"I suppose so."

She pulled out of the hug and bounded up the stairs calling, "Stella, Papa is going to take me riding."

David listened to the echo of her small voice. He needed to see Abigail. He'd never really thanked her for all she'd done. When he finished at the cemetery, he'd go see his mother and find out where she was. He had a lot of fence mending to do.

Stella came to the head of the stairs. "Well, I say it 'bout time yo join ta livin.'"

"You're right. Pack Rosemary's things and ask Hannah to pack mine. We're taking a trip."

* * *

At the cemetery, David tied his horse to the gate. He walked to the family crypt. He stood for a moment, then touched the slab that read *Mariah D. Cranshaw, beloved wife of David S. Cranshaw*. He remembered the day she'd asked him if he thought her tombstone would say *beloved*. Yes, she would always be his, but he'd have to put together some sort of life for Rosemary. He looked up. Arnell and the stone-cutter were approaching.

"Massa, yo not gwine open up dat tomb, is yo? Yo' wife not dere. She done and gone to ta great beyond."

"No. I'm adding another name."

They watched as the stone-cutter etched the words Rosemary Mariah Cranshaw, Born: December 25, 1857. Died: January 1, 1858 into the marble door.

David stepped forward and touched the inscription. "There, my dear wife. The name that claimed your life. Now, may you rest in peace."

"Massa, our little Rosemary back at ta plantation. She jest as 'live as yo and me."

"Before you came to live in the house, Mariah had a child who died. After her nervous breakdown, I tried to keep it from her." He wiped at his eyes. "But lies always come home to roost. I've got something else to take care of. Tell Hannah and Stella, if all goes the way I hope, Rosemary and I will be leaving tomorrow."

* * *

A little while later, David halted in front of his mother's house. She wasn't doing too well. The war and losing Mariah had been hard on her.

He opened the door and called, "Mother, are you home?"

"Here in the kitchen. I'm so glad you're getting out! Stella came by last week, worried sick about you."

"I know. I told my servants that they don't owe me anything, that they're free. They won't listen, just keep on working hard as always."

"Well, you know I never believed in slavery, but I *did* believe in states' rights. That's why I did all I could to help during the war."

David poured a cup of coffee and sat down at the table. "Seems I heard somewhere that you gave Butler and his men a rough time."

"Son, *that* man had this city turned into a madhouse! I fought fire with fire." A satisfied grin covered her face.

"Mother, bless your soul, you opened your home to a group of women whose main purpose was to tease and tantalize the devil out of the Union soldiers."

"You mean '*The Ladies of New Orleans*'?"

"You don't have to play dumb with me. I heard it got so bad that the General gave an order saying any woman found wooing a union soldier would be treated as a woman of the town plying her trade." He chuckled, then grew serious and was quiet for a long time. He knew that his mother lived in her own private hell just as he did, but he needed to know how to find Abigail.

"I went to the cemetery and put our baby's name back on the crypt. Now, Mariah can rest in peace." Peace! Would he ever have any? Maybe, when he'd made things right with Rosemary's mother. "I've come to ask about Abigail. Now that my wife is gone, she should have the opportunity to see her daughter if she likes."

"I haven't heard from her. With postal service shut down, about all the news is word of mouth, but I can tell you where she is." She opened a drawer and pulled out a letter and unfolded it. "Abigail wrote me before she went to the mountains. Here it is. She's in a place called Shady Junction, North Carolina. It's north of Morganton, close to the Virginia line."

"Do you know about the railroad? How far does it go?"

"I believe it goes to Morganton."

He got up to leave. "Thanks, Mother."

"She's a married woman, and she's already been hurt enough. Remember that day when you came rushing over after you found her with the baby? She had feelings for you all along. Please, don't hurt her anymore."

"That's not my intention. I'm learning when a wrong is righted, it doesn't hurt as much." He walked through the house and stepped into the gathering dusk. What was he thinking? He could loss his daughter. Would he be able to survive another loss? But even if it meant losing her, he had to see Abigail.

❧ 43 ❦

Shady Junction: Late Spring, 1865

Abigail finished supper and went to her room to relax. The work at the millinery shop wore her out. She had barely let out her breath when someone knocked.

"Come in."

Amos Ledbetter stuck his head in. "I don't want to disturb you, but there's a gentleman downstairs who says he has to see you. Do you want me to tell him to call back later?"

Dread like she'd never felt before settled in the pit of her stomach. It must be Seth. She'd been expecting him to show up any time to take her home now that the war was over. How was she going to tell him she had no intention of returning to Greenwillow? Tell him that she was *home*? She had a job she liked and people who loved her. She didn't need him. Didn't *want* him.

"Miss Abigail, I've gotta tell him sump'n."

"I guess you can . . . what does he look like?"

"A man, Miss Abigail."

"I mean what color is his hair? Is he tall or short?"

"He's tall. Has dark wavy hair, and he has a little girl with him. Looks to be about five or six."

Could it be her David? No, not *her* David, but *her child*—a child she hadn't seen in six years. What were they doing here? Something had to be wrong. Had the war destroyed the plantation? And Mariah? Had the war pushed her over the edge? She jumped up from the chair, fatigue forgotten.

"Go back downstairs and make them comfortable. I'll be down

shortly." The door closed and she dug frantically through her closet for a dress to wear. Finally, she decided on a mint green one with puffed sleeves, and then she brushed her hair up and pulled a few curls close to her face. Pinching her cheeks and biting her lips, she twirled in front of the mirror. There, not bad.

She descended the stairs with a stomach full of butterflies. She loved children, but what if *this* one didn't like her? It'd hurt more because the child belonged to her. At the door, she stood for a few moments drinking in the sight of the man she'd been in love with for so long. Taking a deep breath, she spoke defensively. "I've outgrown being shut in closets, and stealing my baby wasn't my aim."

David turned at the sound of her voice. "Abigail, I can never tell you how sorry I am. I came to ask you to . . .forgive me."

"I want to hear about my . . . your daughter. Where is she? Amos said you had her with you." She wanted him to tell her that he loved her—wanted him to take her in his arms. But then they were both married and didn't have that right.

He took a step forward. "Mr. Ledbetter has her out in the kitchen giving her milk and cookies. You look good. Mountain air must agree with you."

"I'm learning to take care of myself, Mr. Cranshaw."

"Can't you call me David? We share enough to be on a first name basis, don't you think?"

Slow warmth crept over her. Yes, they did have more in common than most people. And even if he didn't know it, she'd carried a special love for him all these years. A love she'd sealed and tucked away in its own private little place in her heart, the same way she'd harbored love for her child. "I think you're right. Now, tell me what brings you so far north."

"To see you. When I said I was sorry about the past, I meant it."

Abigail's knees went weak. Something must be wrong for him to be here with Rosemary, but what? "Mariah, did you have to…" a lump rose in her throat.

David eased down into a chair. "No, I didn't have to put her away, but I had to bury her. Last year. A while back I went to the cemetery and had our baby's name put back on the crypt. I gave Mariah back the very thing that claimed her life. You see, even though she never remembered the birth, she kept seeing visions of the tomb."

Instinctively, Abigail went to him and placed a hand on his arm. "I'm so sorry. You loved her. I wish I had known that sort of love. I know this is hard, and don't answer me if you feel you can't. I'll understand. But what happened?" She felt the trembling of his body.

He sat with his face in his hands without saying anything for some time. When he raised his tear-streaked face to hers, the cry for help was there for the world to see.

"I came home on leave for Rosemary's fifth birthday. Mariah seemed fine, but the next thing I knew, she was gone. The mirror. Somehow, when she lashed out, a shard pierced her heart."

"And Rosemary, how is she with the loss of her mother?"

I had to leave right after the funeral. Stella has done a good job with her, but I can tell since I've been home that it has affected her."

Abigail's heart ached for the child. Being alone in that big old plantation house with no one but the servants. Being without mother or father. And the war. How had it affected her? When you're little, everything seems so much more serious. Of course, the circumstances *were* bad, but for a young child, it could be devastating. "I'd like to spend some time with her. See if she likes me. You asked for my forgiveness. If you feel you need it, then, I give it to you. I'm not holding you responsible for loving too much." Before she could say anymore, she heard the sound of voices down the hall.

"Well, this pretty little Miss has her tummy full of cookies and milk. And I do believe she's getting sleepy." Amos tickled Rosemary under the chin. "I'll go upstairs and tell Sissy we have company."

Abigail studied the tiny face that looked so much like her own. Love flooded her with such strength that it nearly took her breath away. All the years they'd been apart vanished. She was down on the floor playing with a baby—her baby.

David touched her elbow, returning her to the present.

"Rosemary, I'd like you to meet my friend, Abigail. She used to come to the house when you were a tiny baby and play with you."

"Hello, Miss Abigail. Was that before I remembered, Papa?"

"Oh, I think you remembered then. You've forgotten."

Her forehead wrinkled in a worried frown. "You mean I'm getting old like you said Hannah was?"

David picked her up and hugged her. "When did I say Hannah was getting old, honey?"

"I don't know, but I heard Stella and Hannah talking when they were packing my stuff for this trip."

"Did you hear anything else?"

"No, just Hannah saying that you thought she was old. Is she,

Papa?"

"We're all growing older. Let's see, six weeks ago you became one year older than you were last year. That makes you six, doesn't it?"

Rosemary held up six fingers. "Stella said I'm this many. I told her I didn't need to count. I know how many six is."

Abigail took her from her father and relaxed when she slid her arms around her neck as though she'd always known her. "Seems to me like you're a smart girl. I bet it takes being smart to take care of a papa like yours."

"It sure does. He can be a handfull. Sometimes I have to put my foot down."

"I see that your papa had better march the straight line!"

"Marching is what he did in the army. Now that he's home, we're going to ride."

"Well, little Miss Rosemary, it's time you marched off to bed." David turned to Amos who'd returned and stood in the doorway. "Do you have room for a couple of vagabonds?"

The old man nodded. "Sissy's upstairs. Go on up, and she'll show you."

At the door, David stopped. "We still need to talk, Abigail. Wait, I'll be down as soon as Rosemary's settled."

She watched them go. Should she offer to help put the child to bed? No, not *the* child, *her* child. Her heart beat wildly. The pretty dark headed little girl who'd ascended those stairs was hers. Maybe not legally, but there was no denying it. She felt the emotional ties, and she believed Rosemary felt it too. She'd like nothing better than to be a mother to her.

But what about Seth? She didn't give a *damn* about him. When he came for her, she'd tell him he could find someone else to provide an heir. Tell him why she couldn't. That should finalize things.

"Would you like to go for a walk? It's still light outside. You can show me around the Junction."

Abigail turned to find David watching her. "You're back already?."

"Rosemary and Mrs. Ledbetter took to each other like life- long friends. She's tired. I dare say she's already asleep."

"A walk sounds good. There are some things I need to ask you. Are you sure Rosemary won't cry or something?"

"She'll be fine. Will you need a wrap? It's lots cooler here than New Orleans."

"Yes, I'll get it and meet you on the porch." She disappeared, thinking about their first meeting. He'd told her then that her shawl was too thin. She smiled. Who'd a thought that he'd ever care about her warmth again.

* * *

David stood on the porch of the boarding house, waiting. He glanced around. A few places of business and a post office that was still boarded up, lined the street. The war had brought lots of changes to the country, but it looked as though the closed post office was its only effect here.

"So, what do you think of Shady Junction?" Abigail asked as she came out.

"I can understand why they call it shady. I've never in my life seen so many trees! And what are those blossoms over there? And all those pink and white flowers. They're all over the place."

"The orange is wild honeysuckle. The pink and white ones are

Mountain Laurel and Ivy. If you'd come a little earlier you'd have seen a real treat. These mountains were white with dogwood blossoms."

He tucked her hand under his arm and guided her down the steps. "It seems to me you've grown fond of this place."

"I've never found more peace than I have here. And the people are wonderful. Sissy and I have become the best of friends. She used to work at the Wellington brothel. I've told her all about what happened to me there."

David stopped and looked down at her with a worried frown on his face. "Does she know about Rosemary?"

"Yes, I told her everything, and I couldn't have had a more understanding friend."

"How much does Amos know?"

"He knows Sissy used to work at a brothel, but he doesn't know about my situation. I don't plan on going back to Greenwillow. I have a job here, and I can take care of myself."

A young couple walked by. The man's arm circled her waist and the other was in a sling. He said, "Evening, Miss Abigail." The woman nodded a greeting.

"You're right about friends. The boy, is he a war casualty?"

"Yes, he's the son of a man who owned a plantation called Five Oaks. It's near Greenwillow. Ned Miller, Seth's son-in-law, found him injured in Virginia and brought him back. Sissy, Margaret, Alice, and I nursed him back to health. The blacksmith gave him a job, and he's stayed here with us."

"Could the lady on his arm have anything to do with that?"

"Everything! They married several weeks ago. Margaret's the schoolteacher here. They're so happy. It makes me sad to see how much I've missed."

They walked in silence for a while. David felt the old feeling for her deep inside. She looked so little and determined, exactly like Rosemary had the day she stood on the stairs and demanded that he not leave. He remembered Abigail standing in the middle of the floor back at his mother's, clenching and unclenching her small fists, saying she'd never be used, abused, or accused again. Well, it seemed she'd succeeded. She was making it on her own, and he didn't have the right to upset her. He'd stay a few days, then take Rosemary and go home. He'd fulfilled his moral obligation.

At the end of the street, they stopped on a little bridge over a shallow stream. As they watched the current pulling at some lodged rubbish, he broke the silence. "I have something for you. Hold out your hand, and close your eyes."

Abigail giggled like a schoolgirl and stretched out her hand.

David took a small bundle from his coat pocket and placed it in her hands. "You can open your eyes now."

She ripped open the tissue-wrapped package and her eyes lit up at the sight of the tiny christening dress with the row of pearl buttons down the front.

The joy on her face was enough to make him thankful he'd thought to bring it to her. "I know that you'll never have another child, but since Rosemary wore this and it has your buttons on it, you might like to keep it."

"Oh, David! You couldn't have brought me anything I'd treasure more. But suddenly a worried expression crossed her face.

"What's wrong?" He asked, full of concern.

"I left the button box at the plantation."

"You can always start your own."

"I know. But it won't be the same. I'm the sentimental type."

"That's not such a bad trait. I'm guilty of that myself. I will have to clean out Mariah's things." His eyes clouded. "Some day."

They were both silent for quite a while.

Abigail's nearness made it hard for him to think. All the feelings he'd fought rushed back. It was as though the time they'd been apart had never been. His wife's face had faded into Abigail's many a time. He'd thought his desire for her was lust, but would that sort of thing last this long? Maybe now, a relationship would be possible . . . *if* only she was free of *Seth*.

"I'm going back to the plantation and get my buttons."

David wanted to say, '*and your freedom*,' but held his tongue. He didn't want to assume too much. "What do you think you'll find at the plantation? I heard that Sherman's still in that area. Lee's surrendering doesn't mean that scrimmages have stopped. Rosemary and I couldn't take the train all the way to Morganton because the railroad had been destroyed."

"I don't know what I'll find, but I've got to go. Sullus, one of his slaves, passed through here back in the winter of sixty-three. He said there'd been a fire at the big house, but he didn't say how it happened or how much damage had been done. It must have been bad because Seth hasn't sent for us yet."

"That's too long a trip for a lady to take by herself. Let me go with you."

Abigail looked up at him. "You'd really do that for me?"

David took her hands in his. The last rays of light had turned to dusk. Downstream, the frogs chirped their love song. Baby bunnies scurried to the nearby underbrush. Was it the mountain air that made him dizzy or the company? What difference did it make? He hadn't felt this alive since . . .. It didn't matter. Mariah was gone. He'd never have her back, but could he have the mother of his child? He drew Abigial close. He felt the shiver that ran through her. Gently, he tilted her face up and touched his lips to hers. For a second he thought she'd pull away but instead she returned his kiss. When they drew apart, he held her at arm's length. "Miss Abigail, I'm at your mercy, but I need a few days to get Rosemary settled. Do you think we can get Mrs. Ledbetter to keep her while we're gone?"

She turned away.

Gently, he guided her off the bridge. "I shouldn't have kissed you. You're a married woman and besides I promised my mother . . ."

"You *promised* her what?"

"That I wouldn't hurt you anymore than I already have."

"Oh, David. It was dreams of your kisses that's gotten me through. You've brought me more happiness than I ever dreamed of. And to answer your question. I think Sissy would like keeping her. She loves Sophie and Ned's children."

"Who are Sophie and Ned?"

"She's my stepdaughter. She has four boys and a girl. Rosemary will like playing with them. We'd better get back to the house. We'll talk more tomorrow and make some plans." She turned to leave.

He pulled her back into his arms. "I know I have no right. But you're the mother of my child, and she needs you. If this time together goes well, I'd like to tell her the truth. How do you feel about that?"

"I . . . I've hoped this might happen someday, I've had visions of holding her in my arms as my own. I'd like that very much."

David brushed her cheek with another kiss. He wouldn't push her any further tonight. He had time. He not only planned on telling Rosemary about her mother; he dreamed of winning Abigail's heart.

❧ 44 ❧

Greenwillow: David and Abigail, 1865

Abigail stood in the doorway of the partially burned plantation house. Good Lord, how had all this happened? Sullus said there'd been a fire, but she'd never imagined there'd be this much damage. It didn't look like Seth was here. Maybe the Yankees took him. If they had, that would free her. She watched the Negro children meandering about the yard at will. A few straggly chickens flapped their wings nearby. One rooster crowed as though it hurt his throat. The sultry July sun beat down with a vengeance. She swatted at a fly that buzzed around her head. *Stupid war.* It had lasted four years, taken thousands of lives, and for what?

The smell of collards drifted through the house, and she followed the scent to the kitchen. A woman stood at the stove, punching down greens in a big black pot with a long paddle . . . was it?

"How've you been, Pearl?"

The slave turned and shock registered in her eyes. "Lawd a mercy on mah soul if it not be our missy returned from ta dead!"

The sight of Pearl's shiny face and bright eyes stirred memories of the time spent at Greenwillow. Not good memories, but nothing compared with how bad things were now. Pulling up a stool, she sat down. "Dead? Why'd you believe that?"

Pearl wiped her hands on her apron. "Yo be gone so long and ain't been a word 'bout yo. What else we gwine think?"

"It seems like a life time, but dere not any way to get in touch. I sent a couple of letters by a supply wagon, but I guess day not get through." She looked around. "Where's Seth?"

Pearl went back to stirring the greens. The lines in her face were no longer soft. "Pearl, what's wrong?"

The cook didn't lift her eyes. "What's left of him be out'n ta church graveyard wid his mama."

She jumped from her stool. "What do you mean, 'what's left of him'?"

"After ta fire we find his remains. Nothin' but a few bones left. Outta respect to ta family, we bury him by his mama."

"'We' who?"

"Me and Asa. We ta ones dat find him. Sullus and Sally Mae took off and left when ta fire start. Ta ones of us who stay save what we can."

Slowly, Abigail sat back down, her heart pounding. Poor Seth . . . he'd been a stern man, even cruel at times, but he was a human being, one that could act very loving. At least David's mother had seen some good in him. "My room, is it gone?"

"No, Missy. Everythin' jest like yo leave it."

She sighed with relief. Her button box was safe. The image of Seth burning in a fire was almost more than she could bear. She closed her eyes and tried to blot out her thoughts, but she couldn't clear her mind. She had to know what happened. "How'd the fire start?"

"We not sure. All I knows Sullus found out ta Masta be his daddy, and . . .." She looked away.

"It's all right. I know he slept with women. Corrie, in particular."

"Well then, yo hab to know Tasha done and died, too. She ta one Masta pick to pleasure him after Corrie left. She die when she hab her baby, back in sixty-two." Pearl shoved the pot of collard greens

338

to the rear of the stove and began making a batch of cornbread. Two small boys ran in. She squatted and gathered them to her full bosom. "Missy, dese here be my babies."

If Abigail had been surprised to find out that Seth had died, she was more shocked to see Pearl as a mother. She knelt in front of the boys. "They're beautiful. Asa must be so happy."

"He be dat. Even though . . . oh, my goodness. I stand right here and let my pan catch on fire. Cain't hab ta rest of ta big house burn now dat yo be back." She grabbed a handful of salt and dumped it on the blaze. The boys bounded out the kitchen door. Pearl yelled, "Don't go runnin' off too fer, supper almost ready." She looked back at Abigail. "We ain't got nothin' but cornbread and collard greens, but you be welcome to eat. I serve yo in ta dinin' room. Me and Asa and ta boys eat out here."

"The war's over. We'll all eat out here. That is, if my friend is welcome."

"Course he is, but free or not, it ain't right for yo to eat with us." Pearl poured the bread into the pan she'd rescued and stuck it in the oven.

Abigail took the cook by the shoulders. "Look me in the eye, because I don't want to have to say this again. Once and for all, your people are *not* slaves! You and I, we're the *same* now. That's what the war was all about. Lincoln signed the Emancipation Proclamation back in January of sixty-three. You have been free for two years."

Pearl puckered up her lips. "E-man-sue. I can't say dat word, Missy."

Abigail laughed. "All it means is he put his name on a paper saying that there's no more slavery."

Pearl shook her head. "Dat what Sullus say 'fore he left. I not see nothin' so good 'bout dat. How we gonna live?"

Abigail took plates from the shelf. "Like you always have, except you won't have a master."

"Yo be ta boss now." Pearl reached for the dishes. "Ain't no mistress gwine work in mah presence no matter what dat Lincoln man done and signed. Now, where ta company yo bring?"

"The captain's out looking over the fields. I'll go get him." At the door, she stopped and looked back. She hadn't noticed how really pretty Pearl was. Motherhood *did* agree with her.

* * *

Abigail entered the kitchen on the arm of Captain David Cranshaw. Her dress, the one she'd worn to her welcoming party, was layers of blue taffeta and lace. She felt awkward about dressing for supper, but it'd been so long since she'd had the opportunity. She tilted her face to look into the eyes of the man she'd loved for so long, and her heart skipped a beat. What else could a person want? She glanced at Pearl, who poured water into the glasses, and felt kinship between them. No matter what the color of their skin, they both had a man to love and children to call them mother. This kind of love washed away all the ravages of war. The world was new and at peace again and so was she.

She'd never seen a prettier supper table even though it was in the kitchen. A white cloth hid all the cracks and crevices, and a vase of flowers adorned the center. Napkins were in place with real silver laying on them. Water glasses stood tall. A bowl of steaming collard greens topped with a chunk of fatback graced one end and a plate of cornbread the other.

A smiling Asa hobbled behind his chair. The two boys, scrubbed almost to shining, wiggled and squirmed.

"Mama, can we set now?"

"Company go first." She turned to Abigail and David. "Boys, dis here be ta mistress of Greenwillow, Abigail Turner."

Abigail smiled and asked, "And may I ask your names?"

The boy closest to her said, "Zeke. Now, can we eat?"

"And your brother, does he have a name?"

"Him, Jake. *Now*, can we eat?"

Abigail laughed at his impatience then faced her companion. "Jake and Zeke, I'd like for you to meet my friend, Captain David Cranshaw. He's from a faraway place called New Orleans."

Zeke turned wide brown eyes on David. "Do day hab collard greens dere?'

A slight smile edged its way into the corners of David's mouth.

Abigail wondered if Rosemary had been that full of questions at this age. She must have been an endless bundle of energy. A moment of sadness at having missed so much of her child's young life filled her heart. The sound of David's voice chased it away.

"Yes, son. I suppose they do, but I haven't had any since my grandmother made them when I was small."

"Our Mama, she make ta best collards yo ever hab. Now, can we eat, Mama?"

Pearl ruffled Zeke's fuzzy head and said, "Jest as soon as our company sets."

Zeke ran over and pulled out Abigail's chair. "Set!"

Abigail sat. She sensed a familiar impatience about this boy. Why? Was it the same as all three-year-olds or something else?

Pearl motioned for Asa and the boys to sit, and then she took her seat. "If I had a-knowed yo wuz a-comin' I'd killed one of ta few chickens we hab left."

Abigail remembered the sickly looking birds she'd seen outside and was glad there wasn't one on the table. "Now, don't you go fretting about the food. We didn't expect to intrude on your meal."

David tucked his napkin into his shirt collar. "Yes, Abigail's right. We appreciate your hospitality."

Abigail looked over at Zeke who had taken his napkin and was imitating David. Again, she had the same uneasy feeling there was something about this child that was familiar. Mannerisms, his eyes, the nose, what was it? Asa's voice broke into her thoughts.

"Missy, yo see fightin' in ta mountains?"

"Not much, Asa, just a skirmish here or there. But guess what? Remember Billy Jackson?"

Asa and Pearl both nodded.

"Well, we brought him and his bride home this morning."

Pearl dipped a helping of collard greens on to the captain's plate. "Well, I declare, it shore ta day fer miracles. We heared he killed at Manassas. Day say his mama grieved herself nigh on to death."

"No, Sophie's husband found him way up in Virginia, almost dead. He brought him back to the Junction, and Mrs. Ledbetter, who runs the boarding house, took him in. She and a couple of young women who boarded there nursed him back to health. He married one of the girls. She's a school teacher."

"Is day gwine stay at Five Oaks, or day gwine back to Shady Junction?" Asa asked.

"They'll return to the mountains. His wife is needed as a teacher, and she loves her job."

Pearl reached for the cornbread. "Shore hope mah boys get some schoolin'. I read some, but can hardly make my x on paper."

The captain raised an eyebrow as he took a bite of greens. "Zeke, I have to say, these taste about like my grandmother's used to."

"See? I tell you Mama ta best cook dere ever be."

David looked at Pearl. "With reconstruction, there will come good schools for all."

"Mama, can me and Jake go play?"

"Don't you want some bread puddin'?"

"Yum, bread puddin', but cain't we have it 'fore bed?"

"Yes, and don't you two wander off too fer."

The boys scrambled to get out the door. Abigail's heart skipped a beat. Zeke's gait was strikingly familiar! He walked just like—surely Seth hadn't bedded Pearl with her married to Asa. That son-of-a-bitch! Weren't there enough young unmarried wenches to satisfy him? She looked at David. "I bet Asa would love to show you some more of the fields before it gets dark."

"How 'bout ta bread puddin'?" said Pearl

David grinned. "Can we have it 'fore bed?"

A smile flashed across Pearl's face. "Yo be back soon. I not serve nothin' after dark."

Asa hobbled toward the door. "Yo shore 'bout that, Pearl baby."

"Get outta here, now!" She made a playful shooing motion with her arms as she stepped forward."

"We gwine . . . we gwine," said Asa with a grin.

The only sound left in the room was that of Pearl scraping

dishes. Finally, Abigail spoke. "Tell me about the boys' father. It wasn't Seth, was it?"

The plate clattered to the floor and shattered in a million pieces. Pearl looked up, panic written across her face. "It ain't what yo thinkin'. I swear I not bed Masta."

"Calm down. Come sit here by me."

Pearl sat and wiped at the tears gathering in her eyes.

"You don't have to say anything. I understand."

Pearl took a sip of her coffee, and after a few minutes she cleared her throat. "Yes, I has to tell yo. Yo need to know. Ta truth'll hep yo hab a life with that nice captain."

Abigail felt her cheeks grow warm. Was it that obvious she was in love with David? Someone like Pearl would know. She nodded "Say what you must."

Pearl wiped at her eyes. "Yo hab to know Asa not know what I gwine tell you."

"I know. But talking will help. We all need someone to bare our souls to."

"Well, Tasha carry two babies. One born 'live and one never born. When Seth see ta baby look like him, he say bury it with its mama. He not know 'bout ta other chile."

The collard's tried to work their way back into Abigail's mouth. How could she have lived with such a man? She'd been wrong. He could never be human!

"I was habin' Jake the same night. Sally Mae brin' me ta live baby. Granny take ta baby Tasha not hab outta her. Dat ta baby ta masta see in ta casket. We jest tell folks I hab twins."

"And you never told Asa any different?"

"No. Didn't see no need to."

"But Jake's father can't be Asa. He's too light."

"Dat right. Seth used Sullus to breed ta young nigger gals. He wuz gwine breed me. When McRoy come for me, instead of takin' me ta Sullus, he took me ta my cabin. Asa almost kill him. He believe McRoy ta daddy of bof' my babies."

The whole ugly picture closed in on Abigail. No wonder Seth's empire crumbled. She took a deep breath and slowly replaced her thoughts with those of David.

"Seems we're interrupting on some serious woman talk."

Abigail looked up to find David standing just inside the door with Asa behind him. Had they been there long enough to overhear any of their conversation?

"Mama, we want bread puddin' now." The boys darted past the two men and climbed onto their chairs.

Abigail collected her thoughts as Pearl went to the stove and dished up generous helpings of pudding for everyone, topping it with lots of vanilla sauce. Soon everybody was too busy eating to talk.

David finished first, rubbing his stomach as he pushed back his bowl. "Now that was worth the trip. I haven't had anything like that since before the war."

"I done and told yo Mama make good stuff."

"That you did, Zeke. I would definitely get fat if I ate here all the time." He looked at Abigail and winked. "Can you cook?"

Raising an eyebrow, she said, "I can do whatever I need to, Mr. Cranshaw." She turned to Pearl. "Where can the captain sleep?"

"In Seth's mother's old room. Soon as I clean up here, I make ta bed, bring hot water fer bathin' and fresh towels."

Abigail reached out and took the captain's hand. "That's all right. You've done enough, and thank you. I want to take David up and show him my button box. One of the reasons I came back was to get it"

A frown crossed Pearl's brow. "You mean yo not gwine stay. Dis still yo home, and we here to hep. Like I say, don't matter none what dat Lincoln man signed."

"I don't know what my plans are right now. Things are so different from what I expected. We'll see."

When they reached her old room, David said, "You and Pearl looked so serious when Asa and I returned. Do you two have some sort of secret?"

"Then you didn't overhear what we were talking about?"

"No, but from the looks of things, I'd say it was good I was in front of Asa."

"You're right. There's no reason for anymore hurt."

"And from what I've seen, I'd say Asa isn't the daddy of those boys."

"Oh, he knows the father was McRoy. What Asa doesn't know is that the boys aren't brothers."

"Not brothers? Those collards must have affected your brain. They look like twins to me. You can tell both of them have white blood in their veins."

"Seth was Zeke's father."

David sat down on the bed. "Now, wait a minute! You just said McRoy was the father. He shook his head. "Start over. I'm completely confused."

Abigail sat down and took his hand. "After I left here and went to the mountains with Corrie, Seth took a slave girl to warm his bed. Her name was Tasha. She died giving birth to Zeke. Pearl was having her baby the same night so she took the child and told everyone, including Asa, that she had twins." She went on to explain about Tasha's unborn child and Seth's hateful crime. "Seth had a warped sense of what it meant to be a human. Or a man. He had to have a woman in his bed."

David rose and went to the window. After a while, he turned. "He had someone before Tasha? Besides . . . you?"

She nodded. "Corrie. He bought her after his daughter was born, just for that purpose. I didn't know it, for sure, until we left to go to the mountains. He told me because he wanted me to know what sort of *sacrifice* he was making by letting us both go." She stopped and rubbed her head. It was all too much, and she'd lived it. How could she make him understand? He was such an honorable man. She took a deep breath. "While we're talking about Seth, you might as well know how he died. I still haven't come to terms with all that's happened. Part of me is glad he's gone, but yet . . ."

David reached out and pulled her into his arms. "I know. All this is very hard on you."

For a few minutes, she let herself relax in his embrace. Six years ago she'd never dreamed . . . yes, she had. Dreams of David helped get her through. She withdrew and went to the window. "He died in the fire, by the hand of his own son."

"But you told me he only married you to give him an heir."

"Yes, a *legal* heir. You see, Corrie's son, Sullus, wouldn't be legal."

"Oh, Abigail. You poor thing. How . . ."

"I'm fine." She wanted to say *because I have your love,* but she couldn't, not yet. "Come on, let's not talk about this anymore. I want to show you my button box." She raised the lid of the trunk. The gold leafed box glimmered in the dim light. She removed the top and dipped her fingers into the buttons. She'd heard them call to her before and always knew that somehow they were connected to her future. Now she grabbed a handful. Going back to the window next to David, she held out her hand. "Aren't they beautiful? They remind me of the way the country will be now. We're all like buttons in a box. All shapes, sizes and colors, living together."

David tilted her head and placed a soft kiss on her lips. "You're a dreamer, Abigail. Maybe someday it'll be that way, but I'm afraid there's going to have to be a lot of healing first. In the meantime . . ."

"I have the people I love and my buttons," she said lightly and went back to the trunk and picked up the button box. If she had lived for a million years, she wouldn't have been prepared for what was underneath it. She stood, speechless.

"Abigail, what in the world is wrong? Is something missing?"

She shook her head.

By now David was by her side. "My Lord! Did Seth rob banks, also?"

"I don't know. He said one time that he'd never be poor because of the war. He must have been hoarding these coins for a long time."

"Well, you won't have to worry about reconstruction. From the looks of things you could build your own city!"

She knelt and let the coins slide through her fingers. All the gold in the world was worth nothing without love. She'd learned that lesson the hard way.

David kissed her cheek again. "Seriously, you can rebuild with this money."

"Do you want me to be a tobacco tycoon?"

"What I'm saying is I want you to be happy."

She rose and went to the window, pulled back the curtain, and looked out over the land that once was green with tobacco plants. No, this had never been her home. She was not the rightful owner. This land belonged to Sophie and her children. Now with Seth gone, Ned might consider living here. She had all she needed to rebuild her life. Turning back to the trunk, she knelt and buried her hands in the gold pieces. "I can remember a time when all this gold would have meant . . .." She lifted the coins, enjoying the feel as they slid through her fingers. The years melted away and once again she stood in David's old room at his mother's. All the hurt from the past bubbled forth like an uncapped well. "Damn my stepdaddy . . . he hurt me . . . used my mother . . . The Wellington house . . . That man . . . took me. No where to go . . . into the streets . . . David . . ." She dropped her head and let the tears flow.

David backed toward the door. He'd watched her clench and unclench her fists and stomp her foot, but this—never had he seen her eyes so bright or her face so pale. Oh, God. He'd hurt her just like the others—probably more than anyone. He'd taken part of her and left her to suffer. He had to get out of here. Had to go before . . .. She'd suffered, but so had he. First, losing a child then doing all in his power yet failing to save his wife. He'd fought in a war and come home to an empty house and a daughter without a mother. He had to go because he couldn't take anymore hurt.

"David your love means more to me than all the gold in the

world." Abigail stood and turned, still holding a handful of coins. "Dav . . .." She felt the blood drain from her face. He was gone. She dropped the gold pieces onto the bed and rushed down the stairs.

Pearl was wiping the dishpan as Abigail hurried in. "Did the captain come through here?"

"Yes'um. Jest a few minutes ago."

"Did he say where he was going?"

"No. He jest mumblin' sump'n under his breath. I not make out a-thing he say."

Abigail felt her legs grow weak. Why had he walked out on her? "I'm going to look for him. If he comes back, will you please tell him to wait right here?"

"I shore do dat, Missy."

Outside, Abigail looked at all the devastation. Without David, her life would be just as desolate. She heard a horse nicker in the barn. She had to hurry. She couldn't let him get away! She stepped into the barn as David was throwing a saddle on his horse. "David, what are you doing?"

David tightened the girth. "I'm going back to New Orleans. The Jacksons will see that you get back to the mountains and Rosemary safely." He put his foot in the stirrup and swung into the saddle. Looking down at her, he said, "You deserve to be happy. You have it all now, including your daughter. I'll have my lawyer send you papers granting you custody. Do me one favor. Remind her often that I love her very much."

Abigail didn't try to hold back her tears. She reached up both hands to him. "What do you mean? Don't you know *you're* my happiness? Without you, I don't have anything! I've loved you from that very first day you found me on the street and took me home. I've dreamed of being your wife. It seems impossible, but that helped me through these past years."

The edge of dark crept in and with it the eerie shadows from her past. Fighting the urge to run, she shut her eyes and forced them away. As she fought, the touch of lips brushed her check. Could this be real, or was it just another dream? She kept her eyes closed, afraid it was her imagination. She felt them again, but this time they claimed her lips with a force she'd never dreamed possible. She let her arms slip around David's neck. She opened her eyes and met the gaze of the man she loved.

"Will you marry me, Abigail?"

"Mr. Cranshaw, I'd gladly give up all that gold and what's left of this plantation for you and my child, but there's one thing you need to know about me. I've become a mountain girl."

David kissed her. "Well, there is nothing I'd like better than to marry a mountain girl, but I can't wait until we get back. How about tomorrow? I'd like to take a mother home for Rosemary."

Abigail shut her eyes and remembered all the times she'd thought about becoming Mrs. David Cranshaw. Could this be real? She felt his lips touch hers, again. She returned the kiss eagerly.

Yes, she'd marry him, tomorrow.

www.ingramcontent.com/pod-product-compliance
Lightning Source LLC
Chambersburg PA
CBHW051229260626
47162CB00002B/338